W9-CZX-813

NUMBERED
ACCOUNT

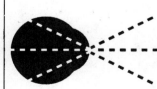

This Large Print Book carries the
Seal of Approval of N.A.V.H.

NUMBERED ACCOUNT

CHRISTOPHER REICH

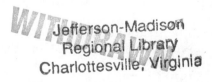
Thorndike Press • Thorndike, Maine

Published in 1998 by arrangement with Delacorte Press, an imprint of Dell Publishing, a division of Bantam Doubleday Dell Publishing Group, Inc.

Thorndike Large Print ® Basic Series.

The tree indicium is a trademark of Thorndike Press.

The text of this Large Print edition is unabridged. Other aspects of the book may vary from the original edition.

Set in 16 pt. Plantin by Juanita Macdonald.

Printed in the United States on permanent paper.

Library of Congress Cataloging in Publication Data

Reich, Christopher.
    Numbered account / Christopher Reich.
        p.   cm.
    ISBN 0-7862-1505-4 (lg. print : hc : alk. paper)
    1. Large type books.   2. Banks and banking —
Switzerland — Fiction.   3. International finance —
Fiction.   4. Switzerland — Fiction.   I. Title.
    [PS3568.E476284N8   1998b]
    813'.54—dc21   98-19325

For Sue,
yesterday, today, and tomorrow

Acknowledgments

I would like to thank the following people for their kind assistance:

Babs and Willy Reich offered only encouragement and support.

Farlan Myers, a longtime family friend, showed his true colors when it counted.

Karla Kuban, Tina Venema, and David Yorkin read early drafts of this book and offered helpful advice.

Sarah Piel of Arthur Pine Associates provided invaluable assistance in whipping the first drafts of the book into shape.

Lori Andiman, also of Arthur Pine Associates, proved to be nothing less than a wizard.

Jacqueline Miller, my editor, lit the way and held my hand through some difficult times.

Carole Baron showed her faith in a new writer.

Most important, I'd like to thank Leslie Schnur for believing in the book and pulling out all the stops. You're the best.

And finally, I offer my heartfelt thanks to my agent, Richard Pine. Onward and upward!

Prologue

Lights. Magnificent lights.

Martin Becker paused before descending the stairs of the bank and gloried in the sea of glowing pearls. The length of the Bahnhofstrasse was festooned with row upon row of Christmas lights, strands of yellow bulbs falling from the sky like warm, electric rain. He checked his watch and with dismay noted that only twenty minutes remained before the last train to the mountains left for the evening.

And still one errand to run. He would have to hurry.

Clutching his briefcase, Becker joined the bustling throng. His pace was brisk, fast even for the dourly efficient executives who, like him, called Zurich their home. Twice he stopped and looked over his shoulder. He felt certain no one was following him, yet he could not help himself. It was a reflex born more of guilt than any perceived threat. His eyes scanned the crowd for a flurry of activity that might justify his apprehension — a guard yelling for him to halt, a determined face forcing its way through the crowd — anything out of the ordinary. He saw nothing.

He had done it and now he was free. Yet

already his exuberance was waning, the triumph of the moment replaced by a fear of the future.

Becker reached the silver doors at the entry to Cartier as the manager was locking up. Frowning good-naturedly, the handsome woman opened the door and ushered him into the store. One more harried banker buying his wife's affection. Becker hurried to the counter. He had his receipt ready and accepted the elegantly wrapped box without ever losing hold of his briefcase. The diamond brooch was an extravagant gesture. A token of his fierce love. And a glittering reminder of the day he had decided to listen to his soul.

Becker slid the box into his pocket and, thanking the jeweler, left the store. Outside a light snow had begun to fall. He set off toward the railway station at an easier pace. Crossing the Bahnhofstrasse, he continued past the Chanel boutique and Bally, two of the city's numberless shrines to luxury. The street was filled with last-minute shoppers like him: well-dressed men and women rushing home with presents for their loved ones. He tried to imagine his wife's expression when she unwrapped the brooch. He could see her lips pursed in anticipation, her skeptical eyes squinting as she removed it from the box. She would mumble something about the cost and saving for the children's education. Laughing, he would hug her and tell her not to worry. Only then would she put it on. Sooner or later, though, she would need a reason. Marty, why such an expensive gift? And he would have to tell her. But how could he reveal the extent of his treason?

He was pondering this question when a foreign hand found the lee of his back and gave him a violent shove. He stumbled forward a few steps, his knees buckling under him. At the last moment, his outstretched arm found a nearby streetlamp, and he averted a nasty spill. Just then a city tram rushed by, passing no more than two feet in front of him. A blast of wind tousled his hair and spit grit into his eyes.

Becker sucked in a lungful of cold air, calming himself, then spun to locate the culprit. He expected an apologetic face eager to lend him a hand or a leering maniac ready to toss him under the next tram. On both counts, he was disappointed. An attractive woman passing in the opposite direction smiled at him. A middle-aged man dressed in a loden coat and matching hat nodded sympathetically and walked by.

Standing straighter, Becker ran a hand over his jacket, feeling the bulge that was his wife's present. He looked down at the pavement, then at his leather-soled shoes. He breathed easier. The snow. The ice. He'd slipped. No one had pushed him into the path of the tram. Then why could he still feel the imprint of another person's palm scalding his lower back?

Becker looked into the stream of oncoming pedestrians. Frantically, he sifted their faces, not knowing what or whom he was looking for, only that a voice deep inside him, some primal instinct, was screaming at him that he was being followed. After a minute, he resumed his course. He had seen nothing, yet his anxiety remained.

As he walked he assured himself that no one could have discovered his theft. Not yet, anyway. He had, after all, taken measures to avoid detection. He had used his superior's access code. To be safe he had waited until the imperious little man had left the office and used his computer as well. There would be no record of an unauthorized request. Finally, he had chosen the quietest day of the year, Christmas Eve. Those that weren't already in the mountains skiing with their families had left the building by four. He'd been alone for hours. No one had seen him printing the files in his superior's office. It was impossible!

Becker tucked the briefcase under his arm and lengthened his stride. Forty yards ahead the tram was slowing as it approached its next stop. A swarm of passengers pressed forward eager to board. He moved toward the gathering, attracted by its promise of anonymity. His walk turned to a trot, and then to a run. He had no idea from where this sense of desperation had sprung, only that he was full in its grip and had no choice but to obey its commands. He closed the distance quickly, sprinting the last few yards, and arrived as the tram groaned to a halt.

Air whooshed, the doors opened, and a pair of steps extended from the undercarriage of the car. Several passengers descended. He forced his way into the rear of the crowd, rejoicing in the crush of bodies against him. Step by step, he neared the tram. His heart rate slowed and his breathing calmed. Secure in the jostling mass, he managed a short dry chuckle. His worry had been for naught. He would make the last train to the mountains. By ten o'clock he would be in Davos, and for the next week there he would remain, safe in the bosom of his family.

The restless crowd climbed one by one into the tram. Soon it was his turn. He placed his right foot onto the metal step. He leaned forward and grasped the iron railing. Suddenly, a firm hand fell onto his shoulder and arrested his movement. He struggled against it, using the railing to pull himself into the tram. Another hand snatched a fistful of his hair and yanked his head back. A cool ball traversed his neck. He opened his mouth to protest, but no sound emerged. He had no air with which to cry. Blood sprayed from his throat, painting the passengers around him. A woman screamed, and then another. He stumbled backward, one hand groping at his ruined throat, the other mindful of its grip on the briefcase. His legs grew numb and he fell to his knees. It was all happening so slowly. He felt another hand on his, prying the briefcase from his grasp. Let go, he wanted to cry. He saw a flash of silver and acknowledged a tear in his stomach, something gnawing at a rib, then breaking free. His hands lost all feeling and the case dropped to the ground. He collapsed.

Martin Becker lay still on the cold pavement. His vision was blurry and he could no longer breathe. A stream of blood touched his cheek, warming him. The briefcase lay on its side a few feet away. He wanted desperately to retrieve it, but he could not will his arm to move.

Then he saw him. The man in the loden coat, the dapper fellow who'd been walking just behind him when he had stumbled. No, dammit, the man who had pushed him! His murderer bent over and picked up the briefcase. For a second their eyes met. The man smiled, then ran into the street, Becker couldn't see where.

Stop, he yelled silently. But he knew it was too late. He rolled his head and stared above him. The lights were so beautiful. Magnificent, really.

Chapter 1

It was the coldest winter in memory. For the first time since 1962 the Lake of Zurich threatened a solid freeze. Already a shelf of blue ice clung to her shores. Farther out a transparent crust floated upon the surface. The stately paddle wheel steamships that called regularly on Zurich and her prosperous environs had taken refuge at their winter harbor in Kilchberg. At ports around the lake storm lamps burned red: danger, conditions hazardous.

The last snow had fallen only two days before, yet the city's roads were immaculate. Muddy piles of frozen slush that might sully the sidewalks of other urban centers had been removed. Recalcitrant patches of ice likewise. Even the rock salt and gravel spread to hasten their decomposition had been neatly swept up.

In any other year, the continuing bout of record low temperatures and unending snowfall would be reason for spirited discussion. Many a newspaper column would be devoted to a thorough tallying of the economic gains and losses to the country. To her agriculture and livestock — losers, as thousands of cows had frozen to death in low-lying barns; to her many Alpine ski resorts — all winners, and about time, after consecutive seasons of insufficient snowfall; and to her precious water table — also a winner, as experts forecast a restoration of the national aquifer after a decade of depletion. More conservative rags might even include a spiteful article pronouncing the much-feared "greenhouse effect" dead and buried.

But not this year. On this first Monday in January, no mention of the severe weather could be found anywhere on the front pages of the *Neue Zürcher Zeitung*, the *Tages Anzeiger*, or even the chronically mundane *Zürcher Tagblatt*. The country was struggling with something far rarer than a harsh winter: a crisis of conscience.

Signs of turmoil were not difficult to find. And Nicholas Neumann, stepping off the number thirteen tram at the Paradeplatz, immediately spotted the most prominent of them. Fifty yards ahead, along the east side of the Bahnhofstrasse, a band of men and women were gathered in front of a drab four-story building that was home to the United Swiss Bank. His destination. Most held signs, which Nick, as he preferred to be called, could read even at this distance: "Clean Up the Swiss Laundry." "Drug Money Is Blood Money." "Hitler's Bankers." Others stood with their hands shoved into their pockets, marching determinedly back and forth.

The past year had witnessed a parade of embarrassing revelations about the country's banks. Complicity in the wartime arms trade with the Third Reich; hoarding of funds belonging to survivors of Hitler's death camps; and the concealment of illicit profits deposited by the South American drug cartels. The local press had branded the banks "soulless instruments of financial chicanery" and "willing conspirators to the drug barons' deadly trade." The public had taken note. And now those accountable must be made to pay.

Worse storms had raged and passed, mused Nick, as he set off toward the bank. He didn't share in the country's self-inculpatory mood. Nor was he sure the nation's banks were solely to blame. But that was as far as his interest went. His concern was focused elsewhere that morning: on a private matter that had haunted the darkest corners of his heart for as long as he could remember.

Nick moved easily through the crowd. He had broad shoulders and stood just over six feet tall. His step was confident and purposeful and, except for a faint limp, commanding. Veterans of the parade ground would note the curled hand laid along the rail of the trousers, the shoulders pushed back a breath more than was comfortable, and immediately recognize him as one of their own.

His face was cast from a serious mold, framed by a crop of straight black hair. His nose was prominent and spoke of a distinct, if unlanded, European heritage. His chin was sturdy rather than stubborn. But it was his eyes that caught people's attention. They were a pale blue and surrounded by a network of fine lines unexpected in someone his age. They offered a furtive challenge. His fiancée said once that they were the eyes of another man, someone older, someone wearier than a twenty-eight-year-old had any right to be. Someone she no longer knew. She'd left him the next day.

Nick quickly covered the short distance to the bank. A freezing drizzle had begun to fall, whipped up by a stiff lake breeze. Flakes of snow darkened his trench coat, but the foul weather did not intrude on his thoughts. Threading his way through the crowd of demonstrators, he kept his eyes fixed on the twin revolving doors that sat before him at the top of a broad flight of granite stairs.

The United Swiss Bank.

Forty years ago his father had begun his employ here. Apprentice at sixteen, portfolio manager at twenty-five, vice president at thirty-three, Alexander Neumann had been on the fast track to the top. Executive vice president. Board of directors. Anything was possible. And everything expected.

Nick checked his wristwatch, then climbed the stairs and entered the lobby of the bank. Somewhere close by, a church bell tolled the hour. Nine o'clock. His stomach fluttered and he recognized the uneasy frisson of a mission at hand. He smiled inwardly, giving silent greeting to the once familiar sensation, then continued across the marble floor toward a lectern marked "Reception" in letters of gold relief.

"I have an appointment with Mr. Cerruti," he said to the hall porter. "I'm to begin work today."

"Your papers?" demanded the porter, an older man resplendent in a navy topcoat with braided silver epaulets.

Nick passed across the counter an envelope bearing the bank's embossed logo.

The porter withdrew the letter of engagement and looked it over. "Identification?"

Nick presented two passports: one navy blue with a golden eagle emblazoned on its cover, the other a bold red with a prim white cross painted upon its face. The porter examined both, then returned them. "I'll announce your arrival. Take a seat, please. Over there." He motioned toward a grouping of leather chairs.

But Nick preferred to remain standing and walked slowly through the great hall. He took in the elegantly dressed customers waiting for their favorite tellers and the gray executives hurrying across the shiny floor. He listened to the stubble of hushed conversations and the whisper of computer-assisted commerce. His thoughts drifted to the flight over from New

York two nights earlier, and then back further, to Cambridge, to Quantico, to California. He'd been headed this way for years, without even knowing it.

A telephone buzzed behind the porter's lectern. The porter snapped the receiver to his ear and nodded crisply in time to his every grunted response. Moments later, Nick was being shown across the lobby to a bank of antiquated elevators. The porter walked ahead with perfectly measured strides, as if determined to establish the exact distance to the waiting elevator, and once there, made a show of sweeping open its smoked glass door.

"Second floor," he said, in his clipped voice. "Someone will be waiting for you."

Nick thanked him and stepped into the elevator. It was small with maroon carpeting, burled wood paneling, and a polished brass balustrade. Immediately, he caught scent of a medley of familiar fragrances: the blunt trail of stale cigar smoke; the nasal pinch of well-polished shoes, and most distinctly, the bracing note, at once sweet and antiseptic, of Kölnisches Wasser, his father's favorite eau de cologne. The masculine odors assaulted his senses, conjuring up a fractured image of his dad: wine black hair cropped unfashionably short; unblinking blue eyes capped by unruly eyebrows; stern mouth locked in a downcast expression of disapproval.

The porter grew impatient. "You must go

to the second floor. 'Second floor,' " he said, this time in English. "You're expected. Please, sir."

But Nick did not hear a word. His back remained to the open door, his eyes staring blindly ahead. He struggled to fit the separate images together, to bind them into a finished portrait. He recalled the powerful feelings of awe and pride and fear he'd experienced when in his father's company, but nothing more. His memories remained incomplete and somehow disjointed, wanting for some essential fabric that he did not possess.

"Young man, are you all right?" the porter asked.

Nick spun to face him, banishing the disconcerting images from his mind. "I'm fine," he said. "Just fine."

The porter placed a foot into the elevator. "You're sure you are ready to begin work today?"

Nick raised his chin and fought the porter's inquisitive stare. "Yes," he said gravely, giving an imperceptible nod of his head. "I've been ready for a long time."

Offering an apologetic smile, he let the elevator door close and pressed the button for the second floor.

"Marco Cerruti is ill. Out with some virus or bug, who knows what," explained a tall, sandy-haired executive well on the downslope to forty, who was waiting for Nick on the second-floor landing. "Probably the lousy water in that part of the world — Middle East, that is. The Fertile Crescent: that's our territory. Believe it or not, we *bankers* did not give it that name."

Nick stepped out of the elevator and offering the required smile, introduced himself.

" 'Course, you're Neumann. Who else would I be waiting for?" The sandy-haired man thrust out his hand and gave a vigorous shake. "I'm Peter Sprecher. Don't let the accent fool you. I'm Swiss as William Tell. Did my schooling in England. Still know the words to 'God Save the Queen.' " He pulled at an expensive cuff and winked. "Old man Cerruti is just back from his Christmas run. I call it his yearly Crusade: Cairo, Riyadh, Dubai, and then off to points unknown — probably a sunny port where he can work on his tan while the rest of us back at head office wilt. Guess it didn't work out as planned. Word's come down he'll be out at least a week. The bad news is you're with me."

Nick listened to the rambling outpouring of information, doing his best to digest it all. "And the good news?"

But Peter Sprecher had disappeared down a narrow corridor. "Ah, yes, the good news," he called over his shoulder. "Well, the good news is that there is a mountain of work to be done. We're a bit shorthanded at the moment,

20

so you won't be sitting on your duff reading a sackful of annual reports. We're sending you out into the blue, pronto."

"Into the blue?"

Sprecher stopped at a closed door on the left-hand side of the hallway. "Clients, chum. We have to put somebody's pretty mug in front of our trusting customers. You look like an honest type. Got all your teeth, do you? Should be able to fool them."

"Today?" Nick asked, ruffled.

"No, not today," Sprecher answered, grinning. "The bank usually likes to provide a little training. You can count on at least a month to learn the ropes." He leaned on the handle and opened the door. He walked inside the small meeting room and tossed the manila envelope he'd been carrying onto the conference table. "Take a seat," he said, flinging himself into one of the quilted leather chairs. "Make yourself at home."

Nick pulled out a chair and sat across the table from his new boss. His momentary panic settled, giving way to the usual vague unease that accompanied his arrival at a new post. But he recognized a new sensation, too — a stubborn disbelief that he was actually there.

You're in, Nick told himself in the admonishing tone that had belonged to his father. Keep your mouth closed and your ears open. Become one of them.

Peter Sprecher pulled a sheaf of papers from

the envelope. "Your life in four lines, single spaced. Says here you're from Los Angeles."

"I grew up there, but I haven't called it home for a while."

"Ah, Sodom and Gomorrah rolled into one. Love the place, myself." Sprecher shook loose a Marlboro and offered the pack to Nick, who declined. "Didn't figure you for a tobacco fiend. You look fit enough to run a damned marathon. Some advice? Calm down, boy. You're in Switzerland. Slow and steady, that's our motto. Remember that."

"I'll keep it in mind."

"Liar," Sprecher laughed. "I can see you've got a bee buzzing about your bonnet. Sit too damn straight. That will be Cerruti's problem, not mine." He lowered his head and puffed on his cigarette while studying the new employee's papers. "Marine, eh? An officer. That explains it."

"Four years," said Nick. He was trying hard to sit more casually — drop a shoulder, maybe slouch a little. It wasn't easy.

"What d'ya do?"

"Infantry. I had a reconnaissance platoon. Half the time we trained. The other half we floated around the Pacific waiting for a crisis to flare up so that we could put our training to use. We never did." That was the company line, and he'd been sworn to keep it.

"Says here you worked in New York. Four months only. What happened?"

Nick kept his answer brief. When lying, he knew it best to stay within the shadow of the truth. "It wasn't what I had expected. I didn't feel at home there, at work or in the city."

"So you decided to seek your fortune abroad?"

"I've lived in the States my whole life. One day I realized that it was time for something new. Once I made the decision, I got out as quickly as I could."

"Wish I'd had the guts to do something like that. Alas, for me it's too late." Sprecher exhaled a cloud of smoke toward the ceiling. "Been here before?"

"To the bank?"

"*To Switzerland.* Someone in your family is Swiss, isn't he? Hard to pick up a passport any other way."

"It's been a long time," said Nick, purposely keeping his answer oblique. Seventeen years, actually. He'd been eleven, and his father had brought him inside this same building. It had been a social visit, the great Alex Neumann poking his head into the offices of his former colleagues, exchanging a few words before presenting little Nicholas as if he were an exotic trophy from a far-off land. "The passport comes from my father's side. We spoke Swiss-German together at home."

"Did you? How quaint." Sprecher stubbed out his cigarette and brought his chair closer to the table so that he sat directly facing Nick.

"Enough small talk, then. Welcome to the United Swiss Bank, Mr. Neumann. You've been assigned to *Finanz Kundenberatung, Abteilung 4*. Financial Client Management, section 4. Our small family deals with private individuals from the Middle East and southern Europe, that is Italy, Greece, and Turkey. Right now we handle approximately seven hundred accounts with assets totaling over two billion U.S. dollars. In the end that's still the only currency worth a damn.

"Most of our clients are individuals who hold numbered accounts with the bank. You might see their names penciled somewhere inside their files. Penciled, mind you. Erasable. They are to remain officially anonymous. We don't keep permanent records regarding their identity in the office. That information is kept in DZ, *Dokumentation Zentrale*. Stalag 17, we call it." Sprecher wagged a long finger at Nick. "Several of our more important clients are known only to the top brass of the bank. Keep it that way. Any inclination you may have about getting to know them personally had better stop now. Understood?"

"Understood," said Nick. The help does not mix with the guests.

"Here's the drill: A client will call, give you his account number, probably want to know his cash balance or the value of the stocks in his portfolio. Before you give out any information, confirm his or her identity. All our clients have code words to identify themselves. Ask for it. Maybe ask their birthday on top of that. Makes them feel secure. But that's as far as your curiosity runs. If a client wants to transfer fifty thousand deutsche marks a week to an account in Palermo, you say, *'Prego, Signore. Con gusto.'* If he insists on sending monthly cash wires to a dozen John Does at a dozen different banks in Washington, D.C., you say, 'Of course, sir. It's my pleasure.' Where our clients' money comes from and what they choose to do with it are entirely their own business."

Nick kept his wry comments to himself and concentrated on keeping straight all the information being tossed his way.

Sprecher stood from his chair and walked to the window, which overlooked the Bahnhofstrasse. "Hear the drums?" he asked, tilting his head toward the demonstrators who paraded in front of the bank. "No? Get up and come over here. Look down there."

Nick rose and walked to Sprecher's side, from where he could see the assembly of fifteen or twenty protesters.

"Barbarians at the gate," said Sprecher. "The natives are growing restless."

"There have been calls for greater disclosure of the bank's activities in the past," Nick said. "The search for assets belonging to customers killed during the Second War. The banks handled that problem."

25

"By using the nation's gold reserves to set up a survivors' fund. Cost us seven billion francs! And still we stonewalled them over direct access to our records. The past is verboten. You can be sure of one thing: Swiss banks must be built of the hardest Bernadino granite, not of porous sandstone." Sprecher glanced at his watch, then dismissed the demonstrators with a wave. "Now more than ever we have to keep our mouths shut and do as we're told. Granite, Neumann. Anyway, that's enough of Saint Peter's pap for now. You're to go to Dr. Schon at personnel to have an identification card made up, get a handbook, and take care of all the other niceties that make our beloved institution such a wonderful place to work. Rules, Mr. Neumann. Rules."

Nick leaned forward, listening carefully while directions to the personnel director's office were given. *Rules,* he repeated to himself. The admonition sent him back to his first day at Officer Candidate School. The voices here were softer and the barracks nicer, but all in all it was the same. New organization, new rules, and no room to mess up.

"And one last thing," said Sprecher. "Dr. Schon can be a little testy sometimes. Americans are not a favorite topic. The less said the better."

From his window on the Fourth Floor, Wolfgang Kaiser stared down upon the damp heads of the demonstrators gathered in front of his bank. Forty years he had worked at the United Swiss Bank, the last seventeen as chairman. In that time, he could recall only one other demonstration taking place on the steps of the bank — a protest against the bank's investments in South Africa. He had frowned on the practice of apartheid as much as the next man, but politics simply didn't factor into a business decision. As a rule, Afrikaners were damned good clients. Paid back their loans on time. Kept a decent amount on deposit. Lord knows they held gold bars up to their eyeballs.

Kaiser gave each end of his mustache a brief tug and moved away from the window. Though of medium height, he was a formidable man. Clothed, as was his custom, in bespoke navy worsted, he could be mistaken only for Lord of the Manor. But his broad shoulders, plowman's back, and stout legs testified to a common upbringing. And of his less than noble parentage he carried a permanent reminder: his left arm, damaged at birth by the enthusiastic forceps of a drunken midwife, was thin and limp, a paralyzed appendage. Despite constant exercise during his early years, the arm had remained atrophied and would always be two inches shorter than the right.

Kaiser circled his desk, staring at the telephone. He was waiting for a call. A brief message that would bring the past into the present. Word that the circle was closing. He could not expel from his mind the message written on one of the crude placards below. "Child Killers," it read. He didn't know what exactly it made reference to, but still the words stung. Damned press! Vultures were thrilled to have such an easy target. The evil bankers so eager to accommodate the world's baddies. Horseshit! If not us, then somebody else. Austria, Luxembourg, the Cayman Islands. The competition was closing in.

The phone on his desk buzzed. He pounced on it in three swift steps. "Kaiser."

"*Guten Morgen, Herr Direktor.* Brunner speaking."

"Well?"

"The boy has arrived," said the hall porter. "He came in at nine o'clock sharp."

"And how is he?" Kaiser had seen photographs of him over the years. More recently, he had viewed a videotape of the boy's interview. Still, he could not stop himself from asking, "Does he look like his father?"

"A few pounds heavier, perhaps. Otherwise, a spitting image. I sent him to Mr. Sprecher."

"Yes, I've been informed. Thank you, Hugo."

Kaiser hung up the phone and took a seat behind his desk. He turned his thoughts to the young man sitting two floors below him, and soon a faint smile pushed up the corners of his mouth. "Welcome to Switzerland, Nicholas Alexander Neumann," he whispered. "It's been so long since we last met. So very, very long."

Chapter 2

The office of the Director of Personnel (Finance Division) was located at the far corner of the first floor. Nick paused outside an open door and knocked twice before entering. Inside, a slender woman was bent over a messy desk, sorting through a collage of white papers. She wore an ivory blouse and a navy skirt that fell one frustrated sigh below her knee. Brushing a wave of hair from her face, she rose from the desk to stare at her visitor.

"May I help you?" she asked.

"I'm here to see Dr. Schon," Nick said. "I've just begun work this morning and —"

"Your name, please? We have six new employees beginning today. First Monday of the month."

Her stern voice made him want to square his shoulders, fire off a salute, and bark out his name, rank, and serial number. That would make her jump. He told her who he was, and recalling Sprecher's comments about his posture, made sure he didn't stand too straight.

"Hmm," she said, suddenly interested. "Our American. Please come in." The woman craned her neck and ran a none too discreet eye over him, as if checking to see what the bank had gotten for its money. Apparently satisfied, she asked in a friendlier voice if he'd had a good flight over.

"Not bad," Nick said, returning her appraising stare. "It gets a little cramped back there after a few hours, but at least we had smooth sailing."

She was shorter by a head with intelligent brown eyes and thick blond hair cut to fall in a slant across her brow. A gracefully upturned chin and a sharp nose conspired to lend her an air of assumed importance. She told him to wait a moment, then stepped through an open door that led to an adjoining office.

Nick removed his hands from his pockets and without thinking wiped his palms on the rear of his trousers. He had known a woman like her before. Confident, assertive, a little too professional. A woman who relied on perfect grooming to improve on nature's careless oversights. In fact, he had almost married her.

"Please come in, Mr. Neumann."

He recognized the stern voice. Poised behind a broad desk sat the woman with the intelligent brown eyes. A testy one, Sprecher had warned, who didn't care for Americans. She had tucked her blond hair behind her ears and found a blazer to match her skirt. A large pair of horn-rimmed glasses rested on her nose.

"I'm sorry," Nick said sincerely, "I didn't

realize . . ." His explanation petered out.

"Sylvia Schon," she announced, standing and extending a hand across the desk. "It's a pleasure to meet you. It's not often the Chairman recommends a new graduate."

"He was a friend of my father's. They worked together." Nick shook his head as if to dismiss the connection. "It was a long time ago."

"So I understand. But the bank doesn't forget its own. We're big on loyalty around here." She motioned for him to sit down and when he had, lowered herself into her chair. "I hope you don't mind my asking a few questions. I take pride in knowing everyone who works in our department. Usually we insist on several interviews before extending an offer."

"I appreciate any exceptions that were made on my behalf. Actually, I did interview with Dr. Ott in New York."

"It was rather perfunctory, I imagine."

"Dr. Ott and I covered a lot of ground. If you're asking whether he went easy on me, he didn't."

Sylvia Schon raised an eyebrow and cocked her head as if to say, "Come now, Mr. Neumann, we both know you're full of shit." She was right, of course. His meeting with the bank's vice chairman had been nothing more than an extended bull session. Ott was a short, fat, unctuous man, an unapologetic arm patter, and it seemed to Nick that he'd been told to paint the sunniest possible picture of life in Zurich and a career at the United Swiss Bank.

"Fourteen months," she said. "That's the longest one of our American recruits has lasted. You gentlemen come over for a European vacation, do a little skiing, take in the sights, and a year later you're gone. Off to greener pastures."

"If there's been a problem, why don't you conduct the interviews yourself?" he asked pleasantly, in counterpoint to her combative tone. "I'm sure *you* would have no problem weeding out the weaker candidates."

Dr. Schon squinted her eyes, as if unsure whether he was a smart-ass or just an exceptionally perceptive individual. "An interesting question. Feel free to ask Dr. Ott next time you visit with him. Interviewing foreign candidates is his department. For now, though, let's concentrate on you, shall we? Our refugee from Wall Street. I don't imagine that a firm like Morgan Stanley often loses one of its best recruits after only four months."

"I decided that I didn't want to spend my career in New York. I've never had the opportunity to work in a foreign environment. I realized that if I wanted to move, the sooner the better."

"So you quit like that?" She snapped her fingers.

Nick was beginning to find her aggressive tone irritating. "First I spoke with Herr Kaiser.

He'd contacted me following my graduation in June and mentioned that he'd like me to come to the bank."

"You didn't consider anywhere else? London? Hong Kong? Tokyo? After all, if you were offered a position by Morgan Stanley, I'm sure there were other firms that went away disappointed. What brought you to Zurich?"

"I'd like to specialize in private banking, and for that Zurich's the place. No one has a better reputation than USB."

"So our reputation led you to our doorstep?"

Nick smiled. "Yes, exactly."

Liar, said a determined voice from a dark corner of his soul. You would've come if the place was buried in shit and the last shovel had just broken.

"Remember, things move slowly here. Don't expect a promotion to the executive board anytime soon. We're less a meritocracy than you Americans are used to."

"Minimum fourteen months," said Nick. "I should just be settling in by then. Getting to know my way around." He smiled broadly to let her know that he wasn't put off by her predictions of a short stay and that she should get used to him. But behind the smile, the determined voice had the final say.

I'll stay, it promised. Fourteen months or fourteen years. As long as it takes to discover why my father was murdered in the foyer of a close friend's home.

Sylvia Schon brought her chair closer to her desk and studied some documents on it. The room fell silent. The tension of a first encounter dissipated. Finally, she looked up and smiled. "You've met Mr. Sprecher, I understand? Everything satisfactory?"

Nick said yes.

"He explained to you, I'm sure, that his department is a little shorthanded."

"He said that Mr. Cerruti was ill. He'll be back next week."

"We hope so. Did he say anything else?"

Nick looked at her intently. She wasn't smiling anymore. What was she tiptoeing around? "No. Just that Cerruti had contracted a virus on his business trip."

Dr. Schon removed her glasses and pinched the bridge of her nose. "I'm sorry to bring this up on your first day of work, but I think it's best you hear it now. I don't suppose you know about Mr. Becker. He also worked in FKB4. He was killed Christmas Eve. Stabbed to death not far from here. We're still very upset. It's an absolute tragedy."

"He was the man killed on the Bahnhofstrasse?" Nick hadn't recalled the name, but he recognized the facts from an article in a Swiss newspaper he'd read on the flight over. The brazen nature of the murder made for front-page news. Apparently, he'd been carrying some expensive jewelry. The police did not

35

yet have a suspect, but the article had clearly stated that robbery was the motive. Somehow USB had managed to keep its name out of the paper.

"Yes. It's appalling. As I said, we're still in a state of shock."

"I'm sorry," Nick whispered.

"No, no. It's I who must apologize. No one deserves to hear such terrible news on their first day of work." Dr. Schon stood and circled her desk. A signal the meeting had come to its conclusion. She forced a smile to her lips. "I hope Mr. Sprecher won't pass along too many of his bad habits. You should be with him only a few days. In the meantime, several other matters need to be taken care of. We'll need a few photographs and your fingerprints, of course. Those can be taken down the hall, three doors to the right. And don't let me forget to give you a copy of the bank's handbook." She brushed by him and walked to a cabinet against the near wall. She opened a drawer, then picked out a blue book and offered it to him.

"Should I wait down here for the ID card to be finished?" Nick peered at the handbook. It was half the size of a phone book and twice as thick. *Rules,* he heard Sprecher saying.

"I don't think that will be necessary," boomed a rich, male voice.

Nick raised his head and looked directly into Wolfgang Kaiser's beaming face. He took a

36

step backward, though if it was from surprise or awe he did not know. Kaiser was his family's grayest eminence: ever watching unseen from somewhere beyond the horizon. After so long, Nick was unsure how to greet him. As the man who had attended his father's funeral and then accompanied the body to Switzerland for burial. As the distant benefactor who surfaced at odd moments across the years, sending congratulatory cards upon his graduation from high school and college and, Nick suspected, checks on the occasions when his mother had navigated them into particularly dire straits. Or as the celebrated icon of international business, the subject of a thousand newspaper articles, magazine profiles, and television interviews. The most recognized face of Switzerland's banking establishment.

Kaiser solved Nick's dilemma in an instant. Wrapping his right arm around his shoulders, he brought him close to his chest for a sturdy bear hug. He whispered something in his ear about the time that had passed and how he resembled his father and finally let him go, but not before kissing him smartly on the cheek.

"At your father's funeral, you told me that one day you would come back and take his place. Do you remember?"

"No, I don't," Nick said, embarrassed. He caught Sylvia Schon gazing at him, and for a second he had the feeling she was sizing him up not as a trainee but as an opponent.

"Of course not," said Kaiser. "What were you? Ten, eleven. Just a boy. But I remembered. I *always* remembered. And now here you are."

Nick grasped the Chairman's outstretched hand. It was a vise. "Thank you very much for finding room for me. I realize it was short notice."

"Nonsense. Once I make an offer, it stands. I'm glad we could lure you away from our American colleagues." Kaiser released his hand. "Dr. Schon putting you through her paces? We saw on your application that you speak our dialect. Made me feel better about the small push I gave on your behalf. *Sprechen sie gerne Schweitzer-Deutsch?*"

"*Natürlich,*" Nick answered. "*Leider han-i fascht kai Möglichkeit dazu, weisch?*" The language felt heavy on his tongue. Nothing like the ease with which it flowed from his mouth in the dozens of silent rehearsals he'd conducted for this moment. He saw a cloud darken Kaiser's animated features, then looked to Dr. Schon and saw the edges of her mouth turned up in a faint smile. What the hell had he said?

Kaiser switched back to English. "Give it a few weeks and it will come back to you. Ott told me that you did some research about the bank. He was impressed with it."

"My thesis," Nick explained, relieved to be back on solid footing. "A paper on the growing role of Swiss banks in international equity offerings."

"Is that right? Remember that first and foremost we are a Swiss bank. We've served our community and our country for over a hundred twenty-five years. Before there was a unified Germany, our headquarters stood on this very spot. Before the Suez Canal was completed, even before a tunnel had been built through the Alps, we were open for business. The world has changed tremendously since that time, and we're still open for business. Continuity, Nicholas. That's what we stand for."

Nick said he understood.

"We've assigned you to FKB4. One of our more important departments. You'll be looking after a great deal of money. I hope Cerruti will be back soon. He worked under your father and was thrilled to learn that you'd be joining us. Until then, do as Sprecher says." He shook Nick's hand again, and Nick had the feeling he wouldn't be seeing him anytime soon.

"You're on your own here," said Kaiser. "Your career is what you make it. Work hard and you'll succeed. And remember what we like to say: 'The bank before us all.' "

Kaiser said good-bye to Sylvia Schon, then marched out of the office.

Nick spun and faced her. "Just one question. What exactly did I say to the Chairman?"

39

She stood casually, arms crossed over her chest. "Oh, it's not what you said. It's how you said it. You addressed the Chairman of the fourth largest bank in Switzerland as if he were your closest drinking buddy. He was a little surprised, that's all. I don't think he gets it much. But I'd take his advice and brush up on your language skills. That's not quite the fluency we expected."

Nick heard the reprimand lurking within her words and felt ashamed for his shortcomings. It would not happen again.

"You have a great deal of advanced billing to live up to," she said. "More than a few people are interested in how you do here. As for me, I just hope you'll stay awhile."

"Thanks. I appreciate it."

"Don't misunderstand me, Mr. Neumann. It's my intention that the finance division demonstrate the lowest rate of employee turnover in the bank. No more. Call it my New Year's resolution."

Nick met her eye. "I won't disappoint you. I'll stick around."

After having his photograph taken — standard convict's pose, front and side views — and allowing himself to be fingerprinted, Nick retraced his steps to the elevator. He punched the call button and while he waited for it to arrive glanced around him. Opposite the corridor from which he had just come were a pair of glass doors. *"Logistik und Administration"* was painted in large block letters at eye level. Nick thought it strange he hadn't noticed the doors earlier. They seemed oddly familiar. Dismissing the elevator, he crossed the landing and placed his fingers on the panes of milky glass. He *had* seen these doors before. He had passed through them with his father on that last visit, so long ago. Room 103, he remembered. They had visited Room 103 to visit an old friend of his father's.

Nick could see himself as a boy, dressed in his gray trousers and blue blazer, hair cut as short as his father's, marching down the endless hallways. Even then, the little soldier. One vivid memory of that day had stayed with him over the years. Pressed up against a giant picture window, he remembered peering down at a busy street, feeling almost as if he were flying above it. "This is my home," his father had said, and he remembered finding it incomprehensible that his father had ever lived anyplace but Los Angeles.

Nick checked his watch. He wasn't expected back at any particular time, and Sprecher seemed easygoing enough. Why not have a look at Room 103? He doubted the same person still worked there, but it was his only point of reference. Decision made, he opened the door and entered a long hallway. Every five steps he passed an office. Stainless steel plates were posted beside each door. A room number was written large across the plates, and below it a four-letter departmental abbreviation followed by several three-letter groupings, no doubt the employees who worked within. In every instance the door was closed. No sounds escaped that might provide a clue as to the work being done inside.

Nick quickened his pace. Ten yards farther on, the corridor ended. The doorways to his left were unmarked. No number; no departmental abbreviation. He tried a handle and found it locked, then hurried on to the end of the hallway. When he saw that the last door on the left sported the number 103, he breathed a sigh of relief. The initials "DZ" were printed under the number. *Dokumentation Zentrale.* The bank's archives. There was certainly no grand view from there. Nick considered going in but thought better of it. What business could a trainee possibly have there on this, his first day on the job?

A familiar voice echoed his precise thoughts.

"What the hell are you doing down here?" demanded Peter Sprecher. He was carrying a load of papers under one arm. "I couldn't have been clearer with my instructions. Follow the yellow brick road, I said. Just like Dorothy."

Nick felt his body tense involuntarily. Sprecher had, in fact, said just that. "Follow the gold carpeting from the elevator to Dr. Schon's office and back again." What reason could Nick give for being at the portal to the bank's archives? How could he tell Sprecher he'd been chasing a ghost? He took a deep breath, willing himself to relax. "I must have taken a wrong turn. I was beginning to get worried that I wouldn't find my way back."

"If I'd known you were such a navigational whiz I would have given you this stack of papers to take for me." Sprecher motioned with his chin to the bulk of papers under his arm. "Client portfolios bound for the shredder. Keep moving. First office round the corner on the left."

Nick was relieved by the diversion. "Can I help you with them?" he asked.

"Not now you can't. Just stay with me and hold on to that handbook. That's work enough. I'll personally escort you back upstairs. It doesn't do to have new trainees wandering about the bowels of the bank."

Peter Sprecher led Nick back to the second floor and accompanied him to a suite of offices situated far along an interior passageway. "This is your new home," said Sprecher. "We call it the Hothouse."

A line of offices divided from one another by glass walls sprang from either side of a spacious central corridor. Executives sat inside several of the offices, engaged on the telephone or with their heads buried in a pile of documents. Nick's critical eye ran from the beige

43

carpeting to the pabulum furniture to the pewter wallpaper. Despite all the glass inside the building, there wasn't a single window looking onto the outside world.

Sprecher laid a hand on Nick's shoulder. "Not the most glamorous of spots, but it does serve its purpose."

"Which is?"

"Privacy. Silence. Confidentiality. Our holy vows."

Nick motioned toward the hive of offices. "Which one of these belongs to you?"

"Don't you really mean which will belong to you? Come on. I'll show you."

Sprecher lit a cigarette and walked slowly down the central corridor, speaking to Nick over his shoulder. "Most of our clients in FKB4 have given us discretionary control over their money. It's ours to play with as we see fit. You're familiar with the management of discretionary accounts?"

"Clients who prefer their accounts to be managed on a discretionary basis transfer all responsibility and authority regarding the investment of their assets to the bank. The bank invests the money according to a risk profile sheet supplied by the customer that defines the client's preference for stocks, bonds, and precious metals, as well as any particular investments he doesn't feel comfortable with."

"Very good," said Sprecher, as if feigning impression at a simple trick. "Dare I ask if you worked here before, or did they teach you that at Harvard Bragging School? Let me add that the client's money is invested according to a strict set of guidelines established by the bank's investment committee. If you have a hot tip about the next screaming IPO on the New York Stock Exchange, keep it to yourself. Our job is to oversee the proper administration of our clients' accounts. Though our title is portfolio manager, we haven't chosen a portfolio on our own in nineteen years. Our biggest choice is whether to invest in Ford versus General Motors, or Daimler-Benz versus BMW. What we do is administer. And we do it better than anyone on God's green Earth. Got it?"

"One hundred percent," said Nick, thinking he had just heard the Swiss banker's official credo.

They passed an empty office and Sprecher said, "That was Mr. Becker's office. I trust Dr. Schon filled you in on what happened."

"Was he a close friend of yours?"

"Close enough. He joined us in FKB4 two years ago. Awful going like that. And on Christmas Eve. Anyway, you'll be taking his office once your training's through. Hope you don't mind."

"Not at all," Nick said.

Sprecher arrived at the last office on the left side of the corridor. It was bigger than the others, and Nick could see that a second desk

45

had been moved into it. Sprecher strolled through the open door and sat down behind the larger of the two desks. "Welcome to my castle. Twelve years in grade and this is it. Take a seat. That's your place — until you learn the ropes."

The phone rang and Sprecher answered immediately, giving his family name, as was customary. "Sprecher speaking." After a moment, his eyes latched on to Nick. He lowered the phone, covering the receiver with his palm. "Be a good chap and run get me a cup of coffee, would you. Back there." He waved sloppily down the open corridor. "If you can't find it, ask somebody. Anyone will be happy to help you. Thanks."

Nick took his cue and stepped out of the office. Not exactly what he'd quit his job and moved four thousand miles across the Atlantic Ocean to do, but what the hell? Every job demanded that dues be paid. If fetching coffee was all this one entailed, he'd be a lucky man. Halfway down the hallway, he realized that he'd forgotten to ask how Sprecher wanted it. Ever the dutiful adjutant, he hustled back the short distance and tucked his head into his superior's office.

Sprecher was sitting with his head cradled in his hand, eyes staring at the floor. "I told you, George, it will take fifty thousand more to bring me over to your side of the fence. I'm not leaving for a nickel less. Call it a risk premium. You fellows are new at this sort of thing. I'm a bargain at that price."

Nick knocked on the glass wall, and Sprecher's head shot up abruptly. "What is it?"

"How do you want your coffee? Black? With sugar?"

Sprecher held the phone away from his ear, and Nick knew he was trying to figure out how much he had overheard. "George, I'll call you later. Have to run." He hung up the phone, then pointed to the chair in front of his desk. "Sit."

Nick did as he was told.

Sprecher drummed his fingers on the table for several seconds. "Are you one of those blokes always turning up where he doesn't belong? First I find you wandering about on the first floor, hanging around in front of DZ like a lost puppy. Now you come back here and stick your nose into my affairs."

"I didn't hear a thing."

"You heard plenty and I know it." Sprecher rubbed a hand along the back of his neck and exhaled wearily. "Thing is this, old boy, we're going to have to work together for the next little while. I trust you. You trust me. Understand the game? No room for tattling on each other. We're all grown-ups here."

"I understand," said Nick. "Look, I apologize for butting my head into your private conversation. You don't have to worry that I picked up something I shouldn't have. I

47

didn't. So please, put it out of your mind. Okay?"

Sprecher smiled easily. "And even if you did, you didn't, right, mate?"

Nick refused the offer of familiarity, guarding a serious tone. "Exactly."

Sprecher pushed back his head and laughed. "You're not bad for a Yank. Not bad at all. Now get the hell out of here and bring me my coffee. Black, two sugars."

Chapter 3

The call came that afternoon at three o'clock, just as Peter Sprecher had promised. One of their section's biggest fish; Marco Cerruti's most important client. A man known only by his account number and his nickname: the Pasha. Called every Monday and Thursday at three o'clock sharp. Never failed. More punctual than God. Or the Swiss themselves.

The phone rang a second time.

Peter Sprecher raised a finger to his mouth. "Just be quiet and listen," he ordered. "Your training officially begins now."

Nick paid close attention, curious as to what could make his boss so edgy.

Sprecher picked up the phone and placed it to his ear. "United Swiss Bank. Good afternoon." He paused and his shoulders stiffened. "Mr. Cerruti is not available."

Another pause while the other party spoke. Sprecher winced, then winced again. "I'm sorry, sir, I cannot tell you the reason for his absence. Yessir, I would be happy to provide you with information legitimizing my employ at USB. First, though, I require your account number."

He wrote a number on a blank slip of paper.

"I confirm your account number is 549.617 RR." He punched in a blizzard of numbers and commands into his desktop computer. "And your code word?"

His eyes scanned the monitor. A pinched smile indicated he was satisfied with the answer. "How may I help you today? My name is *Pee-ter Shprek-her.*" Slowly and clearly. "I am Mr. Cerruti's assistant." His brow furrowed. *"My bank reference?* Yessir, my three-letter reference is S-P-C." Another pause. "Mr. Cerruti is ill. I'm sure he'll be back with us next week. Any message you'd like me to pass on to him?"

Sprecher's pen flashed across the page. "Yes, I'll tell him. Now, how may we be of service?"

He listened. A command was entered into the computer. A moment later, he relayed the information to his client. "The balance of your account is twenty-six million dollars. Two six million."

Nick repeated the sum silently while his stomach dropped to the floor below. Twenty-six million dollars. Not bad, mister. For as long as he could remember he had been living on the tightest of budgets. There had been no fat since his father had died. Pocket money in high school came from part-time jobs at a dozen fast-food joints. Expenses in college were met through scholarships and a job tending bar — even if he had been two years under age. He'd finally earned a decent paycheck in the Corps, but after sending three hundred a month off the top to his mother, he'd been left with only enough for a small apartment off base, a used pickup, and a couple of six-packs on weekends. He tried to imagine what it would feel like to have twenty-six million dollars in his account. He couldn't.

Sprecher was listening intently to the Pasha. He nodded several times while bouncing a pencil off his thigh. Without warning he erupted in a flurry of disparate movements. The phone was tucked under the chin, the chair rolled backward toward the cabinet. Elbows flew, oaths were whispered. Finally an orange file was extracted and laid upon the desk. Still unsatisfied by his exertions, he lowered his head to search, along with five busy fingers, through the second drawer of his desk. Aha! Victory at last. He had found his treasure, in this case a mint green form bearing the words "Transfer of Funds" in bold capital letters, and now he waved it over his head as if he were a newly crowned Olympic champion.

Sprecher placed the phone to his mouth and took a deep breath before speaking. "I confirm that you wish to transfer the entire amount currently in the account, twenty-six million U.S. dollars, to the schedule of banks as listed per matrix three."

The orange file was opened, consulted, then

a five-digit operational code entered into the computer. Sprecher studied the screen as if he had discovered the Rosetta stone. "Twenty-two banks are listed. I will note that the transfer is to be urgent. The money is to be wired out before the end of business this day. Without fail. Yessir, I am aware that you have my bank reference. Not to worry. Thank you, sir. Good-bye, sir."

With a sigh, Sprecher laid the phone in its cradle. "The Pasha has spoken. So shall his will be done."

"Sounds like a demanding client."

"Demanding? More like dictatorial. Know what his message to Cerruti was? 'Get back to work.' There's a good chap for you." Sprecher laughed as if he couldn't believe the client's gall, but a moment later his features darkened. "It's not his manner that bothers me. It's his voice. Bloody cold. No emotion whatsoever. Like a man without a shadow. This is one client whose orders we follow to a T."

Nick was thinking that he wanted nothing to do with this difficult client. Let Cerruti handle him. Then he remembered the few words of Sprecher's conversation he had overheard earlier. *It will take fifty thousand more to bring me over to your side of the fence. I'm not leaving for a nickel less. Call it a risk premium. You fellows are new at this sort of thing.* If, in fact, Sprecher had been talking about leaving the bank, it might fall to Nick to handle the

Pasha in Cerruti's absence. The thought made him sit up a little straighter.

Sprecher asked, "Did you pay attention to the procedure I followed?"

Nick said he had. "No information given to the client until an account number is received and the account holder's identity confirmed."

"Bravo. That is step one, and I might add, the most important one."

"Step two, remove the client's dossier from that filing cabinet."

Turning his chair, Sprecher dragged a finger across the files visible in the open drawer. "The dossiers are filed in numerical order. No names, remember. Inside are his exact wire instructions. The Pasha uses this account strictly as a temporary way station. Money gets wired in at ten or eleven in the morning. He calls at three to check that it's here, then tells us to get rid of it by five."

"He doesn't keep any money on deposit here?"

"Cerruti whispered about him having over two hundred million at the bank — in shares and in cash. I've looked like hell for it, but Cerberus won't reveal a lick of information, will you, darling?" Sprecher patted the top of the gray computer monitor. "Uncle Peter doesn't have high enough clearance."

"*Cerberus?*" Nick asked.

"Our management information system. Guards our client's financial information like the three-headed hound at the gates to hell. Each employee has access only to those accounts the proper fulfillment of his job demands he see. I can look at the accounts in FKB4, but no others. The Pasha may have two hundred million dollars stashed away, but someone somewhere" — Sprecher jabbed a thumb toward the ceiling, indicating the Fourth Floor, where the top executives of the bank resided — "doesn't want me to see it."

"Do the Pasha's transfers always involve such a large sum?" Nick's curiosity was piqued by the likelihood, however remote, that one day he'd be on the receiving end of that phone call.

"Same instructions twice each week. The amounts vary but are never less than ten million. The highest I've seen in eighteen months was thirty-three million. Scoot your chair over here and let's look at his account together. The Pasha has set up seven matrices, each of which specifies the amounts we are to wire — as a percentage of the total sum in the account — and the institutions where they're to go. Look here: matrix three." Sprecher slid the orange file closer to Nick and peeled back the pages, stopping at a pink sheet. "We type each matrix on a different color sheet for easy differentiation. Matrix one is yellow, two is blue, three is pink. Cerberus has them all memorized, but we always double-check with the hard copy. Procedure."

Nick ran a finger along the list of banks: Kreditanstalt, Vienna; Bank of Luxembourg; Commerz Bank, Frankfurt; Norske Bank, Oslo. A numbered account was listed next to each bank. Nowhere on the paper was there an individual's name. "He's certainly well traveled."

"The money is, that's for sure. The Pasha chooses a different matrix each time he calls, and never in order. He skips around. But his instructions are always the same. Confirm the balance of his account. Transfer the entire amount to anywhere from twenty-two to thirty-three financial institutions around the world."

"I guess I shouldn't ask who he is, or why he's transferring his money through a maze of banks."

"And you'd be correct in that presumption. Don't get into any bad habits. All we need is another . . ." Sprecher exhaled. "Forget it."

"What?" Nick bit his tongue a second too late.

"Nothing," said Sprecher curtly. "Just do as you're told and remember one thing: We're bankers, not policemen."

" 'Ours is not to reason why,' " said Nick wryly. He'd meant it as a joke, but somehow in this office it sounded all too serious.

Sprecher clapped him on the back. "A quick learner, indeed."

"Let's hope so." *Keep your eyes open and your*

mouth shut, his father's stern voice reminded him. *Become one of them.*

Sprecher turned his attention back to the transfer of funds slip. He filled in the necessary information rapidly. When he was done, he checked the time, wrote it on the sheet, and finally signed it. "The Pasha requires our immediate and undivided attention. Therefore, it has become our practice to walk the sheet down to Payments Traffic in order to personally deliver it to Pietro, the clerk responsible for international transfers. When the Pasha says 'Urgent,' he means urgent. Come on, I'll show you where you'll be going every Monday and Thursday afternoon at three-fifteen."

After work, Peter Sprecher invited Nick to join him for a beer at the James Joyce pub, a popular watering hole for bankers and insurance executives, owned and operated by one of the United Swiss Bank's larger rivals, the mighty Union Bank of Switzerland. The pub was dark with low ceilings, lit by faux gas lamps and decorated with brass fixtures. Pictures of turn-of-the-century Zurich covered the walls.

Sprecher sat Nick in a corner booth and after quaffing an entire beer, began talking about his twelve years at the bank. He had started as a trainee fresh out of university, not so different from Nick. His first assignment had been a position on the trading floor. He'd hated it from day one. Every trader was held accountable for gains and losses in the investment "book" he managed, be it the Swiss franc versus the dollar, Iowa pork belly contracts, or South African platinum futures. That wasn't for him, he happily admitted. Private banking was where he belonged. The days were hardly pressure filled. Success was determined by your ability to massage the client, to convince him that a four percent annual return really wasn't something to fret about — and the bank took the heat for any poorly advised investments. It was heaven!

"The secret to this game," he pronounced, "is to reckon exactly who your key clients are. The big fish. Take good care of them and everything else will fall into place."

Sprecher hoisted a beer, sure to guard Nick's eye. "Cheers. To your future at USB!"

Nick departed after a third beer, saying he was still jet-lagged from his flight over Friday night. He left the bar and walked the short distance up the Bahnhofstrasse to the Paradeplatz. It was only seven-fifteen, yet the streets were quiet. Few people passed in either direction. The stores were closed, their expensive wares lit only by dim night-lights. Waiting for the tram, he felt as if he were defying a curfew or the last man standing after some terrible pestilence. He stood shivering, bundled tightly in his too thin overcoat. A solitary figure in a foreign land.

Only a month ago he had been a member in good standing of Morgan Stanley's fall batch of executive recruits. One of thirty blessed men and women (culled from a bumper crop of two thousand) who had deemed a starting salary of ninety thousand dollars, a signing bonus of seven thousand dollars, and a future promising untold millions adequate compensation for allowing the savviest brains on Wall Street to daily instill in them their combined and hard-earned knowledge. And not just another member of his class, but a leading one — for he had recently been offered his choice of positions as assistant to the chief of equity trading or junior member of the international mergers and acquisitions team, both plum assignments his fellow trainees would have killed, maimed, or mutilated to obtain.

On Wednesday, November 20, Nick received a call at work from his aunt Evelyn in Missouri. He remembered checking his watch the moment he heard her squeaky voice. Two oh five. He knew right away what she had to tell him. His mother was dead, she said. Heart failure. He listened as in lugubrious detail she chronicled his mother's deterioration these past years. She chastised him for not visiting, and he said he was sorry. Finally, he got the date of the funeral, then hung up.

He received the news stoically. He recalled massaging his chair's cool leather armrests as he struggled to show the proper shock and sadness at the news of his mother's death. If anything, he felt lighter, the proverbial weight lifted from his shoulders. His mother was fifty-eight years old and an alcoholic. Six years had passed since he'd spoken to her last. In a burst of temperance and good intention, she had called to say that she'd moved from California to her hometown of Hannibal, Missouri. A new beginning, she'd said. *Another one.*

Nick found a flight to St. Louis the next day and from the Gateway to the West, rented a car and drove the hundred miles upriver to Hannibal. He had come in a spirit of reconciliation. He would see her buried. He would forgive her her lapses as a parent and as a self-respecting adult — if only to gild his tarnished memory of her.

His childhood had been a record of sudden disappointments, his father's death being the first and of course the greatest. But others had followed, their arrival as regular as the change of seasons. Nick recalled them all — low points of a peripatetic adolescence flickering through his mind like an old, scratched film. His mother's remarriage to a larcenous real-estate developer; his stepfather's frittering away the insurance settlement, but not before delivering the family a financial coup de grâce — losing Alex Neumann's dream house at 805 Alpine Drive to repay a litigious investor; the Haitian divorce that followed.

Then came the "Fall": a downward spiral through the curdled underside of southern California: Redondo Beach, El Segundo, Hawthorne. Another marriage came and went, this one briefer, less expensive — by then there was nothing left to split, settle, or divide. And finally, mercifully, at seventeen, the split from his mother. His own "new beginning."

The day after the funeral, Nick drove downtown to a storage facility his mother had filled with reminders of her past. It was a grim task, sorting through her affairs. Box after box filled with souvenirs of a mundane and failed existence. A chipped piece of china he recognized as his grandmother's gift to the newlyweds; a manila envelope stuffed with grade cards from elementary school; and a box of record albums containing such gems as *Burl Ives' Christmas Favorites*, *Dean Martin Loves Somebody*, and *Von Karajan Conducts Beethoven* — the scratched soundtrack of his early childhood.

At day's end, Nick came upon two sturdy cartons well sealed with brown electrical tape and marked "A. Neumann. USB — L.A." Inside were his father's effects taken from his office in Los Angeles days after his death: a few paperweights, a Rolodex, a calendar showing scenes of Switzerland, and two calfskin agendas for the years 1978 and 1979. Half the agendas' pages were stained a muddy brown, swollen with the Mississippi floodwater that on two occasions had risen high inside the corrugated tin shed. But half were unharmed. And his father's looping script was easily legible almost twenty years after he had written it.

Nick stared, transfixed, at the agendas. He opened a cover and skimmed through the entries. Nervous energy coursed through his body like a weak current. Hands that had mastered the buck of a sawed-off twelve gauge trembled like a schoolboy's at his first communion. And for one quicksilver flash, his father was alive again, holding him on his lap in the downstairs study while a fire burned in the grate and a November rain pelted the windows. Nick had been crying, as he often did after hearing his parents argue, and father had taken his son aside to console him. Nick laid his head on his father's chest and, hearing the heart beating too fast, knew that his father was also upset. His father hugged him tightly and caressed his hair. "Nicholas," he said, his voice barely a whisper, "promise me that you'll remember me all of your life."

Nick stood motionless in the dank shed. The words echoed in his ears and for a second longer he swore he was staring into those cold blue eyes. He blinked, and the apparition, if it had been one, faded.

Once, that memory had been an important component of his daily life. For a year after his father's death, he had replayed it endlessly, hour after hour, day after day, trying to assign some deeper meaning to the words. Tortured by his futile curiosity, he had arrived at the conclusion that his father had been asking for his help, and that somehow he had failed him and was thus himself responsible for his murder. Sometime in his teens, the memory had faded and he had forgotten it. But he never quite absolved himself of his role in his father's death.

A decade had passed since that memory had taunted him. His father had been right to worry. He could hardly remember him.

Nick stayed in the shed for a while longer. He had given up the idea of learning more about his father. To have the opportunity from Alex Neumann's own hand was almost too much to believe. An unexpected gift. But his joy proved short-lived. A receipt acknowledging acceptance of his father's possessions signed by a "Mrs. V. Neumann" was tucked inside the front cover of one of the leather-bound books. His mother had known about the agendas. She had purposely hidden them from her only son.

Nick spent the return flight to New York examining the agendas. He read both from cover to cover, first perusing the daily entries, then, alarmed, slowing to read each page carefully. He found mentions of a slippery client who had threatened his father and with whom, despite this, he had been pressed to do business; a shadowy local company that had merited the attentions of the Zurich head office; and most interesting, one month before his father's death, a note providing the phone number and address of the Los Angeles field office of the Federal Bureau of Investigation. Taken singly, the entries constituted only small worries. Taken together, they demanded explanation. But when set against the backdrop of his father's unsolved murder and his own guilty memories, they ignited a fire of doubt whose flames cast ill-defined shadows on the inner workings of the United Swiss Bank and its clients.

Nick returned to work the next day. His training schedule called for classroom instruction from eight to twelve. An hour into the first lecture — some dry cant about the underpricing of initial public offerings — his attention began to waver. He cast his eye around the auditorium, sizing up his fellow trainees. Like him, they were graduates of America's leading business schools. Like him, they were pressed and coiffed and packaged into tailored designer suits and polished leather shoes. All managed to convey a slight insouciance in their postures while writing down every single word the speaker uttered. They regarded themselves as the chosen ones, and in fact, they were. Financial centurions for the new millennium.

Why then did he hate them so?

The afternoon saw his return to the trading

floor. He took up his position at the elbow of Jennings Maitland, resident bond guru and avowed nail chewer. "Sit yer ass down, shut yer toilet, and listen up" was Maitland's daily greeting. Nick did as he was told and for the next four hours immersed himself in the floor's activity. He paid close attention as Maitland spoke with his clients. He kept dutiful track of the trader's open positions. He even celebrated his boss's sale of ten million bonds to the New York Housing Authority with an airborne high five. But inside him, his guts roiled and he wanted to throw up.

Five days before, Nick would have flushed with pride at Maitland's big score as if his own presence were responsible in some minor, inconstruable way for the sale. Today he viewed the commerce with a jaundiced eye, wishing to distance himself not only from his boss's dumping of ten million bonds ("fuckin' dogs," to quote Maitland, "real bowwows") but from the entire trading operation.

He stood as if to stretch and peered around him. Row upon row of computer monitors stacked three high ran what looked like the length of a football field in every direction. A week ago he had gloried at the sight, thinking it a modern battlefield. He had relished his opportunity to join the fray. Today it looked like a technological minefield, and he wanted to stay the hell away from it. Lord pity the robots who passed their lives glued to bank upon bank of microwave-spewing cathode-ray tubes.

During the long walk home, Nick told himself his disillusion was temporary and come tomorrow he would regain his appetite for work. But five minutes after setting foot inside his apartment, he found himself pasted to his desk scrabbling through his father's agendas, and he knew he'd been lying to himself. The world, or at least his view of it, had changed.

Nick went back to work the next day, and the day after that. He managed to keep up an eager facade, to pay attention in class and to laugh when required, but inside him a new plan was taking shape. He would resign from the firm, he would fly to Switzerland, and he would take the job Wolfgang Kaiser had offered him.

Friday night, he broke the news to his fiancée. Anna Fontaine was a senior at Harvard, a dark-haired Brahmin from the crustiest section of Boston with an irreverent wit and the kindest eyes he'd ever seen. He'd met her a month after beginning his studies. And a month after that they were joined at the hip. Before moving to Manhattan, he asked her to marry him and she'd said yes, without hesitation. "Yes, Nicholas, I want to be your wife."

Anna listened without speaking as he laid out his argument. He explained that he had to go to Switzerland to find out what his father had been involved in when he was killed. He didn't know how long he would be away — a month, a year, maybe longer — he only knew that he had to give his father's life an ending. He handed her the agendas to read, and when she had finished, he asked her to go with him.

She said no. Without hesitation. And then she told him why he, too, could not go. First off, there was his job. It was what he'd been slaving for his entire life. No one passed up a slot at Morgan Stanley. One in seventy. Those were the odds of nabbing a slot as an executive trainee at Morgan Stanley, and that was after you'd made it through college and business school. "You did it, Nick," Anna said, and even now, he could hear the pride in her voice.

But all he had to do was look at the agendas to know he hadn't done anything at all.

What about her family? she asked, her delicate fingers interlaced with his. Her father had taken to Nick like a second son. Her mother couldn't go a day without asking how he was and cooing about his latest successes. They would be crushed. "You are a part of us, Nick. You can't leave."

But Nick could not become part of another family until the mystery of his own was solved.

"And what about you and me?" she asked him finally, and he could see how much she hated to resort to her own attachment to convince him to stay. She reminded him of all the things they'd said to each other: that they were in it for the long haul; that they were the ones who really loved each other; friends forever, lovers who would die in each other's arms. Together they'd take Manhattan. And he'd believed her. Hell, he'd believed all of it because it was true. As true as anything he'd ever known.

But that was before his mother died. Before he found the agendas.

In the end, Anna couldn't understand. Or she just refused to. She broke off their engagement a week later, and he had not spoken to her since.

A sharp wind blew, mussing Nick's hair and bringing tears to his eyes. He had given up his job. Shit, he'd even returned his seven-thousand-dollar signing bonus. He had cut off his fiancée, the one woman he'd ever really loved. He had turned his back on his entire world to track down a phantom lying hidden almost twenty years. For what?

It was at this moment that for the first time Nick felt the unalloyed impact of his decision. And it hit him like a sucker punch to the gut.

The number thirteen tram pulled into the Paradeplatz, metal wheels groaning as the brakes were applied. Nick climbed aboard and had the pick of the entire car. He slid into a seat halfway back. The tram started forward with a jolt, and the abrupt movement refocused his attentions on the memories of the day. The moment of utter panic when for one life-ending second he'd truly believed that in a matter of hours Peter Sprecher was going to stick him in front of the paying public; his being found in front of *Dokumentation Zentrale,* ostensibly lost; and worst, his unforgivable faux pas when addressing Wolfgang Kaiser informally in Swiss-German.

He pressed his cheek to the window and kept his eye on the brooding gray buildings that lined both sides of the Stockerstrasse. Zurich was not a friendly town. He was a stranger here and he'd better remember it. The jar and rustle of the tram, the empty cabin, the unfamiliar environs, all of it only bolstered his uncertainty while amplifying his loneliness. What could he have been thinking, giving up so much to come on this wild goose chase?

Soon the tram slowed and Nick heard the driver's gruff voice announce his stop. *Utobrücke.* He lifted his cheek from the window and stood up, grabbing the overhead safety rail for balance. The tram stopped and he stepped outside, happy to be wrapped in the night's cold embrace. His worries had bound themselves together into a prickly ball and taken refuge in a hollow basin deep inside his stomach. He recognized the feeling. Fear.

It was the feeling he'd had before walking into his first high school dance when he was thirteen, the dread that came from knowing that once you stepped into the auditorium you were putting yourself on display, and one way or the other you had to ask a girl to dance and just pray you wouldn't be rejected.

It was the feeling he'd had the day he'd reported to officer candidate school in Quantico, Virginia. There was a moment when all the recruits were gathered in the processing hall. The paperwork was finished, the physical exams were completed; suddenly, the hall became very quiet. Every man in the room knew that on the other side of the steel fire doors, ten rabid drill instructors were waiting for them, and that in three months they'd either be a second lieutenant in the United States Marine Corps or a washout standing on a street corner somewhere with a couple of dollars in their pocket and a label that they'd never be able to erase.

Nick watched the tram recede into the darkness. He breathed in the pure air and relaxed, if only a little. He had given a name to his uncertainty and its recognition strengthened him. As he walked, he consoled himself. He was on an upward track. College at Cal State Northridge, the Corps, Harvard B-School. He had made something of his life. As far back as he could remember he had promised to pull himself out of the slime into which he'd been thrust. He had sworn to reclaim the birthright his father had worked so hard to give him.

For seventeen years these had been his guiding lights. And on this winter's night, with a new challenge before him, he saw them more clearly than ever.

Chapter 4

One week later, Marco Cerruti had still not returned to his desk in the Hothouse. No further word regarding his condition had been passed along. Only an ominous memo from Sylvia Schon that no personal calls should be made to the sick portfolio manager and the firm instructions that Mr. Peter Sprecher should assume all his superior's responsibilities, including the attendance of a biweekly investment allocation meeting from which he had just returned.

Talk at the meeting had not centered on the ailing Cerruti. In fact, his condition was never mentioned. Since nine o'clock that morning, those present at the meeting, as well as every other living, breathing employee of the bank, had been talking about one thing and one thing only: the shocking announcement that the Adler Bank, an outspoken rival whose headquarters sat no more than fifty yards down the Bahnhofstrasse, had purchased five percent of USB's shares on the open market.

The United Swiss Bank was in play.

Nick read aloud from a Reuters financial bulletin that blinked across his monitor. "Klaus Konig, Chairman of the Adler Bank, today announced the purchase of a five percent stake in the United Swiss Bank. Citing USB's 'grossly insufficient return on assets,' Konig vowed to take control of the board of directors and force a repositioning of the bank into more lucrative activities. The transaction is valued at over two hundred million Swiss francs. USB shares are up ten percent in heavy trading."

" 'Grossly insufficient return,' " said Sprecher indignantly, slamming a fist onto his desk. "Am I losing my mind or did we not report record earnings last year, an increase in net profits of twenty-one percent?"

Nick peered over his shoulder. "Konig didn't say there was anything wrong with our profits. Only with our return on assets. We're not using our money aggressively enough."

"We are a conservative Swiss bank," Sprecher spat out. "We're not supposed to be aggressive. Konig must think he's in America. An unsolicited takeover bid in Switzerland. It's never been done. Is he totally insane?"

"There's no law against hostile takeovers," said Nick, enjoying his role as devil's advocate. "My question is, where is he getting the money? He'd need four or five billion francs before it's all over. The Adler Bank doesn't have that kind of cash."

"Konig might not need it. He only needs thirty-three percent of USB's shares to gain three seats on the board. In this country that's a blocking stake. All decisions taken by the board of directors must carry by two thirds of those voting. You don't know Konig. He's a wily one. He'll use his seats to foment a rebellion. Make everyone's dick hard by bragging about Adler's fantastic growth."

"That shouldn't be too difficult. The Adler Bank's profits have grown at something like forty percent per year since its founding. Last year Konig's bank earned over three hundred million francs after tax. There's a lot to be impressed about."

Sprecher eyed Nick quizzically. "What are you? A walking financial encyclopedia?"

Nick shrugged. "I wrote my thesis on the Swiss banking industry. The Adler Bank is a new breed over here. Trading is their principal activity. Using their own capital to bet on stocks, bonds, options; anything whose price can go up or down."

"Figures then that Konig would want USB. Get his greedy hands into the private banking side of things. He used to work here, you know — years ago. He's a gambler. And a canny one at that. 'A repositioning into more lucrative activities.' I can just see what he means by that. It means betting the firm's capital on the outcome of next week's OPEC meeting or guessing the next actions of the United States Federal Reserve. It means risk spelled in capital letters. Konig wants to get his hands on our assets to increase the size of the Adler Bank's bets."

Nick studied the ceiling as if figuring a complex equation. "Strategically, it's a sound move for him. But it won't come easy. No Swiss bank will fund an attack on one of their own. You don't invite the devil into the house of the Lord, not if you're a priest. Konig would have to attract private investors, dilute his ownership. I wouldn't worry yet. He only holds 5 percent of our shares. All he can do is scream a little louder at the general assembly."

A sarcastic voice smirked from the entryway, "The future of the bank decided by two of its greatest minds. How reassuring." Armin Schweitzer, the bank's director of compliance, marched into the Hothouse, stopping before Nick's desk. "Well, well, our newest recruit. Another American. They come and go once a year — like a bad case of the flu. Made the reservations for your return flight yet?" He was a bullet-shaped man of sixty, all hulking shoulders and gray flannel. He had steady dark eyes and a tight, pained mouth.

"I plan on a long stay in Zurich," Nick said, after he had risen and introduced himself. "I'll do my best to better your impression of American labor."

Schweitzer's meaty hand appraised the stubble of his scalp. "My impression of American labor was destroyed long ago, when as a young man I made the regrettable mistake of

73

purchasing a Corvair." He pointed a stubby finger at Peter Sprecher. "Some news regarding your esteemed superior. A private chat, if you please."

Sprecher rose and followed Schweitzer from the room.

Five minutes later, he returned alone. "It's Cerruti," he said to Nick. "He's out until further notice. A nervous breakdown."

"From what?"

"That's what I'm asking myself. Sure, Marco is high-strung, but with him it's a permanent condition. Kind of like it is for Schweitzer to be an asshole. He can't help it."

"How long is he gone for?"

"Who knows? They want us to run this section as is. No replacement for Cerruti. The first fallout from the good Mr. Konig's announcement: control rising costs." Sprecher sat down at his desk and searched for his security blanket, the red and white pack of Marlboros. "Christ, first Becker, now Cerruti."

And when are *you* out of here? Nick asked silently.

Sprecher lit his cigarette, then pointed the burning embers at his colleague. "Any reason why Schweitzer should dislike you? I mean besides being a cocky American."

Nick laughed uneasily. He didn't like the question. "No."

"Ever meet him before?"

"No," Nick repeated louder. "Why?"

"He said he wants a sharp eye kept on you. He was serious."

"He said what?"

"You heard me. I'll tell you something — you do not want Schweitzer on your tail. He's relentless."

"Why should Schweitzer want you to look after me?" Had Kaiser given him those instructions?

"Probably just because's he's an anal retentive prick. No other reason."

Nick sat forward, ready to protest. The phone rang on his desk. He picked it up on the first ring, happy to be saved from making a disparaging remark about the bank's director of compliance. "Neumann," he said.

"Good morning. Sylvia Schon speaking."

"Good morning, Dr. Schon. How are you?"

"Well, thank you." A dismissal — trainees had no business engaging in pleasantries with their superiors — but then the voice eased. "Your Swiss-German is sounding better already."

"I still need a little time to get it back, but thanks." He was surprised how good the compliment made him feel. He'd been spending an hour every evening reading aloud and having conversations with himself, yet until now no one had remarked on his improvement.

"And your work?" she asked. "Mr. Sprecher providing proper guidance?"

Nick eyed the pile of portfolios sitting on his desk. It was his job to make sure that the investments in each corresponded to the breakdown set forth by the investment allocation committee. Today that breakdown stipulated a mix of thirty percent stocks, forty percent bonds, and ten percent precious metals, with the rest to be kept in cash. "Yes, plenty to do up here. Mr. Sprecher is keeping me very busy."

Across the desk, Sprecher tittered.

"It's a shame about Mr. Cerruti. I suppose you've heard."

"Just a few minutes ago, as a matter of fact. Armin Schweitzer informed us."

"Under the circumstances, I wanted to schedule a time to meet with you to make sure you're settling in all right. I'm holding you to your promise of fourteen months." Nick thought he heard a smile in her voice. "I'd like to suggest a dinner, something a little more informal than usual. Let's say February 6 at Emilio's."

"February 6 at Emilio's," Nick repeated. He asked her to wait one moment, then put the phone on his shoulder while he checked an invisible calendar. "That would be fine. Yes, perfect."

"Seven o'clock, then. In the meantime I need to see you in my office. We have to cover some issues regarding our bank secrecy requirements. Do you think Mr. Sprecher could spare you tomorrow morning around ten?"

Nick glanced at Sprecher, who stared back, a bemused grin screwing up his face. "Yes, I'm sure Mr. Sprecher can do without me for a few minutes tomorrow morning."

"Very good. I'll see you then." Instantly she was gone.

Nick hung up the phone and asked Sprecher, "What?"

Sprecher chuckled. "Emilio's, eh? Can't recall seeing any personnel files in there. But it's bloody good grub and not cheap either."

"It's routine. She wants to make sure I'm not too worried about Cerruti."

"Routine, Nick, is the cafeteria. Third floor, down the hallway to your left. Wiener schnitzel and chocolate pudding. Dr. Schon has something else in mind for you. Don't think for a second she doesn't know of our august chairman's interest in you. She wants to make sure you're well fed and comfortable. Can't afford to lose you, can she?"

"You've got this all worked out, haven't you?"

"Some things even Uncle Peter can figure out on his own."

Nick shook his head in disbelief, laughing. He reached for his agenda and penciled in her name on the appropriate page. His date with Sylvia Schon — check that, his *meeting* with her — would constitute its first entry. He raised his eyes and saw Sprecher typing a letter on his computer. Bastard still had a smirk on his face. *She has something else in mind for you,* he'd said.

Nick ran the words through his mind a second time, and then a third. What exactly had Sprecher meant? As he pondered his colleague's comments, his unsupervised imagination wandered down to the first floor and tiptoed into Dr. Schon's cozy office. He saw her working diligently behind her cluttered desk. Her glasses were pushed into her hair, her blouse unbuttoned a notch lower than perfectly decent. Her slim fingers massaged a chain that dangled from her neck and brushed the swell of her cleavage.

As if reading his thoughts, Sprecher said, "Watch yourself, Nick. They're smarter than we are, you know."

Nick looked up, startled. "Who?"

Sprecher winked. "Women."

Nick averted his gaze, though if it was from guilt or embarrassment he didn't know. The frank sexual nature of his daydream surprised him. He had no doubt where it would have led had Sprecher not interrupted him, and even now he found it difficult to clear his mind of the seductive images.

Two months ago he'd been ready to bind himself to another woman for the rest of his life. A woman he'd loved and respected and relied on more than he ever knew was possible. Part of him still refused to believe that Anna

Fontaine was gone. But as his vivid daydream made clear, another part of him had resolved itself to the fact, and was antsy to move on. One thing, though, was perfectly clear. A relationship with Sylvia Schon was not the place to start.

Nick returned to his task of verifying that their clients' portfolios met the proper strategic asset allocation model. It was a monotonous chore and in theory never ending, for the bank changed its investment mix every sixty days or so, just the amount of time he'd need to make it through every one of his section's seven hundred discretionary clients.

After a week at the bank, his days had assumed a familiar pattern. He rose each morning at six, then forced himself to withstand fifteen seconds of an ice-cold shower (an old habit from the Corps), the theory being that after suffering through the frosty agony the rest of the day didn't look so bad. He left his one-room apartment at 6:50, caught the 7:01 tram, and hit the office by 7:30, latest. Normally he was among the first to arrive. His morning's work invariably concerned gathering a group of client portfolios and studying them for stocks performing poorly or bonds that were due to expire. These noted, he issued sell recommendations that Sprecher approved uniformly.

"Remember, chum," Sprecher was fond of saying, "revenue is paramount. Commissions must be generated. It's the only *true* yardstick of our diligence."

But Nick's activities were not restricted to those set forth by Peter Sprecher. Each day he found time to pursue inquiries of a more private nature. His unofficial duties, he liked to call them, and these involved finding ways to dig into the bank's past, to see what nuggets he might discover about his father's work those many years ago. His first excursion, undertaken on the Wednesday after his arrival, was to the bank's research library, *WIDO — Wirtschafts Dokumentation.* There he scoured old annual reports, documents issued internally before the bank had gone public in 1980. He found a mention of his father in several of them, but only a passing reference or a notation in an organigram. Nothing that might shed any real light on his day-to-day tasks.

Other times, Nick studied the bank's internal phone directory searching for names of executives that sounded familiar (none did) while checking by rank who might have been at the bank with his father. It was a hopeless task. To approach every executive over the age of fifty-five and inquire whether he had known his father was to invite news of his activities to be publicly broadcast.

Twice Nick returned to *Dokumentation Zentrale.* He would slide by the door, daring himself to step inside, dreaming of the miles and miles of retired papers he'd find filed in me-

80

ticulous order. He grew convinced that if his father's murder was tied in any way to his activities on behalf of the bank or its clients, the only extant clues would be found there.

The call came that afternoon at three o'clock, as it had the previous Monday and Thursday. As it had for the past eighteen months, maybe longer, said Peter Sprecher. Nick found himself guessing the amount the Pasha would transfer that day. Fifteen million dollars? Twenty million? More? Last Thursday the Pasha had transferred sixteen million dollars from his account to the banks listed on matrix five. Less than the twenty-six million he had transferred the previous Monday, but still a king's ransom.

Nick thought it odd, as well as inefficient, that they had to wait to check the balance of account 549.617 RR until the Pasha phoned. Rules forbade the perusal of a client's accounts. Why didn't the Pasha just leave a standing order at the bank asking that all moneys that accumulated in the account be transferred out every Monday and Thursday? Why this waiting until three o'clock to call, this causing such a rush to wire the funds out before closing?

"Twenty-seven million four hundred thousand dollars," said Peter Sprecher to the Pasha. "To be transferred on an urgent basis according to matrix seven." He was using a voice he'd labeled the disinterested monotone of the professionally jaded.

Nick handed him the orange file, opened to matrix seven, and silently read the banks listed: Hong Kong and Shanghai Bank; Singapore Trade Development Bank; Daiwa Bank. Some European banks were included: Credit Lyonnais; Banco Lavoro; even the Moscow Narodny Bank. A total of thirty internationally respected financial institutions.

Later, as Nick left to deliver the transfer of funds form to Pietro in Payments Traffic, he thought of the seven pages of wire instructions included in the Pasha's file and the hundreds of banks that were listed. Try as he might, he could not help himself from imagining the scope of the Pasha's activities.

Was there one bank in the world with which the Pasha did *not* maintain an account?

The next morning at ten A.M. sharp Nick presented himself at the door to Dr. Sylvia Schon's office. He knocked once, then entered. Apparently her assistant was either sick or on vacation, for as on the first day he had met her, the office was empty. He made some shuffling noises, then said, "Neumann here. Ten o'clock meeting with Dr. Schon."

She responded immediately. "Come right in, Mr. Neumann. Sit down. I'm glad to see that you are punctual."

"Only when it keeps me on time."

She did not smile. As soon as he was seated, she began speaking. "In a few weeks you'll begin meeting clients of the bank. You'll help them review the status of their portfolios, assist in administrative matters. Most likely, you will be their only contact with the bank. Our human face. I'm sure Mr. Sprecher has been teaching you how to handle yourself in such situations. It's my job to ensure that you are aware of your obligation to secrecy."

The second day on the job, Nick had been presented by Peter Sprecher with a copy of the country's legislation governing bank secrecy — "Das Bank Geheimnis." He had been forced to read it, then sign a statement acknowledging his understanding of, and compliance with, the article. Sprecher hadn't made a single wisecrack the entire time.

"Are there any further papers I need to sign?" Nick asked.

"No. I'd just like to go over some general rules to stop you from developing any bad habits."

"Please, go ahead." This was the second time he'd been warned about bad habits.

Sylvia Schon clasped her hands and laid them on the desk in front of her. "You will not discuss the affairs of your clients with anyone other than your departmental superior," she said. "You will not discuss the affairs of your clients once you leave this building. No exceptions. Not over lunch with a friend and not over cocktails with Mr. Sprecher."

Nick wondered whether the rule of discussing the affairs of his clients only with his departmental superior would supersede the "no discussion over booze" rule but decided to keep his mouth shut.

"Be sure not to discuss any business concerning the bank or its clients over a private telephone, and never take home any confidential documentation. Another thing . . ."

Nick shifted in his seat. His eyes wandered the perimeter of her office. He was looking for some personal touch that might give him an idea about who she really was. He didn't see any photographs or keepsakes on her desk. No vase of flowers to brighten up the office. Only a bottle of red wine on the floor next to the filing cabinet behind her desk. She was all business.

". . . and it's never wise to make personal notes on your private papers. You can't be sure who might read them."

Nick tuned back in. After a few more minutes, he felt like adding "Loose lips sink ships" or "Shh, Fritz might be listening." The whole thing was a little dramatic, wasn't it?

As if sensing his mental opposition, Sylvia Schon stood abruptly from her chair and circled her desk. "You find this amusing, Mr. Neumann? I must say that is a particularly American response — your cavalier attitude about authority. After all, what are rules for, if not to be broken? Isn't that how you look at things?"

Nick sat up stiffly in his chair. Her vehemence surprised him. "No, not at all."

Sylvia Schon perched herself on the corner of the desk nearest him. "Just last year a banker at one of our competitors *was jailed* for violating the bank secrecy law. Ask me what he did."

"What did he do?"

"Not much, but as it turned out enough. During Fastnacht, the carnival season, it's a tradition in Basel to turn off all the town lights until 3:00 A.M. the morning the carnival commences. During this time the Fastnachters congregate in the streets and make merry. There are many bands, costumes. It's quite a spectacle. And when the lights are turned on, the *Stadtwohner,* the persons living in the city, shower the revelers with confetti."

Nick kept his gaze focused. The smart-ass in the back of his mind was sitting in the corner until further punishment was handed down.

Sylvia continued, "One banker had taken home old printouts of his client's portfolios — passed through the shredder, of course — to use as confetti. Come three o'clock in the morning, he threw these papers out the window and littered the streets with confidential client information. The next morning, street cleaners found the shredded printouts and handed them over to the police, who were able

85

to make out several names and account numbers."

"You mean they arrested the guy for using shredded portfolio printouts as confetti?" He recalled the story of the Esfahāni rug weavers of Iran who had painstakingly reassembled the thousands of documents shredded by U.S. Embassy personnel in Tehran just after the shah's fall. But that was a fundamentalist Islamic revolution. In what country did street cleaners burden themselves with the responsibility to inspect their pickings? And worse, rush to the police to report their discoveries?

She blew the air from her cheeks. "This was a major scandal. Aachh! The fact that the papers were unreadable is secondary. It's the idea that a trained banker violated the confidence of his clients. The man was put in jail for six months. He lost his position at the bank."

"Six months," Nick repeated gravely. In a country that didn't prosecute tax evasion as a criminal offense, half a year for throwing shredded papers out the window was a stiff sentence.

Sylvia Schon put her hands on Nick's chair and brought her face close to his. "I am telling you these things for your own benefit. We take our laws and our traditions seriously. You must also."

"I realize the importance of confidentiality. I'm sorry if I looked as if I were growing impatient, but the rules you were reciting sounded like common sense."

"Bravo, Mr. Neumann. That's just what they are. Unfortunately, common sense isn't so common anymore."

"Maybe not."

"At least we're in agreement there."

Dr. Schon returned to her chair and sat down. "That's all, Mr. Neumann," she said coldly. "Time to get back to work."

Chapter 5

On a snowy Friday evening, three weeks after he had begun work at the United Swiss Bank, Nick made his way through the back alleys of Zurich's old town en route to a rendezvous with Peter Sprecher. "Be at the Keller Stübli at seven sharp," Sprecher had said when he called in at four that afternoon, several hours after failing to return to the office from lunch. "Corner of Hirschgasse and the Niederdorf. Old sign banged all to hell. Can't miss it, chum."

The Hirschgasse was a narrow alley whose lopsided brickwork snaked uphill about a hundred yards from the river Limmat to the Niederdorfstrasse, the old town's primary pedestrian thoroughfare. A few lights burned from cafés or restaurants at the top of the street. Nick walked toward them. After a few steps, he was aware of a shadow over his head. Sprouting from the wall of a pockmarked building was a bent wrought iron sign from which chipped gold leaf hung in tatters like moss from a willow. Below the sign was a wooden door with a ringed knocker and an iron window grate. A plaque buried in verdigris bore the words *"Nunc Est Bibendum."* He ran the Latin words through his mind and smiled. "Now is the time to drink." Definitely, Sprecher's type of establishment.

Nick opened the heavy door and entered a dark, wood-paneled watering hole that reeked of stale smoke and spilled beer. The room was half-empty but sported the type of seedy decor that made him think that soon it would be filled to capacity. A Horace Silver tune played wistfully from the sound system.

"Glad you could make it," yelled Peter Sprecher from the far end of an arolla pine bar. "Appreciate your showing at such short notice."

Nick waited until he reached the bar before answering. "I had to juggle my schedule," he said wryly. He didn't have a friend in the city and Peter knew it. "Missed you this afternoon."

Sprecher threw open his arms. "A meeting of great import. An interview. An offer even."

Nick heard at least three beers talking. "An offer?"

"I accepted. Being a man of few principles and unrivaled greed, it was an easy decision to make."

Nick drummed his fingers on the countertop, digesting the news. He recalled the snippet of conversation he'd overheard his first day at work. So Sprecher had gotten his extra fifty thousand. The question now was from whom. "I'm waiting for the details."

"Take my word, you'll need a drink first."

Sprecher drained the glass in front of him and ordered two Cardinals. When the beers arrived, Nick took a decent swig, then set his glass on the bar. "Ready."

"The Adler Bank," said Sprecher. "They're starting a private banking department. Need warm bodies. Somehow they found me. They're offering a thirty percent boost in salary, a guaranteed fifteen percent bonus, and in two years, stock options."

Nick could not conceal his surprise. "After twelve years at USB, you're going to work for the Adler Bank? They're the enemy. Last week you were calling Klaus Konig a gambler and a bastard, to boot. Peter, you're due for a promotion to first vice president later this year. The Adler Bank? You're not serious?"

"Oh, but I am. The decision has been made. And by the way, I called Konig a canny gambler. 'Canny' as in successful. 'Canny' as in wealthy, and 'wealthy' as in extremely fucking rich. If you'd like, I'll put in a word for you. Why break up a good team?"

"Thanks for the offer, but I'll pass."

Nick found it difficult to think of his colleague's action as anything but a betrayal. Then he wondered: Of what? Of whom? Of the bank? Of *himself?* And knowing full well he had hit upon the answer, chastised himself for his selfish thoughts. In their short time together, Sprecher had slipped into the role of irreverent big brother, dispensing advice on personal and professional matters. His easy banter and cynical worldview were welcome antidotes to the rigid bureaucracy of their workplace. They'd continued their relationship after hours, Sprecher leading the way to one bar or another, Pacifico, Babaloo, Kaufleuten. Soon he'd be leaving the bank and giving up his role as a supporting player in Nick's life.

"So you're going to leave the Pasha to me?" Nick asked. Business seemed a sturdy refuge for his disappointment. He remembered Sylvia Schon's admonitions about client confidentiality and realized too late that he'd acted as cavalierly as she had expected. Just another American.

"The Pasha!" Sprecher swallowed hard and slammed his beer onto the counter. "Now there's a rum bastard, if ever was one. Money's so hot he can't leave it in one spot for more than one hour for fear it'd burn through his mum's ironing board."

"Don't be so sure of his wrongdoing," Nick countered reflexively. "Regular deposits of customer receivables, quick payment of suppliers. It could be one of a thousand businesses. All of them legal."

"Suppliers in every goddamned country around the globe?" Sprecher waved his hands, dismissing the suggestion. "Black, white, gray, let's not argue legality. In this world everything is legal until you get caught. Don't misunderstand me, young Nick, I'm not passing judgment on our friend. But as a businessman, I'm interested in his game. Is he looting the coffers of the U.N. — a bent administrator lining his pockets with gold? Is he some tin-pot dictator siphoning off his weekly due from the widows and orphans fund? Maybe he's pushing coke to the Russians? Few months back we sent a bundle to Kazakhstan, I recall. Alma bloody Ata, Nick. Not your everyday commercial destination. There are a thousand ways to skin a cat and I'll wager he's a master at one of them, our Pasha is."

"I'll grant you his transactions are interesting, but that doesn't make them illegal."

"Spoken like a true Swiss banker. 'The Pasha,' " Sprecher announced, as if reading a newspaper headline, "an 'interesting' client makes 'interesting' transfers of 'interesting' sums of money. You'll go far in this life, Mr. Neumann."

"Didn't you tell me that it's really none of our concern what he does? That we shouldn't poke our noses into our clients' business. We're bankers, not policemen. You said that, right?"

"I did indeed. You'd have thought I'd have learned by now."

"What's that supposed to mean?"

Sprecher lit a cigarette before answering. "Put it this way, it's not just more money that's got me leaving the bank. Your friend, Peter, has a dash of self-preservation in him. Cerruti out with a nervous breakdown — might never come back. Marty Becker just plain dead — definitely can't count on him. Survival instinct, you boys in the marines might call it."

It hadn't taken Nick long to question the odds of two portfolio managers from the same department being knocked out of their jobs by sickness or, in Becker's case, murder. After all, his own father's murder was unrelated to his work at the bank. At least officially. Still, he had dismissed Cerruti's illness as a case of personal burnout, and he had never questioned the fact that Becker's murder was a mugging gone awry.

"What happened to them had nothing to do with their work." He hesitated a second. "Did it?"

"Of course it didn't," Sprecher said earnestly. "Cerruti's been a nervous wreck forever. And Becker just had the worst kind of luck. I'm just spooked. Or maybe I've just had one too many a beer." He nudged Nick with an elbow. "In any event, some advice?"

Nick leaned closer. "Yeah, what?"

"Keep your nose clean after I'm gone. I can see that look in your eyes sometimes. Been here a month and every morning you come in like it was your first day all over again. You've got something going. Can't fool Uncle Peter."

Nick looked at Sprecher as if what he'd said

were absurd. "Believe it or not, I like it here. There's nothing going on."

Sprecher shrugged resignedly. "If you say so. Just do as you're told and keep Schweitzer off your back. You know his story?"

"Schweitzer's?"

Sprecher nodded, his eyes opened widely in mock terror. "The London Ladykiller."

"No, I don't." And after thinking about Becker and Cerruti, he wasn't sure he wanted to.

"Schweitzer made his name with the bank trading Eurobonds in London during the late seventies," said Sprecher. "Eurodollars, Euro-petrol, Euroyen — they were halcyon days. Everyone was making a fortune. From dawn till dusk, Schweitzer leaned on his staff to package a maximum of offerings. From dusk till dawn, he prowled London's poshest clubs, dragging an entourage of once and future clients from Annabel's to Tramp. If you couldn't syndicate a double A deutsche mark offering at three A.M., two bottles of Tullamore Dew down the hatch and a quiver of tarts at the by, you shouldn't be in this business: the Schweitzer credo. And it put USB at the top of the rankings."

Sprecher laughed at the thought, then finished off the dregs of his mug.

"One fine spring afternoon," he continued, "Schweitzer arrived a little late to his suite at the Savoy Hotel. The board of directors had reserved it permanently on his behalf. Convinced them he needed a refined setting in which to meet his clients, he had. The office was too small, too busy. So in walks Armin only to find his most recent mistress, a young minx from Cincinnati, Ohio, and his wife arguing like wildcats."

Nick thought the whole thing sounded like a bad soap opera. "So what happened?"

Sprecher ordered another beer, then went on. "What happened next is still foggy. The official version put forth by the bank stated that at some point during the ensuing altercation, the good Frau Schweitzer, mother of two daughters, treasurer of the Zollikon curling club, and wife of fifteen-odd years to a philanderer of notorious repute, removed a handgun from her purse and shot Armin's mistress dead. A single round through the heart. Appalled at her actions, she put the revolver to her own head and fired a bullet into her right temporal lobe. Death was instantaneous. As was the transfer of her dearly beloved back to the Zurich head office, where he was assigned to a post of comparative importance though, I dare say, reduced visibility. Got himself a broom closet in the basement. Compliance."

"And the unofficial version?" Nick demanded.

"The unofficial version found its champion in Yogi Bauer, Schweitzer's deputy at the tragic moment. He's been retired awhile, but

95

you can find him in some of Zurich's seedier watering holes, of which the Gottfried Keller Stübli, I am proud to say, is one. Lives here day and night."

Sprecher looked over his left shoulder and whistled loudly. "Hey, Yogi," he yelled, hoisting a full glass above his head. "Here's to Frau Schweitzer!"

A black-haired figure bent over a table in the darkest corner of the bar raised a glass in return. "Fucking unbelievable," Yogi Bauer yelled. "Only housewife in Europe who could smuggle a loaded handgun through two international airports. My kind of girl! Prosit!"

"Prosit," answered Sprecher, before taking a long pull from his beer. "Yogi's the bank's unofficial historian. Earns his keep regaling us with tales from our illustrious past."

"How much of that one is true?" Nick asked.

"April 19, 1978. Look it up in the papers. Made big news over here. The point is steer clear of Schweitzer. He has a hard-on for Americans. Half of the reason Ott's recruits don't last is because Schweitzer is all over them from day one. Yogi claims the American mistress had called Schweitzer's wife and told her that he was going to ask for a divorce so he could marry her. Ever since, Armin hasn't been a big fan of the Stars and Stripes."

Nick placed both hands in front of him and patted the air gently, as if telling his colleague to slow down. "We're talking about the same Armin Schweitzer. Big guy, nice gut hanging over his belt. You're telling me this guy was a real Casanova?"

"The prick who told you yesterday morning that he'd rather drive a 'Trabi' than a Ford. That's him. The one and only."

Nick tried to smile, to slough off all he had heard, but he couldn't. Somehow being party to Sprecher's inchoate suspicions had altered his perception of the bank. Becker murdered; Cerruti, a basket case unable to cope; and now Schweitzer, a gun-toting maniac. Who else was there he didn't know about?

Suddenly, Nick was accosted by a memory of his parents quarreling. One of countless spats that had poisoned the house the winter before his father's murder. He heard his father's commanding baritone echoing through the hallways and up the stairs to where he sat perched in his pajamas, listening. Eerily, he remembered every word.

"He's left me no choice, Vivien. I keep telling you it's not about my authority. I'd wash the floors if Zurich told me to."

"But you don't even know that this man's a crook. You've told me yourself. You're guessing. Please, Alex, stop fighting this. Don't be so hard on yourself. Just do as you're told."

"I won't work with him. The bank may choose to do business with criminals. I will not."

What criminals had his father meant?

97

"That's why I'm telling you," Sprecher was saying. "Keep your nose clean. Do as you're told and Schweitzer will stay off your back. If rumors about our cooperating with the authorities are true, it will be his job to clamp down on all portfolio managers. He is compliance."

Nick sat bolt upright on his stool, his attention rooted once again in the here and now. "What are you talking about? What rumors?"

"Nothing official," Sprecher said quietly. "We'll find out Tuesday morning. But it seems there's too much hue and cry about our conduct these days. The banks have reasoned that they'd prefer to cooperate voluntarily rather than face some form of mandatory regulation. I don't know the p's and q's of it, but for a little while at least, we'll be helping the authorities gather some information about our clients. Not about everybody, mind you. The federal prosecutor will examine evidence presented him and decide which numbered accounts the authorities have a right to examine."

"Jesus Christ. It sounds like a witch hunt."

"Indeed," agreed Sprecher. "They're looking under every rock for the next Pablo Escobar."

Nick caught his friend's gaze, and he knew they were both thinking the same thing. *Or the Pasha.* "God have mercy on the bank who's hiding him," he said.

"And the man who turns him in." Sprecher raised two fingers at the barman. *"Noch zwei Bier, bitte."*

"Amen," said Nick. But he wasn't thinking about the beers.

Chapter 6

At 8:30 A.M. the following Tuesday, a convocation of portfolio managers was held on the Fourth Floor. The subject was the bank's response to escalating demands it formally cooperate with the United States Drug Enforcement Administration and other international agencies like it. The meeting constituted Nick's first invitation to set foot on the hallowed Fourth Floor, known throughout the bank as the Emperor's Lair — in deference to the Chairman — as well as his first visit to the executive boardroom.

The boardroom was cavernous. The doorway was twelve feet high, the ceiling twenty. Nick walked solemnly across a plush maroon carpet whose borders were inlaid with the symbols of Switzerland's twenty-six cantons. At the carpet's center, under a prodigious mahogany conference table, lay the seal of the United Swiss Bank: a black Hapsburg eagle rampant dexter on a mustard yellow field, its broad wings outstretched and three keys grasped in its talons. A swirling golden ribbon, captured in the eagle's prominent beak, advertised the bank's dictum: **Pecuniat Honorarum Felicitatus.** *Money welcomed gladly.*

Nick stood with Peter Sprecher at the room's far corner, near the windows that overlooked the Bahnhofstrasse. He knew he should feel intimidated, but he was too busy watching the other portfolio managers. To a man, they gawked at the room's trappings like a bunch of nervous tourists — pinching the port leather of the conference chairs, running a discreet hand along the burnished wood paneling, puffing up with pride as they studied the bank's elaborate seal. It was the first visit to the Fourth Floor for many of his colleagues, too.

He shifted his view to the doorway and caught sight of Sylvia Schon entering the boardroom. She wore a black skirt and blazer. Her hair was pulled back severely into a tight bun. She looked smaller than he remembered, though not the least bit vulnerable in this sea of male executives. She moved around the room greeting her colleagues, smiling, shaking hands, and exchanging a hushed word here and there. It was a textbook display of working a room, and he was impressed.

Abruptly, the boardroom fell silent. Wolfgang Kaiser entered and strode to a chair positioned directly beneath a portrait of the bank's founder, Alfred Escher-Wyss. Kaiser did not sit down but stood with one hand placed on the table before him. His eyes traveled the room, a general of the army appraising his troops before a perilous operation.

Nick stared at him intently. At his cold blue eyes, at his indulgent mustache, and at his limp arm that was buttoned to his left coat pocket. He recalled the first time he had met Kaiser, during his father's last trip to Switzerland seventeen years ago. Then, he had been terrified of him. The booming voice. The spectacular mustache. It had been too much for a ten-year-old boy. Now, seeing him surrounded by his peers, he felt proud of his family's association with him and honored that Kaiser had offered him a position at the bank.

Three men followed Kaiser into the room. Rudolf Ott, vice chairman of the bank (with whom he had interviewed in New York), Martin Maeder, executive vice president in charge of private banking, and last, close behind but a continent apart, an unknown gentleman, tall and reed thin, clutching a battered leather briefcase. He wore a navy suit whose stiff lapels cried out American — Nick should know, his own lapels were the same — and brown cowboy boots whose spit shine would have earned a long, low whistle from the toughest D.I.

Rudolf Ott called the meeting to order. He wore wire-rimmed spectacles and stood with the defensive posture of a man accustomed to ridicule. "As this bank's representative to the Association of Swiss Banks," Ott began, his Basler accent lending his words a nasal inflection, "I have in the past days met with colleagues in Geneva, Bern, and Lugano. Our discussions centered on measures that must be taken in light of current unfavorable winds, to avoid formal federal legislation mandating divulgence of certain confidential client information, not only to the office of the federal prosecutor but to a committee of international agencies. While the secrecy afforded our valued clients remains paramount to the Swiss philosophy of banking, a decision has been made to *voluntarily* comply with the demands of our federal government, the wishes of our citizens, and the requests of the international authorities. We must take our place at the table of advanced industrialized Western nations and help root out those individuals and companies using our services to spread evil and wrongdoing across the globe."

Ott paused to clear his throat, and a murmur rose through the assembled ranks.

Nick looked at Peter Sprecher and whispered, "Weren't we advanced and industrialized enough to sit at that table during the Second World War?"

"You forget," Sprecher answered, "during the Second War, there were two tables. We Swiss simply couldn't decide which one to sit at."

Wolfgang Kaiser raised his head sharply, and silence descended on the room with the finality of a guillotine.

Ott lofted a hand in the gangly American's

direction. "The United States Drug Enforcement Administration has provided us with a list of those transactions which they define as 'suspicious,' and likely to be linked to criminal activities — in particular the laundering of money from the sale of illegal narcotics. To give you more detail about our proposed cooperation, I present Mr. Sterling Thorne." He turned to Thorne and shook his hand. "Don't worry, they won't bite."

Sterling Thorne did not appear unreasonably worried, thought Nick, as he watched the American agent face the assembly of sixty-five bankers. Thorne's brown hair was unruly and cut a little too long, as if to say he didn't belong with the pretty boys at headquarters. He had gunslits for eyes, and cheeks that in his adolescence had fought a battle against acne and lost. His mouth was small and weak, but his jaw could break a pickax.

"My name is Sterling Stanton Thorne," began the visitor. "I am an agent for the United States Drug Enforcement Administration, have been for near twenty-three years. Lately, the powers that be in Washington, D.C., have seen fit to appoint me chief of our European Operations. That means that today I'm standing before you gentlemen asking for your cooperation in the war against drug trafficking."

Nick recognized the type if not the exact model. Nearing fifty, lifetime in law enforcement, a civil servant masquerading as a latter-day Eliot Ness.

"Over five hundred billion dollars was spent on illegal drugs in 1997," said Thorne. "Heroin, cocaine, marijuana, the works. Five hundred billion dollars. Of that sum, roughly one fifth, or one hundred billion dollars, made its way up the food chain into the pockets of the world's drug supremos. The big guns. That's quite a sum to be traveling around the world looking for a safe home. Now, somewhere down the garden path a large chunk of that money disappears. Vanishes into a black hole. No individual, no institution, no country ever reports receiving it. It just ceases to exist en route to the *narcotraficantes*. Location unknown.

"Banks all over the world — including plenty in the United States, I'll readily admit — help launder this money, help recycle it, and put it back into play. Phony invoicing, paper companies, unreported cash deposits to numbered accounts. A new way to launder money is being created every other day."

Listening closely, Nick detected a faint country twang, a stubborn reminder of home that had resisted bullying. He thought that if Thorne had been wearing a cowboy hat, he'd tip it back on his forehead right now and raise his chin the smallest bit, just to let us good people know that he was getting serious.

Thorne raised his chin and stated, "We are

not interested in the average clients of this fine establishment. Ninety-five percent of your clients are law-abiding citizens. Another four percent are your small-time tax evaders, bribe takers, lower-level arms traffickers, and bottom-feeding drug dealers. As far as the United States government is concerned, they do not exist.

"Gentlemen," Thorne announced, as if they were now united in cause, "we are going after the big game. The top one percent. We have, after these many years, received a license to go elephant hunting. Now, the rules of the hunt are strict. The Swiss gaming authority doesn't want just any elephant brought down. But that's all right. We at the DEA have a clear idea of which elephants have the biggest tusks, and they're the ones we're after. Not the baby elephants, not even the mama elephants. We're going after the rogue males. See, they've been tagged by you Swiss 'game wardens' at one time or another, so even if you don't admit to knowing their name, you certainly know their serial number." He grinned slyly, but when he spoke next his voice assumed a solemn tone. "What matters is that once we provide you gentlemen with the name or serial number of one of those rogue males, for which I remind you *we have received a license,* you cooperate." Thorne cocked one knee and pointed into the audience. "If you so much as think of protecting one of my rogue males, I give you my word that I'll find your sorry ass and kick it to the fullest extent of the law. And maybe then some, too."

Nick noted more than a few flushed cheeks. The normally calm Swiss bankers were getting pissed off in a hurry.

"Gentlemen, please pay attention," Thorne continued. "This is the important part. If any of the rogue males — hell, why don't we just call them what they are — if any of the *criminals* we're looking for deposits large sums of cash, amounts in excess of five hundred thousand dollars, Swiss francs, German marks, or the equivalent, you people must call me promptly and let me know. If any of these criminals receives wire transfers in excess of ten million dollars or the equivalent, and transfers more than fifty percent of that amount out again, to one, ten, or a hundred banks, in less than twenty-four hours, you gentlemen must inform me, pronto. Keeping your money in one place, that's being a wise investor. Moving it around day and night, that's laundering — and his ass belongs to me."

Thorne relaxed his stance and shrugged his shoulders. "Like I said, the rules of the hunt are strict. You people are not making it easy on us. But I am counting on you to give me your entire cooperation. We're trying out this arrangement as a gentlemen's agreement. For now. Don't play with this one, boys, or it will explode in your face."

Sterling Thorne picked up his briefcase, shook hands with Kaiser and Maeder, then accompanied by Rudolf Ott, walked from the boardroom.

Good riddance, grimaced Nick, as the spasm of a painful memory grasped his spine. He had his own reasons for not liking the man.

For a moment, the room guarded a funereal silence. There seemed to be a sort of collective confusion, whether to stay or whether to go. But as long as Kaiser and Maeder remained no one left the room.

Finally, Wolfgang Kaiser drew a labored breath and rose to his feet. "Gentlemen, a word. If you please."

The bankers drew themselves to attention.

"We are all hoping that our cooperation with the international authorities will be at once brief and uneventful. Mr. Thorne clearly has some unsavory characters in mind when he speaks of going elephant hunting. 'Rogue males' and all that." Kaiser's blue eyes smiled as if to say that he too had seen some interesting customers over the years. "But I am confident that none shall be counted among our esteemed clientele. The foundations of this bank were built upon fulfilling the commercial requirements of the honest businessmen of this country. Over the years, the services we offer to our countrymen, and to the international community, have grown more diverse, more complex, but our commitment to working exclusively with honorable individuals has never wavered."

A collective nodding of heads. Nick's fellow bankers appreciated their Chairman's affirmation of the bank's innocence in any unseemly matters.

Kaiser pounded his fist on the table. "We have no need now, nor shall we ever, to seek profit from the bitter fruit of illegal and immoral commerce. Please go back to your posts confident in the knowledge that while Mr. Thorne may search far and wide for his rogue males, he shall never find what he is looking for within the walls of the United Swiss Bank."

And with that, Kaiser marched from the room. Maeder and Schweitzer followed on his heels like two overgrown acolytes. The assembled bankers milled around for a few minutes, either too shocked or too stunned to say much. Nick maneuvered through their ranks toward the tall doors. He walked out of the boardroom and down the hallway. He shared an elevator with two men he didn't know. One was telling the other that the whole thing would blow over in a week. Nick was only half listening to them. He kept replaying Wolfgang Kaiser's words over and over again. *". . . while Mr. Thorne may search far and wide for his rogue males, he shall never find what he is looking for within the walls of the United Swiss Bank."*

Were they a statement of fact or a call to arms?

Chapter 7

"The terms of our surrender," Peter Sprecher declared the following day as he threw a copy of a memorandum entitled "Internal Account Surveillance List" onto his desk. "Issued by Yankee Doodle Dandy, no less."

"Well, we're safe," said Nick, after studying his own copy of the memorandum. "None of the accounts on this list belong to FKB4."

"It's not *us* I'm worried about," said Sprecher, jamming a cigarette into the corner of his mouth. "It's the bank. It's the whole bloody industry."

The list had arrived earlier that morning, delivered personally by a cheerful Armin Schweitzer. Despite the Chairman's spirited defense of his customers' good names, four numbered accounts belonging to clients of the United Swiss Bank had made their way onto the list.

" 'Any transactions made for benefit of an account listed above must be reported immediately to Compliance, extension 4571,' " Nick read aloud. "This should keep Schweitzer busy."

"Busy?" Sprecher rolled his eyes. "The man has died and gone to heaven. No more niggling over documents without the proper dual signature, no more quibbling over violation of margin requirements. Armin has hit the big time. A servant of *Honesty* and *Decency,* with capital letters. He's answering the call of his nation's government to ensure that our gentlemen's agreement is honorably enforced. Am I the only one here who feels a dire urge to scream?"

"Calm down," said Nick. He wondered if honesty and decency were resident members of the Swiss pantheon, or just visiting. "It certainly beats the alternative."

"The alternative? What's that? Self-immolation."

"Federal legislation mandating cooperation. An act making our voluntary collaboration a matter of public record."

Sprecher circled Nick's desk like a predatory hawk. "Since 1933, we have managed to guard the integrity of our banks. Sixty-five years and now this. An abomination is what it is. A fucking disaster. Yesterday our bank's position with regard to queries about a client's identity and the activity in his account was unyielding. A brick wall. Without a formal federal warrant signed by the president, no information, not even the most inconsequential sliver, would be forwarded to an inquiring party. Not to General Ramos seeking restitution of the billions purloined by the Family Marcos, not to your Federal Bureau of Investigation looking to tamper with the working capital of a certain group of Colombian businessmen, and definitely not to a band of overzealous Zionists howling for the repatriation of funds deposited by their relatives prior to the Second World War."

"It is exactly that intransigence that led to this situation," argued Nick.

"Wrong," shouted Sprecher. "It is that intransigence that built our reputation as the finest private bankers in the world." He jabbed a finger in Nick's direction. "And don't you forget that. Granite, Neumann, not sandstone."

Nick raised his hands above his head. He took no pleasure in defending Sterling Thorne's point of view.

"Anyway, it'll be your problem soon enough," Sprecher said all too quietly. "I'll be departing the premises in ten days."

"Ten days? What about your quitting notice? You're here at least until April 1."

Sprecher shrugged. "Call it a divorce American style. I'm here until Wednesday next. Thursday and Friday, I'll be taken ill. Nothing grave, thank you. Just a dizzy spell or a spot of flu. Feel free to take your pick if anyone should ask. Between you, me, and the fly on the wall, I'll be at Konig's place. Two-day seminar for new employees. I'm to start the following Monday."

"Jesus Christ, Peter. Give me a break. The

Indians are circling the fort and you're tunneling out of here."

"As I recall, the Alamo boasted a very low survival rate. Not a sound career move."

Nick stood and looked Sprecher squarely in the eye. "And what if —"

"The Pasha? Won't happen. I mean, how many clients does the bank have? And after all, according to you he's just a successful international businessman with a crackerjack accounting department. Still, if ever such a situation did present itself, you'd be wise to consider the consequences before acting rashly."

"Consequences?" Nick asked, as if he had never heard the word before.

"To the bank. *To yourself.*" Sprecher loped from the office. "I'm off to the tailor. New job, new suits. Back by eleven. You're on duty this morning. If any new clients arrive, Hugo will phone from downstairs. Take good care of them."

Nick waved good-bye distractedly.

Eight days later, Nicholas Neumann, only son of a slain Swiss banker, former marine lieutenant, unofficially promoted portfolio manager, and if his roster was correct, morning duty officer, arrived at his desk at five minutes past seven o'clock. The office was still dark, as were most of the offices on either side of the ambling corridor that cut a crooked

113

swath through the center of the second floor. Closing his eyes, he flicked on the overhead lights. The intrusion of the fluorescent light never failed to bring back memories of a bad hangover. He walked to the employee pantry, where he hung up his damp overcoat, then laid a plastic bag carrying a freshly laundered dress shirt on top of the coat rack. The clean shirt was for that evening's engagement: dinner with Sylvia Schon at Emilio's Ristorante. Sprecher's words about her plans for him had never really faded. He was looking forward to the dinner more than he cared to admit.

Nick made himself a cup of hot tea, then took a waxed paper sack out of his pocket: breakfast — a *pain au chocolat* fresh out of the oven from Sprüngli. Cup in hand, he returned to his desk to study the *Neue Zürcher Zeitung*'s financial pages and check on the status of the stock markets in Tokyo, Hong Kong, and Singapore.

Once seated, he unlocked his desk and the credenza behind it. He opened his top right-hand drawer and took out his list of "action items," which he updated twice a day. He read it.

"Item one: Review portfolios 222.000–230.999 for bonds that were due to expire before month's end. Item two: Order printouts for accounts 231.000–239.999. Item three: Review preferred equities sheet [a list of stocks portfolio managers were allowed to purchase for the accounts of their discretionary clients]. Highlight companies seen as likely takeover candidates." Item four said simply "15:00."

He stared at the time indicated and wondered why he had written anything at all. Why not: "Item four: Make sure your ass is in your seat at three o'clock when the Pasha calls." Or "Item four: Don't screw the pooch the first day your superior is absent." As if he even needed an "Item four" to remind him!

Nick opened the newspaper to the financial section and checked the daily market commentary. The Swiss Market Index had risen seventeen points to 4975.43. USB shares were up five francs to 338 on heavy buying — Klaus Konig stocking up his war chest in advance of the general assembly to be held in four weeks' time. Nick decided to check on the stock's daily volume since Konig's announcement.

He slid his identification card into Cerberus's access slot and waited for the computer to power up. A stream of yellow words passed along the left side of the screen as Cerberus ran its self-diagnostics. Moments later a brusque voice said *"Wilkommen,"* and the screen blossomed into a dull shade of gray. Nick entered his three-digit identification code, and a rectangular box descended through the center of the screen. Four choices were offered him: Financial Market Information, Reuters News, USB Account Access, and Document Manager. He moved the cursor to

Financial Market Information and hit enter. The screen blinked, then turned a lustrous blue. The same rectangular box appeared. New choices: Domestic or International. He chose domestic, and a yellow ribbon appeared at the bottom of the screen flashing yesterday's closing prices at the Zurich stock exchange. He typed in the symbol for USB, added a ".Z" to indicate the Zurich exchange (prices of major Swiss stocks were also quoted by the Geneva and Basel exchange), and followed it by the coded instructions VV21. A daily summary of USB share price and volume traded for the past thirty days appeared on the screen. Graphical interpretations of the data were shown on the right side of the screen.

The price of USB shares was up eighteen percent since Konig's announcement. Daily volume nearly double. The stock was definitely in play. Traders, brokers, arbitrageurs eager for a little action on the habitually calm Swiss market, had seized upon the United Swiss Bank as an interesting "story," that is, a possible takeover candidate. Still, an increase of eighteen percent in the share price was small, given the higher daily volume, and reflected the unlikelihood of Konig's actually making good on his promise. Then why the rise? A certainty that USB would act decisively to improve its lagging return on assets, and thus profitability, be it through cost cutting or more aggressive trading.

Nick moved to the "Reuters News" section and tapped in USB's symbol to see if any stories had been floated the night before about Konig's foray. The screen blinked. Before he could read the first words, a firm hand was placed on his shoulder. He jolted upright in his chair.

"Guten Morgen, Herr Neumann," said Armin Schweitzer. "How is our resident American managing today?" He pronounced the word *American* as if it were a sour lemon. "Checking on the continued meltdown of your beloved dollar or just having a look at the all-important basketball scores?"

Nick spun in his chair to face the bank's director of compliance, noticing the man's scuffed brogues and his short white socks. "Good morning."

Schweitzer waved a sheaf of papers. "I have the newest warrants from the American gestapo. Friends of yours, are they?"

"Hardly friends," Nick answered, a shade louder than he would've liked. Schweitzer made him nervous. He emanated a kind of palpable instability. A toxic chemical best kept at room temperature.

"You're sure?" asked Schweitzer.

"I resent the intrusion into our bank's affairs as much as anyone. We should be fighting these requests for confidential information by all means possible." Inside, Nick shuddered.

A large part of him actually believed his own words.

" 'Our bank,' is it, Mr. Neumann? Six weeks off the boat and already a claim of ownership. My, how they teach you to be ambitious in America." Schweitzer smiled unevenly and leaned closer. His breath was bitter with the dregs of that morning's coffee. "Unfortunately, it seems that your American friends have left us no alternative but to cooperate. What splendid consolation to know that your sentiments are in the correct place. Perhaps one day you will have a chance to prove such heartfelt loyalty. Until then, I advise you to keep your eyes open. Who knows? One of your clients may be on this list."

Nick caught a glimmer of hope in Schweitzer's voice. So far there had been no bites on the four accounts that had originally been listed; no activity that might fit Sterling Thorne's strict criteria. Nick took the updated account surveillance list and laid it on his desk without glancing at it. "I'll keep my eyes open," he said.

"I expect no less," called Schweitzer over his shoulder as he left the room. *Schönen Tag, noch.*

Nick watched him go before picking up the updated sheet. Six accounts were listed. The four from the previous week plus two new ones. Numbered accounts 411.968 OF and 549.617 RR.

Nick stared at the last number.

549.617 RR.

He knew it by heart. Every Monday and Thursday at three P.M. Set your clock to it. Six digits, two letters. Today they spelled the directions for the quickest route to hell. Ninth circle. First class. Nonstop. "The Pasha," he whispered aloud.

On Monday, Nick had demanded to listen to their notorious client. Though initially opposed, Sprecher had relented, knowing that he wouldn't be in the office next time the Pasha called. "Wait until you hear him," Sprecher had said. "The man is cold." And so while speaking to him on the telephone, he had broadcast his client's voice from a tinny speaker.

The Pasha's voice was low and rough, Nick remembered. Like an empty cardboard box being dragged across a gravel lot. Demanding but not angry. Intonation a tool, not an emotion. Listening to the voice, he had felt a shiver growing at the base of his spine, at that tiniest of nubs where intuition signals the arrival of an unwelcome event.

Now, seated at his cramped desk, he stared at the Internal Account Surveillance List and felt the same curious tingling, the same frisson of anxiety itching at the base of his spine. From all exterior appearances the list was an innocent sheet of USB stationery, "Strictly for internal use" printed in bold letters across the upper left corner, its body sullied only by the four-word heading, the six account numbers below, and an admonition stating "All transactions regarding above accounts must be reported immediately to your superior and/or directly to Compliance, ext. 4571."

In seven hours, the holder of account 549.617 RR would phone. He would inquire as to the balance in his account, then he would ask that it be transferred to several dozen banks around the world. Should Nick transfer the money as asked, he would deliver the Pasha into the hands of the United States Drug Enforcement Administration. Should he delay the transfer, the Pasha would have escaped their grasp — at least for now.

Schweitzer's admonition reverberated in his head: *"One of your clients might be on this list . . ."* And then? Nick asked himself. Would he contact Schweitzer in conformity with the bank's directives? Would he tell him that a client whose account number was on the surveillance list had executed a transaction that required the bank to "voluntarily" inform the United States DEA?

Nick's mind shot back to the Keller Stübli, to Peter Sprecher's wild accusations. *The Pasha: thief, smuggler, embezzler.* Why not add "murderer" and cover all the bases? Four weeks ago, Nick had defended his reputation, and by extension, that of the bank. But hadn't he always suspected, if not the worst, well, then, at least something worse? Something marginally at odds with the laws of Western society?

"The Pasha," he mused. "International criminal." Why not?

Few at the bank even knew the man's identity. One of them, Marco Cerruti, was currently suffering from, and here Nick chose the official terminology, "chronic stress-related fatigue." So much prettier than saying the poor guy had suffered a force-ten nervous breakdown. It was Cerruti who had given the Pasha his nickname; Cerruti who for years had personally handled the account. Had he in his choice of sobriquet provided a clue to the identity of his client? Could he have been referring to the man's nationality, or perhaps, more pointedly, hinting at his character?

Nick rolled the word around in his mouth. *The Pasha.* It oozed a familiarity with corruption. He envisioned a slowly turning ceiling fan scattering clouds of blue cigarette smoke, a whispering palm brushing against a shuttered window, and a crimson fez with a braided golden tassel. *The Pasha.* It recalled the slutty elegance of a once great empire, now tired and dilapidated, and gliding toward the devil with a wicked nonchalance.

The phone rang, waking Nick from his anxious reverie.

"Neumann speaking."

"Hugo Brunner, chief hall porter, here. An

121

important client has arrived without an appointment. He wishes to open a new account for his grandson. Your name has been posted as duty officer. Please come down immediately to Salon 4."

"An important client?" This worried Nick. He wanted to pawn him off on somebody else. "Shouldn't his regular portfolio manager handle it?"

"He is not yet on the premises. You must come immediately. Salon 4."

"Who is the client? I'll need to bring down his dossier."

"Eberhard Senn. The Count Languenjoux." Nick could practically hear the porter's teeth gnashing. "He owns 6 percent of the bank. Now hurry."

Nick forgot all about the surveillance list. Senn was the bank's largest private shareholder. "I'm only a trainee. There must be someone more qualified to meet with Mr. Senn — uh, the count."

Brunner spoke slowly and with a fury that brooked no excuse. "It is twenty minutes before eight o'clock. No one else has arrived. You are the duty officer. Now move it. Salon 4."

Chapter 8

"My grandfather was a close friend of Leopold of Belgium," bellowed Eberhard Senn, the Count Languenjoux. He was a chipper man of eighty dressed in a neat Prince de Galles suit and a sprightly red bow tie. "Do you remember the Congo, Mr. Neumann? Belgians stole the whole damned country. Hard to do that nowadays. Take that tyrant Hussein: Tried to steal the postage stamp next door and got his cheeks waxed."

"Soundly defeated," translated Hubert, the count's grandson, a blond waif of twenty swallowed by a three-piece navy pinstripe. "Grandfather means that Hussein was dealt a crippling defeat."

"Ah yes." Nick nodded, feigning little knowledge of this minor imbroglio. Tactful ignorance was an important component of the successful banker's repertoire. Not to mention speed.

After receiving Hugo Brunner's call, he had raced down the corridor to retrieve Senn's file from his official portfolio manager's secretary. In the two minutes required to reach the ground floor and find Salon 4, he'd reviewed the client's dossier.

"But not to our entire disadvantage, eh Hubert?" continued the count. "Fools lost all their weaponry. Tanks, machine guns, mortars. All of it. Gone. It's a gold mine for us. The secret is Jordan. You'll need a strong business partner in Jordan to ferry the weapons in."

"Of course," said Nick in firm agreement. Senn remained silent a few moments longer, and Nick worried that *he* was being asked to supply the name of such a partner.

"Belgians haven't done a damn thing since they took the Congo," said Senn. "I'm still hoping they'll take it back. Do the place some good."

Nick and Hubert both smiled, each bound by a separate duty.

"And that, Mr. Neumann, is how my grandfather received his title."

"By helping Leopold conquer the Congo?" Nick ventured.

"Of course not." The count guffawed. "He imported European women to make the damned place habitable. Leopold's mistresses wouldn't go near it! Someone had to look after the king's pleasures."

The count's express purpose that morning was to alter the signatures on his existing accounts. His son, Robert, had recently passed away. Nick recalled seeing a few lines in the paper: *Robert Senn, 48, president of Senn Industries, a Swiss manufacturer of light firearms, pres-*

surized aerosol containers, and ventilation systems, died when the plane in which he was traveling, a Gulfstream IV belonging to Senn Industries, crashed shortly after takeoff from Grozny, Chechnya. No speculation was made on the cause of the crash or for that matter on the purpose of Mr. Senn's visit to the war-torn area. Recent history was littered with the corpses of arms merchants cut down by credit-poor warriors. Now the dead man's signature must be replaced by Hubert's. Another generation to be welcomed into the bank. The entire business would take only a few minutes.

Nick opened his leather folder and placed two blank signature cards on the desk. "If you'll kindly sign the bottom of these forms, we can have the account transferred to Hubert by the end of the day."

The count stared at the cards, then lifted his eyes to the young banker across the table. "Robert never wanted to stay in Switzerland. He preferred traveling. Italy, South America, the Far East. Robert was an excellent salesman. Wherever he journeyed he sold our products. There are Senn pistols and machine guns in the armed forces of over thirty nations and territories. Did you know that, Mr. Neumann? Thirty nations. And that's only the *official* tally." Senn directed a conspiratorial wink at Nick, then shifted in his chair to gaze at his irresolute grandson. "You know, Hubert, I told your father, 'Stay away from these funny new countries, Kazakhstan, Chechnya, Ossetia.' 'New frontiers, Papa. New borders', he said. Robert loved our clients."

No doubt best those that paid cash, Nick said to no one.

A cloud passed over the count's wrinkled face. He leaned forward as if puzzling over one last question. His eyes filled and a tear rolled down his cheek. "Why was he so terribly bored, my Robert? Why was he so bored?"

Hubert took his grandfather's hand and gently patted it. "We'll be all right, Grandfather."

Nick kept his eyes on the polished tabletop.

"Of course we'll be all right," the count roared. "The Senns are like this bank: solid, indestructible. Did I tell you, Neumann, that we have been clients of USB for over one hundred years? That Holbein on the wall behind you is a gift from my father. My *Opa*, the first count, started his business with loans from this bank. Can you imagine? The first Senn weapons built with money from this institution. You're part of a great tradition, Neumann. Don't forget that. People rely on this bank. On tradition. On trust. Not enough of it left in the world."

Hubert motioned in the banker's direction, signaling to move on to the business at hand. Nick placed the signature cards in front of his clients. Eberhard Senn signed the two cards and passed them to his grandson. Hubert freed his elbow from the constricts of his jacket and added his signature to one card, then the other.

Nick collected the cards and thanked the gentlemen for coming. He stood to show them the way out. Senn shook his hand vigorously. "Trust, Mr. Neumann. When you get older, it's the only thing that really matters. Not enough of it left in the world today."

Nick escorted Senn and his grandson to the entry, then took his leave. Crossing the lobby he thought about the count and what he had said. Eberhard Senn was an unrepentant arms merchant, the grandson of a white slaver — after all, what woman went peaceably to the Congo, the "heart of darkness," way back in 1880? — a man whose entire family fortune had been amassed through the conduct of morally ambiguous commerce, and here he was going on about the importance of trust and how he relied on the unimpeachable integrity of the United Swiss Bank.

Nick's mind rocketed to the sheet of paper that waited on his desk: the Internal Account Surveillance List. What about every other client who had put his trust in the bank? he asked himself. Didn't they also depend on the bank's guarantee of confidentiality? In a country where absolute secrecy was a bank's defining characteristic, trust meant everything. Surely,

Wolfgang Kaiser would not take exception to that sentiment. What had he said to the collected bankers after Sterling Thorne's remarks? *". . . while Mr. Thorne may search far and wide for his rogue males, he shall never find what he is looking for within the walls of the United Swiss Bank."*

Why wouldn't Thorne find them? Because they didn't exist? Or because Kaiser would do everything within his power to prevent their discovery?

Nick reached the bank of elevators and pressed the call button. He could see Hugo Brunner lecturing a young woman dressed in a neat blue business suit. For some reason he just knew that this was her first day of work at the bank. He imagined himself through her eyes: a serious executive in a charcoal suit traversing the lobby with his head bowed, a "Do not disturb" sign practically flashing above his head. He found the picture amusing. He spun the picture on its axis and his amusement faded. In six short weeks, he had become one of the brooding gray bankers scuttling to and fro he had seen on his arrival. What would happen to him after six years?

Nick stepped into the elevator and punched his floor. Don't worry about six years down the road, he told himself. Worry about today. The Pasha's account number is on the bank's Internal Account Surveillance List. He heard Peter Sprecher's voice telling him to *"mind the consequences. To the bank. And to yourself."*

The uncovering of the Pasha as a criminal pursued by the DEA would not portend well for USB. It didn't take a genius to figure that one out. Just the suggestion of a relationship would send the press into a feeding frenzy. An actual investigation would tarnish USB's precious public image, regardless of the results. Given Klaus Konig's announcement that the rival Adler Bank was moving to gain control of a large block of USB shares in advance of the bank's general assembly, now just a few weeks away, USB could under no circumstance afford any hint of scandal.

Nor could Nick's career.

He could hardly expect a promotion for turning in the Pasha, even if technically he was complying with the bank's directives. On the contrary. Turn in the Pasha and he could expect a lateral move to an eminent position in office supplies management. See how far he'd get with his investigation then.

The Swiss did not lionize the whistle-blower. Eight years ago, in an unprovoked fit of morality, the government had amended its legal tomes to allow any banker to report, without recourse to his superior, acts of an illegal nature he had witnessed during the hours of his employ. In those eight years, hardly more than a dozen individuals had noticed an act of criminal intent or questionable nature that necessitated a call to the authorities. The grand majority of the one hundred seventy thousand employed by the Swiss banking industry chose to remain comfortably silent.

Such a statistic spoke volumes on the politics of the Swiss people but did not begin to describe the reasons that cold-fired in Nick a notion toward willful disobedience. Those reasons could be found in the pages of his father's calfskin agendas, now lying less than two miles away on a top shelf in his small apartment. The agendas had given Nick a way to account for the vagaries of a turbulent life, to say "the Fall" did not come because of a random act of violence. The words were brief, terse even — *Bastard threatened me! I must comply. Man is a crook, out and out* — and they illuminated not only his father's miseries but his own, for Nick was unable to dwell upon his father's death without brooding on the consequences it had unleashed on his own life. The shuttling from town to town. The new schools every five months — ten in six years, if you wanted to count. The battles to ingratiate himself with a revolving slate of classmates, the constant efforts at fitting in, until one day he just gave up and decided that he didn't need any friends.

The drinking came later, and it was the worst. His mother wasn't a loud drunk. She was the other kind. The teary-eyed lush content to sip one cocktail after the other. By nine

130

in the evening she'd have a dozen stiff ones under her belt, maybe more. He'd need a crane to get her out of the BarcaLounger and into bed. Even now Nick wondered how many teenagers had put their mother naked under a cold shower. How many had made sure she had two aspirins each morning with her coffee? And how many had tucked a fresh bottle of Visine into her handbag before she went off to work so that maybe she'd last another day without being fired?

The Internal Account Surveillance List was his chance, then. A skeleton key to the unlit corridors of the bank. The question was how to use it.

The elevator jostled unevenly on its run between floors, and Nick's mind confronted another issue. What about Thorne? asked a crusading voice he thought long dead. What about his mission to arrest the major players in the international drug trade?

Screw Thorne, he answered. Let him pursue his rogues' gallery of drug *supremos* and *narcotraficantes,* but goddamn it, not on my watch. As far as Nick was concerned all government agencies — the CIA, the FBI, the DEA, the whole rotten bunch — operated on some hopelessly stilted agenda. They were motivated as much by the self-serving and entirely human aspirations of their leaders as by a legitimate desire to remedy societal ills. To hell with them all.

Nick returned to his desk at five minutes before three o'clock. The office seemed unnaturally quiet. Sprecher's desk was empty, as was Cerruti's — a desolate stretch of banking highway. He had five minutes to decide how to handle the Pasha, true identity unknown, this day at odds with the laws of at least one Western nation.

Nick tapped his pen on the Internal Account Surveillance List. He had been neglecting his duties for most of the day. To divert his thoughts, or maybe to focus them more clearly, he took out the two modification of account information forms he had filled out that morning and began making the necessary additions. A valiant trumpet sounded the charge from an imaginary battlefield. He recognized the Chairman's air. A call to arms.

Nick hazarded a weak smile and glanced up to the clock. 14:59. And then it was done . . . 15:00. He slid open his top drawer and withdrew a green transfer of funds sheet and a black pen. He laid down both in front of him, sure to cover Schweitzer's surveillance list, and began counting. One . . . two . . . three. He could practically feel the pulses of compressed light firing through the fiber-optic cables. Four . . . five . . . six.

The phone jumped in front of him. Nick stared at the flashing light. The phone rang again. He picked up the receiver and placed it firmly against his ear.

"United Swiss Bank, Mr. Neumann, good afternoon."

Chapter 9

Nick leaned back in his chair and repeated himself. "United Swiss Bank, Mr. Neumann speaking. How may I be of service?"

A brusque hissing erupted from the line.

"Good afternoon. Is anyone there?" His stomach felt empty. A streak of anxiety sparked in his lower abdomen and rose unchecked into his throat.

"Please come to my desert kingdom," said a scratchy voice. "The pleasures of Allah await. I have heard you are a handsome and virile young man. We have many beautiful women, some very, very young. But for you I have reserved something special, something infinitely more pleasurable."

"Excuse me," Nick said. This didn't sound like the man he had listened to on Monday.

"The pleasures of the desert are legion," the voice rumbled on. "But for you, my young friend, I reserve my precious Fatima. Such softness you do not know. Like the down from a thousand pillows. And gentle . . . ahh, Fatima is a kind and loving beast. The queen of all my camels." The voice broke down, trading its shaky Arabic accent for one of English origin. "Please you may fuck her as often as you

134

like," Peter Sprecher blurted out, before bursting into laughter, no longer able to continue his charade. "Am I keeping you from something more important, young Nick?"

"Bastard! You'll pay!" Nick railed.

Sprecher laughed louder.

"Isn't Konig keeping you busy enough? Or are you already buying shares for him? Is he going to make a bid for the entire bank?"

"Sorry, chum, I couldn't tell you. But if I were a betting man, I wouldn't count him out."

"Always full of positive news . . ." Nick halted in mid-sentence. A new light on his telephone had begun blinking. "Gotta run. Our friend is here. By the way, his account is on Schweitzer's surveillance list." He caught the beginning of a loud exclamation before he stabbed the flashing extension. "United Swiss Bank, Mr. Neumann, good afternoon."

"Mr. Sprecher, please." It was him.

"This is Mr. Neumann speaking. Unfortunately Mr. Sprecher is away from the office today, but I am his assistant. May I help you, sir?"

"What is your bank reference?" the gravelly voice demanded. "I know Mr. Sprecher well. I do not know you. Please be so kind as to provide me your full name and bank reference."

"Sir, I would be more than happy to provide you with information legitimizing my employ at the bank; however, first, I need to have either your name or your account number."

The line faded for a second. The quietest of hums cut out, and then was back.

"Very well. My account number is" — he pronounced the numbers slowly and deliberately — "five four nine, six one seven. R. R."

"Thank you. Now I require your code word for this account."

Nick felt oddly empowered by the strict procedure set forth to control the identity of the anonymous individuals holding numbered accounts. For decades all that had been required to open an account at any Swiss bank was a check drawn on an internationally active bank, or for more discreet individuals, a stack of currency freely convertible against the Swiss franc. Proof of identity was welcome but by no means obligatory.

In 1990, Switzerland's banking authorities, no longer willing to advocate a policy that could be viewed as favorable to the desperadoes who used banks as blind coconspirators, passed legislation calling for legitimate proof of a client's identity and country of origin, in the form of a valid passport, to be noted as a vital part of the client's records.

Peter Sprecher claimed that prior to implementation of the "draconian" legislation, many of banking's wiser heads had set aside several thousand numbered accounts to be held in the names of their favored *Treuhänder*, or financial middlemen. These accounts were made available to special clients of the bank interested in keeping their identity a secret — "grandfathered," as it were. The minimum deposit required to obtain such a numbered account, no meddlesome questions asked, was five million dollars. One had to keep the riffraff out.

"The code word?" Nick repeated.

"Ciragan Palace," said client 549.617 RR.

Nick smiled to himself. The Ciragan Palace in Istanbul had been home to the latter Turkish viziers in the nineteenth century. Clearly, Marco Cerruti had been pointing a finger at his client's nationality when christening him the Pasha.

"I confirm, sir, Ciragan Palace," Nick stated. "My bank reference is NXM, the family name is Neumann." He spelled it, then asked his client if he had understood. There was an extended silence punctuated only by a rhythmic liquid clicking. Nick brought his chair closer to his desk and leaned over the Pasha's file, as if physical proximity to his client's paperwork would hasten the response.

"Loud and clear, Mr. Neumann," the Pasha said with renewed vigor. "Now may we proceed to business? Please tell me the current balance of my account, 549.617 RR."

Nick entered the account number into Cerberus, followed by the coded instructions AB30A to request the account's balance. A microsecond later, the display spit forth the results of his inquiry. His eyes widened. The balance had never been this high. "Your account holds forty-seven million U.S. dollars."

"Forty-seven million," the Pasha repeated slowly. If there was any pleasure to be had in finding such an astronomical sum in one's account, the gruff voice did not betray it. "Mr. Neumann, you have all my transfer instructions, yes? Please look at transfer matrix six."

Nick withdrew the sheet from the file on his desk. Matrix six detailed specific instructions to transfer a given sum, today the tidy amount of forty-seven million U.S. dollars, to banks in Austria, Germany, Norway, Singapore, Hong Kong, and the Cayman Islands.

"Matrix six involves the transfer of the entire amount to a total of twenty-two banks," said Nick.

"That is correct, Mr. Neumann," the Pasha answered. "You sound hesitant. Is there any problem? Would you like to review the banks to whom you must wire these funds?"

"No, sir," Nick said. "No problem." His eye caught the corner of the account surveillance list peeking from under the Pasha's file. He did not consider telling the client about the existence of the list or that his account was on it. The bank's cooperation with the authorities was voluntary. And confidential. "But I would like to review the names of the correspondent banks. To ensure we are one hundred percent correct." He began with the first bank on the list. "Deutsche Bank, Frankfurt Head Office."

"Correct."

"South West Landesbank, Munich."

"Correct."

"Norske Bank, Oslo," Nick droned, waiting for the impatient grunt that confirmed each name. "Kreditanstalt of Austria, Vienna . . ." His eyes darted around the office. Peter Sprecher, absent. Marco Cerruti, absent. A quote he'd memorized during an endless Pacific float came to mind. *"Isolation is the sole crucible in which man's character may be forged."* He had forgotten who had written the words, but at this instant, he fully understood their meaning.

"Bank Negara, Hong Kong branch office. Bank Sanwa, Singapore . . ." Nick continued reading the list of banks while the memory of Sterling Thorne's short speech made a surprise entrance onto the stage. *Elephant hunting, rogue males, game wardens.* The words provoked an almost physical revulsion in him. He had met one of Thorne's kind before. Mr. Jack Keely of the Central Intelligence Agency — like Thorne, an overzealous caretaker of his government's sacred rules and regulations, eager to co-opt others into his service. Nick had responded to the call of Keely's bugle. He had stepped forward of his own volition, and he had paid the price for his naive pursuit of glory. Never again, he had sworn when the

139

affair was finally over. Not for Keely. Not for Thorne. Not for anyone.

"I confirm a total of twenty-two institutions," Nick said, in conclusion.

"Thank you, Mr. Neumann. Be sure these funds are transferred by the end of your business day. I am not tolerant of errors."

The Pasha rang off.

Nick replaced the receiver in its cradle. He was on his own now, and a stern voice reminded him that was how he liked it. The decision was his. The clock above Sprecher's desk read 15:06. He moved the transfer of funds form closer, noting the time of the order, then began filling out the necessary details. In the upper left-hand corner, he inscribed the six-digit and two-letter account number. Below it, in a rectangular space requesting the client's name, he wrote "N.A.," not available. Under "wire instructions," he penned "matrix six (per client instructions), see screen CC21B." And in the box marked "value," he wrote a forty-seven followed by six zeros. Two boxes remained to be filled in: "validity date" — when the instructions should be executed — and "initials of responsible employee." He wrote his three-letter employee identification in one box. He left the other box empty.

Nick rolled his chair back from his desk, slid open the top drawer, and laid the transfer of funds form at the far back corner. He had settled on a course of action.

140

For the next two hours, he busied himself checking and double-checking numbered accounts 220.000 AA through 230.999 ZZ for all bonds due to mature in the next thirty days. At 5:30, he refolded the last of the portfolios and stacked them in the cabinet behind him. He collected the remaining papers on his desk and arranged them in some logical order before placing them in the second drawer. All confidential documents were filed away and locked under key for the night. His desk was spotless. Armin Schweitzer rejoiced in patrolling the offices after hours, scouring the deserted building for stray papers carelessly left unfiled or unprotected. Offending parties were sure to catch hell the next morning.

Just prior to leaving the office, Nick opened his top drawer and withdrew the transfer of funds sheet bearing the Pasha's account number and wire instructions. He guided his pen to the single box yet to be filled in, that for validity date, and scribbled the next day's date. His scrawl was unreadable so as to ensure a delay of two to three hours before Pietro in Payments Traffic telephoned for clarification. Given the usual Friday logjam, the transfer would never be made before Monday morning. Satisfied, he walked down the hallway to the department's mail nook and picked up an intrabank envelope. He addressed it to *Zahlungs Verkehr Ausland,* International Payments Traffic, then slipped the sheet inside and carefully secured the figure-eight clasp. He took a last look at the envelope, then dropped it into the cotton gunnysack that held the bank's internal mail.

It was done.

Having willfully disobeyed the clearest instructions of his superiors and defied the orders of a major Western law-enforcement agency to protect a man he had never met and uphold a policy he did not believe in, Nick extinguished the Hothouse's nagging lights, certain that he had taken his first step toward the dark heart of the bank and the secrets that lay behind his father's death.

Chapter 10

Ali Mevlevi never tired of watching the sun set over the Mediterranean Sea. In summer, he would take his place in one of the rattan chairs set upon the veranda and let his thoughts drift out across the shimmering water as he kept careful watch of the fiery orb's descent. In winter, on evenings such as this, he had but a few minutes to enjoy the passing of day through dusk and into night. Looking out over the westernmost edge of the Arab Middle East, he followed the sun as it sank deeper into a nest of billowy clouds huddled close to the horizon. A breeze skittered across the terrace and in its wake spread hints of eucalyptus and cedar.

Through the darkening haze, Mevlevi could make out the slums, the skyscrapers, the factories, and the freeways of a city bordering the sea, five miles to the southwest. Few neighborhoods were without damage, none fully rebuilt — this, years after the real fighting had ended. He smiled while trying to count the trails of smoke drifting into the evening sky. It was his way of measuring the city's slow return to civilization. As long as her residents cooked their suppers over an open fire, squatting in the ruins of bombed-out side streets, he would feel safe and at ease. He stopped counting at fourteen, hampered by the failing light. Yesterday evening, he had spotted twenty-four separate plumes. If ever he were to count fewer than ten, he would have to consider finding a new home.

The Pearl of the Levant was still besieged. Make no mistake. Taking the place of mortars and gunfire were incompetence and lethargy. Water was spotty and power available only six hours a day. Three militias patrolled the streets, and two mayors governed her people. And for this the people crowed like proud parents that their city was reborn. A measure of congratulations he would grant them. Since the billionaire had purchased the reins of power, the country had shifted into first gear. The Hotel St. Georges had reopened her doors. A freeway linking the Christian east and Muslim west sides of the city was practically complete. Flights from major European cities had resumed. And the city's favorite restaurants prospered.

Enterprises of a sufficient scale were not averse to providing the prime minister and his cronies an advisory fee of five percent of their revenues to ensure continued prosperity. When the prime minister briefly resigned, and the currency tumbled, it was rumored that only a mild increase in royalty — to seven percent — had secured his return to office.

The P.M. was not a greedy man.

Beirut. She was the world's whore and he loved her.

Mevlevi held his breath and watched as the sun gave a final bow between a parted curtain of orange cloud and disappeared for the night. The sea grew frothy with the heat of the falling star, but he knew this to be an illusion played on his aging eyes by sunlight, water, and distance. The sun, the sea, and the stars: nothing else inspired in him such awe and majesty. Perhaps in a former life, he had been a mariner, a companion to the greatest of Islamic adventurers, Ibn Batutah. In this life, though, another destiny was promised him. As the agent of the Prophet, he would lead the resurgence of his people and give back to them what was rightfully theirs.

This he knew in his heart.

Later, Ali Mevlevi sat behind his wooden desk studying a map of southern Lebanon and Israel. The map was only a month old, yet it was soft with wear, its creases gray from countless foldings. His eyes found Beirut and the hills where his own compound stood northeast of the city, then moved south across the border. He studied a dozen landmarks, cities and towns, before affixing his eyes to a small dot in the occupied territory of the West Bank. Ariel. A settlement of fifteen thousand Orthodox Jews. Squatters on land that did not belong to them. The town had been built out of the desert. Its nearest neighbor was ten miles in any direction. He opened his desk and found a slim compass. He centered the compass on the settlement, then drew a small circle one inch in diameter around it. "Ariel," he pronounced grimly, then shook his head. He had decided.

Mevlevi folded the map carefully and placed it in his desk. He lifted the telephone and dialed a two-digit extension. A moment later, he said softly, "Joseph, come immediately to my study. Bring the traitor and my pistol. And summon Lina. It would be a shame to waste such an instructive event."

The sharp cadence of a military footstep sounded from afar and grew nearer.

Mevlevi rose from his desk and walked to the entrance to his study. "And so, my friend," he announced loudly enough to be heard across the great hall. "Come now. I am anxious for news of the day."

A compact man wearing fresh olive drab utilities walked briskly across the foyer. He did not speak until he stood at attention four feet from his master.

"Good evening, Al-Mevlevi," said Joseph, giving a crisp salute. "I am grateful for the opportunity to debrief you on the day's activities."

Mevlevi pulled the uniformed man to his chest and kissed him on each cheek. "You are my eyes and ears. You know how I depend on you. Please begin."

Joseph began his recitation with a summary of ongoing security measures. Three-man patrols had been sent out at fifteen-minute intervals throughout the day to survey the compound's perimeter. A scout followed each. No activity was reported. The height of the fences on the northernmost boundary of the compound was to be increased. However, the work crew did not arrive as scheduled. Christians, no doubt.

Ali Mevlevi listened attentively while appraising his chief of internal security. He admired the stiff cast of his shoulders and his formal posture. How well they matched the man's stern appearance: his black hair shorn in a crew cut, his dark face covered with an even darker stubble, and his sad eyes. The eyes of his people.

He had found Joseph in Mieh-Mieh, as he found all his men.

Joseph had been in charge of the labor pool for the southern division of the refugee camp that lay twenty miles southeast of Beirut, a bloody stain on Israel's northern doormat. Fifteen years after the Jews' invasion, the camp still stood, even thrived. Thousands of Palestinians crowded the camp's narrow alleyways, fighting daily over meager rations and squalid quarters. A job that creased a man's hands and crooked his back was the camp's most valued commodity. Cutting slabs of concrete under a merciless sun for ten hours brought two American dollars, enough to purchase a loaf of bread, three strips of lamb, and two cigarettes. Filling craters dug by countless mortars and car bombs, a twelve-hour shift spent under constant threat of hostile fire, brought the princely sum of four dollars. Two men were killed each week while repairing the city's roads. Two hundred clamored to take their places.

Joseph had been brought to Mevlevi's attention by a godless man, a thorny Syrian, Abu Abu by name, slaver by trade. Abu Abu had a sharp and discerning eye for the ruthless and cunning among the camp's inhabitants. Most refugees were arrogant; many were strong. Few were intelligent. Fewer still, clever. At the top of this pile of refuse sat Joseph.

"He is mean as a cobra, yet wise as an owl," said Abu Abu, before telling with glee of the last aspirant to Joseph's position. Eyes gouged out, thumbs severed, and tongue spit into a neighbor's cooking pot, the interloper spent his every day seated on an immaculate Syrian quilt, ten steps from the entrance to Joseph's tent.

"This one is special," whispered Abu Abu. "He has pride."

Joseph had been polite in his refusal to leave, but Mevlevi had convinced him. It had taken time, and, in truth, he had revealed more of his plans than he had thought prudent. He spoke of a new praetorian guard; this time they, not the Romans, would be conquerors. He spoke of a new Jerusalem returned to its sole and rightful possessors, and of a world where devotion to God came first, and to man, second.

Finally, Joseph agreed to join him.

"Were our esteemed instructors able to keep to their course plan?" Mevlevi demanded, after Joseph had completed his summary. "We cannot afford to lose any more days."

"Yes, Al-Mevlevi. All instruction specified for day fifty-seven was carried out. Sergeant Rodenko instructed the men on the proper use of Katyusha rockets in the morning. Emphasis was placed on rapid setup, firing, and deconstruction of the base firing units. So far we have received twenty-one firing platforms. Each assault squadron was able to have a go at it. Unfortunately we were unable to fire live ammunition. Rodenko insisted the heat signature of the rockets would be visible to satellites overhead."

Mevlevi said he understood. Heat signatures, satellite overflies, microwave fences — they were all part of his new vocabulary. The lexicon of Khamsin.

Joseph continued. "In the afternoon, Lieutenant Ivlov delivered a lecture on target selection and the arming of the laser proximity fuses. The men grew bored quickly. They are more comfortable with their Kalashnikovs. They are all anxious to know what use they will put their training to. Ivlov demanded to know once more whether our target would be civilian or military."

"Did he?" asked Mevlevi. Lieutenant Boris Ivlov and Sergeant Mikhail Rodenko had arrived along with the equipment two months ago. Both were burned-out veterans of the Afghan war. Trainers for hire supplied in a package deal brokered by General Dimitri Marchenko, late of the Kazakhstani Armed Forces, now president of the quasi-governmental Surplus Arms Warehouse. One of the new breed of post–cold war entrepreneurs. Like many of his country's wares, Marchenko's trainers were second-rate, prone to breaking down at inconvenient moments. A vodka-induced stupor had already cost two days of training. And now they were asking questions. Not good.

"Your target will be made known to you in due time," Mevlevi said coldly. "We will not be firing blanks much longer. You can be certain of that."

Joseph nodded his head respectfully.

"I am reluctant to inquire about the final matter," said Mevlevi.

"Unfortunately, true. Another hornet buzzing in our nest."

"It's been seven months since Mong's raid. Will the oriental bastard never let up? Not a month has passed when a traitor hasn't been uncloaked, not a week when we haven't had to tighten security." Mevlevi sighed. And not a night when the promise of restful sleep wasn't dashed by the recollection of the Asian's aggressive gambit.

During the predawn still of a July morning, a band of warriors had infiltrated the compound. Fifteen men in all. Their task: Assassinate Ali Mevlevi. Their patron: General Buddy Mong, long Mevlevi's most trusted business partner, commander of some fifteen thousand irregulars massed along the Thai-Burmese border. Or so Mevlevi had guessed. To this day, he did not know what had prompted the attack and so, in the tortured etiquette of the international narcotics trade, had continued to transact business with Mong on a regular basis. Truth be told he could not afford to stop. Not now.

Not with Khamsin so close to fruition.

"Let us give thanks to Allah that we have sufficient strength to guard against further incursions," said Joseph.

"Thanks be to Allah." Mevlevi found it difficult to avoid staring at the terrible scar that ran an unsteady course from the corner of Joseph's right eye to the base of his jaw. The last wish of Mong's assassins. Alone among his aides, Joseph could not be questioned as to his loyalty. The scar would not allow it.

"No mercy can be shown Mong, nor any of

151

his minions. Bring the young Judas to me."

Joseph spun on his heel, and walked from the room, bowing slightly before Lina, who lingered in the doorway awaiting Mevlevi's acknowledgment.

"Lina," Mevlevi commanded. "You will join us. Now."

He wanted his mistress to witness this demonstration of his authority, crude as it might be. The educational powers of punishment were vastly underrated. Though, in retrospect, he had erred in the case of an old acquaintance, Cerruti the banker, who had visited him on New Year's Day. Mevlevi had felt it necessary to extinguish an unwelcome streak of independence the banker had recently exhibited. He could not allow an underling, no matter how far removed, to believe himself capable of issuing his master unilateral instructions. The Swiss had not responded well to a brief course of negative reinforcement, unthreatening as it might have been.

And now there were more developments from the Swiss front. He scoffed at the news that the nation's banks had entered into a secret agreement to cooperate with the DEA. Such cooperation would prove a minor headache, nothing more. But the smugness with which the American authorities had emasculated Switzerland's banks begged defiance. And defy them he would. He would pass before the enemy's eyes unseen, unmolested, and unscathed. The challenge invigorated him.

He took a breath to sober himself. All actions with regard to his holdings in Switzerland must be carried out with the utmost delicacy. The distant mountain democracy was the key to his ambitious plan. It contained the fuel that would power his legions.

The fuel that would ignite Khamsin.

And today, a new contact at the bank. For that he must accept at least partial responsibility. He could not suppress a chuckle at the recollection of poor Cerruti's expression when he was brought to Suleiman's Pool. At first, the banker had refused to believe what lay beneath the pool's surface. He had stared into the water, eyes blinking madly while his head shook from side to side. When Joseph provided him a closer look, it had proved too much. The man had gagged, then fainted. At least the damn blinking had stopped.

Mevlevi walked into the gloom of his office and glanced at the handwritten notes on his desk. He picked up the telephone and pressed a single button programmed with the private telephone number of his partner in Zurich. A husky voice answered after the third ring. "Makdisi Trading."

"Albert?"

"*Salaam Aleikhum.* Hello, my brother. What can I do for you?"

"Routine checkup. An employee of the

United Swiss Bank. Name of Neumann. I don't know the first name. Good English. He might be an American."

"Just routine?"

"Very low-key, if you please. Keep an eye on him for a few days. Invisible, understand. Search his apartment. If necessary, we can offer an encouraging hello. But not yet."

"We'll start today. Call me in a week."

Mevlevi hung up the phone and listened as the patter of Lina's footsteps drifted into the study. "It does my eyes good to see you," he said when she had entered the room.

"Aren't you finished with business for the day?" Lina pouted. She was a young woman, only nineteen. A raven-haired beauty with full hips and a generous bust. "It's nearly seven."

Mevlevi smiled sympathetically. "Almost, *chérie*. One last matter to attend to. I want you to watch."

Lina crossed her arms and said defiantly, "I have no interest watching you pass your hours on the telephone."

"Alas, then you do not have to worry." He stood and hugged his Lebanese tigress. She discarded her rebel's stance and wrapped her arms around him, sighing. He had found her three months ago at Little Maxim's, a nasty establishment in the back alleys of Beirut's waterfront district. A discreet conversation with the proprietor had secured her services on a permanent basis. She stayed with him six nights a week and returned to her mother in Jounieh the seventh. She was a Christian, from a Phalangist family. He should be ashamed. Yet even Allah could not control the heart. And her body took him to realms he had never before discovered.

Joseph strode across the marble entryway and into his study. In front of him, head slack on a sunken chest, stood Kamal, a homely boy recruited only two months before to serve as a member of Mevlevi's private security detail. "He was found in your study, rummaging through your private affairs."

"Bring him to me."

Joseph guided the teenager forward. "He has lost the will to speak."

More likely the ability, thought Mevlevi. With a sack of ripe oranges and an extension of rubber pipe, the dark-skinned devil could make Netanyahu confess his undying love of the prophet Muhammad while leaving the fat Jew's body unmarked.

"He is in the pay of Mong," said Joseph. "He has admitted to as much."

Mevlevi approached the sallow youth and with a firm finger lifted up his chin. "Is what Joseph tells me true? Are you working for General Mong?"

Kamal's eyelids fluttered. His jaw ground upon itself, but he uttered no sound.

"Only the infinite one's love can heal the rift you have torn in the heart of Islam. Surrender unto His will. Know Allah and paradise will be yours. Are you ready to accept His mercy?"

Did the youth nod his head?

Mevlevi motioned for Joseph to lead Kamal outside. The prisoner was marched to a round pillar behind which glowed the faint outline of Beirut.

"Assume the position of supplication to the Almighty."

The teenager kneeled and looked out over the calm expanse of the Mediterranean Sea.

"Let us recite the Ode to Allah."

As Mevlevi spoke the ancient prayer, Joseph withdrew into the house. Lina remained silent at her master's side. The last words of the prayer drifted away on the evening's languorous breeze. A compact pistol was drawn and its silver muzzle laid against the nape of the traitor's neck. For several seconds the gun grazed among the boy's downy hairs. The weapon was lowered. Aim was taken. Three rounds were fired into the prisoner's back.

The boy fell forward, eyes open but unseeing, the torn remnants of his heart bruising the pale stone terrace.

"The punishment for traitors shall be death," proclaimed Ali Mevlevi. "So sayeth the prophet. And so sayeth I."

Chapter 11

Nick bounded down the stairs leading from the employee entrance of the bank, happy to be freed from the fluorescent confines of the Hothouse. He jogged several yards, shaking off the bank's behavioral corset, then slowed to gulp down a lungful of the pure Swiss air. The last two hours had dragged on forever. He'd felt like a thief trapped in a museum, waiting for the alarm to go off after he'd stolen a painting. At any moment, he had expected Armin Schweitzer to storm into his office demanding to know what Nick had done with the Pasha's transfer. Remarkably, no alarm had sounded; Schweitzer had been nowhere to be seen. Nick had escaped.

With an hour until his dinner with Sylvia Schon, he decided to make his way to the head of the Bahnhofstrasse, where the lake of Zurich narrowed and ran into the Limmat River. Bundled in his overcoat, he set off through the alleys that ran parallel to the Bahnhofstrasse. The day's light was fading fast, and patches of ice were rapidly forming. His thoughts, though, were not on the ground in front of him. Like the snow and mist trawling the deserted back streets, his mind cast about in the hazy events of the day, searching for defenses to his actions and calculating the responses that might follow.

According to Sterling Thorne's rules, should any account on the bank's internal account surveillance list receive funds greater than ten million dollars and transfer at least half of that amount to an unrelated financial institution within one business day, the bank would be compelled to report such a transaction to the international authorities. While such cooperation rested on a gentlemen's agreement, USB could ill afford to violate a peace brokered by the president of Switzerland's Bundesrat. Just in case they had any ideas in that direction, the DEA had placed agents full-time in the payments-trafficking department of every major bank.

Nick's decision to delay the transfer of the Pasha's funds by forty-eight hours meant the transaction would not qualify as one of suspect intent. Thorne would no longer have the right to demand all papers pertaining to the account in question. Nor could he call for the account to be frozen pending investigation. The Pasha would elude the grasp of the DEA. And in so escaping, he would protect the United Swiss Bank from scandal.

Nick continued through the dusky alleys, hands dug into the pockets of his overcoat, chin nestled into his scarf. He passed a gaslight lamp long since converted to electricity and watched an elongated shadow take shape on the pitted concrete wall blocking his path. A left turn here should take him to the Augustinergasse, a right turn to the Bahnhofstrasse. He hesitated, not sure of his way, then took off to the left. The pitted wall continued along his right, but as he was no longer in the lamp's path, his shadow disappeared. He began climbing the winding street but slowed when he noticed an odd shadow appear on the wall ahead of him. A man, he guessed, with rounded shoulders and a peaked hat. The tremulous form gave the impression of a southern Klansman backlit by faint candlelight. Nick stopped to watch the distorted shadow grow. Abruptly, the shadow halted, then shrunk back and disappeared. Nick shrugged and continued on to the Augustinergasse.

The alley snaked uphill to the right. He passed a bakery, a jewelry store, and a boutique selling down comforters imported from Scandinavia. Strolling past this last storefront, he stopped short to check on the price of a pair of eiderdown pillows. He took a step backward and bent closer to the window, placing his hand on the glass to deflect a streetlamp's glare. The rhythmic attack of footsteps that he had been sure were just behind him ceased. It was too strange to consider. Was someone following him?

Without a moment's thought, Nick ran back

along the path he had just covered. After ten strides, he pulled up and looked in both directions. His eyes sought out the darkest corners of the alleyway and searched the entries of apartments and businesses alike. Nothing. He was alone. His breath came in bursts, his heart beating faster than the mild exertion demanded. Around him the snow-streaked windowpanes and barren window boxes drew nearer. The alley, filled in the daylight with rustic, inviting merchants, was now dark and forbidding.

Nick turned and walked up the street. A hundred yards farther along, he stopped again. He hadn't heard someone behind him so much as felt him. He darted a glance over his shoulder sure he would catch sight of his stalker. Again, there was no one. He stood as stiff as a pillar, listening to the echoes of his own footsteps carom off the cobblestones and dissolve into the misty evening air. *Christ, he must be getting paranoid!*

Nick hurried down the alley and rejoined the busy street running parallel to him. The Bahnhofstrasse was swollen with thousands of nightly émigrés returning home from their posts with the grand banks and major insurance companies. Trams passed in both directions. Vendors hawked bags of hot chestnuts roasted in iron kettles. He forded the stream of businessmen moving north along Zurich's most famed artery and made his way in the opposite direction, toward the Paradeplatz. Anyone following him would have a harder time of it in the dense pedestrian traffic.

He walked on, head lowered, shoulders slumped forward. Every few steps, he'd peek over his shoulders and scan the crowds. Half-convinced he'd seen the peaked cap some-where in the sea of bobbing heads behind him, he dashed across the street and hurried his pace. A few paces ahead, the door to a brightly lit boutique opened. He veered sharply to his left, sliding by an impatient husband and his dawdling wife, and entered the store.

Nick was surrounded by watches. Shimmer-ing creations of gold, stainless steel, and dia-monds. A touch of class at thirty thousand francs a shot. He had walked into Bucherer, the city's most renowned watch emporium, now crowded with early evening shoppers. Be-hind him the glass door offered an easy view to where he stood. Ahead he saw a flight of stairs.

The second floor was calmer. Four show-cases were positioned in a square in the center of the room. Nick pretended to study their contents as he slowly circled their perimeter. His eyes shifted quickly between the watches displayed below him and the stairwell before him. Most of the watches cost more than his annual salary. An Audemars Piguet Grande Complication was priced at Sfr. 195,000. Around a hundred fifty thousand dollars. You

161

could barely make out the actual time because of all the individual hands, and dials within dials, and days and dates. Probably someone's idea of a masterpiece. He pulled back his sleeve and looked at his own watch — a 1961 Patek-Philippe his father had left him. He thought of how much money it was worth and marveled at how he'd managed to keep it out of his mother's hands.

When Nick looked up again, he noted the arrival of a swarthy man — tall and thick with curly black hair, looking strangely his way. Could be a thug, he thought. Nick glanced up and offered a weak smile, but the ill-shaven man was examining a favorite watch and couldn't be disturbed.

Nick stopped to study a solid gold wristwatch. *Come closer,* he dared him. *If you're a customer, like me, you'll keep walking.* He kept his eyes glued to the gaudy watch — nice if you're a Vegas bookie or a loan shark in Miami Beach. Looking up, he saw that the man had vanished.

"I see that Monsieur is interested in the Piaget," came a polished voice from behind his right shoulder.

Nick turned and stared into a dazzling smile.

"Frankly, I would recommend something more casual," said the swarthy salesman. "Maybe even something a little bit rugged. You appear a man of action, a sportsman, *non?*

Perhaps the Daytona from Rolex? We have a wonderful model in eighteen-karat gold, sapphire crystal, deployment buckle, water resistant to two hundred meters. The finest timepiece in the world for just thirty-two thousand francs."

Nick raised an eyebrow. If he ever had a spare thirty thousand francs, he wouldn't spend it on a watch. "Do you have that model with a diamond bezel?"

The salesman registered gross disappointment. "*Hélas, non.* We have just sold our last such model. But may I propose —"

"Maybe another time then," Nick cut in apologetically before finding the staircase to the ground floor.

He exited the store and headed south toward the lake, staying close to doorways and shop windows. You *are* getting paranoid, he told himself. You didn't see anybody in that alley. You didn't see any peaked cap trailing behind you. The man in Bucherer was a salesman. Nick asked himself who in the world would have the slightest interest in following him. He had no idea. No logical answer suggested itself.

Relax, he told himself.

In front of him, the Bahnhofstrasse widened. The buildings to his right fell away, revealing a large open square, the Paradeplatz. Trams arrived from all four corners, encircling the kiosk and ticket station that sat shyly in the midst of their more commanding neighbors. To his immediate right stood the headquarters of Credit Suisse, a neo-Gothic edifice reflecting the Victorian era's pride in the mastery of detail. Farther across the square sat the Swiss Bank Corporation, a masterpiece of postwar anonymity. Immediately to his left, the Hotel Savoy Baur-en-Ville welcomed many a thirsty banker to Zurich's most elegant watering hole.

Nick crossed the street and turned into the square. He ducked into the entry hall of Credit Suisse where he hid, rather idiotically by his own estimation, behind a potted date tree. Well-dressed eccentrics were apparently quite common in Zurich, for none of the bank's customers, seeking the services of the twenty-four-hour *bancomat*, gave him a second glance. He waited five minutes, then deciding he'd studied the date tree's leaves long enough, left the bank. He paused to allow the number thirteen tram to pull into the Paradeplatz, direction Albisguetli, then trotted across the tracks, daring the number seven, picking up speed rapidly in the other direction, to hit him. With one last stride, he was clear of the tracks and on safe ground. Content that no one was behind him, he walked directly across the square to the Confiserie Sprüngli.

As Nick passed through the pastry shop's doors, he was overwhelmed by a succession of intoxicating aromas, each more seductive than the last. A whiff of chocolate, the tart sniff of lemon, and in a lower register, a note of freshly whipped cream. He made his way to the counter and asked for a box of chocolate *luxembergerli,* confections of meringue and chocolate cream, each no larger than his thumb and lighter than air. He paid and turned toward the exit. *Leave your overactive imagination at the door,* he told himself.

Then, for reasons Nick couldn't quite explain, he turned to take a final look back into the pastry shop. Perhaps he'd wanted to savor the feeling of safety the shop had provided. Or, less sentimentally, and as he would prefer to believe, he had actually felt someone's eyes upon him. But look back he did. There at the opposite entryway stood a middle-aged man of olive complexion and salt-and-pepper goatee, wrapped in a houndstooth cape. He wore an Austrian mountain guide's hat, rugged green with a sandy brush extending from its brim. The hat rose like an incomplete mountain, a shallow cleft interrupting its summit. The caped shoulders were rounded.

Nick had found his Klansman.

The man stared intently in his direction for several moments. When he realized that his subject was returning his gaze, his mouth turned upward in an insolent smile. His eyes narrowed, then he rushed from the store. The bastard was letting him know he'd been following him.

Nick remained where he was for perhaps five seconds. The realization had left him too shocked to move. Moments passed. Bewilderment was replaced by anger. Furious, he raced out the nearest exit to confront his stalker.

The Paradeplatz was jammed with hundreds of people. Nick dashed into a multitude of shoppers, commuters, and tourists. He darted through the crowd, raising himself on his tiptoes to see the people ahead. The evening gloom, the snow and mist, made it impossible to separate one group from the next. Still, he searched for the creased hat, the Holmesian cape. He circled the square twice, looking everywhere for the little man. He had to know why he was being followed. Was the man in the cape just some middle-aged freak with nothing better to do, or had someone put him up to it?

Fifteen minutes later, he decided that further search was futile. His stalker had vanished. Just as bad, sometime during his search, he'd dropped the box of pastries. Nick returned to the Bahnhofstrasse and continued south toward the lake. He noted that the crowds had thinned. Few stores were open. Every tenth step he turned and checked for the presence of his gentlemanly escort. The street was empty. Only the trail of his own footprints in the powdery snow followed him.

Nick heard the whine of an engine approaching behind him. This part of the

Bahnhofstrasse was reserved for trams. Automobile traffic was limited to several blocks going north and south. He checked over his shoulder and confirmed the presence of a late-model Mercedes saloon car: black with smoked windows and consular plates. It appeared to have come from the Paradeplatz. The car gunned its motor and pulled up alongside him. The passenger window lowered and an ungoverned head of brown hair popped out.

"Mr. Nicholas Neumann," called Sterling Thorne. "You're an American, correct?"

Nick took a step back from the automobile. Wasn't he popular tonight? "Yes, I am. *Swiss* and American."

"We've been interested in meeting with you for a few weeks now. Did you know that you're the only American working at the United Swiss Bank?"

"I don't know all the members of the bank," answered Nick.

"Take my word for it," Thorne suggested affably. "You're flying solo." He was wrapped in a suede jacket, collar turned down to expose a lamb's wool lining. His eyes were ringed with dark circles, his cheeks sunken, pocked with a hundred pinpricks.

"How do you like working in that nest of vipers?" he asked. "I mean being an American and all."

"We're a pretty benign group. Hardly vipers." Nick matched Thorne's cordial tone, wondering where this was leading, sure it was nowhere he wanted to go.

"Well, I will agree that you fellas don't look like much, but looks can be deceiving, can they not, Mr. Neumann?"

Nick leaned down to look into the car. One look at Thorne brought back his aversion to agents of the United States government. He thought of the man in the cape with the mountain guide's hat — his stalker. He couldn't link the dignified clothing, the European headgear, the overall refined bearing with Sterling Thorne. The two were oil and water. "What can I do for you? It's snowing. I have a dinner appointment. Mind if we get to the point?"

Thorne stared straight ahead and shook his head. He chuckled in disbelief as if to say "How about that boy's manners?" "Bear with me, Nick. I think it would behoove you to listen to what a representative of Uncle Sam has to say. As I recall, we did pay your salary a few years back."

"All right. But make it brief."

"We've been keeping an eye on that bank for some time now."

"I thought you were looking at all the banks."

"Oh, we are. But yours is my personal favorite. I wasn't kidding when I told you you're working in a viper pit. Your associates are up to a lot of funny business. Unless you think it's normal procedure to accept deposits of a million dollars in precounted packets of tens and twenties. Or if you think it's standard operating procedure for a client to open accounts in Panama and Luxembourg without giving his name, rank, or serial number, and for you to say 'Of course, sir, it's our pleasure. What else can we help you with today?' But it's not. That's what my daddy called doing the devil's handiwork."

Nick looked at Thorne's partner, a chubby man in a charcoal suit. The man was sweating. His hands nervously tapped the steering wheel. He didn't want to be there.

"What's this got to do with me?" Nick asked. As if he didn't know the answer.

"We need your eyes and ears."

"Do you now?"

"If you cooperate with us," said Thorne, "we'll cut you some slack when we bring that house of cards down. I'll put in a word to the federal prosecutor. Get you out of here on the next plane."

"And if not?"

"Then I'll be forced to bring you in with the rest of your buddies." He extended an arm out the window and tapped Nick's cheek twice. "Tell you the truth, it'd probably feel pretty good to corral an arrogant cocksucker like you. But that's your choice."

Nick brought his face closer to the American agent. "Are you trying to threaten me?"

Thorne threw his head back and snorted.

"Why, Lieutenant Neumann, where did you get that idea? I'm only reminding you of your sworn duties. Did you think that oath you took to obey the President and protect your country stopped when you took off your uniform? I got the answer for you: No. It sure as hell did not. You're a lifer. Just like me. You can't hide behind your little red passport. That blue one you got is bigger and stronger."

Nick felt his anger welling up inside of him. He ordered himself to control it. "If and when the time comes, that's my decision."

"I don't think you fully grasp the picture here. We've got your number. We know what you and your pals are up to. This is not a request. It's a standing order. Consider it as coming from the commander in chief himself. You are to keep your eyes wide open and report when ordered. You legally blind pricks at USB and every other fucking bank in this town are helping a lot of dangerous individuals clean up their profits."

"And you're here to save us from them?"

"Put it this way. Without you, Neumann, they wouldn't be sitting in a sixty-foot cabin cruiser off of Boca Raton smoking cigars, getting laid, and planning their next score. You're as guilty as they are."

The accusation incensed Nick. Heat prickled the back of his neck. He clenched his jaw, telling himself to calm down, but it was too late.

"Let me make something clear to you, Thorne. First off, I served my country for four years. I'll carry the oath I took every day for the rest of my life. It's a two-inch piece of shrapnel sitting behind what's left of my knee. Every day it cuts a little more of my tendon, but it's so far in there no one even wants to try to get it out. Second, you want to go chasing bad guys around the world, be my guest. That's your job. But if you can't stop them, don't go running around looking for fall guys. I take my job seriously and I try to do it to the best of my abilities. All I see are a bunch of papers, people putting money in, moving it around. We don't have guys bringing in a million bucks over the counter. That's a fairy tale." Nick put his hands on the windowsill and brought his face close to Thorne's. "And finally," he whispered, "I don't give a good goddamn who you work for. You ever touch me again, I'm gonna haul your skinny ass out of that car and bounce it around the street until there isn't anything left of you but your belt, your boots, and your fucking badge. My leg is still strong enough to do that."

Nick did not wait for a response. He backed away from the car, straightening, grimacing as his right knee gave a sour snap, then set off toward the lake.

The black Mercedes matched his speed.

"Zurich's a small town, Neumann," called Thorne. "Surprising how often you run into your friends. I imagine we'll be seeing each other again."

Nick kept his eyes focused in front of him, vowing not to be baited by this asshole.

"I wasn't kidding about those vipers," Thorne shouted. "Ask Mr. Kaiser about Cerruti. Keep your eyes open, Nick. Your country needs 'em. Semper fi!"

Nick watched the car accelerate down the Bahnhofstrasse and turn left toward the Quai Brucke. "Semper fi," he repeated, shaking his head.

The last refuge for a scoundrel and the first for Sterling Thorne.

Chapter 12

Nick curled his fingers around the railing of the dock and peered into the night. Red storm lamps flickered at the ports of Wollishofen and Kilchberg, and on the Gold Coast, at the Zurichhorn and Küsnacht. Snow swirled in unseen eddies while agitated currents slapped the ice extending from beneath the dock's pilings. He turned his face into the wind, willing the nettly gusts to wash away the memory of Thorne's last words.

Semper fidelis.

Three years had passed since Nick had signed his separation papers. Three years since he had shaken hands with Gunny Ortiga, delivered one last salute, then walked out of the barracks into a new life. A month later he was searching for an apartment in Cambridge, Massachusetts, buying textbooks, pens, and paper, and generally living in another universe. He recalled the looks he had attracted that first semester at business school. Not many students walked across Harvard Yard with a marine crew cut, hair trimmed high and tight, shiny whitewalls and half an inch of fuzz on top.

He had been gung ho from the day he arrived at Officer Candidate School until the day he got out. Loyalty to the Corps went beyond politics and beyond mission. It sat in your gut forever like an unexploded grenade, and even now three years since he last wore a uniform, just hearing another's call of *Semper fi* triggered an unwanted flood of memories.

Nick stared into the snow and cloud that lay on top of the lake like a fleecy blanket. He mulled over the timing of Thorne's contact. Why today? Did Thorne know about the Pasha's biweekly calls? Did he know that Nick handled the Pasha's account? If not, why had he mentioned Cerruti? Or had Nick been contacted only because he was an American?

Nick didn't know the answer to those questions. But the timing of the visit aroused his distrust of coincidence — a distrust bred from experience. The gameboard was extending its field.

"Semper fidelis," Thorne had bidden. *Always faithful.*

Nick closed his eyes, no longer able to fight back the torrent of memories that cascaded before him. *Always faithful.* Those words would belong forever to Johnny Burke. They would belong forever to a steaming swamp on the forgotten corner of a secret battlefield.

First Lieutenant Nicholas Neumann USMCR is sitting in the forward operations center of the assault ship USS *Guam.* The room is hot and cramped and rancid with the sweat of too many sailors. The *Guam*, commissioned from the San Diego Naval Shipyard twenty-seven years before, is moving at flank speed through the calm waters of the Sulu Sea off the coast of Mindanao, southernmost island in the Philippine archipelago. It is five minutes before midnight.

"When is the fuckin' air con gonna be restored on this goddamn boat?" Colonel Sigurd "Big Sig" Andersen yells into a black phone swallowed by his meaty palm.

Outside the air temperature is a mild eighty-four degrees Fahrenheit. Inside the steel hull of the *Guam*, the temperature has not descended below ninety-five for the past twenty-seven hours, when the central air-conditioning unit quit in a spasm of fits and coughs.

"I am giving you until 0600 to fix that unit or else there is going to be a goddamned mutiny and I am going to lead it! Is that clear?" Andersen slams the phone down onto the wall-mounted cradle. He is commander of the two thousand United States Marines aboard ship. Nick has never witnessed a senior officer so completely lose his cool. He wonders if it's the heat that has precipitated the violent discharge. Or if it's the presence of a shifty "civilian analyst" who boarded the *Guam* at their last port of call in Hong Kong, and who has spent the last eighteen hours holed up in the radio room engaging in a top-secret tête-à-tête with company unknown.

Jack Keely sits three paces from Nick. He is smoking a cigarette and nervously pinching the copious rolls of fat that fall over the belt of his trousers. He is waiting to begin his briefing on a clandestine operation Nick has been chosen to lead. A "black op," in the parlance of spooks and their obedient surrogates.

Andersen collapses into a beat-up leather recliner and motions for Keely to get up and begin speaking.

Keely is nervous. His audience numbers only seven, yet he fidgets constantly, transferring his weight from one foot to the other. He avoids eye contact and stares at some fixed point on the wall behind Nick and his fellow marines. Between draws on his cigarette, he provides sketchy details of their assignment.

A Filipino, one Arturo de la Cruz Enrile, has been speaking out against the government in Manila, demanding the usual reforms: honest vote counts, redistribution of land, better medical care. Here on the southwestern corner of Mindanao, Enrile has built a following of between five hundred and two thousand guerrillas. They are armed with AK-47s, RPGs, and RPKs: leftover weaponry from the Russkies' vacation fifteen years ago.

But Enrile's a communist. And he's popular. Not a bad guy, really, but he has Manila worried. Recovery is finally picking up steam. Subic Bay and Olongapo are booming. The

P.I. are back from the dead. There is even talk about re-leasing Subic Bay and Clark Airfield to the Americans, says Keely. And *that* is the clincher. The President will do anything to get back that naval base. One brand spanking new naval installation that will save him five hundred million dollars from this year's defense budget. Big wampum in Washington.

Keely pauses and takes a long drag on his cigarette. He wipes away the rivers of sweat rolling down his forehead, then continues his briefing.

Turns out the firebrand is protected by his uncle, the sheriff of Davao Province, who without his makeup is the local warlord. The sheriff likes the deal because the kid and his troops are working his pineapple plantations. The sheriff is all capitalist. When the government in Manila sent troops to arrest Enrile, they got blasted back to kingdom come. Lost a lot of men, not to mention face.

Keely shifts his feet and grins like he is getting to the good part. He grows excited and motions with his arms, a comedian doing stand-up.

"We are here," he announces, "to sanitize the situation." He smiles when he says it. *"Sanitize"* — like they were cleaning a toilet and not placing a noose around a man's neck.

Major Donald Conroy, battalion S-2 (operations officer), stands and presents an outline of the mission: Nine marines will be inserted onto the beaches of Mindanao, twenty kilometers north of metropolitan Zamboanga. First Lieutenant Neumann will lead eight men along the Azul River through the jungle to a small farm at coordinates 7°10′59″ latitude, 122°46′04″ longitude. There they will establish a firing line and await further instructions. Nick is to take with him a second "looey" from Kentucky named Johnny Burke. Burke is an expert marksman just out of advanced infantry school. He will go ashore carrying only his Winchester 30.06 rifle with fifteen power magnification scope. They call him Quaalude because he is able to slow his pulse to under forty beats per minute and squeeze off rounds between heartbeats. Only a dead man could keep his body stiller. He maxed the range at Quantico from 100, 200, and 500 yards. First time since Vietnam ended.

Nick and his men lie prone in a gravel-strewn gully six kilometers inland. Three hundred yards in front of them stands a clapboard farmhouse in the middle of a dirt clearing, surrounded by jungle. Chickens and pigs wander around the unkempt yard.

Since their landing at 0245, the marines have covered fifteen clicks through uncut jungle, following the winding path of the Azul River, which in fact is no more than a stream.

In some places it is dry and overgrown with jungle foliage. The marines rely on Nick to find the next outcropping of water.

It is 0700. Nick and his men are fatigued and must take salt tablets to combat the loss of water. He double-checks the Magellan Satnav direction finder and confirms they are bang on their coordinates. He tunes in the operational frequency and keys in a double-click to confirm their position, then signals for Ortiga, his Filipino gunnery sergeant, to fall in. Ortiga is a small soldier, five foot five on his best day, and tired after humping through the dense undergrowth. He flops down beside the first lieutenant. Next to Ortiga lies Quaalude, breathing unevenly. He is a pasty white. Ortiga, a former navy corpsman, checks Burke's pulse and heart rate. Pulse is 110, heart fluttering. Heat exhaustion. Lost his conditioning aboard the *Guam*. No way Quaalude can take the shot.

Nick removes the Winchester 30.06 from Burke's back and instructs Ortiga to keep pouring fluids down Burke's throat. Even if Burke can't shoot he'll have to hump out like the rest of them.

Nick's walkie-talkie burps and squelches. Keely. A white pickup will arrive at the farmhouse in fifteen minutes. Arturo de la Cruz Enrile will be alone.

Above the nine marines, the jungle canopy comes to life as the first rays of morning sun warm the uppermost leaves. A red-beaked macaw screams.

Nick hefts the Kentuckian's rifle. It is long and heavy, at least twice the weight of the M-16 with grenade launcher that Nick and his men carry. Burke has carved "USMC," and under it "First to Fight," into the stock of his rifle. Nick raises the weapon to his shoulder and presses his eye to the scope. The magnification is so great that he can zero in on the ear of a sow rooting in the garden.

The morning is hot and calm. Steam rises from the clearing. Nick's eyes burn. The sweat from his forehead has melted the jungle camouflage painted onto his face. He signals for his men to take their weapons off safety. No aggressors reported in this sector, but the jungle has eyes. Burke is feeling better. He pukes into the dry creek bed at his feet. Ortiga gives him more water.

An engine backfires far off in the distance. Nick makes out the road leading to the ramshackle farmhouse at the opposite end of the clearing. In a moment, an ancient Ford pickup rumbles into view. Maybe it's white, but all he can see is rust and the gray of unprotected metal. The glare of the morning sun off the windshield keeps him from noting if the driver is alone.

The pickup stops behind the farmhouse.

Nick cannot see anyone. He hears a voice. Enrile is yelling. He is expecting someone.

Nick can't make out what he is saying. Is it Tagalog?

Enrile comes round the side of the farm-house and walks toward Nick. Through the scope he appears to be less than ten meters away. He is wearing a clean white guayabera shirt. His hair is wet, combed back neatly over his forehead. Dressed for church.

Christ, he's no older than I am, thinks Nick.

Enrile searches the yard. He yells again.

A rooster crows.

Enrile moves skittishly. He dances on his toes and lifts his head, as if straining to see a point one degree below the horizon. He looks behind him. Nervous. Getting ready to run.

Nick's hand closes over the rifle stock. A bead of sweat trickles into his eyes. He tries to keep the crosshairs centered on the doomed guerrilla, but his hand is shaking.

Enrile shields his eyes and looks directly at him.

Nick holds his breath. Slowly, he squeezes the trigger. Arturo de la Cruz Enrile spins. A cloud of pink vapor erupts from his head. Nick feels the rifle kick and there's a loud crack, like a small firecracker, a Black Cat. He was aiming for the heart.

Enrile is down. He is motionless.

The marines lie and wait. The sharp report of the rifle drifts into the air, as fleeting as the morning steam rising from the paddies.

Ortiga scans the clearing and is up, running

to confirm the kill. He removes his K-Bar, raises it high into the air, and brings it down into Enrile's chest.

Abruptly, Nick spun on his heels and buried his face in the shoulder of his overcoat. He squeezed his eyelids and prayed for the machine to stop projecting his relentless nightmare. Momentarily, he was aware of the freezing night air. The snow that had fallen on Zurich for the better part of the day had begun to taper off. The wind had died down.

He had taken a young man's life on that morning. A true believer, like himself. For one minute only, he had believed that his actions had been correct; that his responsibility as commander of the insertion team dictated that he take the shot in place of Burke; that his job was not to question the directives of his government, but to faithfully execute them.

For one minute only.

Chapter 13

Nick stood in the men's room of Emilio's Ristorante, his sweaty hands clutching the sink, and stared into the mirror. His eyes were open wide, unnaturally so. His hair was dripping wet. The walk from the lake had done little to calm him. He was still jittery, his system jerky with adrenaline. He shut his eyes and strengthened his grip on the sink. It's done, he told himself. You can't change the past.

Nick turned on the water and splashed several handfuls in his face. He grabbed a paper towel and dried off his hair, then leaned over the sink, placing his ear next to the running tap, listening to the water fall onto the polished porcelain. He didn't know how long he stayed in that position, maybe five seconds, maybe a minute, maybe longer, but after a certain time his breath came normally and his heartbeat slowed. He lifted his head and looked in the mirror. Better now, but hardly perfect. Remnants of coarse paper stuck out here and there, contrasting sharply with his disheveled black hair. He plucked the flakes free, one by one. "Good evening, Dr. Schon," he rehearsed saying. "Don't mind me. Just a mild case of dandruff. Happens all the time." And seeing himself like that, hair mussed, fingers search-ing for the damp morsels of paper, mouth much too anxious, he managed a laugh, and slowly the tension began to slip away.

"Am I late?" Sylvia Schon inquired, check-ing her wristwatch incredulously.

"Not at all," said Nick, standing and shak-ing her hand. "I got here a little early. I had to get out of the snow."

"You're sure? We did say seven, didn't we?"

"Yes. Seven." He felt calmer now, no small thanks to the double vodka he had finished in several hurried gulps. "By the way, thanks for the invitation."

Dr. Schon looked surprised. "Manners too? I see the Chairman has brought us a gentle-man and a scholar." She slid into the booth next to him, and eyeing the empty highball glass said to the hovering captain, "I'll have the same as Mr. Neumann."

"Ein doppel vodka, Madame?"

"Yes, and one more for my colleague." Then to Nick: "It is after hours, isn't it? One thing I love about you Americans is that you know how to enjoy a decent drink."

"Some opinion you must have about us. A nation of noncommittal drunks."

"A little shy of commitment, yes. Drunks, no." She turned her attention to the stiff nap-kins arranged on the table. She unfolded one and placed it in her lap.

184

Nick turned his attention to Sylvia Schon. Her blond hair fell in a shower onto the shoulders of a maroon blazer, which he guessed to be cashmere. A chiffon blouse was prudishly buttoned just shy of the neck, revealing a strand of pearls. Her hands were a creamy white, unblemished by sun or age; fingers, long and graceful, absent of jewelry.

Since his arrival at the bank six weeks earlier, he had yet to view her in anything but a professional light. In their meetings, she had conducted herself formally. She was instructive. She was attentive. She was even friendly — to a point. But she was always careful to maintain a certain distance. She laughed as if each chuckle was rationed, and she was allowed only one or two an hour.

Now, watching her relax, sensing her shed her shell of harried importance, Nick realized he'd been anxious to see another side of her. Sprecher's words had never really left his mind. *She's got something else in mind for you.* He still wasn't sure how to interpret them — as a sincere warning or a sophomoric aside.

A mustachioed waiter brought their cocktails and proffered menus. Sylvia Schon waved the menus away. "There is only one thing to eat at Emilio's and it is the chicken. A small *Mistkratzerli* roasted with herbs and absolutely doused in butter. It is heavenly."

"Sounds great," said Nick. He was very hungry.

She fired off their order in rapid Spanish. *Dos pollos, dos ensaladas, vino de rioja, y dos agua minerales.* Afterward, she turned toward him and said, "I view every member of the finance department as a personal responsibility. It's my job to make sure you are happy in your position, and by that I mean that you have the opportunity to grow as a professional. Your career is my concern. We pride ourselves on attracting the best talent and on keeping them."

"For at least fourteen months," he butted in.

"At least," she agreed, grinning. "You may have heard my displeasure at some of the American graduates Dr. Ott has brought over in the past, but don't take it personally. My bark is worse than my bite."

"I'll be sure to keep that in mind," said Nick. He was taken aback by her solicitous nature. It was a new color for her and he liked it.

Emilio's was jumping. A stream of waiters in crisp white jackets plied back and forth from kitchen to table. Patrons crowded the banquettes that lined the garish red walls and spoke loudly, effusively to one another. Meals were devoured with relish and abandon, cigarettes smoked with hearty appreciation.

"I had a chance to glance through your papers," said Dr. Schon after she had taken a generous sip of vodka. "You've led an interesting life. Growing up in California, visits to Switzerland. What made you join the marines? They're a tough bunch, aren't they?"

Nick shrugged. "It was a way to pay for college. I had a track scholarship for two years, but when I didn't have quite the spring in my step the coaches expected, I lost it. No way I was going back to waiting tables. I'd had enough of that in high school. The marines seemed like the right idea at the time."

"And your work here? It must seem rather dull to work in a Swiss bank when compared with flying in helicopters and playing with guns."

Dull? Nick asked himself. Today I shielded the assets of a suspect wanted by the international authorities. I was followed through the streets by a guy dressed like Sherlock Holmes, and I was threatened by a rabid drug enforcement agent. Where else can you sign up for those kind of thrills?

"Mr. Sprecher is keeping me busy," he said, keeping to the official line of banter. "He tells me we're lucky this is a quiet time of year."

"My sources tell me that your department is doing just fine. You, in particular, seem to be excelling at your position."

"Any word on Mr. Cerruti?"

"Actually, I haven't spoken to him, but Herr Kaiser thinks he may be improving. Cerruti may assume a calmer post at one of our daughter companies when he's recovered. Probably the Arab Overseas Bank."

Nick saw his opening. "Do you work closely with the Chairman?"

"Me. Good Lord, no. You have no idea what a surprise it was to see him in my office that day. First time in ages anyone can remember spotting him on the first floor. What exactly is his relationship to your family?"

Nick often asked himself the same question. Kaiser's intermittent contacts were alternately professional and paternal. He did not know whether they were motivated by a strict sense of bank protocol or a blurry allegiance to a fallen friend. "I hadn't seen Herr Kaiser since my father's funeral," he explained. "He kept in contact with us periodically. Cards, phone calls, but no visits."

"The Chairman likes to keep his distance," said Sylvia Schon.

Nick was happy the two had the same perception. "Did he ever mention anything to you about my father? He started at the bank a few years after Kaiser."

"Herr Kaiser doesn't mingle with the little people."

"You're a vice president."

"Ask me that question when I'm on the Fourth Floor. That's where the power is. Right now you're better off asking the old timers — Schweitzer, Maeder, why not the Chairman himself?"

"He's done enough for me already."

"You're the first employee he's personally recommended since I've been handling human resources in the finance department. How did you swing that?"

He shook his head. "Actually, he approached me about the job. He first mentioned it about four years ago, when I was getting ready to leave the marines. Called me up out of the blue and suggested that I consider business school. Harvard. Said he'd call the dean on my behalf. A few months before I graduated, he phoned to say that there was a job waiting for me if I wanted one." Nick pasted an angry scowl across his features. "He didn't tell me I'd have to interview for the job."

She smiled at his facetious quip. "Obviously, you managed just fine. I must say you fit right in line with the usual type Dr. Ott manages to lure over. Six feet tall, bone-crunching handshake, and a line of bullshit that would make a politician blush." She raised a hand. "Except for the bullshit, that is. I hope you'll excuse me, Mr. Neumann."

Nick smiled. He liked a woman who wasn't afraid of a little salty language. "No offense taken."

She shrugged. "When his golden boys leave ten months later, it's marked very clearly on my hiring record."

"And that's your problem with him?"

Sylvia squinted her eyes as if appraising his

ability to keep a secret. "So we're being honest with each other, are we? Actually, it's nothing more dramatic than a little professional jealousy. I'm sure you'd find it very dull."

"No, no. Go ahead." Nick was thinking that right now she could talk about the mathematical derivation of modern portfolio theory and it wouldn't bore him.

"Currently, I direct the recruiting of employees who'll work in the finance department of our Swiss offices. But the finance department's biggest area of growth is overseas. We've got a hundred fifty people in London, forty in Hong Kong, twenty-five in Singapore, and two hundred in New York. The sexy stuff — corporate finance, mergers and acquisitions, equity trading — most of that takes place in the world's financial capitals. For me, the next step up is to conduct the recruiting of the professionals who will fill those upper-level positions in our foreign offices. I want to make the deal that brings a partner at Goldman Sachs to the United Swiss Bank. I'd love to lure away the entire deutsche mark team from Salomon Brothers. I've got to get to New York to demonstrate that I'm capable of finding top performers and convincing them to come to USB."

"I'd send you in a second. Your English is impeccable, and with no disrespect to Dr. Ott, you make a much nicer impression than he does."

She smiled broadly, as if the compliment meant something to her. "I appreciate your confidence. Thank you."

At that moment, their waiter arrived, his hands full with two green salads and a basket of fresh bread. He placed them on the table and returned bearing a carafe of red wine and two bottles of San Pellegrino. They had hardly finished their salads when two sizzling chickens were brought for their inspection. Approval was given, and the waiter set about preparing the succulent birds.

Sylvia raised her wineglass and offered a toast: "On behalf of the bank, we are happy to have you with us. May your career be long and successful! Prosit!"

Nick met her eye and was surprised when she held his gaze a moment longer than he expected. He looked away, embarrassed, but a second later looked at her again. He couldn't stop himself. He felt a flush of attraction warm his stomach and spread upward into his chest. The feeling made him uncomfortable. She was his superior. She was off-limits, he told himself.

He couldn't go any further until he had sorted out his feelings for Anna. Two years they'd been together and two months apart. Yet right now it felt like the opposite, and that their separation would be permanent. The first few weeks in Zurich, he had expected her to phone to say she was sorry, and that she understood why he had dropped his life and rushed across the Atlantic. He'd even teased himself with a fantasy of her showing up unannounced on his doorstep. She'd be wearing ratty blue jeans, scuffed boots, and an impossibly expensive camel's hair coat, the collar turned up. She'd cock her head and ask to come in, as if she'd only been driving through the neighborhood and hadn't flown five thousand miles to surprise him.

But she hadn't called. Now he saw that he'd been foolish even to ask her to come. Had he actually expected her to quit Harvard in the middle of her senior year? Had he really thought she'd give up the job she'd lined up on Wall Street just to be with him?

"Your father's been dead for seventeen years, Nick," Anna had said the last time he saw her. "What can you expect to find except more disappointment? Leave him in peace."

"If you cared about me, you'd make the sacrifice," he'd fired back.

"And you —" she cried, "why won't you make the sacrifice for me?" But before he could respond, she answered for him. "Because you're obsessed. You don't know how to love anymore."

Seated in the busy restaurant, Nick wondered if he still loved Anna. Of course he did. Or maybe he should say a part of him did. But time and distance had weakened his love. And every minute he spent in the presence of Sylvia

Schon weakened it further.

Over coffee, Sylvia inquired, "Do you happen to know Roger Sutter? He's the manager of our representative office in Los Angeles. Been there forever."

"Vaguely," said Nick, wondering if forever was longer than seventeen years. "He called our home a few times after my father died. I haven't been back to L.A. for a while. My mother moved away about six years ago. She passed away last year, so I don't have much occasion to visit."

Sylvia met his eyes. "I'm sorry. I lost my mother when I was little, just nine. Cancer. After she was gone it was just my father and my little brothers, Rolf and Erich. Twins. That's probably why I feel so comfortable working in a bank full of men. Some may think I'm a little bossy, but when you have two brothers and a rigid father to contend with, you quickly learn how to fend for yourself."

"I can imagine."

"Brothers? Sisters?"

"Nope. Just me. 'Independent' is how I look at it."

"Best to rely on yourself," said Sylvia, without a trace of sympathy. She sipped her coffee before resuming her personnel director's interrogation. "Tell me what really brought you to Switzerland. No one just ups and leaves a post at one of the top firms on Wall Street."

"When my mother died, it hit me hard that I didn't have any real roots in the world. All of a sudden I felt alienated from the States, especially from New York."

"So you quit and came to Switzerland?" Her voice said she wasn't buying his spiel.

"My father grew up in Zurich. When I was younger we came over all the time. After he passed away, we lost contact with our relatives. I didn't like the idea of letting it all fade away."

Sylvia stared at him a moment, and he could see she was evaluating his answer. "Were you close to him?"

Nick breathed easier, happy to be over that bridge. "My father? Tough question to answer after so many years. He was from the old school. You know, kids should be seen and not heard. No television. In bed at eight o'clock sharp. I don't know if I was ever really close to him. That part was supposed to come later, when I had grown up."

Sylvia raised the cup to her lips and asked, "How exactly did he die?"

"Kaiser never told you?"

"No."

Now it was Nick's turn to size her up. "So, we're supposed to be honest with each other, right?"

Sylvia half-smiled and nodded.

"He was murdered. I don't know by whom. The police never arrested anyone."

Sylvia's hand registered a minor tremor, and a few drops of coffee tumbled from her cup. "I am sorry for prying," she said crisply. "Please excuse my being so rude. It was none of my business."

Nick saw that she believed she'd gone too far, and that she was ashamed. He appreciated her respect for his privacy. "It's all right. I don't mind you asking. It's been a long time."

Both took a sip of coffee, then Sylvia said she had something to tell him, too. She moved closer to him, and for a moment it seemed that the din and roar surrounding them faded. He hoped she didn't have some catastrophic family secret of her own to share. She gave him a puckish smile and he knew his fears were for naught.

"Since the beginning of the evening I've been dying to take these horrid little pieces of paper out of your hair. I was afraid to ask how they got there, then I realized that you must have had to dry your hair — because of the snow. Come on, lean a little closer."

Nick hesitated for a moment, studying Sylvia as she shifted her body on the banquette to face him more directly. She looked at him and a puzzled expression wrinkled her brow. Her eyes were a soft brown, no longer so challenging, and for a moment they held his in their embrace. Her nose crinkled slightly, as if he had asked her a vexing question, and then she smiled and he saw that a small gap separated her front teeth. And in that smile, he spotted — if only for a moment — the girl who had grown into this, perhaps, too responsible executive.

"Don't be afraid. I told you that my bark is worse than my bite. You must believe me."

Nick inclined his head toward her. He came nearer her body, smelling her perfume, then sensing it mix with her own warmth, her own peculiar, feminine scent. He blushed, and as she removed the last pieces of tissue from his hair, he dismissed any worries he had had about her being his superior at the bank. Abandoning himself to her feminine charms, he could barely suppress a sudden and powerful urge to wrap his arms around her and bring his mouth to hers and to kiss her long and deep and hard.

"I think we've cured your rather nasty case of dandruff," Sylvia stated proudly.

Nick brushed the top of his head, not quite ashamed of his secret thoughts. "All gone?"

"All gone," she confirmed, a bright smile gracing her features. And then she added in a tone of hushed confidentiality, "If you ever need anything, Mr. Neumann, I want you to promise me right here that you'll call."

Nick promised.

Later that night, he spent a long time thinking about her final remark and the million and one things it might have meant. But right then, as she spoke the words, he could think of only one thing that she could do that would make him happy. Maybe, just maybe, she would call him by his first name.

Chapter 14

The United States Drug Enforcement Administration chose the first floor of a nondescript three-story building in the Seefeld district as its temporary headquarters in Zurich. Number 58 Wildbachstrasse was a grim affair of plaster stucco and sober disposition, its only extravagance the pair of double-paned French windows that peered from each floor onto the street. Neither terrace, balcony, nor window box prettied its spinster's facade.

Seeing the building for the first time, Sterling Thorne had declared that it resembled a cinder block wearing a bedpan. But the monthly rent of Sfr. 3,250 had been well within budgetary constraints, and the outdated floor plan, which divided the ground floor into six rooms of equal size, three on either side of a central corridor, was ideal for a staff of four or five United States government employees.

Thorne held a telephone close to his ear and stared anxiously out the front window, as if waiting for a tardy agent to cross over from the east. The morning fog, which during winter loitered on the Swiss plateau like an unwelcome houseguest, had at 11:45 A.M.

Friday not yet lifted.

"I heard you the first time, Argus," said Thorne, "but I didn't like the answer. Now come again. Did you find the transfer I told you to look for?"

"We got zip," said Argus Skouras, a junior field agent, from his post in the payments traffic department of the United Swiss Bank. "I was here until they kicked me out last night at 6:30. Came in this morning at 7:15. I have searched through a stack of papers taller than an elephant's ass. Zip."

"That is impossible," said Thorne. "We have it on good sources that yesterday our man received and transferred a huge chunk of money. Forty-seven million dollars cannot just disappear."

"What can I tell you, Chief? If you don't believe me, come over here and we can do this together."

"I believe you, Argus. Don't get yourself all worked up. Settle down and keep doing your job. Give me that officious prick Schweitzer."

A few moments later a gruff voice came through the receiver. "Good morning to you, Mr. Thorne," said Armin Schweitzer. "How may we be of service?"

"Skouras tells me you have no activity to report from the account numbers we supplied you with on Wednesday evening."

"That is correct. I sat with Mr. Skouras this morning. We reviewed a computer printout listing every electronic funds transfer the bank has received and transmitted since the surveillance list was last updated twenty-four hours ago. Mr. Skouras was not satisfied with the summary sheet. He demanded to check each individual instruction form. As we process over three thousand transfers a day, he's been very busy."

"That's what his government pays him for," Thorne said dryly.

"If you care to wait a moment, I will key in the accounts on your list. Our Cerberus system does not lie. Anything specific you are looking for? It might be easier if I had an exact sum, say the amount transferred, to use as a cross-reference."

"Just check all the accounts on your list one more time," said Thorne. "I'll let you know if we find what we need."

"State secrets?" joked Schweitzer. "Fine, I'll enter all six accounts. This will take a moment. I'll pass you Mr. Skouras."

Thorne tapped his foot impatiently and scowled at the miserable weather. Near noon and no sign of sun, no sign of rain, and no sign of snow. Just a quilt of gray cloud sitting on top of the city like a dirty carpet.

Thorne's gaze wandered to the building across the street. From an upstairs window, an elderly woman viewed his men's activity with a bitter eye. Two cars belonging to the DEA were pulled onto the sidewalk. Empty filing boxes were being loaded into the trunk. Like a hungry rat emerging from its hole, the wizened lady leaned far out over the window ledge and surveyed all below.

"Chief, Skouras here. Mr. Schweitzer is checking the accounts now. I can verify that he put in the right numbers. We're waiting on a hard-copy printout."

Without so much as a knock, the door to Thorne's office swung open and rebounded noisily off the wall. The heavy cadence of a single individual's footsteps approached. Thorne turned and stared into the sweating face and knotted brow of a stocky black man.

"Thorne," the visitor spat out, "I'll wait till you get off the phone and then I want an explanation of what in the name of good Christ is going on here."

Thorne shook his head. A knowing smile brightened his features. "The Reverend Terry Strait. Surprise, surprise. Sinners, fall to your knees and repent! Hello, Terry. Here to fuck up another operation, or just to make sure our hallowed rules are properly obeyed?"

Strait pulled on the pockets of his vest and rolled on the balls of his feet while Thorne placed a hand to his lips and motioned to be quiet.

"Mr. Thorne," said Schweitzer. "I am sorry to disappoint you, but we report no activity in any of the accounts on our list."

"Nothing, in or out?" Thorne scratched the

back of his neck and glared at Strait, who remained less than a foot away.

"Absolutely nothing," said Schweitzer.

"You're sure?" Thorne squinted his eyes. *Impossible,* he thought. *Jester's never wrong.*

"Are you suggesting we at the United Swiss Bank are not telling the truth?"

"It wouldn't be the first time. But seeing as how we have Skouras right next to you, I can't exactly accuse you of holding back on us."

"Do not push your luck, Mr. Thorne," said Schweitzer. "The bank is doing its best to extend a courteous welcome to you. You should be content that you've managed to place one of your watchdogs inside our premises. I shall ask my secretary to see that Mr. Skouras continues to receive a copy of every wire instruction given to our payments-trafficking department. If you have any further questions, do not hesitate to call me. In the meantime, good day." Schweitzer rang off.

Thorne slammed the phone onto its cradle. He faced his unannounced visitor. "What in the hell are the desk jockeys doing in Switzerland?"

Terry Strait glared at Thorne. "I'm here to make sure you follow the game plan we established a long time ago."

Thorne crossed his arms and leaned against his desk. "What makes you think I wouldn't?"

"*You,*" boomed Strait. "You never have in the past. And I can see you aren't now." He withdrew a sheet of paper from his jacket pocket, unfolded it, and held it in front of Thorne. *Internal Account Surveillance List* was printed in bold letters across USB stationery. "What the hell is going on? How did this account number get on this paper?"

Thorne took the paper, examined it briefly, and showing no emotion, handed it back to Strait.

"I imagine this is what you were yapping to Schweitzer about," Strait said. "Account 549.617 RR. Am I correct?"

"Righto, Terry. On the ball as usual."

Strait held the surveillance list as if it gave off a foul odor. "I am actually afraid to ask how this account ended up on that bank's watch list. I don't think I want to know."

Thorne stared blankly ahead, one corner of his mouth peaked in a silent smirk. He hadn't told Strait a thing, and already he was tired of explaining. "I hate to break it to you, Terry, but it's legit."

"Legit? Franz Studer allowed you to place this account on USB's surveillance list? You've got to be kidding!" Strait shook his head as if it couldn't be true. "Why, Sterling? Why are you jeopardizing the operation? Why do you want to scare our man out of the net?"

" 'The net'?" Thorne exclaimed in disbelief. "Is that what you think we've set up here? If we've got a net, Terry, then it's got a hole big enough for Moby fucking Dick to swim through, 'cause that's what our man has been doing these last eighteen months."

"You've got to give Eastern Lightning time. Every operation has its own schedule."

"Well, this schedule is coming to an end. Eastern Lightning is my baby. I set her up. I put her into play." Thorne pushed himself off his desk and began pacing the room. "Let me remind you of our tactical goals. One: Staunch the flow of heroin into southern Europe. Two: Force the party responsible, and we know damn well who that is, out of his mountain hideaway and into a Western nation where we can arrest him. And three: Seize the sonuva-bitch's assets so we have sufficient resources to pay for our dream holiday here in Switzerland. After all, every op's got to be self-financing, these days. Am I right so far?"

"Yes, Sterling, you're right, but what about —"

"Shut up, then, and let me finish." Thorne rubbed his forehead and continued his pacing. "How long has this op been green lighted? Nine months? A year? Try twenty months. Two zero months. Hell, it took us a year just to get Jester in place. Since then, what have we got? Have we stopped the flow of heroin into Europe? Even one damned shipment?"

"That's Jester's fault," Strait protested. "Your source is supposed to supply us with details regarding our man's shipments."

"And so far he hasn't. Put the blame on my

shoulders. They may be narrow, but I'll be proud to carry the load."

"This is not about placing blame, Sterling."

"You're right," said Thorne. "It's about getting results. As for our first goal — interdict the flow of heroin — strike one. As for our second — flush the bird from its covey — let me ask you this: Has that sonuvabitch Mevlevi even looked in our direction? Has he even blinked?"

Strait said nothing, so Thorne continued.

"Instead of getting scared, the bastard's hunkering down for the long haul, tightening security, doubling the size of his army. Christ, he has enough firepower up there to take back the West Bank. Jester says he has something big planned. You've read my reports."

"That's what has us scared. You're more interested in broadening the scope of this operation than in bringing its original mandate to a successful conclusion. We passed on your information to Langley. Let them handle it."

Thorne beseeched the ceiling for divine intervention. "Face it, Terry, we aren't ever going to force our man into a friendly nation where we can arrest him. And so we're left with goal number three: Seize the motherfucker's assets. Hit him where it hurts. You know what I'm saying? Grab 'em by the balls and their hearts and minds will follow. That's all we got left going for us. The only information that Jester has given us is regarding our target's finances. Let's use it."

Terry Strait stood very still, refusing to be caught up in Thorne's emotional outburst. "We have discussed this before," he said quietly. "Proper evidence must be submitted to the office of the Swiss federal prosecutor. Evidence that must first substantiate the target's involvement with illegal narcotics —"

"Beyond any reasonable doubt," Thorne cut in.

"Beyond any reasonable doubt," confirmed Strait.

"And that's what I gave him, goddammit."

"You didn't?" Strait's eyes bulged. "That information is classified!"

"Hell, yes I did. We have satellite photos of Ali Mevlevi's compound. The man has his own private army, for Christ's sake." Thorne put a hand to his mouth as if he had mistakenly revealed a secret. "Oh, I forgot, that's Langley's concern. None of our business." He smiled sarcastically. "No problem. There's enough evidence to go around. We have sworn statements as to Mevlevi's involvement in heroin trafficking from his former business partners, two of whom are doing time in the supermax facility outside Colorado Springs. Best of all we've got intercepts from the Defense Intelligence Agency's supercomputing center in San Diego that track the exact sums of money going into and out of Mevlevi's accounts at the United Swiss Bank. That alone is proof of significant money-laundering activity. Put those three together and we have a slam dunk. Even that pansy-assed federal prosecutor Franz Studer couldn't disagree."

"You had no right to submit that information without prior approval from the director. Eastern Lightning has to be given time. Director's orders."

Thorne grabbed the piece of USB stationery from Strait's hands. "I am sick and tired of waiting around until the bad guys figure out we got a hook in their gills and wriggle free. Jester has provided all the information we need. It's my op and I decide how and when to roll it up." He crumpled up the surveillance list and threw it on the floor. "Or do we have to wait until Mevlevi uses that army of his?"

Strait shook his head vigorously. "Would you stop with that army nonsense? Operation Eastern Lightning was designed to capture the man responsible for the trafficking and distribution of thirty percent of the world's heroin and, in the process, to seize a significant amount of contraband. We did not go to all this trouble to freeze a dozen insubstantial bank accounts that hold what for this man amounts to pin money. Or to indulge your hopeful fantasies about stopping some Middle Eastern crackpot."

"Have you read Jester's summary of the matériel Mevlevi's accumulating? He's got a couple dozen tanks, a squadron of Russian

Hind helos, and who knows what else? We don't have a fart's chance in a windstorm of arresting this guy. Success in our game is the art of the possible. The only thing we have left to us is his assets. If you think freezing upwards of one hundred million dollars is 'pin money,' then we must be reading from two different balance sheets." Thorne walked past Strait and looked out the window. The nosy old broad across the way was still checking on his team's activities.

"Freeze his money and he'll be back in business in a year, maybe two," said Strait. "This operation is about drugs, Sterling. We work for the United States Drug Enforcement Administration. Not the CIA, not the NSA, and not Alcohol, Tobacco, and Firearms. We can nail Mevlevi *and* his drugs. But it will take time and patience. Something you're very short of."

"Fine. Forget about the guns. By freezing Ali Mevlevi's accounts, we stop the flow of drugs now. No one in D.C. gives two shits about what happens next year."

"Well, I do. And so does the director." Strait approached Thorne and jabbed a rigid finger into the West Virginian's shoulder. "I'll remind you of one other problem. By convincing Studer to stick that account number on the USB surveillance list, you placed the life of source Jester in great danger. After what happened on Christmas Eve, I'd have thought you'd be a little more careful."

Thorne spun, and as quick as a mongoose grabbed Terry Strait's index finger, bending it backward unmercifully. His guilty conscience didn't need a reminder about his responsibility toward his agents. "That does it. I have tolerated your sanctimonious bullshit long enough. I am going to nail Mevlevi the only way I know how. Stop the money and you stop the man. Is that clear?"

Strait grimaced. "If Mevlevi finds out we know what we're looking for, Jester is in deep shit."

"Did you hear me, Reverend Terry? I asked if that was clear?" Thorne bent the finger further backward. He told himself that Becker's death was a random act of violence, a failed robbery, then laughed at his willful naïveté. He knew better.

Strait stooped forward. His head faced the floor as if he were looking for a lost contact lens. In response, Thorne applied greater force to the distended digit. Strait yelped, then fell to one knee. "Clear, Terry?"

Strait nodded and Thorne let go of the finger.

"You're a schoolyard bully," yelled Strait. He shook his hand to lessen the pain.

"I may be a bully, but I also happen to be running things out here, so watch your mouth."

"Not for long if I have my way. The director

sent me out to keep an eye on you. He had a feeling you'd be getting antsy."

"I already have a shadow," said Thorne.

"Well, now you have two. Consider yourself a lucky man." Strait walked to the couch on the opposite side of the room and slumped onto its lumpy cushions. "Just tell me one thing. Tell me, please, that no activity came across that account."

"It's your lucky day. Yours and Mevlevi's, that is. No activity has come across the account. For months Jester has been calling the transfers into and out of that account like clockwork. The day that account goes on their surveillance list, Jester goes cold. Frankly, it has me wondering."

"Our priority is Eastern Lightning," said Strait. "And Eastern Lightning is about drugs. That's the word from the director. *Is that clear?* I'm just here to make sure you toe the line."

Thorne stared out the window and waved a tired hand in Strait's direction. "Go away, Terry. The op is safe and sound for the time being."

"That is what I needed to hear," Strait said exhaustedly. "From now on, clear any ideas you might have with me. And tell Franz Studer to take that damn account number off his list."

Thorne waved his hand once more. "Fuck off, Terry."

Outside, a white Volvo from the Zurich Police Department had drawn up on the side-walk, behind the DEA's rented vehicles. A young policeman wearing a knee-length black leather topcoat was lecturing one of the junior agents. It was clear from the officer's exaggerated gestures that the improvised parking spaces constituted an infraction of the highest magnitude. Somewhere above breaking and entering but below first-degree murder.

Who sent this joker? Thorne wondered. By instinct, he looked up at the old woman perched at her window. The hag caught sight of him and quickly withdrew into the shadows of her apartment. The window slammed shut a second later.

A bewildered Sterling Thorne shrugged and returned to his desk. "Christ, I hate this place."

Chapter 15

Two hours earlier, Nick Neumann sat in a stiff leather armchair, allowing his eyes to adjust to a dimly lit office on the Fourth Floor of the United Swiss Bank. Iron window blinds built into the walls like a medieval portcullis remained fully lowered. A single lamp sprouting from the left forecorner of the imposing crescent-shaped desk provided the room's only light.

Nick stared across the room at Martin Maeder, executive vice president for private banking. Maeder's head was lowered, his eyes riveted on two pieces of paper lying side by side on his desk — no doubt some report concerning Nick. He'd been sitting this way for the past ten minutes, not saying a word. Nick figured his silence to be a tactic designed to soften up his insides and make him ready to confess to a whole litany of crimes, one or two of which he just might have committed. Grudgingly, he admitted it was working.

Nick guarded his strict posture, determined not to appear nervous in any way. The peaks of his shoulder blades brushed the back of the chair. His elbows rested on the armrests and his hands were folded in his lap, thumbs raised to form a steeple. He examined his shoes, which were spit polished, and his trousers, which sported a razor crease. He studied his hands, which were immaculate and had been ever since the age of nine when his father had started a nightly homework review.

During the fall of Nick's fifth-grade year, it became his father's practice to meet with him every evening at six o'clock in the dining room to review his schoolwork. Nick would put on a fresh shirt and using a fingernail brush his father had given him, wash his hands and nails assiduously. Before presenting his homework for review, he'd show his father his hands — palm up, palm down — while answering the usual questions about how school had been that day. He could still remember the feel of his dad's hands, so large and soft and strong, taking his own little ones into them, turning them over, checking for dirty nails. When the inspection was finished, they'd shake hands, interlocking their little fingers. It was their secret handshake. Then they would begin work. This went on for a year and a half, and during that time Nick convinced himself he hated it.

The first Monday after his father was killed, Nick came down to the dining room table exactly at six o'clock. He had done all his homework, then put on a clean shirt and washed his hands, using his dad's fingernail brush. He waited at the table for an hour. He could hear his mother watching TV in the den, getting up every fifteen minutes to make herself a drink. He came down every evening for the rest of that week. Each night he hoped that she would take his father's place. Each night he prayed that things would be like they'd been before.

But his mother never came to the table. After a week, Nick didn't either.

Martin Maeder lifted his head from the documents. He cleared his throat, then leaned across the desk and drew a cigarette from a sterling silver mug. "So, Mr. Neumann," he said in flawless English, "is Switzerland agreeing with you?"

"More or less," Nick answered, trying hard to match Maeder's easygoing tone. "The work more, the weather less."

Maeder picked up a cylindrical lighter with both hands and lit his cigarette. "Let me rephrase that. Since you arrived, would you say your glass has been half-filled or half-emptied?"

"Maybe you should ask me that question after this meeting."

"Maybe." Maeder laughed and took a long drag. "You a tough guy, Neumann? You know, Sergeant Rock, the howling commandos, the whole nine yards. Oh yeah, I lived in the States. Little Rock, 1958 to 1962. The height of the cold war. We had to practice taking cover under our desks. You know the drill." He clenched his cigarette between his front teeth and clasped his hands behind his head. "Put your head between your knees and kiss your ass good-bye." He removed the cigarette, exhaled a thin stream of smoke, and continued smiling. "You're an army man, you should know."

Nick didn't answer right away. He gazed at Maeder. His hair was slicked back off the forehead in a viscous wave. His complexion was chalky. Bifocals perched at the end of a suspicious nose partially hid his dark eyes while his mouth remained twisted in a kind of perpetual grin. Nick recognized that it was the grin that betrayed the solid jaw and the scholarly spectacles, the grin that gave him the irrevocable impression that Maeder was a trickster. A well-groomed one, to be sure; but a con, all the same.

"Marines," said Nick. "Rock was army. We were more the Alvin York type."

"Well, Nick, army, marines, Boy Scouts, whatever. We have one pissed-off client who doesn't give a fuck if you're the emperor Ming. Get my drift? Just what the hell did you think you were doing?"

Nick asked himself the same question. Any certainty that his actions on behalf of the Pasha would be appreciated had evaporated at 6:15 that morning, when Maeder woke him with an invitation to an informal meeting at 9:30 A.M. Since the summons, Nick's mind had been racing.

How could anyone have learned so quickly of his failure to transfer the Pasha's money? None of the European banks to which he *should have* wired the funds could confirm their arrival or absence until this morning at ten the earliest. While the forty-seven million dollars should have exited USB's accounts last night, the banks to which the funds were wired wouldn't officially credit the money to their client's account until sometime this morning, the overnight float being theirs to enjoy. As two hours were required for the bank to catalogue the past day's transfers, no confirmation of Nick's wire transfer could be given to even the most inquisitive client before 10:00.

But that applied only to Europe. The Far East was seven hours ahead of Zurich, and Nick recalled that matrix six included two banks in Singapore and one in Hong Kong. If he gave them until twelve P.M. local time to credit the funds to the Pasha's account, the Pasha could only have discovered their absence at five A.M. Swiss time. One hour prior to Maeder's call.

Confronted with Maeder's Cheshire grin, he suddenly felt very naive.

"Tell me, Mr. Neumann," asked Maeder, "what is the overnight carry on forty-seven million dollars?"

Nick took a deep breath and glanced at the ceiling. This kind of quick figuring was his specialty, so he decided to give Maeder a little show. "For the client, two thousand five hundred seventy-five dollars. That's at yesterday's rate of two and one half percent. But the bank would credit the money to its overnight money market fund and earn approximately five and one half percent or seven thousand and, um, eighty-two dollars. That would give the bank a positive carry of around forty-five hundred dollars."

Maeder banged at his calculator like a nearsighted typist. Robbed of his thunder, he slid it across the desk and changed tack. "Unfortunately, our client is not concerned about several thousand dollars of accrued interest we failed to credit his account when we added his assets to our overnight float. What concerns our client is your failure to honor his transfer instructions. What concerns our client is the fact that sixteen hours after he gave you, and I quote, 'bank reference, NXM,' an order to wire transfer, sorry, to *urgently* wire transfer, his assets elsewhere, his money is still in Switzerland. Care to explain that?"

Nick unbuttoned his jacket and sat a little easier in his chair, pleased that he was to be given an opportunity to defend his actions. "I filled out a funds transfer form, as usual, but I specified the transaction time as today at three-thirty. I sent the form to payments traffic by internal mail. If the Friday logjam is as bad as usual, the funds should be transferred sometime Monday morning."

"Is that right? Do you know who this client is?"

"No, sir. The account was opened by International Fiduciary Trust of Zug in 1985, prior to the current Form B regulations, which demand proof of an account holder's identity. Of course, we treat all clients with the same respect, whether we know their names or not. They're all equally important."

"Though some more than others, eh?" Maeder suggested, sotto voce.

Nick shrugged. "Naturally."

"I've been given to understand that yesterday was particularly calm in your neck of the woods. No one around to consult with. Sprecher ill, Cerruti out of commission."

"Yes, it was very calm."

"Tell me, Nick, if one of your superiors *had* been with you, would you have consulted him? Better yet, if this Pasha fellow, if he were your own client — say you were Cerruti — would you have acted in a similar manner? I mean given the extraordinary circumstances and all." Maeder held up a sheet of paper and gave it a shake: the Internal Account Surveillance sheet.

Nick looked his interrogator in the eye. *Don't waver. Show them you're a true believer. Become one of them.* "If anyone else were there, I would never have been presented with this dilemma. But to answer your question, yes, I would have acted in a similar manner. Our job is to ensure the safekeeping of our clients' investments."

"What about following your clients' instructions?"

"Our job is also to faithfully execute instructions given by our clients. But . . ."

"But what?"

"But in this instance, execution of this particular set of instructions would have endangered the client's assets and brought unwanted" — Nick paused, searching for the right word to tap-dance around the ugly facts — " 'attention' to the bank. I don't feel qualified to make decisions that may have a damaging effect, not only on the client, but also on the bank."

"But you do feel qualified enough to disobey the bank and ignore the commands of your section's biggest client. Remarkable."

Nick didn't know whether this was a compliment or a condemnation. Probably a little of both.

Maeder stood up and strolled around the side of his desk. "Go home. Don't go back to your office. Don't speak with anyone in your department, including your buddy Sprecher — wherever the hell he is. Understood? The court shall deliver its verdict on Monday." He patted Nick on the shoulder and grinned. "One last question. Why such an urge to protect our bank?"

Nick rose from his chair and reflected before

answering. He had always known that his father's past employ offered him a mantle of legitimacy. No matter his private suspicions, he was the bank's kin. Not quite the dauphin returning to claim his throne, but not a wandering contract laborer — an auslander, to wit — either. Tradition. Heritage. Succession. These were the bank's most hallowed grounds. And it was on these grounds that he would stake his claim.

"My father worked here for over twenty-four years," he said. "His entire career. It's in our family's blood to be loyal to this bank."

The job was done quickly enough. He had been given a key and it didn't take more than thirty minutes to search such a small apartment. He had watched the man leave and before entering the building waited a quarter of an hour until he received confirmation that the mark had boarded a tram, direction Paradeplatz. He knew almost nothing about him, only that he worked at the United Swiss Bank and that he was an American.

He set to work immediately once inside the apartment. First he took instant photographs of the single bed and the night table, of the bookshelf and the desk, and of the bathroom. Everything must appear exactly as it had been left. He started at the doorway and worked his way clockwise around the one-room flat. The closet held no surprises. A few suits — two navy, one gray. Four ties. Several white shirts just back from the laundry. Some blue jeans and flannel shirts. A parka. A pair of dress shoes and two pairs of sneakers. All were neatly arranged: clothing hanging in the same direction, shoes aligned. The bathroom, though cramped, was immaculate. The American had few toiletries — only the necessities: toothbrush, toothpaste, shaving cream, an obsolete double-edged razor, one bottle of American aftershave, and two combs. He found a plastic bottle of prescription medication: Percocet — a strong painkiller. Ten tablets were prescribed. He counted eight still in the container. The tub and shower were spotless, as if wiped down after every bath. Two white towels hung from the rack.

He backed out of the bathroom and continued his tour of the apartment. A pile of annual reports sat on top of the desk. Most were from the United Swiss Bank, but there were others — the Adler Bank, Senn Industries. He opened the top drawer. Several pens and a block of writing paper lay inside. He moved the writing paper to one side and found a letter from the bank. He opened it and read it. Nothing interesting — just a few words confirming the mark's start date and his salary. He moved to the lower drawer. Finally, there was some trace that this guy was a human being. A stack of handwritten letters was bound by a thick rubber band. They were addressed to a Nick

Neumann. He slipped one out of the bundle and flipped it over to see who had sent it. A Mrs. Vivien Neumann from Blythe, California. He considered opening one but saw that the postmark was ten years old and put it back.

There were thirty-seven books on the shelves. He counted them. He skimmed the titles, then removed each and skipped through the pages to see if any papers might be secreted inside. A couple of photographs fell from a thick paperback. One showed a group of soldiers in full jungle camouflage, faces painted green and brown and black, M-16s strapped across their chests. Another showed a man and a woman standing in front of a swimming pool. The man had black hair and was tall and skinny. The woman was brunet and a little chubby. Still, she wasn't too bad. It was an old photograph. You could tell by the white borders. The last two books didn't have a title written on the spine. He pulled them off the shelf and saw they were agendas, one for 1978, the other for 1979. He scanned the pages but saw only what he would consider routine entries. He looked at the date of Tuesday, October 16, 1979. Nine o'clock was circled, and next to it was the name Allen Soufi. Another circle at two P.M. and "Golf" written next to it. That made him laugh. He replaced the agendas as they were.

Finally, he moved to the chest of drawers

near the bed. The top drawer was filled with socks and underwear, the second drawer with T-shirts and a couple of sweaters. Nothing was hidden in the corners or taped to its underside. The bottom drawer held a few more sweaters, a pair of ski gloves, and two baseball caps. His hands delved under the caps and came to rest upon a heavy leather object. Aha! He removed a well-oiled holster and stared at it for a few seconds. It held a Colt Commander .45-caliber pistol. He took the weapon out of the holster and saw that the gun was loaded and that a round was chambered, the safety on. He drew aim on an invisible adversary, then, ashamed of himself, holstered the pistol and slipped it back into its hiding place.

A glass of water and a few magazines sat on the nightstand. *Der Spiegel, Sports Illustrated* — the swimsuit edition — and *Institutional Investor,* which had a mean-looking fellow with a brushy mustache on the cover. He probed the mattress, then lay on the floor and looked under it. Nothing. The flat was clean except for the pistol. That was hardly unusual. Every man in the Swiss Army kept a service revolver at his home. Of course, they probably didn't keep it next to their bed with nine bullets in the butt and a round chambered. Still, he didn't think it strange for the mark to have a gun. After all, Al-Makdisi had called him "the marine."

Chapter 16

Wolfgang Kaiser slammed his hand onto the conference table. "It's in his blood to be loyal. Did you hear him?"

Next to him stood Rudolf Ott and Armin Schweitzer. All three focused their attention on a beige speakerphone marooned in the mahogany sea.

"Knew it all along," said Ott. "I could have told you five minutes into our first interview."

Schweitzer muttered that he had heard him, too, but the tone of his voice said he didn't believe a word.

Kaiser had reason to be content. He had kept an eye on Nicholas Neumann for years. Followed the boy's difficult childhood, the mother's peregrinations from one town to another, his stint in the Marine Corps. But only from a safe distance. Then three years ago, he'd lost Stefan, his only child; his beautiful, doomed dreamer. And soon afterward, he had found himself thinking of Nicholas more and more. He suggested that the boy enroll at Harvard Business School, and when Nicholas agreed, he said aloud what he'd been thinking for over a year: "Why not bring him to the bank?" He'd been disappointed when Nicholas chose a post on Wall Street. He hadn't been surprised, though, when he called six months later, informing him he hated the place. Nicholas had too much European blood in his veins to fall into that go-go lifestyle. And hadn't he just said it? *It was in his blood to be loyal to the bank.*

Yet, despite his contacts over the years, Kaiser had had no idea what Neumann would really be like until just this moment. And by that he meant very specifically that he'd had no idea whether or not he would be like his father. Now he had his answer. And it pleased him enormously.

The speakerphone squawked.

"I hope you were able to follow our conversation," said Martin Maeder. "I had the windows closed and the blinds lowered. It was like the tomb of Ramses. We scared the shit out of the kid."

"He didn't sound too scared, Marty," said Armin Schweitzer, standing closest to the speakerphone, arms crossed over his barrel chest. "His math skills certainly didn't suffer."

"The kid's a wizard," gushed Maeder. "Arrogant as all hell, but a goddamned Einstein!"

"You're right," said Kaiser. "His father was the same way. Worked as my assistant for ten years. We practically grew up together. He was a bright man. Terrible end."

"Gunned down in Los Angeles," added

225

Schweitzer, unable to disguise his glee in the misfortune of others. "The place is a war zone."

"I won't hear your ignorant accusations," shouted Kaiser, his exuberant mood soured. "Alex Neumann was a good man. Maybe too good. We're damned lucky to have his kid."

"He's one of us," said Maeder. "Didn't fidget once in that chair. A natural."

"So it seems," said Kaiser. "That's all for now, Marty. Thank you." He terminated the connection, then looked at Ott and Schweitzer. "He acquitted himself well, wouldn't you say?"

"I would caution against reading too much into Neumann's actions," said Schweitzer. "I'm sure he was motivated more by fear than by any loyalty to the bank."

"Really?" asked Kaiser. "I disagree. I can't think of a better way in which we could have tested his executive mettle, or his loyalty to the bank. It takes balls for a trainee to make that type of decision in the absence of any guidance. Rudy, call Dr. Schon. Have her join us. *Sofort!*"

Ott scrambled to the telephone.

Kaiser took two measured paces toward Schweitzer so that the men were an arm's length apart. His countenance darkened. "It's you with whom I should be concerned, Armin. Isn't it your duty to monitor the surveillance list given us by Mr. Studer and this Thorne character? Of all our numbered accounts, certainly *this one* should have caught your eye."

The director of compliance met the Chairman's gaze. "Franz Studer gave us no warning. I was indisposed Wednesday evening when the list was submitted to us. I didn't have a chance to review the list until yesterday afternoon. When I saw it, naturally I was appalled."

"Naturally," said Kaiser, unconvinced. Schweitzer had two excuses for every missed step, but never an apology. Indisposed? Probably something that could only be cured by a few generous shots of schnapps. He put his hand on the man's shoulder and squeezed. "Don't ever forget at whose behest you serve, Armin."

Rudolf Ott hung up the phone. "Neumann's papers will be here right away," he announced, then glared at Schweitzer. "I can't get over the coincidence of this account number appearing on the list while both Herr Kaiser and I were absent in London. And you, Armin," Ott let the final word dangle, *"indisposed."*

Schweitzer rolled forward onto the balls of his feet. His cheeks colored. Ott took a step backward, cowering. Schweitzer looked at the Chairman, and his stance relaxed. "You've confirmed that Franz Studer did not accidentally allow the account past his desk?" he asked.

"If the account is on the list, it is because Studer put it there," said Kaiser calmly. "Hard to believe even he's joined the Americans. At least we know where he stands." He shook his head and for the first time realized the hairbreadth nature of their escape. He exhaled noisily. "We were damned lucky."

Ott raised his hand shyly as if afraid to be called upon. "Another piece of unfortunate news. Dr. Schon has just informed me that Peter Sprecher is leaving us."

"Not another one," said Kaiser. He didn't have to ask where Sprecher was going.

"To the Adler Bank," said Ott. "Another lion for Konig's menagerie."

"One more reason not to trust Neumann," said Schweitzer, suddenly heartened. "The two are fast friends. Where one goes, the other will follow."

"I think we can rule out Neumann's leaving," Kaiser stated. "He stuck out his neck for all of us. He didn't do it without a reason." He walked slowly over the maroon carpet, his feet traveling from one canton to the next. From the blue and white shield of Lucerne to the bear of Bern to the bull of Uri. "Regardless of Mr. Neumann's motivations, it is clear that we can no longer handle our special accounts as before."

Schweitzer spoke immediately. "Why not have members of my staff, of compliance, handle our special accounts? We can keep perfect track of our clients' commands."

Kaiser said nothing. He had his own notions about who should keep track of the special accounts.

"Why not bring Mr. Neumann into our offices?" suggested Ott. "He's shown a flair for handling this account, and you do require a new assistant. Mr. Feller isn't coping well with the increased workload. Konig's bid is making matters unmanageable."

"I beg your pardon, Herr Kaiser," said Schweitzer hurriedly. "But the thought of bringing Neumann to the Fourth Floor is unconscionable. No thinking man would —"

"No thinking man would have allowed this numbered account to appear on our very own internal surveillance list," said Ott. "Studer be damned! But to calm you, Armin, we can keep a closer eye on Mr. Neumann on the Fourth Floor. He would be ideal to assist in responding to our North American shareholders. We require a native English speaker to pen our rebuttals to the American press."

Kaiser stood between the two men, his head tilted slightly backward as if he were smelling the air. "Very well," he announced, pleased that Ott had beaten him to the suggestion. "Decision made. I want him here Monday morning. No time to lose. We've only four weeks until our general assembly."

Schweitzer stalked from the conference room, ever the jilted suitor. As he reached the door, Kaiser raised his voice. "And Armin . . ."

"*Jawohl*, Herr Kaiser?"

"Keep a sharper eye on the lists submitted to you by Franz Studer. He's on the other side now. Is that clear?"

"*Jawohl*, Herr Kaiser." Schweitzer nodded curtly and closed the door.

"Poor Armin must feel rather the goat today," said Kaiser, sighing.

"I'm disappointed in him," added Ott. "I hope we mustn't question his allegiance."

Kaiser turned on his plump deputy. "Schweitzer has been with us for thirty years. His devotion cannot be questioned." He didn't need to mention what had secured the man's obeisance. Two female corpses, a smoking gun, and a philandering husband made for big news in any country. It had been an expensive affair to keep quiet. But worth it. He'd have his hands wrapped tightly around Schweitzer's balls for the rest of the man's life. He turned his mind to more pressing matters and asked, "Have our friend's assets been located and transferred?"

Rudolf Ott clasped his hands in contrite supplication. "The entire amount was wired out first thing this morning. The transfer of funds form Neumann mentioned was located and removed. It never reached Agent Skouras."

"Christ, it doesn't do to upset a client like

that, two hundred million on deposit and one percent of our shares in his pocket."

"No sir, most unwise." Ott parroted the Chairman like a court eunuch.

"And were we able to route the transaction through Medusa?" Kaiser referred to the online data management system that had become operational only two days before.

"Yes, Herr Kaiser. Sprecher's and Neumann's terminals have been altered to share access with it. No sign of our client's transfer will be detectable."

"Just in time," whispered Kaiser gratefully. He'd been aware for years that the intelligence agencies of several Western nations possessed technology capable of tapping into their main data banks. The Americans were especially crafty. Their first line of attack was the sophisticated communications technology that allowed them to listen verbatim to the interbank conversations carried on between Cerberus and its computer brethren around the world. Transfers of funds made from Zurich to New York or from Hong Kong to Zurich were easily intercepted.

Medusa was the answer to these unwarranted incursions: a state-of-the-art encryption system capable of detecting and defeating any and all on-line surveillance measures. When Medusa was fully up and running, USB would be able to conduct her private banking the old-fashioned way: *privately*. But it had not come cheap. One hundred million francs had been allocated for the development, construction, and implementation of Medusa. And one hundred fifty million spent. What were hidden reserves for?

A firm knock on the oak door interrupted Kaiser's thoughts.

"Good morning, Herr Kaiser, Herr Dr. Ott," said Sylvia Schon. "I have Mr. Neumann's dossier."

Ott walked briskly to meet her and thrust forward his right hand, palm up. "The file please. You may go."

"Not so quickly," said Kaiser. He walked the length of the room and extended his hand. He had forgotten how attractive she was. "Dr. Schon, a pleasure to see you."

She looked questioningly at Ott, then walked past him and handed the file to Kaiser. "Neumann's file as requested."

Kaiser accepted the file. "He's one of your boys. Any word on how he is faring?"

"Nothing but praise from Mr. Sprecher."

"Given his decision to leave the bank, I don't know precisely how to evaluate that. What about you? Had a chance to get to know him?"

"Only briefly. We had dinner last night."

"Where?" He couldn't prevent himself from asking.

"Emilio's."

Kaiser raised an eyebrow. "I see. Maybe

Konig has a point about using our assets better. If you took every one of your recruits there, we'd have to file for bankruptcy within a week."

"I thought the bank should ensure he feels welcome." Sylvia Schon darted a glance at Rudolf Ott.

"I'm hardly one to tell you how to do your job," said Kaiser. "Neumann's special. His father was very close to me. Fine man. Fine son. And how does Mr. Neumann feel about our 'proposed cooperation'? Get a chance to discuss that with him?"

"We touched on the matter. He mentioned in no uncertain terms that he thought it unwise for the bank to cooperate with the authorities. He said 'the walls of the bank should be made of granite, not sandstone.' "

Kaiser laughed. "Did he? How refreshing for an American."

Sylvia Schon advanced a step. "Has he gotten into any trouble? Is that why you wished to see me?"

"On the contrary. Seems our boy has a nose for keeping us *out* of trouble. We're thinking about bringing him to the Fourth Floor. I need another assistant."

"Mr. Feller isn't bearing up under the increased pressure," added Ott malevolently.

Sylvia Schon raised a hand in protest. "Mr. Neumann has been here less than two months. Maybe after a year, he could assume a position on the Fourth Floor. He's hardly begun his employ."

Kaiser knew the promotion would feel like a dagger in the woman's back. No one was more ambitious and in truth, no one worked as hard. She was a tremendous asset to the bank. "I understand your concerns," he said, "but the boy did go to Harvard, and Ott tells me his thesis is brilliant. Knows more about the bank than you or I, right, Ott?"

"Certainly more than *I* do," said the vice chairman. Ott checked his watch. He fidgeted as if needing to visit the men's room. "Herr Kaiser, we are expected in Salon 2. The Hausammanns."

Kaiser tucked the file under his left arm and shook Sylvia's hand. He'd forgotten how soft a young woman's skin could be. "First thing Monday morning, understood?"

Sylvia Schon lowered her eyes. "Of course. I'll inform Mr. Neumann immediately."

Kaiser noted the downcast expression on her face and made a sudden decision. "From now on, I want you, Dr. Schon, to handle our recruiting in the States. Get over there in the next couple of weeks and find us some stars. You've shown a talent for nurturing the employees in your department, eh, Ott?"

But Ott was too busy glaring at Dr. Schon to respond.

"I asked you, Rudy, if you agreed with me?"

Ott said, "Of course," and breaking off his

stare, scurried to the door.

Kaiser stepped closer to Sylvia Schon. "By the way," he asked, as if an odd idea had just popped into his mind, "do you think you could get to know him better?"

"Excuse me?"

"Neumann," Kaiser whispered. "If *urgently* required?"

Sylvia Schon glowered at the Chairman.

Kaiser looked away. Yes, perhaps that was pushing things too far. Best to go slowly. He wanted Neumann around for a long time. "Forget I asked," he said. "One last thing, though. About you telling Neumann — better wait until Monday. Clear?" He wanted Nicholas to sweat over the weekend. He didn't like his subordinates making important decisions without first consulting him. Even if their instincts were correct.

Sylvia Schon nodded.

Rudolf Ott returned from the tall double doors and taking hold of the Chairman's arm, led him from the room. "Good morning, Dr. Schon. Thank you for coming," he muttered.

"We're off, Ott," said Kaiser, as if embarking on a jaunty morning cruise. "Who did you say is on the agenda? The Hausammanns? Slumlords. Amazing who we have to work with to keep Konig at bay."

Sylvia Schon was left standing alone in the empty boardroom. For a long while she stood motionless, staring at the empty space where the Chairman had been. Finally, as if having struggled with a difficult decision, she took a deep breath, buttoned her blazer, and walked briskly out of the room.

Chapter 17

Upon entering the Keller Stübli, Nick was assaulted by the usual mixture of hot air, stagnant smoke, and stale beer. The small bar was crowded beyond its capacity. A sartorially diverse assortment of men and women were packed together tighter than a stack of new hundreds, waiting for a table to clear. Asshole to belly button, they would say in the Corps.

"You're late," Peter Sprecher barked over the maddening roar. "Fifteen minutes and then I'm gone. Nastassia's waiting at the Brasserie Lipp."

"Nastassia?" Nick asked, reaching the far end of the bar, where his friend sat with a stein of beer in his hand.

"Fogal," Peter explained, referring to the pricey hosiery emporium situated two doors down from USB. "The gorgeous bird behind the counter. I'm giving you fifteen minutes of *her* precious lunch break."

"You're a generous man."

"Least I can do. Now, what's the trouble? Spill your guts to Uncle Peter."

Nick wanted to ask him a hundred questions about his second day at the Adler Bank. Had he met Konig? What had he heard about the takeover? Was it simply a bid to drive up the share price and exact greenmail from Kaiser? Or would Konig unleash a full-scale attack? But those questions would have to wait for another time.

"The Pasha," Nick said simply.

"Our most reliable client?"

Nick nodded and for the next ten minutes explained his decision to delay the Pasha's transfer.

"Probably a wise move," said Peter afterward. "What's the problem?"

Nick leaned closer. "I got a call at six this morning from Martin Maeder. He dragged me into his office and asked me one too many questions about why I did it. Did I know the Pasha? How dare I disobey the bank? Regular drill."

"Go on."

"I was ready for the questions. Not quite so soon, to be honest, but that didn't faze me. When it was over, Maeder sent me home. Told me not to go back to the office; that I shouldn't contact you. 'The verdict will be delivered Monday,' he said." Nick rubbed the back of his neck and scowled in self-doubt. "Yesterday I was sure I had done the right thing. Now I'm not so sure."

Sprecher laughed raucously. "Worst you can expect is a transfer to logistics in Alstetten or the new office in Latvia." He slapped Nick's knee. "Just joking, chum. Don't sweat it.

Come Monday, all will be status quo ante."

"This isn't funny," Nick protested. "I don't think for a second that anything will be the same as before."

Sprecher straightened his shoulders and spun on his stool so that he faced his colleague. "Listen, Nick. You didn't lose any money, you steered a client out of trouble, and in doing so, you kept the bank's nose a damn sight cleaner. I'd be surprised if you didn't get the Victoria Cross for bravery under fire."

Nick didn't share his friend's jovial mood. If he was fired, or even transferred to a less important post, his ability to effect any type of meaningful investigation into his father's death would be hindered greatly, if not destroyed.

"And then yesterday," Nick continued, "I was walking toward the lake when Agent Sterling Thorne stopped me."

Sprecher appeared amused. "I take it he wasn't inviting you to happy hour at the American Club?"

"Hardly. He asked me if I had seen anything 'interesting' at the bank, anything illegal."

Sprecher feigned shock. "Good gracious. What else? Did he ask if you were working for the Cali Cartel? Bribing the whole of the Italian Senate? Don't look so surprised, it's been done. Promise me, Nick, that you didn't confess." He lit a cigarette. "The man is pathetic. The DEA has a mandate to get some arrests, to force our banks to cooperate. I'll bet he didn't say anything specific about the Pasha. Right?"

"Nothing specific. But he mentioned Cerruti."

"Did he now? So what? That clown tried to come down on me two weeks ago. I said, *'Sorree, no speakee Ingrish.'* He got bloody pissed at that, I can promise you."

"If he came after you, Peter, and then tried to speak with me, it has to mean he's after the Pasha. No other client in our section came up on the surveillance list."

"Thorne can lick my silver bells." Sprecher raised his mug of beer. "I hope you told him to get stuffed."

"More or less, yeah."

Sprecher nodded his head once. "No worries, mate. Cheers." He drained his stein, lifted his pack of cigarettes from the bar, and threw down a ten-franc note. "Say five Our Fathers, five Hail Marys, and you will be absolved of all sins."

Nick put his hand on Sprecher's shoulder and indicated he should retake his seat on the wobbly stool.

"You mean there's more?" Sprecher slumped against the bar's railing. "Nastassia is going to be very cross with me."

"Tell her that if she wants you, she'll have to fight me first," Nick said sarcastically.

"Go on then, boy. But make it snappy."

Nick hesitated before diving in. He'd told himself before coming to Switzerland that the bank was only a means to an end. That he would do whatever was necessary to dig up any available information about his father and to hell with the rest of it. But today he needed some answers. The events of the past twenty-four hours had stirred up too much in him. The agonizing decision to shield the Pasha, the visit from Thorne, the call from Maeder. He was taking fire from too many angles. He was on the run. From the bank, from his father, and most surprisingly, from himself.

"After my meeting with Maeder, I went back to the office anyway. I had to check out the account, you know, 549.617 RR. Just to see. All the money had been transferred out. No initials anywhere on the computer as to who ordered it done. Aren't you curious to know who this guy is?"

"Keeps me from sleeping."

"Ask yourself what client can rouse an executive vice president of the bank at six in the morning. What client traces his money from bank to bank and doesn't sleep until it arrives? What client has Maeder's private phone number? He might have even called the Chairman."

Sprecher shot off his stool and pointed a finger at Nick. "Only God has a direct line to Kaiser. Remember that."

Nick tapped the bar with his thumb and

forefinger pinched together. "The Pasha's number is on the surveillance list. The DEA is interested in him. He calls Maeder directly. Fuck, Peter, we are dealing with a major personality."

"I applaud your choice of moniker, young Nick. Yes, I am in full agreement. No doubt the Pasha is a 'major personality.' The bank needs as many major personalities as it can find. It's our bloody business, remember."

"Who is he?" Nick demanded. "How can you explain what's going on with that account?"

"Weren't you the one defending him the other night?"

"Your fit of curiosity took me by surprise. Today it's my turn to ask the questions."

Sprecher shook his head in exasperation. "You do *not* question," he said. "You do *not* explain. You close your eyes and count the money. You perform your duties in a professional manner, you take your handsome fee, and you sleep soundly each and every night. Once or twice a year you jump on a plane and fly to a beach where the sun shines more than in this miserable hole and sip a piña colada. Peter Sprecher's recipe for long life, brilliant success, and unsurpassed happiness. A thick billfold and two tickets to St.-Tropez, first class."

"I'm glad you can live with it."

Sprecher rolled his eyes and he grew angry.

"Saint bloody Nicholas seated right here beside me. Another American ready to save the world from itself. Why is it that Switzerland is the only country that has ever learned to mind its own business? The world would be a damned sight better off if more countries followed our example. Butt the fuck out!" He sighed loudly, then signaled for the barman. "Two beers. My friend here plans to cure civilization of its evils. The very thought makes a chap parched."

Neither man spoke until the bartender returned with the two beers.

Sprecher touched Nick's arm. "Look, chum, if you're so bent on discovering who the Pasha is you needn't go any further than Marco Cerruti. If I'm not mistaken, Cerruti paid a courtesy visit to our Pasha during his last trip to the Middle East. 'Course, he's gone round the bend since then. But take my advice. Leave well enough alone."

Nick squinted his eyes in frustration. "The sum total of your years of experience is to close my eyes and do exactly as I am told."

"Precisely."

"Close my eyes and ride headlong into disaster?"

"Not disaster, dear boy. Glory!"

Chapter 18

Nick left the Keller Stübli and headed to the nearest post office, where he tucked himself into a phone booth and began checking local directories for the name of Marco Cerruti. His curiosity was quickly rewarded. *Cerruti, M. Seestrasse 78. Thalwil. Banker.* His profession was listed next to his name — another one of this country's neat quirks Nick had only just discovered.

He took a tram to the Bürkliplatz and transferred there to a bus for the quarter-hour ride to Thalwil. Seestrasse 78 was easy to find. A pretty yellow stucco apartment building sitting on the main road, running parallel to the lake.

Nick found the name he was looking for at the top of a list of six. He pressed the buzzer next to it and waited. Not a soul stirred. He wondered if he should have phoned in advance, then decided that he'd been correct to come unannounced. This was not an official visit. He rang the buzzer again and a clipped voice spurted from the grate.

"Who is it?"

Nick jumped toward the speaker. "Neumann, USB."

"USB?" asked the garbled voice.

"Yes," said Nick, then he repeated his name. A moment later he heard a soft metallic click as the entry's lock was released. He pushed open the glass door and entered the foyer, which smelled strongly of pine antiseptic. He crossed to the elevator and pressed the call button. Next to the elevator door was a small mirror. He leaned down and checked his appearance. Dark circles under his eyes broadcast a lack of sleep. Why are you here? he asked himself. To spite Maeder? To prove wrong Sprecher's amoral drivel? Or was it to honor the unsubstantiated image he held of his father? Wouldn't Alex Neumann have done the same thing?

Nick opened the elevator door and pushed the top button. Several announcements were posted on the wall. One read: *"Please respect your assigned laundry day. No laundry may be done on Sundays. By Federal Ordinance. "* Written in pen, under the declaration, was *"No switching of assigned laundry days permitted. "* And under that, *"especially Frau Brunner!!"*

The elevator buffeted lightly as it reached the top floor. Before Nick realized that it had stopped, the door was flung open and a short man, impeccably dressed in a double-breasted gray suit, fresh carnation pinned to the lapel, was grasping his hand and ushering him into the living room.

"Cerruti, *es freut mich.* Pleased to meet you. Come in, sit down."

Nick allowed himself to be steered through a narrow corridor and into a spacious living room. A firm hand in the lee of his back gave him a polite shove toward the couch.

"Please have a seat. Good Lord, it's about time you arrived. I've been calling the bank for weeks."

Nick opened his mouth to explain.

"Don't apologize," said Marco Cerruti. "We both know Herr Kaiser wouldn't permit it. I can imagine the bank is in an uproar. Konig, that devil. I don't believe we've met. Are you new on the Fourth Floor?"

So this was the mysterious Marco Cerruti. He was an excitable man, mid-fifties by the look of him. His bristly gray hair was cut short. His eyes were neither blue nor gray. Pale washed-out skin hung on his face like a badly done job of wallpapering — tight here, sagging there.

"I don't work on the Fourth Floor," said Nick. "I'm sorry if you misunderstood me."

Cerruti pulled up. "My mistake, I'm sure. You are . . . ?"

"Neumann. Nicholas Neumann. I work in your section. FKB4. I began shortly after you became ill."

Cerruti looked at Nick oddly. He bent his knees and inspected him carefully, like a critic would examine a particularly frantic work of Picasso or Braque. Finally, he placed his hands on Nick's shoulders and stared directly into his eyes. "I don't know how I could have missed it when you walked in. I heard your name but it just didn't register. Yes, of course. Nicholas Neumann. My God, you look so like your father. I knew him. Worked under him for five years. Best time of my life. Sit still and let me fetch my papers. There are so many things we have to talk about. Look, eh? Fit as a fiddle and raring to go." He turned a full circle, then dashed out of the room.

Finding himself alone, Nick surveyed his surroundings. The flat was furnished in somber tones, a style he would call antique Swiss Gothic. The colors were sober to the point of being morose. The furniture was clumsy and wooden. A picture window ran the length of the apartment and where not obscured by heavy calico drapes, offered a magnificent view of the Lake of Zurich. That afternoon a mantle of fog clung to the lake's surface. A light drizzle fell. The world was textured damp, gray, and forlorn.

Cerruti bustled into the room carrying two notebooks and a stack of files. "Here is a list of clients Mr. Sprecher must call. Three or four had scheduled appointments with me before my absence."

"Peter is leaving USB," said Nick. "He's been hired by the Adler Bank."

"The Adler Bank? They'll be the death of us." Cerruti dropped a limp hand on his head and collapsed onto the couch beside his visitor. "Well, what have you brought for me? Let's see."

Nick opened the slim briefcase he had brought with him and extracted a manila file. "Sheikh Abdul bin Ahmed al Aziz has been phoning every other day. He sends his best personal regards. He wants to know how you are, where he can contact you. Insists that only your personal responses to his questions will do."

Cerruti sniffed twice and blinked his eyes in rapid succession.

"The sheikh," Nick continued, "is dead set on buying German governments. He has it on good authority that *Finanz Minister* Schneider will lower the Lombard rate any day now."

Cerruti looked at Nick uncertainly. A great sigh left him, and then he laughed. "Dear old Abdul bin Ahmed. I call him Triple A, you know. Never could read economic data worth a damn. German inflation is rising, unemployment over ten percent, Abdul's uncle is itching to raise oil prices. The only way interest rates can go is up, up, up!" Cerruti stood up and straightened his jacket. He pulled his sleeves from his jacket until a good inch of cuff showed. "You must tell the sheikh to buy German equities, pronto. Sell whatever German bonds he's holding and put him into Daimler-Benz, Veba, and Hoechst. That should cover the major industrial groups and keep Abdul from losing his shirt."

Nick wrote down his instructions verbatim.

Cerruti tapped Nick on the arm. "Neumann? No word from Kaiser's office on my returning. Even on a part-time basis?"

So Cerruti wanted to come back? Nick wondered why Kaiser might be keeping him away. "I'm sorry. I don't have any contact with the Fourth Floor."

"Yes, yes," Cerruti tried unsuccessfully to conceal his disappointment. "Well, I'm sure the Chairman will call me soon and let me know his plans. Carry on then, who's next?"

"Another client is causing a fuss. I'm afraid it's one of our numbered accounts, so I don't know the name." Nick made a show of searching for the account number among the papers on his lap. After all, he was only a trainee, he couldn't be expected to match the mental acuity of Maestro Cerruti. He held up a sheet of paper. "Found it. Account 549.617 RR."

"Can you repeat that?" whispered Cerruti. His blinking had gone haywire.

"Five four nine, six one seven, R R. I'm sure you recognize the number."

"Yes, yes. Of course, I do." Cerruti harrumphed. He fidgeted. His hands mangled each other. "Well, get to it, boy. What's the problem?"

"Not a problem really. More an opportunity. I'd like to convince this client to keep more of his assets with us. In the last six weeks he's transferred over $200 million through our accounts without keeping a dime of it overnight. I'm sure we can make some more money off of him than simple transfer fees."

Suddenly, Cerruti was on his feet. "Stay there, Nicholas. No moving. No budging. I'll be right back. I have something wonderful to show you."

Before Nick could protest, he was gone. He came back a minute later with a spiral scrapbook tucked under his arm. He thrust the scrapbook into Nick's hands and opened it to a spot kept by a leather bookmark. "Recognize anyone?" he asked.

Nick peered down at the color photo on the right-hand page. It was a 5 by 7 of Wolfgang Kaiser, Marco Cerruti, Alexander Neumann, and a stout, jolly-looking fellow with a sweaty brow. A voluptuous woman with frosted blond hair and bright pink lipstick curtsied in front of them. She was a knockout. Kaiser held one of her hands to his mouth, giving it a zesty kiss. Not to be outdone, the jolly little fellow held her other hand in a similar position. The woman's sparkling eyes made it clear she was enjoying the attention. A handwritten caption beneath the photograph read, "California, Here He Comes! December 1967."

Nick stared at his father. Alexander Neumann was tall and slim, hair as black as Nick's, cut in the style of the day. His blue eyes shone with the zeal of a thousand dreams, all of them attainable. He was laughing. A man with the world before him.

Standing next to him, a head shorter, was Cerruti, ever the dandy, sporting a red carnation in the lapel of a dark suit. Wolfgang Kaiser came next, exuberantly smooching the attractive woman's hand. His mustache was, if possible, bushier than today. Nick did not recognize the fourth man or the woman.

"Your father's going-away party," said Cerruti. "Before he left to open the office in Los Angeles. We were some crew, all of us bachelors. Handsome devils, eh? Everyone at the bank came to the party. Of course, we were only a couple hundred back then."

"You said you worked with him?"

"We all worked together. We were the heart and soul of private banking. Kaiser was our divisional manager. I served as an apprentice under your father. Looked after me like a brother, he did. He'd been promoted to vice president that very day." Cerruti tapped the picture. "I adored Alex. I hated to see him go to Los Angeles but for me it was a big step up."

Nick continued studying the photograph. He'd seen few snapshots of his father before he came to America, mostly black-and-white portraits of a tall unsmiling teenager in a strict Sunday suit. He was surprised at how much younger he looked in Cerruti's photo than in his own recollections. This Alex Neumann

251

was happy, really happy. Nick didn't have a single memory of his father being so cheerful, so unrestrained.

Cerruti bounced to his feet. "Come, let's have a drink. What can I get you?"

Nick felt buoyed by Cerruti's enthusiasm. "How about a beer?"

"I'm sorry, I don't touch alcohol. Makes me nervous. Will a soda do?"

"Sure, that's fine." If alcohol made this guy nervous, what calmed him down? Nick wondered.

Cerruti disappeared into the kitchen. A minute later, he returned with two cans of soda and glasses filled with ice. Nick took the glass and poured himself a soft drink.

"To your father," Cerruti toasted.

Nick raised his glass, then took a sip. "I never knew he worked directly under Wolfgang Kaiser. What did he do?"

"Why, your father was Kaiser's number two for years. Portfolio management, of course. The Chairman never told you?"

"No, I've only spoken to him for a few minutes since I arrived. Like you said, he's pretty busy these days."

"Your father was a tiger. There was a lot of competition between the two of them."

"What do you mean?"

"Come now, turn the page. I kept a letter from your father. It will show you what I mean. Actually, it's one of his monthly reports.

An update detailing the business conducted at the Los Angeles office."

Nick turned the page to find a wrinkled memorandum held in place by a transparent plastic sheet. The stationery was headed *United Swiss Bank, Los Angeles Representative Office, Alexander Neumann Vice President and Bureau Manager.* The memo was addressed to Wolfgang Kaiser and cc'd to Urs Knecht, Beat Frey, and Klaus Konig. It was dated June 17, 1968.

The text was uneventful, more notable for the casual tone employed (compared with the formal reports submitted today) than for any important news. Nick's father wrote about three prospective clients he had visited, a deposit he had received for $125,000 from Walter Galahad, "a big shot at MGM," and his need for a secretary. He mentioned that he could not be expected to mimeograph bank documents and then go to lunch at Perino's, blue ink wet on his hands. He planned a trip to San Francisco the next week. Most interesting to Nick's eye was the postscript labeled *"Confidential"* — no doubt a ruse to ensure maximum readership. *"Wolf, am prepared to double our wager. Goal of one million in deposits first year too easy. Don't say I'm not fair. Alex."*

Nick read the memorandum a second time, this time slowly, line by line. He felt as if his father were still alive. Alex Neumann had a plane to catch next week to San Francisco. A bet with Wolfgang Kaiser he was determined to win. A luncheon date at Perino's. How could he be dead seventeen years? He had a marriage, a child, an entire life in front of him.

Nick stared at the words, transfixed. His stomach grew hollow and his shoulders ached with a fatigue that hadn't been there moments ago. One look at the picture, one reading of the memo, and he was ready to fall apart. He was utterly surprised that after so long he could feel so much pain. He flipped back to the picture and looked deep into his father's eyes. He realized at that instant that he'd taught himself not to miss the man, not to miss Alexander Neumann, but to miss the role he played, to miss his father. He had never considered for a second that he'd been deprived of knowing someone special, a man Cerruti had adored. For the first time in his life Nick felt sorry for his father, for the forty-year-old executive who'd had his life stolen from him. He had discovered a new wellspring of sorrow and already its waters were seeping into him, filling him with his own worst memories.

Nick closed his eyes and held them tightly shut.

He is no longer in Marco Cerruti's apartment. He is a boy. It is night. He shudders as the strobe of a police siren lights a dozen shadowy figures dressed in yellow sou'westers. A heavy rain pounds his shoulders. He walks toward the front door of a house he's never seen before. Why is his father staying here only two miles from home? Business? That's the excuse his mother has lamely provided. Or, is it because lately his parents never seem to stop arguing? Inside the doorway, his father lies on his side in his tan pajamas. A pond of blood has gathered between his chest and his out-stretched arm. "Sonuvabitch caught three in the chest," whispers a policeman behind Nick. "Sonuvabitch caught three in the chest, caught three in the chest . . ."

Marco Cerruti placed a hand on Nick's shoulder. "Are you all right, Mr. Neumann?"

Nick shuddered at the touch. "Yeah, I'm okay. Thanks."

"I was so sorry to learn about your father."

Nick tapped the report. "Reading this brought back some old memories. Do you think I might keep it?"

"Nothing would give me more pleasure." Cerruti folded back the sheet and delicately removed the memorandum. "There are more of these in the bank archives. We've never thrown away a single piece of official corre-spondence. Not in one hundred twenty-five years."

"Where would I find them?"

"*Dokumentation Zentrale.* Ask Karl. He can find anything."

"If I have time, maybe one day I'll take a

look," Nick said nonchalantly, but inside him an agitated voice was yelling at him to get his ass down to DZ pronto.

I'm going to find out what happened to my father, he had told Anna Fontaine. *I'm going to learn once and for all whether he was a saint or a sinner.* The memo was what he had come for.

Nick turned back to the picture of his father and Wolfgang Kaiser. "Who's the lady in this photograph?"

Cerruti smiled, as if buoyed by a pleasant memory. "You mean you don't recognize her? That's Rita Sutter. Back then she was just another girl in the typing pool. Today she's the Chairman's executive secretary."

"And the fourth man?"

"It's Klaus Konig. He runs the Adler Bank."

Nick looked closer. The chubby little man kissing Rita Sutter's hand looked nothing like the brash Konig of today. But then, it had been thirty years and Konig wasn't wearing the red polka-dot bow tie that had become his trademark. Nick wondered which of the two men vying for the secretary's attentions had won. And if the other had held a grudge.

"Konig was part of our merry band of thieves," said Cerruti. "He left a few years after your father. Went to America. Studied some kind of mathematics. He needed his doctorate to be better than the rest of us. He came back ten years ago. Did some consulting in the Middle East, probably for the Thief of Baghdad if I know Klaus. Started up his own shop seven years back. Can't fault his success, only his methods. We don't go for terror and intimidation in Switzerland."

"We call it shareholder dissent in the States," said Nick.

"Call it what you will, it's piracy!" Cerruti drained the rest of his cola and moved toward the door. "If that's all you had to discuss, Mr. Neumann . . ."

"We hadn't finished with our last client," Nick said. "We really should discuss him."

"I'd rather not. Take my advice and forget about him."

But Nick was in no mood for forgetting, so he pressed on. "The amounts of his transfers have increased dramatically since you've been gone. There are other developments. The bank is cooperating with the United States Drug Enforcement Administration."

"Thorne," Cerruti mumbled. "Sterling Thorne?"

"Yes," said Nick. "Sterling Thorne. Has he spoken with you?"

Cerruti wrapped his arms around himself. "Why? Did he mention me?"

"No," Nick said. "Thorne circulates a list each week with the account numbers of individuals he suspects of being involved in drugs, money laundering. This week the Pasha's account was on that list. I need to know who the Pasha is."

"Who the Pasha is, or is not, is none of your concern."

"Why is the DEA after him?"

"Didn't you hear me? It's none of your concern." Cerruti pinched the bridge of his nose between thumb and forefinger. His arm trembled lightly.

"It's my responsibility to know who this client is."

"Do as you're told, Mr. Neumann. Do not get involved with the Pasha. Leave that to Mr. Maeder, or better yet to . . ."

"To who?" Nick demanded.

"Leave it to Maeder. It is a world entirely beyond you. Keep it that way."

"You know the Pasha," Nick insisted. He felt reckless and out of control. "You visited him in December. What is his name?"

"Please, Mr. Neumann, no more questions. I am quite upset." What had been a minor palsy bothering Cerruti's arm grew into an uncontrolled spasm shaking his entire body.

"What business is the man in?" Nick asked forcefully. He wanted an answer now. He fought to stifle an impulse to shake the bantamweight until he talked. "Why are the authorities pursuing him?"

"I don't know. And I don't want to know." Cerruti grabbed the lapels of Nick's jacket. "Tell me, Neumann. Tell me you haven't done anything to upset him."

Nick held the little man by the wrists and eased him gently onto the couch. The sight of so much fear in Cerruti's face drained all the anger out of him. "No. Nothing," he said.

Cerruti released the lapels. "No matter what you do, don't upset him."

Nick looked down at the frightened banker and, drawing a deep breath, realized there was no more to be gotten out of him — at least for now. "I can show myself to the door. Thank you for my father's memo."

"Neumann, one question. What have they told you at work about why I'm no longer at the office?"

"Martin Maeder announced that you had suffered a nervous breakdown, but we've been asked to tell your clients that you contracted hepatitis on your last trip. Oh, and I forgot to mention, word is you may come back to one of our affiliates. Maybe the Arab Bank."

"The Arab Bank? God help me." Cerruti gripped the couch's cushions, his knuckles white with tension.

Nick fell to one knee and placed a hand on Cerruti's shoulder. It was clear why Kaiser was delaying Cerruti's return. The man was a wreck. "Are you sure you're okay? Let me call a doctor. You're not looking very well."

Cerruti pushed him away. "Just leave, Mr. Neumann. I'm fine. A bit of rest is all I need."

Nick walked toward the door.

"And Neumann," Cerruti called weakly, "when you see the Chairman tell him I'm fit as a fiddle and rarin' to go."

Chapter 19

Later that evening, Nick found himself standing before an ungainly gray-stone apartment building on a lesser street far from the prosperous center of the city. The temperature had crawled below freezing and the sky had partially cleared. A scrap of paper showed an address: Eibenstrasse 18.

His father had grown up in this building. Alexander Neumann had lived with his mother and grandmother from his birth until he was nineteen in a lousy two-room apartment overlooking a perpetually shaded interior court.

Nick had visited the apartment when he was a boy. Everything about it had been dark and musty. Closed windows covered by heavy drapes. Massive wooden furniture dyed a deep chestnut brown. To a child used to playing on the rolling lawns and sunlit streets of southern California, the apartment, the street, the entire neighborhood where his father had grown up, had appeared evil and unfriendly. He had hated it.

But tonight he felt the need to revisit the place of his father's childhood. To commune with the ghosts of his parents' past and to reconcile the boy who had grown up on these streets with the man who had become his father.

Nick stared up at the grimy building, recalling a day when he had hated his father. Absolutely despised him. When he had wished the earth would crack open and suck him down to the burning nether regions that were undoubtedly his true home.

A trip to Switzerland during the summer of Nick's tenth year. A weekend in Arosa, a mountain village nestled on the hillside of a sweeping valley. A Sunday-morning gathering of the local chapter of the Swiss Alpine Club in a glade situated under the stoic gaze of a monstrous peak, the Tierfluh.

The party of twenty-odd climbers sets out at dawn. They are a mixed lot: at ten, Nick is the youngest; at seventy, his great-uncle Erhard, the oldest. They walk through a field of high grass, past a milky lake as flat as a mirror, then ford a gurgling brook. Soon they enter a stand of tall pines, and the path begins to move up a gentle slope. Heads are bowed, breathing deep and steady. Uncle Erhard leads the pack. Nick stays in the middle. He is nervous. Will they really try to reach the craggy peak?

An hour after the walk has begun, the group stops at a wooden hut standing in the center of a grassy meadow. The door of the hut is pried open and someone ventures in. He returns a moment later, holding a bottle of clear liquid high in the air. A cry goes up. All are invited to enjoy the home-distilled *Pflümli*. Nick, too, is given the bottle, and he drinks down a thimbleful of the plum liqueur. His eyes water and his cheeks flush, but he refuses to cough. He is proud to have been taken into this fine group's company. He vows not to reveal his fatigue. Or his growing fear.

The walk resumes. Again into the trees. An hour later, the path emerges onto a rock-strewn plain and for a while is flatter, but now less sure. Stones crumble beneath every foot-step. Slowly, all vegetation disappears. The trail leads upward as it skirts the side of the mountain, moving deeper into the shadowy saddle that links two peaks.

The line of climbers has strung out. Erhard keeps the lead. He carries a leather rucksack on his back and holds a gnarled rod in his hand. One hundred yards along comes Alexander Neumann. Twenty paces farther back follows Nick. One by one, the climbers pass him by. Each pats him on the head and offers an encouraging word. Soon no one is behind.

Ahead, the trail cuts into a field of summer snow, as white as icing on a chocolate cake. The pitch of the slope increases. Each step forward is one half step higher. Nick's breath is shallow, his head light. He can see his great-uncle far in front, can recognize him only by the walking stick he carries. He can see his father too: a bobbing head of black hair above a sweater as red as the Swiss flag.

Minutes pass. Hours. The trail winds upward. Nick lowers his head and walks. He counts to one thousand. Still the end is no closer. Snow rolls out for miles before him. High above his left shoulder, he can see the sharp rocks that lead to the summit. He notes with alarm the distance that separates him from the others. He can no longer see his uncle. His father is merely a red speck. Nick is alone in a valley of snow. With every step, he grows farther separated from his father and his great-uncle. With every step, he comes closer to the peak that wants to kill him. Finally, he can go no farther and stops. He is exhausted and frightened.

"Dad," he yells. "Dad!" But his thin voice disappears easily in the vast mountain spaces. "Help," he yells. "Come back!" But no one hears. One after another the trail of climbers disappears around the girth of the mountain. And then his father disappears, too.

At first Nick is stunned. His breathing has calmed. His heartbeat has slowed. The constant crunching of snow that has accompanied him for so long has come to a halt. All is quiet. All is absolutely still. And for a child raised in the city there is nothing so terrifying as that first moment when he feels the icy breath of unspoiled nature upon his naked face, when his dulled senses cower at the magnificence of solitude's deafening roar, and when he learns for the first time that he is alone.

Nick falls to his knees unsure of his ability to carry on. Where has everyone gone? Why has his father deserted him? Don't they care? Do they want him to die?

"Dad!" he shrieks.

Nick feels his cheeks flush. His throat tightens uncontrollably. Tears rush into his eyes and his vision grows blurry. With a wrenching sob, he begins to cry. And in the steady flow of his tears come all the injustices, all the petty tyrannies, all the unfair punishments ever bestowed upon him. No one loves him, he says in a garbled tongue, between gulps of air. His father wants him to die up here. His mother probably helped plan it.

Nick cries for his father again. Still, no one comes. The slope ahead is as empty as it was five minutes ago. Soon, the tears dry and the sobbing stops. He is alone with the towering mountains and the slashing breeze and the evil rocks above that want so to kill him. He wipes the dried tears from his cheeks and blows his nose into the snow.

No, he swears, the rocks won't kill me. The mountains won't kill me. No one will. He remembers the hot bite of the *Pflümli* and how he was given the bottle like any other man. He remembers the pats on the head as each climber in turn passed him by. Mostly he remembers the mute plain of his father's back, the bright red sweater that never once looked back to check upon his progress.

I have to go on, he tells himself. I can't stay here. And like a divine gift, the thought forms inside him that he must make it to the summit — that this time he doesn't have a choice. And he tells himself, "I will reach the top of this mountain. Yes, I will."

Nick lowers his head and starts off. His eyes move from one hollow footprint to another. His feet advance quickly along the steep trail. Soon he is almost running. To the beat of his pounding heart, he tells himself he must make it, he cannot stop. And so he climbs. For how long he does not know. His mind is focused only on the empty footsteps of those gone before, knowing that along this path came his great-uncle and his father and all the others who expect nothing more of him than to walk up the mountain.

A high-pitched whistle intrudes on his hermetically sealed world. A whoop, a yell, a cry of encouragement. Nick looks up. The whole group sits on an outcropping of rock, just yards away. They are cheering his arrival. They are standing and clapping. He hears the whistle again and sees that it is his father running down the slope to greet him.

He has made it. He has succeeded.

And then Nick is in his father's arms, held tightly in a loving embrace. At first he is upset. He has walked up this mountain. No one has helped him. It is his victory. How dare his father treat him like a child? But after a few tentative moments, he gives in and wraps his arms around his father. For a long time, they hold each other close. Alexander Neumann whispers something about taking the first steps toward being a man. Nick feels hot and smothered. And for some unexplained reason, he begins to cry. There in the lee of his father's arm, he lets the tears run down his cheeks and he hugs his father as hard as he possibly can.

Nick would always remember that day. He looked up once more at his father's building and felt awash in pride. He had come to Switzerland to get to know Alexander Neumann. To search for the truth about the banker who had died at the age of forty.

Become one of them, his father's spirit had urged him. And he had. Now Nick could only pray that his actions on behalf of the Pasha, whoever he was, had not jeopardized his search.

Chapter 20

Ali Mevlevi slammed his foot onto the accelerator of the Bentley Mulsanne Turbo and pulled into the oncoming lane of traffic. An approaching Volkswagen van carelessly hugging the center line careered to the left, raising a curtain of dust on the highway's shoulder, then toppled onto its side and slid down the unpaved embankment. Mevlevi blared his horn and kept his foot firmly on the gas. "Out of my way," he yelled.

The half-ton pickup that had stubbornly blocked his path scooted to the crest of the highway, allowing him to pass. The decrepit vehicle was loaded far beyond its capacity ferrying a team of migrant laborers, and once on the hardscrabble shoulder it puttered to a halt. Workers jumped from the flatbed, yelling oaths and making obscene gestures at the passing Bentley.

"Miserable beggars," Mevlevi said, his rage waning as he watched the men scramble about in the late-afternoon sun. Under what unfortunate star had they been born? Their time on earth was marked by degradation, penury, and the systematic crushing of their once indomitable Arabic spirit. For these men, he would risk his fortune. For these men, Khamsin must succeed.

Mevlevi returned his attention to the stripe of asphalt before him, but it was not long before his mind wandered back to the dilemma that pressed on his heart like a sharpened dagger. A spy, he thought to himself. A spy is lying nearby.

Hours earlier, he had discovered that the United Swiss Bank had failed to transfer forty-seven million dollars of his money according to his precise instructions. Calls to inquire about the delay had revealed the circumstances of his escape. However, no explanation had been given as to which failure in the bank's systems had resulted in his account number's appearing on a surveillance list established by the United States Drug Enforcement Administration. For now, though, that was of minor concern. For not only had the authorities expected the transfer, they had known its exact amount.

"A spy," Mevlevi said, through clenched teeth. "A spy has been peeking over my shoulder."

Normally, he was thankful for the unerring efficiency of the Swiss. No other country oversaw the execution of a client's instructions with such exactitude. The French were arrogant. The Chinese imprecise. The Cayman Islanders — who could trust that colony of self-serving financial leeches? The Swiss were polite, deferential, and exact. They followed orders to the letter. And so his escape, when analyzed, grew more storied. For it was the disobeying of a clearly defined order that had permitted him to flee the grasp of the international authorities. He was indebted to an American: a United States Marine, no less. One whose brethren's blood defiled the holy land over which he now drove.

Mevlevi could not stifle the laugh rising up from deep within his belly. The self-righteous Americans — policing the world, making it safe for democracy; a planet, dictator and drug free. And *he* was a dreamer?

Mevlevi checked his speed and kept the car pointed south on National Route 1, toward Mieh-Mieh, toward Israel. To his right, barren hillocks of pale alkali grit rose up from the Mediterranean Sea. Occasionally, a settlement dotted the top of a small rise. The low-slung structures were built of cinder block white-washed to deflect the Levant's bleaching sun. More and more sported antennas, some even a modest satellite dish. The Shouf Mountains rose steeply to his left, colored a bluish-gray and shaped like the dorsal fins of a school of sharks. Soon, their slopes would darken into a verdant green as the deciduous trees that flourished on the mountains' slopes sprouted new buds.

General Amos Ben-Ami had led his forces down this very road sixteen years before. Operation Big Pine: the Israeli invasion of Lebanon. American-made tanks, armored personnel carriers, and mobile artillery streamed across the Israeli border in a vomitous wave of Western imperialism. The ill-organized Lebanese militias offered scant resistance. The Syrian regulars scarcely more. Truth be known, Haffez-al-Assad had issued orders to all senior commanders that should the vanguard of Israel's troops reach Beirut, his soldiers were to withdraw to the relative safety of the Bekaa valley. And so when General Ben-Ami led his troops to Beirut and encircled the city, the Syrians were absent. The PLO laid down its arms and was allowed to disembark by sea for camps in Egypt and Saudi Arabia. Eleven months later, Israel withdrew her troops from Beirut, preferring to establish a twenty-five-kilometer security zone on her northern border. A cushion to distance herself from the country of Islamic fanatics who lived to the north.

The Israelis had bought themselves fifteen years, mused Ali Mevlevi. Fifteen years of blemished peace. Their vacation would soon end. In weeks, another army would travel a path parallel to National Route 1, this time traveling south. A secret army under his guidance. A guerrilla force fighting beneath the green-and-white standard of Islam. Like the fabled khamsin, the violent wind that sprang from the desert without warning and for fifty days devoured all in its path, he would rise unseen and rain fury upon the enemy.

Mevlevi opened a sterling case at his side and withdrew a slim black cigarette, a Turkish Sobranie. One last tie to his homeland: Anatolia — *where the sun rises.* And where it sets, he thought bitterly, leaving its inhabitants poorer, dirtier, and hungrier than the day before.

He drew deeply from the cigarette, allowing the acrid smoke to fill his lungs, feeling its potent nicotine invigorate him. He saw before him the rugged hills and salt plains of Cappadocia. He envisioned his father sitting at the head of the rough wooden table that had dominated the living area, serving as workbench, conjugal bed, and on rare occasion, a formal surface for feasting and celebration. His father would be wearing the tall red fez he so treasured. His elder brother, Saleem, too. Dervishes, both of them. Mystics.

Mevlevi remembered their twirling and spinning, their high-pitched chanting, the hems of their skirts bouncing higher as their worship grew more impassioned. He saw their heads tilt back and watched their jaws fall as they cried out to the prophet. He heard their fevered voices urging their fellow Dervs into a state of ecstatic union with the prophet.

For years, his father had implored him to return home. "You are a rich man," he said. "Turn your heart to Allah. Share your family's love." And for years, Mevlevi had laughed at the notion. His heart had turned away from Allah's love. He had abandoned the religion of his father. Yet, the Almighty had not abandoned him. One day his father wrote to him, claiming he had been commanded by the prophet to bring his second son back to Islam. The note included a short verse, and its words had pierced a soul Mevlevi thought long dead.

Come come, whoever you are,
Wanderer, idolater, worshiper of fire,
Come even though you have broken your
vows a thousand times,
Ours is not a caravan of despair.

Mevlevi had dwelled upon the words. The wealth of Croesus was his. He was master of a small empire. Numbered accounts at a dozen banks across Europe sheltered his money. But what had such material success brought him? The same despair, worry, and indirection quoted in the sacred verse.

With each passing day, his mistrust of his fellow man grew. Man was a putrid creature rarely able to govern his lesser desires, concerned only with acquiring money, power, and position. Interested in fulfilling his greed, sating his lust, and dominating all that surrounded him. Each time Ali Mevlevi regarded himself in the mirror he saw a king among such foul creatures. And it made him sick.

Only his identity as a Muslim could provide solace.

Recalling the moment of his awakening, Ali Mevlevi enjoyed a tremor of inspiration. His body was filled with an uncompromising love for the Almighty and a matching contempt for his own earthly ambitions. To what good could he put his wealth? To what use could he bring his experience? Allah alone provided the answer. To the good of Islam. To the greater glory of Muhammad. To the advancement of his people's cause.

Now, on the verge of proving to his father and his brothers that he was capable of showering Allah with a greater glory than they, with their twirling steps and mystic chants, Mevlevi had unearthed a spy, an enemy of God's will who threatened to destroy all he had worked for these past years.

An enemy of Khamsin.

Mevlevi reminded himself that his inquiries must center on those with access to the precise details of his financial transactions. It could not be someone in Zurich. Neither Cerruti, nor Sprecher, nor Neumann could possibly have known the amount of the transfer before it reached the bank. But that the amount was known beforehand was undisputed. His contacts in Zurich had been most specific. A Mr. Sterling Thorne of the United States DEA had been looking for a transfer of forty-seven million dollars.

The spy, therefore, must be nestled close by. The light of inquiry must be directed inside his compound. Who was permitted free passage through his household? Who might overhear a conversation or gain access to his most private documents? Only two persons came to mind: Joseph and Lina. But why would either betray him? What could motivate his lover and his closest manservant to seek his demise?

Mevlevi burst into laughter at his own naïveté. Money, of course. Moral indignation had fled this corner of Western civilization years ago. Only financial gain remained as a plausible motive. And if for financial gain, who was the Caiaphas paying Judas his thirty pieces of silver?

Soon, he would find out. Perhaps even today.

Mevlevi settled into the soft leather seat of his automobile for the remaining drive to Mieh-Mieh. There he would find Abu Abu and discuss with him in a most businesslike manner the details of Joseph's recruitment. His aide's brilliant scar had lost its luster of incorruptibility.

The gleaming black sedan passed Tyre, then Sidon, and after forty-five minutes, the village of Samurad, where it left the highway and descended a gravel road toward a sprawling settlement of whitewashed brick and mud buildings two kilometers distant: Mieh-Mieh.

As Mevlevi neared the entrance to the camp, a crowd began to form. One hundred yards from the gates, he brought the Bentley to a complete stop and the mob surged forward to examine the car. In seconds, the Bentley was awash in the probing hands and curious faces of Mieh-Mieh's forsaken residents. Mevlevi climbed out of the automobile and told two rough-looking youths to guard his car. He gave each a crisp one-hundred-dollar bill. The two took immediate ownership of the vehicle, beating back the mob with a series of slaps, kicks, and when necessary, blows — each accompanied by a derisive glance and an obscene oath. How quickly they forgot that only seconds before they too had been peasants.

Mevlevi made his way into the camp and within minutes was at the headman's residence. He was dressed for his outing in a flowing black *dishdasha* and red checkered kaffiyeh. He drew back the tattered curtain that served as the front door and crossed the home's wooden threshold. Inside, two children stared vacantly at a black-and-white television, its screen filled more by snow and fuzz than any discernible picture.

Mevlevi knelt by the older of the two, a corpulent boy of eleven or twelve. "Hello, young warrior. Where is your father?"

The boy paid his visitor no heed and continued watching the hazy picture.

Mevlevi looked at the girl wrapped in a

hand-sewn blanket. "Does your brother speak?" he asked gently.

"Yes." She nodded dully.

Mevlevi grabbed the boy's ear and lifted him off the floor. The boy screamed for mercy.

"Jafar!" announced Mevlevi. "I have your boy. Come out, you infernal coward. Do you think I come to this hellhole to chat with your children?"

Silently, he apologized to the prophet, explaining that such actions, while harsh, were necessary for the glory of Islam.

A smothered voice called out from a back room. "Al-Mevlevi, I beg you. Do the boy no harm. I arrive presently."

A wooden dresser standing against the room's far wall rattled aside. Behind it, carved out of the wall like a missing tooth, was a dark opening. Jafar Muftilli emerged into the half-light of his living room. He was a crooked figure of forty years. He carried an abacus and a well-thumbed ledger. "I did not know this day would be blessed with so august a visit to our humble residence."

"Do you always pass your days in a cellar hidden from your friends?" asked Mevlevi.

"Please do not misunderstand, your grace. Matters financial must always be conducted with the utmost of care. Unfortunately, my fellow countrymen think nothing of robbing from their own."

Mevlevi snorted with disgust, keeping a

tight hold on the boy and his ear. What "matters financial" could bother this wastrel? Whether to keep his life's savings in a hundred one-dollar notes or twenty-fives? "Jafar, I seek Abu Abu."

The headman nervously stroked his wispy beard. "I have not seen him for days."

"Jafar, today, of all the days I have passed on this wretched planet, I do not wish to be delayed. I must find Abu Abu at once."

Jafar licked his lips and held out his hands in supplication. "Please, your grace. I speak only the truth. I have no reason to lie to you."

"Perhaps not. Or perhaps Abu has purchased your cooperation."

"No, your grace . . ." shouted Jafar.

Mevlevi gave the boy's ear a sharp tug downward, separating it cleanly from the head. The fat child screamed and fell to the ground. Surprisingly, only a thin trickle of blood streamed through the boy's clenched fists.

Jafar fell to his knees. He appeared torn between comforting his hysterical son and beseeching his demanding visitor. "Al-Mevlevi, I speak the truth. Abu Abu is gone. I know nothing of his whereabouts."

Mevlevi withdrew an evil instrument from his robes and held it so Jafar could not mistake its capacity. A blade resembling a silver crescent moon extended from a stubby wooden handle. It was the knife of an opium harvester, an early gift from the Thai general Mong. Mevlevi knelt beside the whimpering youth and taking hold of his long black hair, jerked the child's head upward so that he faced his father. "Do you wish your boy to lose his nose? His tongue?"

Jafar was immobile with rage and fear. "I will take you to his house. You must believe me. I know nothing." He placed his forehead against the floor and cried.

Mevlevi cast down the boy. "Very well. Let us go."

Jafar exited his home followed closely by his insistent visitor. Everywhere they walked, residents of the camp bowed deferentially and withdrew into the shadows of their shanties. The camp itself was a confusing pattern of interlacing alleys and one-way passages, covering an area of five square miles. Once within its walls, a visitor could well be lost for days before finding his way out again. Assuming he was allowed to depart.

After fifteen minutes of navigating a warren of alleys, each narrower than the last, Jafar stopped in front of a particularly foul abode. Wooden postings held aloft a patchwork roof of tin sheeting, discarded plywood, and woolen blankets. Curtains drawn over paneless windows fluttered in and out of the hovel, allowing a malodorous stench to drift into the alleyway. Mevlevi threw back the entry blanket and ventured into the one-room shanty.

Clothing lay everywhere. A bottle of milk was overturned and dried on the pressed-dirt floor. A table stood upended. Above the disorder rested a ripe, overpowering smell that demanded immediate attention. He knew it well. It was the rank scent of death.

"Where is Abu's cellar?" Mevlevi demanded.

Jafar hesitated for a moment before pointing to a rusted cast-iron stove. Mevlevi pushed him ahead and told him to hurry it up. Jafar bent over the stove and placed his arms around its back, as if greeting a long unseen relative. "I'm searching for the release," he said, even as he pulled a lever and the stove swung away from the cinder-block wall.

A short flight of stairs descended into a black void. An inhuman smell flooded out of the unlit cavern. Mevlevi's hands struggled over an uneven wall and found a fat wire that led to a switch. He flicked it and a weak bulb illuminated a dank, low-ceilinged hideaway.

Abu Abu was dead.

No one could have mistaken the fact. He lay before Mevlevi in two pieces. His severed head decorated a copper plate. His unclothed torso lay sprawled nearby, chest down. The earthen floor was covered with what looked like the blood of ten men. The knife utilized for the beheading sat abandoned next to Abu's shoulder, its serrated blade coated with dried blood. Mevlevi picked it up. The handle was of black plastic, crosshatched to improve grip. A Star of David inside a circle was stamped upon its base. He knew the weapon. A K-Bar thrusting knife: standard issue of the Israeli army. He placed his foot under Abu's bloated stomach and turned over the corpse. Both arms draped onto the ground. The thumbs of each hand were missing, and a Star of David was carved into either palm.

"Jews," hissed Jafar Muftilli before rushing to a corner of the room and vomiting.

Mevlevi was nonplussed by the sight of the headless corpse. He had seen far worse. "What has Abu done to offend the Israelites?"

"A reprisal," Jafar answered weakly. "He had special friends among Hamas for whom he worked."

"The Qassam?" Mevlevi asked skeptically. "Had Abu been recruiting for the Qassam?" He referred to the extremist wing of soldiers within the Hamas from whose ranks were drawn the legions of suicide bombers.

Jafar staggered back to the center of the room. "Is this not sufficient proof?"

"So it is." If the Jews had deemed Abu Abu so important a target as to merit the attentions of their finest killers, then he himself must have been a high-ranking member of Hamas, or even the Qassam. His commitment to his Arab brothers could not be questioned. Nor could his skill in evaluating recruits.

Joseph could be trusted.

Mevlevi stared at Abu Abu's head. His eyes were open, his mouth twisted in agony. Hardly a fitting death for a servant of Islam. *Rest in peace,* he said silently. *Your death will be avenged ten thousand–fold.*

Chapter 21

Nick stepped into his apartment and was immediately struck by an odor that hadn't been there that morning. It was a faint smell, not far from the lemon wax he had used to polish mess tables in the Corps. *Not far* — but not it, either. It had a milder flavor, its own distinct signature. He shut the door behind him and locked it, then walked to the center of his one-room palace. He closed his eyes and breathed in deeply through his nose. He caught the elusive scent again but could not recognize it. All he could say was that it was foreign. It didn't belong here.

Nick willed himself to move slowly, to examine every inch of his apartment from carpet to ceiling. His clothing was untouched. His books were in place. If anything, the papers on his desk were stacked too neatly. Still he knew. He could feel it, sure as if they'd slid a calling card under the door.

Someone had been in his apartment.

Nick lifted his nose into the air and sniffed several times. He caught the foreign smell dead on. A waft of men's cologne, something thick and sweet, something expensive. Something he'd never worn in his life.

Nick walked to the dresser where he kept his shirts and sweaters, and opened the bottom drawer. He reached beneath a sweatshirt and feeling the comforting heft of his side arm, allowed himself to relax a little. He had brought his service-issue Colt Commander with him from New York. It had been easy enough. He'd disassembled it and stashed its components in the corners of his suitcase to smuggle it through airport security. The bullets he'd purchased in Zurich. He pulled the holster from the drawer and tossed it onto the bed, then sat down next to it. Drawing the pistol, he checked to see if a round was still chambered. He drew back the slide and peered into the firing breech. The brass jacket of a .45-caliber hollow point smiled back at him. He released the slide and guided his finger inside the trigger guard. His thumb fell to the safety. It was off. Nick stood abruptly. Through habit long ingrained, he kept his pistol "cocked and locked." Hammer back, safety on. He brushed his finger up and down against the safety, seeing if the pinion had loosened, allowing the safety to move to the off position of its own accord. But the switch was firm. Only an intentional flick downward would disarm the safety.

Nick replaced the pistol in its holster, stuck it back in the bottom drawer, then moved to the doorway. He tried to visualize the motions of the person who had been inside his apartment. He could see a phantomlike shape moving from one side of the room to the other. Who had sent him? Thorne and his friends in the U.S. government? Or was it someone from the bank? Maeder or Schweitzer or one of their underlings assigned to check up on the new man from America? Nick crossed the room and sat on his bed. A picture of the green mountain guide's hat and the spare, olive-skinned man wearing it came to him. Had his stalker been the one who'd broken into his apartment?

Nick had no answer to any of his questions. He shuddered as a profound sense of insecurity overcame him. He felt an irrational need to check on the few treasured items he had brought with him from the States. He knew everything would be in its place, but he needed to see them and to touch them. They were the outermost extremities of his own self, and he had to be sure they had not been violated.

Nick hurried into the bathroom and picked up his shaving kit. He unzipped it and looked inside. A small blue box with the words Tiffany & Co. embossed on its lid occupied one corner. He removed the box and opened it. A chamois pouch of the same robin's egg blue rested on a bed of puffed cotton. He picked up the pouch and turned it upside down. A sterling silver Swiss army knife fell into his palm. Engraved on it were the words "Love Forever, Anna." Her good-bye present, delivered on Christmas Eve. Under the bed of cotton, folded into a tight square, was the letter that had accompanied it. He unfolded the letter and read.

My dearest Nicholas,
    The holiday season finds me thinking more and more about all that we had together and all that we could have had. I can't imagine that you're no longer a part of my life. I can only hope that your heart doesn't feel as empty as mine. I remember when I first saw you dashing across Harvard Yard. You looked so funny with that patch of hair on top of your head, walking everywhere as if you were in a race. I was even a little scared of you the first time you spoke to me in front of Dr. Galbraith's econ class. Did you know that? Your beautiful eyes were so serious and your arms were wrapped so tightly around your books I thought you'd crush them. I guess you were nervous, too.
    Nick, know that I never stop wondering how it would have been if I went with you to Switzerland. I know you've convinced yourself I didn't go only because of my career but there was so much more than that. Friends, family, lifelong aspirations. Most of all, though, there was YOU. Our relationship ended when you came back from your mother's funeral. You weren't the same anymore. I'd spent a year prying you out of your

cocoon, making you open up and talk to me like a normal human being. Teaching you to trust me! Convincing you that not every woman was like your mother. (I'm sorry if that still hurts.) I remember seeing you sitting with Daddy at my birthday party in June, you two big lugs drinking beers and swapping stories like old buddies. We loved you, Nick. All of us. When you came back after Thanksgiving, you'd changed. You didn't smile anymore. You retreated into your own little world. Back to being a stupid soldier on a stupid mission that will never change anything about today and tomorrow and what we could have had. We could never have a future together until you stopped living in the past. I am sorry for what happened to your father, but that's over and done. You've got me going on this all over again. You do that to me, Nicholas Neumann.

Anyway . . . I saw this in Tiffany and thought of you.

Love forever,
Anna

Nick folded the letter. Running his fingers over its soft creases he could hear her whispering in his ear as they made love in his third-floor walk-up in Boston. *"We'll take Manhattan, Nick."* He could almost feel her legs wrapped around his back, her teeth biting down on his ear. He could see her under him.

287

"Fuck me, Marine. We're going to the top. You and me, together."

And then the picture changed.

Nick is grasping Anna's slender arms outside his apartment. It is the last time he will see her, and he is fighting to explain himself, frustrated at the insufficiency of words to translate his emotions. "Don't you understand that I wanted everything as much as you, maybe more. I don't have a choice. Can't you see? This has to come first."

Now as then, Anna stared back at him mutely, understanding but not comprehending. His memory faded and he wondered whether he had really said those words. Or if he had just wanted to.

Nick put the knife away and set it inside the shaving kit. Continuing on his tour of bittersweet memories, he left the bathroom and walked the few steps to the bookshelves. He'd only brought his favorites with him, books he'd had for a long time, stories he'd read four or five times. He selected his copy of Homer's *Iliad*, German text, and reading the title on its spine, smiled. Every time he picked up the book he had the same thought: What kind of asshole actually reads this crap? It was just that kind of thinking that had made him attack this book, and dozens of others like it, in the first place.

Nick turned the paperback upside down and shook it. A small photograph fell to the floor.

He picked it up and stared into his past. Squad 3, Echo Company at Jungle Warfare school in Florida. He was standing on the far left, twenty pounds lighter, face greased with jungle cammie. Next to him, a head shorter, stood Gunny Ortiga, skin painted so dark you could only see his pearly whites. And next to him Sims, Medjuck, Illsey, Leonard, Edwards, and Yerkovic. They'd all been with him in the P.I. He wondered what sea they were floating on tonight.

Nick replaced the paperback and drew a volume from the shelf above it. It was a leather-bound book, taller and slimmer than the rest. His father's agenda for 1978. Nick placed it gently on the desk, then went into the bathroom and found an unused double-edged razor blade. He returned to the desk, sat down, and opened the front cover of the agenda. He slid the razor under the upper left-hand corner of the yellow paper lining the inside cover and sawed it slowly back and forth. After three or four passes, the razor cut through the epoxy bond, and the yellow page came free. He folded it back and extracted a wrinkled piece of paper lying under it.

Nick held the police report concerning his father's murder in one hand, the razor blade in the other, and sighed gratefully. His secret admirer hadn't found the report. Thank God for that. He threw the razor blade in the wastebasket and laid the report down so he could take a good look at it. One ear was ripped and there was a perfect brown halo staining the lower half of the paper where a detective had rested his coffee mug. Still, all the facts were there, and Nick was reading them for the thousand and first time before he could even think of stopping himself.

Administrative facts were typed in a series of rectangular boxes across the top of the sheet. Date: January 31, 1980. Detective in charge: W. J. Lee, Lieutenant. Criminal Violation: Code 187 — Homicide. Time of death: approx. 9:00 P.M. Cause of death: multiple gunshot wounds. The box marked "Suspects" held the initials N.S.A. — no suspect apprehended. Below these facts was a large blank area, about a quarter of a page in size, where Detective Lee provided a description of the events. At 9:05 P.M., Sergeants M. Holloway and B. Schiff responded to a call of shots fired at 10602 Stone Canyon Drive. Sergeants Holloway and Schiff found the victim, Alexander Neumann, age 40, lying prone in the entryway to the home. The victim had been shot three times in the upper abdomen by a high-caliber weapon at close range (powder marks visible). Victim was deceased at time of officers' arrival. The front door to the residence was open. The lock was intact. No other individuals were present. No sign of struggle. No determination yet made as to the state of articles in the home. Call requesting immediate dispatch of homicide detectives was made to West Los Angeles police headquarters at 9:15 P.M. Case forwarded to above filing detective.

A red stamp bearing the letters N.F.A. — No further action — and the date July 31, 1980, was emblazoned across the report. Nick had found it among his mother's possessions in Hannibal. He'd called the L.A.P.D. to request a copy of the investigating detective's final report and the coroner's inquest but learned that both had been destroyed in a fire at Parker Center ten years earlier. He even tried calling Detective Lee but found he'd retired and left no forwarding address, at least none for disgruntled relatives of unsolved murder victims.

Nick examined the page for a while longer, reading his father's name over again and again, and the word that followed it: homicide. He recalled the picture of him at his going-away party in 1967, twenty-seven years old, happy as hell to be going to America. His first big step up. He could practically hear the laughter and the revelry. He could feel his father's joy in his own heart. He thought back to those nightly homework reviews, his father cradling his hands. He saw himself hugging his father on that mountaintop in Arosa. He had never felt closer to him than at that moment.

A flashbulb burst and he was standing in the rain looking down at his father's dead body, staring into the pool of blood.

Suddenly, Nick sobbed. A great choking explosion from deep in his gut. He slammed his hand on the desk and held his breath, hoping to rob himself of the very air he needed to give vent to his emotions. But after a moment, he relented, sucking in a deep breath and expelling it just as quickly. "I'm sorry, Dad," he managed to whisper in a voice as wounded as his soul.

Tears fell from his eyes, and for the first time since his father died seventeen years ago, he cried.

Chapter 22

The time was eleven P.M. and for the second time that day, Nick stood in front of an unfamiliar apartment, waiting for the buzzer to sound that would grant him admittance. He had called ahead and was expected — if that's how you could term a halfhearted response to a plea for company late on a Friday night. He pulled his overcoat close around his neck, fending off the insistent cold. Open the door, Sylvia. You know it's me. The poor slob who called an hour ago saying that if he didn't get out of his grim apartment and see a friendly face he'd go crazy.

The buzzer rang and he was inside, tripping over himself to get down the stairs leading to her doorway. The door was ajar. He could see the outline of her face checking if he was shitface drunk or hopped up on drugs. But it was only him. Nicholas Neumann, eager bank trainee, feeling more tired, more uncertain, and more alone than he could remember.

The light went on inside the hallway, and the door swung open. Sylvia Schon stood back and with a wag of her head motioned for him to enter. She was wearing a red flannel bathrobe and heavy woolen socks that drooped low

293

around her ankles, as if ashamed to cover up such gorgeous territory. Her hair was loose around her face, and she had on the heavy eyeglasses that he hadn't seen since his first day at work. The look on her face said she was not amused.

"Mr. Neumann, I am hoping you have something very important to discuss. When I said I'd be happy to do anything for you, it was in reference to . . ."

"Nick," he said softly. "My name is Nick. And you said that if I ever needed anything, to give you a call. I realize this is an odd time to visit and right now I'm standing here asking myself why exactly I'm here, but if we go inside and have a cup of coffee or something, I'm sure we can get this straightened out."

Nick stopped speaking. He had stunned himself. He'd never strung together so many words in a single sentence and not had the slightest idea what he'd said. He stammered, wanting to explain, but a firm hand on his jacket stopped him dead.

"All right, Nick, come in. And since it is eleven-oh-five and I am wearing my most flattering pajamas, I imagine you'd better call me Sylvia."

She turned and walked down a short corridor that gave onto a cozy living room. A brown sofa ran the length of one wall and half of another. A glass coffee table sat in front of it. Bookshelves adorned the other walls, the spaces between hardcover titles filled by framed photographs. "Sit down. Make yourself at home."

She returned with two mugs of coffee and handed him one. Nick took a sip and relaxed. A fire burned in the grate. Soft music played from the stereo. He inclined his head toward the speakers. "Who is that?"

"Tchaikovsky. Violin Concerto in D minor. Are you familiar with it?"

He listened for a moment longer. "No, but I like it. It has passion."

Sylvia sat away from him on the couch, her legs tucked beneath her. She stared at him for a minute, giving him some time to loosen up, letting him know that she was interested in him but that the clock was ticking. Finally, she said, "You seem upset. What's going on?"

Nick looked into the cup of coffee, shaking his head. "The bank's an exciting place. More than most people imagine. Certainly, more than *I* imagined." And with that introduction he recounted to Sylvia the events that had led to his decision to shield the holder of numbered account 549.617 RR, an anonymous client known only as the Pasha, from the scrutiny of the United States Drug Enforcement Administration. His rationale, he explained, was to keep the bank out of trouble and to deny the DEA access to confidential client information. He kept his private reasons to himself, as he did any mention of his gentleman stalker, or of Sterling Thorne's perfectly timed visit. He ended by recounting Maeder's ominous warning that the "verdict would be delivered Monday."

"He wasn't too happy with me," said Nick. "I may have helped the bank in the short run, but I broke some very important rules. I can imagine that Monday morning I may find a note on my desk informing me oh-so-politely that I've been transferred to some squalid little department in charge of counting paper clips."

"So, that's what happened," Sylvia said. "I should have known." Before Nick could question her omniscience, she went on. "Oh, you'll have a transfer. That much I can promise you."

Nick felt the bottom fall out of his stomach. So much for Sprecher's soothing words. Status quo ante, my ass. "Shit."

"You're being transferred to Wolfgang Kaiser's office. You're to be his new executive assistant."

Nick started to mouth a sarcastic aside but the no-nonsense cast to her voice stopped him.

"I wasn't supposed to tell you until Monday," she said. "Now I see why. The Chairman wanted you to stew in your juices for a while. He'd probably be happy if he saw how worked up you've become over this. First thing Monday morning, you'll receive a summons asking you to report to the Emperor's Lair. Ott called me today wanting to see your papers. Seems you've stirred some feathers. The big boys want you upstairs with them. Obviously by protecting this 'Pasha' fellow, you've endeared yourself to Kaiser."

An odd sensation of complete disorientation swept over Nick. All through the day, he'd been preparing himself for a severe reprimand. Even dismissal. Now this! "That's not possible. Why do they want me upstairs?"

"They have their reasons: Konig; the takeover. Kaiser needs someone able to do battle with unsatisfied American shareholders. That's you. You've passed some sort of test in their eyes. I imagine they think they can trust you. But be careful up there. A lot of fat egos walk those halls. Stay close to the Chairman. Do exactly as he says."

"I've heard that advice before," Nick said skeptically.

"And not a word about this," Sylvia ordered. "You're to act surprised."

"I am surprised. I'm shocked."

"I thought you'd be happier," said Sylvia disappointedly. "Isn't that what every Harvard M.B.A. wants? A seat at the right hand of God?"

Nick tried to smile, but inside him, too many rivers had flooded their borders. Relief that he wouldn't be fired. Expectation over the discovery of his father's memorandums. Anxiety over whether he'd be able to live up to the Chairman's expectations. Somehow he managed to say he was thrilled.

Sylvia appeared drained by her revelation. "Is that all, then? I'm glad I was able to put you at ease. You didn't look too good when you walked in here." She stood and walked lazily toward the corridor. Time to go.

Nick jumped to his feet and followed her down the hallway. She opened the door and leaned against it. "Good night, Mr. Neumann. I'm afraid to repeat what I said last night at dinner."

"About calling if I need anything?"

She raised her eyebrows as if to say "Bingo."

Nick looked at Sylvia long and hard. Her cheeks were pale, streaked with a hint of color up high under her eyes. Her lips were pink and full and he wanted to kiss them. His anxiety disappeared. Replacing it was the same rush of attraction, the same nervous jingle in his stomach coupled with the desire to smile like an idiot that had struck him last night.

"Have lunch with me tomorrow," he said. Standing so close to her he felt faintly giddy, as if right now he could do anything and it would be all right.

"I think that might be pushing our luck a bit too far, don't you?"

"No. In fact, I'm sure it wouldn't. Let me thank you for listening to me tonight. Say one o'clock. The Zeughauskeller."

"Mr. Neumann . . ."

Nick leaned closer to her and kissed her. He allowed his lips to linger only a second, just long enough to feel her against him and know that she did not for a moment recoil.

"Thank you very much for tonight." He stepped across the threshold. "I'll be waiting tomorrow at one. Please come."

Chapter 23

The Zeughauskeller reverberated with the cacophony of two hundred patrons consuming their midday meal. In past days a repository for the military arsenal of the canton Zurich, the restaurant's main hall retained the air of a well-kept warehouse. Its high ceiling was straddled by crossbeams of varnished oak and supported by eight grand pillars of cement and mortar. Its stone walls were adorned with the pike, crossbow, and lance. At one P.M. on this winter's day, the place was full up.

Nick sat alone in the center of the room, defending his table against all comers. Every empty seat was fair game. No keeping a table just for yourself. Not in Switzerland. He checked his watch — five after one — then tapped his foot on the floor. *She'll be here,* he told himself. He remembered the touch of her lips, and knowing that God frowned on the cocksure, added a note of prayer to his statement.

From his vantage point Nick could keep an alert eye on the entryways at each side of the restaurant. The door to his left opened. An elderly couple marched in, brushing a light sprinkling of snow from their shoulders. And then behind them a svelte form wrapped in a camel's hair topcoat with a colorful scarf tied around her head. The person turned away from him and the coat came off. He saw a hand tug at the scarf and then a swirl of blond hair. Sylvia Schon scanned the room.

Nick stood from his chair and waved. She saw him and waved back.

Did she smile?

"You're looking better today," said Sylvia when she reached the table. "Get some rest last night?" She was wearing tight black slacks and a black turtleneck to match. Her hair was pulled back into a ponytail. A few strands hung loose to frame her face.

"I needed more than I thought." He'd slept for seven hours without waking. Practically a record. "Thanks for opening your door. I guess I seemed pretty whacked-out."

"New country, new job. I can see that at times it might be overwhelming. I'm glad I could be a friend. Besides, I owed you a favor."

"How's that?"

"Something I didn't tell you last night. Kaiser was very pleased that I'd extended the bank's courtesies toward you."

Nick didn't understand her meaning. He proceeded with caution. "Was he?"

"You see, Mr. Neumann —" she caught herself and started again. "You see, *Nick*, I lied to you about it being a normal practice for me to take my trainees to dinner." She

301

raised her eyes and stared at him. "Just a white lie. I may take them to the bank's dining room, buy them a Coke, but Emilio's is a little out of the ordinary. Anyhow, the Chairman thought it wise of me to have taken you there. He said you were special and that I had an eye for nurturing talent. He ordered Rudy Ott to send me to the States to conclude our spring recruiting. I'll be leaving in two weeks."

Nick smiled inwardly. Sprecher had nailed her motivation dead on. Still, Nick understood her reasoning full well and he found her honesty disarming. "Congratulations," he said. "I'm happy for you."

She smiled broadly, barely able to contain her excitement. "It's not the trip that's so special, it's the vote of confidence. I'll be the first female personnel director permitted to conduct the recruitment of executives overseas. It's as if the ceiling had been ripped off my office and the heavens revealed for the first time."

Or at least a direct route to the Fourth Floor, thought Nick.

After lunch, Nick and Sylvia joined the throngs of men and women strolling up and down the Bahnhofstrasse. Saturday was shopping day and no amount of rain, sleet, or snow could deter the stalwart Swiss consumer from completing his rounds. Exotic foodstuffs could be had at Globus, finer clothing from PKZ, and pastries, of course, from Sprüngli. While Sylvia kept her trained eye on the latest offerings from the fashion houses of Chanel and Rena Lange, Nick examined the opportunities his promotion to the Emperor's Lair might bring. A position as Kaiser's assistant would give him the authority he needed to gain access to the archives. He'd have no problem getting his hands on page after page of reports written by his father those many years ago.

Or would he?

Suddenly, Nick wasn't so sure. Just as Cerberus made careful note of every numbered account accessed by a portfolio manager, so too would it note every file requested by a bank executive. And more menacing than Cerberus's silicon eye were the all too human attentions of Armin Schweitzer and Martin Maeder. Sylvia had made it clear that he would be watched closely. What room Nick might have had for maneuver under Peter Sprecher's lackadaisical supervision had disappeared. His every step would be scrutinized by anxious men who lived and died for the United Swiss Bank; men who would view any question about the bank's integrity as a question about their own — and who would act accordingly.

Nick waited until the two of them were examining a racy gown in the Celine Boutique before broaching the subject of his father's monthly reports.

"Sylvia," he began cautiously, "ever since I got here I've been curious as to the work my father did at the bank. Last week I was talking with some of my colleagues and I learned that as director of the L.A. branch office, he would have sent reports to the bank on a monthly basis."

"Monthly Activity Reports. I receive copies of them whenever one of our foreign branches requests personnel to be sent from Switzerland."

"I'd love to see what kind of matters my father handled. It would be like getting to know him as a business colleague. Kind of man to man."

"I don't see any problem. Go down to DZ and ask Karl to help you find your father's monthly activity reports. Those files are long since inactive. No one will mind."

Nick shook his head gravely. "I thought about doing that, but I don't want Herr Kaiser or Armin Schweitzer to think I'm ignoring my duties just to root around in the past. Who knows how they would interpret my actions?"

"Why should they care?" Sylvia asked playfully. "It's history."

"They might. That's all. They just might."

Nick looked through the store window at a woman struggling to open a stubborn umbrella. This is where Anna had balked, he reminded himself. She had called him selfish and obsessed. Your father's death ruined your

304

life once, she'd said. Don't let it happen again.

He took Sylvia's hand and led her to a quiet corner of the clothing store where he motioned for her to sit beside him on a soft beige ottoman. "No one ever found my father's murderer. He'd been staying at a friend's house when he was killed. He was hiding from someone or some people. The police never even arrested a suspect."

"Do you know who did it?"

"Me? No. But I want to find out."

"Is that why you want the reports? You think his murder was tied to the bank?"

"In all honesty, I don't know the first thing about why my father was killed. But it may have had something to do with his work. Don't you think his monthly activity reports might provide a hint if something was wrong?"

"Perhaps. They certainly would tell you what business he was conduct—" Suddenly, Sylvia stood from the ottoman. A curtain fell over her features. Her caged eyes promised anger where an instant before they had offered sympathy. "You're not saying that the bank was involved in the murder of your father?"

Nick stood. "I don't think it was the bank, itself. More likely, it was someone he knew through work: a client; someone at another company."

"I don't like where this conversation is going," she said coldly.

Nick could feel her pulling back from him,

could sense her own private cast of demons yanking her from his confidences. Still, he didn't give up. "I was hoping those reports might be of some use. There has to be some information in there that will cast a clearer light on just what my father was doing at the time of his death."

Sylvia reddened at his every word. "My God, that's a cheap way to manipulate me. You should be ashamed. If I had any guts, I'd slap you right here in the store. Don't you think I see what you're trying to get me to do? You want me to put my fingerprints over information you're too scared to get for yourself."

Nick placed his hands on Sylvia's arms. "Calm down. You're taking this too far."

Or was it he who had taken things too far? In an instant, he realized he had been foolish to trust her. He had been scared that alone he couldn't come up with a way to get the activity reports. He'd looked into her eyes and mistaken his own affection for hers. Why should she be willing to help? Why should she risk harming her own career for the sake of someone she barely knew? Christ, he was a rube.

Sylvia bristled at his touch, violently shaking off his hands. "Is that why you showed up at my door last night? Were you trying to win my sympathy? Hoping to soften me up so that you could convince me to help you with your wild goose chase?"

"Of course not. I needed to see someone. I wanted to see *you*." He took a breath, hoping a pause would impose some order on things. "Forget I even asked you about the files. I was too presumptuous. I can get them myself."

Sylvia scowled at him. "I don't give a damn what you do about those files, but I'll keep myself well out of any intrigue you may be up to, thank you very much. I can see it was a mistake to extend our relationship outside working hours. I'll never learn, will I?"

She stalked from the showroom, stopping at the entry and calling over her shoulder, "Good luck on Monday, Mr. Neumann. Remember one thing: You're not the only one on the Fourth Floor with his own private agenda."

Chapter 24

Early Monday morning, Nick found himself seated next to Wolfgang Kaiser on a leather couch that ran along the right-hand wall of the Chairman's office. Two demitasses of espresso sat untouched on the table before them. The red light above the Chairman's door was illuminated, indicating he was not to be disturbed. Rita Sutter had been informed to hold all calls, and Kaiser meant all of them, no exceptions. "I have important business with young Neumann," he had explained to his secretary of eighteen years. "The future of the bank, no less."

Kaiser had embarked on a lecture decrying the loss of the well-rounded banker. "Today it's all specialization," he said disparagingly, flicking up the horns of his mustache. "Take Bauer in risk arbitrage. Try asking him about the current mortgage rate and the man will look at you as if you had asked directions to the moon. Or Leuenberger in derivatives. The man's brilliant. He can talk until Christ's second coming about index options, interest rate swaps, the like. But if I had to ask him whether we should loan two hundred million to Asea Brown Boveri, he would panic. Probably shrivel up and die. The United Swiss Bank requires managers who can grasp the finer points of all our bank's activities and fashion a coherent strategic vision from them. Men not afraid to make the difficult decision."

Kaiser reached for the cup of espresso and raising it to his lips, sought Nick's eyes. He took a brief sip, then asked, "Would you like to be part of that management, Neumann?"

Nick paused long enough to dignify the moment. He sat upright, his back as rigid as if he'd been called onto the carpet by the commandant of the Corps himself. He'd been up since five making sure his clothing was spiffed up, his shoes shined, and his trousers properly creased. The invitation to the Chairman's office was a surprise, he reminded himself, his elevation to the Fourth Floor a shock that hadn't worn off yet. And in truth, it hadn't.

He looked the Chairman in the eye and said, "Absolutely, sir."

"Outstanding," said Kaiser, as a preface to slapping Nick on the leg. "If we had the time, I would turn you right around and send you down to Karl in DZ. That's where all our apprentices started. Me. Your father. *Dokumentation Zentrale*. Down there you learned how the bank was structured, who worked where, who did what. You saw it all."

Nick nodded appreciatively. DZ was just the place he needed to be. Cerruti had said the bank hadn't thrown away a paper in over a hundred years. He could only assume that more of his father's memorandums sat on some forgotten aisle gathering dust.

"After those two years, you received your first assignment," said Kaiser. "To be given a posting in private banking was the Golden Fleece. Your father was assigned to me for his first stint. I believe it was in domestic portfolio management. Alex and I took to each other like brothers — which wasn't always easy with your father. He was a feisty one. Spirited, they would say today. Then we called it insubordinate. He was never the type to unquestioningly do what he was told." Kaiser inhaled sharply. "It seems that his blood flows in your veins."

Nick made the appropriate sentimental noises while wondering what Kaiser knew about his father's death, if anything.

"Alex's curiosity made me sharper," continued Kaiser, his far-off gaze betraying a keen interest in his own past. "He helped me get where I am today. His death was a great loss to the bank. And to your family, of course. It must have been difficult to lose your father under such terrible circumstances. But you're a fighter. I can see it in your eyes. You have your father's eyes." The Chairman smiled wanly. After a moment's reflection, he rose and walked to his desk. "That's enough reminiscing for now. We'll all be teary-eyed before long, God help us."

Nick stood from the couch. As he walked

the few steps to the Chairman's desk, he marveled at Kaiser's skills as a thespian. There sat a man who'd probably cried once in his life, and that had been when his bonus failed to meet his expectations.

Wolfgang Kaiser surveyed the stacks of memos, company reports, and phone messages that formed a paper amphitheater around his work space. "Ah! Here's what I was looking for." He picked up a black leather folder and handed it to Nick. "It doesn't do for the Chairman of a *relatively* important Swiss bank to have trainees working for him. No one has thanked you for the actions you took Thursday afternoon. Most men I know would have relied on procedure to absolve themselves of the responsibility you took on your shoulders. Your decision was made for the bank, not for yourself. It required foresight and courage. We need that kind of clear vision, especially in these times."

Nick accepted the padded folder and opened its cover. Inside, on the finest crushed velvet, lay a single sheet of ivory vellum. Hand-painted letters styled in an ornate Gothic script proclaimed that Nicholas A. Neumann was, as of this date, an assistant vice president of the United Swiss Bank, and entitled to all rights and privileges that that position carried.

Kaiser extended his hand across the desk. "I'm extremely proud of your conduct during your brief employment with us. If my own son were here, he could not have done any better."

Nick found it difficult to remove his eyes from the proclamation. He read the words again: "Assistant Vice President." In six weeks, he had achieved a grade not normally assigned for four years. Think of it as a battlefield promotion, he told himself. Konig is attacking on one flank, Thorne on the other. By repelling one, you ended up repelling both.

Nick shook Kaiser's hand. "I'm sure my father would have done the same," he said, once more the investigator.

Kaiser raised an eyebrow. "Possibly."

Before Nick could ask him what he meant, Kaiser was motioning to the chairs facing his desk and talking loudly. "You are now an officer of the bank. Dr. Schon will contact you regarding an augmentation of your salary. Taking good care of you, is she?"

"We had dinner last Thursday." Nick imagined for the first time that she might have reason to be upset that he had been boosted so far, so fast. She'd worked at the bank nine years and stood only a single rank higher than he. Small wonder she'd been so testy about getting the monthly activity reports. It would be difficult to put their relationship back on track. He should never have asked her for the files.

"We'll have to get you out of the bank's

Personalhaus," said Kaiser. "Normally you should go to our educational compound at Wolfschranz for an introductory seminar, but given the circumstances, I believe that can wait."

The mention of the *Personalhaus* jolted Nick in another direction. Not a minute passed when he didn't think about who had been in his apartment Friday afternoon. Maybe having your personal belongings searched was the price of admission to the Emperor's Lair.

A light on Kaiser's telephone began blinking. Nick looked on as Kaiser considered answering. It was like watching an alcoholic consider his first drink of the day. Kaiser looked at Nick, then at the phone, then back again. "Now the work begins," he sighed, then stabbed the flickering button and picked up the phone. "*Jawohl?* Send him in."

The door flew open before Kaiser had replaced the phone in its cradle.

"Klaus Konig has issued a buy order for one and a half million shares of our stock," shouted a disheveled little man far along the path to losing his composure. "The Adler Bank has an open order to buy a full fifteen percent of our shares. On top of the five percent they already own, the purchase will bring their stake to twenty percent. Once Konig is on our board, nothing we do or say will remain private. It will be like the States. Total chaos!"

Kaiser responded calmly. "Mr. Feller, you

may rest assured we shall never allow the Adler Bank to reach a position where they will be entitled to even a single seat on our board. We have underestimated Mr. Konig's intentions. That shall no longer be the case. Part of our efforts will be aimed at winning over our institutional shareholders, many of whom reside in North America. Mr. Neumann, here, will be in charge of contacting those shareholders and convincing them to vote with reigning management at our general assembly in four weeks."

Feller took a step back and looked down at Nick. "Excuse me," he muttered. "The name is Feller. Reto Feller. Glad to meet you." He was short and dumpy and not much older than Nick. He wore thick horn-rimmed glasses that made his dark eyes look like moist, ill-focused marbles. He had a halo of curly red hair on an otherwise bald pate.

Nick stood and introduced himself, then made the mistake of saying that he hoped they would enjoy working together.

"Enjoy?" barked Feller. "We're at war. There'll be no enjoyment until Konig is dead and the Adler Bank gone to perdition." He turned to Kaiser. "What shall I tell Dr. Ott? He's waiting with Sepp Zwicki on the trading floor. Shall we begin our program of share accumulation?"

"Not so quickly," said Kaiser. "Once we start buying, the share price will skyrocket.

First we line up as many votes as possible. Then we commit the bank's capital to fight Konig."

Feller bowed his head and scurried from the office without a further word.

Kaiser picked up the telephone and phoned Sepp Zwicki, the bank's chief of equity trading. He relayed his orders to delay commencement of their share accumulation plan, then asked who could be counted on to sell the Adler Bank large blocks of shares. When talk turned to the effect of Konig's bid on the prices of USB mutual funds, Nick's attention wandered. He swiveled in his chair and for the first time took a thorough look at Wolfgang Kaiser's office.

In size and form, the office resembled the transept of a medieval cathedral. The ceiling was high and vaulted. Four rafters ran its width, their purpose more decorative than structural. Entry was gained through two sets of double wooden doors, which ran from floor to ceiling. The status of the doors mirrored that of the business being conducted within. Open doors allowed all members of the bank's executive board free access without need for advance notice. Should the inner doors be closed, the Chairman could be interrupted, but only by Rita Sutter. She had explained the system to Nick herself, earlier this morning. Should both sets of doors be closed, and the admonition "Do not disturb" given, only a man "desirous of immediate defenestration" would dare venture in. Her words. Presuming, Nick added, he had been capable of bypassing Rita Sutter.

She was hardly the party queen he'd seen in the photograph at Marco Cerruti's apartment. Her hair was a sober blond cut to fall shy of her shoulders. Her figure appeared trim beneath an elegant taupe ensemble, but her blue eyes no longer sparkled as innocently as they had in the photograph. Instead they appraised from a distance. She exuded an unimpeachable sense of control — more a top executive than the Chairman's secretary. Nick thought she probably knew more about what went on inside the bank than Kaiser. He made a point to talk to her about his father.

Visitors to the imperial den had to walk ten paces across a blue carpet to reach the Chairman's desk, which stood directly facing the entryway. The desk was the room's centerpiece, an immovable mahogany altar, and on it sat the objects required for the worship of the Gods of International Business: two computer monitors, two telephones, a desktop speaker, and a Rolodex the size of an impoverished village's water mill.

The desk was framed by a grand arched window that ran from floor to ceiling. Four steel rods vertically intersected the window giving the visitor, in most instances, a secure sense of confinement inside the world's most opulent vault. Or, to those with a guiltier conscience, the dread of being held prisoner inside the barbican of a central European fortress.

Nick followed a beam of sunlight as it penetrated the morning fog and illuminated the recesses of the vast office. Two pictures adorned the wall opposite him. One, an oil portrait of Gerhard Gautschi, who had governed the bank for thirty-five years. The other a Byzantine mosaic whose title could only be the moneychangers in the temple. A kneeling moneylender offered a bag of gold to a mounted Saracen brandishing a jewel-encrusted scimitar. The mosaic was fantastic, and even to Nick's untrained eye, a masterpiece of its kind.

A full suit of samurai armor stood in the corner nearest the Chairman's desk. It was a gift from the Sho-Ichiban Bank of Japan, with which USB shared a two percent cross holding. And on the wall to Nick's left, above the couch where he had sat earlier, hung a small impressionist painting of a wheatfield in high summer. A cloudless blue sky was seared by the sun's oppressive heat. A single farmer worked in the field, his back bent under the weight of cut wheat he carried back to the mill. The artist had left his signature in the lower right-hand corner. Renoir.

Nick pressed his back into the quilting of his chair and tried to find the thread that wound through the decor of Wolfgang Kaiser's office. You could easily be overwhelmed by the beauty of any one of the fabulous items on display. How often do you find a Renoir in a private collection or a sixteenth-century suit of Japanese battle armor? Yet, Kaiser wasn't the type to assemble a meretricious display of vanities, however priceless. He had surrounded himself with souvenirs of his bank's climb to eminence, personal trophies of hard-won battles, and objets d'art that spoke to a private corner of his soul.

Nick felt that there was an order to the eclectic mix of art and antiquities. A message that begged recognition. He looked around the room again, not focusing but feeling; not seeing but absorbing. And then he knew. Power. Vision. Scope. The entire office was a monument to Kaiser's reign. A shrine to the preeminence of the United Swiss Bank and to the man who had brought the bank that glory.

Nick was startled by the crash of a phone being slammed onto the desk.

Kaiser leaned back in his chair and ran a hand through his abundant hair. He fussed with each horn of his mustache. " 'L'audace,' Neumann. 'Toujours l'audace!' You know who said that?" He didn't wait for a response. "We don't want to end up like him, do we? Marooned on an island in the middle of nowhere. Our play must be more subtle. No whiff of grapeshot for the United Swiss Bank. Not if we wish to put an end to this revolution quickly and effectively."

Nick knew better than to correct the Chairman, but in fact, Frederick the Great, not Napoleon, had uttered that famous battle cry.

"Get out some paper. Take down what I say and don't become a frantic rat like Mr. Feller. A general must remain his calmest when a battle reaches its most intense."

Nick grabbed a block of paper that lay on the desk in front of him.

"Feller was right," said the Chairman. "It is a war. Konig wants to take us over, always has, if I read things clearly. He's holding shares worth just over five percent of our outstanding capital and has open orders to buy fifteen percent more. Who knows how many shares his backers are holding, but if he's able to put together a block carrying thirty-three percent of our votes, then two seats on the board are his. With two seats he can influence other board members and forge a blocking position on matters of importance.

"His war cry is that we are stuck in the Middle Ages. Private banking is going the way of the buggy whip, says Konig. Trading is the way of the future. Using your firm's capital to bet on and influence the direction of markets, currencies, interest rates. Anything that he and his cohorts can securitize, they will. Oil futures, home mortgages, Argentinean beef contracts. Any investment that doesn't post gains of twenty percent per year is ready for the slaughterhouse. Not us, by God. Not the United Swiss Bank. Private banking is what made this bank what it is today. I have no intention of abandoning it, or risking our solvency by joining Konig's band of riverboat gamblers."

Kaiser walked around his desk and stood by Nick's chair, placing a strong hand on his shoulder. "I want you to map out which individuals and institutions own major blocks of shares. Find out who we can count on and who will back Konig. We'll have to write up something snappy about our plans to improve our return on assets and increase our shareholders' returns."

Nick saw the pattern of his days developing even as Kaiser spoke. He was in for a long and difficult ride. Any plans he had about using his newly won position to conduct an investigation into his father's death would have to be put on hold — at least until Konig's bid was defeated. Still, he was where he needed to be, "at the right hand of God."

"Where is that son of a bitch getting his financing?" demanded Kaiser. "Over the past seven months the Adler Bank has declared increases in capital three times without ever going to market. That means a number of private groups must secretly be backing Konig. I want you to find out who. Your friend Sprecher is beginning work there today. Use him. And don't be surprised if he tries to use you, especially once he discovers you're working for me."

Kaiser lifted his hand from Nick's shoulder and turned toward the entryway. Nick stood and walked with him toward the massive doors. What about the Pasha? Nick wanted to ask. Who was going to take care of him now? One thing was for certain. If Cerruti knew the Pasha, then Kaiser knew him better.

"We have four weeks until the general assembly, Neumann. That's not a very long time for the work we have before us. Mrs. Sutter will show you your office. And keep an eye on Feller. Don't let him get too flustered. Remember, Neumann: four weeks."

Chapter 25

Sylvia Schon stared at the blue slips on her desk and wondered when he would stop calling. The first note was dated Tuesday evening and read, *Mr. Nicholas Neumann phoned at 6:45, requests that you call back.* The second was taken early this morning. More of the same. She read them both again, recognizing the extension given as belonging to the Fourth Floor, to the Emperor's Lair.

Sylvia laid the messages on her desk and urged herself not to be jealous of his good fortune. In nine years at the bank, she had never seen, or even heard of, an employee moving from the position of management trainee to assistant vice president in the space of five weeks. It had taken her *six years* to gain that rank! Unsure of her chances to rise beyond it, she'd enrolled at the University of Zurich and taken classes three nights a week and on Saturdays toward a doctorate in management. Three years later she received her degree and only this past winter a promotion to full vice president. If Nick excelled at his post alongside Wolfgang Kaiser, there was no reason he shouldn't be elevated to full vice president in nine months' time, in late November when the bank posted its annual list of promotions. Such things happened often to men in the center of power.

Sylvia picked up the blue slips bearing Nick's extension and tossed them into the trash can behind her desk — where she had tossed all the other messages he'd left since Monday. She tried to tell herself that his promotion didn't feel like a slap in the face. That it was just another petty injustice she had to swallow. But she couldn't.

The phone rang. Sylvia craned her neck to see if her assistant was at his desk. The phone rang a second time. Obviously, he wasn't. She picked up on the third ring. "Schon."

"Good morning, Sylvia. It's Nick Neumann. Hi."

Sylvia closed her eyes. This was not what she needed right now. "Hello, Mr. Neumann."

"I thought we had settled on Nick."

She swiveled in her chair, hating herself for hiding in her "Miss Professional" routine. "Yes, Nick. How can I help you?"

"You can probably guess. I'm calling to apologize about the files. I should never have asked for your help. It was selfish of me. I was wrong."

"Apology accepted." She had hardly thought about the files since Saturday. It was his sudden promotion that merited punishment. "How are things with the Chairman?"

"Exciting. Busy. In fact, I'd love to talk to you about it. Are you free for dinner tomorrow night?"

Sylvia took a breath. She'd guessed he'd been calling to set up a date. Hearing his strong voice, she knew her anger was misdirected. She had no right to blame Nick. Still, she needed time to figure out how she felt about him. "I don't think so. In fact, I think it's better if we left this as it was."

"Oh? And how was it?"

"*It* wasn't," she replied testily. His insistence rankled her. "Do you understand now? Look, I really have quite a bit of work to do. I'll stop by when I have some free time. Let's leave it at that."

Sylvia hung up the phone before he could protest. Yet, even as her hand left the receiver, she began criticizing herself for being unspeakably rude — not an easy task given her own demanding standards. I apologize, Nick, she said silently, staring at the phone. Call me back. I'll say I didn't know what got into me. I'll tell you that yes, we had a wonderful time Saturday and that I am still trying to figure out that lovely kiss.

But the phone did not ring.

Sylvia spun her chair and stared into the wastepaper bin. She picked up one of the crumpled message slips, flattened it on her desk, and reread the number.

Nick unsettled her. He was handsome and

confident. He had lovely eyes. Eyes whose unimpeded stare could be frightening one minute and heartbreaking the next. He had no family and she thanked God for that — wished she could be so lucky. Her father was a boorish man, a red-faced tyrant who had never given up trying to run his home as he ran the railway station at Sargans. When her mother died, Sylvia had taken the care of her younger brothers, Rolf and Eric, onto herself, preparing their breakfasts, cleaning their rooms, doing their laundry. Instead of being grateful, the boys had mimicked their father's behavior, ordering her around the house as if she were a maid and not their older sister.

Sylvia thought back on her dinner with Nick. "Independent" was how he'd described himself and she'd jumped on the word. Loved it. Because she was independent, too. Her life was her own. She could make of it what she wanted. She recalled the touch of his lips when they said good night, their cool pressure hiding the warmth close behind. Closing her eyes, she allowed herself to imagine what would come next. His hand brushing her cheek, her body pushing hard against him. She would open her mouth and taste him. She felt a sharp stirring pass through her body, and its stark carnality woke her from her reverie.

Sylvia checked her watch. Seeing that it was already nine o'clock, she set to work updating a list of interviewing requirements for Swiss university graduates. It was a monotonous chore, and to relieve it she reminded herself of the goals that she had set herself earlier in the year.

First, in the spring she would travel to the States to supervise the bank's recruitment of American M.B.A.s. Second, by December 31, the finance department would boast the highest employee retention rate in the bank. The first goal was as good as accomplished. Wolfgang Kaiser had personally assigned her the task. She could thank Nick for that, at least partially, for it was his presence that had allowed her to shine in the Chairman's eyes. The second goal — seeing to it that her department kept its employees — would require her constant attention. The finance department was lagging behind commercial banking but was ahead of trading. If Nick stayed longer than the usual arrogant recruits Rudolf Ott hired, she would be very happy.

You want him to stay for more reasons than that, whispered a naughty voice.

Sylvia tapped her nails on the message slip and picked up the phone. She wasn't seeing anyone at the moment, why not call him back? She reminded herself that he was independent like her, that she could date him without too big a risk of involvement. She preferred her relationships to have a maximum of passion and a minimum of commitment. Special treats she allowed herself once or twice a year. She'd worked too hard for her own freedom to give it up by getting stuck in a relationship — *any relationship*. She expected that someday she'd want something more secure, something for the rest of her life, but for now she was happy with things as they were. Then why, dammit, couldn't she ignore the sentiment tickling deep inside her stomach that he might be the one?

Sylvia dialed Nick's extension. The phone rang once. A male voice answered. "Hello."

"You're supposed to give your family name. You're too friendly."

"Which one of you is this?" Nick asked. "Dr. Jekyll or Mrs. Hyde?"

"I'm sorry, Nick. Forget that call ever happened, would you. You caught me off guard."

"Deal."

A familiar voice drifted in from the hallway. "Fräulein Schon, are you in your office?"

Sylvia bolted upright in her chair. "Nick, I have to call you back. Maybe I'll come up to see your new office. Okay? Gotta run."

She hung up the phone even as his voice said "Bye."

"Good morning, Dr. Ott," she said brightly, already circling her desk to shake hands with the vice chairman of the United Swiss Bank. "An unexpected pleasure." She was not happy to see the rotund form rolling into her office for an unannounced visit. The man was a worm.

"The pleasure is all mine, Fräulein Schon."

Ott stood before her, his hands interlocked on top of his bulging stomach. His lips had the habit of telegraphing his intention to speak three seconds ahead of time. Now Sylvia saw them beginning to squirm, as if disturbed by a weak current. "We have a tremendous amount of work to do," he said. "Many tasks to accomplish before the general assembly."

"Hard to believe that only four weeks remain," she said pleasantly.

"Three and one half, to be precise," corrected Ott. "Letters to your department's personnel regarding the voting of their USB shares at the general assembly must be written today. Be sure you make it exceedingly clear that everyone must vote for our slate of directors, either by proxy or in person. *Everyone.* I'll need a copy by five o'clock this afternoon."

"That's rather short notice," said Sylvia.

Ott ignored her comment. "In one week, you will phone each and every member of your department to learn which way they will vote."

"I don't mean to be impolite, but do you really believe that any of our employees could think it in their interest to vote for Konig?"

Ott bent forward at the waist, as if he had not heard her clearly. "Do I believe that?" he asked. "In the best of all possible worlds, of course not. But that's beside the point. The Chairman has instructed me to ensure that you personally telephone every member of the finance department. You are to encourage all employees to attend the meeting. A half day's leave will be granted. He's under the impression that you're well respected by your charges. You should be thrilled."

"I am. Just pressed for time. I'm leaving for the States next week. I've faxed an interview schedule to all the major schools we've worked with in the past. Harvard, Wharton, Northwestern, a few others."

"I'm afraid your trip will have to be postponed."

Sylvia smiled awkwardly. Had she heard him correctly? "We have to visit these schools before the end of March, or the top graduates will have committed to other companies. The trip will only require two weeks of my time. I planned on sending up a schedule to your office tomorrow."

Ott's lips twitched for a moment, then he spoke. "I am sorry, Fräulein Schon. Surely you can see that the Chairman requires your skills at home. Unless we repel Mr. Konig, we will have no need whatsoever for your crop of M.B.A.s."

Sylvia went to her desk and picked up the itinerary for her recruiting trip. "If you look at my schedule, you'll see that I plan on returning a full week before the assembly. Plenty of time to ensure that all votes will be cast for Herr Kaiser."

Ott brushed away the schedule and lowered

his bulk into a chair. "You're still under the impression that since Herr Kaiser asked you to go to New York in my place, he has taken an interest in your career? My dear, your dining with Mr. Neumann showed admirable foresight. Very clever, indeed. Kaiser was quite impressed. Oh yes, you've poisoned the Chairman against me. That I grant you. I shall not be going to New York. But alas, *Liebchen,* neither shall you."

"Really Herr Doktor. I'm sure we can find a solution acceptable to you and to Herr Kaiser. I can shorten my trip."

"I think not. As I said, your services are too much in demand here."

"I must insist," Sylvia said loudly, unable to keep her desperation from spilling into her voice. "It was the Chairman's wish."

Ott slammed his hand on the table. "There will be no trip. Not now. Not ever! My dear, did you truly believe that your dalliance with the Chairman would insulate you from the rest of us? Did you think it would hasten you along your chosen path?"

"My personal life is no concern of yours. I have never tried to gain any benefit from my relationship with the Chairman, but in this matter I won't hesitate to speak with him directly."

"Do you think you can run back into the arms of Herr Kaiser now? Dear child, the Chairman is finished with you. He is a disci-

330

plined man. Should he require the company of a woman, we will choose someone far less grasping than you. Preferably, a woman with no ties whatsoever to the bank."

"You can't control his heart, who he loves, who he desires . . ."

"Desire is one thing, my dear. Utility, another. The Chairman requires me. Today, tomorrow, and for as long as he shall manage the bank. I am the oil that makes this intricate machine run smoothly." Ott stood, pausing for a moment to glory in his exalted position. He extended a stubby finger in Sylvia's direction. "You didn't actually believe that a Swiss bank would allow itself to be represented in the United States of America by a woman? A child practically?"

Sylvia moved her mouth to respond but nothing came out. Of course, Ott was right. Switzerland was light-years behind England and France and America in its treatment of women. Just look at USB. How many women were on the executive board? None. How many women were executive vice presidents? Still, she knew that things had to change soon. And she had seen herself as the one changing them.

"You did," said Ott, at once incredulous and supremely certain. "I can see it in your eyes. How quaint!" He walked from the office, calling over his shoulder, "Have that letter ready for me by five o'clock this afternoon

331

without fail, Fräulein. We must have our votes."

Sylvia waited a few minutes after Ott had left, then walked to the ladies' rest room. She made her way to the farthest stall, and after shutting the door, collapsed against the tile wall. Ott's words burned like acid in the space behind her eyes. He had won. He had broken her. Another soul vanquished so that he could strengthen his alliance with Wolfgang Kaiser.

Ott was such a bastard! she thought, and then a fresh wave of self-pity swept over her and she cried. She lamented her short affair with Wolfgang Kaiser even as she remembered the day they had met. It had been at the bank's annual picnic on a warm July afternoon almost two years ago. She had never expected to speak with him, let alone flirt. No one at her level even knew the Chairman. There was no telling where the discussion might lead. The chances for disaster were simply too high. So when he drew her aside and asked if she was enjoying herself, she had been reticent, even afraid to meet him in conversation. But instead of hearing some dry rot regarding the bank's newest hiring policies, she had listened as he enthused over the visiting Giacometti exhibition at the Kunsthaus. Instead of a dreaded "do tell" about her colleagues, he had asked if she had ever rafted down the Saanen River, and then related his own trip two weeks before. She had expected a severe but polite functionary but had met a warm and effusive man.

Two weekends at his summer home in Gstaad, that had been the extent of their liaison. He had treated her like a princess. Dinners on the veranda of the Palace Hotel; long walks roaming the grassy hills; romantic and, she still had to admit, passionate evenings drinking exquisite wine and making love. She had never been so blind to think it would continue forever, but neither had she dreamed it might be used against her.

Fifteen minutes later, a becalmed Sylvia ran cold water over her face. She kept her head near the sink and ladled handful after handful of water onto her swollen cheeks. She looked into the mirror for a long time. Trust. Dedication. Effort. She had given her whole being to the bank. Why would they choose to treat her this way?

The United Swiss Bank was an internationally active bank. Should anyone hope to rise to the directorship of the bank's personnel division, *he* — Sylvia wouldn't waste another breath considering herself — would be required to supervise hiring not only in Switzerland but in New York, in Hong Kong, in Dubai. Should that person be blocked by the Chairman's éminence grise from representing the bank abroad, his career would be at an end. That was that.

Sylvia straightened herself up and dried her

face. She needed to unburden herself of the grief that sat on her chest robbing her of oxygen. She needed to escape the confines of her office. But that was impossible. Activity in the bank was running at a fever pitch: every department gearing up for presentations to be made at the general assembly; managers nervous to learn the annual operating results; the Adler Bank hovering ever closer. She couldn't consider taking a day off for at least a month.

Sylvia chided herself for her misplaced loyalties. The avenue leading to a successful future at the United Swiss Bank had been blocked, perhaps permanently, yet she continued to think of nothing but her duty to the bank. She slipped her hand into her pocket and discovered that at some point during her discussion with Ott she had jammed Nick's messages into it. She uncrumpled the papers and memorized his extension. Was she so alone that the only person she could turn to was a younger man she barely knew?

Sylvia looked in the mirror. She was a mess. Eyes swollen, makeup smeared, cheeks redder than a baby's. You're pathetic, she told herself. Allowing the decision of one man to tear apart your dreams; letting a lieutenant tell you the captain's orders. Go to Wolfgang Kaiser. Present your case directly. Convince him that you can represent the bank overseas. Fight back!

She replayed the meeting with Kaiser Friday morning. She recalled the callused grip of the

Chairman's hand. His lingering touch. Instead of desire, she saw in it hunger. Instead of strength, weakness. Weakness of a variety she knew well. Weakness she would exploit to her own advantage.

Sylvia took a tissue from her purse to wipe away a trail of mascara. She dabbed it in cold water and raised it to her face. Halfway to her cheek, she paused and stepped away from the mirror. Something was wrong. She looked at her hand and saw that it was shaking uncontrollably.

Chapter 26

Nick spotted Sterling Thorne loitering under a blinking street-lamp twenty yards from the entrance to the bank's *Personalhaus*. The federal agent was wearing a tan trenchcoat over a dark suit. For once, he looked like part of the landscape rather than a blight on it. When he saw Nick, he raised his hand and offered a faint salute.

Nick had half a mind to take off in the other direction. But it was after ten and he was exhausted. And this, after only his second day working with the Chairman. From eight in the morning until ten at night, Wolfgang Kaiser was on the move. And his newest aide-de-camp, assistant vice president Nicholas A. Neumann, was always somewhere close behind.

The day had begun on the trading floor with Sepp Zwicki, a visit to the front lines for a briefing on Konig's latest sorties. Mid-morning took them to the Emperor's Lair, where Kaiser dished out instructions on what line to give dissenting shareholders, then placed a few calls himself to show how to charm the greedy bastards. Lunch was spent in one of the bank's private dining rooms, veal chops, a '79 Château Pétrus and Cohibas all around for the jolly good fellows from Bank Vontobel and Julius Baer. Both banks held large blocks of USB. During the afternoon, rolls of USB shareholders were reviewed and telephoning chores divvied up between Nick and Reto Feller. At seven, dinner was sent in from Kropf Bierhalle. *Bratwurst mit Zwiebeln.* The three hours since had passed in a flurry of calls to stock analysts in Manhattan. Go, go, go.

And now Thorne. Nick's first instinct was to throw him against a wall and demand whether he'd been the asshole who'd broken into his apartment on Friday.

"Working late, are you, Neumann?" Thorne asked, hand extended in welcome.

Nick kept his hands buried in his pockets. "There's a lot to do these days. The general assembly is coming up soon."

Thorne lowered his hand. "You gentlemen announcing another year of record profits?"

"Are you angling for some inside information? Trying to beef up that government paycheck? I remember how skimpy Uncle Sam can be."

Thorne tried to smile affably but wound up looking like he'd bitten into a rotten apple. Something had soured on his end. Nick was sure of it. Why else the strained courtesy? "How can I be of service to my country this fine evening?"

"Why don't we take it inside, Nick? Get out of the cold."

Nick considered the request. Like it or not, Thorne was an officer of the United States government. He deserved some respect. For now. Nick showed Thorne into the apartment's alcove and led the way up the single flight of stairs to the second floor. He unlocked the door to his apartment and nodded for the agent to go in.

Thorne stepped inside the apartment and looked around. "I thought bankers lived a little better than this."

Nick took off his coat and hung it over the chair. "I've been in worse."

"So have I. You been mulling over our conversation? Been keeping your eyes open?"

"I've been keeping my eyes where they belong. On my work. Can't say I've come across anything that might interest you."

Nick sat down on the bed. He glared at Thorne, waiting. It was his show. Finally, the lanky agent unbuttoned his jacket and took a seat across the room. "I'm letting down my guard tonight because we need your help," he said. "It doesn't happen often, so you'd stand well advised to take advantage of my kind disposition. Won't last long."

"Noted."

"Numbered account 549.617 RR ring a bell to you?"

Nick didn't answer right away. He kept his

face passive, while inside him Thorne's bell clanged mercilessly. Account 549.617 RR. The Pasha.

"It does, doesn't it?" continued Thorne. "Has to be hard for a poor city boy to forget seeing so much money being moved around."

Impossible, if you really want to know, Nick replied silently. "I can't comment on either a client's identity or account activity. You know that. It's confidential information. Bank secrecy and all that."

"Account 549.617 RR," Thorne repeated. "I believe you fellas call him the Pasha."

"Never heard of him."

"Not so quick, Neumann. I'm asking you a favor. I'm as close to falling onto my knees as I'm ever going to get. I'd like to give you a chance to do some good."

Nick smiled inadvertently. He couldn't help it. A government agent doing good was in his experience the most fundamental of oxymorons. "I'm sorry. I can't help you."

"The Pasha is a bad man, Nick. His name is Ali Mevlevi. He's a Turk by birth but lives in a monumental private compound just outside of Beirut. He's an important player in the world's heroin trade. We estimate he's responsible for the importation into Europe and the former Soviet Union of about twenty tons of refined number four heroin — China White, in our lingo — each and every year. Twenty tons, Nick. This is no dilettante we're talking about. Mevlevi is the real thing."

Nick put up both hands in front of him, signaling Thorne to stop. "And so? If he is, what about it? How does that concern me or the bank? Haven't you gotten it through your skull that I am prohibited by law to discuss anything I do for USB with you, or with anybody else for that matter? I'm not admitting that this Pasha fellow is my client. I'm not saying he is, or he isn't. Doesn't matter. I could have Satan calling me twice a day and still I couldn't tell you."

Thorne just nodded his head and kept talking as if the sheer brunt of his evidence would eventually win over Nick's essentially good soul. It was a good strategy.

"Mevlevi's got himself a private army of about five hundred souls in his backyard. Trains them morning, noon, and night. And he's got a mountain of matériel on top of that. Russian T-72s, a few Hinds, plenty of rockets, mortars, you name it. A ready mobile battalion of mechanized infantry. That's what's got us worried. You remember what happened to our boys at the marine barracks in Beirut. Several hundred good men had their lives taken by a lone suicide bomber. Imagine what five hundred of them could do."

Nick leaned closer, the infantry officer in him cognizant of the havoc to be wreaked by such a force. Still, he did not speak.

"We have hard-copy proof of the transfers

Mevlevi's been making to and from your bank for the last eighteen months. Irrefutable evidence that your bank is laundering his dough. Our problem, Nick, is that the Pasha has gone under. Three days after we put his name on your bank's internal account surveillance list, Mr. Ali Mevlevi has stopped making his weekly payments. We were expecting about forty-seven million dollars to hit his account on Thursday. Did it?"

Nick kept his mouth closed. There it was. No more whacking around whether the DEA had the right man or not. They even knew how much he was transferring day in, day out. Mr. Ali Mevlevi — the Pasha — was squarely in their sights. Time to line up the crosshairs. Time for First Lieutenant Nicholas Neumann to help them pull the trigger.

As if sensing Nick's impending acquiescence, Thorne leaned closer, and when he spoke his voice acquired a conspiratorial edge. "There's a human aspect to this case also. We have an agent on the inside. Someone we planted a long time ago. You know the trick?"

Nick nodded, seeing where Thorne was going. He could feel the mantle of responsibility the agent wanted to lay on his shoulders. A second ago he had been ready to sympathize with Thorne, maybe even help him. Now he hated him.

"Our man — let's call him Jester — has also disappeared. He used to call us twice a week to give us Mevlevi's weekly take. I'll let you guess which days. Yep. Monday and Thursday. Jester hasn't called, Nick. E.T. did not phone home. Hear what I'm saying?"

"I understand your dilemma," said Nick. "You've put a man into a hot situation. You're scared he may be compromised and now you can't get him out. In short, you've left him hanging on a two-penny string in a shitstorm and you want me to salvage your operation and save your man."

"That's about right."

"I appreciate the situation" — Nick paused for effect — "but I am not going to spend the next couple of years in a Swiss jail so that you can get your next promotion and maybe, just maybe, save the skin of your man."

"We will get you out of here. I give you my word."

There it was. The lie Nick had been expecting. He was just surprised that it took so long to come. The anger inside him crested. "Your word doesn't mean spit to me. You've got no say over who the Swiss jail or who they release. You almost had me there for a second. Sound the bugle and the loyal marine comes running. I know you guys. Out there playing God, thinking you're doing some good. You're just getting your rocks off, seeing how much power you can exercise over your little slice of the world. Well, forget it. You'll have to count me out. That's not my game."

"You got it all wrong, brother," Thorne shouted. "You can't use me as an excuse to pretend Mevlevi doesn't exist or that you, as his banker, as the man who day in, day out, helps him hide the fruits of his illegal labors, are not responsible. You two are on the same goddamned team. In my world, Nick, there's us and there's them. If you're not one of us, you're one of them. So where do you stand?"

Nick took a while to answer the question. "I guess I'm one of them."

Oddly, Thorne seemed pleased by the answer. "That's too bad. I told you to take advantage of my kindly disposition. Now you've gone and pissed me off. I know about your old friend Jack Keely. What went wrong down there in the P.I. must have been something powerful bad for you to fly off the handle like that. You're lucky you didn't kill that man. So you think long and hard about helping me out, or others will know about your escapade, too. I don't think Kaiser would be too happy to learn that you left the Corps with a dishonorable discharge. I don't think he'd be too keen to learn that you're a convicted felon — maybe in a private military court, but convicted just the same. Hell, maybe I should be afraid of you, too. But, I'm not. I'm too busy worrying about Mevlevi. And about Jester. You may want to piss on guys like me, but I crush guys like you. That's not my job — it's my reason for living. You hear me?"

"Loud and clear," Nick said. "Do what you have to do. Just stay the hell away from me. I don't have anything to say to you. Not now. Not ever."

Chapter 27

Rattling into the Paradeplatz early Thursday morning, Nick was greeted everywhere by headlines trumpeting the improprieties of a major bank. The central kiosk was festooned with flyers from every major daily. *Blick*, Zurich's low-rent scandal sheet, proclaimed, *"Schmiergeld bei Gotthardo Bank,"* Bribe Money at Gotthardo Bank. The *NZZ*, the oldest and most conservative of the city's three daily papers, was equally accusatory: "Shame on Gotthardo." The *Tages Anzeiger* took a more global view: "Swiss Banks in League with Drug Mafia."

Nick hurried from the tram to purchase a newspaper. What had started as a rotten day showed no sign of changing course. His alarm clock had failed to go off at the proper time; the hot water in his building had been turned off, so he'd been forced to endure a full two minutes — not the usual fifteen seconds — under an ice-cold shower; and the 7:01 tram had left at 6:59. Without him! Not that yesterday had been much better, cursed Nick, as he jogged paper in hand down the Bahnhofstrasse.

Klaus Konig had completed his purchase of

over 1.7 million shares of USB stock at eleven A.M. and had followed it with a second order to gobble up an additional two hundred thousand shares at market price. By day's end, the price of USB shares had skyrocketed fifteen percent and Konig held a twenty-one percent stake in the bank, all too near the thirty-three percent threshold that would grant him his coveted seats on the board.

The precipitous rise in share price combined with the Adler Bank's growing stake left the United Swiss Bank more vulnerable than ever. And no one knew that better, or had responded more vigorously, than Wolfgang Kaiser. At noon, the Chairman had descended to the floor of the Borse and personally ordered Sepp Zwicki to buy, buy, buy USB shares at whatever the cost. Kaiser had drawn his line in the sand. In three hours, the bank had picked up a couple hundred thousand shares, and war had been openly declared between the United Swiss Bank and the Adler Bank. Arbitrageurs in New York and in Tokyo, in Sydney and in Singapore, were licking their chops, buying up shares of USB in hopes of a continuing escalation in price.

Nick took a last look at the newspaper in his hand before entering the Emperor's Lair. Scanning the inflammatory headlines, he thought, "Holy shit. Now this."

Kaiser was on the telephone. "*Gottfurdeckel,* Armin," he yelled, "you told me that Gotthardo would wait at least another two weeks before folding. They've known about that drunk Rey for years. Why go public now? This does not put us in a strong position. And Armin" — Kaiser paused, and his eyes found Nick — "this time ensure that your facts are correct. This is the second time in the last week that you've disappointed me. Consider this your last reprieve." He slammed down the phone and turned to his newest assistant. "Sit down, be quiet, and I will be with you in a few minutes."

Nick took a seat on the couch and opened his briefcase. The honeymoon is now officially over, he mused. He placed his copy of the *NZZ* on the table before him and reviewed the facts as reported.

Yesterday, the Gotthardo Bank, a universal bank of roughly USB's size with its headquarters in Lugano, reported to the Swiss federal prosecutor, Franz Studer, that after a lengthy internal investigation, it had discovered evidence of gross impropriety on the part of one of its own executives. For the past seven years, one Lorenz Rey, a senior vice president, had been surreptitiously working for the Uribe family of Mexico to launder money and assist in the international transfer of funds emanating from the sale of illegal narcotics. Rey claimed that only he and two junior members of his department were privy to all details of the account, and thus fully cognizant of the criminality of the acts performed on behalf of their client. Documents given to the federal prosecutor's office indicated that the bank had laundered over two billion U.S. dollars for the Uribes during the past seven years. Included were receipts given the Uribes for cash deposits, made at Gotthardo's Lugano head office, totaling more than eighty-five million dollars, an average of one million dollars per month. Rey further admitted to willfully concealing evidence of the client's activities from his superiors at the bank in exchange for lavish gifts from the Uribe family, including vacations to the Uribe family resort in Cala di Volpe, Sardinia, as well as to Acapulco, San Francisco, and Punta del Este.

A regular Marco Polo, thought Nick.

Franz Studer announced the immediate freezing of the Uribes' accounts pending a full investigation and hailed the Gotthardo Bank as being at the forefront of Switzerland's internal efforts to police the illegal activities perpetrated by foreign criminals. No criminal penalties would be sought against the bank, said Studer.

A front-page photograph showed Rey being led in handcuffs from the D.A.'s office. He had dressed well for his swan song. He wore a stylish three-piece suit and sported a gambler's kerchief, which fell carelessly out of his breast pocket. Worse, the man was smiling.

Nick was hardly a seasoned expert on banking practice. He didn't need to be to realize that if one client had made transfers and deposits totaling more than two billion dollars over a seven-year period, a lot more than three people were going to know about it.

First off, movements in the portfolios of larger clients were examined monthly. Banks liked to curry favor with their larger clients and were constantly on the lookout for increases in funds deposited, facilities granted, or transactions undertaken on their behalf. Letters of solicitation were sent regularly. Encouragement was given that the client's funds would be well cared for, and so on and so forth. An entire protocol existed for the proper wooing and pampering of the wealthy client.

Second, even the humblest portfolio manager can't help bragging about his client's growing presence at the bank. Wasn't he in some small way responsible for the growth in revenues stemming from his client's increased deposits? Shouldn't he benefit in some way? Lorenz Rey, a senior vice president of the Gotthardo Bank, aged thirty-eight, did not look like a selfless monk. Unless, of course, the Franciscan order had taken to wearing Brioni suits, solid gold Rolex wristwatches, and diamond pinkie rings.

Finally, just the act of depositing one million dollars in banknotes every month would beg the attention, if not inspire the conversation, of the bank's sharp-eyed logistical staff. The same portfolio manager arriving at the cash window two, three, maybe four times each month with an armful of greenbacks, always on behalf of the same client, year after year, would be as conspicuous to any and all members of the bank as a woman walking stark naked into its lobby and asking directions to the Basel Zoo.

Nick had trouble suppressing a hoot of laughter as he studied the article. If nothing else, the Gotthardo Bank should be applauded for the brazenness of their claims. And as if to prove the sum total of Nick's suspicions, the paper reported that at the time it was frozen, the Uribes' account held seven million dollars. Here, observed Nick, is an account through which two billion dollars has been laundered, invested, transferred, what have you, and on the day it is closed, it holds what in the currency of the drug trade is pocket change. Chance? Luck? Coincidence? Hardly.

The Gotthardo Bank was buying its freedom from continuing inquiry. The price, seven million dollars and the careers of several replaceable flunkies. The Uribes would be upset; less so when the bank made good on their frozen deposits with a quiet deduction from the institution's hidden reserves.

Nick shifted his gaze to the Chairman, who was engrossed in conversation with Sepp Zwicki. So, Kaiser was upset that the Gotthardo Bank had given up the Uribes so early.

He had taken a sizable chunk out of Schweitzer's ass for having passed on some faulty information. Twice, Schweitzer had screwed up, said Kaiser. What *other* error had recently drawn the Chairman's wrath?

What interested Nick most was the reason for Kaiser's rage. He wasn't pissed off that the Gotthardo Bank had worked with the Uribes — a name that for decades had been linked to organized crime. He showed no concern that Gotthardo's admission might damage Switzerland's reputation for secrecy. His anger was fueled solely by the fact that they had done it *now*. The Chairman was no fool. He knew damn well that the Gotthardo Bank's admission would only increase the pressure on USB to fork over one of its own. In this game, no one was innocent. And no one guilty. But somewhere along the line you had to pay your dues to keep your place at the table. Gotthardo had paid and was now relatively safe from further prosecution. USB could afford no such luxury.

Wolfgang Kaiser hung up the telephone and motioned for Nick to join him. Nick quickly folded the newspaper and walked to the Chairman's desk. On it lay copies of the three Swiss dailies, as well as the *Wall Street Journal*, the *Financial Times*, and the *Frankfurter Allgemeine Zeitung*. Each was opened to an article discussing the Gotthardo Bank investigation.

"A splendid mess, isn't it?" asked Kaiser.

"The timing couldn't be worse."

Nick didn't have a chance to respond. Beyond the closed doors, Rita Sutter's normally calm voice rose to a plaintive wail. A chair was overturned and a glass shattered. Nick sprang from his chair. Kaiser rounded his desk and made for the entryway. Before either could take more than three steps, the double doors were flung open.

Sterling Thorne marched into the office of the chairman of the United Swiss Bank. Rita Sutter followed, clutching at the American's long arm and admonishing him to stop, repeating over and over again that no one was allowed into the Chairman's office without an appointment. Hugo Brunner, the chief hall porter, trotted in behind them, head hanging low like a hound who had failed his master.

"Madam, you can let go of my shirtsleeve if you'd be so kind," Thorne said to Rita Sutter.

"It's all right, Rita," soothed Wolfgang Kaiser, though his eyes conveyed a different message. "We mustn't be impolite to our guests, even if they arrive without an appointment. You can go back to your desk. You too, Hugo. Thank you."

"This man is a . . . a . . . barbarian," shouted Rita Sutter. She relinquished her grasp on Thorne and, giving him a nasty scowl, stalked from the office. Hugo followed.

Thorne shook loose his sleeve. He walked

to Wolfgang Kaiser and introduced himself as if the two had never met.

Kaiser shook his hand, wincing as if to say "Spare me this garbage." "This is a bank, Mr. Thorne. Normally we expect even our most valued clients to schedule appointments. We're not a fast-food establishment where one can simply *drive through*."

Thorne bowed in apology. "Sorry for not following your precious decorum. In America we are taught to take the bull by the horns, or as my daddy used to say, to grab the goat by the balls."

"How charming. Please take a seat. Or would you prefer the floor?"

Thorne sat on the couch.

Kaiser took up position in a chair opposite. "Neumann, join us."

"This is a private conversation," objected Thorne. "I don't know if you want one of your young pups to listen in."

Nick stood and made it clear he was willing to leave the office. The less time spent in Thorne's company, the better.

"It's all right, Nicholas," said Kaiser. "Sit down. I welcome the input of our younger executives, Mr. Thorne. They are the future of the bank."

"Some future," said Thorne, looking at Nick and shaking his head. He redirected his attention at the Chairman. "Mr. Kaiser, I believe we have a mutual acquaintance. Someone we've both known for a long while."

"I find that extremely doubtful," said Kaiser with a polite smile.

"It's not doubtful. It's a fact." Thorne looked at Nick and then back at Kaiser. "Mr. Ali Mevlevi."

Kaiser appeared unfazed. "Never heard of him."

"I'll repeat the name for you. I know some gentlemen begin losing their hearing at your age." Thorne cleared his throat noisily. "Ali Mevlevi."

"I am sorry, Mr. Thorne. The name means nothing to me. I hope you didn't make such a dramatic entrance on behalf of this friend of yours."

"Mevlevi is no friend of mine and you know it. I believe you folks call him the Pasha. Mr. Neumann sure as hell knows him. Isn't that right, Captain America?"

"I never said any such thing," Nick answered calmly. "I thought I made it clear that I'm not allowed to comment on the identity of any of our clients."

"Let me help jog your memory. Account 549.617 RR. Makes transfers every Monday and Thursday. Oh, he's a client of yours. Of that, if nothing else, I'm sure."

Nick, the casual spectator, the man who knew nothing, kept his face a stony blank. He had less success governing his stomach, which like his conscience was growing queasy and increasingly anxious. "I'm sorry. Like I said, no comment."

Thorne reddened. "This isn't a press conference, Neumann. No comment, you say. You, too, Kaiser? Well, I have some comments for you." He withdrew a sheaf of papers from his jacket pocket and unfolded it. "July 11, 1996. A transfer incoming for sixteen million dollars, departs same day to twenty-four numbered accounts. July 15, incoming for ten million, outgoing same day to fifteen banks. August 1, 1997. Incoming thirty-one million, outgoing same day twenty-seven banks. This list goes on and on, like a bad case of gonorrhea."

Kaiser leaned forward, extending one hand. "Did you obtain this information from an official source?" he asked. "If so, may I see it?"

Thorne refolded the papers and jammed them into his jacket. "The source for this information is classified."

Kaiser frowned. "Classified or created from thin air? Neither the name you mentioned nor the figures in which you obviously have so much faith mean anything to me."

Thorne turned again to Nick. "Those figures ring a bell, Neumann? This is your account, is it not? I wouldn't recommend lying to an officer of the United States government. Money laundering is a serious offense. Ask your buddies at the Gotthardo Bank."

Kaiser placed an iron hand on Nick's leg.

"I must interrupt you, Mr. Thorne," he said. "Your zeal is commendable. We, too, share your enthusiasm for putting an end to the illegal practices for which the banks in our country are often used. Really, though, this Alfie Merlani, was it? The name doesn't sound familiar."

"*Mevlevi,*" said Thorne, who by now was growing agitated, shifting constantly in his chair. "Ali Mevlevi. Imports over a ton of refined heroin per month into Europe. Usually through Italy, then into Germany, France, Scandinavia. About a quarter of his stuff ends up right here in Zurich. Look, I'm trying to offer you a deal. A chance to make things right before we blow this case up in public."

"I do not need a deal, Mr. Thorne. This bank has always prided itself on rigorously obeying the laws of this country. Our laws governing secrecy prevent me from disclosing any information about our clients. I am willing, however, to make an exception, just this once, so that we may demonstrate our goodwill. The account number you mentioned was in fact on our internal surveillance sheet last week. And, you are correct that the account was managed by Mr. Neumann, here. Nicholas, tell Mr. Thorne everything you know about this account. I'm absolving you of any responsibility you may have toward our bank under the Bank Secrecy Act of 1933. Go ahead, tell him."

Nick stared into Kaiser's eyes, all too mindful of the Chairman's dissuasive clutch. Willful ignorance was one thing, premeditated obfuscation, quite another. But he was too far along his chosen path to change course now. "I recognize the number," he said. "I remember seeing it on the surveillance list last Thursday. But I don't recall any activity that day. I have no idea to whom it belongs."

Thorne tossed his head back and gave an unpleasant laugh, a horse's whinny. "Well, well. Who do we have here? Edgar Bergen and Charlie McCarthy. I am going to give you one more chance to make a deal with us and spare your company the indignity of seeing its Chairman implicated in the business affairs of one of the world's largest distributors of heroin. I would've thought that a man who had suffered like you — I mean your family's tragedy and all — would be sensitive to the efforts of the authorities to nail a parasite like Mevlevi. He's a big fish for us. We are not going to stop until we've landed him, dead or alive. In fact, I found a snapshot that I thought might inspire you to give us a hand."

Thorne threw a five-by-seven color photograph onto the coffee table.

It landed facing Nick. He looked down at it and grimaced. The photograph showed the corpse of a nude man lying on a silver table. The table was an autopsy platform in a morgue. The man's eyes were open, shaded a

357

translucent blue. Blood ran from his nose. His mouth was open, caked with a milky froth.

"Stefan," gasped Wolfgang Kaiser. "This is my son."

" 'Course it's your son. Wiped out on heroin. Looks like he chased the dragon one too many a time. They found him here in Zurich, didn't they? That means the poison in his veins came from Ali Mevlevi. The Pasha. The holder of account 549.617 RR." Thorne pounded the coffee table. "Your client."

Kaiser scooped the photo off the table and stared at it silently.

Thorne continued, clearly unburdened by any sympathy for Kaiser. "Help me nail Mevlevi. Freeze the Pasha's accounts!" He looked to Nick for support. "Stop his cash and we can stop the drugs. Isn't that a simple suggestion? It's time we protect kids from the same stuff that killed your boy. How old was he anyway? Nineteen? Twenty?"

Wolfgang Kaiser stood as if in a daze. "Please leave, Mr. Thorne. We have no information for you today. We do not know any Mevlevi. We do not work with heroin smugglers. That you would stoop so low as to bring my boy into this is beyond my understanding."

"Oh, I don't think it is, Mr. Kaiser. Allow me to light the last couple of candles on this cake before I leave. I want to make sure you have plenty to think about over the next few days. I know about your time in Beirut. Four years over there, eh? Mevlevi was there, too. Seems he was setting up his operations around the time you arrived. He was a big shot around town, if I'm not mistaken. What I find curious is how you could have lived in the same town for three years and never met the man. Not once, you say. Excuse me, Mr. Kaiser, but wasn't it your job to beg for the scraps of the local gentry?"

Kaiser turned to Nick as if he hadn't heard a word Thorne had said. "Please escort Mr. Thorne from the premises," he said pleasantly. "I'm afraid we've run out of time."

Nick admired Kaiser's self-restraint. He placed a hand on Thorne's back and said, "Let's go."

Thorne spun to knock the hand away. "I don't need an escort, Neumann, thanks all the same." He pointed his finger at Kaiser. "Don't forget my offer. A little information on Mevlevi is all that's required or else I'll take your whole damned bank down with you standing at the wheel. Is that clear? We know all about you. Everything."

He walked away from the Chairman, and as he passed Nick, he smiled and whispered, "I'm not through with you, young man. Check your mail."

As soon as Thorne had gone, Rita Sutter swept into the office, her dignified bearing restored. "That man is a beast. Why, the nerve . . ."

"Everything is all right, Rita," said Kaiser, who looked pale and shrunken. "Would you be so kind as to bring me a cup of coffee and a *Basel Leckerei.*"

Rita Sutter nodded in response to the command, but instead of leaving, came a step closer to the Chairman. She placed a hand on his shoulder and asked tenderly, "*Gehts?* Are you all right?"

Kaiser lifted his head and met her eyes. He shook his head slightly and he sighed. "Yes, yes, I'm fine. The man brought up Stefan."

She scowled, patting Kaiser on the shoulder, then walked out of the room.

When she had left, Kaiser straightened his shoulders, regaining some of his martial bearing. "You mustn't believe the lies Thorne is spreading," he said to Nick. "He's a desperate man. Clearly he'll stop at nothing to capture this man, this Mevlevi. Is it our job to be a policeman? I hardly think so."

Nick cringed at hearing Kaiser fall back to the Swiss banker's standard defense. To his ears, it was a startling admission of the bank's complicity with the heroin dealer, Ali Mevlevi.

"Thorne has nothing," Kaiser was saying, his voice grown vigorous once again. "He's flailing his sword in the wind, hoping to chop down anything he comes in contact with. The man is a menace to the civilized business world."

Nick nodded his head in understanding,

thinking how odd life's random and symmetrical balance could be. He had lost his father. Kaiser had lost his only son. For a moment he wondered if Kaiser had desired his arrival in Zurich more than he himself had.

"I'm sorry about your son," he said softly, before leaving the room.

Wolfgang Kaiser did not acknowledge the condolence.

Chapter 28

Alone in the corridor, Nick breathed a sigh of relief. He began the short walk back to his office confused at what exactly he had just witnessed. He needed to decide who had been telling the truth and who had been lying. Most of what Thorne had said made perfect sense. If Ali Mevlevi had been a big shot in Beirut, Kaiser would at the least have known of him. More likely, he would have actively solicited his business. It was a branch manager's job to circulate among the city's better crowds, insinuate himself in its loftier circles, and at the appropriate time, normally, Nick imagined, after a second martini, suggest that they trust him with a good portion of their assets. Similarly, if Ali Mevlevi was the Pasha — which certainly seemed the case — then Kaiser would also know him. No man became chairman of a major bank by ignoring his most important clients. Certainly not Wolfgang Kaiser.

Hell, Nick thought, everything Thorne said made sense. The Pasha being Ali Mevlevi; his using numbered account 549.617 RR at the United Swiss Bank to launder his profits; that Kaiser must not only know him, but must

362

know him pretty damn well. All of it.

Nick turned a corner and entered a smaller corridor. The ceiling was lower and the hall narrower. He had advanced a few steps when he heard the distinct thud and rattle of a drawer being violently shut. The sound came from an office ahead and to the right. Its door was slightly ajar, and a sliver of light curled from under it onto the carpeted floor. Coming closer, he saw that someone was inside the room searching through a raft of papers that lay on top of the desk. At the same instant, he realized he was peering into his own office.

"I thought you waited until after banking hours to root through an individual's private affairs," Nick said, slamming the door behind him.

Armin Schweitzer continued to rummage through the papers, unfazed. "Simply checking for the list of clients you're to phone. The bank can ill afford for you to alienate its major shareholders."

"I have that list right here." Nick withdrew a folded sheet from his jacket pocket.

Schweitzer put forward his meaty hand. "If you please . . ."

Nick held the copy as if assaying its value, then slid it back into his pocket. "If you'd like a copy, see the Chairman."

"A moment of the Chairman's time would indeed be welcome; alas between you and your close friend Mr. Thorne, it seems that he hasn't a moment to spare." Schweitzer carelessly dropped the papers he held onto the desk. "Coincidental your arriving just when Thorne needs you. You and the American gestapo."

"You think I'm working with the DEA? Is that why you're here?" Nick laughed grimly at the suggestion. "If I were you, I'd spend more time looking after my own affairs. I understand you're the man on the tightrope, not me."

Schweitzer flinched as if he'd been slapped. "You understand *nothing*." He rounded the desk, gathering steam like a runaway locomotive, stopping only when he came within an inch of Nick's chest. "I walk no tightrope here, Mr. Neumann. My blood runs in this bank as deeply as the Chairman's. Thirty-five years of my life, I've given it. Can you even begin to understand such a commitment? You, an American, who flits from one job to another, hoping only for a bigger paycheck and a fatter bonus. Herr Kaiser has never questioned my loyalty to him or my service to the bank. Never!"

Nick stared into Schweitzer's bulging eyes. "Right now, I understand only one thing. This is my office and you should have at least asked my permission before coming in and messing up the place."

"Your permission?" Schweitzer put his head back and laughed. "I'll remind you, Neumann, it's my job to ensure that the bank complies with all legal requirements and that our employees do the same. Anyone who I believe might have reason to do the bank harm warrants my total concern. And any actions I may wish to take are so justified. That includes having a look at your office and your papers whenever I please."

"Do the bank harm?" said Nick, retreating a step. "What have I done to give you that impression? My actions have spoken loudly enough."

"Too loudly, perhaps." Schweitzer placed a hand on Nick's shoulder and spoke softly into his ear. "Tell me, Neumann, whose sins are you atoning for anyway?"

"What are you talking about?"

A bemused expression played across Schweitzer's face. "I told you I've been with the bank thirty-five years. Long enough to remember your father. In fact, I knew him well. We all did. And I can assure that no one on the Fourth Floor has forgotten his embarrassing behavior."

"My father was an honorable man," Nick said instinctively.

"Of course he was. But then again, you wouldn't really know, would you?" Schweitzer offered a malevolent smile and walked to the door. Opening it, he said, "And Neumann? If you think *I'm* walking on a tightrope, perhaps *you* haven't looked down lately. It's a long fall from the Fourth Floor. I'll be watching you."

"Take a number!"

Schweitzer gave a curt bow and left the room.

Nick collapsed into his chair. Peter Sprecher had been right to call Schweitzer dangerous, but he had forgotten to mention paranoid, psychotic, and delusional. What the hell had Schweitzer meant about his father's "embarrassing behavior"? What had his father done to cause the bank distress? Nick knew only the rudiments of his father's career. Alex Neumann had started in the bank at age sixteen and worked as an apprentice for four years. His first real jobs had been as assistant and then full portfolio manager. According to Cerruti, he had worked under Kaiser in both positions. Could his father have done something to embarrass the bank then? Nick didn't think so. Schweitzer hadn't been referring to any lighthearted shenanigans a junior executive might have gotten up to. He'd been talking about something serious, probably something that had happened after Alex Neumann had been transferred to Los Angeles to open up USB's branch office there.

The only clues Nick had to his father's practices in Los Angeles were inside the two agendas he'd found in Hannibal; first there was mention of one Allen Soufi, a private banking client, whose every visit occasioned a stern afterword. One time labeled a *Schlitzohr* —

Swiss slang for crook, another time simply "undesirable." And later, his name underscored by the chilling reminder "Bastard threatened me," written not in his father's usual looping script but spelled out in bold block letters. There was more. A company named Goldluxe that he had visited, apparently in response to a demand for commercial credit, and about which he had written a frank appraisal. "Dirty." "Impossible sales." "Hands off." Yet with which, if his entries were to be interpreted clearly, he had been forced to do business.

Nick brought his head forward and massaged the bridge of his nose. He asked himself how the bank could construe actions taken to protect it from unseemly business interests as embarrassing behavior? He only had to replay Thorne's accusations about Kaiser's long-term relationship with one Ali Mevlevi to know how. The bank *wanted* to do business with those unseemly interests.

Nick sat up straight in his chair. The only place he knew to look for an answer to these questions was in the monthly activity reports his father sent back from Los Angeles. To get those, he'd have to ask Cerberus to generate a request form, which would bear his initials, or find someone willing to retrieve them for him. The first path was too risky, the second closed — at least for now. He'd just have to wait and hope to find another way.

Patience, he told himself in a voice not unlike his father's. *Control yourself.*

Nick had a hard time guiding his attentions back to his job. He unfolded the paper Schweitzer had been so anxious to discover and laid it on the desk. The list contained the names of those shareholders, both institutional and individual, who held significant blocks of USB stock. He smiled when he came to the name of Eberhard Senn, the Count Languenjoux. The old-timer held a block of shares worth over 250 million francs — six percent of the bank. His votes would be crucial.

There were many other names on the list. For those who kept their shares in an account at USB, Nick would request a copy of the client's entire file. This he would study, assimilating a maximum of pertinent detail about the client, before telephoning. Needless to say, those shares of USB stock held in discretionary accounts managed by the bank would be voted in favor of reigning management.

The vast majority of USB shareholders, however, did not hold an account with the bank. In these cases, Nick would contact either the individual shareholder or more frequently, the fund manager responsible for voting the shares, and preach the bank's doctrine of increased profitability. The names on his list were primarily American institutional investors: the New York State Teachers' Retirement Fund, California Employees Retirement Fund, Morgan Stanley European Equity Fund.

Nick grabbed a stack of file request forms and began filling them out. Name of portfolio manager, department, date requested, signature. The paperwork left nothing to chance, nothing unclear. The only spaces missing were for his height, weight, and tipple of choice. Each request was to be signed by Kaiser prior to being forwarded to the responsible executive. Client information was treated as confidentially within the bank's walls as it was outside of them. Nick wondered if he would ever be able to liberate his father's monthly activity reports from *Dokumentation Zentrale*. Not if he needed Kaiser's signature, he wouldn't. Not if Schweitzer was tracking his every move within the bank.

An hour after he'd begun his monotonous travail, Nick was interrupted by Yvan, the postman. Yvan entered his office and handed him several manila envelopes, the medium of internal postage in corporations the world over. Nick signed for them. He recalled Thorne's words, *Check your mail, young man,* and began tearing open the envelopes.

The first held a memorandum from Martin Maeder addressed to all portfolio managers "suggesting" that they consider upping their clients' holding of USB common stock. Obviously, it was a tactic designed to inflate the bank's control over its own shares. Technically, the request bordered on a violation of the sacrosanct "Chinese wall," the invisible boundary that separated the worlds of investment and commercial banking that coexisted under the roofs of all universal Swiss banks. In the world of the managed account, where investments were made with the discretion of the portfolio manager alone, the bank had tremendous power to manipulate the prices of stocks, to ensure the successful underwriting of a bond or equity issue, or to move the value of a currency.

Nick tossed Maeder's memo in the trash bin and opened the second envelope. Inside was a white letter inscribed only with his name and the bank's address. No stamp was affixed, no postmark noted. He slit open the envelope. Inside was a copy of Nick's separation papers from the United States Marine Corps and a one-page ruling from the Board of Inquiry citing the grounds for his dishonorable discharge. Felonious assault with intent to cause grievous bodily harm. *Intent?* Hell, he'd beaten the living tar out of Keely. He'd pummeled the fat-assed motherfucker to within an inch of his worthless life. Payback, Agent Keely, courtesy of First Lieutenant Nicholas A. Neumann USMCR.

Nick threw the papers onto his desk, at once furious and incredulous that Thorne had gotten hold of them. By law, they were to be graded top secret and kept sealed at Headquarters Marine Corps in D.C. He had told no one about his discharge, certainly not Kaiser. The official record accorded him a general discharge. He had served his country well, had done his duty. As a man, he had acted honorably. As a soldier, maybe less so. But it was no one's business but his and Jack Keely's.

He dropped his hand to the underside of his right thigh and massaged the unnatural indentation behind his right knee, where more than a pound of flesh and muscle was missing. Thorne and Keely. Different men, different times, but with the same agenda, the same motivation. Neither could be trusted.

Nick looked at the note from Thorne and squinted as if staring into the rays of a morning sun. He envisioned the dusty clearing where Arturo de la Cruz Enrile lay dead with an American bullet in his brain. He saw Gunny Ortiga bounding across the open space, then spotted the olive bandana that held Enrile's thumb, precious proof of the insurgent's death. And for a second, he swore that he could feel the shuffle of the Gunny's steps as he neared their skirmish line, but in fact, it was only the tread of the postman's footsteps as he shuffled through the hallways.

And then he was back in the jungle. Nothing else existed. Not Thorne, not Schweitzer, not the entire fucking bank. It was just him lying on his belly in the warm red dirt waiting to lead his men back to the USS *Guam*. And with the curse of perfect hindsight, he knew that hell was waiting for him.

Chapter 29

For a few seconds, all is calm. The incessant chatter of the jungle canopy is no more. Ortiga lies sweating behind the dirt berm. "It was a clean shot," he says. "He was dead before he hit the ground."

Nick relieves Ortiga of his grisly trophy, trying hard not to think of the severed thumb wrapped in the sticky cloth. He signals for his men to withdraw into the foliage and form up. A thirteen-mile retreat through the steaming jungle beckons. One by one the marines slide on their bellies backward toward the protective sanctuary of the jungle.

A woman's scream peals through the morning air.

Nick yells for his men to freeze where they are, to keep out of sight.

Again, the woman screams. Her fear dissolves into a guttural cry. Sobbing.

Nick raises his binoculars and scans the clearing but can see only the shape of Enrile's corpse. The sun shines directly on it, and already a circus of flies is congregating near the pool of blood under his head. A small brown woman emerges from behind the white farmhouse. She runs, then falters, then runs again toward the body. Her shriek-ing grows with every step. Her arms flail around her head, then descend to beat her sides. A child totters from the house seeking its mother. Together they stand above the dead man, wailing.

Nick looks to Ortiga. "Where the hell did she come from?"

Ortiga shrugs. "Must've been in the truck. Recon said the house was deserted."

Nick feels a new presence at his side. Johnny Burke is back from the dead. He has appro-priated the binoculars. "Can't tell if the kid's a boy or a girl," he says. "They're both crying themselves to death." Burke raises himself on one knee, still studying the clearing with the binoculars. "You killed that old boy. He's dead, ain't he?"

Nick pulls on the newbie's shirt. "Get your ass down flat."

Burke resists. "Ain't nobody but that poor mother and her little kid out here in the jungle, Lieutenant. Nobody but that woman and . . ." His face is pale. Nick realizes he is delirious. "You killed her husband, Lieutenant."

Timber cracks. Halos of dust spring from the berm to Nick's right and left. Puffs of smoke appear in the jungle like quickly bloom-ing flowers. A smattering of small arms fire pours from the dense wall of foliage opposite the skirmish line.

Burke is standing and screaming, "Hit the

dirt, lady! Get your kid down! Lie down, god-dammit!"

Nick grabs the seat of Burke's pants and orders him to fall behind the berm. The young officer knocks away the offending arm and continues beseeching the lady and her child to lie down on the ground.

A wet slap lands in Nick's ear.

Burke drops to one knee. A sheet of blood spreads rapidly across his tiger-striped utilities. He is gut shot. He coughs and a gob of blood arcs from his mouth.

"Heads down! Do not return fire," yells Nick, who then lifts his own head above the berm. The woman and child stand motionless next to the corpse, their own heads covered by their arms.

"Get down," Nick wheezes, his cheek pressed into the warm dirt. "Goddamn you, get down!"

Bullets whiz by, some pounding into the dirt, others passing inches overhead. Burke is moaning. Nick looks at him, then jumps to his feet, his hands cupped to his mouth. "Get down!" he yells. "Lady, get down!"

A bullet slices the air near his ear and he drops to the ground. Still, the woman and child refuse to move. They stand like statues, cowering above Enrile's body.

Then it is too late.

Nick hears the shots that kill them. A collage of pops and bangs no different from the others, but suddenly, the two are no longer standing. They lie sprawled on the dirt near Enrile. Bullets pound into their bodies. Mother and child twitch with the entry of each slug.

Nick signals the retreat. He looks at Burke. Blood pours from his mouth. His shirt is wet and black. Ortiga pulls it open and applies a sulfa bandage. Frowning, he shakes his head.

High noon in the Philippine jungle. Nick and his men have covered eight miles along the path to their extraction point. They are pursued by an unseen foe. The only testament to the marauders' presence is the occasional crackle of ammunition fired in the marines' direction. Now the men must rest, Nick most of all. He lays Johnny Burke on the slope of what the map signifies as the Azul River. Burke is conscious and momentarily lucid.

"Thanks for the ride, Lieutenant," he tells Nick. "I ain't gonna be going much farther. You just as well oughta leave me here."

"Keep that mouth of yours wired tight," says Nick. "We're gonna get you home. Just keep squeezing my hand. Let me know you're still here."

Nick scrambles to his "0330," a corporal charged with carrying the team's radio. He takes the compact transmitter and keys in their operational frequency, hoping to raise the *Guam.* Three times he's tried to contact the ship to set up an emergency helo extraction.

Again, the *Guam* is silent. Nick changes the frequency and picks up the tower at the Zamboanga Airport. The equipment is not faulty. His calls are being ignored.

Four o'clock in the afternoon. The strip of beach that will serve as their extraction point lies a quarter mile ahead through a clump of tangled undergrowth. Burke is still alive. Nick kneels next to him. His entire being is painted with his comrade's blood. His ear monitors the wind, seeking the faint wash of two landing craft inbound from the *Guam*. An hour ago, he had managed to contact the ship by speaking with an air traffic controller in Zamboanga, who on an open frequency relayed his call to Colonel Sigurd Andersen.

All there is left to do is sit and wait. And pray that Burke will survive.

Ortiga spots the boats one half mile out. A shout goes up from the exhausted men.

Johnny Burke looks to Nick. "Semper fi," he says weakly.

Nick squeezes the Kentuckian's hand. "You're home, kid. Be on board in no time."

Ortiga orders "A" squad to form up. The men must remain inside the line of vegetation until the boats are on the sand. As they move out, a hailstorm of fire erupts from a grove of bent palms to their left. More shots come from a stand of rubber trees behind them. The marines are caught in a classic enfilade, effectively cut off from the beach.

Nick yells for his men to dig in. "This is the last dance! Fire at will!"

Eight marines loose the fury of their weapons at the hidden enemy. The air is afire with exploding shells. Ortiga launches a grenade from the snout of his rifle. Nick empties a clip into the grove and advances toward the beach. He can hear the scream of his enemy above the shooting. He rejoices in the tumult.

The first landing craft is on the beach. "A" squad sprints toward it, free hands clamping helmets to their heads. Nick and Ortiga provide covering fire. The first landing craft is away, the motor opened to full throttle, white wake trailing.

A second craft slides onto the sand. Nick pulls Burke onto his shoulders for the final dash to the beach. Emerging from the underbrush, he stumbles in the sand. Ortiga motions for him to hurry, putting the M-16 to his shoulder and spraying the jungle with disciplined bursts of fire. Nick grunts as he pushes his boots into the fine white sand. He sees the craft, waves to the skipper. He is there. And then he is sailing through the air, a hot wind lashing at his back. He has been swallowed by a mighty roar, enveloped in a blast furnace of fire and grit. Air is sucked from his lungs. Time stops.

Nick's face is buried in the sand. Ortiga is lifting his shoulder. "You kicking, sir?"

"Where's Burke?" Nick yells. "Where's Burke?"

"Ain't nothing left of him," Ortiga screams. "We gotta get to the boat, Lieutenant. Now!"

Nick looks to his right. Burke's torso sprawls in a patch of sand black with blood. His legs and arms are missing, cropped off neatly at the trunk. His back is pocked with chunks of shrapnel, flesh sizzling with molten lead. The smell makes Nick vomit. He tells himself to hustle to the boat, to get off his butt and motor to the landing craft, but his legs refuse to obey his commands. There is something wrong with him. He looks at his right knee. Oh God, he thinks. I've been hit. The fabric of his uniform is torn in a hundred places, the flesh ripped into too many jagged strands and burned black as coal. Blood, this time his own, jets in a small but determined geyser. A band of moist cartilage glimmers in the afternoon sun. Nick grabs the Kentuckian's rifle and rams the barrel into the sand, an impromptu crutch. He stands and sees only white, and then a fuzzy curtain of gray. An internal shrieking more deafening than any noise he has ever heard fills his ears. Ortiga's arm is around him. Together they stagger the last paces to the landing craft. The craft's skipper drags the black stump that is Burke's body to the rubber dinghy.

They are away.

The shooting has stopped.

The pain begins a hundred yards to sea.

Lying in the prow of the craft, Nick dodges unconsciousness for the long ride to the *Guam*. Every wave crested means a spasm of agony, every swell, a rip current of nausea. His right knee is torn apart. His lower leg shattered. A shard of ivory bone pushes through the flesh as if anxious to test the warm afternoon air. Nick does not moan. For a few minutes the pain clears his mind. It allows the implications of the day's events to take form.

The assassination of Enrile. The murder of his wife and daughter. The failure of the *Guam* to respond to Nick's emergency calls. All were planned. All were preordained.

Nick envisions Keely hidden inside the radio room for eighteen hours; he hears Keely relaying news of Enrile's arrival, promising that the insurgent would be alone; he imagines Keely turning off the radio, refusing to respond to the rescue call of nine marines, one gravely wounded. Why? Nick screams. Why?

Rocking in the prow of the bucking craft, he vows to find the answers. He promises to make responsible those who have sanctioned the murder of Enrile and the betrayal that took the life of Johnny Burke.

At first, Nick did not hear the light knock on his door. His eyes were open, staring at the papers on his desk, but he saw only blurred images of his past. When the knock came a second time, this time louder and more insistent, he blinked and told the visitor to come in. He looked up to see the door to his office already open, and the blond head of Sylvia Schon peering anxiously round the corner.

"Are you okay? I've been knocking for ten seconds."

Nick rose to greet her. "I'm fine. Just have a lot on my mind. You can imagine. Come on in." He wanted to tell her it was nice to see her and that she looked great — but he was afraid of appearing overly friendly. He didn't know what to make of her phone call yesterday morning. First she'd acted like she hated his guts, her voice barren. Then she'd called back to apologize, sounding sincere. Before she cut him off, that was.

Sylvia closed the door behind her and leaned against it. She was carrying a faded yellow file under her arm. "I wanted to say I'm sorry about the way I acted yesterday morning. I know I sounded crazy. It's hard for me to say this, but frankly, I'm a little jealous. I don't think you know what you've got here."

Nick swung an arm around the windowless office. It measured eight feet by ten feet. Bookshelves covered two walls and a credenza the third. "What, this?"

"You know what I mean. The Fourth Floor. Working with the Chairman."

He knew exactly what she meant. "I guess I'm pretty lucky, but right now we're so busy

I haven't had time to congratulate myself."

"Consider this a present to celebrate your promotion." She took the yellow folder from under her arm and tossed it playfully on his desk.

"What is it? Don't tell me. A questionnaire to be filled out in triplicate asking how I like my furniture?"

She smiled impishly. "Not exactly."

"A listing of every school I attended, days absent, and what I did for every summer vacation."

She laughed. "Now you're getting closer. Take a look."

Nick picked up the file and turned it sideways to read its title. *United Swiss Bank, Los Angeles Office. Monthly Activity Reports 1975.* "I should never have asked you to get these for me. I wasn't thinking of your position here at the bank at all. It was unfair and rude. I don't want you to put yourself in a bad spot for me."

"Why not? I told you I owed you a favor and besides I want to."

"Why?" he asked, a little louder than intended. He was afraid one day she'd help him and the next turn him in.

"It was me who was being selfish the other day, not you. Sometimes, I can't help it. I've worked so hard to get here that even the smallest bump frightens me." She raised her head and addressed him in a forthright tone.

382

"Frankly, I'm embarrassed about my behavior and that's why I hadn't called you back. I thought about what you asked me and I decided that a son has every right to know as much as he possibly can about his father."

Nick appraised this providential turn of fortune. "Should I be suspicious?"

"Should I?" She took a step closer and laid a hand on his arm. "Just promise me one thing: that soon you'll tell me what this is all about."

Nick laid the dossier on his desk. "All right. I promise. How about tonight?"

Sylvia looked taken aback. "Tonight?" She bit her lip and stared directly at him. "Tonight would be wonderful. My place at seven-thirty? You remember where it is, don't you?"

"Deal."

A minute after she had gone, Nick stared at the place where she had stood as if her presence had been an illusion. On the desk lay a faded yellow folder with a neatly typed title, and next to it, a bin number and a coded reference.

All neat.

All proper.

And for the next twenty-four hours, all his.

Chapter 30

At the same time that Nick received the files from Sylvia, in a warmer location some three thousand miles to the east, Ali Mevlevi inched his Bentley along the rue Clemenceau, happy to be within shouting distance of the Hotel St. Georges, where he had been due for lunch fifteen minutes earlier. Ahead, the white porte cochere of the hotel beckoned as an oasis from the noxious exhaust that fleeced the center of town at midday. Beirut had grown so civilized as to boast a noontime *bouchon* equal to her more fashionable sisters of Paris and Milan.

Mevlevi tapped his foot furiously on the automobile's floorboard, exhorting the vehicles in front of him to progress another fifty feet so that he could offer his car to the hotel valet. Rothstein would hate him for being late. The proprietor of Little Maxim's was famed for his slavish devotion to habits long ago adopted. Mevlevi had practically begged to join him for his weekly lunch at the St. Georges. The memory of his pleading brought a sour taste to his mouth.

You did it for Lina, he reminded himself. To clear her name. To prove once and for all that she cannot be the spy cosseted in your nest.

Mevlevi gave himself up to the unmoving traffic, relaxing momentarily. He thought of Lina. He remembered the first time he had seen her, and he smiled.

Little Maxim's sat like a worn piece of clothing at the far end of Al Ma'aqba Street, two blocks from the waterfront. The place was done up like a seedy bordello on the Barbary Coast. Velvet couches and leather ottomans were spread throughout the room. In front of each grouping rested a glass table, invariably soiled with the spit olive pits and spilled *mezza* of the party just departed. But if Max gave little attention to his furnishings, the same could not be said of his girls. Scattered about the room like loose diamonds on a mountain of coal were two dozen of the world's most alluring women.

That night, Mevlevi had wandered in around two, ragged from working his phones. He chose his usual table and had only just sat down when a slim Asian girl, lacquered pageboy and bursting lips, sauntered over and suggested she join him. He politely declined. As he declined a full-bottomed redhead from Tbilisi and a platinum man-eater from London whose oversize breasts were on display through a mesh blouse. He required not overwhelming beauty, not refined sexuality, but a carnal revelation: raw and primal. An atavistic reincarnation of primordial desire.

It was a tall order, granted.

But he had not been prepared for Lina.

A thumping beat signaled the commencement of the evening's entertainment. The music was near violent in its attack, and despite his normal distaste for American rock 'n' roll, he found himself energized, anxious as to what the song might bring. When Lina walked onto the stage, muscles sinewy, black hair tumbling about her sculpted shoulders, he felt his heart fall into a chasm. She danced with the fury of a caged panther, and when the music demanded that she "walk this way," her responding strut fired a bolt of hormonal lightning through his loins. Watching her remove the leather brassiere that supported her generous breasts, his mouth turned dry as the Gobi. She walked to the end of the runway and lifted her arms above her head, gathering her hair into her hands while swaying her sensuous hips to the music's savage beat. She stared at him longer than appropriate, for even Max had his rules. Her eyes were black, but an untamed light shone within them. And when her gaze fell upon him, he felt as if she were staring into the core of his being. And that she desired him, as he desired her.

A flurry of horns drew Mevlevi back to the present. He moved his car a few meters forward, then stopped. "Be damned," he cursed at the stationary cluster of automobiles. He honked his horn twice and stepped out of his car. Leaving the motor running, he snaked through the traffic toward the hotel. A liveried attendant spotted him and ran down the easy slope onto the main avenue. Mevlevi shoved a hundred-dollar banknote into his hand and told him to keep the car near the entryway.

Beirut. Improvisation in the face of adversity was one's daily chore.

"Max, I thank you so much for letting me join you. And on such short notice. I should be honored."

A spry gray-haired man rose from his chair. He was extremely thin and extremely tan, and wore a silk shirt unbuttoned halfway to his navel. "You're a charmer, Ali. Now I know I'm in big trouble. We have a saying, 'When the lion smiles, even its cubs flee.' Waiter, check!"

Ali Mevlevi and Max Rothstein broke into a healthy laugh.

"You are looking well, Maxie. It's been a while since I saw you in daylight."

Rothstein dabbed at his eyes with a crisp white napkin. "All right for an old kvetch. You look worried. Do you want to get right into it?"

Mevlevi forced a smile. Silently, he recited a homily from the Koran. "Verily, those who show patience will see the Kingdom of Allah."

Easier said than done. "I've come to eat with an old friend. Business can wait."

A captain arrived with menus bound in green leather.

"Glasses," ordered Rothstein, his voice raised. A bulky man at an adjacent table leaned over and handed his patron a pair of bifocals.

"The usual?" asked Mevlevi, casually eyeing the muscle assembled at the next table.

"You know me," said Max, smiling. "I'm a man of habit."

The captain returned and took their orders. Mevlevi selected the Dover sole. Rothstein, a half-pound hamburger patty, well done, with a poached egg on top. He had been eating the same vile concoction for lunch and dinner for as long as Mevlevi had known him.

Maxim Andre Rothstein. German in name, Lebanese by upbringing, the rogue was as slippery as a sturgeon on ice. He had ruled over a major part of the gambling and vice in Beirut for as long as Mevlevi could remember. Certainly since well before his own arrival in 1980. Even at the height of the civil war, Max had kept the doors to his club open. No soldier would risk the reprisal of his chieftains should any harm come to Max or his girls. To ensure that such affectionate feelings were long-lived, Max had sent out teams of croupiers to all factions, determined to bring craps, roulette, and baccarat to soldiers on both sides of the

Green Line. And, of course, to extract his cut from every wager.

In a time when nearly everyone in Beirut lost not only members of their family but a large part of their material wealth, Max Rothstein grew enormously wealthy. The presence of his well-attired bodyguards attested to the fact that the bastard had felt safer during the war than since its conclusion. And added to Ali Mevlevi's growing insecurity at being alone and unprotected in the center of a city never more than a car bomb away from anarchy.

The two men chatted amiably about the host of problems that still befell Lebanon. Neither offered firm opinions. Both knew it was best for businessmen to express their allegiance to whichever faction was in power. Yesterday, Gemayel. Today, Hariri. Tomorrow . . . who knew?

A tray of desserts was brought to the table, and both men made their choices. Mevlevi took a chocolate éclair. Rothstein, the tapioca pudding.

Mevlevi took a bite of his éclair and after confessing his delight, lowered his fork and asked Rothstein a question. "Cars or camels, Maxie?"

"Run that by me one more time."

Mevlevi repeated his question. He thought it wise to refer to his problem in metaphorical terms for the time being. That way should Rothstein grow upset, he could extricate himself diplomatically.

Rothstein looked to his table of bodyguards, then eyed the heavens and gave a whimsical shrug. "Cars," he said. "I've never taken to animals. I don't even have a dog."

Rothstein's retinue laughed dutifully. Mevlevi joined in.

"I have a small problem with my car," he began. "Maybe you can help me."

Again the weary shrug. "I'm no mechanic, but go ahead. What are you driving?"

"A beautiful machine. Dark body, clean, sexy lines, and what an engine. I bought it about nine months ago."

Rothstein spread his hands and smiled sagaciously. "I know what model you're talking about."

"Now let's say, Maxie, that I bought this car new."

"Well, there's new and then, there's new. Sometimes new is new, and sometimes new is almost new, and sometimes new is — " Rothstein chuckled and threw up his hands, "well, sometimes new can be pretty old."

"So what if the car that I thought was new was in fact old? Let's say a trade-in. Maybe something you were selling for a friend?"

Concern blossomed on the wrinkled face. "Would I sell you, one of my oldest customers, a used car?"

"Please, Maxie, it is no matter. That is not the issue today."

"You having troubles with this model? Send it back. If it's the one I'm thinking of, I could find another buyer in an instant."

"I never send back what belongs to me. You know this, Maxie. My purchases are always final. What I no longer need, I discard."

Rothstein ladled a spoonful of tapioca pudding into his mouth. Half dribbled onto his bib, half from his chin. He paid the mishap little mind. "Then what is the problem? Is she losing a little horsepower?" He laughed for the benefit of his coterie, and his four thugs joined in.

Mevlevi felt his patience slipping away. He tightened his grip on the hidden corner of tablecloth. "That is of no concern to you. Where did you find this car? The answer is worth more even than the car itself."

A thick envelope was passed across the table. In it was a stack of one hundred one-hundred-dollar bills. Rothstein inserted a thumb and eyed the bills.

"Ali, I took this car in as a favor to an old friend. The friend told me the car needed a home. A place where she might get the attention she deserved. High-class, you get my drift. The car required a single owner. Definitely not a rental."

"A fine idea," said Mevlevi. "But there are not many gentlemen, even among us, who can afford such a car."

"A few," said Rothstein cagily.

"Who might this old friend be who was so kind as to bring to you such an outstanding automobile?"

"He's a close friend of yours. Not that I put my ear to the ground, but I believe he may be one of your associates. It's only because you two know each other that I can tell you. After all, partners shouldn't keep secrets from each other."

"Ah, Max. As usual, you are a man of reason."

Mevlevi leaned forward and listened as Max Rothstein whispered the name of the man who had brought Lina to Little Maxim's. When he heard the name, he closed his eyes and willed his tears to fire. He had found his traitor.

Chapter 31

Nick arrived at the entrance to Sylvia Schon's apartment precisely at 7:30. He had traveled the same route only six nights before, yet since boarding the tram at the Paradeplatz he had felt as if he were making the journey for the first time.

Sylvia lived in a modern apartment building on top of the Zurichberg. An open field fronted the building, and a dark forest lay in back of it. It had taken him ten minutes to walk up the steep hill from the tram stop on Universitätstrasse. Do that twice a day and he'd live to be a hundred.

He pressed the button next to her name and waited for her to ring him inside. He had come directly from the office and carried his brief-case in one hand and a bouquet of colorful flowers in the other. He hadn't planned on the flowers. The idea had popped into his head as he passed a florist on the way to the tram. Even now, he felt foolish holding them, like a teenager on a first date. Suddenly, his anticipation turned sour. He wondered who'd be standing in front of Anna's door tonight with a bouquet of flowers. None of your business, he told himself, and after a moment his jealousy left him.

The door buzzed and Sylvia's voice told him to come downstairs. Sylvia opened it immediately. She was wearing faded blue jeans and a green Pendleton shirt. She had her hair parted in the center. He thought she was trying to dress like an American. Her eyes passed from him to the flowers, then back again. "They're beautiful. What a lovely idea."

Nick fumbled for an excuse. He could feel himself blushing. "I saw them in a window. It's not polite to arrive empty-handed." *Not twice, that's for sure.*

"Come in. Come in." She kissed him on the cheek and relieved him of the flowers, then led the way to the living room. "Take a seat while I put these in some water. Dinner will be a few minutes. I hope you like peasant fare. I've made *Spätzele mit Käse überbacken.*"

"That sounds great." Nick ambled to the bookshelves and looked at a few pictures before sitting down. In several of them, Sylvia stood with her arm around a tall athletic blond man.

"My brothers," she said, coming into the room with a vase full of flowers. "Rolf and Eric. They're identical twins."

"Oh, really," said Nick. He was surprised to feel relief at her words. He'd been thinking more about her than he liked to admit. He strolled to the sofa and sat down. "Where do they live? In Zurich?"

"Rolf is a ski instructor in Davos. Eric's a lawyer in Bern." Her words were clipped and he guessed she didn't want to talk about them. She set the flowers on the table. "Like a drink?"

"A beer would be great."

Sylvia walked to the terrace and opened the sliding glass door. She leaned down and took a bottle from the six-pack. "Löwenbräu okay? Our own from Zurich."

"Yeah, great." Nick placed his arms on the cushions and settled into the sofa. She had a very nice apartment. The floor was polished wood, covered by two Persian carpets. A small dining nook led off the living room. Two place settings and a bottle of white wine adorned the table. He felt he was seeing her real side and he liked what he saw. He turned his head and looked down a short hallway. A door was closed at the end of it. Her bedroom. If it ever came to it, he wondered which Sylvia would show up in bed: the calculating professional he knew from the office or the casual country girl who had greeted him at the door with a kiss and a smile. The thought of either one excited him.

Sylvia came into the living room carrying two beers. She handed one to Nick, then sat down on the far end of the couch. "So are you enjoying yourself so far in Switzerland?"

Nick laughed, almost spilling the beer.

"What's so funny?"

"That's exactly what Martin Maeder asked me on Friday."

"Well, are you?"

"Actually, I am. It's a lot different than I remembered it. Better, really. I appreciate how everything runs according to schedule, how everyone has pride in their work — from the garbage hauler all the way up to —"

"Wolfgang Kaiser."

"Exactly. We could do with more of that back home." He took a sip of beer. Discussing his point of view made him uncomfortable. He wanted to hear about her. "Tell me why *you* came to the bank. Do you like it as much as you seem?"

Sylvia appeared taken aback by his question, at least the second part of it. "I answered an ad posted at the university, originally. At first, I didn't think I wanted anything to do with a stodgy old bank. I was aiming more for advertising or public relations. You know, something glamorous. Then I was invited for a second interview, this time at the bank. I got a tour of the building, the trading floor, the vault. I never knew so much went on behind the teller's windows. Look at what we in the finance department are doing. We manage over a hundred billion dollars in investments. We underwrite bonds that help companies grow and countries develop. It's so dynamic. I love it."

"Whoa, horsie! Remember, Sylvia, I already

work there. You're preaching to the converted." He found her enthusiasm contagious and remembered that those were exactly the reasons he had gone to work for an investment bank on Wall Street.

Sylvia covered her mouth, embarrassed. "I guess I got ahead of myself. I suppose another reason is that there just aren't many women in banking, even today. Not high up at least." She leaned over the coffee table and picked up a sheaf of papers that Nick hadn't noticed. "I got my itinerary for the States today. I'll have to wait until after the general assembly to go, which will make my job harder. Still, it's better than nothing."

She handed Nick the sheet. He read it, and all the worries of business school recruiting came back to him. She would travel to New York, see grads from NYU, Wharton, and Columbia. Then she was off to Harvard and MIT. Finally she'd fly to Chicago to visit Northwestern. "That's a lot of travel just to hire one or two graduates."

Sylvia took back the itinerary. "We take finding the right personnel very seriously. That's why you better stay. You Americans have to start setting a better example."

"Don't worry, I'm staying. Do you think I'd do anything to mess up your employee retention rate?"

"Devil!" She slapped his leg playfully, then stood up and announced that she had to finish preparing dinner.

Ten minutes later, their meals were on the table. Golden brown bite-size dumplings covered with melted Swiss cheese and sprinkled with paprika. Nick ate heartily, thinking he hadn't tasted anything so good since he'd arrived over six weeks ago. He prodded Sylvia to tell him about her childhood. At first she was a little shy, but once she got started her reticence vanished. She had grown up in Sargans, a small town eighty kilometers southeast of Zurich. Her father ran the local railway station. He was a prominent member of the community. A pillar of civic virtue, she called him. He had never remarried after his wife's death. Sylvia had taken care of the household, assuming complete responsibility for the raising of her younger brothers.

"Sounds like you were close," said Nick. "You were lucky."

"We were miserable," she blurted, then laughed. "I'm sorry."

"Don't be. Why were you so miserable?"

Sylvia put her hands in her lap, bunching up her napkin, and stared at Nick as if deciding whether his interest was earnest or just flattery. She looked away from him, then said, "My father was a difficult man. He spent his whole life working for the railway, so everything had to be perfectly organized — just like a train schedule — or he wasn't happy. I think that's why he never got over losing my mother.

He hadn't approved it. God hadn't asked whether he could take her from him. You can imagine who bore the brunt of his discontent. Me. Mostly it was because he didn't know how to handle a little girl."

"What'd he do?"

"Oh, he wasn't a bad man. He was just very demanding. I had to get up at five to fix his breakfast and prepare a sack lunch. Then, of course, there were the twins, who were four years younger than me. I had to get them up and out the door in time for school. That's a tall order when you're nine years old. When I look back on it, I don't know how I did it."

"You were strong. You still are."

"I'm not sure if that's a compliment."

Nick smiled. "I was the same way. After my dad died, I always felt like I had to catch up. I worked hard in school. I tried to be the best at everything I did. Sometimes at night, I'd get out of bed, take out my books, and check if my homework was where I had put it earlier. I was scared someone had stolen it. Crazy, huh?"

"I didn't have that problem. What I hated was having to be this perfect little family. Sargans was a small town. Everyone knew my father. Naturally we had to be on our best behavior. We couldn't show that our life was any harder without having a wife or a mother around. Maybe I was the only one who wasn't happy. My brothers had it great. I tidied their rooms, washed their clothes, helped them with their homework. They had a full-time servant."

"They must love you for that."

"As Rudy Ott said to me a few days ago, 'in the best of all possible worlds, of course.'" She gave Nick a sardonic smile. "Unfortunately, they followed their father's example and took me absolutely for granted. They thought I didn't go out on Friday nights because I didn't want to, not because I was too tired. I think they even believed I enjoyed changing their beds every week."

"You're not close to them?"

"Oh, I make the usual efforts, birthday cards, Christmas presents. But I haven't seen Rolf or Eric in three years. It's easier that way."

"And your father?"

Sylvia raised a finger. "Him, I still see."

Nick nodded his head, reading in her expression that she had gone as far as she would on that subject. He looked away and spotted his briefcase in the hallway. Inside was the faded yellow binder she had given him earlier in the day. He had become so enraptured in his discussion with Sylvia that he had forgotten he'd brought it with him. He smiled inwardly, feeling warm and content. He had forgotten the pleasure of spending time with an interesting, attractive woman. He had missed it.

After dinner, Nick laid the binder on Sylvia's

dining room table and threw open its cover. Inside, filed in chronological order, were monthly activity reports submitted by his father for the period January through June 1975.

The monthly activity report for January 1975 was divided into four sections. First, a summary of fee-producing business; second, an evaluation of new business opportunities; third, a request for additional personnel and office supplies; and last, a section entitled "Miscellaneous Items of Interest."

Nick read the report.

I. Business Activity Summary for the period 1/1/75–1/31/75

A. Deposits of $2.5 million received, of which $1.8 from new clients (see attached client profile sheets).
   1. Fee Services: Trade Financing fees of $217,000 accrued.
   2. Pro forma Financial Statements for fiscal 1975.
B. New Business:
   Swiss Graphite Manufacturing, Inc.
   CalSwiss Ballbearing Company
   Atlantic Maritime Freight
C. Proposal to increase staff from seven (7) to nine (9) persons.
   1. Request for new
   IBM Selectric Typewriters (4).
D. Miscellaneous: Dinner at
   Swiss Consulate (see report).

Nick lifted his head from the binder. Nothing in the contents hinted at anything untoward, but he hadn't expected to find anything of interest in reports written five years prior to Alex Neumann's death. Still, he was determined to read each and every page of the report. This particular set might not hold the information he needed, but he was on the right trail. More important, he had a willing guide.

The patter of footsteps approached from the hallway.

Sylvia placed her hand on Nick's shoulder. "What are you looking for?"

He sighed and rubbed his eyes. "You really want to get involved in this?"

"You promised that you'd fill me in on what you were looking for. I mean, that's why we're here, isn't it?"

Nick laughed, but behind the smile a tightness gripped his throat. The time for truth had arrived. The time for trust. He knew he couldn't go any further without Sylvia's help and deep down, he wanted it. Maybe because with every passing minute he was growing fonder of her golden hair and more dependent on her crooked smile. Maybe because he saw so much of himself in Sylvia: the child forced to grow up too quickly, the tireless striver never satisfied with his accomplishment. Or maybe just because Anna hadn't given a damn.

"I'm looking for two things," Nick said.

"Mention of a client named Allen Soufi — a shady character who did some business with the bank in Los Angeles. And, any reference to Goldluxe, Incorporated."

"Who's Goldluxe?"

"I don't know the first thing about them. Just that my father's decision to end a commercial relationship with them caused a small uproar at the head office in Zurich."

"So they were clients of the bank?"

"For a while, at least."

"What drew your attention to Mr. Soufi and to Goldluxe?"

"Some things my father said about them. Wait here and I'll show you."

Nick walked into the hallway to retrieve something from his briefcase. He returned carrying a slim black book. He set it down on the table and said, "This is my father's agenda for 1978. It came from his office at USB in Los Angeles."

Sylvia eyed it warily, sniffing at it as if its contents were as suspect as its odor. "It doesn't smell like it came from an office."

"Floodwater," said Nick, matter-of-factly. He'd gotten used to the smell of mildewy leather a long time ago. "Believe it or not, I found it in a U-Rent-It storage facility. It was on top of a pile of old junk my mother had kept for years. The place flooded twice during the time she rented it. Everything stacked below three feet was completely destroyed.

When she passed away, I flew back to take care of her effects and to make the necessary arrangements. That's when I found this book. There's one for 1979, too."

He opened the first agenda and leafed through the pages, stopping to point out several of the entries that had merited his attention. *"Oct 12. Dinner with Allen Soufi. Undesirable." "November 10 — Soufi in office."* And beneath it, *"Credit check"* followed by an incredulous *"Nothing?!"* And finally, the infamous notation of September 3, *"Bastard threatened me"* — florid commentary to a twelve o'clock lunch engagement at the Beverly Wilshire Hotel with the oft-appearing Allen Soufi.

"There's more like this in the next agenda. You'll see."

"You only have the two of them?"

"They were the only ones I could find. Luckily, they were the last two he kept. My father was killed on January 31, 1980."

Sylvia drew her arms around herself, as if suddenly chilled. Nick stared into her warm brown eyes. Once he had found them remote and selfish. Now he found them caring and sympathetic. He leaned back in the stiff wooden chair and stretched his arms. He knew what he had to say, knew that he had to tell the whole story. He was suddenly struck by how few people he had actually told about his father's murder: a few kids from school after it had happened, Gunny Ortiga, and, of course, Anna. Normally the prospect of sharing the story left him antsy and uncomfortable. But tonight, sitting close to Sylvia, he felt calm and at peace. The words came easily.

"The worst part of it was the ride over," he began softly. "We knew something had happened to him. The police had called. They said there had been an accident. They sent a squad car for us. My father wasn't living at our house at the time. I think he knew someone was after him."

Sylvia sat as steady as a rock, listening.

"It was raining that night," he went on, speaking slowly as the images came back to him. "We drove up Stone Canyon. My mother was holding on to me so tightly. It was late and she was crying. She must have known he was dead. Her intuition, whatever. But I didn't. The police hadn't wanted me along, but she'd insisted. Even then she wasn't very strong. I looked out the police car's window, watching the rain fall, wondering what had happened. The radio was squelching all the time, that clipped police jargon. Somewhere in there I heard the word *homicide* and the address where my father had been staying. The policemen up front didn't say a word to us. I expected them to say, 'Don't worry,' or 'Everything's going to be fine.' But they didn't say anything."

Nick leaned forward and laced his hands in

Sylvia's, bringing them to his chest. He saw that tears had formed in her eyes, and for a few seconds he was mad at her. Seeing another person cry prompted in him a disdain for that person's weakness. He knew his anger was bred out of a fear of confronting his own emotions and that he was wrong to have it. Still, it sat there for a minute and he had to wait until it played itself out before going on.

"You know what I felt sitting there? That everything was going to be different. I knew *right then* that my world was going to turn upside down and nothing would be the same."

"What happened?" Sylvia whispered.

"The police figured that someone came to the door of the house at around nine o'clock that night. My dad knew whoever it was. There was no sign of forced entry. No sign of a scuffle. He opened the door, led the killer inside the house a few steps, probably talked to him for a while. He was shot in the chest. Three times from close range, just two or three feet. Someone looked my father straight in the eye and killed him. You'd never know a man has so much blood in him. I mean, that whole entryway was red. The police hadn't covered him up yet. They hadn't even closed his eyes." Nick allowed his own eyes to wander to the broad picture window and stared outside, seeing nothing but darkness. He blew out a breath of air and let go of the memory. "Boy, it was raining that night."

Sylvia placed her hand on Nick's cheek. "Are you okay?"

"Yeah, I'm all right." He half smiled, and nodded to show that he was in fact okay, that a marine never cries, that he was hardly deserving of her compassion. "So my father is dead. That's it, right. That's the sad part. Obviously, I'm wondering who did it. There's the regular investigation, but no witnesses, no murder weapon. The police didn't have a thing to go on. Six months later, case closed. Life goes on. Chalk it up to a random act of violence. The cops will tell you it happens all the time in a big city like Los Angeles." Suddenly, he pounded his hand on the table. "But goddammit, it doesn't happen all the time to me."

Nick slid his chair away from the table and asked if she minded if he stepped outside for a moment. He crossed the living area, then opened the sliding glass door and stepped into the icy night air. A perfect semicircle was carved from the snow so that one could stand on the terrace and look out at the curtain of forest. The night's cold embrace could not stifle the scent of pine and oak. He breathed deeply and watched as the vapor of his condensing breath cut a swath out of the darkness. He willed himself to think of nothing, to make his mind a blank, to breathe and watch and feel the world around him as if this were all there were.

"It's beautiful here."

Nick jumped at the sound of Sylvia's voice. He hadn't heard her approaching. "I can't believe we're still in the city," he said.

"Just out the front door and down the street."

"I feel like I'm in the middle of the mountains."

"Mmmm," she agreed. She looped her arms around him and drew herself against his back. "Nick, I'm so sorry."

He placed his hands over hers and held them tightly against him. "So am I."

"So that's why you came here?" she whispered, more answer than question.

"I guess so. Once I found the agendas I didn't really have a choice. Sometimes I tell myself that there's no way in the world I'm going to find anything." He shrugged. "Maybe I will, maybe I won't. I just know I have to try."

For a while neither spoke. Gently, he rocked back and forth, enjoying the warmth of her body and the mix of her perfume with the crisp air. He turned to Sylvia and lowered his face toward hers. She touched his cheek and as their lips met, he closed his eyes.

Inside, Sylvia asked Nick what the next step was.

"I need to see my father's activity reports for 1978 and 1979."

"There are eight volumes. Four for each year."

"So be it," he said.

She replaced a strand of hair behind her ear and nodded as if summing up a daunting task. "I'll do my best. I really do want to help. But, Nick, it's been so long. Who knows what your father might have written in those reports? Please don't expect too much. You'll only be disappointed."

Nick made his way around her living room, stopping to examine a picture here, a knick-knack there. "Someone once told me that every man and woman could easily choose how happy they wanted to be. The whole thing boiled down to a simple equation. Happiness, he said, equaled reality divided by expectation. If you don't hope for much, then reality will almost surely beat your expectations, therefore you'll be happy. If you expect the world, you'll always be disappointed. The problem is for folks who always want to be happy, the dreamers who put a big ten on the bottom of that equation."

"What do you expect, Nick?"

"When I was young, I wanted the ten. We all do, I guess. After my father died and things took a turn for the worse, I would have been happy with a three. Now I'm more optimistic. I want a five, hell, I'll take a risk, give me a six. If six days out of ten are good, I'll be all right."

"I mean, what do you really expect? What do you want to do with your life?"

"Well, obviously I'd like to put my father's murder behind me. After that I'm not sure. Maybe I'll stay in Switzerland for a while. Fall in love. Have a family. Mostly, I want to feel like I belong someplace." A feeling of intimate complacency fell over Nick as he spoke to Sylvia, almost as if he were yielding to a mild opiate. He barely knew her, yet already he was sharing his innermost feelings, dreams he had held for a future with Anna. Dreams for another world, he reminded himself. And another lifetime. "What about you?"

"I change from day to day, from minute to minute. When I was growing up, I wasn't very happy. I always wanted my mother to come back. I would've taken a four. When I first began at the bank, a nine. Anything was possible. Today, with you sitting in my dining room, I still want a nine. I'd rather be a little disappointed than not have wished at all."

"What do *you* really want?"

"That's easy. To be the first woman on the executive board of USB."

Nick ended his tour of her living room and fell into the overstuffed couch. "A dreamer, eh?"

Sylvia sat down next to him. "Why else would I help you with these binders? They're darned heavy to carry around."

"Poor Sylvia, what will we do with her?"

Nick rubbed her back. "Bad back?"

She nodded her head. "Uh-huh."

He lifted her legs onto his lap and massaged her calves. "And your legs. They must be killing you?" Running his hands along her smooth legs sent a current of desire through his body. He had forgotten the touch of a woman's body, forgotten seduction's joyous impatience.

"As a matter of fact, yes." Sylvia pointed to a spot that needed particular attention, and he obliged. "That feels much better."

"And your feet?" Nick threw off her loafers. "To think they had to carry around such an enormous load."

"Stop," Sylvia cried. "That tickles. Stop it now."

"What, this tickles?" He ran his fingers lightly over her stockinged toes. "I don't believe it."

"Please stop." But her command dissolved into laughter. "I'm begging you."

Nick paused momentarily, allowing Sylvia to place her feet on the floor.

"What will you give me?"

She smiled coyly. "How about I try and elevate your top number?"

"I don't know. That's pretty serious stuff. How high do you think you can get it? An eight?"

"Definitely higher." Sylvia gently bit Nick's lower lip, then caressed his neck.

"A nine?"

She straddled him. Slowly, she unbuttoned her shirt until it hung open before him. "Higher."

"Higher than a nine? Nothing's perfect."

Sylvia unsnapped her brassiere and gently rubbed each breast in turn across his open mouth. "Take that back."

Nick closed his eyes and nodded his head. He had decided to go for the ten.

Chapter 32

Nick arrived at the office the next morning, eager to begin work on a document that would be sent to institutional shareholders — naturally, under the Chairman's name — detailing steps the bank would take to cut costs, increase efficiency, and better operating margins. All were measures designed to improve financial performance over the next five years. He set to work drafting an outline, but after only a few minutes he discovered it impossible to concentrate. Images of Sylvia flooded his mind. He saw the curve of her waist. He felt her firm belly. He ran his hands over her endless legs. Without speaking, she made him smile; without moving, she made him wince; without breathing, she made him pant.

Abruptly, Nick rolled his chair away from the desk. He rubbed his hands slowly on his thighs, requiring some physical assurance that it was him having these thoughts — the same man who only two months before had left behind a woman who loved him and whom, he was afraid to admit, he might still love. You're a cad, he thought, jumping at the first woman who comes your way. You betrayed her. No, a calmer voice objected, Anna belongs to your past. She's safer there.

At half past nine, Rita Sutter tucked her head into his office.

"Good morning, Mr. Neumann. You arrived early this morning."

Nick looked up from his work, surprised. He hadn't seen her outside Kaiser's suite of offices once in the four days he'd been on the Fourth Floor. "Not much choice, if I want to keep up with the Chairman."

"He brings out the best in us all," she said, venturing a foot inside. She was wearing a navy blue dress, a strand of pearls, and a white cardigan, and carrying a sheaf of papers. She managed to look chic, mature, and a little bit sexy all at the same time. "I haven't had the chance to congratulate you on your promotion. You must be very excited."

Nick sat back in his chair, confused by her solicitous approach. She was hardly the kind to engage in idle chitchat. Her primary responsibility was the ordering of the Chairman's day, and she performed her task with a mastery worthy of a seasoned military staff officer. Nothing reached Kaiser without her prior knowledge and approval. No phone calls, no letters, and certainly no visitors. (Sterling Thorne being the exception.) No matter how hectic the day became, she kept Kaiser focused and on schedule, all the while retaining a composed, unflappable air. Nick wondered what she wanted.

"It's an honor to be here," he agreed. "Though I wish the current circumstances were a little different."

"I'm sure Herr Kaiser will manage just fine. He won't let go of the bank without a fight."

"I don't imagine he will."

Rita Sutter came closer to the desk. "I hope you don't mind if I tell you how much you look like your father."

"Not at all." He had been curious to learn how well she had known him but hadn't yet found the right moment to ask. "Did you work together?"

"Why yes, of course. I started at the bank a year after he did. In those days we were a small group, about a hundred of us. He was a good man."

"About time someone confessed to liking him," he said under his breath, then stood and motioned to the chair opposite his desk. "Please have a seat — that is, if you have a few minutes free."

Rita Sutter sat down on the edge of the chair, fingering her pearls. Her tentative stance suggested a brief visit. "Did you know that we all came from the same neighborhood, Herr Kaiser, your father, and myself?"

"You lived on Eibenstrasse too?"

"Manessestrasse. Around the corner. But Herr Kaiser lived in the same building as your father. They were never close as children. Your father was a much better athlete.

415

Wolfgang kept to his books. He was still quite shy in those days."

"The Chairman, shy?" Nick imagined a small boy with a limp arm dangling uselessly at his side, no thousand-dollar suits to camouflage it. Then his thoughts turned to his father, and he fought to locate some memory of him as an athlete. Sure his dad had played golf, but he had never once thrown a baseball or kicked a soccer ball with Nick.

"We don't talk about the past very often here," she said. "I felt, though, I had to tell you how much I admired your father. He had a very positive influence on my life. He was a strong believer. To him anything was possible. Sometimes I ask myself if I wouldn't be working for Alex instead of Wolfgang, if your father were still . . ." She let her words drift off, then smiling suddenly, brought her attention to Nick. "He was the one who pushed me into getting my degree at HSG — the Hochschule St. Gallen. I'll always be grateful to him for that. Though I don't think he would have liked how I used it."

Nick was impressed. HSG was Switzerland's most respected business school. "You practically run the bank," he said, meaning it. "That's pretty good, isn't it?"

"Oh, I don't know, Nicholas. I haven't seen Rudolf Ott fetching the Chairman coffee and biscuits." She stood up and patted her skirt into place.

Nick circled the desk, accompanying her to the door. He had wanted to work the conversation around to his father's duties at the bank. Now it seemed there wouldn't be time. "Can I ask you something about my father?" he said awkwardly, hating to broach this subject out of the blue. "Did you ever hear of him doing anything that might have harmed the bank? Something that might have hurt USB's reputation?"

Rita Sutter stopped abruptly. "Who told you that? No, don't tell me. I can imagine." She turned so her body brushed against Nick and looked him in the eye. "Your father never did anything to tarnish this bank's good name. He was an honorable man."

"Thanks, I had just heard that —"

"Shhh." She brought a finger up to her lips. "Don't believe everything you hear on this floor. Oh, and about that letter you're drafting for the Chairman, he asked that you keep the proposed staff cuts to a minimum. Here are his ideas."

She handed him the sheaf of papers and left the office. He glanced down at the topmost sheet. It was entirely in her writing.

An hour later, Nick arrived at a final draft of the Chairman's letter — including Rita Sutter's suggestions on how to minimize any proposed staff cuts. He was rereading the document, deciding if it was satisfactory, when the phone rang.

"Neumann speaking."

"What, no secretary, young Nick? One would expect better for the king's equerry."

Nick threw down his pencil and tipped back his chair. A broad smile creased his face. "*I* work for an emperor. *You,* my friend, work for a lowly king."

"Touché."

"Hello, Peter. How are things on the other side?"

"The other side?" Sprecher chuckled. "Of what? The Maginot Line? Damned busy, actually. A sight too much activity for these weary bones. And you, no fear of heights? My, my, the Fourth Floor. All this time I thought you were a worker bee."

Nick missed his colleague's lazy patter and his dry sense of humor. "I'll tell you about it over a beer. You'll have no trouble affording one now."

"Agreed. Keller Stübli at seven o'clock."

Nick scanned the pile of work on his desk. "Make it eight, and I'll see you there. Now, what can I do for you?"

"You mean you can't guess?" Sprecher sounded genuinely surprised. "I'm looking to buy a packet of your bank's shares. Wouldn't happen to have a couple thousand lying around your desk?"

Nick played along with his friend's joke. "Sorry to disappoint you, Peter, but we're fresh out. Saving for a rainy day, you might say. As a matter of fact, we're shorting Adler shares."

"Give me a few weeks and I'll be happy to personally cover them for you. I've been looking for the means to buy a new Ferrari."

"Good luck but . . ."

"Can you hold one second?" Sprecher interrupted. "I have another call."

Before Nick could answer, Peter cut the line. Nick picked up a pen and tapped it on the desk. He wondered what Sylvia was up to right now. No doubt fretting over her all-important employee retention rate. Or better yet, dreaming about her trip to the States after the general assembly.

A faint squawk and Sprecher returned. "Sorry, Nick, an emergency. Always is, eh?"

"Since when are you on the trading desk? I thought you were hired to help start a private banking department."

"Things change quickly around this place. You might say I'm following the Neumann plan. I've been jacked upstairs onto Konig's acquisition team."

"Jesus Christ," said Nick. "So you're not joking. You're a point man on the USB deal? Scouring the market for our shares."

"Don't take it personally. Konig thought I might know where I could dig some up. You might say he's making the best use of the tools at his disposal. As a matter of fact, we hustled a few thousand shares from your own boys yesterday."

"So I heard," said Nick. "I wouldn't count on it happening again."

The story was that several United Swiss Bank portfolio managers more eager to lock in a double-digit return on their clients' investments than see to the security of the bank had sold shares of USB, which were trading at an all-time high. Word of their behavior quickly reached the Fourth Floor, enraging the Chairman. Kaiser stormed their offices, personally firing each on the spot.

Sprecher adopted a serious tone. "Listen, chum, some of our guys want to talk to you . . . *privately*." He let the last word hang in the air. "They'd like to suggest some sort of an arrangement."

"What for?" Suddenly, Nick recalled the Chairman's warning that Sprecher would be quick to exploit their friendship. At the time, he'd found the idea ridiculous.

"Must I be so obtuse? Guess."

"No," said Nick, his disbelief turning to fury. "You tell me."

"What I asked you about earlier. Blocks of shares. Preferably, big blocks. We want to put this deal on ice before the general assembly. You know who's holding the largest stakes. Tell us their names and we'll make it worth your while."

Nick could feel the nape of his neck flush.

First Schweitzer pawing about his desk for the list of shareholders, and now Sprecher. "You're serious?"

"Deadly."

"Then I'll say this once, Peter, and *please,* don't take it the wrong way. Go fuck yourself."

"Easy, Nick. Easy."

"How low do you think I'd stoop?" Nick asked.

"There is no honor in loyalty," said Sprecher earnestly, as if disabusing a child of a foolish notion. "Not anymore. At least not to corporations. I'm in this game for a paycheck and a pension. You should be too."

"You worked at this bank for twelve years. Why are you so eager to see her go down?"

"It is not a question of one bank dying so the other can live. This will be a merger in the truest sense: United Swiss Bank's strength in private banking combined with the Adler Bank's proven trading skills. Together, we can control the entire Swiss market."

Nick didn't find the prospect so thrilling. "I'm afraid the answer is no."

"Do yourself a favor, Nick. If you help us, I can promise you a position here after USB's been swallowed. Otherwise your head will be on the chopping block with everyone else on the Fourth Floor. Get with the winner!"

"If the Adler Bank is so awash in cash," Nick demanded, "why don't you just make a bid for the whole company?"

"I wouldn't believe every rumor you hear. Hold on a second, chum." He cupped a hand over the mouthpiece, but Nick could still make out the muffled words. "Hassan, throw me that price sheet. No, the pink one, you bloody wog. Yes, yes, that's it." Sprecher released his hand from the mouthpiece. "Anyway, Nick, think about our proposition. I'll tell you more tonight. See you at eight, right?"

"I don't think so. I only drink with my friends."

Sprecher started to protest, but Nick had already hung up.

At 12:35, Nick headed to the Chairman's office with a final copy of his letter in hand. He sauntered lazily down the quiet hallway. At this hour even the biggest grinds were eating lunch. The floorboards squeaked under his lolling step. Suddenly, he felt the presence of someone behind him.

"Tired or drunk, Neumann?" Armin Schweitzer barked.

Nick was sick of being afraid of Schweitzer. Shaking the papers in his hand, he turned and said, "I couldn't get the words to flow right, so I took a wee taste of Scotland's finest. A dram of single malt does wonders for finding the muse."

Schweitzer smirked. "A smart-ass, no less. Well, on this floor we keep our backs straight and our step spirited. You can *wander* in the park, if you like. What do you have there?"

"Some ideas the Chairman had for whipping the bank into shape. It's a letter to be sent to the shareholders." Nick handed Schweitzer a copy. Why not extend an olive branch? He still wanted to find out what the bastard meant by his father's "embarrassing behavior."

Schweitzer skimmed the letter. "Dark days, Neumann. We can never fit Konig's model of a bank. He prefers machines. We still like the living, breathing variety, thank God."

"Konig doesn't stand a chance. He'll need a mountain of cash if he wants to take us over."

"Yes, he will. But don't underestimate him. I've never met a greedier man. Who knows where he's put his mitts? He's an embarrassment to all of us."

"Like my father?" Nick asked. "Tell me, what exactly did he do?"

Schweitzer pursed his lips, as if considering how to answer. He sighed and put his hand on Nick's shoulder. "Something you are much too intelligent to even contemplate, my boy." He handed the letter back to Nick. "Run along now. I'm sure the Chairman is eager to see his puppy dog."

Nick rose on his toes, flushed with anger. He bit his tongue but couldn't resist a parting jab. "My office is open if you're interested. Help yourself. Never know what you might find there!"

Chapter 33

A war council had convened in the executive boardroom. Four men in progressive states of unease were scattered around the immense chamber. Reto Feller stood against the far wall. His arms were folded across his chest, and the heel of his foot was rapidly wearing a hole in the carpet. Rudolf Ott and Martin Maeder sat at the prodigious conference table, the very picture of conspiracy. Each faced the other with hunched back and lowered head, whispering. Armin Schweitzer paced the length of the room. A sheen of perspiration matted his heavy features. Every few steps, he withdrew a handkerchief from his hip pocket and with an unashamed stroke dried his forehead. They all awaited the arrival of their master. On this ship, there was only one captain.

At precisely two P.M., Wolfgang Kaiser threw open the tall mahogany doors and entered the boardroom. He walked briskly to his usual chair. Nick followed him and took an adjoining seat. Ott and Maeder straightened their backs. Feller dove into the nearest chair. Schweitzer alone remained standing.

Kaiser dispensed with all formalities. "Mr.

Feller, what is the status of the Adler Bank's share purchases?" His voice was dry and grim, as if assessing the damage of an artillery barrage.

Feller answered in a shrill voice. "Twenty-eight percent of shares outstanding. Another five percent and Konig will automatically be granted two seats on the executive board."

"*Scheisse!*" came an unattributed response.

"Rumor has it the Adler Bank will make a fully funded takeover bid," said Schweitzer. "Bastards don't want two seats, they want the whole damned show."

"*Quatsch,*" said Maeder. "Nonsense. Look at their balance sheet. No way they can take on that much debt. Their assets are fully leveraged to cover their trading positions."

"Who needs debt when cash will suffice?" squealed Feller.

"Mr. Feller is correct," said Wolfgang Kaiser. "Klaus Konig's buying power has hardly dwindled. Where in God's name is that son of a bitch getting his cash? Doesn't anybody know?"

No one spoke. Maeder and Ott bowed their heads, as if shame were ample excuse for their ignorance. Schweitzer shrugged. Nick couldn't remember when he had ever felt more ill at ease. He was profoundly aware of his inexperience. I don't belong in this room, he kept telling himself. I shouldn't be sitting here with the bank's top brass. What the hell do

425

they want with me?

"More disturbing news," said Ott. "I've learned that Konig is wooing Hubert Senn, the count's grandson, to accept a seat on Adler's executive board. I don't need to remind anyone here that Senn Industries has long been an ardent supporter of current management."

"And that they control shares worth six percent of outstanding votes," said Kaiser. "Votes we have counted as our own until now."

Nick recalled the pale young man dressed in his baggy navy suit. Hubert Senn's name was indeed on the count's primary account. The boy's signature would be required to vote their shares for USB. One more obstacle.

Feller raised his hand as if in elementary school. "I'll be happy to phone the count and explain the bank's restructuring plan. I'm sure —"

"I think the Chairman should speak with the count," Nick said brusquely, cutting off his ass-kissing associate. "Senn is at an age when tradition means everything. We should arrange a personal meeting with him."

"The count will remain loyal," stammered Schweitzer as he mopped his brow. "Right now let's concentrate on buying up our own shares."

"With what, Armin, your life savings?" Kaiser shook his head. "Neumann's right. I should see the count personally." He turned to Nick and said, "Set it up. Just tell me where to be."

Nodding his head, Nick felt something inside him relax. He'd been blooded. He'd made a suggestion and it had been accepted. From the corner of his eye, he could see Reto Feller reddening.

Kaiser drummed his fingertips upon the table. "At this juncture, there aren't many options left to us. First and foremost, Neumann and Feller must continue contacting our most important shareholders. Marty, I want you to join in. Talk to everyone holding more than five hundred shares."

"The list is endless," complained Maeder.

"Do it!" ordered Kaiser.

"*Jawohl.*" Maeder lowered his head.

Kaiser went on. "Still, I feel that our efforts in that regard may come up short. What we need is cash and we need it now."

There was a collective nodding of heads. Nick noted that all present were only too aware of the bank's lack of liquidity.

"I have two ideas in mind. The first involves the participation of a private investor — an old friend of mine; the second, the creative use of our own customers' accounts. It's a plan a few of us have been batting around these last days. Daring, perhaps, but we have no other choice."

Nick glanced around the table. Maeder and Ott appeared relaxed enough, hardly curious about what was to come. Schweitzer, though, had stopped pacing and stood at attention, as rigid as a statue. So, the big boys have left you out of the loop. Poor Armin, what have you done to lose your place at the top table?

"Our only way out," said Martin Maeder, standing and gripping his seat back with both hands. "Our managed portfolios."

Schweitzer bent forward as if he hadn't properly heard. He muttered a single word over and over again: *"Nein, nein, nein."*

"We have over three thousand accounts under our discretionary management," continued Maeder, ignoring his colleague's fretful mumbling. "Over six billion Swiss francs of cash, securities, and precious metals under our direct control. We can buy and sell on the client's behalf as we please. Simply stated, we must reconfigure the portfolios of our discretionary clients. Sell off some underperforming stocks, get rid of some bonds, and use the proceeds to buy every last share we can find of our own stock. Pump those portfolios full of United Swiss Bank class A equity."

"We can never do such a thing!" protested Schweitzer.

Maeder granted Schweitzer a single sidelong glance, then went on as before. "Most of our discretionary clients ask that all mail be held at the bank. If they visit the bank, it's once, maybe twice a year. They'll have no idea what we've done with their accounts. By the time they check their portfolios, we'll have defeated the Adler Bank, sold off our own shares, and reconfigured their portfolios just as they were before. If one of them does find out, we'll just say it was a mistake. An administrative error. It's not as if they can contact another account holder. They're anonymous — to the outside world and to one another."

Nick shuddered involuntarily. What Maeder was proposing was grossly illegal, fraud on a gargantuan scale. They were taking all their clients' chips and betting them on black.

Schweitzer removed his jacket. His shirt was soaked through and clung to the crook of his back. "I am this bank's director of compliance and I forbid it. Such actions constitute a violation of the most fundamental of banking laws. The funds in a discretionary account are not ours to do with as we please. They belong to our clients. Our duty is to invest their money as if it were our own."

"Why, that's exactly what I'm proposing," said Maeder. "We're investing their money as if it's our own. And right now, *we* need to buy shares of USB. Thank you, Armin."

Ott pulled an oily grin at his cohort's sarcasm.

Schweitzer appealed directly to Kaiser. "To appropriate their funds to buy up our own shares is madness. They're trading at an all-time high. Their value is grossly inflated.

When we defeat Konig, the share price will plummet. We must follow the strategic investment guidelines promised our clients. It's the law."

No one paid Schweitzer's argument an ounce of attention. Least of all Kaiser. The Chairman averted his gaze from the offending party. He didn't say a word. Nick imagined Sylvia sitting at the table with them. What would she say? Would she be in favor of going this far? Several times he'd caught a glint of steel in her eye — something unmerciful, cruel even — and he thought that maybe she might. Another image of Sylvia provoked in him a sudden, intense flush of sexual excitement, and because of his surroundings, it both thrilled and annoyed him. Sylvia sat astride him, slowly moving up and down. He saw his hands on her breasts. He caressed them gently and felt her nipples harden under his touch. He was deep inside her. She drew his hand to her mouth and longingly licked his fingertips. She moaned again, louder this time, and he was lost in her pleasures.

Feller's voice interrupted his reverie. "One question. After we defeat the Adler Bank, don't we risk losing many of our clients if we're unable to show a gain in the value of their portfolio?"

Maeder, Ott, and then even Kaiser broke into a hearty laugh. Feller looked to Nick, who returned his mystified gaze.

Maeder answered the question. "True, we're expected to report modest gains, but preservation of capital is our real goal. Growth beyond the rate of inflation of each portfolio's base currency is . . . well, let's say growth is an afterthought. After we defeat Konig, our shares may suffer a temporary decline. I'll grant Armin that much. Consequently, we may be forced to report a minor loss in the value of our clients' portfolios. Not to worry. We'll assure them that next year promises to be much better."

"We may lose a few clients," said Kaiser. "But it's a damn sight better than losing them all."

"Well said," chipped in Ott.

"And if the Adler Bank wins control of the bank?" demanded Schweitzer, unappeased. "Then what?"

"Win or lose, we'll set the portfolios back to how they stand today," explained Maeder flippantly, to everyone but Schweitzer. "If Konig wins, the share price will remain high. He can take credit for the gains his takeover provided his newest clients. For him, it will be icing on the cake!"

Kaiser slammed his hand ferociously upon the table. "Konig will not win!"

For a few moments, everyone was silent.

Ott lifted his scholarly head, speaking as if to remind his assembled colleagues of a minor inconvenience. "Should word of our activities leak, I need not mention the consequences."

Schweitzer laughed rudely. Down but not defeated.

"Three square meals a day, a few hours of exercise, and a well-heated room, all at government expense," joked Maeder.

"Nothing could be worse than being owned by the Adler Bank!" exclaimed Feller, gleeful in his role as coconspirator.

"You idiots," Schweitzer spat out. "A two-year stint in the St. Gallen penitentiary is hardly the vacation Marty describes. We'd be ruined. Disgraced."

Kaiser paid no attention to his director of compliance. "Rudy has brought up an important point. Word of our plan can never leave this room. All buy and sell transactions will be routed through the Medusa system. Our eyes only. Can I rely on every man here to guard his silence?"

Nick watched each man nod, even Schweitzer. The sum of their surroundings — the cavernous room occupied by so few men, the haunting echo of their voices, the imposing table at which they sat bunched up in a tight arc — cast a mantle of evil on their planning that far exceeded the first whispers of fiscal larceny, no matter how sophisticated. Suddenly, he found the full bore of their eyes upon him. He clenched his jaw to mask the doubt lurking so close behind his eyes. He nodded his head once.

"Good." Kaiser's eyes remained fixed upon Nick. "This is a time of war. Keep in mind the punishment for treason. Believe me, it stands."

Nick felt the man's cold eyes drilling into him. As the newest member of Kaiser's inner circle, he knew that the words were directed at him.

The Chairman expelled a heavy sigh, then continued in a lighter tone. "As I mentioned, I'm in touch with an investor who may be willing to purchase some shares on the bank's behalf. He's an old friend and I feel confident he can be convinced to take a five percent stake. The cost, however, will be high. I'm proposing we guarantee him a ten percent gain over ninety days."

"Forty percent per annum," shouted Schweitzer, again at odds with his Chairman. "That's extortion!"

"That is business," said Kaiser. He turned to Maeder. "Call Sepp Zwicki on the trading floor. Begin a program of share accumulation. Hold the shares for two-day settlement."

"Will two hundred million francs' worth do the trick?" asked Maeder.

"It's a start."

Maeder grinned at Nick and Feller, clearly excited by the challenge before them. "We'll have to sell off one shitload of stocks and bonds to reach that amount."

"We have no alternative," said Kaiser. He

shot up from his chair, beaming like a man given a last-minute reprieve. "And Marty, tell Zwicki to short Adler shares. A hundred million worth. That ought to give Konig a minute to think. If he loses this battle, his investors will crucify him!"

Chapter 34

How did I get drawn in so deep?

Nick stood on the rotting planks of an abandoned jetty, asking himself the same question over and over again. The green waters of the river Limmat swirled below him. Across the river, the twin spires of the Grossmunster cathedral rose into the mist. It was five o'clock and he knew he shouldn't have left the office. Martin Maeder had wanted to begin instructing his "boys" — as he now called Nick and Reto Feller — on the intricacies of the new Medusa computer network.

"Medusa tells it all," Maeder had gushed, as if describing the bells and whistles of a high-end stereo. "Direct access to every account." And then, like a drunk whose loose tongue had revealed one secret too many, he had grown surly and defensive. "And I'll remind you of the promise you made to the Chairman. You'll guard these secrets with your life."

Maeder was probably looking for Nick even now, anxious to begin issuing sell orders and generate the cash that would keep Wolfgang Kaiser's hand firmly on the bank's tiller. Nick wished he could tell Maeder the truth. "Sorry,

435

Marty, I needed some fresh air to help me figure out what in the hell I'm doing to my life" or "Gee, Marty, give me a few minutes and let me figure if there's a way off of this bucket of bolts. What did you say her name was? The *Titanic*?" He had a dozen pithy excuses to explain his flight from the constricting corridors of the bank. In the end, he had simply told Rita Sutter that he was running out for a quick errand.

He hadn't mentioned that it was his soul he'd be searching for.

Looking out over the snow-covered roofs of the old town, Nick felt the realization creep over him that he had gone too far, that in his quest to locate information that might shed light on his father's murder he'd strayed from the boundaries of decent behavior. When he'd first taken Peter Sprecher's place, he had justified his actions by saying he was just doing as others before him had done. Shielding the Pasha from the DEA had simply been an extension of that philosophy, though secretly he had hoped that such an act would gain him the confidence of his superiors. He had rationalized his behavior by arguing that he had had no idea as to the true identity of the man who held numbered account 549.617 RR and that his disobeying of the instructions spelled out on the account surveillance sheet was a reaction to his bitter experience with Jack Keely.

But he could no longer permit himself such

moral leeway. The scope of the larceny proposed at this afternoon's meeting obliterated any remaining doubt. Nicholas A. Neumann was standing on the dark side of the legal fence. He couldn't lie to himself anymore. He had willingly abetted a criminal wanted by the drug enforcement authorities of several Western nations. He had lied to an agent of the United States government working to bring that man to justice. And now he stood on the brink of helping a bank commit an act of financial fraud unparalleled in recent history.

No more, Nick swore to himself. Like a bowstring drawn too far, he would spring reflexively in the opposite direction. He would make up for what he had done wrong. He thought for a minute about resigning his post, about running to the Swiss authorities. He imagined himself arriving at police headquarters brimming with good intentions, so eager to expose the corruption that was at this moment, Officer, devouring the United Swiss Bank. Nick laughed at himself. Some ploy! The word of an employee at the bank all of seven weeks, a foreigner in spite of his Swiss passport, pitted against that of Wolfgang Kaiser, the nearest thing to a folk hero this land of gold and chocolate had to offer.

Proof, young man! Where is your proof?

Nick laughed disconsolately, realizing that only one course of action was left open to him. He would have to stay at the bank and conduct his investigations from within. He would partition his soul and show Kaiser its dark side. He'd slip deeper into the evil tapestry being woven inside the Emperor's Lair. And all the while, he'd keep an alert eye peeled for his moment. He didn't know how or when. Just that he had to do everything within his power to obtain enough evidence of wrongdoing to warrant the freezing of the Pasha's accounts.

Nick spun on his heels and walked up the rickety gangway. A pair of hungry swans and a lonely mallard followed him. He raised his head and noticed a black Mercedes sedan lolling at the curb. Before long, the passenger door opened and Sterling Thorne stepped out. He was wearing his trench coat, collar turned up against the cold.

"Hello, Neumann." Thorne's hands remained conspicuously in his pockets.

"Mr. Thorne."

"Call me Sterling. I think it's about time we became friends."

Nick couldn't smother a smile. "That's okay. I'm happy with our relationship the way it is."

"Sorry about that letter."

"Does that mean you'll take it back? Maybe toss in an apology?"

Thorne smiled grimly. "You know what we want."

"What? To crucify the man I work for? To help sink United Swiss Bank?" Saying the words, knowing that yes, they were exactly what he himself had pledged to do, made Nick feel tired. Tired of defending the bank from Konig's takeover. Tired of Thorne's persistent interference. Tired of his own nagging doubts. Still, as if allergic to Thorne, he said, "Sorry, that isn't going to happen."

"I made myself a promise that we're going to stay calm today," Thorne said. "We aren't going to argue like a couple of alley cats. You heard what I told Kaiser the other day. I saw by your eyes that you believed me."

Christ, Nick thought, the guy never said die. "That was some scene you made up there. Uncle Sam would be real proud of you."

"Sounded like an encyclopedia, didn't I? All those dates and figures. Only stating the truth. I don't enjoy hound-dogging you like this. It's just my job."

"Is blackmail part of your job, too?"

"If necessary," said Thorne innocently, as if blackmail were just another form of friendly persuasion. "I'm sorry to hurt your feelings, but your pride means a damn sight less to me than getting my hands on Ali Mevlevi. I told you the other night about Jester — the agent we had in place next to Mevlevi."

"Has he turned up yet?" Whoever Jester was, Nick felt for him. He'd been in the same lousy position.

"He hasn't and we're worried about him. Before he went under, Jester swore that your

439

boss and Mevlevi were real close. Apparently, they go way back. Seems Mevlevi was one of your boss's first clients in Beirut when Kaiser was setting up the bank's office over there in the Middle East. I think I remember hearing Kaiser deny that, don't you? How do you like your boss palling around with one of the biggest smugglers of heroin in this hemisphere?"

Nick didn't like it one bit, but he'd be damned if he'd let Thorne know. "Let me stop you right here," he said, placing a hand on the agent's jacket.

Thorne grabbed his wrist and stepped closer to him. "You are working for a man who kisses the ass of the scum who killed his son! A low-life bastard who values money over his own blood. You are aiding and abetting the worst men on the face of this planet."

Nick pulled his hand free and retreated several steps. His position was untenable. "Maybe you're right, this guy, Mevlevi, the Pasha, whoever, is a major heroin smuggler and he does his banking at USB. I agree, that stinks. I'm on your side here. But do you expect me to rifle through the bank's papers, to request duplicates of his transfer confirmations, to steal his mail from his post box?"

Thorne looked deeper into Nick's eyes, as if he had spotted the glimmer of something promising. "I see you've been thinking about it."

Nick's carefully constructed defenses were crumbling. "It can't be done," he said. "Not by me, not by anyone, except Kaiser or Ott or one of that group. And even if I did get you the info, it's illegal for me to turn it over. I'd go to jail."

"We can get you to America on the next plane."

"So you told me. And then what? I hear whistleblowers are warmly welcomed by corporate America."

"We'd keep your name secret."

"Bullshit!"

"Dammit, this is about more than your career at the bank."

Thorne had never spoken truer words. "And what about Mevlevi himself, or his cohorts?" Nick asked. "You think they're going to just let me go? If he's as bad as you say, he's not going to let me walk away, free and easy. If you want this guy so badly, why don't you just get out there and arrest him?"

"I'll tell you why. Because Mr. Mevlevi lives in Beirut and never comes out. Because we can't crawl within ten miles of the Lebanese border without violating a dozen treaties. Because he's got himself holed up in a compound with more firepower than the First Marine Division. That's why! It's a shitty situation. The only way we can get him is by freezing his money. We need your help to do that."

Nick had already decided what needed to

be done, but he sure as hell wasn't going to invite Thorne along for the ride. Thorne was his cover. Nick didn't want to be treated like one of the good guys. "Sorry, no go. I am not ruining my life so you can nail one of ten thousand bad guys out there. Now excuse me, I have to go."

"Dammit, Neumann, I'm giving you the word of the United States government. We will protect you."

The word of the United States government.

Nick tried to find an answer that would put off Thorne once and for all. But he had lost his concentration. He couldn't stop Thorne's pledge from reverberating in his head.

The word of the United States government. We will protect you.

He stared at Sterling Thorne and for just a second, he swore he was looking into the slack-jowled face of Jack Keely.

"Neumann, it's good to see you here," says Jack Keely. He is nervous, fidgeting on the balls of his feet. "Colonel Andersen called my superiors, said something about you augmenting. You want to be a lifer, eh? Congratulations. Said you're interested in Intelligence? Maybe a liaison position between Quantico and Langley?"

First Lieutenant Nicholas Neumann sits at a table in the visitors' entry hall at the headquarters of the Central Intelligence Agency in

Langley, Virginia. It is a large room with a high ceiling and fluorescent lighting. On this hot June day, the air conditioners labor to keep the building cool. Nick wears his class A "alpha" dress greens. Two new ribbons adorn his breast — one for duty in the Pacific theater of operations, the other for meritorious service. The second is a surrogate for the Bronze Star awarded for valor in combat during an operation that never officially took place. He balances a black cane in his right hand. The cane is a step up from the crutches he wore out during his four-month stay at Walter Reed Hospital. The truth is that he has been declared NPQ — not physically qualified — for further duty. He cannot become a career officer, even if he wanted to. In ten days he will be discharged from the United States Marine Corps. Colonel Sigurd Andersen, of course, knows this. As he knows about all of Keely's intrigues.

"Thanks for finding the time to see me," says Nick, motioning as if to stand.

Keely waves him down. "So your wounds have healed?" he asks lightly, as if a quarter pound of shrapnel, like a bad haircut, is only a temporary nuisance.

"Getting there," says Nick. He rubs his leg gingerly to show that there is still a long way to go.

Keely relaxes, now that he has assessed Neumann and found him not to be a physical threat. "Any specific posting you have in mind?"

"I'm interested in assuming the type of role you played aboard the *Guam*," says Nick. "Coordinating incursions onto foreign soil. Marines are more comfortable having one of their own run an operation. I thought maybe you could talk to me about what it takes to do that kind of a job. I mean, since you did such a fine job with my team."

Keely grimaces. "Boy, that was a screwup. I'm sorry I couldn't talk to you about it more aboard ship. Regulations. Of course, you were hardly in a condition to speak with anyone when they hauled you aboard."

"Sure," says Nick, squinting his eyes, remembering.

"Radio malfunction," continues Keely. "I'm sure Colonel Andersen told you. We didn't pick up your distress signals until you were patched through the open airport communications channel. In the future, remember to guard that as a last resort. Not a secure com link."

Nick swallows his hatred of this man. His anticipation grows. He tells himself it won't be long now. "We had a man down," he says evenly. "We were being pursued by a superior enemy force. Operations command had not responded to our signals in over seven hours. Does that count as enough of a *last resort?*"

Keely rummages in his breast pocket for a

cigarette. He slumps in his chair, assuming his usual arrogant posture. "Look, Lieutenant, no one likes to dredge up the past. The basic intel was on the money. You took out Enrile. We achieved the mission goal. We still don't have a clue as to who set up the ambush. Anyway, your boys fucked the extraction. It was a navy job to maintain the ship's communications equipment in proper working order. If one of your radios was on the fritz, what was I supposed to do about it?"

Nick smiles and says that he understands. Behind the smile, he maps out the progress of his assault. He plans every blow that he will deliver to this man's lying body. He has chosen Langley for an express purpose — so that Keely will never feel safe again, so that for the rest of his life he'll cower before turning a corner and hesitate before opening a door, so that he'll always wonder who'll be there to meet him and pray it won't be Lieutenant Nicholas Neumann.

"What's past is past," Nick says amicably. "The reason I came, Mr. Keely, is to get a tour of the navy liaison facility. I'm sure Colonel Andersen mentioned it. I thought maybe you'd give me some pointers about which channels would be most receptive to my requests for duty."

"Sure thing, Neumann. Follow me." Keely throws the butt of his cigarette into a cold cup of coffee, which had been left on the table. He stands up and tucks his creeping belly into his pants. "You okay on that leg?"

Nick follows Keely down a featureless corridor: linoleum floor, eggshell walls, all strictly government issue. They are returning to the visitor center after having visited the Satellite Imaging Department — run by a former marine named Bill Stackpole, a close friend of Colonel Andersen's.

"Jack, I've got to use the head," says Nick as they approach a rest room. "I might need a hand." The visit has gone well. Nick and Keely are now friends. Keely insists he be called by his first name.

"A hand?" asks Keely, and when Nick offers an embarrassed grin, Keely obliges. "Sure thing . . . *Nick.*"

Nick waits until Keely is inside the rest room, then moves quickly. He drops the cane, then turns and grasps the unsuspecting man by the shoulders, spinning him around while throwing an arm around his neck to pin him in a headlock. Keely yelps in fear. Nick seeks the carotid artery, and with his free hand, blocks the flow of blood to the brain for five seconds. Keely collapses to the floor, temporarily unconscious. Nick removes a rubber doorstop from his pocket and wedges it under the door. He knocks twice and hears the same signal given in return. A sign stating that the rest room is out of order has been placed on the door. Stackpole has delivered.

Nick limps to Keely's prostrate body. Despite the pain from his leg, he bends over to slap the ruddy face twice. "Get with it," he says. "We have a hot date."

Keely shakes his head, instinctively avoiding a third strike. "What the hell is going on? This is a secure government facility."

"I know it's a secure facility," says Nick. "I fucking secured it. You ready?"

Keely raises his head and asks, "For what?"

"Payback, brother." Nick's right hand flashes downward and catches Keely across the cheekbone, sending him sprawling onto the floor.

"It was the fucking radio," gasps Keely. "I told you already."

Nick draws back his left foot and kicks the agent in the face. Blood splatters across the tile floor. "Give me the good news," he says.

"Forget it, Neumann. It's beyond you. We're talking realpolitik, policies that influence the well-being of millions of people."

"Fuck your realpolitik, Keely. What about my team? What about Johnny Burke?"

"Who the fuck's Burke? That green looie who got shot in the gut? That was his fault, not mine."

Nick reaches down and grabs a patch of Keely's scalp. He brings the man upright so that he can stare into his eyes. "Johnny Burke was a man who gave a shit. That's why he died." He butts Keely with his forehead, crushing the older man's nasal cartilage and breaking his nose. "You're dirty," he says. "I smelled your stink back in the ops room of the *Guam* before we went in, but I was too fucking naive to do anything about it. You set us up. You knew about the ambush. You sabotaged the radios."

Keely pushes both hands to his nose, trying to stanch the flow of blood. "No way, Neumann. It wasn't like that. It's bigger than you think."

"I don't care how big it was," says Nick, towering over Keely's quivering body. "You set my men up and I want to know why." He draws back his boot and freezes, suddenly sickened by his bloodlust. For nine months he has dreamed of this moment. He has imagined the crunch of his fist against Keely's cheek. He has told himself that his actions will constitute only revenge and that Johnny Burke deserves at least this measure of satisfaction. But now looking at Keely's prostrate form, ropes of blood hanging from his nose, he is no longer sure.

"Yeah, all right," says Keely, throwing his hands to his face in an impotent gesture to ward off the blow that does not come. "I'll give you the story." He drags himself to a corner of the rest room and puts his back to the tiled wall. He blows a clot of blood from his nose and coughs. "The Enrile hit was sanctioned by the NSC, the National Security Council — we wanted to show the Philippine government we were behind them in their efforts at building a long-lasting democracy in the American tradition. I mean without all the Marcos cronyism and corruption. Understand?"

"So far."

"But some members of the Philippine government didn't think the plan was sufficient. It wasn't enough to accomplish their goals."

"Sufficient for what?" asks Nick.

"To bring back the U.S. in a bigger way to the Philippines. You know, like the old days. Capital investment, new business, a spigot of dough opened full bore. They needed an excuse to bring America charging back into the Philippines."

"And that excuse was American blood?"

Keely sighs. "A plea from a fellow democracy. Our boys killed planting freedom's flag. Christ, it works every time. If you heroes had just died like you were supposed to, we'd already have ten thousand servicemen back in Subic Bay where they belong. We'd have a squadron of F-16s sitting pretty at Clark Airfield and half the Fortune 500 bursting down the doors trying to get back in the P.I."

"But that was *your gig*, wasn't it? Setting us up. The NSC didn't know shit about that. Right, Keely? That was between you and your pals in the P.I.?"

"It was a win-win proposition. Some of us over here made a little extra money, all the poor devils in the P.I. would make out a lot better, too."

"*Win-win?* Did I hear you spouting that bullshit, you miserable fuck? You set up nine United States marines to die so you could feather your own lousy nest. You got one good man killed and another permanently disabled. I am twenty-five years old, Keely. I'll have this leg for the rest of my life."

Keely's moral complacency drains the pond of mercy that had begun to form inside of Nick. Qualms about physical retribution and the purposeful infliction of pain vanish. His world turns to black, and then very distinctly, he hears something inside him snap. He sees Burke's smoldering torso splayed on the Philippine sand; he recalls the ragged crater carved from the back of his right leg, can feel himself gagging at the sight, not believing that is *his leg;* he hears the plush tones of the doctor's voice telling him that he will never walk properly again and relives in a microsecond the painful months of rehabilitation to prove him wrong. He spins and lashes out with his strong leg, whipping the hardened toe of his boot with all his force into Keely's exposed crotch. Keely expels his breath and keels over onto his side. His face is a deep crimson and as he vomits, his eyes look as if they will pop from his skull.

"Payback, Keely. That one was for Burke."

Nick's memories faded as quickly as they had come. Only a second had passed. Maybe less.

"I'm sorry, Thorne. I just can't be of service to you. That's all there is to it."

"Neumann, don't make it hard on yourself. Once I tell Kaiser about your discharge, he's going to have to fire you. He can't have a convict working as his assistant. The way I see it, you don't have much of a career left in this business anyway. Might as well do some good while you're still there."

Nick brushed past the federal agent. "Nice try. Do what you gotta do. So will I."

"I didn't have you figured for a coward, Neumann," Thorne shouted. "You let the Pasha get away once. His crimes are on your soul!"

Chapter 35

The office was dark, except for a halo of light focused on a stack of papers in the center of his desk. The building was quiet. No footsteps scurried through the hallways. Only the hushed electronic breathing of the computer disturbed the pall of silence that surrounded him like a fertile cocoon.

Wolfgang Kaiser was alone.

The bank once again belonged to him.

Kaiser stood with his cheek pressed against the glass, staring out the arched window behind his desk. The object of his attention was a stout gray building fifty yards up the Bahnhofstrasse: the Adler Bank. No lights glowed from behind its shuttered windows. Squat and ominous it sat, eyes closed for the night. The predator, like its prey, was asleep.

Kaiser peeled his cheek from the cold window and circled his desk. For twelve months he had been aware that the Adler Bank was accumulating USB's shares. A thousand here, five thousand there. Never enough to upset the average daily volume. Never enough to bid up the price. Just small blocks. Slow and steady. He had guessed Konig's intentions, if not his means. In response, he had conceived a modest plan to permanently cement his own position as Chairman of the United Swiss Bank.

Twelve months earlier the bank had celebrated its one hundred twenty-fifth birthday. A celebratory dinner was given at the Hotel Baur au Lac. The collected members of the board of directors and their ladies were invited. Toasts were made, achievements recognized, and perhaps a tear was shed, but only by one of the pensioned board members. Kaiser's active colleagues remained far too concerned with the evening's final announcement to praise the labors of their predecessors. Their hearts were on money. Specifically, on how much of it they'd get their grubby hands on before the evening was over.

Kaiser recalled the greedy glow that lit those ratlike faces that evening. When he had announced that each member of the board was to receive an anniversary bonus of one hundred thousand francs, he was greeted by silence. His guests were incapacitated, man and woman alike. For several seconds, they sat as still as the dead, perched on the edge of their seats. The pressure from a lone mouse's fart would have sent them sprawling onto the dining room floor. And then came the applause. A thunderous barrage of hand clapping. A standing ovation. Cries of "Long live USB!" and of "To the Chairman!"

How could he have doubted that the board

was comfortably in his pocket?

Kaiser allowed himself a self-pitying laugh. Less than a year later, many of the executives so content to pocket a cool hundred grand had joined Klaus Konig's snarling wolf pack, eager to denounce his own "antiquated" management strategies. The future lay with the Adler Bank, they argued, with aggressive trading in options and derivatives, with controlling stakes in unrelated companies, with leveraged wagers on the directions of foreign currencies.

The future, Kaiser summarized, lay with the inflated value of USB shares a takeover by the Adler Bank would bring.

The Wild, Wild West had arrived in Zurich. Gone were the days of negative interest rates, when foreigners anxious to deposit their funds in a Swiss bank would not only forgo interest but actually pay the bank account-management fees to accept their money. Switzerland was no longer the only safe haven for capital "in flight." Competitors had raised their banners both near and far. Liechtenstein, Luxembourg, and Austria all offered stable, discreet institutions rivaling their Swiss neighbor's. The Cayman Islands, the Bahamas, and the Netherlands Antilles each provided sophisticated banking services catering to the harried businessman in need of a secure hiding place for funds spirited from under the blind eyes of a trusting partner or the vengeful maw of a wronged spouse. Swiss banks weren't the only game in town.

In this hostile environment, Wolfgang Kaiser had struggled to maintain USB's position at the top of the private banking hierarchy. And succeeded. True, accounting measures of the bank's profitability were down. Key indicators of the bank's financial strength — its return on assets and return on equity — had suffered as internal investment was funneled toward those areas that would ensure continuing supremacy in private banking. Still, net profits would increase for the ninth consecutive year: a gain of seventeen percent over the past year was expected. At any other time such gains would be admirable. This year they were deemed a failure. How could you compare a rise of seventeen percent against the two hundred percent increase registered by the Adler Bank?

Kaiser slapped his hand against his thigh in frustration. His course for the United Swiss Bank was sound and correct. It respected the bank's history and played aggressively to her strongest points. For its first hundred years the bank had prospered as one of a dozen medium-size local institutions that catered domestically to the commercial requirements of Zurich's smaller concerns and internationally to the discreet demands of those foreign neighbors, who wanted to place their earnings in an atmosphere of maximum security and minimum scrutiny. When deciding where to deposit these newly gotten gains, more than a few educated heads turned toward the far-off safety of Switzerland and to the private banking division of the United Swiss Bank. Others followed.

Kaiser stood alone in the center of his dark office, savoring the past. He swore he would not allow Klaus Konig and his damned Adler Bank to take USB. Yet the situation was not encouraging. Even USB portfolio managers eager to lock in a decent return on their clients' managed assets had taken to selling shares of USB stock. Meanwhile, the Adler Bank continued its purchase of shares on the open market, if at a calmer tempo. Was it too soon to hope that Konig's inexhaustible supply of cash had dried up?

The Chairman returned to his desk, sat down, and looked at his neatly stacked papers. The lacquered ear of a photograph protruded from the bottom of the pile. He pulled it out and gazed at its lifeless subject. Stefan Wilhelm Kaiser. Sole fruit of an acrimonious and short-lived union. His mother lived in Geneva, remarried to another banker. Kaiser hadn't spoken with her since the funeral.

"Stefan," he whispered aloud to the ghosts hovering in his office. His only son had died at nineteen from an overdose of heroin.

For years, Kaiser had shielded himself from the pain of his death. *His son* was still ten years old. *His son* loved skating at the Dolder Ice Rink. *His son* clamored to swim at the local *hallenbad*. He did not know this man on the slab, this unkempt ruffian with the matted hair and acned skin. This drug addict who had exchanged a soccer jersey for a leather jacket, who preferred cigarettes to ice cream cones. This man he did not know.

Now Kaiser had a second chance. The son of a man he had known as well as a brother might replace Stefan. The thought of young Neumann on the Fourth Floor comforted him. The boy's resemblance to his father was uncanny. Glimpsing him each day was like glimpsing the past. He saw every opportunity he'd taken and every one he'd missed. Sometimes when he looked at Nicholas he felt like grabbing him and asking him whether all his work had accomplished anything. And he could see in Neumann's eyes that the answer would be yes. A resounding yes. Other times he felt as if he were staring at his own conscience, and he prayed for it never to betray him.

Kaiser turned off the light. He leaned back in his chair and wondered where it all was going to end. He didn't care for the image of his tired body lying on the slag heap of deposed corporate chieftains. He'd give his last franc to remain Chairman of the United Swiss Bank until his death.

Kaiser closed his eyes and willed himself not

to feel, but to be. He was the bank. Its granite walls and impenetrable vaults; its quiet salons and frenetic trading floor; its imperious directors and ambitious trainees. He was the bank. His blood flowed in its veins and his soul was mortgaged on its behalf.

"The Adler Bank shall not pass," he declared aloud, taking the words of another embattled general. "They shall not pass."

Chapter 36

"I am positively sated," declared Ali Mevlevi, allowing a last forkful of braised lamb to fall to his plate. "And you, my darling?"

Lina puffed her cheeks. "I feel like a balloon filled with too much air."

Mevlevi examined her plate. Most of her midday meal had gone uneaten. "You did not enjoy it? I thought lamb was your favorite."

"It was very good. I am simply not hungry."

"Not hungry? How is that? Not enough exercise, perhaps?"

Lina smiled wickedly. "Perhaps too much exercise."

"For a young woman like you? I think not." Mevlevi slid his chair back from the table and walked to the broad picture window. He had devoured her that morning. Acted like a man just released from prison. One last time, he had told himself. One last moment in her arms.

Outside, an army of clouds surrounded his compound. A weak storm from the Mediterranean advanced over the Lebanese coastal plain, gathering against the low foothills. Pockets of wind swept rain across the terrace and rattled the windows.

Lina joined him, locking her arms around his stomach and rubbing her head against his back. Normally, he enjoyed her attentions. But the time for such enjoyment was past. He unclasped her hands. "I can see clearly now," he declared. "The way ahead is shown to me. The path illuminated."

"What do you see, Al-Mevlevi?"

"The future."

"And?" Once more, Lina laid her head against his back.

He turned and pushed her arms to her sides. "Surely you know what it must bring."

Lina met his eyes. He could see she thought his behavior odd. Her innocence was disarming. Almost.

"What?" she asked. "Do *you* know what it will bring?"

But Mevlevi was no longer listening. His ears were attuned to the staccato snap of Joseph's footsteps, sounding from a distant hallway. He checked his watch, then walked out of the dining room and through the house to his office. "Do join us, Lina," he called over his shoulder. "Your company would be most welcome."

Mevlevi entered his study and brought himself face-to-face with his chief of security. Joseph stood at attention, eyes drilled to the fore. My proud desert hawk, thought Mevlevi.

Lina padded in a moment later and settled herself on the sofa.

"News?" Mevlevi asked Joseph.

"Everything is as according to plan. Sergeant Rodenko has two companies training on the south pitch. They are working with live grenades. Ivlov is giving a lecture on the deployment and detonation of antipersonnel claymore mines. Sentries report no activity."

"All quiet on the western front," said Mevlevi. "Very good." He sidestepped the soldier and began pacing the room. He clutched the back of his chair, then straightened a few papers on his desk. He moved to the bookshelf, where he selected a novel, examined its cover, frowned, then replaced it. Finally, he placed himself directly behind Joseph. "Has your affection for me waned?" he asked.

Lina began to answer, but a quickly raised hand stopped her. He repeated the question, this time as a whisper in Joseph's ear. "Has your affection for me waned? Answer me."

"No, sir," the desert hawk replied. "I love and respect you as I would my father."

"Liar." A sharp blow to the kidneys.

Joseph fell to one knee.

Mevlevi wrenched his ear and lifted him to his feet. "No father could be more ill served by a son. No man more disappointed. How could you fail me so? Once you would have given your life for me." A finger traced the crooked scar that creased the hawk's cheek. An open palm slapped the hawk's face. "Would you still?"

"Yes, Al-Mevlevi. Always."

A fist fired into the stomach.

Mevlevi glared at his retainer. "Stand up. You're a soldier. Once you protected me. Saved me from a suicide raid by Mong's killers. Once you were proud and hungry to serve. And now? Can you not defend me?"

Lina grabbed a pillow and clutched it to her chest.

Mevlevi placed his hands on the bodyguard's shoulders. "Can you not save me from an asp in my household? One so close to my bosom?"

"I shall always do my best."

"*You* will never betray me."

"Never," said the desert hawk.

Mevlevi grasped Joseph's jaw with his right hand and with his left caressed his minion's closely shorn hair. He kissed him on the lips — a hard, sexless embrace. "Yes, in my heart I know this. *Now I know this.*" He released him and walked with measured steps to the couch where Lina sat. "And you, *chérie?* When will you betray me?"

Wide-eyed, she stared at him.

"When?" Mevlevi whispered.

Lina jumped to her feet and ran past him into the hallway.

"Joseph," the Pasha ordered. "Suleiman's Pool!"

Fifty yards from Ali Mevlevi's principal residence stood a low rectangular building, unremarkable in all aspects. Its cement walls had recently been whitewashed. Its terra-cotta roof was common to the region. Trellises laced with dormant bougainvillaea decorated its bland facade. A quick inspection, however, would yield several curious observations. No approach was cut from the manicured lawn surrounding the building. No door interrupted its plain exterior. Blackout curtains were drawn inside double-paned, soundproof windows permanently secured by a row of four-inch nails. But nothing was stranger or more inescapable than the odor that seeped from the house. It was an invasive smell that caused the eyes to water and the throat to burn. "An astringent or a cleanser?" one might ask. "A detoxicant?" Not exactly. Just the nastiest bits of all three.

As he walked through the subterranean passageway, Ali Mevlevi kept his head bowed and his step pious. He wore a white *dishdasha*, thonged slippers, and an embroidered Muslim prayer cap, inlaid with pearls and golden thread. In his hand he carried the Koran. The holy book was opened to a prayer appropriate for the occasion — the Exaltation of Life — and he read aloud from it. After a single verse, he approached the end of the tiled passageway. His eyes began to tear — a natural reflex to the abrasive odor that stung his nasal passages

— and he stopped reading. He dismissed his discomfort as necessary to further the work of almighty God, Allah, and climbed the concrete steps leading to the hall.

Before him lay Suleiman's Pool: legacy of the greatest of Ottoman rulers, Suleiman the Magnificent. Thirty yards long and fifteen wide, the pool was filled with a brackish mixture of water, formaldehyde, and sodium triphosphate. For centuries, Turkish rulers had enjoyed preserving for months, even years, the youthful bodies of particularly treasured concubines. Somewhere during the twists and turns of history, the vagaries of corrupt Eastern rulers had turned from worship to torture, and from torture to murder. One was but a hop, skip, and jump from the other.

"Al-Mevlevi," Lina shrieked upon seeing him enter the pavilion. "I beg you. You are mistaken. Please . . ."

Mevlevi guarded his devout pace and walked slowly to Lina, who was seated nude in a high-backed rattan chair. Her hands and feet were bound with sisal. He stroked her fine black hair. "Tsk, tsk, my child. No need to explain. You asked of your future. Behold it now."

Mevlevi averted his gaze from Lina and looked at the pool. He could make out the outline of a dozen heads below the surface. Hair meandered from the corpses like undersea plant life on a tropical reef. He followed the bloated shapes downward to where bound feet were attached to dark oblong stones.

Lina gasped and began anew. "Al-Mevlevi, I do not work for the Makdisis. Yes, they brought me to the club. But I never spied on you. I never told them anything. I love you."

Mevlevi laughed mirthlessly. He relegated his heart to a far corner of his soul. Devotion to a higher calling replaced it. "You love me? The Makdisis would be disappointed. I, though, am charmed. Should I believe you?"

"Yes, yes. You must." Her tears stopped. She was pleading desperately for her life. Sincerity remained her sole currency.

"Tell me the truth, dear Lina. Only the truth. I must know everything." Normally, Mevlevi enjoyed these last moments. The teasing and taunting. The luring of last hopes. But not today. He kissed her and found her lips hard and dry. He removed a handkerchief from his caftan and wiped the tears from her cheeks.

"Tell me the truth," he said again, this time softly, as if lulling her to sleep.

"Yes, yes. I swear it." Lina nodded her head furiously. "The Makdisis found me in Jounieh. They spoke first with my mother. They offered her much money. One thousand dollars American. My mother took me aside and told me of their offer. 'What do such men wish me to do?' I asked her. One of the Makdisis answered. He was a short, fat man with gray hair and very big eyes, eyes like oysters. 'Lina, we want you only to look. To watch. To learn.' 'What am I to learn?' I asked. 'Just watch,' he said. 'We will contact you.'

"They wanted nothing specific?"

"No. Just for me to watch you."

"And?"

Lina licked her lips and opened her eyes as wide as they might stretch. "Yes, I watched you. I know you begin work at seven in the morning and that often you remain in your office until I go to sleep. Sometimes, you do not recite the mid-morning prayers. I think it is because they bore you, not because you forget. On the rest day, you watch the TV. Soccer all day."

Mevlevi was surprised at the alacrity with which she revealed her crimes. The girl actually believed herself innocent.

She said, "Once, I swear only once, I looked through your desk when you were not at home. I am sorry. But I found nothing. Nothing at all. I do not understand so many numbers. What I saw meant nothing to me."

Mevlevi brought his hands together as if to pray. "An honest child," he exclaimed. "Thanks be to Allah. You spoke of numbers. Please go on."

"I do not understand so many numbers. What is there to see? You work, work, work. On the telephone all the day long."

Mevlevi smiled as if her confession pleased him. "Now, Lina, you must tell exactly what you reported to the Makdisis."

"Nothing, I swear." She cast her eyes to the floor. "Only a little. Sometimes on Sundays, when I visited my mother, he would call."

"Who?"

"Mr. Makdisi. He wanted to know what you do all day long. What time you get up, when you eat, if you go out. Nothing else. I swear."

"And this, of course, you told him," Mevlevi suggested as if it were the most reasonable thing in the world.

"Yes, of course. He paid my mother so much money. What harm could it do?"

"Of course, darling. I understand." He stroked Lina's soft tresses. "Tell me now, did he ask you about my money? About banks? About how I pay my partners?"

"No, no, he never asked that. Never."

Mevlevi frowned. He was certain that it was Albert Makdisi who had fed information about his transfers to the American DEA. Makdisi had long wanted to go direct to Mong. Eliminate the middleman. "Lina, I prefer it when you tell me the truth."

"Please, Al-Mevlevi, you must believe me. No questions about money. He only wants to know about where you spend the day. If you travel. Nothing about money."

Mevlevi pulled a silver Minox camera from his pocket. He passed the camera before Lina's eyes, then under her nose as if it were a fine cigar. "And so darling, what is this?"

"I don't know. A small camera? Maybe I have seen one in stores."

"No, *chérie*. You have never seen one like this in any store."

"It is not mine."

"Of course not," he cooed. "And this charming little device?" He presented for her inspection a casing of matte black metal, no larger than a deck of cards. From one end he pulled a blunt rubber antenna.

Lina stared at the metal object. "I do not know what this is," she said indignantly. "You tell me."

"Me tell you?" Mevlevi peered over his shoulder at Joseph. "She wants us to tell her?"

Joseph looked on impassively.

Mevlevi said, "I'll let you in on a secret. When Max Rothstein told me that Albert Makdisi had brought you to Little Maxim's, I went with Joseph to search your quarters. You see, my dear, Max's word simply wasn't good enough. Not to condemn you, it wasn't. I had to be sure for myself. We found this pretty device — it's a radio, actually — along with the camera in that clever hole you fashioned in the flooring under your bed." Mevlevi held the small transmitter beneath her eyes. "Tell me about your radio. So petite, so compact. Frankly, I'd have thought such a toy far beyond the Makdisis' clumsy grasp."

Lina grew agitated. She fumbled with her hands and ground her ankles together. "Stop it!" she screamed. "There is no hole in my room. That camera doesn't belong to me. Neither does the radio. I've never seen them before. I swear it."

"The truth, Lina." Mevlevi's voice assumed a velvety monotone. "Here we speak only the truth. Come now. You were doing so well just a few moments ago."

"I am no spy. I never listened to that radio. I own no camera."

Mevlevi drew nearer Lina. "What did you say?" His voice was filled with an urgency until now absent, his posture suddenly rigid.

"I never listened to the radio," moaned Lina. "If I want music, I go to the living room. Why would I need a transistor radio?"

Mevlevi regarded her anew. "A *transistor* radio," he said appreciatively. *"She never listened to the transistor radio."* He glanced at Joseph, then back at Lina, as if momentarily unsure with whom to speak. The device he held in his hand was as far from a transistor radio as modern science allowed. It was an ultra-high-frequency single-band two-way radio capable of plucking from the ether the faintest cobweb of a signal — but only one sent on its preset frequency. It could not be used to find commercial radio transmissions.

"Charming," he said to Joseph. "And well trained. Don't you think? For a moment, I

469

nearly believed her. Women often make superb plants. They are naturally emotional. One tends to mistake their hysteria for honesty. If a man cries, it is only because he is guilty and pitying himself."

Joseph said nothing. He nodded once resolutely as if he knew exactly what his patron was speaking of.

Mevlevi placed himself behind the rattan chair and ran his hands over Lina's body. He gently squeezed her powerful shoulders and caressed her firm breasts. A morose fog fell upon him. "Lina, the time has come for us to part ways. You go now on a transcendent path. I am sorry I cannot join you, but my work is not yet completed. Soon, though, we may be reunited. Truly, I loved you."

Lina faced him with her eyes closed. She cried quietly. "Why?" she asked between sniffles.

For a moment, Mevlevi asked the same question of the Almighty. Why must I lose one who means so much to me? One who has brought only light and joy into my life. She is but a child. An innocent. Surely, she should not suffer so for her crimes. And then he felt his resolve stiffen, and he knew it to be Allah speaking through him.

"You were brought to test me. If I can part with you, my sweetest creature, I can part with life itself. Allah demands sacrifices of us all."

"No, no, no," she whispered.

"Adieu, my love." He stood and nodded to Joseph.

Joseph approached Lina slowly and asked her to be calm. "Go serenely," he counseled. "Go with grace. It is the way of Allah. You must not resist." And when he cradled her in his arms, she went without fighting.

Joseph carried her to a low bench at the far end of the building. An oblong stone, twenty inches long and ten inches high, lay below the bench. The stone weighed exactly thirty pounds — easily enough to anchor a small woman's body to the pool's bottom. He unbound Lina's feet and placed each one in a shallow depression molded into the stone. Stainless steel manacles extended from a brass eye screw that protruded from between her feet. He locked a cuff around each foot.

"Why are you doing this?" Lina asked. Her tears had dried. Her swollen eyes were clear.

"I must obey Al-Mevlevi. He is inspired by a greater purpose than either of us."

Lina tried to slap Joseph's face with her bound hands. "I do not believe you. It is you, the liar. You put the radio under my bed. You!"

"Shhh!" Joseph knelt and offered her a cup of wine. "It contains a powerful tranquilizer. Al-Mevlevi did not wish you to feel any pain. Look into the water. You don't want to die like that, not while you're fully conscious."

"This is the end of my life. I must feel every moment."

Hastily, Joseph raised her to her feet.

Ali Mevlevi stood at the opposite end of the pool, his head tilted toward the heavens, a muted prayer playing from his mouth. He stopped and looked at Joseph, then nodded and resumed his incantations. Truly, he had loved her.

Lina struggled against her bonds. She whimpered at her inability to move her feet or to free her hands.

Joseph whispered in her ear that Allah would love her forever. He carried her onto a narrow span that bridged the pool, and when he stood over the water, he lifted her as high as his strength would permit and threw her into the pool. Her scream mixed with the tumult of the splashing water, and for several seconds after she had fallen below the surface, her voice echoed through the vaulted pavilion.

Outside, a Bell Jet Ranger helicopter sat with rotors turning at idle on the main lawn of the compound. The sky was bleak. A light drizzle fell.

Mevlevi walked toward the chopper, his hand on Joseph's shoulder. "Lina jeopardized Khamsin. You understand there was no other solution."

"Of course, Al-Mevlevi."

"I am growing to be a sentimental fool. I felt for her. It is harder to live without emotion at my age." He paused and in a rare loss of temper, cursed the Almighty. "Our priorities are clear. Khamsin must be allowed to take shape. You must leave at once to take responsibility for our latest shipment. You will fly to a freighter steaming in the Adriatic, near Brindisi, off the Italian coast."

"May I gather my belongings?"

"No. I'm afraid you may not. No time."

For once, Joseph protested. "I only need a few minutes."

"You will leave immediately," Mevlevi commanded. "Take this bag. Inside you will find a passport, some clothes, and five thousand dollars. Once you are safely on board, I will contact you with further instructions. The profit from this transaction is essential. Is that clear?"

"Yes, Al-Mevlevi."

"Very good." Mevlevi wanted to tell Joseph more. He wanted to tell him that in two days his men would begin moving south toward the Israeli border; that they would travel in two groups, each three hundred strong; that they would move under cover of darkness, between the hours of two and six when American satellites did not have the region of southern Lebanon in their purview. Mostly, he wanted to tell Joseph that without the profits from this transaction, and the far greater sums those profits would almost immediately make available, Khamsin would surely fail — yet one more vainglorious, and ultimately suicidal, border incursion. But alas, such knowledge was his to bear alone.

"The men who will meet you in Brindisi . . ."

"Yes?"

"I no longer know if they can be trusted. They may be with the Makdisis. Take precautions. Our shipment must reach Zurich as soon as possible. Once the merchandise is unloaded, accept no delays."

Joseph reached for the athletic bag. He grasped the handle, but Mevlevi refused to give it up. He stared deep into his retainer's eyes. "You will not betray me."

Joseph stood straighter. "Never, Al-Mevlevi. I am beholden to you. You have my holy word."

Chapter 37

Marco Cerruti sat up in his bed. His breath came fast and shallow. He was soaked with perspiration. He opened his eyes as widely as possible, and slowly the room came into focus. Shadows looming in the dark took form. Phantoms sought refuge behind heavy curtains and antique dressers.

Cerruti untangled his legs from the covers and turned on the bedside lamp. He was confronted with a portrait of his mother staring at him from the confines of her beloved armchair. He turned the picture facedown on the table and rose from the bed. He needed a glass of water. The cold tile of the bathroom floor sent a wash of clean sensation through his body, restoring his nerves. He drank a second glass of water, then decided upon a quick inspection of the apartment. Best to ensure he'd properly locked the windows and secured the elevator door. This done, he returned to bed, first arranging the sheets and covers. He climbed in, fastened the top button of his wool pajamas, then slid under the covers. His hand reached for the lamp but stopped midway there. He recalled the dreadful nightmare. Maybe it was smarter to leave the light burning a little longer.

Cerruti laid his head on the pillow and stared at the ceiling. For weeks, the dream had not come. His recovery had progressed. Night was no longer a time to be feared. A return to work was hardly out of the question. And then the visits from Thorne.

The American frightened him. So many questions. Questions about Mr. Mevlevi, about the Chairman, even about young Mr. Neumann, whom he had met only once. Cerruti had been polite, as he was with all his guests. Had offered the rude man a Coca-Cola and some biscuits. Had answered his questions respectfully. Of course, he had lied. But he had done it diplomatically, and with what he hoped was aplomb. No, Cerruti had sworn, he did not know a man by the name of Ali Mevlevi. No, he did not know a client at the bank nicknamed the Pasha. A supplier of heroin to the European continent? The bank did not work with such people.

"You have a moral responsibility to assist us in our investigation," Thorne had argued. "You are not just an employee of a dishonest bank. If you insist on keeping your mouth closed, you're also an employee of Ali Mevlevi, a criminal just like him. I don't plan on resting until I stop him. And after he's sitting in a black hole forty feet underground, I'm coming after you. Count on it."

Funny, Thorne so concerned about Mevlevi

being a big wheel in the heroin trade. Didn't he know about the guns? Cerruti was a major in the Swiss Army — intelligence, of course — but he knew his way around the standard armaments of a light infantry battalion. He had never imagined that a private individual could purchase the monumental store of arms and munitions, the near mountain of matériel he had seen only two months ago at the Pasha's compound: crates of machine guns, ammunition, pistols, grenades — both anti-personnel and incendiary. And that was the small stuff. He had seen several Stinger ground-to-air missiles, three anti-tank guns, and at least a dozen mortars, some large enough to lob a projectile five kilometers. Enough, Cerruti concluded, for a very messy little war.

He reached for the glass of water on his night table. Recalling his last visit to Ali Mevlevi's compound in the foothills above Beirut led inexorably to the root of his distress, the cause for his psychic dysfunction. Suleiman's Pool.

He had never in his life borne witness to so horrific a sight. He winced at the memory of the smell: the rank odor of a hundred midnight laboratories. He shut his eyes against the recollection of the pale bodies drifting in the pool. He covered his ears to muffle the laugh. Mr. Mevlevi howling with glee as poor Marco fainted.

Cerruti sat up in his bed for the second time that night. Perhaps Thorne was right. Perhaps Mevlevi did have to be stopped. The guns, the pool, heroin, too, according to the DEA. What more did he need to recognize a villain?

Cerruti clutched the sheets to his chin as the nightmare returned. The black water. The demons lurking just beyond the periphery of his vision. He couldn't go back to sleep with the dream awaiting him. Instead, he rocked gently back and forth moaning "Suleiman's Pool." He repeated the words like a mantra. *Suleiman's Pool*. Switzerland had a law for just such a situation. And even though it remained more or less untested years after its inclusion in the country's legal tomes, he knew that no one qualified more aptly as "a client whose activities lead the employee to infer illegal business practices" than Mr. Ali Mevlevi.

Cerruti drew in several deep breaths. Tomorrow morning he would call Mr. Thorne and show him the papers that sat in his desk. He would turn over evidence of the Pasha's accounts at the United Swiss Bank and confirmations of the transfers made twice each week. He would help the international authorities bring the scoundrel Mevlevi to justice.

"No, Mr. Thorne, I am not a criminal," he declared aloud to the silent walls, and then quietly to himself, "I don't want to go to prison."

Cerruti sat upright in his bed, proud of his decision. Slowly, though, the faint smile faded. He couldn't make such a momentous decision alone. Discussion was required. But whom could he share his feelings with at this late hour? He had no relatives, none at least who would understand such complex issues. Friends? None. Colleagues? He wouldn't consider it.

Cerruti lay in his bed thinking, and soon a damp sweat bathed his entire body. There was only one man with whom he could talk about this. The man who had helped him make so many of the major decisions in his life. Only he could help Marco rid himself of the nightmare.

For the second time in a quarter of an hour, Cerruti turned back the sheets and rose from his bed. He padded to the closet and pulled out a terry-cloth robe. He walked through the apartment turning on all the lights, stopping last in his small study, where he sat himself down behind his desk. He opened the drawer and removed a slim gray book — his personal phone directory — which he laid on his desk beside the telephone. His hand shook only a little as he found the proper page and located the number. He stared at the book, and though the apartment was heated to a mild seventy degrees, he began to shiver. For while he recognized the first number listed on the page, and had in fact called it on a hundred occasions during his long career, he had never called the second number. *For emergencies, Marco,* he heard the stentorian baritone tell him. *For the closest of friends in the direst of times.*

Cerruti pondered his decision — whether this was an emergency, whether it was in fact the direst of times — and when after a few minutes of this he found himself unable to fight back an onslaught of tears, he knew he had his answer.

At 1:37 A.M., he picked up the telephone and dialed his savior.

Wolfgang Kaiser picked up the phone on the second ring.

"Now what is it?" he asked, keeping his head on the pillow and his eyes closed. A dial tone answered noncommittally. Nearby, a phone rang again.

Kaiser dashed off the bedcovers and swung his feet to the floor. Kneeling, he grasped the handle of the bedside cabinet and flung open the door. A black telephone sat on a sliding drawer. His hand found the receiver as the phone rang once more.

"Kaiser," he announced in a gruff tone.

"Please engage now." A command.

Kaiser pressed a transparent cube on the base of the special phone, engaging the Motorola Viscom III Scrambler. Static tickled his ear. The line bulged with white noise. A moment passed and the line regained its clarity.

"Kaiser." This time he spoke quietly, deferentially.

"I will be arriving in two days," said Ali Mevlevi. "Make the usual arrangements. Eleven A.M. Zurich Airport."

Kaiser placed the phone on his left shoulder, using his right hand to cover the mouthpiece. "Out," he hissed to the lump on the far side of his bed. "Go to the bathroom, shut the door, and turn on the bathwater. Now!" He removed his hand from the phone. "Eleven A.M.," he repeated. "Unfortunately, I cannot be there to welcome you."

"I would not dream of disturbing the day of such an influential man. I hope I am not disturbing your night." A hoarse laugh.

Kaiser pressed the phone against his chest and grunted at the form next to him, "Hurry up. *Raus!*"

A woman rose from the bed and walked unclothed to the bathroom. He watched her go. After all this time, he still enjoyed her lush figure. The woman closed the door without a backward glance.

Kaiser said, "Ali, this is a crazy time to come to Zurich. Thorne and his team are sure to be maintaining surveillance on the bank."

"Thorne is a nuisance easily disposed of. Surely you don't view him as a threat?"

"The man is a representative of the United States government. Any other time, we could shoo him away. Today?" Kaiser sighed. "You

481

know too well the situation we are in."

"No matter. He must be neutralized."

"You don't mean . . ."

"Growing squeamish, are we?" Mevlevi asked. "Don't lose the qualities I used to admire in you. Ruthless. Relentless. Remorseless. You were unstoppable."

Kaiser wanted to say that he still possessed these qualities. But such a response would be construed as defensive and thus weak. So he said nothing.

"Get this man off of my back," said Mevlevi. "I don't care how you choose to do it. If you prefer a more genteel method, so be it. But make no mistake, he is your responsibility."

Kaiser could imagine the Pasha sitting in his study at five in the morning, smoking his filthy Turkish cigarettes, musing about the future. "Understood. And regarding your arrival, I'll have Armin Schweitzer meet you at the airport."

"No. Send Mr. Neumann. I'm anxious to meet the young firebrand. Did you know that he has been seeing Thorne? Or, Thorne has been seeing him. I haven't yet decided how to interpret the meetings."

"He's been seeing Thorne?" asked Kaiser, unable to mask his surprise.

"Three times by my count. But he is resisting. Nothing to worry about. Not yet, anyway. Send Neumann. I simply wish to ensure that he's one of us."

"I still need him," said Kaiser firmly. "See that no harm comes to him."

"That will be my decision. You must have plenty of other stallions in your stables."

"I said I require Neumann. He's instrumental in our drive to win over undecided shareholders."

Mevlevi coughed. He said distractedly, "I repeat, that will be my decision."

Kaiser responded angrily. "Sometimes you lead me to believe you welcome the bid from Adler Bank."

"Be content that I'm concerned. Consider it a display of my respect for our long relationship." Mevlevi cleared his throat and asked, "Other news?"

Kaiser rubbed his eyelids. How did the man know? How could he have learned so quickly — in the space of only minutes? "We have a problem. Cerruti has broken. You scared him witless. It seems that Thorne has been pressuring him."

"Cerruti is weak," said Mevlevi.

"True. But he is a trusted colleague. He has given his life to the bank."

"And now? Does he wish to clear his conscience? Is he seeking absolution at the hands of the United States Drug Enforcement Administration?"

Kaiser said reasonably, "I thought we would send the poor fellow to Grand Canary. I have an apartment there. It is far away and my staff can keep an eye on him."

"A short-term solution to a long-term problem. Not at all like you, friend."

Kaiser looked toward the bathroom, listening for the muted gurgle of water running in the tub. What would she think of all this if she knew? After so long together, would she be surprised that he was beholden to another?

"What is the status of this renegade bank?" Mevlevi asked.

"Very tight. Adler has a limitless source of cash. Every dollar they receive goes toward buying USB shares. Have you considered my proposition?"

"Two hundred million Swiss francs certainly ranks as greater than a proposition."

"A loan. We'd repay the full amount in ninety days. Interest at forty percent per annum. A ten percent gain on your outlay in three months."

"I'm hardly the Federal Reserve."

Kaiser had difficulty guarding an objective tone. "It is crucial we repel the Adler Bank."

"Why?" asked Mevlevi playfully. "Isn't that the natural scheme of affairs in your financial world? Engulf and devour? It's hardly more civilized than mine."

Kaiser exploded, the strain of the past days quivering in his voice. "This is my life's work, dammit."

"Calm yourself," ordered Mevlevi. "I understand your predicament, Wolfgang. I've always understood it, haven't I? Now listen to me carefully, and I'm sure we can find suitable accommodation for all." The voice lowered a tone, losing all hint of humanity. "If you wish for me to consider extending to you a temporary credit facility of two hundred million francs, you will take care of Mr. Cerruti before my arrival. A long-term solution. You will also devise a plan to remove Thorne from my back for good. Understood?"

Kaiser closed his eyes tightly. He swallowed painfully. "Yes."

"Good." Mevlevi laughed, once again innocence and joy. "Do these small chores for me and we will discuss the loan when I arrive. And don't forget Neumann. I'll expect him at the airport."

Christ, it was easy to take orders once you got used it, lamented Kaiser. "Yes, of course."

"Good night, friend. You may ask your companion to rejoin you now. Sleep well."

Chapter 38

Nick planned his excursion for ten A.M. sharp, at the height of the morning rush. Throughout the bank it was a time of rehearsed chaos. Secretaries hurried from one office to another on missions of dubious importance. Apprentices filed back to their posts after a mandated fifteen-minute break. Reptilian executives conspired in ill-lit corridors. The bank bustled with activity, and he would lose himself in it.

Nick left his office one minute early. He strode past the entrance to the Chairman's anteroom and continued down the corridor until he reached the entry to the interior stairwell. Careful not to show the least hesitation, he swept open the door and stepped inside. He descended the stairs, head lowered, hugging the outside wall. Several people passed him, but he didn't notice them. He wasn't making this trip. At least not officially.

Nick slowed his pace as he neared the first-floor landing. He stopped next to the unmarked iron door and gathered his breath, steeling himself for the task ahead. When he was ready, he tucked his chin into his neck, cast his eyes downward, then pulled open the heavy door and stepped into the corridor. The hallway was as endless as he remembered. He walked quickly toward his destination — one more harried worker on his daily rounds. His footsteps echoed off the walls. The numbers inscribed on the small metal plates beside every door declined. Finally, he passed a series of unmarked entries. He was there. Room 103. *Dokumentation Zentrale.*

He opened the door and stepped inside. The office was full of people. Two neat lines were formed in front of a Formica counter behind which stood a twisted old man with a shock of white hair. The famous Karl, dungeon master of DZ.

Waiting in line, Nick thought of his father working in this same office forty years ago. The place looked as if it hadn't changed an iota. Metal desks of prewar vintage were arranged in twin columns of four behind the counter. Scuffed linoleum flooring peeled near the walls and under the radiators. Maybe the lighting had improved — if you could call fluorescent bulbs an improvement. The room smelled of decay, and Nick was sure it had smelled no different in 1956 when Alex Neumann had begun his career here. He pictured his father hefting files to the highest shelves, scooping up request forms and patrolling the miles of stacks in search of one document or another. Two years he'd spent working for Karl. Two years in this dustbin. Step one of his education. The first rung up the ladder.

The woman in front of Nick received her files and left the office. Nick stepped forward and handed Karl the account request form. He stared at the old man and began counting down from ten, waiting for the bomb to go off.

"You don't say please?" Karl barked as he slipped on a pair of bifocals hanging from a tarnished iron chain around his neck.

"Please," said Nick. Seven, six, five . . .

Karl brought the request to his eyes. He sniffed.

Four, three, two . . .

Karl dropped the form on the counter as if it were worthless currency. "Young man," he huffed, "this request has no personal reference. It does not show *who* wants the files. No reference, no file. I am sorry."

Nick had prepared an explanation, though it was weak and had not been tested under live fire. He checked over his shoulder, then leaned across the counter and whispered, "These forms were generated by a new computer system. It isn't initialized yet. Only on the Fourth Floor. I'm sure *you* know about it. *The Medusa system.*"

Karl stared at the paper. His bushy eyebrows bunched together. He looked unconvinced. "No reference, no files. I am so sorry."

Nick pushed the request form under Karl's eyes. Time to up the stakes. "If you have a problem, call Herr Kaiser immediately. I just left his office. His extension is —"

"I know his extension," declared the dungeon master. "No reference, no file. I am so —"

"So sorry," Nick said in unison. He had expected such obstinacy. He had known a few master sergeants in the Corps who made Karl look like a pussycat, and he had learned through trial and error that the only way to make them circumvent sacred routine was to use a technique he had developed named the shove and hug. A discreet but firm hint of a threat, followed by a show of respect for their position and a heightened appreciation for the favor they were about to grant. At best, it worked half the time.

"Listen to me carefully," Nick began. "Do you know what we're doing upstairs? We're working night and day to save this bank from a little man down the street who has every intention of buying us. Do you know what will happen if he takes us over?"

Karl didn't seem to care.

"No more papers. Every file in here will be scanned, digitized, and saved on a computer disk. They'll cart off all your precious documents, all this —" Nick gave a wide sweeping gesture to encompass the entire room, "and store them in a warehouse in Ebmatingen. We'll never see them again. If I need to access a document, I'll sit at my desk on the Fourth Floor and call it up on my own monitor."

The shove rendered, Nick kept a sharp eye on Karl, watching the old man absorb the information. Before long his wrinkled face fell. "And what about me?"

Gotcha, thought Nick. "I'm sure Klaus Konig would find a position for you. If, that is, he values experience and loyalty as much as Herr Kaiser. But all this will be gone." Onto the hug. "I apologize for not having put the proper reference. But Herr Kaiser is waiting for the information in this file. I know he would greatly appreciate your help."

Karl straightened out the request form and picked up a pen off of the green countertop. "Your three-letter reference?"

"S . . . P . . . R," said Nick, enunciating each letter as if it were its own word. If there were ever an inquiry, using Peter Sprecher's personal reference would gain him two, maybe three hours. At that point, who knew? It might be enough time to get him off the premises. Then again, it might not. Regardless, there was no way he was going to leave his own fingerprints all over this file.

Karl wrote the three letters on the request form. "Your identification, please?"

"Of course." Smiling, Nick reached into his coat pocket. His smile turned to surprise, then dismay. His hands rummaged through his pants and again in his jacket. He frowned apologetically, at once angry and contrite. "Looks like *I* made the mistake this time. I must have left my I.D. upstairs. Get that file for me while I run and get it."

Nick hesitated a moment, then turned and made his way to the door. All the while, he shook his head vigorously, as if chastising himself for his forgetfulness.

"No, no," said Karl. "Stay. Client dossiers belonging to a numbered account may not be removed from this room anyhow. Sit over there and wait where I can keep an eye on you. For the Chairman, I make an exception." He stared past Nick and pointed to a small table with two chairs on each side of it. "Over there. Go and sit. You will be called when it is retrieved."

Nick breathed easier and did as he was told. He walked sheepishly to the table, still shaking his head at his careless behavior. He was probably overacting.

The activity in the office had increased. Eight or nine people waited in line. Still, the room was absolutely silent. "Church mice," Nick would have said to his infantry platoon when silent running was an operational necessity. Only the shuffling of paper and one secretary's itchy throat marred the calm.

"Herr Sprecher?"

Nick jumped to his feet, fearful that someone might recognize him. He scanned the room. No one looked at him oddly.

Karl held a sepia folder in both his hands. "Here is your file. You may not remove any of its contents. You may not leave it unattended, even if you have to go to the toilet. Bring it directly to me when you are finished. Understood?"

Nick said he understood. He took the file from Karl and started back to the reading table.

"Herr Sprecher?" Karl asked unsurely. "That is correct, isn't it?"

Nick turned. "Yes," he answered confidently, waiting for someone to call him an impostor.

"You remind me of a boy I used to know a long time ago. He worked with me. Name wasn't Sprecher, though." Karl shrugged his shoulders and went back to work.

It was a thick file, as big as a textbook and twice as heavy. Nick turned the folder horizontally to check the tab. 549.617 RR was typed in heavy black script. He relaxed and opened the cover. Signature sheets were stapled to the left-hand side. The sheets listed the names of the bank executives who had previously requested the file. Cerruti's name was written on ten or eleven lines, interrupted once by Peter Sprecher's. The name Becker popped up half a dozen times all within a six-month period. Then Cerruti again and before him, something illegible. Lift the sheet and go back in time, mid-eighties. Another page, more names. Back again. And finally, at the top of the first page, a signature he knew well. The date: 1980. He traced the bold curves of the signature with his pen. Wolfgang Kaiser. Chalk up another run in Sterling Thorne's column, thought Nick. Irrefutable proof the Chairman knew Mr. Ali Mevlevi.

Nick turned his attention to the manila folder marked "client mail" sitting loose on top of the right-hand page. The folder held a pile of unclaimed correspondence: official confirmations of every transaction completed for benefit of the Pasha's account. As was common for numbered accounts, all mail was held at the bank until such time as the account holder wanted to review it. The stack wasn't very thick. Marco Cerruti must have delivered a bundle during his most recent visit. Nick counted approximately thirty envelopes. One corresponding for each incoming and outgoing wire transfer plus two month-end statements, the one for February dated only yesterday.

Nick closed the manila folder and slid it onto the signature sheet. A sheaf of transaction confirmations two fingers in height was attached to the right outermost cover of the file. Perusing them, he saw that the stack contained a record of all confirmations sent to the holder of account 549.617 RR. Every incoming wire, every outgoing wire since the account was opened. At the bottom of the stack was a copy of each of the seven matrices listing the name of every bank and every account number to which the Pasha's funds were to be wired. To Sterling Thorne, the matrices would prove more valuable than any treasure map, more inculpatory than any confession. With them, he could trace the flow of funds from USB to fifty or sixty banks around the world. Sure it was only one step in what was no doubt a circuitous route. But it was the first step, and as such, the most important.

Nick studied the incoming wire transfers for the final three months of the previous year. Rules forbade the copying of any information in the files. It was strictly "for his eyes only." As well as he could, he memorized the amounts that arrived on each Monday and Thursday. He totaled the dollar value of the transactions for each week and set them in a column inside his head. When he got as far back as October, his mind failed him. It was as if a screen went blank, a momentary short circuit. He began again, reading in reverse chronological order the transfers made from December 31 back through September 30, totaling the figures weekly. Thirteen numbers stood out clearly in his mind. He ran his mind's eye down the column, summing the eight-digit figures. Finished, he memorized the sum. In three months, $678 million had passed through the Pasha's account.

Nick raised his head and found Karl staring unabashedly at him. "Who are you, really?"

he seemed to be asking.

Nick returned his attention to the folder. He had come to steal the unclaimed transaction confirmations. The envelopes held hard-copy proof that the client was violating the rules against money laundering as prescribed by the DEA. They also proved that USB knowingly facilitated such contraventions. In his jacket pocket were a dozen envelopes identical to those in the file below him. He had typed the Pasha's account number on every envelope and placed a folded sheet of blank paper inside. Keeping his eyes glued to the papers below him, he slid the phony confirmations out of his pocket and tucked them under his leg. Now he had to wait for a person to enter and divert Karl's attention.

Nick checked the time. It was 10:35. He should be at his desk selling off shares. Feller would have noticed his absence by now. The little zealot had adopted the habit of phoning every fifteen minutes to keep a running tally of the dollar value of shares Nick had sold. Just this morning, Nick had generated sell orders for over eight million dollars and had issued buy orders for a corresponding amount of USB shares. Maeder's plan was going off without a hitch.

Time passed slowly. DZ was deserted. Ten minutes ago, the room had been packed. Now it was empty. Where in the hell had everybody gone? He couldn't wait here forever. Nick snuck a glance at Karl. The old coot was still staring right at him.

A few minutes later, the door creaked halfway open and then closed. False alarm. Nick blew out his breath anxiously. The last thing he needed was for Feller to start searching all over the place for him. He had to get back to the Fourth Floor. A single bead of sweat formed at the top of his spine. He could feel it roll the length of his back. He lifted his hand from the desk and saw that he had left a moist imprint. He wiped his palm on the seam of his pants.

At 11:05, a dark-haired man walked into the room. He was a clerk returning from the lavatory. Nick waited until he approached the service counter, then counted to three and extracted the transaction confirmations from the Pasha's dossier. Sure not to raise his head, he brushed the unmailed letters into his lap. With his right hand, he removed the dozen surrogate confirmations from under his thigh and placed them into the dossier. Still keeping his head immobile above the dossier, he arranged the stolen letters into a neat stack and in one assured motion deposited them in the inside pocket of his jacket. Every letter slid in smoothly. Except one. One envelope protruded from his jacket for all the world to see. Nick flung his elbow in a wide arc and repeatedly jammed the envelope into his jacket. Three times he tried to stuff it into his jacket.

On the fourth try the letter slipped in.

Nick waited for the alarm to sound. Karl must have noticed. One of the secretaries had to have seen his bungled burglary. Nothing happened. Daring a glance toward the counter, Nick saw that Karl was staring directly at him. Why hadn't the old codger spotted his brazen theft?

Nick rearranged the Pasha's dossier so that all was neat and orderly. As he approached the counter, he looked past Karl and saw that the young secretaries behind him were laughing. Nick returned his eyes to the keeper of *Dokumentation Zentrale.* He was leaning over the counter, his chin resting comfortably on his palm. His bifocals sat precariously at the end of his nose, and his eyes were closed.

Karl was snoring.

Nick left the office that evening at seven on the dot. He hurried up the Bahnhofstrasse to the Paradeplatz, hoping to catch the next tram. A light snow was falling, and tonight it made Zurich the prettiest city in the world. His step was light and energetic, buoyed by a sense of purpose he hadn't known since his first day at the bank eight weeks ago. He passed the tram stop that would take him to his grim apartment in the USB *Personalhaus* and crossed the square, arriving just in time to board the number two, heading in the opposite direction.

Nick chose a seat near the doorway and settled in for the short ride. He repeated Sylvia's address in his head as the tram bucked and jostled its way up the Universitätstrasse. He hoped she wouldn't mind his showing up unannounced — if she was even home. He had tried to call her earlier, but her assistant had said she would be out for the day. A rush of well-being came over him, and he smiled. He didn't know why he felt so exhilarated. Maybe part of it was because he had pulled off his petty theft; maybe part because he was keeping his word, taking concrete steps to make amends for his poor conduct. Whatever the reason, he felt alive and vital — full of piss and vinegar, his father would have said — and he needed to see Sylvia. He needed to see someone who understood the foreign world into which he had delivered himself.

Nick arrived at the top of Frohburgstrasse twenty minutes later and caught his first glimpse of Sylvia's apartment. A light was burning in her window. He had a hard time keeping himself from running the short distance to her doorway. Two weeks ago, he'd asked himself what it was about her that he found so attractive and he hadn't been able to fashion an answer. Yet tonight, he knew it without thinking. She was the first person he'd ever met who kept a tighter rein on her life than he kept on his. For once, he could be the one to let go, to be a little crazy, even whimsical, and relax doing it, knowing that she was in control. It was a role he'd never played before, and he liked it. Then, of course, there was the sex. He didn't like to admit it, but at first he had enjoyed the taboo implicit in seducing his older female superior. And he thought she did, too. When he was with her, the whole world stopped turning. Everything beyond their immediate periphery ceased to exist. She made him feel complete.

Nick reached the entry to her apartment and pressed the call button. He prayed Sylvia would be at home. He felt too good to be left alone on a Friday night. He tapped his foot nervously. *Come on, answer,* he said to himself. *Open the goddamned door.* He pressed the buzzer again, and his spirits began to fade. He took a step back. A voice came from the intercom. "Who is it?"

Nick felt his heart skip a beat. He was nervous and excited at the same time. "It's Nick. Let me in."

"Nick? Are you all right?"

He laughed. She was probably wondering if he was as frazzled as he'd been that Friday night not so long past. "Yes, of course."

The door buzzed and he rushed inside the apartment. He took the stairs two at a time, forgetting all about his sore knee. He just wanted to see Sylvia. She was waiting for him at the door as he came down the final few stairs. She was wearing a white terry-cloth bathrobe, toweling her hair dry. He stopped for a second to stare at her. Her skin was flushed from hot water. Her face was damp and moist. He walked slowly the last few steps, feeling like he needed her more than he'd needed anyone else before in his life. Not knowing why and not caring.

"I was just in the bath. You sur—"

Nick slid an arm inside her bathrobe and drew her toward him. He kissed her firm and hard on the lips. She resisted, trying to wedge a hand in between them. He wrapped his other arm around her back and held her tighter. She relaxed, allowing her head to fall back and opening her mouth to taste him. She moaned. He closed his eyes and drifted to a warm place.

Nick released her and they stepped into the apartment. He shut the door and pulled back to stare into her soft brown eyes. He saw a flicker somewhere inside them, and he knew she was asking herself what he was doing there, why he had kissed her like that. He expected her to speak, maybe even to tell him to get out, but instead she remained silent, standing inches away from him. He could feel the warmth of her body and her slow, heavy breathing. She raised a finger to his lips and brushed it slowly across them. He grew aroused. She turned and led him by the hand down the corridor and into her bedroom. She pushed him down onto the bed and peeled the bathrobe back from her shoulders, allowing it to drop to the floor. He looked at her nude body. He longed to run his hand along every curve, wanted to brush his lips across her stomach and then lower. He lifted his hands and cupped her breasts, running a thumb around her nipples until they hardened. Her breathing slowed and grew shallow. She reached down and touched him, rubbing her hand back and forth over the swelling in his trousers. Then she lowered herself to her knees, and ran her face back and forth across him. She pushed his jacket from his shoulders, then anxiously unbuckled his belt and pulled down his trousers. She caressed him for a moment, her tongue tasting him, then took him into her mouth.

Nick watched her, his pleasure forcing his hips off the bed. He wanted her to take more of him, all of him. He wanted to be inside her, to hold her next to him, to share the same breath.

Sylvia released him and climbed onto the bed. She straddled him, guiding him slowly into her, taking him out, then bringing him in deeper. Her eyes were closed and she moaned each time he touched her. Nick held on to the bed, balling up the sheets in the palms of his hands. He struggled to breathe slower, to feel less. Finally, she lowered herself onto him and shuddered. Nick sat up and wrapped his arms around her. He kissed her ravenously. Her mouth was hot and wet with desire. His entire body stiffened, and when he could hold back no longer, he let himself go, arching his back and thrusting himself deep into her. She lowered her head to her chest and her body quaked, an uneven humming drifting from her mouth. Her tremors increased and she laid both hands on his chest, breathing heavily. Then suddenly her body relaxed. She exhaled loudly, then fell onto the bed.

Sylvia lay down beside him. After a while her breathing calmed and she laughed huskily. She raised herself on an elbow and ran a cool nail down his chest. "Better get some rest, Tiger. We have the whole weekend to get through."

Chapter 39

Sterling Thorne could not erase the grin from his face. He knew he must look like an idiot, smiling and laughing like a six-year-old boy, but he couldn't help it. He was reading the text of the charges that had been filed against First Lieutenant Nicholas Neumann USMCR for the first time in its entirety. And he was enjoying it. One section was of particular interest, and this he read again and again.

"... *whereby defendant did willfully and with malice aforethought batter the plaintiff. Said plaintiff did suffer severe bruising to the lower back and hip, two ruptured disks at the 14th and 15th vertebrae, a class-one subdural hematoma, gross swelling of the testicles and concomitant edema.*"

That last one made Thorne fidget in his chair. "*Gross swelling of the testicles and concomitant edema.*" Old Jack Keely had got himself a thorough going-over; his back was half broken, his skull near fractured, and worst, his balls had been throttled so hard they were swollen the size of grapefruits. Not only that, the fucker's *cojones* were leaking.

Thorne flipped to the next page, and then back again. Nowhere in the file did it specify the reason for the attack. Nowhere did it say what had gotten Neumann so riled at this man Keely, whom the record listed as a "civilian defense contractor." Read "spook," Thorne corrected.

Earlier in the day he had finally received the full copy of Neumann's military personnel file. A buddy had FedExed it over from Headquarters Marine Corps in D.C. The same guy had faxed him a copy of Neumann's discharge and the final ruling of the board of inquiry that he'd used to set the kid running. Frankly speaking, Thorne wished he'd gotten his eyes on the whole dossier before he'd started putting pressure on the kid. The last thing he needed was a list of injuries like those suffered by Mr. Jack Keely.

Thorne closed the file. Once more he ran the highlights through his head. Neumann had zoomed through OCS, finishing as honor graduate. During Basic School, he had maxed every physical fitness test he'd taken and gotten himself a billet to U.S. Army Ranger school. He'd finished the course, naturally, and earned his tabs. Not at the top this time, but in a class that boasted a seventy percent attrition rate, just finishing the damn thing in one piece was impressive. Next came an assignment to active duty at Camp Pendleton as executive officer of an infantry platoon. That lasted a year. Then he disappeared. No word on his actions for three years. No fitness reports, no senior officer appraisals, no requests for transfer, no nothing. Just the board of inquiry's summary and a copy of his separation papers. Dishonorable discharge. No wonder the kid came overseas. Probably couldn't get a job in the States with that monkey on his back.

Thorne grinned in anticipation. Once Wolfgang Kaiser read this report, he'd be too frightened for his physical safety to keep Neumann working by his side. Who cared about the dishonorable discharge? It paled in comparison to Neumann's capacity to inflict bodily injury. In theory, Thorne had Nick by the short and curlies. All he had to do was tighten his grip. With it, Neumann could be cajoled, convinced, coerced, whatever, into helping him nail Ali Mevlevi. Or could he? Thorne was beginning to realize that Neumann was just as stubborn as he was. A frontal assault might not work.

A door behind him swung open and clattered against the wall.

"Sterling Thorne, good evening," said Terry Strait. "Or should I say good morning, seeing as how it's after midnight." He stood with his hands on his hips and a monstrous shit-eating grin on his face.

Thorne swung around in his chair and stared at the beaming figure in the doorway. Didn't the guy know how to knock? "Hello, Terry. Back so soon?"

"Afraid so. Mission accomplished."

"And what mission might that be? To burrow your nose as far into the ambassador's snatch as possible before she paws you away?"

"She sends you her best regards too." Strait walked in and sat himself down on Thorne's desk. "We enjoyed a lively evening together. A glass of sherry at the embassy, dinner at the Bellevue Palace. We were joined by one of our Swiss counterparts, Franz Studer."

"Counterpart, my ass. That man is the tightest-lipped, slowest-moving prosecutor I have ever come across."

"Slow moving? Maybe. Tight-lipped?" Strait shook his head. "You must not know him very well. Tonight, Mr. Studer was positively gabby. In fact, he couldn't *stop* talking."

"No doubt you plan on passing on his words of wisdom?"

"You were his favorite topic of conversation. He had a few good yarns up his sleeve. An unannounced visit to the Chairman of the United Swiss Bank. Hijacking an elevator, brutalizing a secretary, and then attempting to blackmail Wolfgang Kaiser. He felt strongly that this was a violation of the accord between his government and ours. Madam Ambassador was in full agreement."

Thorne leaned back in his chair and rolled his eyes. Best let the good reverend have his moment in the pulpit. "Go on."

"Was that your intention? To expose his son's death from an overdose of heroin unless he gave up Ali Mevlevi? And I thought you didn't like *me*."

"To be honest, I don't."

Strait squinted incredulously. "What is wrong with you? Are you at war with the entire world?"

Thorne laughed. "You just might have a point there. Maybe I am at that."

Strait laughed, too. "I hope you won't mind too much, but since Madam Ambassador's spirits were already flagging and the evening more or less ruined, I couldn't resist firing a couple broadsides of my own. The best time to finish a man off is when he's down on his knees and begging. No mercy. Right, Thorne? Isn't that one of your maxims?"

"Well, Terry, you got me horny with anticipation. I'm sitting here all hot and bothered. So either fuck me or tuck that big dick back into your pants and get the hell out of here."

"With pleasure. I think I'll opt for the former choice, so stand up and bend over. That is the way you country boys like it, isn't it?"

Thorne jumped from his chair and thrust an open hand at Strait's throat.

Strait deflected the outstretched arm and hopped away from the desk. He slid a chair between himself and the irate agent. "Just so we're clear on things, Thorne, let me recite the charges. One, strong-arming one of this country's most respected businessmen. Two, convincing Studer to place Mevlevi's account number on the USB surveillance list without the approval of the director. And three, something else I learned yesterday, harassing a U.S. citizen on foreign soil. A Mr. Nicholas Neumann."

The name stopped Thorne in his tracks. He hadn't figured on the kid being a tattler.

Strait said, "I have it on good authority that twice you've stopped and harassed this individual with the sole intent of gathering information on Ali Mevlevi."

"Whose authority is that? Did Neumann call you up and cry on your shoulder?"

Strait looked surprised. "Neumann? Of course not. The kid is probably scared stiff. You need to look a little closer to home." He offered Thorne a smug smile. "Your driver, Agent Wadkins. Next time, make sure you choose your accomplices with greater care. Is it a surprise to learn that your fellow agents don't share your zeal for flouting the laws of the country in which you're stationed? That they don't like disobeying orders?"

Thorne was relieved that Neumann hadn't ratted him out. The kid represented his last chance at nailing Mevlevi. As for Wadkins, he'd kick his pansy ass later. "Is that what this is about? Breaking a few rules to get a job done?"

"No, Sterling. This is about Eastern Lightning. We won't let you put the operation into more danger than you already have."

"More danger?" Thorne felt like falling to his knees and clawing the ground. These boys would never understand what it took to get a job done. "It seems to me I am the only man trying to save this op. You're ready to sit on your hands for the next six months praying that someday you'll receive a speck of information about his shipments."

"And you're ready to flush all our work down the toilet so you can nab a few guns and crow about stopping the next Colonel Qadhafi. This is about drugs, Sterling, not arms, and it's our opinion that you're out of control. This operation does not belong exclusively to you. You don't have the patience necessary to see it out."

"Patience?" cried Thorne, as if he possessed carloads of the stuff. "Bullshit. I'm a realist. The only one for miles around."

"We haven't heard from Jester for ten days. If he's been compromised, if he's dead —" Strait took a breath, "and I pray to the Lord that is not the case — it is because of you and you alone."

"Jester is my agent. I've run him since he went in eighteen months ago. Any decision I make, he knows about. He can cover his ass when the time comes."

"Like Mr. Becker covered his?"

Thorne bit his lip. Only the sharp pain kept him from beating the living hell out of Terry

Strait. "He was only doing what his conscience told him."

Strait smiled smugly. "Believe that if you want to. From this moment onward, Eastern Lightning is officially my baby. Per the director's instructions. Not only will I handle communications with Jester, I'll be running the whole show." He withdrew an envelope from his jacket and tossed it onto the desk beside Thorne. "From now on we're doing things my way. If you're caught talking to Neumann or anyone else at USB, you're getting a one-way ticket back to the States. Destination of your choice 'cause you're history."

Thorne picked up the white envelope and looked at it. He knew what the letter would say. Take a step down the ladder. Do as we tell you and keep your big yap closed. He slid his thumb under the flap and tore it open. A fax from the director's office. Shit, not even a letter. He read the text. It confirmed what he suspected, what he should have guessed the second he saw Strait's grinning mug. Demotion to second banana.

Thorne tossed the letter into the trash. "So this is how it's going to be?"

"No," answered Strait. *"This is how it is."*

"Congratulations, Terry. Welcome back to the field." Thorne offered his hand. "Or have you ever been out of admin before?"

Strait waved away the hand. "Clear out of *my* office now. Get your crap and move.

There's a desk for you across the hall. The one next to the trash can."

"Terry, you can be a real s.o.b.," Thorne said mockingly.

"It'll do you good to take orders again. And believe me, I have plenty for you. Tomorrow, I'm seeing Franz Studer to go over how we might patch up the mess you've made."

"Be sure to give him your bank account in case any of his buddies want to give you an early Christmas present."

"Fuck you, Thorne."

"Careful now, Terry. God won't let you into heaven if you use the *F* word."

Strait stalked out of the office.

Sterling Thorne placed his hands behind his head and looked out the window. Snow fell, dusting the cars parked along the street. A low cloud cover gave the night a downy softness. For a moment, he considered packing it in. Strait wanted Eastern Lightning, let him have it.

"No, goddammit!" Thorne said out loud, crashing his fist onto the desktop in booming punctuation. "The Pasha is mine."

Thorne watched as the good reverend shuffled down the pathway, afraid to lift a foot too high off the walk for fear he'd discover a hidden sheet of ice. Slow and cautious. Mr. Routine. Move him to Zurich, give him responsibility for the operation, what's that going to get you? A surefire recipe for disaster. If Jester wasn't in danger before, he sure as hell was now.

One thing was for certain. He would not work under Terry Strait. No sir-fuckin'-ree Bob!

So deep was he in his thoughts that he didn't hear the telephone in the other room until it had rung a second time. He walked into Wadkins's office and picked up the phone.

"Yeah," he answered, too tired to wonder who the hell was calling at one in the morning.

"Sterling Thorne, please."

"This is Thorne." He heard money being added to a pay phone.

"Agent Thorne, this is Joe Habib."

Thorne felt as though he'd been struck by lightning. "*Jester?* That you? You're alive?" Thought Mevlevi had taken care of you, he almost added. "Why the hell haven't you checked in? You've missed two call-ins."

"I don't have enough coins to talk for a long time, so listen. I am in Brindisi, Italy. We're unloading over two tons of product. It's been secreted into a shipment of cedar paneling. We are bringing it over the border in two or three days' time. Through Chiasso and then to Zurich."

"Slow down, boy." Thorne checked the window again. Strait rounded the corner and disappeared from view. "Joe, take this number. It's for my private phone. Don't call the main number again. Ever. The line may not be secure. We have to chance it with a cellular. Contact me directly. Is that clear?" Thorne read off the number to his cellular.

"Why? I was told in case of emerg—"

"Don't argue with me, Joe. Do as you're told."

"Yes sir, I understand."

A bell bleated repeatedly in Thorne's earpiece. Jester was running out of change. "Now tell me again about this shipment. What are you doing in Italy?"

"It's Mevlevi. He doesn't trust the Makdisis anymore. I'm supposed to be his watchdog. Thorne, we finally got our break. The shipment is coming to Zurich."

"Where is he?" Thorne asked, unable to keep the desperation from his voice. "Where is Mevlevi? What about his army?"

"Mevlevi is —"

"Joe?" The line was dead.

Thorne put the phone down. And though he hadn't been able to question Jester about Mevlevi or the arms, he felt as if God had just whispered in his ear. A shipment was coming into Zurich. Hallelujah!

Thorne ran to his office and set to work with a determined glee. Working methodically, he gathered all the papers he would need. Transcripts of Jester's messages, historical files on Mevlevi, "top secret" intercepts from the Defense Intelligence Agency confirming wire transfers, both incoming and outgoing, to and from Mevlevi's accounts at USB. Anything and everything that might be useful in the coming days was crammed into his worn brief-case. This done, he scribbled a note to Strait stating his decision to voluntarily retire from the case. "Adios, Terry," he wrote. "She's all yours."

Thorne threw on his overcoat, grabbed his tired briefcase, and marched down the narrow path leading from Wildbachstrasse 58. As he walked, one word buzzed and crackled in his head. It rang sweet and clear in his ears, and tasted even better on his lips. It promised him the world. It gave him another chance at Neumann and a final shot at Mevlevi. Oh, God, how he loved that word!

Redemption.

Chapter 40

Nick had been seated at his desk exactly three minutes when Reto Feller telephoned.

"The Adler Bank has crossed over thirty percent," came the frantic voice.

"I hadn't heard."

"Get in at a decent hour. Everyone knows."

Nick checked his watch. It was five minutes past seven. The bank was deserted. "Bad news."

"A disaster. Konig needs three percent to get his seats. We have to stop the bastard. Have you started selling?"

"I'm starting now."

"Get to it. Call me at ten. Let me know how many orders you have on the floor."

Feller hung up before Nick could answer.

Three hours later, Nick's eyes were burning from the glare of the computer screen. One stack of portfolio printouts sat on the floor, rising as high as his desktop. Another stack sat directly in front of him. Each portfolio belonged to an investor who had given the bank discretionary power to trade his account. Nick's job was to sell fifty percent of the Swiss franc value of the equities in each of these portfolios and issue an order to buy USB shares for the equivalent amount. So far that morning he'd "liberated" — as Martin Maeder encouraged him to think of his task — over twenty-seven million Swiss francs from seventy numbered accounts. That came out to twenty-three accounts an hour, or one every two minutes forty-five seconds. Essentially, it was piecework once you got the hang of it.

Nick reached across his desk and picked off the next portfolio. This one had a name. Surprise, surprise. An Italian, one Renato Castilli. Nick flipped the pages. He would sell off Metallgesellschaft, Morgan Stanley, Nestlé, and Lonrho. Two of them were dogs. No harm done. He typed the sell orders into Medusa and passed them to the floor. In two minutes he had liberated over Sfr. 400,000 from Signor Castilli's portfolio. An order to purchase a corresponding amount of USB shares was duly entered. *Finito!*

Nick pushed back his chair and stretched his frame. He needed a break. His eyes were watery and his back was stiff. Five minutes. Visit the bathroom, get a drink of water. Then back to the mill. He was a machine.

A conference call with Hambros Bank in London was set for eleven. Hambros held roughly ten million pounds' worth of USB stock. Nick had the spiel memorized cold by now. USB would cut costs by offering early retirement and firing nonessential staff, up ef-

516

ficiency through increased computerization, create a merchant banking division, and expand its trading operations. The result: an increase of between two and four percent to their operating ratios within twelve months. After that, who knew? Bankruptcy or a banner year.

At twelve, he had a lunch date with Sylvia. She had promised to bring more monthly activity reports filed by his father from the Los Angeles office. The first binder she had supplied had been a bust. Nineteen seventy-five was too long ago. He needed everything she could find for the period from January 1978 through January 1980. She seemed to be having no problems getting ahold of the reports. If she was scared about being asked why she needed them, she hadn't told him.

Nick closed his eyes and for a second was blessed with the scent of her skin. He returned his gaze to the monitor in front of him, but instead of perusing the holdings of a numbered account, he was watching Sylvia all over again, replaying the golden moments of their weekend together, already three days and half a century past. He saw her reflection in the Chronometrie Beyer as she pointed to an obscenely expensive diamond-encrusted wristwatch and raised her eyebrows in comic disbelief, though he was sure he spotted a glimmer of envy, too; he was standing next to her in Teuscher as she popped a *petite gour-*

mandise into her mouth and proclaimed it *wunderbar;* he was lying against her warm body among the tousled sheets of her bed after they'd made love, counting the shades of blond in her hair. He was staring transfixed at the perfect curve of her naked breasts as she writhed and whispered, and then collapsed onto him, suddenly silent.

Nick had been seeing Sylvia for two weeks now. He kept expecting his infatuation with her to die down. But that hadn't happened. Each time he saw her, he suffered a moment of sheer anxiety, scared that she might inform him that their relationship was over. Then she would smile and kiss him on the cheek, and his fears would subside. She was constantly on his mind. If he heard something funny, he wanted to share it with her; if he read an interesting article, he wanted to call her and tell her to read it, too. But despite their intimacy, he was often unable to figure how she looked at things. Like him, Sylvia guarded a part of herself hidden, a part he knew he'd never discover.

The phone rang. It was Felix Bernath from the floor of the exchange. "You have a fill on five thousand shares of USB at three seventy," he said. Nick thanked him and picked up another portfolio. He flipped back the cover page and began looking for likely sales candidates, category Q–Z. The phone rang again and he answered it immediately.

"Another fill for me, Felix?" he said sarcastically.

"What's that, Nick? Filling sandbags, are you?"

Nick recognized the insouciant patter. "Hello, Peter. What do you want? I'm busy."

"Expiation, chum. I'm calling to make up. I was dead wrong to ask you what I did. I knew it then and I know it now. I'm sorry."

Nick had lost his capacity for forgiveness. "That's nice, Peter. Maybe we can get together when this contest is over. Until then, forget it. Keep your distance, okay?"

"Such the hard-liner. I expected as much. I didn't call just to chat. I have something for you. I'm sitting here enjoying a double espresso at Sprüngli, second floor. Why not come and join me?"

"What, are you kidding? You expect me to skip out of here because you have *something for me?*"

"I'm not really asking. I'm telling you. This time you have to trust me. I assure you it's in your best interest. And the bank's, for that matter — Kaiser's, not Konig's. Meet me here as quickly as possible. It took me three minutes to walk here; it will take you four. On your mark. Get set. Go."

Four minutes later, Nick's snow-capped head mounted the stairs leading to Sprüngli's main dining hall. The room was filled with

519

midday habitués, mainly women of a certain age, impeccably dressed and bored to distraction. An old rumor suggested that women breakfasting alone on Sprüngli's second floor between the hours of nine and eleven were seeking the company of gentlemen for pursuits rather less genteel than shopping.

Sprecher signaled to Nick from a corner table. An empty demitasse sat in front of him. "Espresso?"

Nick remained standing. "What's on your mind? I can't be away from my desk for long."

"First, I'm sorry. I want you to forget that I ever asked about those blasted shares. Konig said you were too good a target to pass up. He hit on me to give you a call. Point me in the right direction and I march. That's me. The loyal soldier."

"That's a pathetic excuse."

"Come on, Nick. First couple of days on the job. Eager to do anything to please the wallahs upstairs. Surely, you know what I'm talking about. Christ, you practically did the same thing yourself."

"I didn't try to betray a friend."

"Look, it was a vulgar proposition. Case closed. Won't happen again."

Nick pulled out a chair and sat down. He ran a hand through his hair, and flakes of snow tumbled onto the table. "Let's get to it. What do you have for me?"

Sprecher pushed a white sheet of paper toward him. "Read this. I found it on my desk this morning. I'd say it evens the score between us."

Nick pulled the sheet closer. It was a photocopy and not a very good one. The sheet listed the names of five institutional shareholders of USB stock, their approximate holdings, the portfolio manager, and his telephone number. He raised his head abruptly. "I typed this sheet."

Sprecher smiled, victorious. "Bingo. Your initials are at the top. 'NXM.' Whoever copied this did a shoddy job. You can see half of the USB logo."

Nick looked at Peter skeptically. "Where did you get this?"

"Like I said, it fell on my desk." Sprecher fumbled for a cigarette. Something in his face weakened. "If you must know, George von Graffenried threw it at me. He's Konig's right-hand man at the bank. George mumbled something about an investment finally yielding a dividend. It seems, chum, you have a very naughty mole in your organization."

"Jesus Christ," Nick muttered under his breath. "This sheet is from my desk. Only a few people have seen it."

"Only takes one."

Nick counted off the names of those he knew had copies of the sheet: Feller, Maeder, Rita Sutter, and of course, Wolfgang Kaiser. Who else might have seen it? Immediately,

Nick recalled the guilty expression of a lumbering prowler caught *in flagrante* stealing a glance at his papers. Armin Schweitzer had been so emboldened — or so desperate — as to even request a copy of this very sheet. Nick's cheeks colored with anger and embarrassment.

Peter took back the sheet, folded it neatly, and replaced it in his jacket pocket. "I'll have to contact these investors. No way around that, is there? But, I've got a feeling a few of these chaps may be tied up this morning. Best wait until later this afternoon or early tomorrow. You know these intercontinental connections. Devilishly poor at times."

Nick stood and put out his hand. "Thanks, Peter. I'd say this evens the score."

Sprecher shook it uneasily, an odd expression straining his features. "Still haven't figured out whether I'm a hero or a whore."

Nick rushed back to the bank, his mind boiling with conspiracy. He passed Hugo Brunner without so much as a hello and took an elevator reserved for clients directly to the Fourth Floor. "Two can play at this game," he whispered to himself.

Inside his office, Nick made a beeline for his desk. He shoved the endless stack of client portfolios to one side and positioned himself squarely before the computer. He exited Medusa and logged on to Cerberus, where he accessed the word-processing software. The noble struggle to "repatriate" shares of USB would have to wait a few minutes. He had a more urgent calling: ferreting out a traitor.

First he accessed the list of institutional shareholders holding blocks of USB shares. It was the same list now in Peter Sprecher's possession — the list that he was certain had been taken from his desk. Once it was on the screen, he erased the date and all pertinent shareholder information: name, phone number, address, and finally contact person. He typed in today's date and moved to the area reserved for shareholder information. In this space, he added the name of a heretofore unknown shareholder — a group Martin Maeder, Reto Feller, and he had failed to locate during their initial screening. He chewed on his pen, trying hard to recollect the institution's name. Ah, yes, he had it. *The Widows and Orphans Fund of Zurich.* He typed in the name and next to it wrote "140,000 shares held in trust at J. P. Morgan, Zurich. Contact Edith Emmenegger."

Happy with this piece of fiction, Nick inserted a piece of USB stationery into his laser printer and printed the document. He took it in his hands and reviewing the information, saw that he had forgotten to list the phone number of the good Mrs. Emmenegger. Whose number could he use? His own was out of the question. The prefix for the USB

Personalhaus was the same as the bank's. Only one other number came to mind. He called it and waited for the answer. As he hoped, a machine picked up. A woman's voice said, "You have reached 555-3131. No one can take your call at this time. Please leave your name, phone number, and any message after the tone. Thank you."

"*Thank you,* Sylvia," Nick whispered. "Or should I say 'Frau Emmenegger'?" He typed in her phone number and reprinted the document. Once more he held it up for examination. Everything was in place. To authenticate it, he jotted some notes in the margin. "Called at 10 and 12." He added yesterday's date and "No answer. Message left." It was complete. He marched around his desk paper in hand, surveying where to put it for best effect. Somewhere obvious, but not out of place. He settled on tucking the document under the bottom left side of the telephone so that only the U and the S of the letterhead were visible. He stepped away from the desk and admired his *petit chef-d'oeuvre,* his little masterpiece. His gem of misinformation.

Wolfgang Kaiser circled his office, enjoying a Cuban cigar while listening to Nicholas Neumann relate how he had convinced Hambros Bank to vote with the USB slate of directors at the general assembly. "That is wonderful news," he said when his assistant had finished.

"Where does that leave us, then?"

Neumann's voice blurted from the speaker-phone. "At around forty-five percent. Feller will have the exact tally. Adler passed thirty percent this morning, but it looks like their purchasing power has begun to dry up."

"Thank God for that," replied Kaiser, eager to align the deities on his side. "And the count? Have you arranged the meeting?"

"Bad news. The earliest date he's available is the morning of the assembly. Can you give him a half hour at ten o'clock?"

"Out of the question. I have a breakfast with the board at eight sharp." Senn had always been a pain in the ass. The gall of the man! Even to suggest a meeting the same day as the assembly.

Neumann said, "He's in America until a few days before. The count says ten o'clock."

Kaiser realized he had few options open. "All right, then, ten o'clock. But keep on him. See if you can't move it up a day or two."

"Yessir."

"And Neumann. I need to see you privately. Come down in ten minutes."

"Yessir."

Kaiser terminated the call. The boy was a wizard. Nothing less. Hambros committing this morning; and yesterday afternoon, Banker's Trust — the cagiest outfit on the street. Neumann had argued to the rocket scientists in Manhattan that USB shares — given current management, of course — were an effective hedge against Banker's Trust's own volatile earnings. They'd swallowed his argument hook, line, and sinker. It was nothing short of miraculous. One of Konig's fire-spewing brethren, disciples of the "lose a hand, double the next" school of trading, and they had committed to the boring old farts at USB. Kaiser whooped. A fucking miracle!

He picked up the phone and called Feller to obtain an exact vote count. He wrote the figures on his desktop blotter. USB forty-six percent. Adler thirty point four percent. Christ, it would be close. Mevlevi's loan would end all speculation. Kaiser was prepared to do all demanded of him to see that his Turkish friend coughed up the money required to keep the United Swiss Bank free from Klaus Konig's grip. If it was necessary for Neumann to shepherd the man about his business, then so be it. That was the least problematic of Kaiser's devoirs.

Kaiser sat in his chair, considering how to tell Neumann about his relationship with Mevlevi. Getting around Sterling Thorne's accusations would be difficult. Had Neumann's father been witness to Kaiser's blatant, even theatrical mendacity, the man would have resigned on the spot. In fact, he had on two occasions. Both times, Kaiser's silver tongue had been required to assuage Alex Neumann's wounded conscience. "A genuine misunderstanding. We had no idea the client was dealing in stolen armaments. It will never happen again. Faulty information, Alex. Sorry."

Kaiser frowned at the memory. Thank goodness, Nicholas was more pragmatic. Damned difficult to get from strenuously denying one's knowledge of an individual, even going so far as to purposely mispronounce his name, to professing a twenty-year business relationship with him. But Kaiser had only to think of the actions Neumann had taken to protect Mevlevi from Thorne's surveillance list to feel better. If the young man was half as smart as anyone thought, he'd have guessed it already.

A buzzer sounded on his telephone. Rita Sutter's mellifluous voice informed him that Mr. Neumann had arrived. He told her to send him in.

Wolfgang Kaiser greeted Nick in the center of the office. "Fantastic news this morning, Neumann. Just great." He laced his good arm around Nick's shoulder and guided him to the couch. "Cigar?"

"No thank you," said Nick. Alarm bells sounded in his head.

"Coffee, tea, espresso?"

"Mineral water would be fine."

"Mineral water it is," Kaiser enthused, as if no answer could have pleased him more. He walked to the open doors and told Rita Sutter to bring a mineral water and a double espresso.

"Neumann," he said, "I need you to run a special errand for me. Something very important. Requires your gifted touch." Kaiser seated himself on the couch and blew out a cloud of smoke. "I need a diplomat. Someone with manners. A little worldly experience."

Nick sat down and nodded unsurely. Whatever Kaiser was up to had to be big; Nick had never seen him so friendly.

"An important client of the bank is arriving tomorrow morning," said Kaiser. "He'll require a chaperon to help him transact his business throughout the day."

"Will he be coming to the bank?"

"At some point, I'm certain he will, yes. First, though, I'd like you to greet him at the airport."

"At the airport?" Nick rubbed the nape of his neck. He didn't feel well. Too long in front of the computer. "You're aware that we've only just begun implementing Martin Maeder's sales plan. I've got another five hundred dossiers to get through."

"I understand," Kaiser said graciously, "and I appreciate your diligence. Continue on that for the rest of today. You can finish off tomorrow evening, day after that, all right?"

Nick wasn't thrilled at the prospect, but he nodded his assent anyway.

"Good. Now then, some details about the

man you'll be meeting." Kaiser took a long drag off the cigar. Several times, he began to speak and then stopped, first to pluck a speck of tobacco from his mouth, next to adjust his position on the couch. Finally, he said, "Nicholas, I'm afraid I lied to you the other day. Rather I lied to that bastard Thorne. There was no choice, really . . . given the circumstances. Should've told you earlier. Don't know why I didn't. I know you would've understood. We're cut from the same cloth, you and I. We do what's necessary to get the job done. Am I right?"

Nick nodded once, enthusiastically guarding the Chairman's eye. Kaiser was suffering under the mounting pressure. Like a worn truss, his face betrayed a constant interior strain. His eyes, normally clear and confident, were puffy and decorated by dark circles etched into his chalky skin.

"I know Ali Mevlevi," said Kaiser. "This man Thorne is after. The man you call the Pasha. In fact, I know him well. One of my first clients in Beirut. I wouldn't expect you to be aware that I opened our representative office in Beirut a very long time ago."

"Back in seventy-eight, wasn't it?"

"Exactly." Kaiser smiled briefly and Nick knew he was flattered. "Mr. Mevlevi was then, and is to this day, a well-respected business-man in Lebanon and throughout the entire Middle East."

"Sterling Thorne accused the man of being a heroin smuggler."

"I've known Ali Mevlevi for twenty years. I've never heard the slightest hint that he was involved with drugs. Mevlevi is active in commodities, rugs, and textiles. He's a well-respected member of the business community."

That's the second time you've said that, thought Nick, suppressing a sarcastic grin. Marco Cerruti certainly respected Mevlevi — to the point of suffering a petit mal seizure upon the mention of his name. Sterling Thorne respected Mevlevi — so much that he came charging into the bank like a wounded bull rhino. How the hell did the people act who *didn't* respect him?

"No need to apologize," said Nick. "It's best to keep the confidence of your clients. It's certainly none of Thorne's business."

"Thorne wants us all as members of his private constabulary. You saw the picture of my son. Do you think I could work with a fiend who gained his living from the international commerce of death? Thorne's mistaken about our Mevlevi. I'm sure you'll learn that tomorrow when you meet the man. Remember, Neumann, it's hardly our job to be policemen."

Not that old chestnut, thought Nick. Now he was really feeling sick. And sicker still when he heard himself mutter, "I agree fully." The defender of the faith had spoken.

Kaiser puffed his cigar and patted him on the knee. "I knew you'd see things clearly. Mevlevi will be arriving by private jet tomorrow morning at eleven o'clock. You'll be there to meet him. Car and driver provided, of course. I'm sure he'll have plenty of errands to run."

Nick stood, eager to get back to his own cloistered den. "Will that be all?"

"That's all, Neumann. Get back to Maeder's project. Have Rita order you some lunch in. Anyplace you like. Why not try the Kronenhalle?"

"I have plans . . ." Nick began.

"Oh yes, I completely forgot," Kaiser said. "Well then, back to work for us all."

As Nick walked out of the grand office, he asked himself when he had mentioned his luncheon plans to the Chairman.

Chapter 41

"Were you able to get the reports?" Nick asked as he crossed the threshold to Sylvia Schon's apartment. It was eight o'clock and he had come directly from the bank.

"What? No hello? No 'How was your afternoon?' " She gave him a kiss on the cheek. "It's nice to see you, too, Mr. Neumann."

Nick walked down the hallway, taking off his overcoat. "Sylvia, were you able to get the monthly activity reports?"

"I said I'd help you, didn't I?" Sylvia picked up the polished briefcase leaning against her sofa. She unbuckled the cover and drew out two thick binders, colored the same faded yellow as the one they had read several nights before. She handed one to him. "Satisfied? I'm sorry I forgot to get them in time for lunch."

Nick lifted one and read the coding on its spine. *January through March 1978.* He shot a glance at the other file. It was entitled *April–June 1978.* At least one thing had gone right today. "I'm sorry if I was rude."

Nick was tired and irritable. His only break the entire day had been the scant half hour he'd spent lunching with Sylvia at Kropf Bierhalle. Time to consume a sausage, french fries, and two Cokes, but hardly enough to get around to asking her if she had mentioned their lunch date to someone. They had agreed it best to keep their relationship quiet. Not secret — for *secret* was a dirty word. Just quiet. Neither had thought to ask what answer should be given if someone were to question them about their seeing each other. Or if they had, they hadn't dared ask it.

Sylvia stood on her tiptoes and rubbed his cheek. "Want to talk about it? You don't look so great."

Nick knew he looked haggard. He'd been getting by on five hours of sleep a night. When, that is, he could sleep at all. "Just the regular grind. Things are pretty crazy up on the Fourth Floor. The general assembly is only five days away. Konig's biting at our heels."

"What does Kaiser have you doing?"

"The usual," Nick explained, aware that he was doing everything but. Regardless of his feelings for Sylvia, he couldn't bring himself to confess the larceny being perpetrated on the Fourth Floor. Some things he had to keep to himself. "Lining up votes. Answering phone calls from investment analysts. We're all feeling the pressure. It's crunch time."

"*Everyone* is feeling Konig's pressure," she said. "Not just you big shots on the Fourth Floor. No one wants Konig to get his seats. Change is frightening, especially for the little guys underneath the Emperor's Lair."

"Too bad we can't order every employee of the bank to purchase a hundred shares of our stock," Nick said. "If they don't have the money — no problem. We can subtract it from their future salaries. That would go a long way toward fending off the Adler Bank. At least then I wouldn't have to —" He bit off his words in mid-sentence.

"Then you wouldn't have to what?" asked Sylvia. Her eyes flickered, and Nick could see the scent of scandal was rich in her nose.

"Then *we* wouldn't have to fight so damned hard against Konig," he shot back, not missing a beat.

"How does it look?"

"Forty-six percent for the good guys, thirty percent for the bad guys. Just keep your fingers crossed Konig doesn't launch a full-scale hostile bid."

"What's stopping him?"

"Cash. Or lack of it. He'd have to offer a significant premium to the market price, but if he did, enough shares are in the hands of the arbs that he'd have no problem capturing sixty-six percent of the votes. Even our supporters would defect to Konig. That would give him full control of the board. A one-way ticket to Valhalla for Wolfgang Kaiser."

"And for the rest of us?" demanded Sylvia. "What about us? You know very well the first jobs cut after any merger are overlapping staff functions: accounting, treasury, logistics. I can't imagine that the Adler Bank will have any need for two personnel directors in their finance department."

"Sylvia, don't worry. The battle we're fighting is to keep Konig off the board. No one is talking about an outright takeover."

"Not yet they're not." She squinted her eyes as if she didn't like what she saw. "You'll never understand what this bank means to me. The time I've put in. The hope I've wasted on this stupid job."

"Wasted?" he asked. "Why wasted?"

"You wouldn't understand," she said disgustedly. "You can't. It's that simple. You can never know what it's like to work twice the hours of your male colleagues, to consistently do better work, and to see everyone around you promoted quicker because they have hair on their chest and speak with a deeper voice. Imagine, being passed over for client meetings, just so men can lie to each other about who they've seduced. Imagine what it's like having to endure a hundred compliments a day about how nice you look — *'Isn't that a new scarf?' 'Why, Fräulein Schon, you look particularly fetching today.'* Or, to be asked your opinion about a proposed project, and when it doesn't quite jibe with Mr. Senior Vice President's, have it dismissed with a polite smile and a wink. A wink, dammit! Has Armin Schweitzer ever winked at you?"

Stunned by the verbal barrage, Nick dug his

chin into his neck and said "No."

"I have to go twice as far, twice as fast. You make a mistake and the powers that be say, 'Of course, happens all the time.' I make a mistake, they say, 'Typical woman. What'd ya expect? Chuckle, chuckle, yuck, yuck.' And all the time they're thinking 'My, wouldn't I like to have a go at her?' "

Sylvia met Nick's eyes and gave him a smile of dignified resignation. "I haven't put up with this nonsense for nine years only to have some bastard come along and kick me out my own front door. If Konig takes over USB, my life is shot."

For a few seconds, there was silence between them. Then she said, "I'm sorry. I didn't mean to come on so strong."

"Don't be sorry. The scary thing is, everything you said is true."

"I'm glad you realize it. You're probably the only one at the bank. The boys on the Fourth Floor prefer their women like Rita Sutter. She's been Kaiser's secretary forever, making his lunch appointments, fixing his coffee. She should be a senior vice president. How can anyone put up with that kind of abuse for so long?"

"People make their own choices, Sylvia. Don't feel sorry for Rita Sutter. If she's there, it's for a reason." He recalled the photo he had seen in Marco Cerruti's apartment. Kaiser kissing Rita Sutter's hand. Maybe he had beaten out Klaus Konig for her affections.

"I don't feel sorry for her. I just wonder what she's getting out of it."

"That's her concern. Not ours."

Nick walked to the sofa and sat down. "Christ," he said sharply. "I almost forgot."

Sylvia came over to him. "Don't scare me. What is it?"

"If you get a funny message on your phone machine tomorrow, don't erase it." Nick went over his meeting with Peter Sprecher and the discovery that a mole at USB was supplying the Adler Bank with information crucial to the successful defense of the United Swiss Bank. He shared his suspicions as to the culprit's identity.

"If it is Schweitzer," Sylvia declared angrily, "I swear I will personally kick him in the you know where."

"If it is him, you have my permission. For now, though, save any message that sounds funny. You'll know it when you hear it."

"I promise."

After dinner, Nick retrieved the files from the living room and laid them on the dining room table. He waited for Sylvia to rejoin him, then brought out his father's agenda for 1978.

Nick said, "The first time I read through my father's entries, it was just out of nostalgia, you know, to see if he had left any personal notes that might help me get a handle on who he really was. He didn't — which was just like my dad. He was all business. It was only after I'd looked at the agendas a few times that I picked up on the vibe of fear that ran through the last pages of 1979. Going back through them, I saw that the only places where my father indicated any type of emotional response to his work were in reference to a Mr. Allen Soufi and this company Goldluxe."

"Are the two related?"

"No. At least, I don't think so. Soufi was a private banking client, a guy who maintained a numbered account with the bank. He wanted my father to help with some iffy business proposition. I don't know any more than that."

"Let's look for Soufi then," Sylvia suggested.

"The first mention of Soufi is on April 15, 1978." Nick flipped open the agenda to that date. His father had written, *"Dinner. A. Soufi. The Bistro. 215 Canon Dr."*

Sylvia looked at the page. "Is that all?"

"Until later, yeah." Nick thought of the indignant comments left by his father, *"Soufi is undesirable. Bastard threatened me,"* then opened the file containing the monthly activity reports for the period January through March 1978. "Regardless, we've got to start at the beginning of the year. There might be a mention of him earlier. My father had to send the head office copies of new account information for every client he brought in. If he brought in Soufi, there'll be copies of account registration, name, address, signature cards, the works."

"And Goldluxe?"

"They don't show up till later."

Nick read the January activity report from first page to last. He learned that the results for the L.A. rep office for 1977 were thirty-three percent above forecast; that in 1978, a newly hired secretary could expect to earn $750 a month; and that the U.S. prime rate was sitting up in the stratosphere at sixteen percent.

The activity report for February contained a revised pro forma budget, a third request for greater office space, and a proposal to open a two-man San Francisco office.

Nick pinched the bridge of his nose. "Where is he, Sylvia? Where is Soufi?"

Sylvia rubbed his back. "He'll be here, sweetheart. Be patient. We're almost finished with this month's report."

They returned to the section highlighting new business. Sylvia ran her finger down the list of names listed as new clients. A Mr. Alphons Knups, a Max Keller, a Mrs. Ethel Ward. Suddenly, she shouted, "Look, there it is." She pointed to the last name on the list.

Nick pulled the file closer. Sure enough, there it was. *Mr. A. Soufi.* A star had been placed next to his name. Nick found the star at the bottom of the page and read that Soufi was a referral from Mr. C. Burki (VP) in USB's London branch office.

"Bingo," said Nick. "We found him." He flipped to the back of the report for the supporting documentation that accompanied every new account. A sheet topped by Allen Soufi's name was attached. However, neither occupation, business, nor home address was provided. At least there was a signature. Soufi had signed the sheet in an expansive looping script. Under "Comments" was written: *"Cash deposit $250K."*

Nick checked the client profile sheets filled out by other new customers. Each one had given full biographical information: name, address, date of birth, passport number. Only Soufi had left his sheet blank. He nudged her shoulder. "My question is, who is C. Burki in London?"

Sylvia removed her glasses and wiped them on the hem of her shirt. "If he was in London, it's more likely than not that he was a member of the finance department. Offhand, I can't say I remember the name. I'll check our personnel records. Maybe something will turn up."

"Maybe." Nick kept his doubt to himself. He'd looked up Soufi first on Cerberus and then Medusa, and found nothing.

For the next two hours, Nick and Sylvia read through the remaining reports and cross-checked the agenda. Numerous references were made to budgetary matters: actual versus projected revenues, a running tab of selling, general and administrative expenses. A steady stream of new corporate clients appeared each month. And, of course, there was mention of new private banking clients, always by name, always accompanied by a meticulously completed client information sheet. Nick asked himself again why Soufi hadn't filled his out.

Nick finished reading the report for May and looked over at Sylvia. Her eyes were closed and her head was bobbing unsteadily. He felt as tired as she looked.

"Sylvia," he whispered. "Time to call it quits." He closed the binders as quietly as possible, then took his father's agenda and shuffled into the corridor to place it in his briefcase.

"Don't go," came a weak voice. "You can stay here."

"You don't know how much I want to, but I have a big day tomorrow. I can't." He thought about how good it would feel to fall asleep with her back nestled close to his chest. He considered changing his mind but held firm. At eleven A.M. tomorrow, he'd be shaking hands with Ali Mevlevi, the Pasha, and extending the fullest courtesies of the bank to an international drug trafficker — sorry, to a "well-respected businessman." He intended on getting a solid night's rest. "I have to run if I'm going to make the last tram."

"Nick . . ." she protested sleepily.

"I'll call you in the morning. Can you return the binders and get the next six months of reports?"

"I'll try. Should I set a place for you tomorrow night?"

"I don't think that'll work. Kaiser has a full day and night planned for me."

"Call me if you change your mind. Remember Saturday, I'm going to my father's."

Nick knelt beside her and placed a strand of hair behind her ear. "And Sylvia . . . thanks."

"For what?"

He looked at her a few seconds longer, wanting desperately to spend the night. He kissed her lightly. She reached an arm up and tried to bring him close for another kiss. He moved her arm gently back to her side. One more kiss would doom him. "Just thanks."

Chapter 42

Wolfgang Kaiser gunned the twelve-cylinder engine of his BMW 850i along the expanse of the General Guisan Quai. To his right, lights burned from the windows of Zurich's century-old concert *haus,* the Tonhalle. To his left, a skirt of ice extended thirty meters from the lake's shore. Past it, the surface of the lake was ruffled by a strong north wind.

Kaiser shivered involuntarily, glad he was warm and dry inside the automobile with the heater roaring. Things were looking up. Thanks to the rapid implementation of Maeder's share accumulation plan, the bank had picked up three percent of its outstanding votes today. Young Neumann had added another one percent to the kitty, sweet-talking Hambros into committing their shares to current USB management. Perhaps most encouraging, the Adler Bank had been silent the entire day. Their traders had stood by passively as USB snapped up all available shares of its own stock: a packet valued by market's close at over one hundred million Swiss francs. Maybe Konig was finally tapped out. Was it too much to hope for? Poor Klaus. An auction's really no place to be without a checkbook in hand.

Kaiser allowed himself a moment of silent elation. He turned onto the Seestrasse, accelerating down the two-lane straightaway that would carry him to Thalwil, fifteen kilometers along the lake's western shore. He checked the car's digital clock. It read 9:08. He was late.

And now a chore. A task. A wayward baron's final errand to secure his fiefdom.

Once completed, there was no reason Mevlevi shouldn't turn over the two hundred million francs Kaiser required. The funds would guarantee his continued stewardship of the bank and doom Klaus Konig's gamble to ignominious defeat.

First, one chore.

Kaiser appraised the clumpy object wrapped in oilskin that sat on the passenger seat. He had been surprised at its weight when he withdrew it from his private vault. It seemed much heavier than when he had last used it. But he had been a younger man then.

One task.

Kaiser checked the rearview mirror for traffic and found another man staring back at him. A man with dead eyes. His elation smoldered. Self-loathing replaced self-congratulation. How did this come to pass? he asked the unfeeling man. Why am I driving to Thalwil with a loaded pistol in the seat next to me? Why am I going to the home of a man who has worked by my side for thirty years, my only intention to fire a bullet into his skull?

Kaiser returned his gaze to the road. The automobile whisked past the turnoff to Wollishofen. He shrugged, disposing of his self-pity. The answer's simple, he said, explaining his predicament to the weaker man. My life belongs to Mr. Ali Mevlevi, the distinguished trader from Beirut. I handed it to him years ago.

"I require the services of a Swiss bank."

Patrolling the night, Kaiser hears the words as clearly as if they were spoken by an invisible passenger. They are words from another era, another lifetime. Days long past when he was a free man. He recalls the dashing figure of Ali Mevlevi, some twenty years ago. And instead of negotiating the final stretch of the slick road that leads to murder, he is at its beginning, and the road, like the weather, is dry. For no longer is he in Switzerland, but Beirut, and the year is 1978.

"I require the services of a Swiss bank," says the dapper client, dressed like a British gentleman in a navy blazer, cream slacks, and rep striped tie. He is a youngish man, no more than forty, with thick black hair and a razor-sharp nose. Only his skin betrays him as a native.

"At your disposal," answers the newly arrived branch manager, eager to be of service.

"I would like to open an account."

"Of course." A smile now. Show the client

he has been wise to follow his instincts by choosing the United Swiss Bank as his financial partner, by entrusting the young and not yet altogether polished Wolfgang Kaiser to safeguard his money. "Will you be wiring funds to the account or making deposit by means of a check?"

"Neither, I'm afraid."

A frown. But only fleeting. After all, there are many ways to begin a business relationship, and the new manager is the model of ambition. "Did you wish to make a cash deposit?"

"Precisely."

A problem. Cash deposits to foreign institutions are not permitted in Lebanon. "To our office in Switzerland, perhaps?"

"To your office at 17 Al Muteeba Street, Beirut."

"I see." The branch manager informs his fastidiously groomed client that he cannot accept a cash deposit. Such an act would put his company's banking license in jeopardy.

"I will be depositing a trifle over twenty million dollars."

"Well, that is a large sum." Kaiser smiles. He clears his throat but stands firm. "Alas, my hands are tied."

The client continues as if he hasn't heard. "The entire amount is in American banknotes. Primarily hundred-dollar bills. I am sorry but you will find some fifties and some twenties.

Nothing smaller. I promise."

What a reasonable man, this client, this Mr.
. . . Kaiser consults the silver tray that bears
the prospective client's *carte de visite,* this *Mr.
Ali Mevlevi.* No tens. No fives. He is a saint.
"Should you wish to deposit this amount in
Switzerland, I'm sure arrangements could be
made. Unfortunately . . ." The manager motions with his good arm that he appreciates
the opportunity but in this instance must let
it fly away.

Mr. Mevlevi is undaunted. "Did I mention
the fee I am willing to pay for you to accept
this deposit? Is four percent adequate?"

Kaiser cannot hide his astonishment. Four
percent? Eight hundred thousand dollars.
Double his projected profit for the entire operating year! What is he to do? Pack it in his
suitcase and transport it to Switzerland himself. The thought crosses his mind, lingering
a moment longer than wise. His throat has
dried and he requires some water. He forgets
to offer a glass to his fabulously wealthy client.

Mevlevi pays the faux pas no heed. "Perhaps
you should discuss how you wish to treat the
deposit with your superiors. Will you join me
this evening for a late supper? Mr. Rothstein,
a close friend, manages a charming establishment. Little Maxim's. Do you know it?"

Kaiser smiles graciously. Does he know it?
Every man in Beirut short of the hundred-
dollar entry fee and the clout to gain admit-

tance knows Little Maxim's. An invitation? The branch manager does not hesitate. The bank would insist he accept. "It would be a pleasure."

"I hope to have a favorable response by then." Mevlevi offers a soft handshake and departs.

Little Maxim's at the height of the Lebanese civil war. A sultry Friday evening. Wolfgang Kaiser is wearing his favorite garment, a tailored silk dinner jacket, its ivory color chosen to offset his burnished skin, suitably darkened by the Levantine sun. A burgundy kerchief flares from his breast pocket. His hair is rich with brilliantine, his mustache impeccably groomed. He waits at the side entrance. His appointment is for ten P.M. He is twelve minutes early. Timeliness outranks godliness on the banker's list of virtues.

At the appointed hour he mounts the stairs. The club is dimly lit, some corners nearly obscure. His eyes swallow a dozen objects at once. The voluptuous blonde on stage twirling quite naked around a ceiling-high silver pole. The hostess walking to greet him whose scant silver tunic covers only one breast. The tuxedoed gentleman drawing deeply from a hookah of gigantic proportions. He stares until a rough hand lands on his shoulder and guides him to a smoky corner of the club. Ali Mevlevi remains seated, gesturing to an unoccupied chair across the table.

"Have you spoken to your colleagues in Zurich? Mr. Gautschi, I believe."

The young branch manager smiles nervously and unbuttons his jacket. Mevlevi is well informed. "Yes, I reached them late this afternoon. I am sorry to say that we cannot help you in this instance. The risk of losing our banking license is simply too great. Believe me, it is painful for us to pass up the opportunity to initiate a business relationship with an eminent businessman such as yourself. Should you, however, wish to deposit your funds in Switzerland, we would be more than happy to assist your banking needs."

Kaiser fears his host's response. He has asked around about Mevlevi. It seems he is involved in all manner of activities, some of them even legitimate: money brokering, real estate, textiles. But rumor suggests his primary means of income derives from the international transport of heroin. In no uncertain terms, he is a dangerous man.

"The money is here!" Mevlevi brings a hand down on the table, upsetting a glass of Scotch. "Not in Switzerland. How am I to take my money to your bank? Do you think your customs officials welcome a Turk from Lebanon with open arms?" He scoffs. "You think we are all members of the Black September. I am an honest businessman. Why do you not wish to help us?"

Kaiser has delivered his canned response. He is at a loss for words. Mevlevi's unflinching gaze tears into him. He fumbles for something to say, and when he speaks his tongue has reacquired the clumsy accent of his country. "We must follow regulations. There are so few alternatives."

"You mean *no alternatives.* Do you expect me to leave my money with this bunch of thieves?"

Kaiser shakes his head no, confused. It is his first lesson in the topsy-turvy calculus of Middle Eastern business practice.

Mevlevi leans across the table and grabs Kaiser's withered arm. "I can see that you wish to help me."

Kaiser is shocked at the affront to his deformity. But it is his eyes, not his arm, that feel Mevlevi's grasp, and as if hypnotized, he nods yes.

Mevlevi calls for a waiter and orders a bottle of Johnnie Walker Black Label. The Scotch arrives. He proposes a toast. "To the spirit of enterprise. The world belongs to those who fashion it in their image!"

An hour or two or three later, Kaiser enjoys the attentions of a slim young woman. A waif, he would call her. Long black hair frames a sensuous face. Frail dark eyes flash from under thick lashes. Another drink and the strap of a sequined cocktail dress dangles off a soft but well-muscled shoulder. Her English is impeccable. She asks in a throaty voice for him to move closer. He cannot draw himself away from her probing fingers and her sweet breath. She insists on saying the nastiest things.

Mevlevi is smoking another of his filthy Turkish cigarettes. Black tobacco bombs expelling rivers of blue smoke. His glass is full. Isn't it always?

The raven-haired waif has insisted that Kaiser accompany her to her apartment. Who is he to deny? After all, it is only three blocks from the club, and the grand Mevlevi has given his benediction, a fraternal pat on the back and a sly wink that all would be taken care of at Little Maxim's. The girl asks for a drink and points to the bar. Kaiser splashes liberal helpings of Scotch into two glasses. He knows he has drunk too much but is not sure if he cares. Perhaps recklessness becomes him. She puts the glass to his lips and he takes a sip. She swallows the rest in one fearsome gulp. She staggers and searches the folds of her handbag. Something is awry. An unpleasant cast crosses her features. Suddenly, she is smiling. The problem is resolved. An immaculate pile of white powder sits on the underside of a perfectly manicured fingernail. She sniffs and then offers the like to her evening's companion. He shakes his head, but she insists. He bends forward and sniffs. "The white pony," she giggles and offers him another pile.

The banker from Zurich is growing disoriented. He has never felt such a roar of blood through his veins. The pressure builds in his head, only to be replaced a moment later by relief. His chest tingles. Warmth suffuses his entire body. He wants only to sleep, but a greedy hand rouses him, its kneading grip drawing the heat from his chest to his loins. Through glazed eyes, he sees the lovely woman from Little Maxim's undoing his pants and taking him into her mouth. He has never been harder. His vision blurs and he realizes he has forgotten her name. He opens his eyes to ask. She is before him, her dress peeled down to her waist. Her chest is flat, her nipples too small and pale and surrounded by tufts of black hair. Kaiser sits up, yells for this woman . . . for *this man* to stop, but another pair of hands holds him back. He struggles drunkenly, vainly. He neither sees nor feels the needle that enters the prominent blue vein running across the top of his shrunken left hand.

"If you'll sign at the bottom of the paper, we can put this messy situation behind us."

Ali Mevlevi hands Wolfgang Kaiser a receipt issued by the Beirut representative office of the United Swiss Bank for the sum of twenty million U.S. dollars. Where he has procured the official paper is a mystery. As is so much else.

Kaiser meticulously refolds his handkerchief and places it in his pocket before reaching forward to accept the document. He places the receipt on top of a stack of color photographs, eight by tens. Photographs of which he, Wolfgang Andreas Kaiser, is a prominent subject, one might even say the star. He and a horribly mutilated transvestite he has learned carried the name Rio.

Kaiser signs his name to the document, knowing with each loop of the pen that this "messy situation" will never be behind him. Mevlevi watches with detached interest. He points to three worn duffel bags stuffed to bursting slumped in the entryway. "Either you discover a way to deposit the money within three days or I will report it stolen. Your country looks rather harshly upon bank fraud, does it not? Lebanon is no different. But I fear her jails are not so comfortable as your own."

Kaiser straightens his back. His eyes are puffy and his nose stuffed. He tears off the top copy of the receipt, places it in an empty plastic tray, then gives the yellow copy to Mevlevi. The Swiss banker's refuge is order; procedure, his sanctuary. The pink copy, he says, will stay in this office. The white copy will go to Switzerland. "With the money," he adds, managing a smile.

"You are a remarkable man," says Mevlevi.

"I see I have chosen the proper partner."

Kaiser nods perfunctorily. Now they are partners. What torture will this relationship hold in store for him?

Mevlevi speaks again. "You may tell your superiors that I have agreed to pay a special fee of two percent of funds deposited to handle the administrative costs of opening my account. Not bad. Four hundred thousand dollars for a day's work. Or should I say a night's?"

Kaiser does not comment. He strains to keep his back pinned to his chair. If he loses contact with the hard surface, if the pressure against his spine slackens, he will go mad.

The next morning the branch manager boards a flight to Zurich, via Vienna. In his four suitcases he has packed twenty million one hundred forty-three thousand dollars. Mevlevi had lied. There were three one-dollar bills.

At passport control, Kaiser is waved through. At customs, though pushing a cart laden with a mountain of bulging suitcases, he does not receive a second glance. The passenger following him, while carrying only a small valise, is detained. Kaiser signals his understanding to the immigration official. What else is one to do with a dirty Arab?

Gerhard Gautschi, chairman of the United

Swiss Bank, is too stunned to speak. Kaiser explains that he could not turn down the opportunity to generate so substantial a profit for the bank. Yes, there was a risk. No, he cannot envision committing such a foolhardy act again. All the same, the money is safely deposited in the bank. A sizable commission has been earned. Better yet, the client wishes to invest in securities. His first purchase? Shares of the United Swiss Bank.

"Who is he?" asks Gautschi, referring of course to Kaiser's new client.

"A well-respected businessman," answers Kaiser.

"Naturally," laughs Gautschi. "Aren't they all?"

Kaiser leaves the Chairman's throne room, but not before Gautschi has a last word.

"Next time, Wolfgang, let us send the plane for you."

A smattering of snow slapped the windshield and brought Wolfgang Kaiser back to the present. A sign ahead indicated that he had reached Thalwil. Seconds later he sped through the shadow of the Lindt and Sprüngli chocolate manufacturer, an industrial monstrosity painted a lavender blue. He slowed the car, lowering his window and extinguishing the heat. A numbing cold invaded the cabin.

Sick of him, aren't you? Kaiser asked himself, referring of course to Ali Mevlevi, the man who had destroyed his life. *Of course I am. I'm sick of the midnight calls, of the tapped phones, of the unilateral orders. I am sick of living under another man's heel.*

He sighed. With luck, that might soon change. If Nicholas Neumann was as willful as he estimated, if he was as mean-spirited as his military records indicated, Mevlevi might soon be a memory. Tomorrow young Neumann would be introduced to the guileful ways of Ali Mevlevi. Mevlevi himself had stated that he planned to make sure Neumann was "one of us." Kaiser could well imagine what those words meant.

For the past month, he had allowed himself the fantasy of using Nicholas Neumann to get rid of Mevlevi. He knew that Neumann had spent time in the Marine Corps, but his record of service was a mystery. Some of the bank's better clients were higher-ups at the U.S. Department of Defense — procurement analysts. Rich bastards. A little digging had yielded some startling answers. Neumann's military record had been officially sealed, labeled "Top Secret." More interesting, the boy had received a dishonorable discharge. Three weeks prior to his discharge on medical grounds, he had ruthlessly attacked a civilian defense contractor named John J. Keely. Beaten the man senseless, apparently. Rumor said it was retribution for a failed operation. All very hush-hush.

No more information was forthcoming, but to Kaiser it was more than enough. A soldier with a bad temper. A trained killer with a short fuse. Of course, he could never ask the boy outright to kill another man, a client, to boot. But he could see to it that someone with a bent toward mayhem came up with the idea himself.

After that, it had been easy. Assign Neumann to FKB4. Give him some time working with account 549.617 RR. Cerruti's illness and Sprecher's departure had been marvelous coincidences. The arrival of Sterling Thorne, even better. Who better to prime Neumann on Mevlevi than the United States Drug Enforcement Administration? And now Mevlevi actually coming to Zurich. His first visit in four years. If Kaiser were a religious man, he would call it a miracle. Being a cynic, he called it fate.

At 9:15, Kaiser parked the car in a private lot abutting the lake. He placed the weighty oilskin in his lap and turned it over and over until the weapon's silver skin flashed in the darkness. Cupping the pistol in the craw of his left hand, he drew back the slide and chambered a round. With his thumb, he clicked the safety to its off position. He looked in the mirror and was relieved to find the man with dull, lifeless eyes staring back at him.

First, one chore.

A block from the apartment building, Kaiser slowed his pace and sucked in the brittle air.

Lights burned in every corner of the penthouse. Was that a shadow crossing the window? He lowered his head and walked on. His hand stroked the smooth metal object in his pocket, as if like some magical talisman it might deliver him from this circumstance. He reached the door too soon. The voice that blurted from the speaker was nervous and high-strung. Kaiser could already see the blinking eyes.

"Thank God you're here," said Marco Cerruti.

Chapter 43

Ali Mevlevi sat alone in the spacious cabin listening to the pilot announce their initial descent toward Zurich Airport. He put down the sheaf of papers that had held him in their embrace the past three hours and tightened his seat belt. His eyes burned and his head ached. He wondered if it had been a smart idea coming to Switzerland, then dismissed the question outright. He hadn't had a choice. Not if Khamsin was to succeed.

Mevlevi returned his attention to the papers in his lap. His eye wandered from top to bottom. It began with the heading, written in large Cyrillic script and emblazoned in maroon ink across the top of the page. He knew it to read "Surplus Arms Warehouse." A polite introductory paragraph written in English followed. "We sell only the finest new and used armaments, all in perfect operating order." He half expected to see a disclaimer informing him that he could return the merchandise after thirty days if he was in any way dissatisfied. The Russians were giving international commerce their best shot. He turned the page and reviewed the list of the material he had purchased.

Section I: Aircraft. Item 1. Hind Assault Helicopter Model VII A (the winged beast of Afghan fame). Price: $15 million per copy. He'd taken four. Item 2. Sukhoi Attack Helicopter. Price: $7 million. He'd taken six. Item 3. Unpronounceable air to ground missiles at fifty thousand a pop. Two hundred sat in his hangar. Turn the page. Section II: Tracked Vehicles. T-52 Tanks at $2 million apiece. He had a damned fleet of them, twenty-five in all. Mobile Katyusha Rocket launchers. A bargain at half a million per. He'd taken ten. Next to item seven, page two, the Zhukov armored personnel carrier with rear-mounted quad .50-caliber machine guns on sale at $250,000 per, there was a star and a handwritten addendum: *"Still in use by the Russian Armed Forces — spare parts available!!!"* He'd taken a dozen. The list went on and on. A devil's cornucopia of deadly toys. Field artillery, mortars, machine guns, grenades, mines, t.o.w.'s. Enough weaponry to fully equip two reinforced companies of infantry, a company of armored cavalry, and a squadron of attack helicopters. Six hundred men in all.

And to think they were only a diversion.

Mevlevi laughed slyly while he turned to the final page of the document. The main event, as it were. He moved his eyes across the page. The words leaped up at him as if it were the first time he had seen them, and not the hundredth, causing his scrotum to tighten and his skin to bristle with goose bumps.

Section V. Nuclear Ordnance. *1 Kopinskaya IV two-kiloton concussive bomb.* Mevlevi's mouth grew dry. A battlefield nuclear weapon. An atomic device no larger than a mortar shell carrying one tenth the destructive power of the Hiroshima bomb with only one fiftieth the radioactivity. Two thousand tons of TNT with hardly a stray atom.

It was the only item he had not been able to purchase. It would cost him roughly eight hundred million Swiss francs. He would have the money in three days' time. And the bomb in three and one half.

Mevlevi had chosen the target with great care. Ariel — an isolated settlement of fifteen thousand Jews in the occupied West Bank, constructed even as the Israelis proclaimed their good faith in negotiations concerning their withdrawal from that exact area. Did they think the Arab stupid? No man builds a town he will leave in one year. Even the name was perfect. *Ariel* — no doubt in honor of Mr. Ariel Sharon, the Israelis' most belligerent Arab hater, the beast who had personally supervised the massacres at Shatila and Sabra in 1982.

Ariel — the name would come to symbolize the Jews' woe.

Mevlevi yawned unexpectedly. He had risen at 4:00 A.M. to conduct a predawn review of his men on the main training field. They had looked magnificent, clad in their desert warfare utilities. Row upon row of inspired warriors, ready to advance the work of the prophet; ready to give their life for Allah. He walked their ranks, offering words of encouragement. *Go with God. Inshallah. God is great.*

From the field, he continued on to the two immense hangars he had had carved into the hills at the south end of his compound five years ago. He entered the first hangar and was deafened by the roar of twenty battle tanks conducting final checks on their transmission and drive trains. Mechanics swirled around the mighty beasts, asking drivers to rev the engines and rotate the turrets. Last measures of petrol were added to the lumbering giants, jerricans strapped to their steel hulls. He stopped to admire the immaculate paintwork. Moshe Dayan would turn over in his grave. Every tank had been painted to the exact specifications of the Israeli Army. Each carried an Israeli flag to be raised at the moment of the attack. Confusion was a raider's greatest ally.

Mevlevi walked to the second hangar, which housed his helicopters. "Death from above," cried the Americans and their Israeli vassals. Now they'd learn firsthand. He looked at the Hind choppers, their stout wings bent under the weight of so much ordnance. And the sleeker Sukhoi attack helicopters. Just staring at these instruments of destruction sent a chill down his spine. The helicopters had also been painted the dirty khaki tones of the Israeli armed forces. Three of them carried Israeli transponders captured from downed craft. When the birds crossed the Israeli border, they would activate the transponders. For all the world, or at least every radar installation in the Galilee, they would appear to be friendly forces.

Mevlevi's last stop before climbing aboard the aircraft to Zurich had been to the operations center, a reinforced underground bunker not far from the hangars. He wished to conduct a final review of the tactical situation with Lieutenant Ivlov and Sergeant Rodenko. Ivlov summarized the plan of battle: At 0200 Saturday, Mevlevi's troops would cross into Syria and move south toward the Israeli border. Their movement was timed to coincide with the beginning of an anti-Hezbollah exercise conducted by the South Lebanese Army. Syrian reconnaissance would be expected. Intelligence confirmed that no satellites would be overflying the operational area at this time. One company of infantry would take up position three miles from the border near the town of Chebaa. The other company, working in concert with the armored cavalry, would travel seven miles east to Jazin. The tanks themselves would be transported to the staging area by seven lorries normally used to deliver tractors. Each lorry could take up to four tanks. All troops would be in position by dawn Monday.

They would attack on their master's command.

Mevlevi assured Ivlov and Rodenko that the plan would go forward as set forth. He didn't dare tell the two Russians that their incursion across the border to destroy the newest Israeli settlements of Ebarach and New Zion was only a feint, a bloody charade designed to lure the Jews' attention away from a small flight corridor above the northeasternmost corner of their homeland. To be sure, a few hundred Hebraic settlers could count on losing their lives. It wasn't as if Ivlov's attack would have no positive consequences. Just insignificant ones.

Mevlevi dismissed the Russian mercenaries, then descended a spiral staircase to the communications facility. He asked the clerk on duty to leave and, when he was alone, locked the door and moved to one of the three secure telephone lines. He picked up the phone and dialed a nine-digit number.

A groggy voice at the Surplus Arms Warehouse in downtown Alma-Ata, Kazakhstan, answered. *"Da?"*

"General Dimitri Marchenko. Tell him it is his friend in Beirut." Mevlevi expected Marchenko to be sleeping. However, this was his private line, and the general was proud to offer twenty-four-hour service, a concept he had no doubt picked up during one of his military exchanges to the United States. Besides, he was one of the general's better customers. So far he had paid him and his sponsors in the Kazakh government $125 million.

Two minutes later Mevlevi's call was transferred to another line.

"Good morning, comrade," boomed Dimitri Marchenko. "You are an early riser. We have a Russian proverb, 'The fisherman who —' "

Mevlevi interrupted him. "General Marchenko, I have a plane waiting. Everything is in order for our last piece of business."

"Wonderful news."

Mevlevi spoke using the agreed-upon code. "Please bring your baby to visit. He must arrive no later than Sunday."

Marchenko did not speak for a few seconds. Mevlevi could hear him lighting up a cigarette. If the general pulled off this deal, he would be a patron saint to his people for generations to come. Kazakhstan had not been blessed with abundant natural resources. Her land was mountainous and her soil barren. She had some oil, a little gold, and that was about it. For the essentials, wheat, potatoes, beef, she had to rely on her former Soviet brethren. But wares were no longer distributed according to a centrally mandated five-year plan. Hard currency was required. And what better place to begin than with her national armory? Eight hundred million Swiss francs would turn around his impoverished country's balance of payments overnight. Not exactly beating swords into plowshares, but close enough.

"That is possible," said Marchenko. "However, there is still the small matter of payment."

"Payment will be made no later than noon on Monday. I guarantee it."

"Remember, he cannot travel until I give him his final instructions."

Mevlevi said that he understood. The bomb would remain inert until a preprogrammed code was entered into its central processing unit. He knew Marchenko would enter this code only after he had learned that his bank had received the full eight hundred million francs.

"*Da,*" said Marchenko. "We will bring our baby to your house on Sunday. By the way, we call him Little Joe. He is like Stalin. Small but a mean sonuvabitch!"

Recalling the conversation, Mevlevi silently corrected the general. *No, its name is not Little Joe. It is Khamsin. And its devil wind will hasten the rebirth of my people.*

Chapter 44

Nick watched from the backseat of the bank's Mercedes limousine as the Cessna Citation taxied through the falling snow. The roar of its engines oscillated, alternately whining and growling, as they drove the jet off the skirt of the runway toward an empty patch of tarmac. Abruptly, the jet braked, bouncing off its front wheel as it came to a complete halt. The engines were cut and their purring faded. The door of the jet shuddered and collapsed inward. A flight of stairs descended from the fuselage.

A lone official from customs and immigration climbed the stairs and disappeared into the aircraft. Nick opened the car door and stepped onto the tarmac. He prepared his best welcoming smile while rehearsing his greeting to the Pasha. He felt curiously detached from himself. He wasn't really going to spend the day playing tour guide to an international heroin smuggler. That was someone else. Another former marine whose knee was so stiff that every step felt like broken glass grinding into his joints.

He walked to within ten yards of the aircraft and waited. The man from customs reappeared a few seconds later. "You may go aboard," he said. "You're free to exit the airport directly."

Nick said thanks, wondering why he had never cleared customs so quickly.

When he turned his head back to the plane, the Pasha was standing at the open door. Nick straightened his shoulders and covered the distance to the plane in four quick steps. "Good morning, sir. Herr Kaiser extends his sincerest greetings, both personally and on behalf of the bank."

Mevlevi shook the extended hand. "Mr. Neumann. We finally meet. I understand thanks are in order."

"Not at all."

"I mean it. Thank you. I commend you on your sound judgment. Hopefully during my stay I can find some better way of expressing my gratitude. I try not to forget those who have done me a service."

"Really," said Nick, "it's not necessary. Please come this way. Let's get out of the cold."

The Pasha was hardly the hardened criminal Nick had expected. He was slim and not very tall — maybe five eight or five nine — and weighed no more than one hundred sixty pounds. He was dressed in a navy suit, a bloodred Hermès tie, and polished loafers. In the manner of an Italian aristocrat, he had draped an overcoat over his shoulders.

Put me in a crowd next to this man, thought Nick, and I would take him for a high-ranking executive or the foreign minister of a Latin American country. He could be an aging French playboy or a prince of the Saudi royal family. He did not look like a man who made his business peddling thousands of kilos of refined heroin to the greater European continent.

Mevlevi drew the coat around him and shivered theatrically. "I felt the chill even at thirty thousand feet. I have only two bags. The captain is taking them from the cargo hold."

Nick showed Mevlevi to the car, then returned to the plane to retrieve the suitcases. The bags were stuffed full and heavy. Lugging them to the limousine, he recalled the Chairman's orders to do exactly as Mevlevi instructed. In fact, only one appointment had been fixed for the Pasha's visit. A meeting with the Swiss immigration authorities in Lugano, three days from now, on Monday morning at ten. The subject: issuance of a Swiss passport.

Nick had arranged the meeting at the Chairman's request but had no interest in attending. The same day he had spent hours cajoling Eberhard Senn, the Count Languenjoux, into moving his discussions with the Chairman forward by at least one day. The count had finally been won over. Monday at eleven would be fine, but only if the meeting could take place at the small hotel he owned on the Lake of Lugano where he made his winter residence. Kaiser agreed, saying that Senn's six percent were easily worth the three-hour drive to the Tessin. Nick had wanted to be in on the meeting. The Chairman, however, was intractable. "Reto Feller will accompany me in your place. You will escort Mr. Mevlevi. You've earned his trust."

Nick climbed into the limousine, ruing the day he'd taken the actions that had earned him that trust. It didn't take a genius to know why Kaiser could never escort Mevlevi anywhere. Thorne's accusations were true. Every one of them.

"First, we go to Zug," announced Mevlevi. "International Fiduciary Trust, Grütstrasse 67."

"Grütstrasse 67, Zug," Nick repeated to the chauffeur.

The limousine set off. Nick didn't feel like indulging in the usual pleasantries. He'd be damned if he'd kiss the ass of a drug smuggler. Mevlevi remained quiet. For the most part, he kept his eyes directed out the window. Every so often Nick would catch the Pasha staring at him, not unkindly, but from a distance, and he knew he was being sized up. Mevlevi would offer a faint smile and avert his gaze.

The limousine sped through the Sihl valley. The road wound steadily uphill through an endless pine forest. Mevlevi tapped Nick on the knee. "Have you seen Mr. Thorne lately?"

Nick looked him squarely in the eye. He had nothing to hide. "Monday."

"Ah," said Mevlevi, nodding his head contentedly, as if they were discussing an old friend. "Monday."

Nick glanced at Mevlevi, turning the simple question over in his mind, allowing its myriad implications to confirm what he should have known weeks ago. A man like Mevlevi wouldn't be satisfied keeping an eye only on Thorne. He'd want to know what Nick was up to also. An American in Switzerland. A former United States marine. No matter what Nick had done on his behalf, he hardly merited his trust. And then Nick knew why Mevlevi had really asked the question. Thorne wasn't the only one being followed. He belonged in the same boat himself. Mevlevi had sent the dapper man in the mountain guide's hat. Mevlevi had ordered his apartment searched. Mevlevi had been watching him the entire time.

The International Fiduciary Trust was housed on the third and fourth floors of a modest building in downtown Zug. A simple gold nameplate above the doorbell indicated the businesses housed here. Nick pressed the buzzer, and the door swung open immediately. They were expected.

A bent stick of a woman in her late forties asked them to come in and led them to a conference room overlooking the Zugersee. Two bottles of Passugger sat on the table. A glass and coaster, an ashtray, a tablet of paper, and two pens had been placed in front of every chair. The woman offered coffee. Both men accepted. Nick had little idea as to the subject of the meeting. He would sit and listen. Kaiser's yes-man.

A polite knock and the door opened. Two men entered. The first, tall and jowly with a ruddy complexion. The second, short, thin, and bald, except for a strand of black hair twirled on top of his head like a sticky bun.

"Affentranger," announced the heavy-set fellow. He approached first Nick and then Mevlevi, offering each a business card and a handshake.

"Fuchs," said the smaller man, following his partner's example.

Mevlevi began speaking as soon as all four men were seated around the table. "Gentlemen, it's a pleasure for me to work with you again. A few years ago I worked with your associate, Mr. Schmied. He was of great assistance in opening a number of corporations for me in the Netherlands Antilles. A sharp man with figures. I trust he's still with you. Perhaps I could say hello?"

Affentranger and Fuchs exchanged concerned glances.

"Mr. Schmied died three years ago," said Affentranger, the jowly one.

"Drowned while on vacation," explained Fuchs, the runt.

"No . . ." Mevlevi placed the back of one hand to his mouth. "How terrible."

"I had always thought of the Mediterranean as a calm sea," said Fuchs. "Apparently it gets quite rough off the coast of Lebanon."

"A tragedy," opined Mevlevi, his eyes smiling at Nick.

Fuchs brushed the insignificant matter of his colleague's passing aside. He smiled broadly to dispel any lugubrious thoughts. "We hope our firm can still be of service, Mr. . . ."

"*Malvinas.* Allen Malvinas."

Nick gave his complete attention to Ali Mevlevi, or rather to *Allen Malvinas*.

Mevlevi said, "I am in need of several numbered accounts."

Fuchs cleared his throat before replying. "Surely, you realize that you can open such an account at any one of the banks just down the street from us."

"Of course," Mevlevi responded politely. "But I was hoping to avoid some of the more unnecessary formalities."

Affentranger understood perfectly. "The government has grown much too intrusive as of late."

Fuchs concurred. "And even our most traditional banks, not as discreet as they once were."

Mevlevi opened his hands as if to say such is the world we live in. "I see we are in agreement."

"Unfortunately," Fuchs complained, "we must abide by government regulations. All clients wishing to open a *new* account of any type in this country must provide legitimate proof of their identity. A passport will do."

Nick found the emphasis Fuchs had placed on the word *new* strange.

Mevlevi, though, jumped on the word as if it were the cue he had been looking for. "*New accounts,* you said. Of course, I understand the need to follow regulations should one wish to open a *new* account. However, I would prefer an older account, perhaps one registered in the name of your company that you don't use on a day-to-day basis."

Fuchs looked to Affentranger. Both men then looked at Nick, who kept a concerned expression on his face. Whatever it was they were seeking from him, he supplied it, for the next moment, Affentranger began talking.

"Such accounts do exist," he said cautiously, "but they are very expensive to obtain. A dwindling resource, so to speak. Banks insist on certain minimum conditions being met before we are allowed to transfer a numbered account originally opened by our office to a client."

"Naturally," said Mevlevi.

Nick felt like telling Fuchs and Affentranger

574

to name their price and get on with it.

"Do you wish to open just the one account?" asked Fuchs.

"Five to be exact. Of course, I have proper identification." Mevlevi removed an Argentinean passport from his jacket and laid it on the table. "But I prefer to have the account remain anonymous."

Nick eyed the navy passport and choked down a smile. Mr. Malvinas of Argentina, *Malvinas* being the Argentinean name for the Falkland Islands. Mevlevi thought himself a pretty clever customer. Sure, he was clever — his men at USB had informed him that the DEA had compromised account 549.617 RR — but he must be desperate too. Why would he leave his safe haven in Beirut and risk arrest to straighten out a banking problem that could just as easily have been remedied by someone here? Kaiser, Maeder, even Nick alone, could have made this trip to Zug. It was hardly adequate reason to flee the security of his prickly nest.

Fuchs asked, "Would accounts at the United Swiss Bank be of interest?"

"No finer institution in the land," replied Mevlevi, to which Nick just nodded.

Fuchs picked up the phone and instructed his secretary to bring in several account transfer forms.

Affentranger said, "The minimum amount the United Swiss Bank has set for granting a client a preexisting numbered account is five million dollars. Of course as you need five accounts, we can discuss terms."

"I propose placing four million dollars into each account," said Mevlevi.

Nick could see Affentranger and Fuchs calculating their commission, somewhere between one and two percent. On this one transaction the august International Fiduciary Trust would garner fees of more than two hundred thousand dollars.

Fuchs and Affentranger answered in unison. "That would be fine."

Conversation ebbed as Mr. Malvinas drank his coffee and the necessary paperwork was filled out. Nick excused himself and walked down the corridor to the rest room. He was joined immediately by Affentranger.

"A big fucking fish, that one, eh?"

Nick smiled. "It appears so."

"You're new at the bank?"

Nick nodded.

"Usually Kaiser sends Maeder. Don't care for him much. He bites too hard." Affentranger slapped his own fat ass. "Right here. Get my drift."

Nick murmured his understanding. "Oh."

"And you? You're okay?" Affentranger asked. Which meant did Nick expect a commission on the business?

"I'm fine."

Affentranger looked puzzled. "Fine, then. And remember, if you've got any more like him, send 'em our way."

Inside the conference room, Fuchs rifled through the paperwork. Mevlevi sat at his side and together they filled in the pertinent information, or didn't fill it in, as was the case. No name was placed on the accounts. Nor an address. All mail for the accounts was to be held at the United Swiss Bank, Main Office, Zurich. All that was required from Mr. Malvinas was two sets of code words. These he gave happily. The primary code word would be Ciragan Palace. The secondary, his birthday, November 12, 1936, to be given orally as day, month, and then year. A signature was required for verification of any written requests he might have, and this Mr. Malvinas kindly supplied. A seismic scrawl was duly inscribed at the bottom of the form. And then the meeting was finished, adjourned with smiles and handshakes all around.

Nick and his client remained quiet as they took the elevator to the ground floor. A Cheshire grin peeked from the corners of Mevlevi's mouth. And why not? thought Nick. The man held five account transferral receipts in his hand; he possessed five clean numbered accounts to use as he saw fit. The Pasha was back in business.

In the limousine en route to Zurich, Mevlevi

finally spoke. "Mr. Neumann, I will need to use the bank's facilities. I have a small amount of cash that needs to be counted."

"Of course," Nick answered. Now the other shoe drops. "How much, approximately?"

"Twenty million dollars," Mevlevi said coolly, staring at the bleak landscape. "Why do you think those suitcases were so damned heavy?"

Chapter 45

At 11:30 the same morning, Sterling Thorne took up position fifty yards from the employee entrance to the United Swiss Bank. He stood inside the pillared entryway of an abandoned church, a drooping concrete assemblage of right angles, more sump house than place of worship. He was waiting for Nick Neumann.

His ideas about Neumann had changed drastically during the last twenty-four hours. The more he thought about it, the more he was sure Neumann was on his side. Out there by the lake, he swore he'd seen a spark of willingness in the kid's eye. Neumann was this close to jumping on board the *Fuck Mevlevi* express. He'd tell him about Becker if and when he did. Not that there was much to tell.

Thorne had approached Martin Becker in mid-December for no other reason than that he worked in the section that handled Mevlevi — intercepts from the Defense Intelligence Agency noted the bank's internal departmental reference, FKB4 — and that he looked like a weak-willed paper pusher who might actually have a conscience. He was a smiler, and smilers usually liked a cause. Becker didn't need much prodding to cooperate. He said he'd been thinking about it for a long time and that he'd do his best to bring out papers that would give irrefutable evidence of Mevlevi laundering his money through the United Swiss Bank. A week later he was dead: throat slit ear to ear and no trace of any papers that might help the DEA. Thorne would tell Neumann about him at the right time. No point in scaring the boy off.

A few employees began trickling out of the bank, alone and in pairs, mostly secretaries. Thorne kept his eyes nailed to the stairs, waiting for his boy to show. The fact that somewhere out there Jester was rolling along with a major shipment of refined heroin bound for the Swiss market was terrific, but Neumann's help would be essential if he wanted to demonstrate USB's complicity in Mevlevi's affairs. He thought of Wolfgang Kaiser breezily lying to him about not knowing Mevlevi. *Alfie Merlani?* he had asked. Arrogant sumbitch. With a start, Thorne realized that he wanted Kaiser's ass as much as Mevlevi's. And it made him feel good.

Twenty wasted minutes later, the cellular phone attached to Thorne's belt rang. The dull electronic chirping took him by surprise, sending a jolt of adrenaline down his spine. He fumbled with the buttons on his leather coat. Jester, he prayed, let that be you. Come through for me, buddy. He freed the phone from his belt and pressed the answer button.

"Thorne," he said calmly.

"Thorne," Terry Strait yelled. "I want you back in this office immediately. You have taken property belonging to the United States government. Files on running operations are never, I repeat *never*, to be removed from secure premises. Eastern Lightning is . . ."

Thorne listened to the good reverend rant and rave for another five, maybe ten seconds, then hung up on him. Worse than a wood tick in your belly button.

The phone rang again. Thorne hefted the compact plastic unit, weighing it as if to judge who might be on the other end. Keep dreaming, Terry. You wanted me out of your hair — I'm out. But one day soon I'm going to intercept a mother lode of refined no. 4 heroin without your help and I am going to put away the Pasha. Eastern Lightning will be a bigger success than any of us thought possible. I'll be back. And I'll be gunning for your sorry ass.

The phone rang a second time. What the hell? thought Thorne. If it was Strait, he'd just hang up again. A third ring. "Thorne, here."

"Thorne? This is Jester. I'm in Milan. At a house belonging to the Makdisi family."

Thorne nearly crossed himself and fell to his knees. "Good to hear from you. Can you talk? Do you have some time?"

"Yeah, a little."

"Good boy. Have you got a schedule for me?"

"We're crossing at Chiasso, Monday morning between nine-thirty and ten-thirty. Far right-hand lane. We're in a two-trailer rig with British plates. A transnational *routier*. It has the blue shield on the front bumper saying T-I-R. Gray canopies covering the load. The inspector is looking for us. We'll get a free pass."

"Go on."

"Then I guess we're coming to Zurich. The Makdisis' boys are driving. We'll be taking it to their usual drop point. Near a place called Hardturm. I think it's a soccer stadium. I'm caught in the middle of something here. Everybody is looking at me funny. A lot of phony smiles. I told you I'm only along for the ride because Mevlevi suspects the Makdisis of double dealing. Too big a shipment to let go without a friend nearby. We're looking at a couple of thousand pounds minimum, maybe more. He is desperate that this go through."

Thorne interrupted Jester. "Getting our hands on that much product is damned good work, but we have to tie it to Mevlevi, otherwise he'll just send a bigger load in two weeks' time. I don't want a cargo of contraband without the man responsible. I don't want the bullets without the gun, you understand. The Makdisis don't mean shit to me."

"I know, I know . . ." The connection weakened and static filled Thorne's ear. Jester's voice came through a garbled mess.

"What did you say? What about Mevlevi? Can you hear me, Joe?"

Jester's voice returned. ". . . so like I said there will never be a better chance. We can't miss out on this opportunity."

"Speak up. I lost you for a second."

"Jesus," Jester rasped, sounding out of breath. "I said he's in Switzerland."

"Who?"

"Mevlevi."

Thorne felt as though he had been punched in the stomach. "You're telling me that Ali Mevlevi is in Switzerland?"

"He arrived this morning. He called the house where I'm staying to make sure everything was all right. Told me that after the load came through safely he'd build me my own house at his compound. He's got a big gig planned for Tuesday. The bank's meeting. He's in deep with that bank, I told you a dozen times."

Thorne pleaded. "You've got to give me more than that. What about his army?"

"Khamsin," said Joseph. "Mevlevi's operation. He's moving his men out tomorrow at 0400. He's kept the target quiet, but I know they're going south toward the border. He's got six hundred fanatics revved up for something big."

"0400 Saturday," Thorne repeated. "No target, you say?"

"He told no one. Just south. Use your imagination."

"Dammit," whispered Thorne. Not now! What was he supposed to do with that information? He was a defrocked government agent, for Christ's sake. He'd kept a buddy at Langley apprised of his suspicions. He'd give him a call, maybe fax him the latest. He'd have to make it their problem and pray. He just hoped that six hundred men showed up as more than a dot in the midst of all that military traffic on the Lebanese-Israeli border.

Thorne's mind returned to the problem at hand. "Super work, Joe. But I need something to nail him here."

"Keep your eye on the bank. He'll probably stop by some time. I told you he and Kaiser are tight. They go way back."

Thorne watched a Mercedes limo drive up to the gate and stop. "Never. Mevlevi knows we're on to him. You think he has the balls to drive right past me?"

"That's your call. But you have to let me know how you're going to handle this. I don't want to be with these guys when the heat comes down. It'll get ugly fast."

"You hold tight and give me some time to set something up. We have to arrange a welcoming committee on this end."

"Hurry it up. I can't call every hour. I got one more chance before we move out of here."

The gate clanged, stopping at its fully opened position. The limousine advanced into the courtyard of the bank.

"Stay calm, Joe. You give me until Sunday and we'll set up a nice reception. Take you out of the fire without getting you burned. I have to figure some way to take that product off the streets and still nail Mevlevi. You call me Sunday."

"Yeah, all right. If that's the way it's gotta be." Jester hung up.

"Hang in there," Thorne said to the dead line. He exhaled and dropped the phone to his side. "You're almost home, kid."

Inside the courtyard of the United Swiss Bank, the taillights of the Mercedes flashed red as the limousine drew to a halt. Thorne looked on as the rear door of the automobile swung open and the top of a head emerged. The gate began closing: a long curtain of black metal rolling along a steel track. He recalled Jester's words. *He and Kaiser are tight. Keep your eye on the bank.*

The first man out of the limousine was the chauffeur. He adjusted his jacket, then put on his cap. The back left door opened on its own. A head of black hair peeked out, then dipped back below the smoked glass.

Thorne dipped his head, trying to see past the moving screen. A pair of shiny loafers hit the pavement. He could hear the brush of the heels on the cement. Again the head popped up. The man was turning toward him.

Just a second longer, he begged. *Please!*

The gate crashed into place.

Thorne jogged toward the bank, curious to learn who had been inside the limousine. A laugh drifted over the wall. A voice said in English, "I haven't been back for ages. Let's have a look at the place." Funny accent. Italian maybe. He stared at the gate for another minute and wondered, *What if . . . ?* Then he smiled and turned away. No way. Couldn't be. He had never believed in coincidence. The world's small. But not that small.

Chapter 46

"I purchased this piece thinking of you, Wolfgang," said Ali Mevlevi as he stepped into Wolfgang Kaiser's office. His arm was pointing at the fabulous mosaic of the mounted Saracen brandishing his sword above a one-armed moneylender. "I don't get to see it often enough."

Wolfgang Kaiser strolled to the door of his private elevator, his broad smile bursting with all the bonhomie in the world. "You must make it a habit to stop in more often. It has been a while since your last visit. Three years?"

"Nearly four." Mevlevi grasped the outstretched hand and drew Kaiser in for a hug. "It's more difficult to travel these days."

"Not for much longer. I'm pleased to say that a meeting has been arranged on Monday morning with a colleague of mine, a man well placed in the naturalization department."

"A civil servant?"

Kaiser raised his shoulders as if to say "Who else?" "One more who never quite got accustomed to living on his salary."

"Doing your bit for privatization, are you?"

"Unfortunately, the fellow is located in the Tessin, in Lugano. Neumann scheduled the meeting for ten A.M. It will mean an early start."

"You will be joining me, Mr. Neumann?"

Nick said yes and added that they would be departing at seven Monday morning.

He had just presided over the counting of twenty million dollars in cash. For two and a half hours, he had stood in a small, antiseptic room two floors underground helping break the seals on slim packets of one-hundred-dollar bills and handing the money to a portly clerk for the counting. At first, the sight of so much cash had left him giddy. But as time passed and his fingers grew smudged with the U.S. Treasury's ink, his giddiness grew to boredom and then to anger. He could not continue the charade much longer.

Mevlevi had watched it all, never once growing restless. Funny thing, Nick thought, the only ones who didn't trust the Swiss banks were the crooks who used them.

Kaiser took his favorite seat under the Renoir. "If a Swiss passport is strong enough to protect Marc Rich against the wrath of the United States government, I'm sure it will do for you."

Mevlevi sat on the couch, dapperly pinching the knees of his trousers. "I must accept your word on this."

"Rich hasn't been bothered by the American authorities since he set up his domicile in Zug," enthused Kaiser.

Before becoming a fugitive from justice, Marc Rich had been president of Phillipp Bros., the world's largest commodities trading corporation. In 1980, he had found the sub-market oil prices offered by the newly installed fundamentalist government of Iran irresistible, and despite the American government's strict embargo on trading with the Ayatollah Khomeini, had bought as much of the stuff as he could. He sold the lot to the Seven Sisters' traditional customers at one dollar below the OPEC floor and made a killing.

Soon afterward, the U.S. Treasury Department traced the orders to buy the restricted oil back to New York and from there to the offices of one Marc Rich. Rich's lawyers kept the government at bay for over two years, agreeing to fines as high as fifty thousand dollars a day to keep their client out of jail. But soon it became clear that the government's case was rock solid, and that if tried, Rich would take an extended vacation behind the bars of a federal country club. Discretion, and in this instance, self-preservation, being the better part of valor, Rich skedaddled to Switzerland, a country holding no extradition treaty with the United States for crimes of a fiscal or tax-oriented nature. He set up his new company's headquarters in the canton Zug, where he hired a dozen traders, put some local big shots on the board, and made several generous donations to the local community. Soon afterward, Rich was awarded a Swiss passport.

Kaiser explained that Mevlevi suffered from a similar problem. Sterling Thorne was attempting to have his accounts frozen on grounds that he had violated statutes prohibiting money laundering, an act that Switzerland had only recently declared illegal. Generally speaking, no Swiss prosecutor would freeze the account of a wealthy citizen based solely on charges of money laundering brought by a foreign authority, however well supported by hard evidence. First, the suspect had to be tried and convicted. And lest any rash measures be taken, an appeal granted. Holding a Swiss passport would thus effectively prevent the U.S. DEA from obtaining a warrant to freeze Ali Mevlevi's accounts. In one week, Sterling Thorne would be just a bad memory.

"And our other problem?" Mevlevi asked. "The nagging one that threatened to do us so much harm."

Kaiser glanced at Nick. "Effectively resolved."

Mevlevi relaxed. "So much the better. This trip has already freed me of a great many worries. Onward then? Do we have some time to review my account?"

"Of course." Wolfgang Kaiser turned to his assistant. "Nicholas, would you mind running down to DZ and picking up Mr. Mevlevi's mail. I'm sure he would like to take it with him." He picked up the phone sitting on the coffee table and dialed a four-digit extension. "Karl? I am sending down a Mr. Neumann to pick up the file for numbered account 549.617 RR. Yes, I know one isn't allowed to remove it from DZ. Indulge me this one time, Karl. What's that? The second favor this week. Really?" Kaiser paused and looked directly at Nick. Nick could tell he was wondering what in the world the first favor had been. But this was no time for dawdling and in a second Kaiser continued his conversation. "Thank you, that's very kind of you. His name is Neumann, Karl. He may look familiar to you. Call me if you recognize him."

Nick was worried. Yes, he had anticipated that Mevlevi might want to review his file. Yes, he had been sure to bring back all the transaction confirmations he'd stolen from Mevlevi's file three days ago. But, like a fool, he'd left them in his office, taped to the underside of the top drawer of his desk. Now he had one chance to replace the transaction confirmations in the file before the Pasha discovered them missing. His only hope was to return to his office after retrieving the file and exchange the dummy envelopes for the real ones.

And therein lay his problem.

To retrieve the letters, he would have to pass the entrance to Kaiser's outer offices with Mevlevi's compendious file in hand. Rita Sutter might see him. Or Ott or Maeder, or any one of the executives who frequented the Chairman's antechamber. Of course that wasn't the only problem. During his call to Karl, Kaiser had referred to Nick twice specifically by name. The Chairman had even served up a riddle as to his identity. *"Call me if you recognize him,"* he'd said. Only three days ago, Nick had presented himself to Karl as Peter Sprecher. Now what would the old geezer think?

Nick waited for the elevator, frustrated at his lack of alternatives. He was scared. If Mevlevi discovered that his mail was missing, his crime would be discovered in a second. And then? Immediate dismissal if he was lucky. And if he wasn't? Better not to think of it.

Nick decided that speed would be his only ally. He'd rush into DZ, grab the dossier, and rush out. Similarly, when he returned to the Fourth Floor, he would dash past the Emperor's Lair and replace the stolen letters before anyone saw him. Carl Lewis was better suited to run this errand.

On the first floor, Nick strode briskly through the hallway until he reached the entry to DZ. He placed his back against the steel door, drew in three deep breaths, then opened it and marched to Karl's counter.

"I'm here to pick up the file for account

549.617 RR for Herr Kaiser."

Karl responded to the commanding edge of Nick's voice. He spun, picked up the thick dossier, and handed it to the Chairman's assistant in one fluid motion. Nick placed the dossier under his arm and turned to leave the office.

"Wait," cried Karl. "The Chairman asked if I could recognize you. Give me a minute!"

Nick rotated his shoulders to the left and gave Karl his profile. "I'm sorry. We're very busy. The Chairman expects to receive this dossier right away." With that he exited the office as quickly as he had entered. The entire visit had lasted fifteen seconds.

He hit the stairwell running, taking the steps two by two. He held the dossier in his left hand and the banister in his right. After five upward strides, his knee gave out. He could raise the leg, but only if he was willing to endure a severe lick of pain. So much for speed. Now he had to make sure he suppressed a limp.

Nick rested when he reached the entry to the Fourth Floor. He could not imagine walking into Wolfgang Kaiser's office and handing Ali Mevlevi a dossier from which privately addressed mail had been stolen. What would the man do when he opened up letters supposedly containing confirmations of his many deposits and transfers only to find blank paper?

The consequences were unthinkable. Yet

593

only seconds from happening.

Nick opened the door that led to the Fourth Floor hallway and walked directly into Rudolf Ott.

"Excuse me," said Ott, eyes wide with shock.

"I'm in a hurry to see the Chairman," Nick blurted without thinking. As Ott was directly facing him, there was no way to judge in which direction the man was heading. If he was going to see Mrs. Sutter, Nick would have no choice but to accompany him.

Ott blinked anxiously through his thick glasses. "I thought you were with him right now. Well, what are you waiting for? Get moving."

Nick sighed with relief and set off down the hallway. He could already see the wide entryway leading to the Chairman's anteroom. Rita Sutter sat just inside and to the right. She would be expecting his return any minute and unless he practically ran by, she would see him. He had no choice but to lower his head and walk past the entryway. He told himself to disregard any remark he might hear. His own office was down the corridor and to the left. Fifteen seconds, twenty max, were all he needed to replace the Pasha's correspondence.

Nick walked down the hallway, conscious of keeping an even gait. He was in a great deal of pain. Three steps and he would be in Rita Sutter's view. Two steps. The double doors were wide open, just as they'd been when he had left a few minutes ago. His peripheral vision told him that Kaiser's doors were shut and that the red light above them was illuminated. Do not disturb. Period!

Nick kept his head down and powered past the entryway. He thought he saw someone speaking with Rita Sutter but he couldn't be sure. Anyway, it didn't matter now. Another few steps and he would be around the corner, out of her sight. He slowed his pace and straightened his back. His worry had been for naught.

"Neumann," a deep voice yelled.

Nick kept walking. One more stride and he was around the corner. If necessary he could lock his office door.

"Goddammit, Neumann, I called for you," Armin Schweitzer boomed. "Stop this second."

Nick slowed. He hesitated.

Schweitzer lumbered down the hall after him. "My God, man, are you deaf? I called your name twice."

Nick turned on his heel. "The Chairman is expecting me. I need to get a few papers out of my office."

"Bullshit," said Schweitzer. "Rita told me where you've been. I see you have what you were sent for. Now get in there. You probably wanted to call a girlfriend, right? Make plans for a Friday night. It doesn't do to keep the Chairman waiting."

Nick looked down the corridor toward his office and then toward Schweitzer, who was extending an eager hand, ready to personally drag him back to the Chairman's office. The choice between Ali Mevlevi and Armin Schweitzer was easy to make. "I said I have to get something out of my office. I'll be with Herr Kaiser in a minute."

Schweitzer was taken aback. He took a step toward Nick, then stopped. "Suit yourself. I'll be sure to inform the Chairman later."

Nick turned his back and continued to his office. Inside, he locked the door behind him and bustled to his desk. He opened the top drawer and felt under it for the Pasha's correspondence. Nothing was there. Had he forgotten where he had taped the letters? He opened the drawers on his right, first one, then the second, even the third, though he knew he hadn't hidden the letters there. Nothing was under any of the drawers. Someone had found the stolen correspondence.

Entering the Chairman's anteroom, Nick saw that Rita Sutter was engaged on the telephone.

"I'm sorry, Karl, but the Chairman cannot be disturbed." She punched a button, disconnecting the call, then motioned for him to stop at her desk. "Karl just asked me if a Mr. Sprecher had come down to DZ in your place."

"Really?" Nick pried open a brittle smile.

He had been sure he'd escaped scot-free.

"I don't know how he confused you with Mr. Sprecher. You two don't look anything alike. Poor Karl. I don't like to see him getting older. We're following close behind." She dialed a two-digit number and after a moment said, "Mr. Neumann is back from *Dokumentation Zentrale.*"

"Send him in," barked Kaiser, loud enough for Nick to hear.

Nick waited for Rita Sutter to pass on Karl's quip to the Chairman, but she hung up the phone, then inclined her head toward the double doors.

Nick walked into the Chairman's office. He was struck once again by its overwhelming size. The massive mahogany desk beckoned like a medieval altar. Dim light filtered in through the grand arched window. He looked through it, surveying the busy scene below. Trams passed one another. Pedestrians crowded the sidewalks. A large square flag bearing the blue and white shield of Zurich was strung above the street. He hadn't noticed it before. He looked closer at the flag. Suddenly, it struck him that he knew this view. It was the one vivid memory from his father's last visit to the bank, seventeen years ago. He imagined himself as a child, nose pressed to the window, marveling at the busy street scene below. Nick had been in the Emperor's Lair when he was ten years old.

Kaiser and Mevlevi were still seated around the long coffee table. They paid no attention to his slow approach.

"How have my investments fared of late?" demanded the Pasha.

"Rather well," said Kaiser. "As of yesterday afternoon's close, your investment has earned twenty-seven percent in the last ten months."

Nick listened, wondering what Kaiser had put the Pasha's money into.

Mevlevi asked Kaiser, "And if this Adler Bank gains seats on your board?"

"We will not allow that to happen."

"They're close, no?"

Kaiser looked up at Nick, only now registering his return to the office. "Neumann, what's the official tally? Take a seat. Here, give me that dossier."

Reluctantly, Nick handed Mevlevi's file to Wolfgang Kaiser. "The Adler Bank has stalled at thirty-one percent of outstanding votes. We are holding fifty-two percent. The rest are uncommitted."

Mevlevi pointed to the dossier sitting on Kaiser's lap. "And what percentage of the votes do I control?"

"You hold exactly two percent of our shares," said Kaiser.

"But an *important* two percent. Now I understand why you need my loan so badly."

"Think of it as a guaranteed private placement."

"Loan, placement, call it what you like. The terms you are offering still stand? Ten percent net after ninety days?"

"For the full two hundred million," Kaiser confirmed. "The offer still stands."

Nick grimaced at the usurious terms the Chairman so blithely offered.

Mevlevi asked, "Would this loan be used to buy shares?"

"Naturally," said Kaiser. "It will raise our holdings to sixty percent. Konig's bid will be effectively blocked."

Mevlevi crinkled his brow, as if he had been misinformed. "But should the Adler Bank's offer unravel, the price of your shares would plummet. I may stand to earn the ten percent you are offering on the two hundred million, but the value of my shares will decrease. We both stand to lose a good deal of money."

"Only temporarily. We've taken steps to drastically improve our operating ratios and lift the year-end net profit. As soon as they're in place, the price of our shares will far surpass their current level."

"You hope," cautioned Mevlevi.

"Markets are unpredictable," said Kaiser, "but seldom illogical."

"Perhaps I should sell my shares while I'm ahead." The Pasha motioned toward his private file. "May I?"

Kaiser extended it halfway to his client, then drew it back. "If arrangements for the loan could be made this afternoon, I would be most grateful."

Nick held his breath. His eyes were riveted to the dossier, while an inner chorus demanded to know who had discovered the transfer confirmations beneath his desk.

"This afternoon?" said the Pasha. "Not possible. I have pressing business. Mr. Neumann will be required. I'm afraid I can't give you a response until Monday morning. Now, I'd like to take a moment and leaf through my papers. See what mail I've received."

Kaiser handed Mevlevi the dossier.

Nick rubbed his forehead. His eyes examined the carpet under his feet. All his senses were directed inward. He listened to his heart beating steadily. Surprisingly, his pulse was hardly elevated. His fate was sealed.

Mevlevi opened the dossier and picked up an envelope, one of Nick's phonies. He flipped it over and placed his thumb under the flap, digging a smooth nail along the seal.

Nick watched him intently. He could hear the envelope being opened. He could feel the paper tearing. Then he shut his eyes. He was not aware of Rita Sutter's presence until she was halfway into the Chairman's office.

Kaiser rose sharply to his feet. "What is it?" he asked.

Rita Sutter appeared shaken. Her skin was gray and her face cast with grim resolve. As she neared, she extended her hand as if seeking a wall to steady herself.

"What is it, woman? What in God's name is the matter with you?"

Rita Sutter took a step back, visibly hurt by his brusque indifference. "Cerruti," she whispered. "Marco Cerruti. He's killed himself. The police are outside."

Like two deer caught in an automobile's headlights, Kaiser and Mevlevi stared at each other for one interminable second, and the acknowledgment of conspirators passed between them.

Suddenly, the room was in motion. Mevlevi threw the half-opened letter into the dossier and closed the cover. "This will keep for another time."

Kaiser gestured toward the private elevator. "We can speak this evening."

Mevlevi walked with measured strides to the concealed elevator. "Perhaps. I may be busy with other matters. Neumann, come with me."

Nick hesitated. Something told him not to leave the bank. Cerruti was dead. Becker was dead. Hanging around the Pasha did not improve your life expectancy.

Rita Sutter hugged her chest as if to console herself. "I can't understand it. You told us Marco was getting so much better."

Kaiser paid the disconsolate woman no heed. "Nicholas," he ordered. "Go with Mr. Mevlevi and do as he says. Now!"

Nick stopped considering whether or not to go. The defender of the faith had no choice. He walked to the elevator and slid in alongside Mevlevi. The door closed and he caught a last glimpse of Wolfgang Kaiser. The Chairman had draped an arm around Rita Sutter and was speaking softly to her. Nick could only make out a few of his words.

"My dear friend, Marco," he was saying. "Why would he do such a thing? I wouldn't have thought him capable of it. Did he leave a note? A terrible tragedy."

And then the elevator door slammed shut.

Chapter 47

For the next quarter of an hour, Nick's life passed in a blur. He was presented with a succession of hazy images, as if watching a separate self through the fogged window of a fast-moving train. Nick descends in the cramped elevator with the Pasha; Nick climbs into the waiting limousine; Nick offers appropriate noises while Mevlevi issues the first in a string of hollow laments over Marco Cerruti's death. And when the Pasha instructs the chauffeur to take them to the Platzspitz, instead of voicing his concern, Nick remains silent. He is too busy replaying in his mind's eye the interplay between Wolfgang Kaiser and Ali Mevlevi at the moment Rita Sutter informed them of the unfortunate banker's death. He is convinced of their complicity.

The limousine sped down Talackerstrasse. Nick sat in the backseat watching the city pass by. As they drove past the *Hauptbahnhof*, he took note of the Pasha's instructions and running them once more through his head, spoke up. "The Platzspitz isn't open to the public anymore," he said. "The gates are locked. It's off-limits."

The chauffeur pulled the limousine to the

curb, then turned in his seat to offer a like opinion. "This is correct. The park has been closed for eight years. Too many bad memories."

The Platzspitz was Zurich's infamous "needle park." Ten years ago the place had been a junkie's paradise. An assembly point for the forlorn and forgotten of Europe. The Pasha's private gold mine.

"I've been assured we'll have no problem entering," said Mevlevi. "Give us forty minutes. We just want to have a stroll through the grounds." He climbed out of the car and walked to a gate cut into the heavy wrought iron fence that surrounded the park. He tried the handle and the gate swung open. He cast a last glance at Nick. "Come on, then."

Nick jumped from the car and followed. He had a presentiment that something bad was going to happen. What business could bring Mevlevi to the park? Who had assured him the gate would be open? And been right?

Nick passed through the gate and followed the Pasha along a gravel pathway bisecting triangular patches of grass dusted with snow. Giant pines towered above their heads. Behind them loomed the Gothic tower and cleft battlements of the Swiss National Museum.

Mevlevi paused long enough to allow him to catch up. "You decided to join me."

"The Chairman asked that I accompany you," said Nick evenly, though to his own ear

604

he lent his words a combative ring. In his heart he had given up the amoral preserves of banking for the riskier estates of law enforcement. If he couldn't intervene directly, then he would bear witness, he would record, he would make himself a living testament to this man's crimes. And if that meant he had to become an accomplice, and later pay the necessary price, then so be it.

"Ordered you was more like it," said Mevlevi as he set off at a leisurely pace. "Still, he thinks highly of you. He told me your father was at the bank before you. You respect your heritage, following in his footsteps like a good son. My father always wished for as much, but I could never be a derv. The spinning, the chanting. I was only interested in this world."

Nick walked alongside the Pasha, barely hearing his words. His mind was filled only with plans and plots and schemes to end the man's reign.

Mevlevi said, "Family is important. I've come to think of Wolfgang as a brother. Without my help I doubt the bank would have grown at such a rapid pace. Not because of my money. What I gave him was the spark to succeed. Without the proper encouragement it's surprising what an intelligent man *cannot* do. All of us are capable of great acts. It's the motivation we so often lack, don't you agree?"

Nick suppressed a caustic grin and managed

to say yes, though he was certain his definition of "great acts" differed wildly from the Pasha's. What spark had Mevlevi provided Kaiser to succeed? What did he have in store for Nick?

Mevlevi said, "Soon it will be time for the next generation to see to the bank. It's a pleasure to know that some of that responsibility may fall on your shoulders, Mr. Neumann. Or may I call you Nicholas?"

"Mr. Neumann is fine."

"I see." The Pasha waved a finger at Nick as if scolding him. "More Swiss than the Swiss themselves. A good strategy. I know it well. I've lived in other men's countries my entire adult life. Thailand, Argentina, the States, now Lebanon."

Nick asked where he had lived in the States.

"Here and there," said Mevlevi, as if it were the title of a catchy tune. "New York, California." Suddenly, he walked faster. "Ah, my colleagues have arrived."

Ahead, on a park bench facing the river Limmat sat two heavily dressed men. Shadows cast by the boughs of an overhanging pine masked their faces. One was short and stocky, the other larger, plain obese.

"This shouldn't take long," said Mevlevi. "Feel free to join me. In fact, I insist. Kaiser expects me to provide you with a bit of a business education. Consider this the first lesson: How to maintain a proper relationship between supplier and distributor."

Nick steeled himself. Be silent, he told himself. Be vigilant. And above all, remember every goddamned word spoken.

"Albert, Gino, I am thrilled to see you again. *Salaam Aleikhum.*" Ali Mevlevi kissed each man three times — left cheek, right cheek, left cheek — all the while pumping their hands.

"*Salaam Aleikhum,* Al-Mevlevi," each said in turn.

Albert was the smaller of the two men, a tired accountant one audit past his prime with wiry gray hair and mottled yellow skin. "You must tell us the latest news of our homeland," he said. "We have heard encouraging reports."

Next to him, Gino, a lumbering giant going three hundred pounds easy, nodded his head as if he had also wanted to ask the question.

"Most is true," said Mevlevi. "Skyscrapers going up everywhere. A new freeway nearing completion. And still the traffic is absolutely terrible."

"Always," laughed Albert, too loudly.

"Perhaps the nicest development has been the reopening of the St. Georges. Better than before the war."

"Tea dancing?" Gino asked in a voice barely louder than a whisper.

"Speak up," exhorted Albert. He averted his gaze from his brother and spoke to an invisible gallery in the sky. "The size of an elephant and he talks like a mouse."

"I asked if tea dances were still held at the St. Georges?"

"More splendid than ever," said Mevlevi. "Thursdays and Sundays at four on the esplanade. A wonderful string quartet."

Gino smiled wistfully.

"There, you've made my brother happy," said Albert. He put a hand on the Pasha's shoulder and whispered in his ear.

"Yes, of course," replied Mevlevi. He took a step backward and placed his hand in the lee of Nick's back, nudging him forward. "This is a new member of my staff. Mr. Nicholas Neumann. In charge of financing for our operations. Neumann, meet Albert and Gino Makdisi, brethren long absent from Lebanon."

Nick stepped forward and shook each man's hand. He knew who they were. A corner of the local papers was practically reserved for their portraits. And it wasn't the society column.

Albert Makdisi guided the group toward the river. "We spoke this morning with our colleagues in Milan. All is well. Monday at this time the shipment will be in Zurich."

"Joseph tells me your men appeared nervous. 'Skittish,' he said. Why?"

"Who is this Joseph?" asked Albert. "Why do you send a man to accompany your shipment? Look at me, Al-Mevlevi. We are not nervous. We are thrilled to see you once again. It's been too long. Nervous? No. Surprised? Happily!"

The Pasha lost his easy banter. "Not as surprised as I, when I learned that you had sent the lovely Lina to Max Rothstein. You knew I had an eye for her sort, didn't you? You always were a clever one, Albert."

Nick could feel the tension between the two men ratchet up a notch.

Albert Makdisi dabbed at the corner of his eyes with a white hankie. Both lower eyelids sagged horribly, revealing vitreous crescents. "What are you talking about? Lina? I don't know a woman named Lina. Tell me about her."

"With pleasure," said Mevlevi. "A spirited girl from Jounieh. A Christian. She came to live with me these last nine months. Alas, she has recently departed. I understand you spoke together every Sunday."

Albert Makdisi grew red in the face. "Utter nonsense. Who is Lina? Really, this is beyond any of my imaginings. Let us talk sense. We have a shipment due in. Business to discuss."

Gino huffed his agreement, keeping his eyes locked on his brother.

Mevlevi adopted a conciliatory tone of voice. "You're right, Albert. Very important business. It is to that end that we must dedicate ourselves. Personal differences? Let's put them in the waste bin. I'm willing to give you an opportunity to apologize for your past actions. I want us to restart our business relationship on its former solid ground."

Albert spoke to Gino as if no one else were present. "Here is a real gentleman. He proposes to return to us that which we have not yet lost." He gave a dyspeptic grunt. "Go on, Al-Mevlevi. We await your proposition with open assholes."

Mevlevi pretended not to have heard the insult. "I am asking you for a prepayment of forty million dollars for the shipment that is due to arrive Monday. The full amount must be transferred to my account at the United Swiss Bank before the end of business today."

"Do you expect me to run to my bankers and sit with them while they rush to make this payment?"

"If necessary."

Gino prodded Albert. "Perhaps, older brother, we should take a moment and discuss the proposition. We do have the cash. It's only a question of two or three days."

"Nonsense," Albert Makdisi spat out. "With such sound advice we would be bankrupt three times over." He took a step forward and addressed himself directly to Mevlevi. "We will never prepay for a shipment of merchandise. This is forty million dollars we are discussing. If anything should happen to the cargo, then what? Once it is in our warehouse, properly weighed, its quality assayed, payment shall be made. Until then, I am sorry."

Mevlevi shook his head slowly from side to side. "I thought I might rely on a small favor after our many years of business. I thought I might overlook your indiscretions. Lina? Your poisonous flower." Finally, he shrugged. "What am I to do? There is no one else with whom I can work in this territory."

Albert Makdisi crossed his arms over his chest and stared hard at Mevlevi. He dabbed nervously at the corner of each eye.

"Your final word?" asked Mevlevi, clearly hoping that Makdisi might reconsider.

"The very last."

The Pasha stared back. "The right of refusal is often a man's final victory."

"I refuse."

Mevlevi lowered his eyes and looked over both shoulders. "Cold, isn't it?" he said to no one in particular. He removed a pair of driving gloves from a pocket and carefully pulled them on.

Gino Makdisi said, "It's been a miserable winter. Never have we had such weather. Storm after storm after storm. Don't you agree, Mr. Neumann?"

Nick nodded distractedly, unsure what he was supposed to do. What the hell had Mevlevi meant about the right of refusal being a man's final victory? Hadn't Albert Makdisi caught the veiled threat?

Albert looked at Mevlevi's gloves and said, "You'll need better than those to keep your hands warm."

"Oh?" Mevlevi stretched his hands in front of him as if admiring the fit of the gloves, pulling first one and then the other tight. "No doubt you are correct. But I don't intend to use them for warmth." He reached into his jacket pocket and drew out a silver nine-millimeter pistol. With surprising speed he wrapped his left arm around Albert Makdisi's shoulder and pulled him near. At the same time, he drove the barrel of the weapon deep into the folds of the man's overcoat and pulled the trigger three times in rapid succession. The blast of the pistol was muffled, sounding more like a harsh cough than a discharging firearm. "Lina said you had eyes like wet oysters, *habibi*."

Albert Makdisi collapsed to the ground, his watery gray eyes open wide. A trail of blood fell from the left corner of his mouth. He blinked once. Gino Makdisi knelt at his brother's side. He put a hand inside the coat and it came away smeared red. His porcine face was frozen in shock.

Nick stood motionless. He hadn't seen this coming. His senses left him, overloaded by all he had seen and heard that day.

Mevlevi advanced a step toward Albert Makdisi's corpse. A symphony of hate played across his features. He ground the heel of his shoe onto the dead man's face until the nasal cartilage collapsed and blood rushed forth. "Stupid man. How dare you?"

A wisp of smoke rose from the barrel of the pistol.

"Here, Neumann," Mevlevi called. "Catch." And with that he tossed the gun to his escort.

Four feet, maybe less, separated the two men. Before Nick could stifle his reflexes, he had caught the gun in his bare hands. Instinctively, he placed his finger through the trigger guard and raised the pistol so that it pointed at Mevlevi's haughty face.

The Pasha spread open his arms. "Now's your chance, Nicholas. Feeling out of sorts? Seen too much for one day? Not sure banking is the right profession for you? I bet you didn't think it would be this exciting, did you? Well, here's your chance. Kill me or join me forever."

"You've gone too far," Nick said. "You shouldn't have brought me down into your filthy world. What choice have you left me? Have others seen as much and kept quiet?"

"Worse. Far, far worse. You'll guard your silence, too. It will be our bond."

Nick lowered the gun so that it aimed at the Pasha's torso. Was this the spark Mevlevi had provided Wolfgang Kaiser? Making the Chairman an accessory to murder? "You're wrong.

There's no bond between us. You've pushed me too far."

"No such place. I've spent my life pissing in the darkest corners of men's souls. Believe me, I know. Now give me the gun. After all, we're on the same side."

"What side is that?"

"The side of business, of course. Free trade. Unrestricted commerce. Healthy profits and healthier bonuses. Now let's have the gun, chop-chop."

"Never." Nick allowed his finger to caress the polished metal trigger. He enjoyed its promise of swift and final judgment. The grip was warm and the smell of burned powder tickled his nose. It was all coming back to him now. He tightened his grip on the pistol and smiled. Christ, this would be easy.

Mevlevi lost his jocular mien. "Nicholas, please. The time for games has passed. There is a corpse behind you and your fingerprints are all over the murder weapon. You've made your stand. As I said before, I am most impressed by you. I see defiance runs in your veins, too."

Had Kaiser also defied the Pasha? Nick wondered. Or was he talking about somebody else? "I'm taking this gun with me and leaving. Don't expect to see me Monday morning. About this" — he motioned his head toward the lifeless body of Albert Makdisi — "there's only one thing I can do. I'll have to explain best I can."

"Explain what?" said Gino Makdisi, who had pulled himself to his feet and taken a position next to Mevlevi. "That you killed my brother?"

Mevlevi said to Gino, "I am so very, very sorry. I did as you requested. I gave him a last chance to apologize."

"Albert?" scoffed Gino. "He never apologized to anyone."

Mevlevi returned his attention to Nick. "I'm afraid it appears that you, my friend, killed Albert Makdisi."

"Yes," agreed Gino Makdisi. "Two witnesses. We both saw you do it."

Nick laughed grimly at his predicament. Mevlevi had bought off Gino Makdisi. A wild thought came to him. Fuck it all, then. One man's death was already on his soul. Why not two? Why not three? He stepped toward the Pasha and firmed his grip around the pistol's steel butt. He raised his arm and drew a bead on Ali Mevlevi's face, suddenly absent its smug smile. You killed Cerruti, you son of a bitch. You murdered your partner in cold blood. How many more men have you killed before that? Becker too? Was he snooping around a little too much? And now you want to frame me?

Nick's world narrowed to a tight corridor. His periphery grew dark. Anger spread through every inch of his being. Unconsciously, he increased his pressure on the trigger. The muscles in his forearm contracted and his shoulder hardened. This is what it feels like to do some good, he told himself.

Do some good.

"Think of your father," Mevlevi said, as if reading Nick's mind.

"I am." Nick extended his arm and pulled the trigger. The gun clicked. He pulled it again. Metal struck metal.

Ali Mevlevi exhaled noisily. "Quite some feat. I must admit it requires real courage to stare down the barrel of a gun even when you know it to be empty. For a moment there, I forgot how many shots I had given Albert."

Gino Makdisi took a snub-nosed revolver from his jacket and pointed it at Nick. He looked to Mevlevi for instructions. Mevlevi lifted a hand and said, "I'm deciding." Then to Nick, "Please give me the gun. Slowly. Thank you."

Nick looked away from the men to the river running below them. The dry firing of the pistol had shattered the rage pounding inside his skull. He had expected the gun to buck in his hand, to feel the crack of the bullet, to hear the tinkling of the spent shell as it hit the ground. He had expected to kill a man.

Mevlevi tucked the silver pistol back into his jacket. He knelt and collected the spent shell casings. Standing, he whispered in Nick's ear. "I told you this morning that I wanted to thank you. What better way to show my gratitude than to make you a member of my family? Cerruti's passing has left a convenient opening."

Nick stared through him. "I'll never be a member of your family."

"You have no choice. Today, I let you live. I gave you life. Now, you'll do as I ask. Nothing serious. At least, not yet. For the moment I simply want you to do your job."

Gino Makdisi said, "Remember the gun, Mr. Neumann. It carries your fingerprints. I may be a criminal, but in court my word is as good as the next man's." He shrugged his shoulders as if things weren't so bad, then twisted his bulk toward the Pasha. "Can you drop me at the Schiller Bank? We'll have to hurry if we're to make the transfer this afternoon."

The Pasha smiled. "Not to worry. Mr. Neumann is an expert at processing late-arriving transfers. Every Monday and Thursday at three o'clock, right, Nicholas?"

Chapter 48

Peter Sprecher drummed his fingers on top of his desk and told himself in a stern voice that he must count to ten before exploding. Silently, he invoked Almighty God, the King James variant, thank you, to pacify the jabbering crowd gathered around the hexagonal trading desk adjacent to his own. He heard Tony Gerber, a rat-faced options specialist, rave about the "strangle" he had put on USB shares. If the shares stayed within five points of their current level, he'd take down a two-hundred-thousand-franc profit in just thirty days. "Go ahead and annualize that return," he heard Gerber brag. "Three hundred and eighty percent. You try and beat it."

Sprecher reached seven before deciding he could stand it no longer. He slid his chair back and tapped his neighbor Hassan Faris, the bank's chief of equities trading, on the shoulder. "I know it is a quiet Friday afternoon but if you wish to continue this infernal racket, take your pack of thieves off to another corner of the cave. I've another dozen calls yet to make and I can't hear myself think."

"Mr. Sprecher," answered Faris over the continuous buzz, "you are sitting in the center of the trading floor of a bank that derives its entire income from buying and selling financial instruments. If you have a problem hearing, I'll be happy to order you a headset. Until then, mind your own fucking business. Okay?"

Sprecher grumbled something about not being an operator and slid his chair back to his desk. Faris was right, of course. The place was supposed to be a hive of activity. The more frenetic, the better. A moving market meant someone somewhere was making money. He scanned the floor. Like bumpers on a snooker table, seven hexagonal desks sprang from the green baize floor. Around them, men stood in varied positions of action. He heard someone fire off an order for a thousand OEX contracts at the market. Beside him, Alfons Gruber was whispering feverishly into his handset, "I know Philip Morris is up twelve percent in the last week, but I still want to short the sucker. I hear the jury's ready to convict. I'm telling you, short it!"

Sprecher felt lost. This was not his world. It was everything he had rebelled against. A trader's career was nasty, brutish, and short. He did not enjoy phoning ladies and gentlemen with whom he had no prior acquaintance and hectoring them to put in their lot with Klaus Konig and the Adler Bank. It made him feel cheap. In his heart he was still a USB man, and probably would be until the day he died.

Sprecher returned to the task at hand. Officially stated, his job was to rally the votes of those institutional shareholders holding sizable blocks of USB stock to the Adler Bank's cause. It had been a difficult task, confidential shareholder lists pirated from USB notwithstanding. Holders of Swiss bank stocks tended to be a conservative lot. The Adler Bank was having little luck winning votes based on its past returns. Too risky, too aggressive by half, stammered the stodgy investors. With days remaining until USB's general assembly, he was convinced that the sole route open to capture two seats on the board of the United Swiss Bank was straightforward share accumulation: cash purchases on the open market.

There was only one problem. The Adler Bank's cash reserves had dried up. The bank had leveraged its assets beyond any prudent measure to secure its current position of thirty-two percent of USB's outstanding shares, a stake valued as of yesterday's close at 1.4 billion Swiss francs. God forbid Konig failed to gain the deciding one percent: the price of USB stock would collapse, and the market value of Adler's portfolio would drop between eighteen and twenty percent overnight.

Sprecher spotted a tall man waving to him from across the room. It was George von Graffenried, Konig's number two and head honcho on the bond desk. He waved back and began standing but Von Graffenried motioned for him to stay seated. A few moments later he was squatting by Sprecher's side.

"I've just received another surprise from our friends at USB," Von Graffenried said quietly, handing him a sheet of paper. "Get on it. A block of one hundred forty thousand shares. Exactly the one percent we need. Find whoever runs this Widows and Orphans Fund of Zurich and get your butt over there as quickly as possible. We have to capture their votes!"

Sprecher picked up the photocopy of USB stationery and brought it closer to his eyes. *The Widows and Orphans Fund of Zurich. Fund manager Mrs. F. Emmenegger.* He smirked. His American friend's ploy had obviously worked. Such was the pressure to surpass the thirty-three percent vote barrier that neither Konig nor Von Graffenried, despite never having heard of the fund, had bothered to research its authenticity.

"I'll expect an answer by tomorrow," said Von Graffenried. "We'll be here all day long."

Sprecher slapped the paper onto his desk and withdrew a pen. He read the sheet, suppressing an urge to laugh aloud. Look at the handwritten notes Neumann had inscribed: *Called at 10:00, called at 12:00. No answer. We must not fail!!* Young Nick, earnest to the last.

Dutifully, Sprecher picked up the phone and rang the number written on the sheet. An answering machine responded after the fourth ring. The voice sounded familiar but he couldn't place it, and upon hearing the beep, he left a brief message. "This is Mr. Peter Sprecher calling on behalf of the Adler Bank. We would very much like to speak with you as soon as possible regarding the voting of your block of USB shares at the general assembly on Tuesday. Please feel free to call me back at the following number. Mr. Konig and Mr. Von Graffenried would personally enjoy meeting with you to discuss the Adler Bank's famed investment strategies and to point out how the value of your shareholding would greatly increase with benefit of the Adler Bank's wise counsel."

"Very well done," applauded Hassan Faris. "This is Mister Peter Sprecher. Send out your wives and daughters. Trust us. We want only to ravage and enslave them. Do not worry."

Hassan's troop burst into laughter.

A light on the equity trader's desk lit up. Faris jabbed at the lit button and brought the phone to his ear. He plugged his finger into his other ear, then motioned for his charges to be quiet.

"Shut up!" yelled Faris. He swept his hands through the air, and his followers dispersed.

Sprecher sat up and took note. He rolled his chair closer to his neighbor while inclining his head so as best to eavesdrop on Faris's conversation.

"Wait a moment, sir, I must write this all down," said Faris. "I never make a mistake on so big an order . . . Yes, sir, that is why you hired me . . . For-tee million . . . Is that U.S. dollars or Swiss francs? . . . Dollars, yes sir . . . At the market . . . One minute . . . Mr. Konig, our cash account shows only two million dollars . . . Yes, of course I can arrange for settlement on Tuesday . . . No, we aren't required to say anything . . . Well, technically, yes, but we'll just pay twenty-four hours late, that's all . . . On Tuesday morning at ten . . . Will the money have arrived by that time? . . . Yes, sir . . . I repeat: An order to buy forty million U.S. dollars of USB shares at the market for settlement Tuesday. The entire purchase to be booked into the Ciragan Trading Account."

Sprecher eased his chair back another few inches. He wrote down the words exactly as Faris had spoken them.

"Yessir, I will call with a fill before the day is out . . . We may have to work on the aftermarket . . . I will keep you informed." Faris slammed down the receiver.

"What is the Ciragan Trading Account?" asked Sprecher. Best to pry while the trader was occupied tending to the details of the call.

Hassan scribbled Klaus Konig's instructions onto his order block. "What's that, Sprecher? *Ciragan?* It's Konig's private account."

"Konig's? That doesn't sound like the name of a Swiss trading account. Surely it doesn't belong to the Adler Bank proper."

"It is the account of his largest investor. Most of the USB stock we have purchased is being held in Ciragan Trading. We hold proxy over all shares in that account. They're as good as ours." Hassan looked up from his writing. He wrinkled his brow in annoyance. "Why am I telling you? It's none of your fucking business. Go back to your work, whatever the hell it is you do all day."

Sprecher watched Faris call down to the floor of the Zurich stock exchange. The trader excitedly relayed the "open to buy" for forty million U.S. When the order was filled, the Adler Bank would pass the thirty-three percent barrier. It could, for all intents and purposes, count on winning two seats on the board of the United Swiss Bank. Kaiser would be finished. Nick too.

Ciragan Trading, Sprecher whispered. He'd heard that word only once in his life. *Ciragan Palace.* The password for numbered account 549.617 RR. The Pasha.

Zurich wasn't a big enough town for it to be a coincidence.

He picked up the telephone to call Nick. The whine of Faris's voice reminded him that calling from the Adler Bank was no longer wise. He grabbed his cigarettes and his jacket. Time for a late lunch. "Be a good chap, young

Nick," he whispered to himself, "and keep your bloody ass firmly planted behind your desk for the next ten minutes."

Chapter 49

Nick trudged up the steep hill. The sidewalk was as slick as a wet bar of soap, cobbled with fissures of ice. Normally, this kind of walk would put him into a dark mood. Tonight, he found a grim enjoyment to it. Anything to divert his mind from the events he'd been party to that afternoon. Three hours ago, he had tried to murder a man. He had willed himself to pull the trigger and take the consequences. Even now, part of him wished he'd been successful.

Nick slowed and rested against a barren tree. He was content to hear his heart beating and see his breath's vapor wash. But after a second, another chorus of sound and light took their place. He heard the muted crack of Mevlevi's pistol as it fired three bullets into Albert Makdisi's chest. He caught the Pasha's contemptuous sneer as Rita Sutter announced Cerruti's death. He saw Albert Makdisi's wrecked face, its crushed nose and accusing eyes and he imagined his own face replacing it. Suddenly, he felt sick. He dropped to his knee and heaved. His empty stomach produced a trickle of bile that burned his throat. He gasped, sucking in the cold night air. He had become Mevlevi's pawn. He was in hell.

After leaving the Platzspitz, Mevlevi had ferried him back to the bank. Kaiser was out. The Emperor's Lair was quiet. Three messages from Peter Sprecherg lay on his desk. He ignored them. Reto Feller called once, saying that he'd taken the remaining portfolios Nick had not yet "liberated," and that USB now controlled fifty-eight percent of its outstanding votes. The Adler Bank was mired at thirty-two percent.

Pietro from payments traffic called at 4:15 to inform him that a newly activated numbered account (one of the five Mevlevi had obtained from the International Fiduciary Trust that morning) had received a transfer from the Schiller Bank. The amount: forty million dollars. Nick followed the Pasha's instructions and immediately transferred the full amount to the banks specified by matrix one. Immediately afterward, he left the bank.

Nick resumed his slow walk to Sylvia's apartment. He hadn't wanted to go home after work. He couldn't face the cramped one-room apartment. He thought of it as a cell and of Mevlevi as his jailer. Arriving at the crest of the hill, he paused and turned to study the slope behind him. His eyes skimmed hedges and fences, trees and entryways. He was looking for a phantom he knew must be somewhere behind him — a shadow sent by Mevlevi with instructions to stop any sudden and ill-advised flight to the police.

Nick was exhausted when he reached the entrance to Sylvia's building. Cold, confused, and out of breath. He checked his wristwatch and saw it was only 5:30. He doubted she would be home but rang the buzzer anyway. No one answered. She was probably still at work. He longed to be inside the glass door where he could wait in the warmth and relative comfort of her hallway. Sighing, he closed his eyes and pressed his back against the wall, then slid down until his bottom rested on the crusty snow. Sylvia would be home any minute, he told himself. Relax. His shoulders sagged.

Just a few minutes more till she gets home.

Somewhere over the horizon the earth was shaking. The ground rent itself into towering slabs of concrete that threatened to topple onto his prostrate form. A blunt object poked him in the ribs. Someone shook his shoulders. "Nick, get up," his mother called. "You're blue."

Nick opened his eyes. Sylvia Schon was hunched over him. She felt his cheek with her warm hands. "Are you all right? How long have you been here? My God, you're frozen stiff."

She had too many questions to wait for any one answer.

Nick shook himself and stood up. His back

was sore and his right knee a rock. He checked his wristwatch and groaned. "It's almost seven. I sat down at five-thirty."

Sylvia clucked like a mother hen. "Get inside right now and take a hot shower. Get those clothes off." She gave him a quick kiss. "You're cold as ice. You'll be lucky not to catch pneumonia."

Nick followed her into the apartment. He took note of the faded yellow dossiers she carried under her arm. "You were able to get more activity reports?"

"Of course," Sylvia said proudly. "I have the rest of 1978 and all of 1979. We have the entire weekend, don't we?"

Nick smiled and said they did. He marveled at the facility with which Sylvia checked information into and out of the bank. He wondered briefly if she had told Kaiser about their lunch yesterday, then dismissed the thought. It had probably been Rita Sutter or that asshole Schweitzer — either one of them might have overheard his conversation. Be happy you have at least one person on your side, he told himself. He started to thank her for the reports, but before he could she began peppering him with questions. Where had he been all day? Had he heard the dreadful news about Marco Cerruti? Why hadn't he called if he had planned on joining her for dinner?

Nick sighed and allowed himself to be led into the bathroom.

The watcher stood fifty yards from the apartment hidden in a copse of tall pines. He punched a number into his cellular phone, keeping his eyes pasted to the entry of the apartment building. The desired party answered after a dozen rings. "Where is he?"

"With the woman. She just came home. He's inside with her now."

"Just as we thought." A knowing laugh. "At least he's predictable. I knew he wouldn't go to the police. By the way, how does he look?"

"Exhausted," said the watcher. "He slept in front of her apartment building for an hour."

"Go home," said Ali Mevlevi. "He's one of us now."

Nick huddled beneath a fierce shower, enjoying the needles of hot water that pounded his skin. Another hour in here and he'd feel human again. He savored the warmth, willing it to take away his despair. He thought about that afternoon. He had to look at it analytically, to divorce himself from what he had witnessed. He wanted desperately to talk about it with someone, probably just so that he could proclaim his innocence. He considered confiding in Sylvia but decided against it. Knowledge of the Pasha's actions would serve in the long run only to incriminate her. He didn't want to share his troubles.

Nick turned his face upward, allowing the

bristling water to massage his eyelids and tickle his nose and his mouth. Suddenly, a memory stirred deep inside his confused brain — a souvenir from earlier that afternoon. He closed his eyes and concentrated. A word or two flickered — something sparked by his interest in the activity reports. He tried to coax it out, sure for a split second that he had a letter or two. But no, it kept itself hidden, swimming just below the surface. He gave up. Still, he knew something was there, and its presence fired in him a fierce desire for its discovery.

A dinner of veal scaloppini and spaetzle went mostly to waste. Nick couldn't find his appetite. He told Sylvia that plain fatigue had caused him to fall asleep outside her apartment. He just couldn't keep up with the Chairman. She accepted the explanation without comment, or for that matter, interest. She was too busy replaying her colleagues' reactions to Marco Cerruti's suicide. No one could begin to understand why he had taken his own life.

Nick did his best to share her feelings of bewilderment and anguish. "He must have been a brave man. Shooting yourself requires a helluva lot of courage."

More than Cerruti had, that was for certain.

"He'd been drinking," Sylvia explained. "Drink enough and you'll do anything."

Cerruti drink? The hardest stuff he touched

631

was classic Coke. "Where did you hear that?"

"That he'd been drinking? Nowhere. Some-one at the bank mentioned it. Why?"

Nick pretended as if his conscience had been offended, not his memory. "It's a nasty thought, isn't it? As if that explains it all. The guy juiced himself up and capped himself in the noggin. I'll buy it. Now we can forget he even existed. Our consciences are spotless. None of us to blame."

Sylvia frowned. "I wish you wouldn't talk about the poor man like that. It's tragic."

"Yeah," Nick agreed. "A crime."

A heap of yellow folders covered the dining room table. Each one contained three monthly activity reports submitted by Alex Neumann. Nick selected the folder dated July through September 1978 and drew it toward him. Sylvia slid a chair from the table and sat down. She held the agenda from 1978 close to her chest. "I checked our personnel records on Mr. Burki, first initial C — the executive at USB London who referred Soufi to your father. His name is Caspar Burki. He retired from the bank as a senior vice president in 1988."

"Still alive?"

"I have an address in Zurich. That's all. I can't tell you whether it's current."

Nick took his father's agenda from Sylvia and opened it to the month of April. He turned to the fifteenth of the month and found the first mention of Allen Soufi. Suddenly, the hidden recollection shot to the surface. He saw himself walking alongside Ali Mevlevi in the Platzspitz earlier in the day. He heard the Pasha's voice complaining about his father: *I could never be a derv. The spinning, the chanting. I was only interested in this world.*

Nick stared for a moment at his father's handwriting. *"A. Soufi."* He repeated the name several times and felt a jolt of adrenaline fire through his chest. The elusive memory was close. Mevlevi's voice echoed louder.

"Sylvia, do you know anything about dervs? You know, whirling dervishes?"

She eyed him suspiciously. "Are you serious?"

"Humor me. Do you?"

Sylvia put her hand to her chin in a pose of classic cogitation. "Not a thing. Except that they wear some very funny hats." She lifted her hand high above her head to indicate the height of a fez.

"Do you have an encyclopedia?"

"Just one on CD-ROM. It's in my p.c. in the bedroom."

"I need to look at it. Now."

Five minutes later, Nick was seated at a desk in Sylvia's bedroom. He stared at the opening screen of the encyclopedia and under "Search" typed in the word *dervish*. A short definition appeared. "A monastic sect founded by the disciples of Jalāl ad-Dīn ar-Rūmī, considered the greatest of Islamic mystic poets, who called themselves whirling dervishes. The basis of Islamic mysticism, called Sufism in Western languages, is to attempt by meditation to capture the nature of . . ."

Nick stopped reading. His eyes returned to the top of the screen, rereading the entry. His eyes stopped again at the same place. "The basis of Islamic mysticism, called Sufism in Western languages . . ."

Taking a breath, he ordered himself to review everything he knew about Ali Mevlevi. The man was a Turk. He had chosen the code word Ciragan Palace for his numbered account — the Ciragan Palace in Istanbul being the home of the last Ottoman sultans during the late nineteenth century. He carried an Argentinean passport that gave his family name as Malvinas and just that afternoon had admitted to living in Argentina. Malvinas, of course, was the Argentinean name for the Falkland Islands. He used the first name Allen as an alias. Allen was the anglicization of the Muslim Ali. And finally the last piece. Mevlevi's father was a whirling derv, and the dervs belonged to the Sufi sect of Islam, *ergo the name Soufi.*

Nick swallowed hard. Keep cool, he told himself. You're not there yet. Still, he could discern a pattern emerging. Ali Mevlevi constantly wove elements of his real life into his fictitious one. Allen Soufi. Allen Malvinas. Ali Mevlevi. The behavior fit. Hadn't the Pasha also mentioned that he had lived in California? Throw all the facts together in a blender, stir violently, and what came out? Could Nick conclude that eighteen years ago Alexander Neumann had entertained Allen Soufi, better known as Ali Mevlevi, as a client of the Los Angeles branch of USB? Or was it simply a whole lot of coincidence?

It was nothing, Nick told himself. You've never believed in coincidence. But for once his skepticism deserted him. He ran the facts through his head one more time, daring himself to believe it. Strangely, part of him was scared to accept his own hypothesis. It reeked of fate and karma and all the things he had fought against his whole life. It was just too improbable.

But was it? If he really thought about it, no. Many clients work with a single bank their entire lives. Many sons work for the same company as their father. He stared at the name written in his father's script and tossed aside his remaining doubts. "Sylvia," he said excitedly, "we've got to keep looking for this Allen Soufi."

"What is it? What have you found?"

"Confirmation that he's our man." Nick paused to temper his certainty. Humility demanded a modicum of doubt. "At least, I think. It's still a little iffy. Let's get back to the monthly activity reports. The answers we need are in there."

Nick and Sylvia returned to the dining room table. He pulled her chair close to his, and together they scanned the contents of the remaining reports. Each report began with a mention of deposits made by new and existing clients. A description of corporate loan facilities granted and those under consideration followed. Third came logistical questions: salaries, personnel reports, office expenses. And last, a section for miscellaneous information. It was in this final section of the March 1978 activity report that Nick had first found mention of Soufi. He scoured his father's reports, praying to find further word of the mysterious client. There had to have been a sound reason, a business necessity, that Soufi wished to work with USB Los Angeles.

Nick read through the June report. No mention. July, no mention. August, no mention. He reached for the next dossier. September, nothing. October. He slammed his hand on the table. "There. We've got him," he cried. "Sylvia, October 12, 1978. What does the agenda say?"

Sylvia thumbed through the pages energetically, sharing Nick's adrenaline rush. She found the correct date, then pushed the agenda closer to him.

The entry for October 12 read: "Dinner at Matteo's with Allen Soufi. Undesirable." The word *undesirable* was underlined three times and a box drawn around it. Nick looked at the writing and repeated the word. *Undesirable.* It had been one of Dad's pet phrases and he had misused it mercilessly. Dessert was undesirable. Anything lower than a B on a report card was undesirable. Television on weeknights was undesirable.

Allen Soufi was undesirable.

"What does the activity report say?" Sylvia demanded.

Nick passed her the notebook. His finger rested on the page at Section IV: Miscellaneous. Item 5.

Sylvia read aloud: "Third meeting held October 12 with Mr. Allen Soufi. Credit facility of $100K offered to Goldluxe, Inc. Additional trade financing as required okayed per instructions USB ZRH. AXN notes for record his opposition to the extension of the credit. Overruled by WAK — division manager."

Nick held his breath. Allen Soufi was connected to Goldluxe. Alex Neumann had mentioned visiting Goldluxe stores sometime during the early months of 1979. Nick picked up the agenda for 1979 and skimmed through the pages, finding the first referral to Goldluxe on March 13, 1979. Just an address. *22550 Lankershim Blvd.* He picked up the yellow dossier containing that month and found the corresponding monthly activity report. A related item immediately caught his eye. Under

"Trade Financing," letters of credit totaling over one million dollars had been opened by Goldluxe in favor of El Oro de los Andes, S.A. of Buenos Aires, Argentina.

Allen Malvinas from Argentina.

Nick swallowed hard and kept reading. A note under Goldluxe's name said, "See attached letter to Franz Frey, senior vice president of international finance." The subject was listed as a company visit to Goldluxe, Inc. Nick searched the entire report but couldn't find the letter. It had either been lost or stolen.

Fast-forward to Alex Neumann's agenda. April 20, 1979. "Dinner with Allen Soufi at Ma Maison," accompanied by the word *Schlitzohr* — the familiar words were made clearer by a matching entry in the April activity report. Alex Neumann calling for the suspension of credit facilities to Goldluxe. A return letter from Franz Frey follows. Frey agrees that USB should sever relations with Goldluxe, but suggests AXN (Alex Neumann) obtain approval of WAK (Wolfgang Andreas Kaiser). The letter contains a handwritten note from Frey. "Interpol trace of A. Soufi located nothing."

Nick stopped at the mention of Interpol. What had his father found out about Goldluxe that warranted contacting Interpol?

Fast-forward to the June activity report. Wolfgang Kaiser responds in writing. "Continue business with Goldluxe. No grounds for concern."

Sylvia searched the agenda, stopping on July 17. She held the book out for Nick to read. Four words filled the page. *Franz Frey, dead. Suicide.*

Jesus, No! thought Nick. How had they killed off Frey? Gunshot wound to the head, slashed his throat, take your pick.

Fast-forward to August. The activity report lists letters of credit issued on behalf of Goldluxe amounting to three million dollars. The beneficiary, the same El Oro de los Andes. Cash balance listed as sufficient to cover the full amount. No outstanding debt. Why then was his father so against working with them? What the hell was Goldluxe's business, anyway? Obviously they imported large quantities of gold into the United States, but then what? Did they sell gold to jewelry manufacturers or did they make jewelry themselves? Did they mint some type of coin? Were they wholesalers or retailers?

Fast-forward to September. The first of several entries in his father's agenda that Nick had found frightening. "Lunch at Beverly Wilshire with A. Soufi" and directly below it, written in a forceful hand brimming with rage, "Bastard threatened me!"

November 12. "Soufi to office. 2 P.M." On the same page, a number for the Los Angeles office of the FBI and the name of Special

Agent Raylan Gillette.

Sylvia stopped Nick from turning the page and asked, "When you first saw this entry, did you call the FBI?"

"Only about ten times," said Nick. "No information given to civilians without proper authorization. Sound familiar?"

November 19. "Head office calls. Keep relations with Goldluxe open at all costs."

November 20. "Evans Security. 213-555-3367."

Sylvia pointed at the number. "What about Evans Security? Did you call them?"

"Of course. Evans Security supplies professionally trained limousine drivers, bonded couriers, and personal bodyguards. I figure my father was interested in the bodyguard service. I called them up but they don't keep records going so far back."

"Your father seriously thought about employing a bodyguard?"

"Not seriously enough, he didn't."

Nick snapped his fingers. He remembered the bait he had left for Armin Schweitzer. "Sylvia, I need to see your phone. I mean your answering machine." He rose from the table and found the phone. An old dual-cassette answering machine sat next to it. A red light flashed intermittently. "You have some messages. Come over here and play them."

"They may be private," she answered fussily.

Nick frowned. "I won't tell any of your secrets. Now come on, I need to know if the trap I set yesterday afternoon worked. Come on, come on, come on. Let's see who called."

Sylvia rewound the machine. The first message was from a squeaky-voiced girlfriend, Vreni. Nick tried not to listen. He tapped his foot impatiently while Vreni spoke. The machine beeped. "This is Mr. Peter Sprecher calling on behalf of the Adler Bank. We would very much like to speak with you as soon as possible regarding the voting of your block of USB shares at the general assembly on Tuesday. Please feel free to call me back at the following number."

Nick and Sylvia listened to the entire message. The machine beeped. A gruff voice spoke. "Sylvia, are you there?" Sylvia hurriedly turned off the machine. "My father," she explained. "I think I'll listen to that one alone."

"Fine. I can see it's personal." The voice echoed in Nick's head. He decided Sylvia's father sounded a lot like Wolfgang Kaiser. "Did you hear Peter Sprecher? I was right. Someone at the bank stole the piece of paper I had left on my desk and gave it to the Adler Bank."

Sylvia fiddled with the machine. "Do you really think it was Armin Schweitzer?"

"My gut feeling says it's him, but I can't be sure. Any one of four or five people could walk in my office when I'm not there. I wanted to hear his voice on that machine. Dammit."

"Schweitzer," she scowled. "Selling out his own bank."

"We can't be sure it's him," cautioned Nick. "Not yet. I need to talk to Peter Sprecher first. See if he knows who gave the list to the Adler Bank."

"Talk to him," she commanded.

Nick tried to call Peter Sprecher, but there was no answer. He suggested to Sylvia that they move back to the table and return to their work.

Nick read through the contents of the activity reports for October, November, and December 1979. There was no further mention of Allen Soufi or Goldluxe. Nothing. He closed the dossier and reread his father's entries for the last days of 1979.

December 20: "A. Soufi in office. 3:00 P.M."

December 21: "Christmas party, Trader Vics, Beverly Hilton."

December 27: "Move out. 602 Stone Canyon Rd."

December 31: "New Year's Eve. Next year will be better. It has to!"

When Sylvia excused herself to go to the loo, Nick closed the book and traced the golden numbers on its cover with his fingernail. His stomach felt hollow. He was beyond exhausted. He fell into a kind of reverie, where his past, his present, and what might be his future all mingled together. "Burki," he whispered to himself, recalling the name of the USB executive who had referred Soufi to his father. "The key to this game is Burki."

Nick laid his head on the cool wooden surface. He shut his eyes. "Burki," he said. "Caspar Burki." Over and over he repeated the name, as if during the night he might forget it. He thought of his father and of his mother. He remembered Johnny Burke and Gunny Ortiga. He recalled the awe he felt as he mounted the steps of the United Swiss Bank eight weeks ago. He replayed his first meeting with Peter Sprecher and he laughed. Then his thoughts melted into one another and the world around him darkened. Peace was what he sought. And soon he had it.

Chapter 50

Two hundred miles due east of Beirut at a remote military air base deep in the Syrian desert, a Tupolev-154 cargo jet touched down and taxied the length of the runway before laboring to a halt. The flight had lasted only three hours, yet all eight engines were overheated. Fresh oil had not been added for two hundred flying hours — twice the maximum allowable period. The turbine coolers responsible for maintaining a stable running temperature had worked only intermittently. In fact, somewhere over the Caucasus Mountains one engine had failed for fifteen minutes and the pilot had insisted on returning the plane to Alma-Ata. General Dimitri Sergeivitch Marchenko had been firm in his instructions to continue to the Syrian air base. The cargo could not be delayed.

The Tupolev cut its engines and lowered its rear cargo hatch. Four vehicles rumbled down the loading ramp and onto the warm concrete tarmac. Marchenko followed them, greeting the Syrian commander who waited nearby.

"Colonel Hammid, I presume."

"General Marchenko. It is an honor. As ordered, I am happy to provide you with a

644

platoon of our finest infantrymen for the trip to Lebanon. I understand the shipment is highly sensitive."

"Classified electronics for the regional headquarters of the Hamas. Surveillance gear." Marchenko had never thought highly of his Arab allies. As soldiers, they were impostors. They'd lost every war they'd fought. They should, however, pass muster as escorts for his small convoy into Lebanon. They were fearless supporters of other men's battles.

Marchenko walked to the six-ton truck carrying his precious cargo. He was a short man, stout and heavyset around his jaw and neck. He carried his weight well, using it to add extra swagger to his step. He lifted the canvas canopy and climbed aboard, inviting his Syrian counterpart to join him. Together, they checked that straps securing the crates had been properly tightened. The crates were filled with obsolete radio transmitters, polished up and triple wrapped in plastic to make them look new. The Kopinskaya IV was packed in a reinforced steel container welded to the truck's flatbed. A sophisticated antitampering switch had been attached to the container. If someone attempted to remove the container from the truck, or to forcibly open it, a small packet of Semtex explosive would be ignited and the bomb would be destroyed. No one would steal Little Joe.

Marchenko flopped his rump on the tail of

the truck, then jumped to the ground and made his way forward to the command jeep. The idea to sell a small percentage of his nation's conventional armaments had not been his own. The Kazakh government had embraced it early on, believing it was acting no differently than the former Soviet government. From there, talk moved naturally to another of the republic's salable assets: her nuclear arsenal. No one had ever considered selling off one of the big birds, the SS-19s or SS-20s — missiles equipped with a twenty-megaton warhead and a six-thousand-mile flight span. At least, not seriously. The Kazakhs were a moral people. Besides, the logistics were overwhelming.

Attention had focused on how to profitably dispose of the stockpile of enriched plutonium kept in the vaults of the Lenin Atomic Research Laboratory, one of the former Soviet Union's most secret installations, located forty kilometers outside Alma-Ata.

Until 1992, the installation had been guarded by a division of mechanized infantry. Over five hundred men patrolled the compound and the surrounding woods twenty-four hours a day. Six separate checkpoints had to be cleared before reaching the maze of buildings that made up the laboratory itself. Since that time, however, security had become considerably more lax. Today a single post stood at the compound's entry. A smile and a flash of one's military identification were all that was necessary to gain admittance.

Marchenko scowled, recalling events from the recent past. The Americans had also known about the Lenin Laboratory and the airtight rooms filled with lead canisters holding fissionable materials. Their covert agents had easily penetrated the compound's porous security and had reported back that a paperboy could con his way in, fill his pockets with uranium, and pedal out again. In the summer of 1993, a joint inspection team of CIA and KGB officers landed in Alma-Ata and made directly for the Lenin Atomic Research Laboratory. The operation, code-named Sapphire, had been a complete success. Almost. The interlopers removed over two tons of enriched weapons-grade uranium-235 and plutonium from the Lenin Laboratory and shipped it west. But they had missed a few items.

Marchenko was not a stupid man. He had imagined such an event, if tardily, and had moved with haste on learning of the Americans' plans. He and his colleagues had pinned their hopes on a small weapons manufacturer inside the grounds of the Lenin Laboratory; a factory charged with overseeing the construction of next-generation weapons prototypes. Among the items being developed for introduction into the armed forces was a highly mobile, easily launchable low-yield nuclear device. A battlefield nuclear weapon.

Hours ahead of the Americans, he had stolen his way into the laboratory and removed the existing functional prototypes. Two Kopinskaya IV concussive bombs, each possessing a two-kiloton load. His country's true patrimony.

Marchenko climbed aboard the jeep. The deal is almost done, he said to himself. And though his face retained its veneer of stolid dissatisfaction, inside he was as giddy as a fifteen-year-old. He tapped the driver on the shoulder and ordered him to move out. Up and down the line, motors turned over as the small convoy got under way. It would be an eight-hour drive to their destination. Closing his eyes for a moment, he enjoyed the warm desert wind that tickled his face. Sure that no one could see him, he smiled.

It was time someone else suffered.

Chapter 51

The number 10 tram lurched out of the morning mist like an arthritic serpent. Its blunt blue snout and reticulated body rattled through the curtain of dew, groaning and sighing as it drew to a halt. Doors jerked open. Passengers got off. Nick lifted a hand to help a stooped old lady whose slow descent threatened the punctuality of the entire transit system. The witch batted it away with her bent umbrella. He dodged the blow and stepped aboard. So much for starting the day on the right foot.

Nick shuttled down the aisle looking for an empty seat. Gray faces sagging with the burdens of living in the world's wealthiest democracy greeted him. Their unsmiling countenances shoved him with a thump out of Sylvia's bed and back into the real world. The world where he was an accessory to murder, conspirator to fraud, and prisoner of a man who might very well have had a hand in murdering his father.

Nick sat down at the rear of the tram. An elderly man in front of him was reading *Blick*, the country's daily scandal sheet. He had the paper open to the second page. A photograph of Marco Cerruti slumped in a leather recliner occupied the upper left-hand corner. The headline read "Despondent Banker Takes Life." The text was short, included so to dignify the lurid photograph. Cerruti looked peaceful enough, sleeping except for a small black crater carved into his left temple. His eyes were closed and a fluffy white pillow was propped on his stomach.

Nick waited for the old man to finish reading the paper, then asked if he might have a look. The man eyed him long and hard, as if assessing his creditworthiness. Finally, he handed him the paper. Nick stared at the picture for a while, wondering how much cash the paper had slipped the police photographer, then directed his attention to the brief article.

"Marco Cerruti, 55, vice president of the United Swiss Bank, was found dead at his home in Thalwil early Friday morning. Lt. Dieter Erdin of the Zurich Police classified the death as a suicide and listed the cause as a self-inflicted gunshot wound to the head. Officials at the United Swiss Bank reported that Cerruti had been suffering from nervous exhaustion and had not worked on a daily basis since the beginning of the year. A memorial scholarship in his name will be established by the bank at the University of Zurich."

Nick studied the picture closely. It took him a few seconds to locate the detail that irked him — the bottle of Scotch upended in his lap. Cerruti didn't drink. He didn't even keep a bottle for guests. Why didn't the police know that?

Nick closed the paper, frustrated at the police's incompetence. Headlines emblazoned across the front page caught his eye. "Crime Boss Gunned Down in Platzspitz." A color photograph of the crime scene showed Albert Makdisi's corpse lying on the ground next to a stone wall. He folded the newspaper and handed it back to the man in the next row, thanking him for his kindness. He didn't need to read the article. After all, he was the killer.

Nick unlocked the door to his apartment and stepped inside. Every time he came home, he wondered if someone might have been snooping around during his absence. He didn't think anyone had broken in since the day three weeks ago when he had smelled the traces of a sickly sweet eau de cologne and found that his gun had been tampered with. But he could never be sure.

He leaned forward to open the dresser's bottom drawer, then ran his hand under his sweaters until he felt the smooth crease of his holster. He grabbed ahold of it and set it down in his lap. He withdrew the Colt Commander and held it snugly in his right hand, staring at it as if it were an extension of his own person.

The familiar heft of the gun allowed him to relax for several seconds. It was a false comfort and he knew it. Still, he had to take what he could get.

Nick stood and walked to his desk. He removed a chamois cloth, spread it out, then laid his gun down on top of it. He set about taking apart and cleaning his pistol. He hadn't fired a round in months, but right now he needed to fall back on the rigorous order of his past. He wanted to reside in some distant universe where rules still existed for everyday conduct. As far as he knew there was still only one way to clean a Colt .45-caliber pistol. No one could tamper with that.

Nick ejected the clip and popped out the bullets. All nine of them. He locked back the slide and turned the gun on its side, allowing the chambered round to fall onto the beige cloth. His hands assumed a rhythm of their own, following steps ingrained in his memory long ago. But only half his mind supervised the cleaning of his pistol. The other half damned him for his selfish actions.

His willful deceit had led him to be a participant in fraud and a witness to murder. If he hadn't delayed the Pasha's transfer, Mevlevi's accounts would have been frozen; the bank, under severe scrutiny, would not have embarked on its insane plan to manipulate its customers' discretionary accounts; the Pasha would not have dared come to Switzerland; and, most important, Cerruti would still be alive.

Maybe . . .

Nick fought a sudden rush of heat that flooded his neck and shoulders. He tried to concentrate harder on his weapon, willing the tide of emotion to recede. But it was no good. Guilt won. It always did. He felt guilty for shielding the Pasha and guilty for Cerruti's death. Hell, he felt guilty for every fucking thing that had happened since he'd come to Switzerland. He wasn't just an innocent by-stander; he wasn't even an unwilling accomplice. He was a one-hundred-percent willing participant in this mess.

He unscrewed the gun barrel and raised his eye to it, checking for any oil residue. The grooves were clean, dulled by a sheen of lubricant. He put the barrel on the cloth, then paused in his work. Yesterday's actions came back to him in an instant. He stood helpless as Albert Makdisi crumpled under the force of three shots point-blank to the chest. He watched stunned as the Pasha tossed him the pistol and he caught it. His muscles twitched with the recollection of raising the gun and pointing it at Mevlevi's leering face. Even now, eighteen hours later, he felt a feral desire rise in him to kill another man.

Nick held the chassis of the pistol in his hand. The last thought he'd had as he pulled the trigger had been of his father. Arm extended, aim taken, standing there with no doubt in his mind whatsoever that he was going to willingly end the life of a bad man, he had looked to his father for approval.

Nick moved his gaze from the gun to the window. A Slavic woman walked briskly down the street, dragging her young son roughly by the hand. She stopped suddenly and raised a finger at the boy, chastising him loudly.

Nick replaced her muted shouts with the plaintive strain of his own mother's voice. "Do as you're told," she had said to his father. "You said yourself you didn't really know if he was doing anything wrong. Stop making such a big deal about it!"

Dammit, Dad, Nick demanded, why *didn't* you do as you were told? Why did you have to make such a big deal about it — whatever "it" was? You'd probably still be here today. Alive. We could have been a family. Fuck the rest of it! Your discipline, your dignity, your integrity. What good has it brought any of us?

Nick slammed the gun down on his desk. He heard a voice telling him that all his life he'd been doing what other people had wanted him to. That the marines was just another excuse not to have to make his own decisions. That a degree from Harvard Business School and the high-paying career it promised would have made his father proud. And that abandoning his career to come to Switzerland to investigate his father's murder would have been Alex Neumann's only recommended course of action.

As Nick stared out the window into the bleak morning sun, a strange sensation took hold of him. He felt as though he were seeing himself from a distance. He wanted to tell the man standing in the dim apartment to stop living for yesterday, and that while finding his father's murderer might make the past easier to deal with, it wouldn't provide any magic path into the future. He'd have to find that path for himself.

Nick nodded, taking the advice to heart. He finished cleaning the components of his pistol, then put the Colt back together again. He screwed the barrel back in, reracked the slide, shoved home the clip, and chambered a round. He couldn't sit back and watch anymore. He had to act.

Nick raised the gun and took aim at a ghostly figure only he could see — a shadowy silhouette looming in the dusky middle distance. He would clear his own path into the future. And Ali Mevlevi was standing right in the middle of it.

The phone rang. Nick holstered his weapon and put it away before answering. "Neumann speaking."

"It's Saturday, chum. You're not at work, remember?"

"Good morning, Peter."

"I suppose you've heard the news. Just saw

the papers myself. Didn't think the jumpy bastard had it in him."

"Neither did I," said Nick. "What's up?"

"Since when don't you return phone calls? Three times I called yesterday. Where the hell were you?"

"I wasn't in the mood for a drink last night."

"I sure as hell wasn't calling about a drink," complained Sprecher. "We need to talk. Serious business."

"I heard your message. That was Sylvia's number you called."

"I wasn't calling about the shareholder lists. It's a damn sight more important than that. Something came up yesterday that I —"

"Keep it short, Peter. To the point." Nick imagined that if his place had been searched, his phone had probably been bugged. "Let's keep our conversation private. Follow?"

"Yeah," Sprecher replied hesitantly. "Okay, I follow. Maybe what you were saying about our best client wasn't entirely off base."

"Maybe," answered Nick noncommittally. "If you want to talk about it, go to our favorite watering hole in two hours. I'll leave instructions where to meet me. And Peter . . ."

"Yeah, chum?"

"Dress warmly."

Two hours and fifty minutes later, Peter Sprecher staggered to the highest deck of the steel observation tower, two hundred fifty feet above the crest of the Uetliberg. "You've a helluva nerve," he puffed, "bringing me all the way up here in this weather."

"It's a beautiful day," Nick said. "You can almost see the ground from here." He had taken a circuitous route to their rendezvous, ducking through the back alleys of the old town until he reached Central. From there, he took a tram first to the Stadelhofen train station, and then to the zoo. Certain no one was behind him, he assumed a direct course to his destination. The entire trip had taken two hours — including forty minutes to climb the path up the mountain to the crest of the Uetliberg.

Sprecher leaned his head over the safety railing. The tower disappeared into the mist fifty feet down. He reached into his jacket pocket for a Marlboro. "Want one? It'll keep you warm."

Nick declined. "I should ask you for some identification. I didn't recognize the man who called me earlier. Since when have you grown so inquisitive, O cynical one?"

"I blame any recent changes in my condition on one too many a beer in your company. My time in England made me sympathetic to the plight of the underdog."

"Thanks," Nick said. "I guess. So what have you learned about Mr. Ali Mevlevi that has you spooked so badly?"

"I overheard something very disturbing yesterday afternoon. In fact, right after I called the Widows and Orphans Fund of Zurich." Sprecher inhaled, then pointed the ember of his cigarette at Nick. "You're a clever lad. Next time, though, do spice it up a bit. We may want to take off the bag to see who we're fucking."

There wouldn't be a next time, thought Nick. "Who slipped your team my notes?"

"No idea. They were in Von Graffenried's possession. He intimated that they came at a bargain price."

A strong wind blew and the tower swayed like a drunken sailor. Nick grabbed hold of a railing. "Any hint that it was Armin Schweitzer who gave them to you?"

"Schweitzer? That's who you think is stealing your notes?" Sprecher shrugged his shoulders. "Can't help you there. Anyway it doesn't matter a shit. Not anymore. Yesterday afternoon, right after calling your specious fund management company, I overheard my neighbor on the trading floor, Hassan Faris, take a call from Konig. A large buy order was sent to the exchange. An order for one-hundred-odd thousand shares of USB. You're sharp with figures; do your math."

Nick tallied up the cost of a hundred thousand shares of USB going at four hundred twenty Swiss francs each. Forty-two million francs. Something about the sum sent a dagger into his gut. "Once you capture those shares, your holdings will top thirty-three percent."

"Thirty-three point five percent, to be exact. Not including the Widows and Orphans Fund."

Nick could not rid himself of the nagging figure. Forty-two million francs. About forty million dollars at the current exchange rates. "You'll get your seats. Kaiser's reign will be history."

"It's his successor who worries me," Sprecher said. "Listen carefully, young Nick. Eighty percent of all USB shares we own are held in a special account that belongs to the Adler Bank's largest investor. Konig exercises proxy over the shares, but he doesn't own them. The name of that account is Ciragan Trading."

"Ciragan Trading?" Nick asked. "As in Ciragan Palace? As in the Pasha?"

Sprecher nodded. "You don't think me daft for assuming it to be the same man? I don't fancy either the Adler Bank or USB being owned by — what did you call him? A major heroin supplier? If your friend Thorne is correct, that is."

Oh, he's correct all right, Nick wanted to say. That's the whole problem.

"You say the buy order was for a hundred thousand shares? Around forty million dollars? Would you believe me if I told you that I transferred that exact amount out of Mevlevi's account yesterday at four P.M.?"

"Not happily, I wouldn't."

"To the banks listed on matrix one. The Adler Bank's nowhere on that list. How could you have already received the money?"

"I didn't say we had received the money. As a matter of fact, Konig asked Faris to ensure that settlement won't be made until Tuesday. We'll claim an administrative error on our part. No one will care if payment is twenty-four hours late."

Nick ran his hands along the guardrail and peered into the mist. He played with the question of why Mevlevi would be backing the Adler Bank's takeover of USB but gave up after a few seconds. The realm of possibilities was too great. Another idea came to him. "There is an easy way for us to confirm if the Pasha has been behind all of Adler's purchases. Match his transfers through USB with the Adler Bank's purchases of USB shares. If every week Konig bought shares worth the amount Mevlevi transferred through USB, we've got him. Of course, that assumes that Mevlevi followed the same pattern as yesterday."

"The Pasha is nothing if not a creature of habit," said Sprecher. "Never missed a transfer in the eighteen months I worked with Cerruti — God rest the poor bugger's soul."

Nick sighed heavily. "Peter, there's more to this than you can imagine."

"Shoot, sport."

"You don't want to know."

Sprecher stamped his feet on the metal platform while vigorously rubbing his arms. "Yesterday, the day before even, you'd be right. Today I want to know. Let my reasons be my own. Now out with it."

Nick looked Sprecher in the eye. "I know where Mevlevi's getting the forty million dollars."

"Pray tell?"

"A shipment of refined heroin is due in on Monday morning. Mevlevi arranged to be prepaid for the merchandise by Gino Makdisi."

Sprecher looked skeptical. "May I inquire as to the source of your information?"

"*I* am the source," said Nick, giving vent to the full range of his frustrations. "My eyes. My ears. I watched Mevlevi murder Albert Makdisi. In return for his battlefield promotion, Gino transferred the money for the shipment up front. Forty million bucks. New terms on trade, says the Pasha. Don't like 'em? Bang bang, you're dead. Termination effective immediately." Nick wiped at his nose. "Jesus, Peter, my life is royally fucked."

"Calm down. You sound like you're a member of the Cosa bloody Nostra."

"Not yet, I'm not. But he's trying like hell to pull me in."

"Go easy, Nick. Who's trying to pull you in?"

"Who do you think? The Pasha. He owns

Kaiser. Don't know how, don't know why, or for how long, but he owns him, lock, stock, and barrel. And what about Cerruti? He didn't drink. You know that. Did you see the picture in the paper? Whoever killed him left the bottle right on his lap. And what about that pillow? It was from his bedroom, for Christ's sake, and I bet there's a bullet hole smack dab in the middle of it. Can you see it? Cerruti is drunk as all hell, ready to blow his brains all over the living room wall, but he's still concerned not to disturb his neighbors. Boy, he's a real saint. Mr. Considerate till the very end."

Nick broke off his tirade and circled the restricted platform. He stared at Peter, and Peter stared back. A sharp wind whistled through the trestles of the observation tower, blowing with it a smattering of frozen rain and the smell of damp pine.

"So why kill him?" Sprecher asked finally. "What does he know now that he hasn't for the last five years?"

Nick halted his pacing. *What about our nagging problem?* Mevlevi had asked Kaiser yesterday afternoon. *The one that threatens to do us so much harm.*

"The way I see it, Cerruti was going to talk to Sterling Thorne or to Franz Studer. Mevlevi got wind of it and had him killed."

As Sprecher shook his head in disbelief, Nick explained his predicament with the conviction of the damned. He told Sprecher everything that had happened during the past two weeks. Maeder's plan to liberate the equity shareholdings of USB's discretionary clients, the theft from DZ of the Pasha's correspondence, how he'd foolishly put his own fingerprints on the pistol that shot and killed Albert Makdisi. Finally, he told Sprecher about his true reasons for coming to the bank. He explained how his father was murdered. He described his interest in the USB Los Angeles rep office monthly activity reports and underlined his growing certainty that Mevlevi had been involved in his father's killing. He left nothing out.

Sprecher whistled long and low. "You really believe the Pasha had a hand in your father's death?"

"If Mevlevi is Allen Soufi, then I'm sure of it. What I have to discover is why my father felt so strongly about not working with him. What was Goldluxe up to? The only person who can tell us is Caspar Burki."

"Who?"

"Allen Soufi was recommended to my father by a portfolio manager out of USB London. His name was Caspar Burki. He'd have known what Soufi and Goldluxe were up to. You've been at the bank twelve years. Name ring a bell?"

"I don't know anyone by that name in our London office."

"He retired in 1988," said Nick. "Used to live in town. I have his old address. I went by before coming to see you. The place was deserted."

Sprecher shifted his gaze from Nick to the panorama of drizzle that enveloped the tower. He fished for another cigarette. "Can't say I know a Caspar Burki. Only fellow I know who dates from that period is Yogi Bauer. In fact, we both know Yogi."

"Both of us?" Nick raised an eyebrow. "I don't know anybody named Yogi."

"*Au contraire, mon chére.* You've even bought the man a drink. At the Keller Stübli. Fat bloke with greasy black hair, white as death. We toasted Schweitzer's talented wife."

Nick remembered him. "Some luck. The guy's a full-blown alcoholic. He can't remember how he gets to the bar every day, let alone a stranger from twenty years ago."

"Yogi Bauer worked in the London branch of USB. He was Schweitzer's assistant. If Burki was there at the same time, Bauer is bound to have known him."

Nick laughed at their situation. "Are you getting the feeling that this is a pretty tangled web we're caught up in?"

Sprecher lit the cigarette that had been dangling from his mouth. "I'm sure the authorities can unravel it just fine."

"The authorities won't be of any help. We have to take Mevlevi down ourselves."

"Far beyond our domain, I'm afraid. Tell the proper authorities. They'll see to it that all is set right."

"Will they?" Nick was incensed by Sprecher's willful naïveté. "Any documents we show the police will incriminate us. The bank will press charges that we stole them. Violation of bank secrecy laws. I can't see nailing the Pasha from the inside of a jail cell."

Sprecher was unconvinced. "I don't think the federal government will be keen to learn that two of its most important banks were being controlled by a Middle Eastern drug lord."

"But, Peter, where are the drugs? Mevlevi's been convicted of no crime. We have numbered accounts, money being laundered, maybe even a tie to the Adler Bank. But no drugs. And, I might add, no name. We have to do this ourselves. Do I have to mention what happened to Marco Cerruti? Or to Marty Becker?"

"Please don't," said Sprecher, blanching.

Nick thought he was finally getting through. "You agree that we can match Konig's purchases of stock to the Pasha's transfers through USB?"

"Theoretically, it's possible. I'll grant you that. I'm afraid to ask what you want of me."

"Get me hard-copy evidence that the Ciragan Trading account holds eighty percent of the USB shares. It's got to be clear that the shares do not belong to the Adler Bank, but that they are only being voted on their behalf. We need a historical record of Adler's accumulation of USB shares through that account: dates, quantities, and purchase prices."

"Should I bring you back Cinderella's glass slipper while I'm at it?" Sprecher's tone was as flip as ever, but Nick could see that his jaw was set and his eyes harder than before.

Nick smiled. For a split second he felt that they might even have half a chance. "I've got to get a copy of all the transfers made for account 549.617 RR since last July, when Konig began accumulating shares. Plus a copy of the Pasha's banking instructions. Our records show where the money went on its first leg. Your records will show which bank it came from on its last leg. Together that's a pretty good map."

"Maps are all well and good. But who are we going to show it to?"

"We don't have much choice. There's only one man reckless enough to move while Mevlevi is in Switzerland."

"Besides you and me, you mean. Who is it?"

"Sterling Thorne."

Sprecher looked as if someone had just stolen his cigarettes. "You're joking? I don't disagree that the man is reckless. The portrait you've painted makes him sound absolutely possessed. But what of it?"

Nick was careful to hide his own misgivings. "Thorne will do anything to get his hands on the Pasha. He's the only one who can use any evidence we manage to steal. If he knows that Mevlevi is in this country, he'll put the full efforts of the DEA behind our plan. I bet Thorne will bring in a fucking Ranger A-Team to kidnap the Pasha and take him back to the States."

"If he can find him . . ."

"Oh, he can find him. Monday morning at ten A.M., I'll be escorting the Pasha to a meeting in Lugano with an employee of the Federal Passport Office. Seems Kaiser has arranged for Mevlevi to obtain citizenship in this fine country as a way to get the DEA off his back."

"Kaiser set that up?" Peter gave a soft laugh. "Like you said, 'lock, stock, and barrel.' So how does one go about finding our Mr. Thorne?"

Nick patted his pocket. "I've got his card. Didn't he give you one too?"

"He did, but I'm a smart lad. I threw it away." Sprecher shivered suddenly. "All right, mate, let's make the plan. It's too cold up here to continue our little parley."

Nick thought of what he needed to do that afternoon. He wouldn't be free until six at the earliest. "Let's hook up at the Keller Stübli tonight at eight," he suggested. "I'm looking forward to seeing Yogi."

"Keep your fingers crossed," said Sprecher.

"Hope that Bauer hasn't quaffed one too many beers."

Nick placed his palms together and brought them up to his chest. "I'm praying."

Chapter 52

Nick arrived at the Paradeplatz at five past two, anxious to get to the bank. It had taken him over an hour to slog down the icy path from the Uetliberg and catch a tram into the center of the city. An hour that he did not have. The game had a time limit now. Monday, Gino Makdisi would take possession of the Pasha's merchandise. Tuesday, Konig would officially be voted his seats on USB's board of directors. Nick could not allow either to take place.

The sky had darkened in the last hour. Ominous clouds rolled in from the north like an advancing army and hovered low overhead as if preparing to lay siege to the city. Oblivious of the weather, a throng of shoppers flocked up and down the Bahnhofstrasse. Smartly dressed men and women attacked their errands with a brio as joyless as it was efficient. Nick sliced through their ranks, impatience dampening his fear of what he was about to do.

He passed the front entrance to the bank and peered up at the gray building. A row of lights burned from the windows on the Fourth Floor. The lights enlivened the building's sterile facade and offered passersby the impression that here stood an institution unmatched in its commitment to its clients. The model of industry and enterprise. He shook his head in disgust. Nothing could be further from the truth.

Nick walked to the rear of the bank and climbed the short flight of stairs leading to the employee entrance. He was dressed in a charcoal suit and navy overcoat, his workaday battle gear. He entered the bank, flashing the security guard his identification as he slid through the turnstile. The guard saw his dark suit and waved the card away. Anyone crazy enough to work on a weekend deserved easy entry.

On the Fourth Floor, Nick was hit with the sounds of an office in uproar. Phones rang, doors were slammed, and voices were raised, though none louder than Wolfgang Kaiser's.

"Dammit, Marty," Nick heard him shout from the far end of the corridor, "you promised me two hundred million in buying power. Where is it? Five days I've been waiting. So far you've produced only ninety million."

A response was mumbled and Nick was surprised to hear his own name mentioned.

Kaiser said, "If I needed Neumann for a day or two, you should have taken his place and liberated the shares yourself. That's what leadership means. Too late to teach you, I see."

Rita Sutter scurried from the Emperor's

Lair and bustled down the hallway. When she saw Nick, a worried expression crossed her features. "Mr. Neumann. I didn't expect you here today."

Nick wondered why not. It looked like everyone else was here. "I need to speak with Herr Kaiser."

Rita Sutter nibbled on a slender finger. "It's a bad day. Terrible news from the exchange. Mr. Zwicki and Mr. Maeder are with the Chairman now. You've heard?"

"No," he lied. "What is it?"

"Klaus Konig has picked up another one percent of our shares. He will have his seats."

"So it's finally happened," said Nick, mustering whatever disappointment he could.

"Don't mind the Chairman," Rita Sutter counseled. "He has a sharp tongue. He doesn't mean the half of what he says. Remember, he likes you very much."

"Well, where is he?" Kaiser asked when Nick walked through the set of tall doors, this afternoon flung open to admit the Chairman's counselors. "Where's Mevlevi? What have you done with him?"

Rudolf Ott, Martin Maeder, and Sepp Zwicki stood in a semicircle around the Chairman. Only Schweitzer was missing.

"Excuse me?" said Nick. The question was preposterous. *No one did anything to the Pasha.*

"I've been trying to reach him at his hotel

since last night," said Kaiser. "He's disappeared."

"I haven't seen him since yesterday afternoon. He was a little preoccupied with his business's distribution network. He had a falling-out with one of his partners."

Kaiser took note of his colleagues. "Tell me more when I'm finished with these two. Stay," he commanded and snapped his fingers toward the couch. "Sit over there until I'm through."

Nick settled into the couch and listened as Kaiser vented his anger at his subordinates. He accused Zwicki of a catastrophic failure to communicate and of allowing Konig to scoop up the shares without so much as a peep. Zwicki tried unsuccessfully to defend himself, then bowed his head and fled.

Kaiser turned his attention to Maeder. "What is Feller doing now?"

Maeder melted under the Chairman's burning glare. "Finishing up the last of the discretionary portfolios. We've managed to scrape up another fifteen million." He adjusted his necktie and squeaked out a question. "No word yet on the loan from . . ."

"Obviously not," barked Kaiser. "Or we would have purchased those shares instead of Konig." He dismissed Maeder and found a place on the couch next to Nick. Ott followed suit.

"No idea where he is?" asked the Chairman

again. "I leave you with the man who owes me two hundred million francs and you let him disappear."

Nick didn't recall the Pasha owing Kaiser anything. Mevlevi had given his word to consider the loan. Nothing more. Clearly, he was keeping his whereabouts secret to avoid just this sort of confrontation. "You might find him with Gino Makdisi. Probably taking the place of his older brother. Cementing a new relationship."

Kaiser stared at him queerly, and Nick wondered if he knew what had transpired yesterday at the Platzspitz. Or if that was to be the Pasha's little secret.

"Your responsibility was to guide Mr. Mevlevi around Zurich," said Kaiser. "*At all times.* An easy task, or so I would have thought. Instead you show up at the bank at half past three, a zombie from what Rita Sutter tells me, and sit in your office waiting to do that bastard's bidding. Forty million he received. Forty million you transferred out. You had the good sense to delay his transfer once. Why didn't you think to do it again?"

Nick met Kaiser's intense gaze, knowing it was wiser not to answer. He was sick and tired of Kaiser's constant bullying. At first he had found it a mark of the Chairman's decisiveness, his will to succeed; now he saw it as pure bluster, a means to shift the blame for his own mistakes onto his subordinates. Nick knew that even with the two-hundred-million-franc loan, it was too late. Konig had his thirty-three percent. And the cash for his purchases had come from Ali Mevlevi. Tough luck, Wolfgang. There'll be no loan from the Pasha, no last-minute dispensation granted by your unholy savior.

"What have you come in for today?" Kaiser asked. "More lazing around? Three weeks at the top and you're exhausted. One more soldier who couldn't cut the mustard."

"Don't get upset at Mr. Neumann," said Rita Sutter, who had entered the room with a stack of photocopies. "I'm sure he has been doing his job as best he can. You told me yourself Mr. Mevlevi can be diffi—"

Kaiser attacked her venomously. "No one asked for your opinion. Put the papers down and show yourself out!"

Rita Sutter smiled tremulously, blinking back tears as she retreated.

Rudolf Ott kept his fists bunched to his chest and snickered. "You were saying, Neumann?"

"I came in to help Reto Feller with the portfolios. I hadn't heard that Konig had reached the thirty-three-percent barrier."

In fact, Nick had no intention of helping Feller liberate more shares. His days as a willing accomplice were over. He had come for one reason only: to steal the Pasha's file from DZ.

"He may have his thirty-three percent," Kaiser said, "but I won't allow him his seats on the board. Not while I command this bank. To think that at one time he worked with us. The traitor!"

"And not the only one among us," hissed Ott.

Kaiser ignored him. "I won't permit it!" he said. "I simply won't!"

Nick averted his eyes from the Chairman. He knew Kaiser wouldn't give up until the final vote had been cast at the general assembly. But the truth was that once Konig had purchased this last block of shares, the battle was over. Kaiser would fight the changes in management Konig's presence would bring, but in the end he would lose. Public sentiment was in favor of any measure that might result in a company's rapidly increasing its earnings. The Chairman was the last of the old school; the last of the men who believed that long-term growth was more important than short-term results. In the end he was too Swiss, even for the Swiss.

Kaiser turned his attention back to Nick. "Get down to Feller's office and find out where our holdings stand. I want a list of all the votes we can count on from our institutional shareholders and —"

Ott placed a pale hand on the Chairman's shoulder. Kaiser stopped speaking and followed his lackey's gaze to the entryway. Armin

Schweitzer walked slowly into the room. His face was waxen, damp with sweat.

"I arrived as quickly as possible," he said to Kaiser and Ott. His eyes avoided Nick.

The Chairman rose from the couch and strolled to his director of compliance. "Armin, I am sorry to drag you out of bed. Rudy tells me you are suffering from the flu. Remember, rest is the only cure."

To Nick, he just looked badly hung over.

Schweitzer nodded weakly. He appeared confused by the Chairman's solicitous nature. "I'll be sure to heed your advice."

"You've heard the news, I take it?"

"Mrs. Sutter informed me. Our next fight is to oust Konig from the board. We should look at this as only a temporary setback. With your leadership, I have no doubt that we'll succeed in getting rid of him."

"I thought you'd be pleased," said Kaiser.

"How could I be pleased?" Schweitzer laughed awkwardly, looking for support to Ott, and in a sign of his confusion, to Nick.

"The Adler Bank," said Kaiser. "You were close to Klaus Konig at one time, weren't you? Both from the trading side of the firm. Both wheelers and dealers."

"I was a bond man myself. Klaus concentrated on equities and options."

"But you got along?"

"He was a decent sort. Before he went to America, that is. He came back with his head stuffed with all kinds of financial garbage."

"Still, it is exciting what Konig is pulling off these days," Kaiser said begrudgingly.

"Excitement has no place in the world of investments," declared Schweitzer. "It belongs in the gaming halls of Monaco. I think Klaus has become addicted to risk."

"You used to share the same appetites, didn't you?" Kaiser suggested in a salacious tone. "New York? London? Those were heady days for you."

Schweitzer dismissed the suggestion outright. "Another lifetime."

"But one to which no doubt you wish to return."

"Absolutely not. I'm happy where I stand today."

"Come, Armin, you mean you don't fancy a return to the trading side of the family? Compliance must be a dull racket for a man of your proven skills."

"If we are talking about a possible transfer, then perhaps we should do so in private." Schweitzer glanced around him, visibly uncomfortable discussing his present situation. A select audience had gathered in Kaiser's office. Nick sat perched on the couch. Ott stood by his master's shoulder. Rita Sutter crept closer, step by cautious step. Only she prevented Reto Feller from carelessly bounding headlong into the escalating pas de deux.

"Armin Schweitzer," boomed Kaiser, like a

man envisaging his own promotion, "executive vice president for bond trading." He
paused and asked in a good-natured voice, "Is
that what Konig has promised you? A new title
with the Adler Bank?"

Schweitzer replied meekly. "I beg your pardon?"

"I asked what Konig has promised you. In
return for your espionage?"

"What are you talking about, Wolfgang?
There's been no offer. I would never speak
with Konig, let alone work for him. You know
that."

"Do I?"

Kaiser advanced on Schweitzer, stopping
when he stood only a foot away. He ran his
fingers along the lapels of the doomed man.
Without warning, he drew back his hand and
slapped the larger man across the face. "I res-
cued you from the bowels of another country's
prisons. I made a place for you at the summit
of this bank. I gave you a life. And now this?
Why, Armin? Tell me why."

"Stop!" shouted Schweitzer. He put a hand
to his inflamed cheek. For a moment the room
was still. All motion suspended. "Stop," he
repeated breathlessly. "What in God's name
are you talking about? I would never betray
you."

"Liar!" Kaiser shouted. "What has Konig
promised you in return for your cooperation?"

"Nothing! I swear it. This is insanity. I have

nothing to hide." Schweitzer stepped forward and pointed his finger at Nick. "Who's cast these stones against me? Was it him?"

"No," Kaiser stated sharply. "It wasn't him. But have no worry, my source is impeccable. You only think it was Neumann because you stole the list from him, don't you?"

"What list? What are you talking about? I've never given Konig a thing."

Rudolf Ott slithered to his master's side. "How could you, Armin?"

"Whatever you've heard, they're lies," said Schweitzer. "Garbage, pure and simple. The bank is my home. I've given you thirty years. Do you think I'd ever do anything to endanger it? Be serious, Wolfgang."

"Oh, I am, Armin. Deadly serious." Kaiser paced in a circle around the accused man. "I saved you once. If this is how you choose to repay me, fine. Enjoy your new post at the Adler Bank. Your stay here is at its end. Next time you see me on the street, cross to the other side. Next time we happen to dine in the same restaurant, you'll leave immediately, or else I'll stand up and publicly accuse you of these crimes. Do you understand me?"

Schweitzer's eyes were open wide and he blinked wildly to clear them of tears. "You can't mean this. This is a mistake. I never —"

"No mistake has been made, save yours to work for Konig. Good luck to you, Armin. Now get out of my bank." Kaiser's arm pointed stiffly toward the hallway.

Still, Schweitzer refused to leave. He took a few off-balance steps as if walking on the rolling deck of a seagoing vessel. "This is madness. Please, Wolfgang — Herr Kaiser — at least give me the opportunity to clear my name. You have no right to —"

"I said *now*, dammit!" yelled Kaiser, in a baleful voice Nick had never before heard. "Leave!"

The indignity was complete, the Chairman's cavernous office as silent as a tomb. Schweitzer turned and walked from the room under the bewildered stares of his colleagues.

"And the rest of you," the Chairman commanded, "go back to your posts. We haven't lost her yet."

Chapter 53

The witnesses to Schweitzer's dismissal gathered in the anteroom to the Emperor's Lair and exchanged expressions of disbelief. Ott and Feller appeared energized by what they had seen. Nick thought they could barely keep the smiles from their faces. Rita Sutter, though, sat behind her desk in a sort of stunned silence, shell-shocked. Nick waited until Feller had left the office, then approached Rudolf Ott.

"I've been asked by the client I was escorting yesterday, account number —"

"Mr. Mevlevi," Ott cut in. "I know the man's name, Neumann."

"He asked me to deliver all correspondence from his account being held at the bank." Nick had wanted to broach the issue with the Chairman, but Schweitzer's arrival — and departure — had prevented him from bringing it up. Now he was stuck playing to Ott.

"Is that right?" Ott stepped closer to Nick and like a courtier eager to catch up on the latest rumors, linked arms with him and set off down the corridor. "I understood he reviewed his file yesterday afternoon."

"He was interrupted." Nick jostled his arm,

trying without success to remove it from Ott's clutch. "News of Cerruti's death."

"Ah." Ott nodded as if now he understood what had transpired. "When does he want it?"

"This evening before seven. I had planned on asking the Chairman but . . ." Nick let the sentence drift off.

"A wise decision," said Ott. "This is hardly the time to bother him with administrative matters. As for Mevlevi, can't he wait to read his correspondence while at the bank?"

"I suggested the same to him. He says he wants to review his mail before we drive to Lugano Monday morning."

"Wants it by seven tonight, does he?" sniffed Ott. "And he expects you to bring it to his hotel?"

"That's right. To the Dolder. I'm supposed to leave it with the concierge."

"Well, Herr Kaiser will be relieved to know where he can contact Mevlevi, won't he? Though he can hardly risk a visit. Much too public to be seen with one of Mevlevi's sort. Especially now." Ott looked up at Nick, who stood a head taller. "All righty then. Let me give security a call. Be at DZ in ten minutes. That's three sharp."

Nick extricated himself from the man's clinging grip. He had taken only a few steps when Ott called after him. "And Neumann, be sure to take Mr. Feller with you. He spent a year with Karl. He'll help you find what you're looking for much faster."

Nick returned to his office, cursing his luck at being saddled with Feller's obnoxious presence. He closed the door and locked it, then circled behind his desk and opened the second drawer of his filing cabinet, taking out a battered sepia folder. He set the folder on his desk and began filling it with random memos and out-of-date papers until it approximated the girth of the Pasha's file. Halfway through his task, he stopped and opened his top desk drawer. As he had done yesterday, he felt along its underside, hoping that the Pasha's transaction confirmations might have magically reappeared. His fingers scraped unsanded wood. Nothing more. He had no idea who might have taken them, or why. Yesterday their loss had seemed a disaster. Today he dismissed it as small potatoes. The confirmations of the Pasha's transfers into and out of the bank would hardly paint as bold a picture as Mevlevi's entire file. It was the file he wanted. The signature cards, the originals of all seven transfer matrices, the names of the portfolio managers — most important, Wolfgang Kaiser's — who had supervised the account. The whole damned thing.

Nick closed the drawer and shifted his attention back to the task at hand. He slipped off his jacket, slid the surrogate file into the back of his pants, then adjusted his belt so that it was held firmly in place. This done, he put his jacket on and left his office.

"Did you see his face, Neumann? Did you?" Feller asked, as the two men waited for an elevator to take them to the first floor. "I've never seen a grown man cry. An executive vice president of the bank, no less. My God. He was blubbering like a child. No, like a baby!"

Or like an innocent man, Nick thought.

The elevator arrived and both men stepped inside. Nick pressed the button for the first floor and kept his gaze directed at his feet. He found Feller's glee irritating and inappropriate.

"What did Kaiser mean about the shareholder list?" Feller demanded. "I didn't quite catch that."

Nick said he didn't quite catch it himself.

Feller repeated his question. "What did he do, Neumann? Tell me. Lately, you've been spending more time with the Chairman than I have. Fill me in."

"I can't," Nick said, lying to get the nervous twerp off his back. "I don't know myself."

He knew the details of the crime, but he didn't know its motivation. Why would Schweitzer betray the bank that had been his home for thirty years? Had the promise of a return to his former duties as head of a trading desk been that tempting? More money, a new title with an aggressive and extremely profitable bank. Nick didn't think so. At USB,

Schweitzer was a member of the Chairman's inner circle, privy to daily decision making at the highest level of the bank. Heady stuff — even if officially he was director of compliance. He could hardly hope for as much at the Adler Bank.

Moreover, Peter Sprecher had made a point of repeating Von Graffenried's words that the list of institutional shareholders had come at a bargain price, practically for free. That didn't jibe with the careerist treachery of which Schweitzer now stood convicted. On the contrary. It reeked of the basest of human motivations. Revenge.

Feller rapped his knuckles against the wall in a nervous tattoo. "What kind of turncoat would provide information to the enemy in the midst of a battle, eh, Neumann? I ask you that."

Nick didn't answer, choosing only to grunt in general agreement. Feller's questions had forced his mind back to an unwelcome suspicion that had been scratching at the base of his skull these past few minutes. Who had whispered in the Chairman's ear that it was Schweitzer who had given the list of institutional shareholders to Konig? Nick had set the trap by himself, and he had told just two people about it.

In a distant world, Feller was continuing his tirade against Schweitzer. "God, did you see him crying? To think he's almost sixty. It was like seeing your father break down. *Unglaublich.*"

Nick turned on Feller. "Schweitzer's life is ruined, don't you see that? What kind of pleasure do you get out of glorying in his destruction?"

"None," answered Feller, momentarily abashed. "But if the bastard stole confidential information pertaining to our defense and gave it to the Adler Bank, I hope he burns in hell. Look at you, Neumann. You would never for an instant consider doing anything to hurt the bank, to harm the Chairman. It's unthinkable!"

Nick felt the heft of the false dossier pressing against his spine. "Absolutely," he said.

A security guard was waiting at the entrance to *Dokumentation Zentrale*. Nick and Feller flashed their identifications and the guard admitted them to the bank's central archive. The room was deserted and pitch-black. Feller walked inside and turned on a bank of fluorescent lights. The guard took a seat at the reading table.

"Like old times," said Feller, ambling to Karl's customary position behind the worn green counter. He leaned against it and asked in a palsied voice, "What can I do for you, young man? Want a file, do you? Well then fill out the form, you cretin. You young pups are all alike. Lazy, stupid, and slow. I don't know how the bank will survive. Haven't you finished writing up your request yet?" He pretended to take one from Nick. "No reference — no files. Moron."

Nick laughed. The imitation wasn't half bad. Apparently he hadn't been the first guy ever to ask for files without giving his proper personal reference. Feller motioned for him to come behind the counter.

"I need the file for numbered account 549.617 RR," Nick said.

Feller repeated the number and set off down the central path that ran between the rows and rows of shelves. "Five four nine, what was the rest?"

"Six one seven."

"All right, come right this way."

They walked a few yards farther, then took a right turn down a row of shelved materials stacked fifteen feet high. Like street signs, numbers were posted at every corner. Feller moved quickly through the narrow aisles. After a break in the shelves, he turned left down a narrower corridor, hardly wide enough for two persons to stand side by side. Suddenly he stopped. "Here we are then, 549.617 RR. What do you need from this file?"

"Just the uncollected correspondence."

"Up on the fourth shelf." Feller pointed above Nick's head. "I can't reach it."

"Don't you have a ladder for this?"

"There's one here someplace. Quicker just

to climb up the shelves. We used to have races to see who could touch the ceiling first."

"Really?" said Nick. He needed exactly such a distraction to occupy Feller. He stood on his tiptoes, and the fingers of his right hand just reached the Pasha's file. "You think you still have it in you?"

"Naw, I'm too used to life on the Fourth Floor," said Feller, patting his belly.

Nick spotted his cue. "I don't believe that for a second, Reto. Give it a go. I'll let you practice a few times and then I'll whip you myself."

"You? With your leg? I'm not a cruel man." But Feller was already removing his suit jacket. "Not in normal circumstances, anyway. But hey, if you want a thrashing, no problem." He turned his back to Nick and trained his eyes on the small spaces and gaps in each shelf that might serve as his footholds.

Nick withdrew the file from his back and laid it on an empty section of shelf. Tiptoeing, he stretched to reach the Pasha's file.

A terrible racket echoed through the hallways as Feller clambered up the shelves and touched the ceiling. "See, Neumann," he called, glowing with pride from his perch between the shelves. "That took about four seconds."

"Damn quick," said Nick with appropriate awe. He glanced down to be sure that his body was blocking the shelf where he had laid the surrogate file. It was.

"Are you kidding?" asked Feller, caught up in revisiting his old haunts. "On a good day, I could make it up *and down* in four seconds. Here goes again." He clattered down the shelves, and before Nick could worry that he might spot the file, he turned around and climbed right back up again. He had made it halfway up to the top when the security guard yelled from across the room. "What are you two doing back there? Come here at once."

Feller froze where he was, back turned to Nick.

Nick grabbed the edge of the Pasha's file and freed it from its bin. He opened its cover and took out the pile of fake correspondence he had made up a few days before. Then, he rammed the file — which was much thicker than he had remembered — into the back of his pants, pulling his jacket down to cover the bulge. Christ, it felt like he had an anvil strapped to his waist.

The guard called once again across the room. "Hurry up and come back here. What are you doing?"

Feller answered with an irreverence Nick hadn't known he possessed. "We're climbing the walls, what do you think?" He looked over his shoulder at Nick and winked.

"Hurry up, then," replied the guard. "Zurich Grasshopper is playing Neuchâtel Xamax.

You damn suits will make me miss the kick-off."

Nick tapped Feller on the leg and handed him the surrogate file. "Put that back for me, will you. You can reach the bin from where you are."

The security guard popped his head around the corner. His regard went from Nick to Feller.

Feller replaced the dossier and dropped to the ground. "Looks like our race will have to be rescheduled. Got everything you need?"

Nick held up the counterfeit bundle of the Pasha's correspondence. "Everything."

Chapter 54

Nick walked into the Keller Stübli that evening at a few minutes past nine. His neck and shoulders bristled with tension, but it was a tension born of impatience, not desperation. For once, he was acting instead of reacting. His plan to steal the Pasha's file had come off brilliantly. A quick glance at the file's contents proved that everything was still in its place: the bank's copies of every transfer confirmation, the matrices specifying the name and accounts where his funds were wired every Monday and Thursday, the names of the portfolio managers who had so modestly administered his account. And along with the file, he had managed to bring something of his own out of the bank. A scheme to nail both Mevlevi and Kaiser. The knowledge that he might be able to regain control of his future sent a current through his system, fueling the tightness that had settled around his shoulders. Good news from Sprecher and the day would be complete.

Nick let his eyes wander the room. He didn't believe he'd been followed at any time that day, but he couldn't be certain. Walking to the bar, he had kept an eye behind him, stopping frequently at shop windows and searching their reflections for the shadow of a man or woman moving a shade too slowly. That he had neither seen nor felt another's presence was no guarantee of his security. A team of professionally trained surveillance artists could shadow him for days without his knowing it. And so, he could not afford to let his guard down.

The bar was filling up rapidly. Customers crowded the score of wooden tables that lined the walls. A jazzy backbeat pounded from the loudspeakers. Sprecher, lit cigarette in hand, occupied his usual place at the far end of the bar.

"Any luck?" Nick asked. "Could you pull up any data on the Ciragan Trading account?"

"The place was a zoo," said Sprecher. "Konig handed down a case of Dom Pérignon to the traders to celebrate our victory. Manna from heaven."

"A little early, isn't it?"

"Konig's pulled out all the stops. He's had a secret weapon all along. Seems that conditional on his passing the thirty-three-percent barrier, a couple of big American banks had agreed to provide him bridge financing to make a cash bid for all the shares of USB he doesn't own. Monday morning at eight o'clock, he'll announce an offer to pay five hundred francs for every share not in his possession. That's a twenty-five-percent premium to yesterday's close."

"That's three billion francs." Nick closed his eyes for a second. Talk about overkill! "Kaiser will fight it."

"He'll try, but so what? How many of the shares you're counting on to vote with current management do you actually own? Twenty-five, thirty percent?"

Nick did his sums. Even after Maeder's liberation plan, USB owned only about forty percent of its shares outright. The other shares belonged to institutions they'd convinced to stick with Kaiser. "A little more than that," he said.

"No matter," replied Sprecher. "By Tuesday at one P.M., Konig will have over sixty-six percent of the bank in his pocket. Who can turn down that kind of premium?"

"Kaiser will find a white knight."

"He won't have the chance."

Nick realized Sprecher was right. The assembly had attracted so much publicity that portfolio managers from New York, Paris, and London were flying in to attend. One whiff of the price Konig was offering and they'd jump ship. Hambros, Banker's Trust — all the groups Nick had spent so much time wooing would vote their shares with the Adler Bank. And why not? Just two months ago, USB shares were trading at three hundred francs. No one could resist that kind of return.

"You can imagine the frenzy," Sprecher

went on. "Everyone at the Adler Bank has been working a long time toward this moment. It was near to chaos. A man couldn't move in there, let alone try and steal something. And it's going to be the same tomorrow. Konig ordered all the troops back at ten A.M. — a last push before the assembly Tuesday."

Nick raised his eyes dejectedly. "So you're telling me you couldn't get the info on Ciragan Trading?"

Sprecher patted him grimly on the shoulder as if to offer his condolences. Suddenly, he grinned. "I never said any such thing." He drew an envelope from his jacket and ran it under Nick's nose. "Every last detail your little heart desires. Uncle Peter wouldn't let his —"

"Oh, shut up, Peter, and give me that thing." Nick ripped the envelope out of Sprecher's hand and they both began laughing.

"Go ahead. Open it. Unless you feel the forces of darkness have us in their sights."

Reflexively, Nick checked over his shoulders. The crowd hadn't grown in the last ten minutes. He spotted no one paying him undue attention. Meanwhile, the envelope was burning the flesh of his fingertips. He glanced once at Sprecher, then slid a thumb under the fold and tore open the envelope. On the Adler Bank's engraved stationery was printed a weekly accounting of shares of the United Swiss Bank purchased for benefit of account E1931.DC — Ciragan Trading. Purchase date, settlement date, price, commission, number of shares — it was all there.

"You didn't just type this up, did you?" Nick asked, joking.

"Couldn't if I wanted to. See there at the lower left-hand corner. Those four numbers followed by the letters AB. That's our internal reference for the operation I requested to print out these shares. Somewhere in our database there is a record of my little theft."

Nick finished for his friend. "So if we call up that record, we'll get the exact same info as you have."

"Natch," said Sprecher, and then he winked. "It was too damned easy. Like I said, the place was bloody chaotic. Faris, our equities guru, sits with his back to me at the next station over. I knew where to look, I just needed the opportunity. Filled the good man's glass with bubbly, Uncle Peter did, and voilà, presto magico. Off he went for a pit stop and off I went to his desk. It's not as if he logs into and out of his computer each time he gets up. I sat my bottom down as if I ruddy well belonged there. Didn't look over my shoulder once. Just tapped in the account name, requested a historical record of all movements into and out of the account for the last eighteen months, and hit 'Print.' And don't worry, Nick, I returned the computer to the screen it was on when I sat down — currency cross rates or some such. He never knew I was there.

And you, Nick. How did thee fare?"

Nick knew he'd have a hard time matching Sprecher's joyous recitation, so he decided on a low-key performance. "The Pasha's file in its entirety." He tapped the briefcase at his side. "With what's inside and the list you gave me, we can check if Mevlevi's transfers match Konig's purchases."

"Good boy. Of course, you I never doubted."

"For now, I'm turning the file over to you. Too dangerous to keep it at my place."

Sprecher eyed the briefcase, then said gravely, "Do not fold, spindle, or mutilate."

"And besides that, keep it in good condition."

Nick had tried to reach Sylvia twice prior to leaving the bank, hoping to wangle an invitation to spend the night at her place. She hadn't been home either time and only belatedly had he remembered a mention of her visiting her father in Sargans. He wondered if the Pasha's file would be any safer at Sylvia's than at his place. He'd assembled a list of questions for her, and now as he reviewed them his stomach burned with a sour fury. Who had told Kaiser about the theft of the shareholder lists and their delivery to Klaus Konig? Who had informed him that Armin Schweitzer was the man behind their theft? How had Kaiser known about their lunch date Thursday? Who had left the message on her machine last night?

Had it been the Chairman's voice he'd heard?

He wanted desperately to assure himself that there was no chance that Sylvia was the responsible party. He wished he knew her so well that he could answer his own misgivings with an unequivocal no. But she had always kept a part of herself hidden from him. He knew it was true, because he had done the same. Until today he had enjoyed exploring the limits of their relationship, never knowing what he might find behind a veiled glance or a furtive sigh. Now he had to ask himself if her diffidence had merely been obfuscation.

Nick turned his attention toward the hopping establishment. "Any sign of our man?"

Sprecher stood and scanned the entire room. "Don't see him."

"I'll check the floor. Maybe I can spot him. You keep your eye on that briefcase." Nick left his stool and walked a few steps into the crowded room. He remembered Yogi Bauer as a hunched gray man in a dark suit. So far he didn't see anyone who matched that description. Clusters of men and women stood drink in hand, every last one smoking a cigarette. He moved through their ranks searching the tables that ran along each wall. No luck. After a few minutes he returned to the bar and found Sprecher nursing a beer.

"Didn't see him?" Sprecher asked, lighting another cigarette.

Nick said no and ordered a beer for himself.

Sprecher leaned back on his stool, grinning sardonically. "What did you say you did in the marines?"

"Recon."

"That's what I thought. Must've been one sad unit." He laid his cigarette in the ashtray and swung around on his stool, lifting a casual finger toward the darkest corner of the bar. "Next to the potted palm, far corner. You might consider investing in a good pair of specs."

Nick looked to where Sprecher was pointing. As if on cue, a clutch of attractive women parted company offering him a clear view of a small man, beer stein in hand, dressed in a wrinkled three-piece charcoal suit. It was Yogi Bauer. Just one problem. Ten empty mugs littered the table in front of him. "He's legless."

Sprecher was signaling the bartender. "Barman, give us another round and whatever Mr. Bauer over there is drinking."

The bartender looked over Sprecher's shoulder. "*Mr. Bauer?* You mean Yogi. Beer or schnapps should do the trick."

"One of each," volunteered Sprecher.

The bartender left to pour their beers and when he returned, said, "Go easy on him. He's been in since noon. He may be a little surly, but remember, he's a paying customer."

Nick picked up two beers and followed his colleague through the crowd. He doubted they'd get anything out of this guy. When they reached Bauer's table, Sprecher pulled out a chair and sat down. "Mind if we join you for a pint? Name's Peter Sprecher and this is my pal, Nick."

Yogi Bauer straightened his arms and adjusted his frayed cuffs. "Nice to see our young ones still have manners," he said, lifting the stein to his lips. His dyed black hair was matted and in need of a trim. His maroon tie sported a stain the size and shape of a small African country. His eyes were rheumy. Bauer was the textbook definition of an aging alcoholic.

He finished off half of his beer, then said, "Sprecher, I know you. Did a little time in Blighty, if I'm not mistaken?"

"Exactly. I did my schooling at Carne in Sussex. In fact, we wanted to ask you a couple of questions about your time in England, when you were with USB."

"When I was with USB?" Bauer asked. "When *wasn't I* with USB? When weren't *all of us* with USB? I've already told you Schweitzer's story. What else do you want to know?"

Nick leaned forward ready to fire away, but Sprecher placed a calming hand on his shoulder, so he eased back and let his colleague bait the lure.

Sprecher waited until Bauer set down the beer. "You were at USB London for how long? Two years?"

"Two years?" said Bauer, as if shortchanged for time spent before the mast. "More like seven. We opened her up in seventy-three and I left in seventy-nine. Got the heave-ho back to the main office. That was a black day, I can tell you."

"So it was a small branch?"

"Small enough, at least early on. Armin Schweitzer was the branch manager. I was his assistant. Why the interest? You heading back?"

"*Heading back?*" asked Sprecher, caught off guard momentarily. "Yes, yes, in fact I was thinking of transferring there. London's the place these days. By the way, how many staffers were you?"

"Started with three of us. When I left we were thirty."

"Must've known everyone?"

Bauer shrugged and grunted in a single well-choreographed movement, as if to say "Of course, you stupid fucking idiot." "We were a family. Of sorts, that is."

"There was a man named Burki there at the same time, wasn't there? Vice president. I believe his name was Caspar. Surely, you must have known him."

Yogi Bauer's eyes darted from the empty beer mug to the full glass of schnapps.

"Caspar Burki?" Sprecher repeated.

"Of course, I remember Cappy," blurted Yogi Bauer, more forced confession than idle reminiscence. "Hard not to know a man when you work in the same office for five years."

Nick said, "Burki was a portfolio manager, right? You were a trader?"

Bauer shifted his attention to Nick. "Cappy was on the client side of the firm. What about it?"

Sprecher touched Bauer's arm and inclined his head toward Nick. "My pal's father knew Burki, too. We wanted to find him, you know, say hello, shoot the shit, catch up on old times." He slid the schnapps across the table.

Yogi Bauer grimaced, not liking what he heard. He picked up the schnapps and polished it off in one messy gulp.

"He is still alive, isn't he?" asked Nick.

"Hell yes," gasped Bauer, eyes watering at the burn of the peppermint liqueur. "Cappy's still kicking."

"And what does he do these days? Enjoying his retirement like you?"

Bauer shot Nick a dirty glance. "Yes, he's enjoying himself fine. Just like me. We're making the most of our golden years. Sitting in front of roaring fires with grandkids on our knees. Vacations to the South of France. Wonderful existence." He lifted an empty stein. "Cheers. What did you say your name was again?"

"Neumann. My father was Alex Neumann. Worked out of the L.A. branch office."

"I knew him," said Bauer. "Piece of bad

luck, that. Condolences."

"It's been a long time," said Nick.

Bauer eyed him warily, then asked in a newly sympathetic voice, "So you're looking for Caspar Burki? Not a good idea. Listen to Yogi. Forget about him. Anyway, I haven't seen him in months. Don't know where to set eyes on the man."

"But he still lives in Zurich?" Nick asked.

Bauer laughed, sounding like a horse whinnying. "Where else would he go? Has to stay near the source, doesn't he?"

Nick sagged. *The Source?* Was that the name of a bar? Was Burki another geriatric alky? "Know where we can find him?" he pressed. "He doesn't live at the address he had given to the bank."

"He moved a while back. I don't know where to reach him, so don't ask me. It's not a good idea, anyway. He's down on his luck. A pension's not what it used to be."

Nick looked at Bauer's exhausted suit and the grimy ring circling his collar. Not if you spend it all on booze, it isn't. He placed his hand on Yogi's arm. "It would mean a lot to me if you could tell me where I could see him. Sure you don't know where he is?"

Bauer shook his arm loose. "Calling me a liar, are you? Caspar Burki is gone. Doesn't exist anymore. At least not the man your father might have known. He's vanished. Leave him alone. And while you're at it, leave me alone."

He shifted his unsteady gaze between Nick and Peter as if by sheer brunt of his will he could force them to leave the table. But like most drunks, he grew tired of his efforts in a hurry and instead, belched loudly.

Nick walked round the table and kneeling, spoke in Bauer's ear. "We're leaving now. Don't want to wear out our welcome. When you see Burki, tell him I'm looking for him. And that I won't quit until I find him. Tell him it's about Allen Soufi. He'll know who I mean."

Nick and Peter returned to the bar and struggled to clear a hole in the crowd to ask for a beer. A pair of stools opened up next to them, and Sprecher hopped aboard one with a cheerfulness Nick could not fathom.

"He was lying," said Sprecher, once Nick had taken his seat. "He knows where Burki is. They're probably drinking pals. Just didn't fancy telling us."

"Why?" asked Nick. "Why try to discourage us from finding him? And what the hell did he mean by 'the source'?"

"Only the guilty have something to hide. Seems we ruffled his feathers. I'd call it a success."

Nick wasn't so sure. So what if they knew that Burki was alive? So what if Bauer was a friend of his? They possessed neither the time nor the resources to keep an eye on Bauer with the hopes that one day he might lead them to

703

Burki. As far as Nick was concerned, it was a failure. Allen Soufi was as far away as ever.

Sprecher nudged him in the ribs. "Over yon shoulder, chum. Like I said, we ruffled his feathers. Now let's see where he flies."

Not three stools down from where they sat, Yogi Bauer poked his head through the wall of patrons and yelled at the bartender for change of a ten-franc note that he waved in his right hand. The bartender flicked the note from his hand and poured a few coins into his palm. Bauer looked to his right, then to his left. Oblivious of Nick's inquisitive regard, he retreated.

Nick told Sprecher to wait at the bar and hold on to the briefcase, then eased himself off the stool and followed Bauer toward the bathroom. The older man weaved his way through the crowd, careering into unsuspecting parties. He left two spilled beers in his wake and for his troubles received a deftly administered cigarette burn in the seat of his trousers. Finally, he made it to the rear of the Keller Stübli, disappearing down a flight of stairs that led to the rest rooms. Nick peeked his head round the corner before descending. Bauer was halfway down the staircase, both hands wrapped around the wooden banister. He took the stairs one at a time and when he reached the bottom, paused to root in his pocket for a piece of change, then stepped to his left out of sight. Nick flew down the stairs.

He stopped at their base and leaned forward to see around the wall. Bauer was on the telephone. He stood with his head lowered and the receiver pressed against his face.

Nick waited for what seemed like an eternity but was probably no more than fifteen seconds. Suddenly, Bauer lifted his head. "*Hoi. Bisch-du daheim?* Hey, you at home? I'm coming over in fifteen minutes. Too bad. Then get your ass out of bed. They've finally come for you."

Nick and Peter stood hidden in a dark corner across the street from the Keller Stübli waiting for Yogi Bauer to come out. The usual Saturday-night parade of unfortunates rambled along the Niederdorf, vocally denouncing the status quo while swilling every imaginable brand of beer and wine. Ten minutes passed. And then another ten. So much for Yogi keeping to his schedule, thought Nick.

Sprecher huddled in his trench coat, guarding the briefcase under one arm. "If you want to play your hunch that Yogi Bauer is going to walk out of the Keller Stübli and lead you right to Caspar Burki, that's fine," he said. "He may have said he was leaving right away, but my money says he stays in there until closing, then goes home to his dirty little bed and passes out. It's past eleven. I'm tapped out."

"Go home," said Nick. "No reason for both

705

of us to wait. I'll see you tomorrow morning, say Sprüngli, nine o'clock? If you get up early, check those numbers. And bring the briefcase. I've got some ideas to run by you."

"I'll be there at nine," said Sprecher. "But about those ideas, Nick? Leave them at home."

Yogi Bauer emerged from the Keller Stübli a few minutes after Peter Sprecher had left. He walked pretty well for a man who'd been drinking since noon that day. Occasionally, he teetered this way and lurched that, but his determined posture and forward motion combined to right his listing. Nick followed at a prudent distance, praying that Bauer was going directly to Caspar Burki's.

Bauer scuttled down the Niederdorf hugging the buildings that ran to his right. He turned left at the Brungasse and disappeared from view. Nick hurried to catch up and when he turned the corner, nearly stumbled onto him. The Brungasse was a steep alley paved with slick cobblestones. Even the soberest pedestrian would have trouble walking up it. Bauer kept one hand on the building to his left, the other flailing the air, and managed to climb the hill, step by painful step. Nick waited until he had disappeared over the crest, then entered the alley and walked briskly up the incline. He paused at the top of the hill and tucked his head around the corner. He was rewarded with a perfect view of Yogi Bauer jamming his finger into the doorbell of a building a little ways down the left-hand side of the street.

Nick held his position and kept watch. Bauer attacked the buzzer while muttering a string of obscenities. When no one answered, he turned his attentions to a shuttered window on the second or third floor. He leaned his shaggy head back and entreated Caspar Burki to come out this instant. It was important, he was saying. They're after you, Cappy. *Sie sind endlich hier.* They've finally come.

Suddenly, a window flew open and a gray head popped out. "Damn you, Bauer. It's midnight. You said you'd be here an hour ago." The door buzzed and the man in the window yelled, "Come in, then."

Bauer shuffled up the steps and into the apartment house.

Nick let a minute pass, then walked to the doorway. He studied the names of the tenants, each posted in perfect script next to a black doorbell. The name *C. Burki* was taped next to the button for apartment 3B. Gotcha, thought Nick. He acknowledged a tremor of genuine elation, then noted the street and the address. Seidlergasse 7. He would come back tomorrow. He would speak to the man who lived in apartment 3B. He would meet Caspar Burki and he would find out just who Allen Soufi really was.

Chapter 55

As the tempo of their lovemaking quickened, the bed began to rock in a steady rhythm. The wooden headboard slapped the wall. The Victorian mattress heaved and sighed. A man moaned, his throaty voice rising in counterpoint to the bed's increasingly violent motions. A woman cried out, her rhapsodic pleasures serenading them. The tempo grew more frenzied, less rhythmic. The man arched his back as the woman's hair cascaded onto his chest like a cool summer shower. He expelled a hot breath into the dark, listening room, then lay still.

A clock in a far part of the house tolled the midnight hour.

Sylvia Schon raised her head from Wolfgang Kaiser's heaving chest. "How can you sleep with that ringing all night long?"

"I've grown to like it. It reminds me I'm not alone."

She ran an ivory hand across his chest. "You're definitely not alone right now."

"Not tonight, at least." Kaiser placed his hand behind her head and guided her down to kiss him. "I haven't thanked you yet for the news about Armin Schweitzer."

"Did he confess?"

"*Armin?* Never. Denied everything. Held his ground to the end."

"Did you believe him?"

"How could I? Everything you told me made perfect sense. I fired him on the spot."

"He should count himself lucky to get away with such a light punishment. You could have had him thrown in jail."

Kaiser grunted. Doubtful, he thought, but let her be content with her victory. "We were together thirty years."

"You talk about him as if he were a woman," she said, teasing him.

"True, but then thirty years is a long time. You've been with us what, nine years? Your entire life is in front of you. I don't know what Armin has left." Kaiser pulled the sheet over his chest. For a moment he felt a pang of remorse.

"He brought it on himself," said Sylvia. "No one forced him to give our secrets to Klaus Konig. Nothing is lower than spying on your own."

Kaiser laughed. "Do you believe Neumann holds a similar view?"

She stared at him harshly, then turned away. "He arrived two months ago. That hardly makes him one of our own. Besides, I'm spying for you."

"You are spying for the bank." Kaiser fondled her buttocks while silently explaining to her that if she had known Nicholas's father, if she could see how alike the two were, in appearance and in manner, she'd know that Nicholas was definitely one of their own. "You haven't finished telling me what you've learned."

Sylvia lifted herself on an elbow and brushed the hair from her face. "Nick wants to find a Caspar Burki. Burki was a portfolio manager in our London branch who recommended a man named Allen Soufi as a client to Nick's father. Did you know him?"

"Who, Burki? Of course, I knew him. I hired the man. He was an odd type. Kept to himself, as I remember. He retired a while ago. Disappeared from sight."

"I meant Allen Soufi."

Kaiser shook his head, feigning ignorance, though his heart had jumped at the name. "Soufi? Can't recall. How do you spell it?"

Sylvia spelled the name and Kaiser denied having ever heard of it. Soufi was a ghost from the past — a man whom everyone would prefer to remain dead.

"Burki still lives in Zurich," Sylvia pointed out. "Nick has a hunch he knows who this Soufi is. He's sure that Burki can tell him if he's right or wrong."

"You didn't give him the address?"

"I did," she said defiantly.

Damn! thought Kaiser. He felt like slapping her across the face, but he was careful to control his raging emotions. His anger subsided, and he realized that his first concern had been about losing young Neumann, not about the unmasking of Allen Soufi. *Strange.* When Sylvia had come to him three weeks ago with news that Nicholas was interested in checking the bank's archive for clues about his father's killer, he had felt that no harm could come from letting the boy have a look at his father's moldy reports. If Nicholas were to assume a position of importance on the Fourth Floor, any questions about the bank's role in his father's death had to be put to rest.

"Alex Neumann was scared that someone was after him," Sylvia said, apparently anxious to make up for her error in judgment. "He looked into getting a bodyguard."

"A bodyguard?"

"Yes. He even called the FBI."

Good Lord, this was getting worse by the minute! Kaiser sat up in bed. "How do you know all this?"

Sylvia pushed herself away from him. "Nick told me."

"But who told him? His father died when the boy was ten years old."

"I'm not sure. I can't remember exactly what Nick said."

Kaiser grabbed her shoulder and shook her once. "Tell me the truth. It's obvious you're hiding something. If you want to help me keep the bank free from Konig, you'll tell me at once."

"You don't have to worry. You're not in-volved in this."

"Let me be the judge of that. Tell me this instant how Neumann found out this non-sense about Allen Soufi and about the FBI."

Sylvia lowered her head. "I can't."

"You can and you will. Or maybe you'd prefer that I follow Rudy Ott's advice and cancel your trip to the States. I'll make damn sure you spend the rest of your career where you are now — a lousy vice president. You and a hundred fifty other losers."

Sylvia stared at him hatefully. Her cheeks were flushed, and he noticed that a tear had fallen from one eye. "You've fallen in love with him, haven't you?"

"Of course not." She sniffled, blinking back a few tears, then took a deep breath and said, "Alex Neumann kept a daily agenda. Nick found two of them when he cleaned up his mother's affairs after her death. For 1978 and 1979. That's how he knew about Soufi and the FBI."

Kaiser massaged his neck in a futile attempt to lessen his growing anxiety. Why was he learning about an agenda only now?

"The FBI?" he asked. "Sounds like the man really was in trouble. What exactly did he write in this agenda of his?"

"Just the name of a special agent and the telephone number. Nick was never able to get any information out of them."

Thank God for that. "My name wasn't anywhere, was it?"

"Only on the activity reports."

"Naturally. I was head of the international division. I was copied on every report submitted by all of our representative branches. It's the agenda I'm interested in. You're sure my name was not in it?"

She wiped her cheek with the bed sheet. She was looking better now. The girl had obviously realized where her priorities lay. "Maybe a few times," she said. " 'Call Wolfgang Kaiser.' 'Dinner Wolfgang Kaiser.' That's all. Nothing to worry about. If you weren't involved with this Mr. Soufi, it doesn't matter what Nick finds out."

Kaiser gritted his teeth. "I'm only worried for the bank," he said in his most professional voice. But inside his head another voice chided young Neumann. Damn you, Nicholas! I wanted you at my side. Seeing you walk into my office that day was like seeing your father all over again. If I could have convinced you to stay at my side, then I would have known that the course I set for the bank, the actions I undertook to ensure we reached our destination, however extreme, were correct. It was your father who was mistaken, not me. The bank is bigger than one man. Bigger than a friendship. I thought surely you would have recognized that. Now, what am I going to do with you?

"Nicholas doesn't know the half of his father's death," he said, inventing wildly. "Alex Neumann was responsible for his own murder. He had been involved in drugs. Using cocaine on a daily basis. We were about to fire him for embezzling from the Los Angeles office."

Sylvia sat up straighter, letting the sheet fall from her chest. "You never said anything about this before. Why haven't you told him these things?"

"We kept it from the family. It was Gerhard Gautschi's decision at the time. We felt it was the least we could do to comfort them. I don't want Nicholas to find out. It would open too many wounds."

"I think Nick should know. It would give him a reason to end this silly search. He won't stop until he finds out something. I know him. Even if it is bad news, he'll want to know. It's only fair. It was his father, after all."

Christ, now the girl had a conscience. "You will not repeat a word of what I've told you to Neumann."

"But it would mean so much to Nick to know. We can't hide this from —"

"Not a word," Kaiser shouted, unable to master his mounting anxiety. "If I learn you've told him, you won't have to worry about Konig eliminating your post. I'll fire you myself. Is that clear?"

Sylvia flinched. He had scared her. "Yes," she said softly. "It's very clear."

Kaiser stroked her cheek. He had over-reacted. "I apologize, darling, for raising my voice. You can't imagine the strain we're under. We can't allow any harm to come to the bank in these next days, not the slightest innuendo of misdoing. My concerns are for the bank, not myself."

Sylvia nodded her head in understanding.

Kaiser saw that her heart was divided. She needed a reminder of what the bank could do for her. "About the promotion. To first vice president?"

Sylvia raised her eyes to him. "Yes?"

"I don't see why we'll have to wait much longer. We can finalize things right after the general assembly. It'll give you some more clout with the big boys in New York City."

"You're sure?"

"Of course I'm sure." He lifted her chin with an outstretched finger. "But only if you'll forgive me."

Sylvia considered the request for a moment. Then she laid her head on his chest and sighed loudly. Her hand delved under the covers and soon it was massaging him. "You're forgiven," she whispered.

Kaiser closed his eyes, abandoning himself to her touch. If only Nicholas Neumann were so easily bought.

Chapter 56

General Dimitri Marchenko arrived at the gates to Ali Mevlevi's compound at ten o'clock Sunday morning. The sky was a magnificent royal blue. Hints of cedar danced in the air. Spring was practically here. He stood in his jeep and signaled the line of trucks behind him to halt. A uniformed sentry fired off a crisp salute and opened the gate. Another sentry jumped onto the running board of his command jeep, pointing the way forward with an outstretched arm.

The convoy thundered into the compound, climbing a gentle incline that paralleled a playing field. The trucks crossed an asphalt parade ground and stopped in front of two large doors cut into the face of a hundred-foot cliff. Marchenko stared at the two enormous hangars, impressed by the feat of engineering. Inside the hangar to his right sat two helicopters: a Sukhoi Attack Model II and a Hind Assault. He had sold them to Mevlevi three months ago. The sentry directed the jeep toward the helicopters, then dropped his arm, indicating they should stop.

Colonel Hammid jogged to Marchenko's jeep. He pointed into the hangar. "Order the truck carrying the 'communications gear' to go there. Then you must advise us which chopper is better suited to carrying such sensitive 'eavesdropping equipment.' "

Marchenko grunted. Evidently, Hammid knew the true nature of the cargo being transported. It figured. No one could keep a secret in this part of the world. "The Sukhoi. It is faster and more maneuverable. The pilot will need to climb sharply after deploying the weapon."

The Syrian commander offered his oiliest smile. "You do not know Al-Mevlevi's troops. The pilot will not return. He will set the bird down and then detonate the weapon. This way there will be no failure."

Marchenko simply nodded and climbed out of the jeep. He had never understood the roots of fanaticism. He walked to the driver of the truck that carried the Kopinskaya IV and said a few words to him in Kazakh. The driver nodded brusquely and when Marchenko stepped back, drove the truck into the hangar, stopping it near the sleek Sukhoi helicopter. Marchenko marched to the next truck in line and ordered his soldiers into the hangar. Twenty men poured from its bay and marched at double time toward the helicopter.

Marchenko wanted to attach the Kopinskaya IV to the helicopter as soon as possible. If there was any problem with the device, he wanted to know now, while time remained to remedy it. There was little risk of a renegade stealing the chopper with the bomb attached. Hammid clearly had orders to protect the weapon at all costs. Marchenko had given his soldiers the same instructions. To be safe he would order the hangar doors closed until five minutes prior to the helicopter's departure.

Marchenko supervised the unloading of the Kopinskaya IV device. After the crates filled with outdated radio equipment had been removed, he climbed into the bay and deactivated the explosive antitampering device. He took a set of keys out of his pocket and, selecting one, inserted it into a lock drilled into the chassis of the truck. He turned the key sharply to the right, withdrew it, then pulled open the container's door. A wooden crate no different from the others littering the hangar floor sat inside it. He yelled for his men to take it out and set it down near the chopper.

Marchenko found a crowbar in the back of the truck and opened the crate. He peered inside. A stainless steel canister three feet high and two feet in diameter rested in a bed of foam rubber. He slipped a hand under one end and eased it from its housing. The canister weighed just thirty pounds. He grunted as he lifted it from the crate and set it down on the smooth hangar floor.

The bomb itself was not much to look at. Marchenko thought it resembled a large tear gas canister with one end domed and the other flat. Height: twenty-eight inches. Diameter: nine inches. Weight: eleven pounds. Its casing was made from unpolished high-tensile steel. It was an altogether unimpressive-looking object.

But it could kill.

The Kopinskaya IV carried four hundred grams of enriched plutonium 238 that when detonated had the explosive force of two thousand tons of high-grade TNT. A measly throw weight in terms of the big birds, but devastating nonetheless to any object, either living or inert, within a one-mile radius of ground zero. Anything within five hundred yards would be instantly vaporized. Inside of a thousand yards the bomb achieved a ninety-five-percent kill rate at detonation. The other five percent would die within two hours from a lethal dose of gamma radiation. The kill rate tapered off dramatically at a mile out. At three thousand yards, only twenty percent would be killed by the detonation, and those mostly by the debris blown outward from the epicenter: shards of glass, splinters of wood, chunks of concrete all propelled through the air at speeds over a thousand miles an hour. A city provided its own shrapnel.

Three latches held the canister closed. He opened them one at a time, then carefully removed the lid. He gave it to a soldier, then returned his attention to the bomb. The plutonium core was housed in a titanium casing.

A chain reaction necessary to detonate the fissionable material could be initiated only when the firing rod had been inserted into the plutonium core, and the firing rod could be inserted only after the proper code had been entered in the bomb's central processing unit. Marchenko would not enter the proper code until he had received acknowledgment that Mr. Ali Mevlevi had transferred eight hundred million Swiss francs to his account at the First Kazakhi Bank in Alma-Ata.

Until then the bomb was worthless scrap.

He took the bomb in his hand and turned it upside down. The soldier assisting him removed six screws at the base of the weapon. Marchenko put the screws in his pocket, then lifted off the inferior lid. He was pleased to see a small dot at the bottom right-hand corner of a red liquid crystal display winking at him. Below the LCD was a keypad with nine digits. He entered in the number 1111 and waited as the unit performed its self-diagnostics. Five seconds later, a green light lit up in the center of the keypad. The bomb was functioning perfectly. All he needed to do now was program the detonation altitude and key in the seven-digit code that would activate the device.

Marchenko replaced the inferior lid, carefully screwing in each of the six titanium screws. He closed the device and set it down in its foam-rubber casing. He stopped his work and listened. It was quiet here. Almost serene.

He looked over his shoulder, suddenly expecting to hear the shrill whistle of a squadron of Israeli F-16s swooping in to obliterate the compound. His soldiers stood casually around him, their weapons hanging loosely on their chests. Colonel Hammid loitered a few paces away, his gaze held by the dull metallic weapon sitting on the hangar floor. He laughed at his paranoia, then turned his thoughts down more promising avenues.

Marchenko imagined his portrait hanging in every government office in Kazakhstan. He reminded himself that in less than twenty-four hour she would have brought his country a princely sum in hard currency. And himself a small one percent commission — eight million Swiss francs. Maybe this is what the Americans meant when they said "rags to riches."

Chapter 57

The phone rang a second time.

Nick shot up in bed. It was dark and the room was cold. Still too early for the central heating to be turned on. He looked at his watch, squinting a second as the hands came into focus. Barely six. His hand fumbled for the receiver, finding first the bedside lamp, then a glass of water, before falling on the phone. "Hello."

"Hi, you. It's me."

"Hey you," he responded groggily. "Whatcha doin'?" It was their greeting and he was surprised to discover it still a reflex after three months. He swung his legs over the edge of the bed and scratched at his hair.

"Just wanted to call," said Anna Fontaine. "See how you were doing. It's been a while."

He was awake now, her voice reverberating inside of him, coming at him from a dozen directions. "Um, let me check," he said. "I don't know yet really. It's only six o'clock over here."

"I know. I've been trying to reach you for a week. I figured if ever you'd be home, it would be now."

"You didn't try the office? Remember where

I work, don't you?"

"Of course I remember. I also remember a very serious former marine who would not appreciate social calls interrupting his work."

Nick could imagine her sitting cross-legged on her bed, the phone in her lap. It was a Sunday, so she'd be wearing ratty blue jeans, a black T-shirt, and a white button-down untucked. Maybe even one of his. "Come on," he protested, "I wasn't that serious. You can call me anytime at work. Deal?"

"Deal," she answered. "And how is it? Work, I mean?"

"Fine. Busy. You know, the usual trainee stuff." He stifled a sarcastic laugh. Jeez, Anna, if you only knew the shit I was up to . . .

"What about your dad?" she asked, cutting off his self-mocking commentary. "Is that panning out?"

"Could be," he said, not wanting to get into it with her. "I might know something real soon. We'll see. And how are you? How are things at school?"

"Just fine," she said. "Midterms in two weeks. Then the final push to the end. I can't wait."

"Well, you'll have a couple months off before you start in New York. You are still taking the job down there?"

"Yes, Nick, I am still taking the job. Some of us still think it's a decent place to work."

He heard hesitation in her voice, like she

wanted to get around to something but she didn't know exactly how. Might as well help her along. After all, there could be only one reason she was calling. "You're not working too hard, are you? I don't want you pulling all-nighters."

"No, and by the way, you were the one to pull all-nighters. I was the organized one who studied ahead of time."

"Are you getting out any?" There it was, a fastball right down the middle.

Anna paused. He heard a batch of white noise fill the line. "Actually, that's why I'm calling. I've met someone."

Nick was suddenly alert. "You have. That's good. I mean, if you like him."

"Yes, Nick, I like him."

Nick didn't hear her answer. He sat still, looking around his room. In that instant, he had become acutely aware of his surroundings. He could hear the bedside clock ticking and the radiator groaning as it sprang to life. He could make out the rustling of the pipes in the ceiling above him as another early riser ran a bath. He suddenly noticed that his boxers were chafing at the waist and he decided that he really did have to lose some weight. Yes, the world was still there. But somehow his position on it had been altered.

"How serious?" he asked suddenly, interrupting her.

"He's asked me to go to Greece with him

this summer. He's working for an insurance company in Athens while he gets his master's degree in international relations. Actually, you may know him. His name is Paul MacMillan. Lucy's older brother."

"Yeah, Lucy. Sure. Wow." It was a robot talking. Not him. He remembered no such person and she knew it. For some reason, she'd decided a degree of social proximity was necessary, as if a partial acquaintance might be more palatable than a total stranger. Her way of not wanting to break it to him too hard. Why was she calling anyway? Did she want his approbation? Did she expect a ringing endorsement of Mr. Paul MacMillan, some schmuck who thought he could provide for a girl like Anna by working in Greece?

Nick tried to find more grist for his enmity, but his fuel had run dry. He was aground on his single bed, sitting in the darkness in his one-room apartment. The time was 6:02. He was marooned in Zurich.

"Anna," he started. "Don't . . ."

"Don't what?" she asked, too quickly, and for a second he wasn't sure if he'd heard hope in her voice. Or maybe it was just annoyance.

Nick didn't know what he wanted to say. He was aghast to find that she had retained such a large claim to his heart. It was none of his business whether she went to Greece with Paul MacMillan or Paul McCartney, and it was a little late to think he still had a claim on her.

"Don't forget to study hard for your test," he said. "Gotta keep that four-point average. You still have to get into a decent business school."

"Oh, Nick . . ." Anna didn't continue. It was her turn to leave him hanging.

"I'm glad you met someone," he said, without feeling. *I gave you up and it was the hardest thing I've ever had to do. You can't come back now. You can't reappear at the precise moment when I need to be my strongest.* But in his heart, he was mad only at himself. He knew that she had never really left.

"Are you there?" she asked, and he realized he hadn't spoken for a few seconds.

"Just don't do anything stupid, Anna. I have to go now." He hung up the phone.

Nick spotted Peter Sprecher walking toward Sprüngli from the kiosk in the Paradeplatz. He was carrying a newspaper in one hand and his briefcase in the other. He wore a dark suit under a navy overcoat and had a white scarf wrapped around his neck. "Don't look so surprised," he said, by way of greeting. "It's not a holiday, is it? I mean, we are going to work."

Nick patted him on the back, checking his own garb in return. Blue jeans, a sweatshirt, and a forest-green parka. "Depends on what kind of work you had in mind." He opened the door to Sprüngli for his friend and followed him up the stairs to the main dining room. They chose a table in the far left corner, not far from the lavish breakfast buffet. They waited until a waitress arrived to take their orders before getting down to business.

Nick shot a glance at the briefcase. "Did you take a minute this morning and compare our man's transfers through USB with the purchases made for the Ciragan Trading account?"

"Did better than that." Sprecher opened the briefcase and withdrew a ledger sheet. He had drawn a line down its center and written the words *USB transfers* to the left and *Ciragan Trading Purchases* to the right. He handed Nick the sheet, saying, "We're close, but it's not a hundred percent. Mevlevi transferred over eight hundred million through his account at USB since last June."

"And Konig's purchases of USB stock?"

"Started small in July and kicked into full gear in November. I'm surprised Kaiser hadn't taken note of someone snapping up such large blocks of shares."

"Could've been anyone. Pension fund managers, mutual funds, individual investors. How was he to know?"

Sprecher raised an eyebrow, not ready to dismiss Kaiser's gaffe. "Anyhow, we're a hundred million off in total."

Nick studied the sheet. "Yeah, but look. For twenty-odd weeks, the value of shares purchased by the Adler Bank exactly matches

Mevlevi's transfers. Maybe the final tally's not a hundred percent, but it's darned close."

Nick continued to examine the ledger. He was excited to have obtained what he believed would pass for proof that Mevlevi was behind the Adler Bank's takeover of USB. Yet, he realized that so far nothing had truly been accomplished. Yes, he had the ammunition he needed. But the real battle would take place tomorrow . . . *if* the proper generals arrived at the proper battlefields at the proper times. Three skirmishes would be fought across two fronts separated by forty kilometers, and the one enemy could not be engaged before the other had been vanquished. The time for celebration was far off.

"I don't fancy being in Klaus's shoes," said Sprecher, "not when his ship gets taken out from under him. Do you think he knows exactly who the Pasha is?"

"Of course he knows," Nick said. "Everyone knows. The secret is pretending you don't, and keeping a straight face when you deny it."

"I suppose you're right."

"Come on. Mevlevi's fingerprints are all over the Adler Bank. My only fear is not knowing exactly what he's trying to pull off. Why does Ali Mevlevi want to control the United Swiss Bank?"

"Why does he want to control the Adler Bank?" Sprecher countered.

" 'Banks. That's where the money is.' Willie

Sutton said that. Back in the twenties, he was a pretty decent bank robber."

Sprecher spread his arms and tilted his head toward Nick as if to say "Case closed." "Tack on sixty years, change the color of the passport, and update the wardrobe. Voilà: it's still the same man. One more well-dressed hood."

Nick wasn't convinced. "So the Pasha is a bank robber? If that's the case, this has to be the most sophisticated heist in history. Not to mention the most expensive!"

"Look at it this way, put up a billion francs in order to get back ten billion. Call me old-fashioned, but that's a fair return on your investment."

"Not possible, my friend. Not possible." But as Nick peered through the window at the clothing stores that quilted the Bahnhofstrasse, boutiques selling cashmere sweaters at three thousand francs a shot and Italian leather handbags at twice that amount, he asked himself, "Why not?" Maybe Ali Mevlevi was a thief, a glorified holdup artist? Was it possible to plunder the resources of a bank from within its own walls? Could the Pasha empty the vaults of his own bank under official pretenses? And what if he didn't give a damn for official pretenses?

Nick turned his mind to a more troubling area of inquiry. What would Mevlevi do with the money? He recalled Thorne's rant about the arms and matériel Mevlevi had accumulated at his compound near Beirut. If Mevlevi has that much equipment now, imagine what he could purchase with funds diverted from the Adler Bank and USB.

Since the end of the cold war, arms dealers had been willing to sell their wares to any breathing soul with hard currency. Damn the politics! Mevlevi had only to pick up a telephone to have his choice of the deadliest weapons currently manufactured.

"Simply not possible," Nick assured Peter, if only to allay his own fears. "The Pasha's a pirate all right, but that might be going too far. Anyway, it doesn't matter why he wants it. With what we've got in our possession, we can drop him cold." He enumerated the evidence on the fingers of his right hand. "Proof of his transfers into and out of USB. Signature cards from when the account was first opened, including code words written in his own hand. Copies of the matrices that show to which banks he wires his funds. And now proof of his involvement with Konig and the Adler Bank."

"And what about Thorne? Without him, all we have is a lot of paper and a crazy theory."

"He's solid," said Nick, coaxing himself to believe his own words. "I got ahold of him this morning and he's ready to work with us." Nick didn't bring up the personal leap of faith required to call Sterling Thorne and offer his services. After his dealings with Jack Keely, he had sworn never to work with another agent of the United States government again. But his current situation forbade the luxury of prejudice. Like it or not, Thorne was all he had.

"Fill me in then," said Sprecher. "What have you worked out with him?"

For the next fifty minutes, Nick outlined the rudiments of his plan to Sprecher. He didn't know what to make of his friend's frequent guffaws and laments, but when he had finished, Sprecher extended his hand and said, "I'm in. We've got no better than a fifty-fifty chance, mind you, but you can count on me. First time in my life I feel like I'm doing something worthwhile. It's a new sensation. Can't decide if I like it or not."

Nick paid the bill and both men walked outside. "You've got enough time to make your train?"

Sprecher checked his watch. "Loads of it. Eleven-thirty now. I'm on the 12:07 via Lucerne."

"And you've brought your friend?"

Sprecher winked and patted a slight bulge beneath his arm. "Standard issue of every officer in the Swiss Army. I am a captain, don't forget."

Nick switched to another topic. "How much do you think it will take to convince the front office manager to give you that suite?"

"Top floor, lake view? Five hundred minimum."

"Ouch!" Nick said. "I owe you."

Peter buttoned his coat and tossed the scarf over his shoulder. "Only if I end up with a tag on my toe. Otherwise, consider it my membership fee in your world of responsible and civilized nations."

Caspar Burki lived in a grim block of buildings. None was higher than four stories, and each was painted a different color along some invisible boundary. The first was yellow — or had been twenty years ago. The next a glum brown. Burki's building had faded to a mottled dishwater gray. All of them were streaked with soot and caked with dirt washed from their mansard roofs.

Nick took up position in the doorway of a store selling antique furniture across the street from Burki's building. He settled in for a long wait, scolding himself for not having arrived sooner. He had accompanied Peter Sprecher to the main railway station after lunch and while there, had made two telephone calls, one to Sylvia Schon, the other to Sterling Thorne. Sylvia confirmed that their dinner engagement was on as planned. He was to arrive no later than 6:30 — she had a roast in the oven and would take no responsibility for its condition should he arrive late. His conversation with Thorne was briefer. As instructed, he had identified himself as Terry. Thorne said only two words: "Green light" — which meant that

Jester had checked in and that everything was on as planned.

Nick peered at the sad building. He didn't know whether to ring the bell and wait for an answer or to hide in the shadows in the hope that Burki would come out and be somehow recognizable. Meanwhile Yogi Bauer's words seeped into his mind. *"Don't look for him. Has to stay near the source, doesn't he?"*

A commotion in the vestibule of Burki's apartment building caught Nick's eye. He made out two men grappling each other inside the glass doorway. It was impossible to tell what was going on, so he took a step into the alley to get a better view. Just then, the two men stumbled from the building. The taller of the two, a thin man with gaunt cheeks and sunken eyes, supported the short man, a wan figure in a dark Sunday suit. Jesus Christ, Nick whispered, the short one was Yogi Bauer. He could hear him swearing and cursing as he stumbled out into the alleyway.

"Du kommst mit? You're coming with me, right?" Yogi asked over and over.

Nick retreated into the doorway of the antique shop and pretended to study a Louis XVI chaise. He watched out of the corner of his eye as the taller, gray-haired man, who he figured was Caspar Burki, led Bauer down the street. He bet he knew where they were going. Sure enough, they headed straight for the Keller Stübli. Nick followed at a safe distance, not wanting to confront Burki with Yogi Bauer present. But then a strange thing happened. When the two men reached the Keller Stübli, Burki refused to go inside. He stood there for a few minutes, hearing Bauer's abusive epithets and vehement protestations until Bauer gave up and went inside alone.

Caspar Burki adjusted his overcoat, gathering it tightly around him, then set off at a rapid pace down the Niederdorf. Destination unknown.

Chapter 58

Casper Burki had an appointment to keep. That much Nick knew for certain. The old man walked with his head bowed and his shoulders pressed forward as if fighting a rising wind. The rhythm of his feet assumed a perfect cadence, and Nick fell into his step, matching him stride for stride. He listened to the steady tap of his own feet on the wet cobblestones and remembered learning to march at Brown Field in Quantico, Virginia. He could practically hear the sergeant instructor's strained voice yelling at him, even now.

What are you, Neumann? A walkie-talkie? Keep your mouth shut and your eyes straight ahead. That's right, troop. Hands cupped to the crease of your trousers, heels to the ground! Left, left, left right left.

Nick maintained a cautious distance, imagining a taut fifty-foot rope strung between him and Burki. He followed the spindly man down the Niederdorfstrasse toward Central, and from there across the bridge toward the Bahnhofplatz. He was sure Burki was heading for the main station, but then Burki veered to the right toward the Swiss National Museum. His path skirted the Platzspitz, taking him north along the banks of the river Limmat. Nick had no idea where Burki was going.

The city took on an unsettled feeling. Nick passed an abandoned factory, windows broken and doors boarded up, and a deserted apartment building wrapped in colorful graffiti. He hadn't known Zurich hid such run-down neighborhoods. Clusters of kids, mostly in their teens, cropped up on the sidewalk. Some were headed in the opposite direction, and they stared at Nick, with his short hair and clean clothing, with undisguised contempt. The sidewalk grew dirtier, littered with empty candy wrappers, crushed soda cans, and a million cigarette butts. Soon, he wasn't able to walk without stepping in a pile of refuse.

"He has to be near the source," Yogi Bauer had said.

Nick slowed as he saw Caspar Burki cross a wooden footbridge that spanned the Limmat. A ragged assortment of lowlifes crowded the railing. Ill-shaven men wrapped in scarred leather coats, grubby women bundled in frayed sweaters. Burki hunched his shoulders, as if trying to make himself thinner, less obtrusive than he already was, and walked between them. Nick could hear the planks rattle under the old man's tread, and in their staccato stamp he felt the fluttering of his own hollow stomach. He knew where the bridge led. Letten. The city's public shooting gallery. *Caspar Burki's source.*

Nick crossed the bridge, working hard not to appear as anxious as he felt. A stubby, bearded man stepped in his path. "Hey, Johnny Handsome," the man said to Nick, "you sure you're in the right place? We don't give manicures around here." He smiled, revealing a dingy set of teeth, then stepped closer. "Fifty francs. That's as low as I'll go. You won't find any better. Not today. Not when there's a drought."

Nick jabbed two fingers into the man's chest, ready to take him down. "I'm already taken care of. Thanks anyway."

He retreated easily, lifting his arms in surrender. "When you come back, it'll be seventy francs. Don't say I didn't warn you."

Nick walked past him, concerned that he might lose sight of Caspar Burki. He asked himself what he was doing here. What could he expect to learn from a junkie? He inched by a teenage girl squatting on her haunches at the top of the far steps. She held a syringe in her hand and had just found a vein to slide the needle into. Drops of blood fell from her arm, spattering the cement. He descended the steps at the far side of the bridge and took his first look at the abandoned station.

It was a picture as foreign as the surface of the moon.

A restless tide of shabby men and women ambled back and forth across a wide cement platform. There were around a hundred of them, maybe more, and they were arranged into small encampments of five or six persons. Here and there, fires burned from rusted oil barrels. A swamplike haze hovered between platform and ceiling. Above his head, spray painted in cheap black Krylon, were the words *"Welcome to Babylon."*

The place was squalor. It was death.

Nick saw that Burki had reached his destination — a circle of doddering addicts his own age at the far end of the station. A scrawny hen of a woman was preparing a dose of heroin for a man who didn't look much different from Burki. Shorter maybe, but just as thin and with that same starved look to his eyes. The "nurse" rolled up the man's sleeve and laid his bony arm across a slapdash wooden table. She tied a short length of rubber tubing around his arm, snapping at his veins to make them stand out more prominently. Satisfied, she popped the needle into his arm. She pulled back the syringe to allow his blood to mix with the opiate, then patiently pumped the drug into his arm. With maybe an eighth of the bloody payload remaining, she withdrew the syringe from the addict's arm, balled her fist, then jabbed the needle into her own arm. A second later, she pressed the plunger, mixing the addict's opiated blood with her own. Finished, she tossed the used needle into a white plastic bag with a Red Cross decal on it. The "nurse" raised her forearm to her bicep, as if she had just received her annual flu shot, said a few words to the addict, then leaned over and gave him a polite peck on each cheek. Decorum. The addict lurched away from the makeshift table, and Caspar Burki stepped forward to take his place.

Nick hung back for a long second. He realized that it wouldn't be any good talking to Burki after he'd gotten his dose and fixed. His only hope was to move quickly and get ahold of the old man before he shot up. He wasn't sure how to intervene. He'd figure it out when he got there.

Nick crossed the platform as quickly as he could. He tried hard not to look at the hollow-eyed men and women combing their bodies for veins firm enough to fix in. Still, with a fascination he could only label macabre, he was unable to shut his eyes. A teenager had tapped out a vein on his lower neck and was showing his buddy where to put the needle. A middle-aged woman had lowered her pants and sat legs splayed on the cement floor while she shot up in the crook of her thigh. A waifish girl of five or six sat next to her. Helluva place to bring your kid on a Sunday afternoon.

A squad of policemen loitered at the far end of the station — *Sondercommandos,* by the blue riot gear they sported. They smoked, arms resting easily on the butts of their submachine guns, backs turned to their charges. This wasn't their battle. The city preferred to gather its addicts in one place where it could keep an eye on them. Containment without confrontation: the Swiss way.

Nick reached the unsteady table just as Burki was taking off his jacket and rolling up his sleeve. He took a hundred francs from his wallet and handed it to the wrinkled woman administering the shots. "This is for my friend Caspar. That should be good for two fixes, right?"

Burki looked at him and said, "Who the hell are you?"

The woman snatched the bill from Nick's hand and said, "Are you crazy, Cappy? The boy wants to buy you a present. Take it."

Nick said, "I need to talk to you for a few minutes, Mr. Burki. About some mutual friends. It won't take long, but I'd prefer to speak with you before —" his hands searched the air for the right words, "before you do this. If you don't mind."

Burki hesitated for a moment. His eyes shifted between Nick and the scraggly woman. "Mutual friends? Like who?"

"Yogi Bauer, for one. I had a few drinks with him last night."

"Poor Yogi. Pity what alcohol will do to you." Burki squinted his eyes. "You're Neumann's boy. He warned me about you."

Nick said yes, he was Alex Neumann's son, and in a calm voice introduced himself. "I work at the United Swiss Bank. I have a few questions about Allen Soufi."

Burki grunted. "Don't know the man. Now run along and get out of here. Be a good boy and go home to your mommy. It's nap time."

The "nurse" laughed hysterically. Nick told her to give him his money back and when he had it, grabbed Burki by the arm and backed him up a few steps. "Listen, you either talk to me now and take advantage of my goodwill, or I'm going to drag you over to the boys in the blue and tell them you're a thief." Nick crumpled up the hundred-franc note and stuffed it into Burki's hand. "Understand me?"

Burki spat in his face. "You're a bastard. Like your father."

"Believe it," said Nick, and wiping the saliva from his cheek, he took his first close look at Burki. The man's skin was a decaying parchment, dotted with open sores and stretched tight across his skull. His eyes were sunken blue orbs. His upper lip was split, and a tooth black with rot shone beneath it. He was a long way down the track.

Suddenly, Burki relaxed and shrugged his shoulders. "Give me a little taste now and I'll talk to you. I'm afraid I can't wait much longer. Wouldn't be any good to you then, would I?"

"You've got your hundred. You can wait. Maybe I'll throw in a little extra because I appreciate what a good memory you have. Deal?"

"Do I have a choice?"

"Sure, go home, take a hot shower, and curl up with a good book. I'll walk you back to make sure you get there safely."

Burki swore under his breath, then grabbed his coat from the wooden trestle and put it on. He motioned for Nick to follow him and led the way to the back wall of the station. He cleared away a spot with his feet and sat down. Stifling his every survivor's instinct, Nick cleared his own small patch and sat down.

"Allen Soufi," Nick repeated. "Tell me about him."

"Why do you want to know about Soufi?" Burki asked. "What brought you to me for God's sake?"

"I've been checking some of the papers my father wrote just before he was murdered. Soufi figures prominently in them. I saw that you recommended him as a client to the Los Angeles branch of USB. I thought that you might have known him pretty well."

"Mr. Allen Soufi. That goes back a ways." He reached into his jacket and took out a pack of cigarettes. His hand shook as he lit one. "Smoke?"

"No, thanks."

Burki inhaled for a full five seconds. "You're a man of your word, are you? You'll keep your end of the bargain?"

Nick took out another hundred-franc note, folded it, and slipped it into his own breast pocket. "Your reward."

Burki hesitated, eyeing the bill, then began talking.

"Soufi was one of my clients," said Burki. "Kept a good-size chunk of his fortune with us. Around thirty million francs, if I'm not mistaken."

"What do you mean he was one of your clients?"

"I was Allen Soufi's portfolio manager. Of course, he held a numbered account — but I knew his name."

Nick thought back to the list of portfolio managers attached to Mevlevi's file. He could not recall having seen the name Burki, or the more distinctive Caspar.

Burki said, "One day my old boss comes in and asks me to recommend Soufi to your father. Told me Soufi wanted to do business with the Los Angeles branch."

"Who was your boss?"

"He still works at the bank. His name is Armin Schweitzer."

"Schweitzer told you to recommend Soufi to my father?"

Burki nodded. "Right away I knew not to ask why. I mean, there could only be one reason for Armin to call me." He spread his hands in a great arc. "Distance. Separating the old man from the client."

"The old man?"

"Kaiser. I mean, who else got him out of

the mess back in London town? Schweitzer was Kaiser's boy. He got all the nasty jobs."

"You're saying Schweitzer asked you to recommend Allen Soufi to my father just to distance Wolfgang Kaiser from the entire affair?"

"Benefit of my superb hindsight. At the time I didn't know what the hell was going on. I just found it a little strange that Soufi hadn't asked me for the introduction. He never said a word about Los Angeles."

Of course, he didn't, thought Nick. The big plans went through Kaiser.

"Well, I didn't make a stink of things. I did what I was told and forgot about it. Wrote a letter: 'Dear Alex, following individual is a client of mine, someone who has worked with the bank in the past, please extend your full services to him. Any questions or references please revert back. Sincerely, Cap.' End of letter. I was happy to be of service. Loyal soldier, that's me."

"And that was the end of it?" Nick asked, knowing full well it wasn't.

Burki didn't answer. His eyelids closed and his breathing slowed. Suddenly, he jerked violently and his eyes opened. He brought his cigarette to his mouth and inhaled desperately.

Nick looked away, seized by a profound sense of the absurd. His entire world was off-kilter. Sitting in a decrepit shooting gallery, freezing his ass off, talking to an aging junkie, and actually entertaining hopes that he might get a measure of truth from him. Anna had been right, hadn't she? He was obsessed. How else could he explain bringing himself to this place?

"If only," Burki snorted, unaware of his lapse. "Six or seven months passed. One day your father rings me up directly. He was curious if I knew more about Allen Soufi than I had mentioned in my introductory letter. 'What's the problem?' I asked. 'He's doing too much business,' said your father. I wondered, 'How could anybody do *too much* business?' "

Nick was puzzled, but only for a moment. "My father was referring to Goldluxe?"

Burki smiled queerly, as if displeased that Nick knew so much. "Yes, it was about Goldluxe."

"Go on." Dusk was falling. More people streamed into the abandoned station.

"Allen Soufi owned a chain of jewelry stores in Los Angeles: Goldluxe, Inc. He wanted USB to be his bank of record. Take deposits, pay his bills, establish letters of credit to finance imports. Alex asked me what exactly I knew about Soufi, and I told him everything — well, almost everything. Soufi was a Middle Eastern client with around thirty million francs on deposit at the bank. Not a man to toy with. I told your father to do as he says. But, Alex, him listen? Never! It wasn't long before Schweitzer called and started pounding me for information about your father. 'What did Alex Neumann say about Soufi? Did he mention any problems?' I told Schweitzer to get off my back. I said your dad had called once, that was it."

"What was Goldluxe up to?"

Burki ignored the question. He took out his pack of cigarettes and tried to extract one. He couldn't. His hand was shaking too violently. He dropped the pack of cigarettes, then looked at Nick. "Kid, you can't keep me waiting. Now's the time. Understand?"

Nick picked up the pack of cigarettes, lit one, and put it in Burki's mouth. "You've got to stay with me a little longer. Just till we get to the end of this."

Burki closed his eyes and inhaled. Buoyed by the blast of nicotine, he went on. "Next time I was in Zurich, Schweitzer and I went out for a night on the town. Armin didn't have anyone to go home to — that was *his* choice. My wife had divorced me long before. We started at the Kronenhalle, ran down to the Old Fashioned, and ended the night at the King's Club, totally bombed, a couple of fancy women on our arms. It was November 24, 1979, my thirty-eighth birthday."

Nick looked at Burki more closely. The man was only fifty-eight years old. My God, he looked seventy if he looked a day. Despite the cold, a sheen of perspiration matted his features. He was starting to hurt.

"We'd already had a couple drinks when I brought up Soufi. 'Whatever happened between him and Alex Neumann?' I asked. I wasn't really curious one way or the other, just making conversation. Well, Schweitzer turned red, and then green, blew a fucking gasket. Alex Neumann this, Alex Neumann that, arrogant bastard, elitist, above the rules, doesn't take orders from anyone, out of control. On and on, for an hour. Jesus, did he have a hard-on for your father! Finally, I calmed him down and got the whole story out of him.

"Seems your father met with Soufi once, thought he was okay — no more crooked than the next guy — and set him up with a numbered account. A little later he took on Goldluxe as a standard commercial account. Goldluxe sold gold jewelry, mostly small stuff — chains, wedding rings, pendants, cheap crap. For a while, everything went swimmingly. But soon Alex noticed that these four stores were generating over two hundred thousand dollars a week in sales. That's eight hundred grand a month, near ten million if they kept it up for the year. I guess your dad went down to the stores, introduced himself, and had a look around. After that, the jig was up PDQ."

Nick recalled his father's entry regarding a company visit to Goldluxe. "Weren't the stores selling jewelry?"

"Oh sure," said Burki. "They were selling

jewelry — a few necklaces here, a bracelet there. But if you want to sell two hundred thousand dollars a week of gold trinkets, you have to move some serious merchandise. These were rinky-dink little stores, maybe a thousand square feet each."

"So Goldluxe was a front?"

"Goldluxe was a sophisticated operation for laundering large amounts of cash. Now give me my fucking fix, would you? You're hurting me bad. Just go on up to Gerda and ask her to make me a dose. I can give it to myself."

Nick was growing cold and impatient. His butt felt like it was frozen to the ground. No way he was going to give Burki a fix now. That would be the end of their conversation. He took out the folded one-hundred-franc banknote and handed it to the heroin addict. "Hold on, Cappy. Keep giving me what I need. We're almost there. Tell me how the operation worked."

Burki fingered the crisp note. His dead eyes showed a spark of life. "First you have to realize that Goldluxe was sitting on a mountain of cash that they didn't know what to do with. They needed a long-term setup that would allow them to deposit all their cash as it came in. Got it?"

"Got it."

"Here's how it worked: USB opened a letter of credit on behalf of Goldluxe to a supplier of gold in Buenos Aires for, say, five hundred

748

thousand dollars — that means that when the South American company sends the gold to Goldluxe in Los Angeles, the bank promises to pay them for the shipment. The company in Argentina exports the gold all right, but not five hundred thousand dollars' worth. Oh, no. They only send about *fifty* thousand worth."

"But fifty thousand dollars' worth of gold is going to weigh a lot less than five hundred thousand worth," Nick protested. He remembered seeing the company name El Oro de los Andes.

"Very good," said Burki, raising a finger as if to say "Point, Neumann." "To make up the difference in weight for our friends in customs, the company in Buenos Aires threw in some lead. No problem. Shipments of precious metals aren't normally examined by customs authorities. As long as the papers match, and the receiving party verifies that the shipment is good, the bank is cleared to make payment of the letter of credit."

"So why does Goldluxe want to pay a company in Buenos Aires five hundred thousand dollars for gold they didn't receive?"

Burki tried to laugh but ended up coughing violently. After a minute he was able to say, "Because Goldluxe has too much cash. They're naughty boys. They need a way to clean it up."

"I don't exactly follow."

"It's actually very easy. Remember what I

told you before — Goldluxe is sitting on a million dollars in cash. They start by importing fifty thousand dollars' worth of gold. That's their inventory."

Nick was beginning to catch on to the game. "But on their books they list the cost of inventory as five hundred thousand dollars. Just like the import documents say."

Burki nodded. "Goldluxe has to make it look like their stores are selling a million dollars' retail worth of gold jewelry. So they mark up the value of the inventory to a million dollars and sell it out the door. By selling, I mean they generate a stack of bogus sales receipts a mile high. Remember they only really have fifty thousand dollars' worth of gold at cost. About a hundred thousand at full retail markup. They take the phony sales receipts and record them in the general ledger. With their books showing sales of one million dollars, they can take their cash to the bank and legitimately deposit it."

Nick shuddered, seeing how simple the plan was. "Where was the money coming from?"

"I've only seen two businesses that generate that kind of cash: casino gambling and drugs. I've never heard of Allen Soufi in Las Vegas, have you?"

Nick smiled grimly. "So the idea is to piggyback the laundering operation on top of the legitimate business."

"Bravo," said Burki. "Once the million dollars is in the bank, USB pays off the letter of credit to the company in Argentina — which Soufi, naturally, controls. And the other five hundred grand is banked as Goldluxe's profit. Soufi wired as much as he wanted to his accounts in London and Switzerland twice a week."

"*Twice a week?*" asked Nick.

"He was a punctual bastard, I'll give him that much, your *Allen Soufi.*"

"And my father?"

"Alex blew the whistle. He asked too many questions. When he figured out what they were doing, he threatened to close the account. Two months after my dinner with Schweitzer, your father was dead." Burki pointed a finger at Nick. "Don't ever tell a man like Soufi, a professional running a very serious operation all over the world, to fuck off."

"His name wasn't really Allen Soufi, was it?" Nick asked, knowing the answer, but wanting to hear it, needing to have another human voice tell him he wasn't crazy.

"What do you care?" asked Burki, pushing himself shakily to his feet. "That's it, kid. Now get the fuck out of here and let me get on with my business."

Nick put a hand on his shoulder and brought him back down to the ground. "I mean you said he was *my* Allen Soufi. You said I could call him that if I wanted to. What was his real name?"

"Cost you another hundred francs. A man's gotta live."

Or die. Nick pulled out his wallet and gave Burki his money. "Give me his name."

Burki crumpled it up into his left hand. "No one you've ever heard of. A Turkish thug. Mevlevi was his name. Ali Mevlevi."

Chapter 59

Beneath her cosmopolitan fringe, Zurich kept hidden a mantle of brooding solitude and introspection that was, in fact, her true self. A devotion to commerce that bordered on pious, an attention to community that ran to the intrusive, a worship of self that one could only call vain: all these conspired during the week to mask her spinster's heart. But on a midwinter Sunday, when those with families retreated to the familiar confines of stolid churches and cozy kitchens, and those without cosseted themselves in a comfortable nook of their comfortable apartment, her streets were left bare and her buildings stripped of their pretentious facades. With a soft gray sky as witness, Zurich let down her veil of pomp and prosperity, and shed a single tear. And Nick, walking through the silent streets, glimpsed her lonely nature and smiled inwardly, for he knew it was his own.

He had come to Switzerland to uncover the circumstances surrounding his father's death. He had forsaken his every moral precept to learn what his father had done to unknowingly precipitate his own murder. Yet now, having put flesh on a framework of conspiracy and deceit, he felt none of the emotions that should crown so difficult a journey. His neck didn't bristle with rage at the crimes of which Wolfgang Kaiser was guilty. His back didn't stand straighter for having put Mevlevi's face to Allen Soufi's name. And worse, his heart had unleashed no secret reservoir of filial pride as the nobility — or was it merely obstinacy? — of his father's resistance came to light. In all, he felt neither triumph nor relief, just a cold determination to put an end to this game, once and for all.

Nothing meant a goddamm thing if he didn't stop Ali Mevlevi.

Nick stood at the center of Quaibrucke. A crust of ice extended unbroken over the Lake of Zurich. The paper said it was the first solid freeze since 1962. A chill breeze grazed his cheeks and took with it his private melancholy. He turned his thoughts away from himself and concentrated on the Pasha, and how after tomorrow Ali Mevlevi would no longer be a force in this world. Nick felt a warm glow in the core of his stomach at the prospect of cutting short his reign of terror, and he knew it was his striving self coming back to the fore. He banished his doubt and his sorrow to a faraway place, wishing he could destroy them forever, but knowing at the same time that they were a part of him, no matter how strong he willed himself to be, and that he had to live with them as best he could.

Nick knew then that the world had changed for him. He wasn't fighting for his father anymore. Alex Neumann was dead. Nothing he could do would bring him back. Nick was fighting for himself. For his life.

Soon, he was thinking only about the Pasha. About the pearly smile and the dismissive laugh. About the serpent's eyes and the confident swagger.

He wanted to kill the man.

Early that evening, Nick climbed the familiar path to Sylvia Schon's home. The road was shorn of ice, and he made good time up the hill. Too good, in fact, for soon he found himself shortening his steps, trying to delay his arrival at her doorstep. Since yesterday afternoon, he had been plagued by a festering doubt concerning Sylvia's true nature. Why had she helped him locate his father's files? Was it because of her affection for him? Had she found deep inside her a need to see justice done, even if it was for a perfect stranger who had died almost two decades ago? Or had she been the Chairman's spy? Keeping tabs on Nick's every move inside the Emperor's Lair? Helping Kaiser for reasons he knew all too well?

He didn't have the answers to any of his questions, and he dreaded finding out. To ask was to admit suspicion, and if he was wrong he would destroy the trust that acted as the foundation of their relationship. *"Trust,"* he heard Eberhard Senn, the Count Languenjoux saying. *"It's the only thing left in this world."*

Nick kept returning to the voice he had heard on Sylvia's answering machine Friday night. The gruff, demanding voice that he was sure belonged to Wolfgang Kaiser. He would have to ask Sylvia straight out if she had told Kaiser about Schweitzer. Yet, he already knew that her words alone could not convince him. He had to hear the tape.

Nick was greeted at the door to her apartment with a kiss on the cheek and a grand smile. For the first time, part of him wondered how much of her welcome was for real.

"How was your father?" he asked, stepping inside the warm hallway.

"Lovely," Sylvia answered. "Curious about who I'm spending my time with. He was interested to hear about my new beau."

"You have a new beau? What's his name?"

Sylvia wrapped her arms around him and stood on her tiptoes so that her eyes almost matched his. "I can't remember offhand. He's a cocky American. Some might say too much for his own good."

"Sounds like a bum. Better dump him."

"Maybe. I haven't decided yet if he's the right man for me."

Nick chuckled as expected of him. It was difficult keeping up an easygoing front. His mind kept returning to Kaiser's office, to the moment when the Chairman had flogged his colleague of thirty years with the barbed accusations of being a spy for the Adler Bank. He asked himself for the hundredth time how Kaiser could have known about Schweitzer's treachery. For the hundredth time, he came up with the same answer, and he hated himself for it.

"Take off your jacket," said Sylvia, leading him by the hand into the living room. "Stay awhile."

Nick unfastened the belt of his jacket and slipped it from his shoulders. He tried to keep from looking at her, wanting to guard a distance between them, but she had never looked more beautiful. She wore a black cashmere turtleneck, and her wheat-colored hair was pulled back into a ponytail. Her cheeks were flushed red. She looked radiant.

Sylvia took the jacket from him and put a hand to his cheek. "What's the matter? Is something wrong?"

Nick lowered her hand from his cheek and stared into her eyes. He had rehearsed the lines a hundred times, but suddenly his mouth was empty of words. This was more difficult than he'd expected. "Yesterday afternoon I was with the Chairman. There was a group of us: Ott, Maeder, Rita Sutter. There was a crisis atmosphere around the place — every problem magnified to three times its real size, everyone at each other's throats. Armin Schweitzer was brought in and questioned about the tips the Adler Bank had received. You know, the phony information about which of our shareholders were still undecided."

Sylvia nodded.

"Kaiser accused him of being the culprit, of secretly providing Klaus Konig with that information. He fired him. Practically kicked Schweitzer out of the office himself."

"Kaiser fired Armin Schweitzer?"

"On the spot."

Sylvia appeared stunned. "The creep deserved it. You told me so yourself. You were convinced he was stealing papers from your office."

"Sylvia, no one but you, me, and Peter Sprecher knew that the Adler Bank had a spy inside of USB. What we felt about Schweitzer, that he was the one responsible, that was only a suspicion, a guess."

"So? If Kaiser fired him, obviously we guessed right."

Nick shook his head in frustration. She wasn't making this any easier. "Did you tell Kaiser that it was Schweitzer who was passing shareholder information to Klaus Konig?"

Sylvia laughed, as if the suggestion were absurd. "I could never phone Herr Kaiser directly. I barely know the man."

"It's okay if you told him. I can understand why you'd feel motivated to protect the bank.

All of us want to stop Konig."

"I told you. No, I did not."

"Come on, Sylvia. How else could the Chairman have found out?"

"I believe you're accusing me, Mr. Neumann." Her cheeks grew redder, though now with anger. " 'How else?' you ask. How else do you think? Schweitzer is guilty. Kaiser discovered it himself. Caught him red-handed. I don't know. Do you think Konig's the only one with spies? The Chairman doesn't need you to protect him. He doesn't need me. He's run that bank for as long as any of us can remember." Sylvia brushed by him. "And I sure as hell don't have to explain myself to you."

Nick followed her into the living room. He was certain she was lying. Sylvia and her devotion to the bank. Sylvia and her employee retention rate. She'd used the assumption of Schweitzer's guilt as a fulcrum with which to lever her career up a notch. Why did she have to lie about it?

"What about your answering machine?" he asked.

"What about it?" she shot back.

"On Friday night, when we were checking your messages, I heard Wolfgang Kaiser's voice. You know I heard it. I saw you. You were scared that I might have figured out who it was. Tell me the truth."

Sylvia recoiled from him. "The truth? Is that

what this is all about?" She ran to the answering machine and rewound the tape, stopping every few seconds to listen to the voice speaking. She found the section she was looking for and pressed play. "You want the truth? I wasn't scared. I was embarrassed."

Peter Sprecher's voice rose from the machine. "Call me at the Adler Bank as soon as possible. We're very interested in meeting with you. Thank you." A pause. A beep. Then the next message. A rough voice spoke from the recorder. "Sylvia, are you there? Pick up, please. All right, then, just listen."

The voice was unsteady and, Nick suspected, drunk.

"I want you at home this weekend. You know what we like to eat on Saturdays. It was always the boys' favorite. On the table by seven, please. You're a good girl, Sylvia, but I'm afraid your mother would have been disappointed — you so far away, leaving your father to grow old by himself. Well, anyway, I'll manage. Be sure to tell your brothers. Get them here on time. Seven o'clock or we'll start without them."

Nick walked to the machine and turned it off. It was not Wolfgang Kaiser's voice.

Sylvia dropped into a chair, her head slumped to her chest. "My brothers haven't come to the house in three years. It's just my father and me. Last night, he spent five minutes berating me for having forgotten to tell them. I just nod and say I'm sorry. So are you satisfied? Happy now that you know all about my daddy's love of beer? How I've abandoned him to grow old alone?"

Nick walked to the dining room table and sat beside her. He felt utterly distraught. His carefully constructed case lay in shambles, a house of cards toppled by a single breath. How could he have been so stupid? How could he have doubted her for a minute? He had distrusted Sylvia when it really counted, insulting her instead of showing his faith in her. Look at her actions. She's been helping you every step of the way. Why can't you just accept that she likes you? That she wants to give you a hand? Why can't you learn that it's okay to rely on somebody else?

"I'm sorry," he said. "I didn't mean to embarrass you."

Sylvia wrapped her arms around herself like a distressed schoolgirl. "Why didn't you believe me when I told you the first time? I wouldn't lie to you."

Nick placed his hands on her shoulders. "I'm sorry. I can't really explain why . . ."

"Don't touch me," she cried. "I feel like a fool. I didn't tell Wolfgang Kaiser about Armin Schweitzer. If you don't like that answer, get the hell out of here."

Nick tried again to gently cup her shoulders. This time she allowed herself to be touched and then drawn to his chest. "I believe you," he said quietly. "But I had to ask. I had to know."

Sylvia buried her head in Nick's chest. "I took it for granted he would be caught. I always expected it to happen. That doesn't mean I opened my mouth like an indiscreet teenager, blabbing to everyone who might have an interest in what Peter Sprecher had discovered." She laid her head back so that she could see his eyes. "I would never betray your confidence."

Nick held her close to him for a while longer. He smelled the clean scent of her hair and delighted in the drape of her cashmere sweater. "These last weeks have been tough. It's as if I've been under water, swimming with a straitjacket. If I can make it through tomorrow, maybe we'll come out of this all right."

"Is it about your father? You didn't tell me if you found Caspar Burki."

"Oh, I found him all right."

"And?"

Nick held her at arm's length, deciding what he could tell her. Was her knowing part of the bonds that lovers share or simply an admission of his own weakness — a foolish gesture to assuage his guilt at having wounded her fragile heart?

"Tell me, sweetheart," she pleaded. "What did you find out?"

"A lot of things are happening. Things you wouldn't believe . . ."

"What are you talking about? The take-over?"

"Konig has his thirty-three percent. He's lined up outside financing to make a full bid for the shares he doesn't own. He wants the whole bank. And that's the good news."

Sylvia sagged visibly. "The *good* news?" Her bewildered expression made it clear she didn't want to hear the *bad* news.

Nick looked into her eyes and told himself he saw compassion and love. He was tired of being alone, of shouldering life's burden without someone else's help. Tired of suspecting. Why not tell her the rest of it?

"Kaiser is working for Ali Mevlevi," he said, "the man we call the Pasha. He's been helping him launder money for years. Lots of it. Mevlevi is a drug lord operating out of Lebanon, and Kaiser is his man in Switzerland."

Sylvia raised her hand to stop Nick. "How do you know these things?"

"You'll have to take my word. All I can say is that everything I'm telling you I've seen with my own eyes."

"I can't believe it. Maybe this Mevlevi is blackmailing the Chairman; maybe Herr Kaiser has no other choice?"

"Kaiser's crimes aren't limited to his dealings with Mevlevi. He was so desperate to stop Konig from obtaining his seats that he ordered several of us on the Fourth Floor to sell off a large percentage of stocks and bonds held in our clients' discretionary portfolios and to re-invest their money in USB stock. He's violated the trust of hundreds of clients who placed their money in numbered accounts at the bank. He's broken dozens of laws. No one made him do that!"

"But he's only trying to keep the bank free from Konig. It's his, after all."

Nick grasped her hands in his own. "Sylvia, the bank does not belong to Wolfgang Kaiser. He's a salaried employee like you and me. Sure he's spent his life building it up, but he's been hugely rewarded. What do think a guy like that makes? Over a million francs a year easy. On top of that, I wouldn't be surprised if he's received options for thousands of shares of company stock. The bank is owned by its shareholders. It's not Kaiser's private fiefdom. Someone has to stop him."

"You're scaring me with that talk."

"You *should be* scared. We all should be. Kaiser is as bad as Mevlevi. Neither of the bastards have the least respect for anybody's law. They kill to see that their will is done."

Sylvia spun away from Nick, walking to the picture window that led onto her terrace. "I don't believe you," she said stubbornly.

"Who do you think killed my father?" Nick argued bitterly. "It was Ali Mevlevi. Only then he called himself Allen Soufi, just like now he's calling himself Allen Malvinas. Maybe Kaiser didn't pull the trigger, but he knew what was going on. He tried his best to force my father into working for Mevlevi, and when my father refused, he didn't do a damn thing to stop Mevlevi from killing him. You saw the activity reports. 'Continue business with Soufi. Do not end relations.' Why didn't Kaiser warn my father? They grew up on the same street, for Christ's sake. They'd known each other their entire lives! Why didn't Kaiser do anything?"

Nick stopped speaking as a terrible realization flooded his senses. He'd known all along why Kaiser hadn't done anything. He'd known since Marco Cerruti had talked about the competition between the two men; since Rita Sutter had mused whether if his father were alive today she might be working for him instead of Wolfgang Kaiser; since bearing witness to Armin Schweitzer's unflagging jealousy of Nick's elevated position inside the Emperor's Lair. Alexander Neumann was the only man who could keep Wolfgang Kaiser from ascending to the chairmanship of the United Swiss Bank. It was about a job. Kaiser had simply done nothing to prevent the elimination of his fiercest rival. It was all just business.

"Those are terrible accusations," said Sylvia. She looked crestfallen, as if she had been the one charged with the crimes.

"It's the truth," Nick railed, buoyed by the certainty that he had forged the last link of a twisted and sordid chain. "And I'm going to make both of them pay for it." He was sick of everyone's offended sensibilities, sick of Sprecher's willful naïveté and of Sylvia's stubborn loyalty to the bank. His father had died to assure another man's position. The banality of it nauseated him.

Sylvia put her arms around Nick and drew herself close to him. "Don't do anything crazy. Don't get yourself in trouble."

In trouble? He already was in trouble. More trouble than he'd known in his entire life. Now he had to get out of it.

"Tomorrow morning I'm driving to the Tessin with Mevlevi. I'm going to . . ." Nick hesitated. He had an urge to tell Sylvia his entire plan, to lay it out for her and pray that she would think it viable, maybe even give him her blessing. But her opinion wouldn't change things one way or the other. Grudgingly, he acknowledged the real reason that prevented him from revealing his scheme. The specter of too many unanswered questions kept tapping his shoulder, taunting him with her guilt. No matter how much he wanted to tell her, he couldn't.

"And I'm going to put an end to this business," he said simply. "If Mevlevi escapes tomorrow, you can measure the rest of my life on a stopwatch." *Along with my ashes.*

Later, Nick and Sylvia walked through the forest that ran from her back door. A new moon sat high in the northern sky. A carpet of snow glowed in the faint light. Neither of them spoke, the dry crunch of the snow fitting punctuation to their silent conversation.

That night, he stayed with Sylvia. He held her in his arms and together they warmed the oversize bed. They made love slowly and with great care. He moved with her and she with him, each devoted only to the other. Lying so close to her body, the magic of their shared intimacy filling the room, Nick knew his feelings were undiminished by his lingering suspicions. He told himself that love was about caring for another person without ever really knowing all of them. But deep down he wondered if this was just an excuse, and if he was staying with Sylvia only to spite Anna.

Nick realized then that there was no point thinking any longer about the past or the future. All he had to do was get to the other side of tomorrow alive. Beyond that he didn't know. And so for one night, he let himself go.

Chapter 60

"Bring us another bottle," Wolfgang Kaiser ordered, grimacing at the ferric aftertaste. "This wine has turned. Tastes like piss and vinegar."

The Kunststube sommelier inclined his head in mute query and poured a sample of the Corton-Charlemagne 1975 into his sterling tasting cup. He sipped the wine, swishing it across his palate, then swallowing it. "I do not share Monsieur's opinion. It is rare for a Corton to turn. Rarer still for two bottles of different vintage. I beg Monsieur to clean his palate with some fresh bread and try the wine again."

"Balls!" retorted Kaiser after sipping the wine. "Tastes like it was poured from the barrel of a gun. Bring us another." He was drunk and he knew it. Scotch never sat well with him, and he had finished two straight up while waiting for Mevlevi to show his face. The gall! Disappearing from his hotel for the entire weekend. Telephoning on a Sunday afternoon to suggest a private dinner, just the two of them, then arriving an hour late.

The sommelier's eyes shifted to the door of the kitchen, seeking the approval of the restaurant's owner and chef, Herr Petermann, and when he received it said, "Right away, sir."

"Shameless bastard," said Kaiser to the sommelier's retreating back, though in his heart he directed the comment at the man seated across the table.

"Bad news, Ali. Friday afternoon Klaus Konig secured a large packet of our shares. He's standing at the portal of the bank with his boarding party. I can hear their swords being drawn even now." He attempted a light-hearted chuckle, but his thick tongue managed only a nervous titter.

The Pasha dabbed at the corners of his mouth. He was his usual elegant self, dressed in a double-breasted navy blazer, a silver ascot adorning his throat. Not a worry in the world. "Mr. Konig cannot be as bad as all that," he said, as if referring to a pesky neighbor.

"He's worse," Kaiser grunted. "The man is an insolent raider. Well-financed, but a pirate all the same."

Mevlevi raised an eyebrow. "Surely you have the resources to repel his advance?"

"You'd think that controlling sixty percent of the bank's shares would guarantee me a healthy margin of comfort. Not in democratic Switzerland. We never expected to be bested by one of our own countrymen. Our laws were written to keep the barbarians beyond the pale. As for ourselves, we Swiss are saints, one and all. Today it's the enemy *within* we have to defend against."

"What exactly do you need, Wolfgang? Is this about your loan?"

What the hell else did he think it was about?

"The terms stand," said Kaiser in his politest voice. "Ninety days is all we require. You'll have your cash back with a ten percent kicker. Come, Ali, that's not just reasonable, it's damned generous."

"Generous it is." Mevlevi reached a hand across the table to pat the Chairman's arm. "Generous you have always been, my friend."

Kaiser pushed his shoulders back and offered a humble smile. What charade was this he must play? The utter pretense of it made him ill. Acting as if all these years he had sheltered the Pasha's income of his own volition.

"You must understand," Mevlevi continued, "that if I had such a bountiful reserve of cash at this time, it would be yours. Damn the interest, I'm no shylock. Unfortunately my cash flow is dreadful at this time of year."

"What about the forty million that passed through your accounts on Friday afternoon?"

"Already spoken for. My business does not allow for credit."

"The full two hundred million isn't necessary. Half of that amount would be sufficient. We must have an order to buy on the floor tomorrow morning when the exchange opens.

I cannot risk the Adler Bank's purchasing any more shares. They have their thirty-three percent as it is. More, and it will appear a mandate on my tenure at the bank."

"The world is changing, Wolfgang. Perhaps it's time for younger men to have a go at it."

"Change is anathema in the world of private banking. Tradition is what our clients seek; security is what we at USB offer best. The Adler Bank is just another hustler on the street."

Mevlevi smiled as if amused. "The free market is a dangerous place."

"It shouldn't be the floor of the Colosseum," Kaiser argued. "A loan of seventy million francs is the least we could accept. Don't tell me that with your substantial investments, you can't commit to such a small sum."

"Small sum, indeed. I should ask you the same question." Again the amused grin. "If you recall, a good deal of my assets are already in your hands. Two percent of your outstanding shares, no?"

Kaiser leaned closer to the table, wondering what Mevlevi found so damned funny. "Our back is to the wall. It's time for old friends to come to the fore. Ali," he pleaded, "a personal favor."

"My poor cash flow dictates that I say no. I'm sorry, Wolfgang."

Kaiser smiled wistfully. Sorry, was he? Then

why was he so fucking delighted by USB's imminent demise? Kaiser reached for his glass of wine but stopped halfway there. He had one last chip. Why not burn it with the rest of them? He lifted his eyes to his companion's and said, "I'll throw in young Neumann."

Mevlevi tucked in his chin. "Will you? I didn't realize he was yours to throw anywhere."

"I've come across some interesting information. Our young friend is quite the investigator. It seems he has some questions about his father's past." In his mind, Kaiser apologized to Nicholas, saying he was sorry but that he'd been left no choice, that he'd done everything he could to make a place for him by his side but that unfortunately he had no room for traitors. He'd told his father practically the same thing nearly twenty years before.

"That should concern you more than me," said Mevlevi.

"I don't think so. Neumann believes that a Mr. Allen Soufi was involved in his father's death. That is not my name."

"Nor mine." Mevlevi sipped his wine. "Not any longer."

"Neumann's learned about Goldluxe as well."

"Goldluxe," Mevlevi cried in jest. "A name from another century. Another epoch. Let him learn all he wants about Goldluxe. I don't think the authorities will show much interest in a laundering operation shut down eighteen years ago. Do you?"

"Of course, you're right, Ali. But, personally, I wouldn't be comfortable knowing that such a bright young man with so much to make up for was looking closely at my past. Who knows what else he's found?"

Mevlevi pointed an inquisitive finger at Kaiser. "Why are you telling me this now?"

"I found out myself only last night."

"Do you expect me to be afraid of these revelations? Should I cower in front of you with my purse held wide open? I have Neumann in the palm of my hand. Like I have you. Neumann's prints are all over the gun that killed Albert Makdisi. If he mentions one word about me to the police, he'll be arrested and placed in protective custody while I line up some reliable witnesses who can put him at the scene of the crime. Neumann is mine. Just like you. Do you really believe he has the courage to cross me? He's seen the consequences of betrayal close up. You tell me Nicholas Neumann is looking into my past. I say fine. Let him look." Suddenly Mevlevi laughed. "Or maybe you're just trying to scare me, Wolfgang."

A tuxedo-clad maître d' appeared with a white-jacketed waiter at his side. The captain supervised the serving of a grilled Chilean sea bass in a black bean sauce. All conversation ceased until the plates were set down and both waiters out of earshot.

"My duty has always been to look after your best interests," continued Kaiser. "To be honest, I thought bringing you this information would be worth at least forty million francs. That amount should buy us one full percentage point."

" 'One full point?' " Mevlevi repeated. "You're giving me Neumann for one full point? Tell me what else he might know. If you'd like me to evaluate your proposition, I need to hear it all."

"Ask him yourself. It's not what Nicholas knows, but what his father knew. And wrote down. Some mention of the FBI, I believe. The boy has his father's diary."

"Why are you so smug?"

Kaiser lied smoothly. "I've seen the pages. I'm in the clear."

"If Neumann uncovers Goldluxe, you will be hurt worse than I."

"If I am going to lose the bank to Klaus Konig, I don't give a damn. Twenty years ago you robbed me of any other life I might have had. If the bank is going down, let me go down with it."

"You never wanted any other kind of life. If you prefer to use my actions to soothe your guilty conscience, go ahead. In your heart you know you are no different from me." Mevlevi pushed his plate toward the center of the table. "I am sorry, Wolfgang. Banking is your business. If you can't protect yourself from those more competitive, perhaps even more competent than yourself, I can't be to blame."

Kaiser could feel his face flushing as his desperation increased. "Dammit, Ali. I know you have the money. You've got to give me it. You owe me."

Mevlevi slammed his hand on the table. "I owe you nothing!"

Kaiser's eyes bulged and his neck grew crimson. He felt as if the floor had been ripped out from under him. How could this be happening?

Mevlevi sat back in his chair, once again the picture of cool restraint. "Still, in appreciation of your telling me the news about young Neumann, I will try and make arrangements. I'll phone Gino Makdisi tomorrow. He may be able to come to your assistance."

"Gino Makdisi? The man is a hoodlum."

"His money is as green as yours. *Pecunia non oelat.* Practically your country's anthem, isn't it? Money hath no odor. He'll be pleased to accept your generous terms."

"Those terms are for you only. We could never do business with a member of the Makdisi family."

Mevlevi gave an exasperated sigh, then dabbed at his mouth. "All right, then, I'll reconsider the loan. But frankly, I don't see where I'm going to get the cash. I'll make some calls. I can have an answer for you tomorrow at two P.M."

"I have an important meeting with one of our oldest shareholders. I won't be back in the office before three." Kaiser knew not to expect a reprieve, but couldn't help himself from jumping at the offer. Hope was difficult to kill.

Mevlevi smiled graciously. "I promise to have an answer for you by that time."

Ali Mevlevi packed a half-sotted Wolfgang Kaiser into his automobile, then returned to the restaurant's lounge and ordered a Williams aperitif. For a few seconds he actually pitied the poor fool. *One percent,* Kaiser had practically slobbered, hoping to sell young Neumann like he was chattel slavery. Neumann was worth the price of a single bullet, no more, and that's how much he'd spend on him.

Give me my one percent.

Mevlevi was tempted to give it to the man, if only to appease his own conscience. After all, *even he* needed to be reminded now and again he possessed one. Chuckling at the thought, he took a long sip of the strong liqueur. Kaiser and his one percent. Young Neumann the investigator. The world was much larger than that, wasn't it?

In Ali Mevlevi's view, the world, and his place in it, was infinitely larger.

He finished his drink, paid, and walked into the cold night. He raised his hand and immediately a car started its motor. A silver Mercedes drove forward. He got in the car and shook hands with Moammar-al-Khan, his Libyan majordomo. "You know where you're going?"

"It is not far. Another few kilometers along the lake and then into the hills. We will make it in fifteen minutes." Khan brought the gold medallion he wore around his neck to his lips and kissed it. "The prophet willing."

"I have every confidence," said Mevlevi, smiling. He knew he could rely on Khan. It had been Khan who had discovered that the heroin being sold in Letten by the Makdisis had not been his own.

Fourteen minutes later, the Mercedes approached a lone cabin at the end of a rutted track deep inside a dark and snowy forest. Three cars were parked in front of the cabin. Lights burned from the front window.

"One of them has yet to arrive," said Khan. "I don't see his car."

Mevlevi guessed who the tardy man was but did not begrudge him his theatricality. He was simply practicing his new role a few days in advance. After all, a chief executive should always be the last to arrive.

Mevlevi stepped from the automobile and crossed through the snow to the cabin. He knocked once, then entered. Hassan Faris was standing by the door. Mevlevi kissed him on each cheek while pumping his hand.

"Faris, tell me the good news," he said.

"Chase Manhattan and Lehman Brothers

have signed a letter of intent for the full amount," said the svelte Arab. "They've already syndicated the loan."

A taller man approached from the crackling fire. "It's true," said George von Graffenried, vice-chairman of the Adler Bank. "Our friends in New York have come up with the cash. We have bridge financing in place for three billion dollars. More than enough to buy every last share of USB stock we don't already own outright. You kept us waiting until the last minute, Ali. We almost came up a few pennies short."

"George, I always keep my word. Or Khan keeps it for me."

Von Graffenried wiped the ridiculous grin off his face.

Mevlevi waved to a thin man standing by the fire. "Mr. Zwicki, it is nice to finally meet you. I appreciate your involvement in our little project. Especially your help these last few days." On his command, Zwicki, chief of USB's equity department, had slowed his bank's purchases of its own shares to a trickle, thus effectively declawing Maeder's vaunted "liberation plan."

Sepp Zwicki stepped forward and bowed his head. "A pleasure."

"We are awaiting your colleague, Dr. —"

The door to the cabin opened suddenly and Rudolf Ott bustled inside. "Mr. Mevlevi, good evening. Sepp, Hassan, George, hello." He drew Von Graffenried close and whispered, "You received my last memo. Did you contact the Widows and Orphans Fund yet?"

"We're hoping to know tomorrow, Herr Dr. Ott. I'm sure you won't be disappointed."

"Good evening, Rudolf." Mevlevi detested the smarmy man, but he was the most important member of their team. "Is everything in place for tomorrow?"

Ott removed his glasses and wiped away the condensation with a clean handkerchief. "Naturally. The loan documents have been prepared. You'll have your money by noon. Eight hundred million francs is a decent sum. I don't know if we've ever lent so much to an individual."

Mevlevi doubted it. He had collateral, of course. Approximately three million shares of USB held at the Adler Bank, not to mention another couple hundred thousand at USB itself. In the future, though, calls for collateral would disappear. That was why he was taking the reins of the bank, wasn't it? The purpose of this entire exercise. Time to become legitimate.

Tomorrow morning Klaus Konig would announce his cash bid for USB: 2.8 billion dollars for the sixty-six percent of USB he didn't yet control. Tuesday, at USB's general assembly, Ott would announce his support for the Adler Bank's bid. He would call for the immediate resignation of Wolfgang Kaiser, and the executive board would support him. Each board member held a hefty packet of USB shares. No one could turn down the huge premium offered by the Adler Bank. For his loyalty (or his betrayal, depending from which side one looked at it), Ott would be installed at the helm of the newly consolidated bank: USB-Adler. Day-to-day operations would be handled by Von Graffenried. Zwicki and Faris would share the equities department. Klaus Konig would retain the nominal position of president, though his real tasks would be confined to fashioning the combined banks' investment strategy. The man was much too impulsive to head a universal Swiss bank. If he didn't like it, he could have a heart-to-heart with Khan.

Over time, new employees would be brought in to fill key posts: global treasury operations, capital markets, compliance. Men of Faris's ilk. Men of Mevlevi's choosing. New appointments would be made to the executive board. The combined assets of the United Swiss Bank and the Adler Bank would be his. Over seventy billion dollars at his disposal.

The thought brought a broad smile to Ali Mevlevi's face, and everyone around him smiled too. Ott, Zwicki, Faris, Von Graffenried. Even Khan.

Mevlevi would not abuse his power. At least not for a while. But there were so many good uses to which he could put the bank. Corporate loans to worthy companies in Lebanon, shoring up the Jordani dinar, slipping a few hundred million to his friend Hussein in Iraq. Khamsin was only the first. But in his heart it was the most important.

Mevlevi excused himself and stepped outside to place a call to his operational headquarters at his compound near Beirut. He waited while he was patched through to General Marchenko.

"*Da?* Mr. Mevlevi?"

"General Marchenko, I'm calling to inform you that everything is proceeding according to plan on this end. You will have your money no later than noon tomorrow. The baby must be ready to travel at that time. Lieutenant Ivlov's attack is to begin simultaneously."

"Understood. Once I have received confirmation of the transfer, it will be only a matter of seconds before the baby can be airborne. I look forward to hearing from you."

"Twelve o'clock, Marchenko. Not a minute later."

Mevlevi folded the cellular phone and put it in his pocket. He breathed in the chill night air, enjoying its bite. He felt more alive than ever before.

Tomorrow, the Khamsin would blow.

Chapter 61

Nick left Sylvia's apartment at five-thirty in the morning. She accompanied him to the door and sleep still in her eyes, made him promise to take care of himself. He brushed off the concern in her voice, preferring not to wonder if this might be the last time he'd see her. He kissed her, then buttoned up his coat and set off down the steep hill toward Universitätstrasse. Outside the temperature was well below freezing. The sky was as dark as ink. He caught the first tram of the day and arrived at the *Personalhaus* at five past six. He ran up a flight of terrazzo stairs to the first floor and hurried to his apartment. Inserting the key, he found the door to be unlocked. He pushed it open slowly.

The apartment was a shambles. A thorough hand had ransacked the place.

The desk was overturned. Annual reports and assorted papers were strewn across the floor. The closet was open, every suit chucked onto the carpet. The dresser drawers had been emptied, then discarded. Shirts, sweaters, and socks were everywhere. His bed rested on its side, the worn mattress lying askew, sheets and blankets tangled up in each other. The bathroom was no better. The mirror on the medicine cabinet was shattered, the tile floor littered with broken glass.

Nick saw all of this in a moment.

And then he spotted his holster. It lay in the far corner of the room cached beside the bookshelves. A gleaming black leather triangle. Empty. Side arm missing.

Nick stepped inside the apartment and closed the door behind him. Calmly, he began sorting through his clothing, hoping to feel the hard plane of his gun's rectangular snout or the stubble of its crosshatched grip. Nothing. He picked up a T-shirt here, a sweater there, praying to catch a glimpse of the dull blue-black sheen of the Colt Commander. Nothing. He grew frantic. He shuffled around the apartment, running his hands along the floor. He lifted the mattress and threw it across the room. He upended the bed frame. Nothing. Shit!

Abruptly, something strange caught his eye. A pile of books lay next to the desk arranged sloppily like a kind of unlit bonfire. In the center of this pile sat a textbook from business school — a large book, *Principles of Finance* by Brealy and Myers. Its cover was open; the pages had been ripped from its spine. Nick picked up another textbook. It had received a similar trashing. He selected a paperback, *The Iliad*, his father's favorite. Its soft covers were bent backward and its pages fanned. He dropped it on the floor.

Nick stopped searching. He stood up straight, alone in his silent apartment. Mevlevi had been here — or one of his men — and he'd been looking for something specific. What?

Nick checked his watch and with a start saw that a half hour had passed. It was 6:35. He had ten minutes to shower, shave, and put on clean clothes. The limo was scheduled to arrive at 6:45. He was due at the Dolder at seven. He grabbed two dirty dress shirts, fell to his knees, and swept the bathroom floor of glass. Finished, he balled them up and threw them into his closet. He stripped and stepped gingerly across the tile floor. He took a navy shower — thirty seconds under freezing cold water. He shaved in record time, ten swipes of the razor, to hell with anything left over.

Outside, a car honked twice. He brushed back a curtain. The limousine had arrived.

Nick walked to his overturned desk, grabbed two of its legs, and brought it onto its side. He ran a hand along each leg, seeking a small indentation he had made a few weeks ago. He found it, then unscrewed the round metallic foot at its base. He inserted the tips of his right thumb and forefinger delicately into the leg. He felt the tip of a sharp object and breathed easier. He grasped the metal blade and withdrew the knife. His marine issue K-Bar. *Jack the Ripper.* Serrated on one side, razor sharp on the other. Years ago, he had wrapped athletic tape around its handle to reduce any slippage. The tape was stained with age, mottled with sweat and dirt and blood.

Nick rummaged through the debris scattered on the bathroom floor until he found a roll of similar tape. He used it to keep the brace he wore on his right knee in place when he exercised. Working quickly, he cut four strips of tape and laid them on the table's edge. Then he picked up the knife and pressed it flat (handle down) against a damp patch of skin below his left arm. One by one, he grabbed the lengths of tape and secured the K-Bar to his body, but not too tightly. A firm downward tug would free the knife. The ensuing motion would rip out a man's guts.

Nick flitted through his scattered belongings looking for some clean clothes. He came up with a shirt and suit just back from the laundry. Despite their mistreatment, they were relatively unwrinkled, and he put them on. One tie remained in his closet. He grabbed it, then bolted from the apartment.

Inside the limousine, Nick checked his watch over and over again. Morning traffic was heavy, slower than it had ever been. The black Mercedes rolled past Bellevue and climbed the Universitätstrasse. It mounted the Zurichberg and passed through the forest. The dovecote tower of the Dolder Grand appeared high above his left shoulder. His heart beat faster.

Calm down, he told himself. You're on.

Nick forced himself to wait until the limousine had made a full stop before opening the door. He was livid with himself for being late. Only ten minutes — but today timing was everything. He climbed the maroon carpeted stairs two at a time and rushed through the revolving door. He spotted the Pasha at once.

"Good morning, Nicholas," the Pasha said quietly. "You're late. Let's make a quick start. Mr. Pine, the night manager, informs me that snow may be on the way. We do not want to be caught at the Gotthardo in a blizzard."

Nick advanced a step and shook Mevlevi's hand. "There shouldn't be any problem. The St. Gotthard tunnel is always open, even in the worst conditions. The driver assures me we should have no problems making it to Lugano in time. The car has four-wheel drive and chains."

"It will be you helping to attach the chains, not me." Mevlevi smiled, then climbed into the backseat of the limousine, nodding once to the chauffeur, who manned the rear door.

Nick followed suit, allowing the chauffeur to shut the door behind him. He was determined to be the perfect functionary. Polite, amiable, never intrusive. "Do you have your passport and three photos?" he asked the Pasha.

"Of course." Mevlevi handed Nick both. "Have a look. Friends of mine at British Intelligence passed it along to me. They tell me it's the real thing. The Brits prefer to use the Argentinean variety. Add a little salt to open wounds. I chose the name myself. Clever, don't you think?"

Nick opened the Argentinean passport. It was the same one used at International Fiduciary Trust in Zug on Friday, issued in the name of one Allen Malvinas, resident of Buenos Aires. Home to El Oro de los Andes. "Didn't you say that you had lived in Argentina?"

"Buenos Aires. Yes, but only briefly."

Nick handed the passport back without further comment. *Soufi, Malvinas, Mevlevi. I know who you are.*

Mevlevi slipped the passport into his jacket pocket. "Of course, it's not the only name I've ever used."

Nick unbuttoned his jacket, and his arm brushed against the forged steel blade. He smiled to himself. *And you know I know.*

An early-morning silence enveloped the car as it sped through the Tal Valley. The Pasha appeared to be sleeping. Nick kept one eye on his watch and the other on the passing scenery. The sky had faded from its earlier pale blue to a paler, watery gray. Still, no snow fell, and for that he was grateful.

The Mercedes hummed along nicely for another hour, its powerful engine sending a comforting vibrato through the chassis. The sleek automobile passed through the quaint lakeside village of Küssnacht before climbing onto a narrower road that followed the steep northern rim of the Vierwaldstätter See toward the St. Gotthard Pass. A few low-lying clouds blanketed the lake. From Nick's vantage point high above its misty surface, he had the impression of a schooner's mainsail torn by a hurricane wind into a thousand tattered strips. It made him think of a shipwreck. If he were a superstitious man, he would consider it a bad omen. Seconds later the car passed into the first of a series of isolated showers, and the lake was lost from view.

At the same time that Nick was passing through Küssnacht, Sylvia Schon tucked the telephone under her chin and dialed the Chairman's home number for the fourth time. The line connected immediately. The phone rang and rang and rang. Twenty-seven times she allowed it to sound before banging the receiver into its cradle. Tears of frustration streamed down her face. Twice during the night, she had crept from her bed to call. Neither time had there been an answer.

Where were you, Wolfgang Kaiser, at three o'clock on a Sunday morning?

Sylvia stalked into the kitchen and rummaged through her drawers for a cigarette. She found a crushed pack of Gauloises and pulled one from the wrinkled blue sheath.

She puffed madly on the harsh cigarette, desperate to rid her apartment of Nick's lingering scent. I'm not betraying you, she explained to his memory. I'm saving myself. I could have loved you. Can't you understand that? Or are you too wrapped up in your personal crusade to notice that I have one of my own? Don't you know what will happen if Kaiser is arrested? Rudolf Ott will take over. Ott — my rival for the Chairman's affection. Ott — who tried his best to deny me my chance to move up. It's him, Nick. He's the one responsible.

Sylvia acknowledged a pang of guilt but wasn't sure who it was for. For Nick. For herself. Anyway, it didn't matter. She had chosen her path a long time ago.

Sylvia stubbed out her cigarette and checked her watch. Another ten minutes until Rita Sutter arrived in the office. She was like a clock, Kaiser had said. In at 7:30 on the dot every day for the past twenty years. His most obedient servant. Rita Sutter would know where to find the Chairman. He didn't do anything without telling her.

Sylvia pinched the bridge of her nose and shuddered, suddenly nauseated from the unfiltered nicotine. She consulted her watch yet again. And though it was eight minutes too early, she picked up the phone and called the Emperor's Lair.

The road had assumed a gentler incline. It rose along the icy banks of the river Reuss and wandered up a majestic valley leading deep into the craggy heart of the Swiss Alps. Nick glanced out the window, numb to the beauty around him. He was keeping his fingers crossed it would not snow, wondering where Thorne was right now. He prayed that Kaiser had left Zurich on time to make his eleven o'clock meeting with the count. A sign for Altdorf flashed past and then ones for Amsteg and Wassen, these last small villages made up of a dozen stone houses sitting alongside the highway.

Approaching the village of Göschenen, Ali Mevlevi asked the chauffeur to leave the highway so that he might stretch his legs. The driver obliged, following the next exit off of the highway and driving into the center of a picturesque village, where he halted the automobile next to a gurgling water fountain. All three men climbed out.

"Look at the time," the Pasha said, making an elaborate show of examining his wristwatch. "At this rate we'll arrive an hour ahead of schedule. Tell me once again what time our meeting is set for."

"Ten-thirty," answered Nick, instantly on edge. He hadn't foreseen any stops. This was supposed to be the express train. Nonstop intercity.

"Ten-thirty," Mevlevi repeated. "We have over two hours. I do not wish to sit in an overheated room twiddling my thumbs waiting for this flunky. I can promise you that right now."

"We can phone Mr. Wenker, the man from the passport office, and ask him to meet us earlier." Nick had dreaded the prospect of being late. So much so, in fact, that he had never stopped to consider what might happen if they were early.

"No, no. Best not to disturb him." Mevlevi appraised the gray sky. "I have another idea. I say we take the old route over the top. I've never been through the pass itself."

Over the top? That was insane. It was a skating rink up there.

"The road is extremely dangerous," Nick said, trying to keep a docent's steady tone. "Steep, curvy. There's likely to be quite a bit of ice. It's not a good idea."

A shadow crossed the Pasha's brow. "I think it is a wonderful idea. Ask the driver how long it will take."

The chauffeur, who had been casually smoking a cigarette by the water fountain, volunteered an answer. "With no snow, we can be up and down in an hour."

"See, Neumann," the Pasha said enthusiastically. "One hour. Perfect! We can add a little

791

scenery to the trip."

A shrill warning bell sounded in Nick's head. He gazed at the dramatic panorama. The Alpine valley rose steeply on both sides of them, its walls lined with outcroppings of rock and stands of snow-covered pines. Jagged peaks of a dozen lesser mountains stared down through swirling mist and cloud. He had never seen a more spectacular vista. Yet now the Pasha wanted to see even more "scenery." Out of the fucking question!

"I have to insist that we stay on the highway. The weather can change suddenly in the mountains. By the time we reach the pass, we could be trapped in a blizzard."

"Neumann, if you knew how rarely I leave my arid little country, you would gladly allow me this pleasure. If we keep Mr. Wenker waiting a little, so be it. He won't mind — not for the fee Kaiser is undoubtedly paying him." Mevlevi walked to the chauffeur and clapped him on the back. "Can we make it to Lugano by ten-thirty, my good man?"

"No problem," came the driver's answer. He crushed the cigarette under his boot and adjusted his cap.

Nick smiled nervously at the Pasha. Tardy arrival to the meeting with Mr. Wenker of the Swiss Passport Office was a luxury they simply did not possess. The entire plan depended on precise timing. Nick and the Pasha were due at 10:30. And at 10:30, they must arrive.

He opened the car door, pausing for a final breath of air before climbing in. Mevlevi had planned this detour. The chauffeur was one of his. Had to be. No one in his right mind would drive on the old road to the Gotthard Pass in this weather. A midwinter ascent was folly. The road would be icy and ungroomed. Worse, the weather was threatening. It could begin snowing at any second.

Mevlevi strode to the automobile. Before climbing inside, he looked Nick in the eye and tapped the roof of the car twice. "Shall we go then?"

Sylvia Schon screamed at the female operator manning the bank switchboard, "I don't care if the line is busy. Put me through on another extension. This is an emergency. Do you understand?"

"Mrs. Sutter is occupied on the telephone," the operator explained patiently. "You may call back later. *Auf Wiederhören.*"

The line went dead.

Exasperated but not defeated, Sylvia found a new dial tone and tried the Chairman's secretary for the third time. Finally, she heard the clipped ringing she so desired.

"*Secretäriat Herr Kaiser,* Sutter."

"Mrs. Sutter," Sylvia began, "where is the Chairman? I must speak with him at once."

"I take it this is Fräulein Schon," answered a cold voice.

"Yes," Sylvia responded. "Where is he?"

"The Chairman is out. He cannot be reached until this afternoon."

"I must know where he is," Sylvia blurted. "It's an emergency. Please tell me where I can find him."

"Of course," Sutter answered, ever formal. "You may find him in his office this afternoon at three P.M. Not before. May I be of service to you?"

"No, dammit. Listen to me. The Chairman is in danger. His safety and his freedom are in jeopardy."

"Calm yourself, young lady," Rita Sutter ordered. "What do you mean by 'in danger'? If you wish to help Herr Kaiser, you must tell me. Or would you prefer to speak with Dr. Ott?"

"No!" Sylvia pinched her arm to remain calm. "Please, Mrs. Sutter. *Please, Rita.* You have to believe me. You must tell me where I can reach him. It's for the good of us all that I find the Chairman."

I'm sorry, Nick, she explained to the persistent shadow that would not leave her shoulder. *This is my home. My life.*

Rita Sutter cleared her throat. "He will be back in the office this afternoon at three o'clock. Good-bye."

"Wait," Sylvia Schon screamed to the dead receiver.

Nick maintained a light hold on the armrest

while looking out the window. The bleak morning had taken on a dusky gloom. He was dismayed to see tufted gray clouds gathering. Snow wasn't far off. He shifted his gaze down the mountain and spotted a single car climbing the tortuous road far below them. It moved with surprising speed, accelerating rapidly along the short straightaways before braking to negotiate the unforgiving hairpin turns. So they weren't the only ones crazy enough to try the pass. He turned his head toward Mevlevi. The frequent sharp turns and constant acceleration and deceleration had turned his complexion yellow. His eyes were focused on the passing landscape. His window was rolled down a crack to allow a stream of freezing air to soothe his confused equilibrium.

Mevlevi leaned forward in his seat and asked the driver, "How much farther to the top?"

"Five minutes," the driver replied. "Almost there. Don't worry. This storm won't hit for a while."

Yet, no sooner had the words escaped the chauffeur's lips than the Mercedes entered a dense cloud bank. Visibility fell from five hundred feet to twenty in the snap of a finger. The car braked sharply.

"Scheisse," whispered the chauffeur in a voice loud enough to alarm his passengers, or at least Nick. The Pasha, however, appeared strangely pleased. The jaundiced tint to his skin had vanished instantly. He tilted his head

against the headrest and looked over at Nick.

"Willful disobedience," he stated, as if throwing out a topic for discussion. "It runs in your family, doesn't it? The urge to tell everyone around you to piss off. Do things your own way. You should have made a career on my side of the fence."

Nick smirked. So now even drug dealers had careers? "I like it on my side," he said.

The Pasha smiled broadly. "I have it on good authority that you've developed quite an interest in the bank's files. Mine for one. And others. Files containing information about your father's work at the bank. *Monthly activity reports,* I believe they are called. Am I correct? Did you need them to corroborate those agendas of his?"

Time stopped. The car no longer moved.

For a moment Nick wondered if he would ever draw another breath. And in that moment, his mind exploded with a thousand questions. Who had told Mevlevi he had been looking at his father's files? Who had mentioned his interest in the file for account 549.617 RR? How did Mevlevi know about the agendas? And why was he confronting Nick now?

Nick told himself to pay the questions no mind, that his sole task was to deliver the Pasha to the Hotel Olivella au Lac where Mr. Yves-Andre Wenker, an underpaid government functionary, would interview him for an hour about why he wished to obtain Swiss citizenship. Get the Pasha to the hotel and the rest of the plan would take care of itself. But the questions remained, cutting into his mind like a dull razor.

"Alexander Neumann," mused Mevlevi. "I knew the man. But I understand you know all that. Did your precious activity reports tell you why he was murdered?"

Nick shot up in his seat. He felt the K-Bar chafing his side. Keep your mouth shut, he wanted to shout. You have no idea how badly I can hurt you. Give me an excuse. Please. Another voice ordered him to remain calm. Let it bounce off of you, it said. He's testing you, seeing what you know. It's all a trick. *It can't be Sylvia who told him.*

"Shot, wasn't he? Do the reports tell you if it was a single bullet that did the trick, or was it several? Three shots, perhaps? I find that to be the most effective. Never seen a man survive who took three bullets to the chest. Use dumdums. They'll tear his heart out."

Nick only half heard the words. A geyser of anger spurted through his body. His neck flushed and his hands tingled. He saw the world through a crimson veneer. And all the while the K-Bar remained taped beneath his arm, crying, *"Use me. End it quickly. Kill him."*

He drew back his right arm to deliver a sharp jab to Mevlevi's chin but stopped halfway there. Mevlevi held a silver nine-millimeter pistol in his hand and it was pointed at Nick's heart. He was smiling.

Sylvia Schon marched into the Chairman's anteroom and presented herself to Rita Sutter.

"Where is he?" Sylvia demanded. "I have to see him right away."

Rita Sutter glanced up sharply from her typing. "Didn't you pay the slightest attention to what I told you on the phone? I informed you clearly that the Chairman will not be back until mid-afternoon. Until then, he cannot be disturbed."

"He must be disturbed," Sylvia said petulantly. "If you plan on coming to work tomorrow for the same man, I have to speak with him."

Rita Sutter rolled her chair back from her desk and removed her reading glasses. "Calm yourself. The office of the Chairman is no place for hysterics. Or threats."

Sylvia pounded the desk with her fist. She was at her wit's end. "Give me his phone number now. If you care about him or about the bank, you'll tell me where he is."

Rita Sutter flinched at the insult. She flew from her seat and rounded her desk, grasping Sylvia tightly by the forearm and forcing her to a grouping of sofa and chairs huddled low against the wall. "How dare you speak to me that way? What could you know about the feelings I have for the bank? Or for Herr Kaiser? Tell me this instant what's gotten into you."

Sylvia swung her arm free of the secretary's firm grip and sat down on the sofa. "Herr Kaiser is going to be arrested this morning. Happy? Now tell me where he's gone. Somewhere in the Tessin. Is it Lugano or Locarno? Bellinzona? We have offices in all those cities."

"Who is going to arrest Herr Kaiser?"

"I don't know. Probably Thorne — the American."

"Who has done this? Is it Mr. Mevlevi? I've always known he was a bad man. Has he implicated Wolfgang?"

Sylvia stared at the older woman as if she were mad. "Mevlevi? Of course not. He's going to be arrested with the Chairman. It's Nicholas. Nicholas Neumann. He's arranged it all. I think he's working with the DEA."

Rita Sutter smiled incredulously; then she shook her head and her features sagged. "So he knows? Oh, dear. What has he said?"

"That Kaiser helped Mevlevi kill his father. That he's going to stop both of them." Sylvia clenched her fists, willing the older woman to action. All she cared about was getting Wolfgang Kaiser away from the police and ensuring that no matter what, Rudolf Ott did not succeed him as Chairman of USB. "Tell me where we can reach him."

Rita Sutter snapped back to attention. "I'm

afraid we'll have to wait," she said. "At least a while. They're in Mr. Feller's car and I don't have the number. They should be in Lugano in an hour. The Chairman has a meeting scheduled with Eberhard Senn, the Count Languenjoux."

"Where is the meeting taking place?"

"At the Hotel Olivella au Lac. The count lives there during the winter."

"Give me the number," Sylvia snapped. "Quickly."

"It's on my desk. What do you plan on saying?"

"I'm going to tell the receptionist that Herr Kaiser must phone us as soon as he arrives. When did you say he should arrive?"

"Wolfgang left my house at seven-fifteen," said Rita Sutter. "If it's not snowing, they should be there by ten-fifteen or ten-thirty."

Sylvia was certain she had not heard properly. "Excuse me?" she asked. "Herr Kaiser was with you last night? He spent the night at your home?"

"Why are you so surprised?" Rita Sutter asked. "I've loved Wolfgang my entire life. You asked whether I cared about the bank — of course I do. It's Wolfgang's." She found the phone number of the Hotel Olivella au Lac and held it out in front of her.

Sylvia snatched the number from Sutter's hand. She picked up the phone and dialed the number. When the hotel operator answered she said, "Give me the receptionist. It's an emergency."

Nick kept his eyes on the barrel of Mevlevi's pistol as he lowered himself to one knee. Snow enveloped the asphalt lot crowning the Gotthardo Pass. The limousine was somewhere behind him, the chauffeur waiting at its side. Visibility was near zero. They had arrived less than a minute before. Dutifully, he'd followed Mevlevi's instructions to step from the car and advance several paces into the mist. He knew he should be afraid, but he couldn't get past feeling stupid and ashamed. He'd been presented with a dozen clues and ignored them all. He'd let his heart blind him. No wonder Sylvia had had such easy access to his father's activity reports. No wonder Kaiser had accused Schweitzer. No wonder Mevlevi knew about his father's agendas. The source for their information was all too clear: Dr. Sylvia Schon. Nick applauded their efficient chain of communication.

Mevlevi stood above him, leering. "Thank you for giving me just cause to abandon you here on this inhospitable mountaintop. I trust you'll find your way home. But don't bother trying the restaurant. Its doors remain closed until May. And the phone," he shook his head, "I am sorry. I think you'll find it doesn't work."

Nick stared at the gun. It was the same pistol

used to kill Albert Makdisi.

"You see, I can't have a man who cares so little for himself working for me. You really should be a bit more selfish. Kaiser was perfect. Our goals were always the same. It took so little to make him move in the right direction. I imagine he spoiled me."

Nick blocked out the Pasha's rambling soliloquy and his own self-abusive thoughts. He concentrated on when to use the knife, how to distract Mevlevi, and what to do with the chauffeur afterward.

"I thought you'd make a fine soldier," Mevlevi was saying. "Or I should say, Kaiser thought so. He was so pleased at being given the chance to seduce the son of the man who had threatened to betray him. You know the rest. And we can't have that, can we? It is a disappointment. As for Kaiser, I imagine he'll get over your loss soon. Probably Tuesday, when the Adler Bank takes over USB and he's out of a job."

The Pasha leveled the gun at Nick. "I'm sorry, Nicholas. You were right about this morning. I can't be late. I require my Swiss passport. It's my final protection against your compatriot Mr. Thorne."

He stepped forward, placing his shiny loafer directly below his intended victim's jaw. Nick didn't look up. He heard the distinct metallic click of the safety being released. And then he moved. His right hand swept under his shirt, seeking the heft of the knife, finding it, ripping it downward and outward. His arm cut the air in a vicious arc. The knife slashed through the Pasha's trousers, slowing only to open a gash on the man's shin. A bullet was fired and ricocheted. The Pasha fell to a knee and cursed. He brought the pistol up for another shot. Nick sprang to his feet and ran. The chauffeur tried to block his path. He had an arm inside his black jacket. Now it was emerging. A gun.

Nick headed directly for him. He spun the K-Bar in his hand so that the serrated edge saluted the ground. He drew his right arm across his chest and slashed upward, dragging the blade across the man's shoulder, rending the arm from his body. The knife impaled itself on bone, and Nick released it. The chauffeur collapsed, screaming.

Nick ran as fast as he could, the blast of the wind drawing tears from his eyes, freezing them on his cheeks. He heard the crack of a bullet fired, and then another and another. Four. Five. He lost count. He urged his legs to pump higher, to run faster. His lungs burned with the cold air. He tilted his head back and screamed at his body to move.

And then he was falling. His right leg collapsed under him like a broken reed. His body tumbled sideways. His shoulder bounced off the asphalt and he was down.

Suddenly all was quiet. Nothing moved behind the snowy curtain. Nick heard only the pounding of his heart and the whistle of the soulless wind as it skittered across the deserted lot. He stared at his twitching leg, recognizing the pain even before he saw the blood.

He was hit.

Chapter 62

Nick stared into the white void.

He waited for the sandpaper shuffle of footsteps to approach from out of the mist and the sarcastic laugh that would follow. He waited for the valedictory exclamation that once again the Pasha had taken his foe. Any second he expected to hear the staccato whine of the nine-millimeter slug as it entered his chest and cauterized his naive, believing heart.

But nothing came. He couldn't hear a thing above the chop of the gathering storm. Just the howling wind.

Nick looked at his leg and saw that the outflow of his blood had slowed. The pool of blood that had formed seconds after he hit the ground had stopped growing. He felt his leg and located the entry wound. He slid a hand under his thigh and it came away slick with blood. The bullet had passed through his leg. No arteries had been severed. He would live. The thought brought a thin smile to his lips and with it, a new realization. He couldn't wait for the Pasha to show himself. To wait was to die, to be an accessory to his own execution. He had to move.

Nick removed his necktie and tied it twice

around his upper thigh in an impromptu tourniquet. He took a handkerchief from his jacket pocket, folded it once and then once again, so that it was its thickest, then wedged it as far into his mouth as possible without inducing an involuntary choking reflex. He closed his eyes and took three deep breaths.

One. Sylvia's earnest reply when he had asked her why she was helping him to find his father's activity reports: *"I was the selfish one. Every man has a right to learn about his father."*

Two. Her astonished voice, laughing, *"I could never phone Kaiser directly. I barely know the man."*

Three. "Sylvia!"

Nick bit down on the handkerchief and thrust himself to a sitting position. His leg screamed at the motion, though he had only moved it an inch. His vision dimmed and for a second all he saw was a buzzing, electric blackness. He spit out the handkerchief and sucked in the mountain air.

Once more, he told himself. One more try and you'll be on your feet.

He could see the restaurant Mevlevi had mentioned behind him. It was a low-slung building with pockmarked concrete walls. Washed-out letters advertised its name: Alpenblick. The parking lot and the road sat somewhere ahead of him, and beyond that, oblivion — a sheer granite cliff. Somewhere inside the pale of snow stood the Pasha with a neat gash in his leg. Bastard was lucky he hadn't caught the serrated side of the blade.

Nick took several breaths and readied his next move. He heard the door of the limousine slam and its engine rev to life. He sat still and turned his ear into the wind. The Mercedes' motor ran in idle for several seconds, then revved anew and accelerated. The wind picked up, drowning the sound of the car.

Nick remained where he was, not fully believing that Mevlevi had just up and left. Why would the Pasha leave him here? To freeze? To bleed to death?

The cough of another engine interrupted his thoughts. The car came closer, now somewhere just beyond the mountain's crest. Its engine whined, straining in second gear as it climbed the final incline.

Nick recalled seeing a car from the limousine window. It had been far below on one of the short straightaways that separated the endless series of hairpin turns. Was this that same automobile? Had its pending arrival prompted the Pasha to get the hell out of there?

Nick didn't know. But he needed someone to find him in a hurry. He didn't have gloves or an overcoat. He could survive a few hours, maybe until night. Longer than that he couldn't guarantee. His leg was already stiffening. Left without any treatment, it would freeze up and he would be incapable of moving it. He required medical attention, someone to swab out the wound and dress it with sulfa and gauze bandages. Most of all, he needed a car to go after the Pasha. He would not allow the sonuvabitch to get away.

Nick heard the screeching of the car's tires as it made its way around the last hairpin turn. The engine fired more confidently as the incline lessened. He rolled to his right so that he could place his left leg under himself. Thousands of shredded nerve endings ignited. Tears came to his eyes. And then he froze. He asked himself who else would be so foolish to come up this road in the dead of winter, braving a wild snowstorm? Was it just some adventurous tourist? Or a local so familiar with the roads that even near whiteout conditions did not daunt him? He didn't think so. Odds were it was a chase car sent by Gino Makdisi to clean up after his business partner.

Nick turned over the situation in his mind. He had to allow the driver to find him. If it was a local, he'd be safe and on his way in a few minutes. If it was a cohort of Mevlevi's, the solution might be messier. One thing was certain: he needed a car to follow Mevlevi.

Nick ran his hands over the asphalt searching for a stone or rock that he might be able to use, if necessary. The lot was scattered with loose gravel. Spotting a decent-size rock — probably a piece of granite from the underlying rock strata — he pulled himself a few feet to his left and grabbed hold of the stone. Then he scooted back to where he had fallen. He ran his hand through the puddle of blood and wiped it across his white shirt. After only a few passes, even he was sickened by the gory sight. His shirt was pasty and crimson — like his father's, the last time he had seen him.

Nick laid down on the ground as the car forded the crest of the mountain. He rested his cheek on the asphalt and focused his eyes on an iron safety pylon intermittently visible through the swirling snow. Keeping his gaze thus directed, he couldn't see what type of car it was that was approaching so slowly. Only that it was red. He tensed as the headlights brushed his eyes. He thought they flashed to bright, then returned to normal but could not be sure. The engine died, and the car came to a halt at the edge of his peripheral vision.

A door opened. Steps approached. Nick kept his eyes glued to the iron pylon. Dead man's stare. He breathed shallowly. It was hard as hell, seeing as how his heart was doing at least a hundred a minute. He was scared and powerless. He waited for a second door to open, but the sound didn't come. Whoever was standing ten feet away from him had come alone.

The steps recommenced. A shape took form in his periphery. Medium-size man. Dark clothing. Approaching cautiously. Why don't you say something? Nick asked himself. Ask me how I am, if I'm alive. He tightened his grip on the rock cupped beneath his hand. The man took another step. Now he was leaning over Nick's body. He jabbed a foot into Nick's lower back.

Definitely not a local.

Nick kept his gaze on the pylon. His eyes itched terribly, and he needed to blink. Still, no voice. The man bent down lower. Nick knew he was staring at his bloody shirt and sizing up his lifeless gaze. Any second now he'd put his hand in front of Nick's mouth and feel the warm breath, and then he'd know. The face was directly above him. Nick smelled expensive cologne. Could almost make out the features. Gray beard, closely cropped. Thick eyebrows.

Then Nick saw the hat. The man held it in his right hand, which had fallen directly in front of Nick's eyes. It was a rugged, dark green affair. A pinsel brush extended from its band.

An Austrian mountain guide's hat.

Nick snapped his head to the right and stared into the surprised face of his gentleman stalker. The man yelped. But before he could rise, Nick's hand arced through the air, delivering the stone to his cheek. The man gasped, then tumbled onto his side, unconscious. He held a snub-nosed revolver in his left hand.

Nick sat up and stared at the damaged face. He had no doubt it was the same man who had pursued him up the Bahnhofstrasse four weeks ago. He could practically see the cocky smirk the man had offered him that night in Sprüngli. He picked up the gun and put it in his pocket, then rummaged through the man's pockets. No wallet. No cellular phone. No car keys. Just a few hundred francs in currency.

Nick leaned to his right and drew his left leg under him. Somehow his anger had lessened the pain. Grimacing, he stood, then limped to the car. A Ford Cortina. The keys were in the ignition. Thankfully it was an automatic. He leaned into the driver's seat, peering around the interior for any sign of a first-aid kit or a telephone. He opened the glove compartment and checked inside. Nothing. A hump on the console behind the rear seat gave him hope. He hobbled backward and opened the passenger door. Lowering himself to the rear seat, he opened the small compartment and found an unused first-aid kit. Inside was adhesive tape, gauze, Mercurochrome, and aspirin. Not bad for a start.

Fifteen minutes later, Nick had cleaned and bandaged his leg. The stalker lay on his side, immobile. Probably had a fractured cheek and a few broken teeth. That would be the least of his problems once he'd discovered he'd been left up here without a car. Nick took a survival blanket from the first-aid kit and threw it at the prostrate form. The Mylar blanket would keep him warm enough until he figured out a way down. Nick might even call the police later and report a pedestrian stranded at the St. Gotthard Pass. Then again, he might not. Right now, though, he had more important matters to tend to.

Nick moved to the front door of the Ford and lowered himself delicately into the driver's seat. He would have to drive with his left leg. He started the engine. The gas tank was three-quarters full. He checked his watch: 10:30. The Pasha was thirty minutes ahead of him.

Time to fly.

Chapter 63

Ali Mevlevi arrived at the Hotel Olivella au Lac at 10:40. The weather was clear and cool, hazy sunshine pushing its way through a thin stratus of cloud. The temperate Mediterranean winds that lapped against the southern wall of the Alps brought to the Tessin mild, comfortable winters, not altogether different from those of Lebanon. In Zurich, it was said, you spent the winter huddled behind the double-paned windows of overheated offices, while in Lugano you buttoned up your sweater and took only a single espresso outdoors in the Piazza San Marco. Certainly, that was the case today — but there would be no time for espresso.

Mevlevi slammed the front door of the limousine and walked deliberately into the hotel, taking care to conceal his limp. He had wrapped his leg with a bandage he had found in the limousine's first-aid kit. It would hold until he could get to a proper doctor and have the ugly gash stitched up. He approached the reception area and asked the clerk in which room he could find Mr. Yves-Andre Wenker. The clerk checked the register. Room 407. Mevlevi offered his thanks and directed himself to the elevators. He clenched his jaw, biting back the pain. One thought consoled him. By now, Neumann should be buried deep in the mountain snow, his disappearance to be solved only by a late spring thaw. There is no nobility in being honest and dead, Nicholas. That is a lesson you should have learned from your father long ago.

Mevlevi took the elevator to the fourth floor. He found Room 407 and rapped twice on the door. One lock disengaged, then a second. The door swung open revealing a tall gentleman in a gray pinstripe suit. He wore pince-nez spectacles and had the terminal stoop and begrudging squint of a deskbound clerk.

"*Veuillez entrer.* Do come in, please," the slim man beckoned. "*Monsieur . . .*"

"Malvinas. Allen Malvinas. *Bonjour.*" The Pasha extended his hand. He detested speaking French.

"Yves-Andre Wenker. Swiss Passport Office." Wenker pointed the way toward an expansive sitting area. "You're alone? I was told you would be accompanied by a Mr. Neumann, an assistant to Herr Kaiser."

"Alas, Mr. Neumann could not join us. He was taken ill quite suddenly."

Wenker frowned. "Is that so? To be frank, I was beginning to doubt whether you would arrive at all. I expect my clients to respect our scheduled meeting times regardless of the weather. Even if they are referred to me by so eminent a businessman as Herr Kaiser."

"Rain, sleet, poor visibility. We had a long ride from Zurich."

Wenker eyed him skeptically, then showed him into the sitting room. "Herr Kaiser informs me you are a native of Argentina."

"Buenos Aires." Mevlevi eyed him uncomfortably. There was something vaguely familiar about this man. "Do you by any chance speak English?"

"I am sorry, but no," Wenker replied, inclining his head deferentially. "I favor only the Romance languages of the European continent. French, Italian, a little Spanish. English is such a vulgar language."

Mevlevi said nothing. He knew the voice, he was sure of it, but its provenance eluded him.

"*Eh bien.* Shall we get down to business?" Wenker checked his watch and sat down on the sofa. He had laid out a succession of manila folders on the coffee table in front of him. Tabs indicated their contents as "Work History," "Residence," and "Financial Information." "The usual application process requires seven years provided proof of Swiss residence has been established. As we're hastening the process, quite a few documents will have to be filled out during our meeting. Please try to be patient."

Mevlevi nodded, though he was hardly listening. His thoughts were an hour behind him, stranded atop the misty mountaintop. He had hit Neumann with at least one of the shots. He had heard the boy cry and fall down. Why, then, hadn't he gone after him? Had he been surprised that the boy had put up a little resistance? Not at all like his father, who had stood as if hypnotized, staring into the barrel of the gun. Had he been scared that somewhere in the blanket of mist he might find Neumann all too alive, and not like what the boy had in mind for him? Neumann was, after all, a marine. Where else did one learn to chop off a man's arm with a single blow? Not that the chauffeur would need it any longer. He'd had to put him out of his misery. Bastard should be thankful. Didn't feel a thing. Slug to the back of the neck. Bang, it's over.

"Have you brought three photographs with you?" Wenker asked again.

"Of course." Mevlevi reached into his briefcase and withdrew his passport and a wax paper envelope holding three small portraits.

Wenker examined them quickly. "You must sign the back of each one."

Mevlevi hesitated, then bowed to the man's demands. The damned Swiss — punctilious to a fault, even in their most corrupt dealings.

Wenker accepted the signed photos and placed them in an open folder. "May we begin with the questions?"

"Please," the Pasha answered gallantly. He turned his head to look out at the lake. The view of dappled palms swaying in the morning breeze did little to dispel the unease chewing at his stomach. He could not relax until he had word about Neumann.

Thirty kilometers south of Lugano, a tangled braid of traffic slowed to a crawl as it neared the southernmost Swiss border at Chiasso. The border crossing was considered the country's busiest, one of only three portals through which the industrial output of northern Italy could reach the mighty economies of Germany and France. Trucks of every size, shape, and vintage traversed the flat stretch of superhighway. Among their number this morning was an eighteen-wheel Magirus rig bravely hauling two trailers. Her cab was painted a royal blue. Her chrome grille sported a white badge with the letters TIR. *Trans Internationale Routier.*

Joseph Habib sat inside the truck's cabin, wedged uncomfortably between two mafiosi, low-level thugs who worked the Italian side of things for the Makdisi family. Eighteen months he'd been under. Eighteen months since he'd tasted his mother's spicy *mezza.* Just a few more minutes, keep these hotheads calm until the rig pulls into the checkpoint, and it would go down like clockwork. He only wished he could be there to see Ali Mevlevi's face when he learned he'd lost his shipment.

The portico came into view a few hundred

yards ahead. Traffic was stop-and-go.

"I told you to pull into the right lane," Joseph said to Remo, the driver. "Do as I say."

"It's backed up halfway to Milano. You want I should take that lane, we never get to Zurich." Remo was a young tough, black hair pulled into a ponytail, shirtsleeves rolled up to show off his chiseled biceps.

Joseph turned his shoulders toward him. "I'll tell you one more time. The right lane or we turn around and go home. Why do you insist on disobeying Mr. Makdisi's orders?"

The traffic stopped. Remo lit a cigarette. "What does he know about crossing this border?" he asked, blowing smoke into the cramped cabin. "I've done it a thousand times. No one has ever given us a second look."

Joseph shifted his gaze to the slovenly man in the passenger seat. "Franco, tell your friend. We go to the right or we go home." He knew Franco was scared of him. The unkempt slob was always looking over at him, his eyes practically swallowing the scar on his cheek. You could see the man shudder, wondering how he had gotten it.

Franco leaned across Joseph and tapped the driver on the arm. "Remo. Right lane. *Pronto.*"

"How much time?" asked Remo.

"Twenty minutes," said Joseph. "No problem. Our man doesn't leave the booth until ten-thirty."

"What's taking so long this morning?"

Remo asked, tapping the giant steering wheel impatiently. "Take a look."

Franco reached for a leather case holding a pair of binoculars that sat on the floor. He grunted. The girth of his stomach prevented him from reaching it. He smiled at Joseph. *"Per favore."*

Joseph unlatched the box and handed him the field glasses. This was crunch time. Stay calm and the others will stay calm, too.

Franco rolled down the passenger window. He labored to place his head and shoulders outside the cab of the eighteen-wheeler.

Remo sucked on his cigarette. "Eh?" he inquired loudly.

"Only two lanes open," answered Franco, after pulling his body inside the cabin.

Remo tapped his forehead. "Two lanes. This explains why we go so slow."

"Which one is closed?" asked Joseph coldly. Say it's the left one. Keep everything according to plan.

"The left one," said Franco. "Everybody is being funneled into the center and right lane."

Joseph exhaled.

Remo blasted his horn and drew the big rig into the right lane.

Thirty meters behind the juggernaut, an undistinguished white Volvo turned on its blinker and followed suit. The driver played with a small gold medallion hanging from his neck. "Almost there," Moammar al Khan whispered, bringing the medallion to his mouth and kissing it lightly. "*Inshallah*, God is great."

"Your name?" asked Yves-Andre Wenker. He sat primly on the couch, forms splayed across his lap.

"Allen Malvinas. Must I introduce myself twice? The essentials are there, in my passport. You have it on the table."

Wenker eyed the travel document resting on the coffee table. "Thank you, Mr. Malvinas. However, I prefer a personal response. Date of birth?"

"November 12, 1936."

"Present address?"

"It is in the passport. On the third page."

Wenker made no move to pick up the passport. "Address?"

Mevlevi scooped up the passport and read off the address. "Satisfied?"

Wenker kept his head lowered and painstakingly filled out his precious form. "Years at this address?"

"Seven."

"Seven?" Sharp blue eyes peeked out from behind the thin spectacles. A strand of blond hair fell across his brow.

"Yes, seven," Mevlevi insisted. His leg was killing him. Suddenly, he was unsure. He swallowed hard and rasped, "Why not seven?"

Wenker smiled. "Seven is fine." He returned his attention to the paper resting in his lap. "Occupation?"

"Import and export."

"What exactly do you import and export?"

"I concentrate on precious metals and commodities," said Mevlevi. "Gold, silver, the like." Hadn't Kaiser told him a damned thing? This drab functionary was beginning to get on his nerves. Not the questions, so much, but the decidedly nasty tinge to his voice.

"Income?"

"That is none of your concern."

Wenker removed his eyeglasses from the bridge of his nose. "We do not sponsor wards of the state to immigrate to Switzerland."

"I hardly qualify as a ward of the state," Mevlevi objected loudly.

"Of course not. Regardless, we must have —"

"And who said anything about immigrating?"

Wenker slapped the stack of forms onto the coffee table. He lifted his chin, ready to deliver a stern rebuke. "Mr. Neumann told me specifically that you wished to purchase property in Gstaad in order to establish a permanent residence in this country. While on certain occasions we make exceptions for the granting of a Swiss passport, permanent residence is an absolute requirement. Are you, or are you not, planning on maintaining a permanent residence in Switzerland?"

Ali Mevlevi coughed, then poured himself a glass of mineral water from a bottle set upon the table. He preferred a country where a bent official at least had a little respect. "I misunderstood you. Mr. Neumann was absolutely correct. I shall be making Gstaad my principal residence."

Wenker sat lower in his chair. He offered Mevlevi a starched smile while he scribbled away at his form. "Income?"

"Five hundred thousand dollars per annum."

Wenker raised his eyebrows. "Is that all?"

The Pasha stood up, his face flushed and his lips quivering. "Isn't that enough?"

Wenker remained unruffled. His pen slid across paper. "That is enough," he said to his questionnaire.

Mevlevi grimaced and returned to his seat. He sensed his wound tear. A warm trail of blood inched down his leg. Just a little longer, he told himself. Then you can walk to the telephone, call Gino Makdisi, and find out what you already know — that your precious cargo is safely across the border and that Nicholas Neumann is dead.

Wenker glanced offhandedly at his wristwatch and then returned his attention to the form spread across his lap. He cleared his throat noisily. "Communicable diseases?"

Remo jerked his head into the cabin of the

truck. His eyes played between Joseph and Franco. "They are checking every truck," he said. "No one is getting a free pass."

"Calm down," Joseph ordered, as much for his nerves as theirs. "Listen, both of you. Everything is going as planned. Who gives a good goddamn if they are checking manifests? Maybe they do it every Monday morning. We've got our man in the far right booth. He is looking for us. Relax and we'll get through this."

Remo looked out the window. The peaks of the Swiss Alps loomed before them like a distant gray specter. "I am not going back inside," he said. "Three years was enough."

Two trucks separated them from the probing eyes of the customs inspectors. All incoming vehicles were forced to pass under a broad portico designed primarily to measure the height of freight carriers entering Switzerland. A small office built from sturdy blue steel sat to the right of each lane. A customs inspector, walkie-talkie in hand, stood next to each office, waving the next trucks forward.

Joseph scanned the booths and beyond. He felt his shoulders tighten. Ten police cars were parked on the shoulder of the highway about two hundred yards up the road. Why so much firepower for a simple bust? he wondered. Three men and a lousy truck. What were they expecting? An army?

The gasoline tanker in front of them roared

forward, belching exhaust.

Remo considered the empty space in front of his rig.

Joseph nudged him in the ribs. "Go on. Don't make us look conspicuous."

Remo eased his foot onto the accelerator, and the truck groaned forward, foot by foot.

The customs inspector jumped onto the running board of the gasoline tanker directly in front of them. He thrust his head inside its cabin and emerged a moment later, cargo manifest in hand. He used the antenna of his walkie-talkie to skim the manifest. He was a tall, thin man wearing a green jacket. He had unruly brown hair and pitted cheeks. He shot a casual glance at their rig, and Joseph spotted the dark rings under his eyes. Sterling Thorne looked as crappy as ever.

Thorne returned the manifest to the driver of the truck currently in bay and directed his attention toward the blue Magirus eighteen-wheeler bearing British license plates and a white TIR tag, next in line. He raised the walkie-talkie to his mouth and issued what appeared to be heated instructions.

Franco shot forward in his seat, pointing a finger at Thorne. "He eyeballed us. He's got us picked out already."

"Keep calm," said Joseph. He could feel the tension ratcheting up inside their cabin.

"I saw it, too," said Remo. "The fucker at the booth. He's got us pegged. Christ, it's a setup. They know exactly what they're looking for and it's us."

"Keep your mouths closed," shouted Joseph. "We've got nowhere to go but forward. There's no other way out. We are holding a legitimate manifest. We are transporting a legitimate cargo. It would take a genius to find our merchandise."

Remo stared at Joseph. "Or a tip."

Franco kept his arm pointed at Sterling Thorne. "The cop at the booth. He took one look at our rig and scrambled his team. And look! Look up there! They got ten cruisers ready for us."

"You're wrong," said Joseph. "They're not scrambling anything." He had to keep these losers calm until they didn't have any other choice but to give up peacefully. Get the truck under the portico. Just another minute or two. "Just sit back and shut up."

At that moment, both rearview mirrors lit up with revolving red and blue lights. A brace of police cars drew up twenty yards in back of them. The tanker ahead was waved through. When it cleared the portico, a team of twelve policemen rushed forward forming a tight phalanx behind Sterling Thorne. Each policeman wore dark blue body armor and brandished a blunt submachine gun.

"We're screwed," said Remo, hysteria cracking his voice. He was rocking off the steering wheel like a hyperactive child. "I told you. No more unpaid vacations. I can't go back."

"Listen to me," Joseph pleaded. "We have to call their bluff. That's our only chance of getting out of here."

"There is no chance of getting out of here," exploded Remo. "Someone has set a trap and we're the catch."

Joseph thrust a finger into Remo's chest. "We have two tons of my boss's merchandise sitting in the back of this rig. I won't allow us to lose it because your nerves can't stand a little heat. We are not caught until they slam the cuffs on our wrists."

Remo wiped his nose, staring at the empty space in front of them and at the tall inspector waving them forward. His fear was palpable. "We're caught," he yelled. "I know it and Franco knows it. Why the fuck don't you?" He cocked his arm and threw an elbow, which caught Joseph in the temple. "You don't know it because you want us to pull into that little party they've set up for us, you fucking sand nigger. The Makdisis told me not to trust you. They were right. You've done this, haven't you?" Another elbow flew, this one smashing the bridge of Joseph's nose, crushing bone and cartilage and releasing a violent stream of blood. " 'Right lane,' you said. 'Right fucking lane.' Well, here we are and it's the *wrong* fucking lane."

Remo rammed his foot onto the accelerator

and the eighteen-wheeler jerked forward.

Franco uttered a whooping war cry.

Sterling Thorne stood in front of the juggernaut, his arm extended and his palm upraised. Through a veil of refracted light, Joseph saw Thorne's expression turn from surprise to confusion, and finally, terror, as the rig advanced on him. Thorne froze, unable to decide which way to move. The twenty-four-cylinder engine roared. Remo blasted the horn. Thorne dove under the chassis of the diesel monster.

Joseph grabbed at the steering wheel. He kicked at the gear shift with his right leg and thrust the fingers of his left hand backward into Franco's face, seeking his adversary's eyes. Franco bellowed madly, screaming for his friend to free him of the crazed Arab. Remo yelled "Kill him" as he put the rig back into gear.

Gunfire erupted to the rear of the truck. Tires exploded as bullets passed through coiled rubber and punctured pressurized inner tubes. The giant truck listed to the left. Still, Remo accelerated. Bullets showered the rear trailer, sounding like a sheet of rain passing over a tin roof. The policemen found their mark, and the benign rain turned to a murderous hail. A curtain of lead struck the driver's door. The windshield shattered in an ejaculatory burst of glass.

Joseph dug his fingers into Franco's eyes. He sheared an eyeball from its optic nerve and dashed it to the floor. Franco screamed louder and brought both hands to his ravaged face. Joseph reached over the wounded man's heaving belly and pushed open the passenger door. He lowered his shoulder and shoved him out of the cabin.

Remo was wounded. Cables of rosy phlegm dangled from his mouth. A bullethole in his gut spurted blood. His face was dotted with a dozen pinpricks where burs of glass had torn the flesh. Still, he concentrated on the road before him with the blind fury of a wounded bull.

Joseph wedged one arm against the dashboard and the other against the seat back. He swung his legs up and lashed out at Remo's head. The heels of his work boots caught the ailing driver flush in the jaw and slammed him against the steel door frame. Remo made a last effort at defending himself, throwing his right arm weakly in his attacker's direction. Joseph dodged the blow. He recoiled and brought his legs up to batter the injured mafioso. Again he landed a solid kick to the driver's head. Remo tottered in his seat. He spit out a patch of blood before falling forward against the steering wheel, either dead or unconscious.

The truck gained speed. It veered precipitously to the right, accelerating toward the column of police cars camped on the dirt shoulder. Joseph lifted Remo's inert body off of the steering column and fought to dislodge his leaden foot from the accelerator. The constant jostling of the truck rendered every effort ineffective. Each thrust served only to pinion Remo's foot more tightly onto the accelerator.

The line of police cars drew nearer. Twenty yards separated the renegade juggernaut from the automobiles. Ten, five . . .

Joseph realized that no action could prevent the truck from striking the cars. He threw open the passenger door and launched himself from the cabin. He landed running and managed to place both feet on the ground before momentum swept him forward and propelled him across the pavement.

The juggernaut plowed into the first police car. Its tires crushed the automobile's hood and thrust the truck skyward. The rig rolled on, careering over one car and then another. Windows shattered, metal tore, and sirens exploded. The downward force with which one gasoline tank was crushed provoked an incendiary spark, instantaneously igniting its contents. The blast lifted the automobile off the ground, overturning the truck's rear trailer and setting off a chain reaction of high-octane explosions as gasoline tank after gasoline tank succumbed to the fireball. The smuggler's rig toppled onto its side and was itself engulfed in flame.

Police surrounded Joseph. Sterling Thorne broke through the circle of officers and bent down beside him. "Welcome back to civilization," he said.

Joseph nodded. He didn't appreciate being at the business end of twelve automatic rifles.

"You have something for me," Thorne asked.

Joseph looked up at Thorne, remembering all over again what an asshole he was. The guy didn't even ask if he was okay. He fished in his pocket for a scrap of paper. It read "Ali Mevlevi. Hotel Olivella au Lac. Room 407. USB account 549.617 RR." Exactly as Thorne had dictated.

Thorne took the scrap of paper from Joseph, raising the walkie-talkie to his lips even as he read it. "We have conducted a search of the suspect and discovered evidence of an incriminating nature. We have probable cause to believe that a suspect involved in the importation of a large shipment of heroin is currently residing at the Hotel Olivella au Lac in room four zero seven. Proceed with caution."

A last gas tank exploded on the road behind them. A fireball rose into the morning sky.

Thorne covered his head. He extended his hand and helped Joseph to his feet. "You didn't have to make my job so much harder," he said. "A lot of very convincing evidence is going up in smoke."

Moammar al Khan stared transfixed at the black and orange plume. He fumbled for the cellular phone, his right hand blindly patting the passenger seat. Look at that smoke, he thought to himself, cringing. A ton of Al-Mevlevi's product in flames. Allah have mercy.

A customs inspector banged the hood of the car and motioned for him to pass through the portico. Khan offered an Italian passport, but it was waved away.

"Drive. Don't look," said the customs official before moving off down the line of stalled automobiles.

Khan ignored his instructions, slowing the car to a crawl as he passed the flaming wreckage. A circle of policemen had surrounded a lone man lying prostrate on the ground. The man was injured. Blood poured from his nose. His clothing was torn, his face blackened by smoke. It was Joseph. He was alive. *Inshallah! God is great!* A gangly man wearing the green jacket of the customs inspectors broke through the circle of policemen. He bent himself upon one knee and spoke to Joseph.

Khan leaned over the passenger seat to look closer.

Thorne. The American agent. There was no mistaking it. The hair. The gaunt face. The DEA had intercepted Al-Mevlevi's shipment.

And then something strange happened. Thorne offered a hand to Joseph and hoisted him to his feet. He gave Joseph a pat on the shoulder, then leaned his head back and laughed. All the policemen were smiling, too. Their guns were lowered. Even Joseph was grinning.

Khan pulled the gold pendant from his shirt and kissed it.

Joseph is an informant.

Khan accelerated madly, driving for two minutes before pulling to the shoulder of the highway and stopping the car. He picked up the cellular phone and dialed the number Mevlevi had given him in case of emergency. Three rings passed. Finally, a voice answered.

Khan pressed the phone to his mouth. He drew in several sharp breaths, not knowing where to begin. Only one phrase came to mind.

"Joseph is one of them."

Chapter 64

Ali Mevlevi was angry. He'd been cooped up with this snit of a bureaucrat for far too long answering inane questions. Did he wish to establish his business in Switzerland? If so, how many employees would he be hiring? Would he avail himself of the tax credit offered to newly registered corporations? Would his relatives be coming to live with him? Now he had had enough. For whatever sum Kaiser was paying him, Wenker could fill out the forms himself. Let him *invent* the goddamned answers.

Mevlevi stood from the couch and buttoned his jacket. "I thank you for your help in this matter, but I'm afraid I'm the victim of a rather pressing schedule. I had been led to believe that this meeting was but a formality."

"You were misinformed," snapped Wenker. He waded through a stack of papers on the table, then turned his attention to a leather satchel lying next to him on the sofa. Giving a sigh of relief, he produced a thick manila envelope and handed it to Mevlevi. "A short history of our country. As a Swiss citizen, you will be expected to respect our long democratic tradition. The country was founded in

1291 when three forest cantons, Uri, Schwyz, and Unter—"

"Thank you very kindly," Mevlevi said brusquely, accepting the sealed envelope and sliding it into his briefcase. Did this jackass actually think he had time for a history lesson? "If we are finished, I must take my leave. Perhaps I can hear the fascinating history of this land at another date."

"*Encore un instant.* Not so quickly, Mr. Malvinas. I have one last paper that you must sign — a release from military service. It's obligatory, I'm afraid."

Mevlevi threw back his head and sighed. "Please hurry it up."

Just then, a shy chirp emanated from his briefcase. Thank God, thought Mevlevi. Gino Makdisi calling to tell me everything is going according to schedule. He took the cellular phone out of his briefcase and walked to the far side of the salon before answering. "Yes."

"Joseph is one of them," came the harried voice. "I watched it all. The truck was surrounded by police. The driver attempted to escape. He had no chance. Only Joseph lived. Everything is in flames."

Mevlevi placed a finger in his ear, as if the connection were poor and he could not make out his correspondent's words. But the connection was clear. And so were the words.

"Calm yourself, Khan," Mevlevi said in Arabic, checking to see if Wenker was listening. The bureaucrat appeared disinterested. "Repeat that again."

"The shipment was intercepted at the Chiasso border. As soon as the truck pulled into the inspection bay, it was surrounded by police. They were expecting it."

Mevlevi felt the hairs on the nape of his neck stand tall. The sum of his life rested in the voice at the other end of the telephone. "You said the shipment was destroyed, not captured. Make yourself clear."

"The driver, Remo, made a run for it. He did not get far. He lost control of the lorry and it exploded. The merchandise was destroyed. More than that I don't know. I am sorry."

"And what of Joseph?"

"He survived. I saw him on the ground. The police, they helped him to his feet. I saw an officer hug him. It was he, the informant."

Not Joseph, Mevlevi screamed mutely. It was Lina. She was the Makdisis' contact. She helped the Makdisis set him up with the American DEA. Joseph, my desert hawk, is ever loyal. He alone can be trusted.

Khan said, "You must leave the country immediately. If the DEA knows about the shipment, they certainly are aware that you are in Switzerland. Joseph would not tell them one thing without the other. Who knows when they will spring?"

Mevlevi could not speak. Joseph was an informant for the United States Drug Enforcement Administration.

"Did you hear me, Al-Mevlevi? We must secure you safe passage out of the country. Get to Brissago. On the Italian border, outside of Locarno. Be there in one hour. The main square."

"Yes, Brissago. Main square. One hour." He hung up the phone.

Wenker was staring at him unabashedly, a look of keen revulsion souring the bureaucrat's features. Mevlevi followed his gaze to the floor. To his own feet.

A pool of blood was growing steadily on the ivory Berber carpet.

Downstairs, a forest-green Range Rover drew into the circular forecourt of the hotel. The car's tires squealed painfully as it negotiated a one-hundred-eighty-degree turn and slid to a halt in front of the main entry. The passenger door swung open, and an imposing man in a three-piece charcoal suit descended. Wolfgang Kaiser straightened his jacket and smoothed his bristly black mustache. He checked his reflection in the passenger window and satisfied as to his appearance, marched into the lobby.

"Time?" he called over his shoulder.

"Eleven-fifteen," answered Reto Feller, rushing to join him.

"Fifteen minutes late," complained Kaiser. "No doubt the count will be impressed. For that I can thank you, Mr. Feller. And your new automobile." The fucking car had gotten a flat tire in the middle of the St. Gotthard tunnel. It was a miracle they hadn't choked to death on the exhaust fumes.

Feller scurried ahead to the front desk, where he rang the arrival bell twice. "We are looking for the Count Languenjoux," he announced breathlessly. "What room can we find him in?"

A hotelier in black morning coat delivered himself to the polished walnut counter. "Whom may I announce?"

Kaiser presented his business card. "We are expected."

The hotelier discreetly read the card. "Thank you, Herr Kaiser. The count is in Room 407." He leaned closer, and in a gesture of implied intimacy, spoke softly from beneath a furrowed brow. "We've received a number of calls for you this morning. All extremely urgent. The caller insisted on waiting on the line until you arrived."

Kaiser arched an eyebrow. He glanced over his shoulder. Feller stood three paces behind him, taking in every word.

"A woman from your office in Zurich," said the hotelier. "Shall I check if she is still on hold?"

"Do you know her name?" Kaiser asked.

"Fräulein Schon."

"By all means, please check." How had she

found him here? He had told no one of his trip except Rita.

"Sir, the count is waiting," said Feller.

Kaiser could imagine the little weasel's impure thoughts. "Then go keep him company," he ordered. "I'll be up in two minutes."

The hotelier returned to the desk. "The lady is still on the line. I'll have the call transferred to one of our private cabins. Directly behind you, Herr Kaiser. Booth number one, the first glass door on the left."

Kaiser thanked the hotelier and walked rapidly to the booth. He closed the glass door and sat down on a stool facing the telephone. The phone jangled in an instant. "Kaiser."

"Wolfgang, is it you?" asked Sylvia Schon.

"What's going on? What's so important that you demean the good name of the bank by calling this hotel in a frenzy? Word will certainly get back to the count."

"Listen to me," Sylvia commanded. "You must leave the hotel immediately."

"Don't be ridiculous. I've only just arrived."

"It's Nicholas Neumann. He's arranged some sort of trap. I've been trying to reach you all night."

What nonsense was this? wondered Kaiser. "Nicholas is with an important client of mine," he said sternly.

Sylvia's voice grew frantic. "Nick thinks that your friend, Mr. Mevlevi, killed his father. He said you knew all about it. He told me he has

838

proof, but he wouldn't say any more. Now listen to me and get out of that hotel this second."

"Who has proof?" demanded Kaiser. The girl was rattling on at a hundred kilometers an hour, and he didn't care for the gist of her argument.

"Just leave the hotel," she pleaded. "They're going to arrest you and Mr. Mevlevi."

Kaiser took a deep breath, unable to decide if her ranting had merit. "I have an appointment with one of our bank's most important shareholders. His votes could be crucial to our long-term ability to keep Konig from enacting his plans. I can't just come back."

"Haven't you heard?"

Suddenly Kaiser felt very alone. The concern had fallen from her voice. Pity had replaced it. "What?"

"The Adler Bank has offered five hundred francs a share for the bank. Konig announced it on the radio this morning at nine. A cash bid for all the shares he doesn't own."

"No, I hadn't heard," Kaiser managed to whisper after a few seconds. Reto Feller had insisted on listening to the Brandenburg Concerto on his new car's hi-fi. He would kill him.

Sylvia said, "Konig is going to ask for a vote of confidence from the executive board at tomorrow's general assembly."

"Oh," said Kaiser halfheartedly. He was no longer listening. A commotion was brewing in front of the hotel. He could hear car doors slamming and instructions being issued in a flat military tone. Several members of the hotel staff hastened toward the revolving door at the front entry. He brought the phone closer to his ear. "Sylvia, be quiet for a few moments. Stay on the line."

He pushed open the cabin's glass door a crack. Outside the hotel, a heavy motor rumbled closer, then quit. Commands were given in excited Italian. A parade of jackbooted feet hit the ground. A bellboy ran into the lobby and disappeared behind the front desk. A moment later the hotel's general manager appeared, senatorial in dress and demeanor. He nearly jogged to the revolving door and went outside. Seconds later, he returned accompanied by two gentlemen, one of whom Kaiser recognized as Sterling Thorne. The other man, identifiable from countless photos in the daily papers, was Luca Merolli, the Tessin's crusading prosecuting attorney.

Thorne stopped in the center of the hotel lobby. He bent over the hotel manager and announced in his booming provincial accent, "We're going to send a dozen men up to the fourth floor. They have loaded guns and their captain's permission to fire. I don't want anybody to interfere with them. Understand?"

Luca Merolli repeated Thorne's words and gave them his own authority.

The general manager bobbed excitedly on

his toes. "*Sì.* We have the elevator and the interior stairwell. Come, I show them to you."

Thorne turned to Merolli. "Bring in your men right away. Kaiser's up there this very second with Mevlevi. My two rats are sitting in a gilded cage. Hurry up, goddammit. I want both of them."

"*Sì, sì,*" shouted Merolli as he ran out of the lobby.

"Wolfgang?" came a faraway voice. "Are you there? Hello?"

Kaiser stared dumbfounded at the receiver in his hand. She was telling me the truth, he whispered. I'm to be arrested with Ali Mevlevi. Curiously, his concerns were not for himself, but for the bank. What will become of USB? Who'll protect my beloved institution from that bastard Konig?

"Wolfgang, are you there?" asked Rita Sutter. "Listen to Fräulein Schon's warnings. You must come home immediately. For the good of the bank, get out of there now."

Rita's calm voice awoke in him a rational sense of self-protection. He took stock of just where he was and what was happening. He realized that not only did he have a full and unimpeded view of Sterling Thorne, but that the odious American had an equally unobscured view of him. One glance in his direction and Thorne would spot him. Kaiser removed his foot from the sill of the door, letting it close. He shifted on the velvet stool so that his body faced the interior wall.

"Rita, it appears you were correct. I'll try and get back as soon as possible. If anyone calls for me, press, television, simply say that I am out of the office and cannot be reached. Do I make myself clear?"

"Yes, but where will you go? When can we expect —"

Kaiser replaced the receiver and shielded his face as best as possible with his right arm. He didn't dare look toward the lobby. He focused his gaze on a patch of carpeting near his left foot, where the embers of another guest's cigarette had burned a neat round hole. Staring at this petty ingratitude, he cringed in expectation of the sharp knock against the transparent door. He imagined the leering visage of Mr. Sterling Thorne staring at him through the window, beckoning him with a crooked finger to give himself up. Wolfgang Kaiser's life would end at that moment.

But no sharp knock came at the cabin window. No American voice demanded that he vacate the booth. He heard only the orderly procession of a large number of men crossing the marble floor. Tic tac, tic tac, tic tac. Thorne yelled more instructions. Then, thankfully, there was quiet.

Ali Mevlevi looked up from his bleeding leg and said, "I'm afraid I must go immediately."

Yves-Andre Wenker pointed at the pool of

blood. "You can't go anywhere bleeding like that. Take a seat. Let me get you medical attention. You need to see a doctor."

Mevlevi limped across the room. He was in terrible pain. "Not today, Mr. Wenker. I haven't the time." The leg was the least of his worries. Khan, while frantic, had been every bit justified in his worry. If Joseph was in fact an informant of the DEA, there was no end to what he might have told Thorne. Mevlevi must assume the worst. All his operations in Switzerland had been compromised. His relationship with Gino Makdisi. His control over Wolfgang Kaiser. And most important, his funding of the Adler Bank's takeover of USB.

Khamsin was in jeopardy.

"I'm not asking you," said a visibly agitated Wenker. "I'm telling you. Take a seat. I'll call down to reception. The hotel is very discreet."

Mevlevi ignored him. He stopped beside the coffee table and threw his phone into the briefcase. He looked back at the trail of bloody footprints he had left on the carpet. He was losing a great deal of blood. Damn you, Neumann.

"At least take the time to sign this last document." Wenker waved a form in the air. He looked nervous. Sweat was forming on his brow. "Civil service is obligatory. I must have a waiver."

"I don't think I will be needing a Swiss

passport as soon as I had previously anticipated. Get out of my way. I'm leaving." Mevlevi secured his briefcase, then swept past Wenker and made his way down the short corridor toward the door. Blood sloshed from his Italian loafers.

"Dammit, Mevlevi," Wenker yelled in English. "I said you're not leaving this room." The lanky bureaucrat charged into the corridor, brandishing a compact pistol. "What the hell have you done to Nicholas Neumann?"

Mevlevi stared at the gun, then at the man. He had been right in suspecting he knew the voice. It belonged to Peter Sprecher, Neumann's former superior at USB. He didn't think a banker would shoot an unarmed man. He, on the other hand, would be fully justified in using his pistol. A case of self-defense. But before he could draw his gun, the banker was coming at him, an enraged expression drawn across his features. Sprecher slammed him against the wall, asking again what he had done with Neumann.

Mevlevi was momentarily stunned. He let his body go slack under the larger man's grip. "I told you, Mr. Sprecher. Neumann was taken ill. A cold. Now let me down. There's no reason we can't be civil about this."

"You're staying here until you tell me what you've done to Nick."

Mevlevi bucked his left knee into Sprecher's groin and brought his forehead down upon the man's nose. It was a neat trick. He'd learned it as a young stowaway on an out-bound steamer to Bangkok.

Sprecher reeled and fell against the wall. The pistol dropped to the floor. Mevlevi deftly kicked it away while reaching into his jacket and withdrawing his own Beretta nine milli-meter. Bad business to leave bodies behind in a five-star hotel. Changing the linens daily was one thing. Disposing of corpses, quite another. He picked up the briefcase in his left hand and leveled the gun in his right. But Sprecher ap-peared to have seen this coming. The hand that had been nursing his broken nose shot forward and arrested the pistol's downward path. The other hand latched on to the brief-case.

Mevlevi grunted and urged the pistol lower, stopping when its muzzle grazed Sprecher's shoulder. He pulled the trigger and a bullet blew Sprecher across the narrow corridor. His back slapped against the wall. His face regis-tered the greatest surprise. Yet one hand re-mained fixed to the briefcase, forcing Mevlevi to advance a step. Mevlevi rammed the pistol into Sprecher's chest, feeling its snout jab the sternum.

Never had a man take three shots and survive, he had told Neumann.

He pulled the trigger twice more in rapid succession. Both times, the chamber clicked on empty. Out of shells. Mevlevi spun the gun in his hand, accepting the warm muzzle as a grip, and raised it high above his head. A few smacks on the cranium would do the trick nicely.

A sharp knock on the door froze his motion.

Sprecher, all too much alive, yelled, "I need help. Come in. Now."

The door flew open and Reto Feller barged in. He looked at the scene, muttering confusedly, "Sprecher? Where's the count? Does the Chairman know you're here?"

Mevlevi's eyes shifted from one man to the next. With a whiplash snarl, he crashed the pistol's steel butt across the chubby interloper's face. The interloper fell to the floor, slamming onto Mevlevi's injured leg.

Mevlevi yelped and tried to jump back, but Sprecher's stubborn hand remained in a death grip upon the briefcase handle.

"Bastard," mumbled Sprecher, who by now had crumpled onto the floor, arm seemingly glued to the briefcase. "You're staying here."

Retreat, Mevlevi heard a voice urge him. Get the hell out of here. To Brissago. To the main square. One hour. The situation was messy. A gunshot had been fired. A man had yelled for assistance. The door to the hallway remained open.

Retreat.

Mevlevi extricated his foot from the florid man's inert body. He gave the briefcase another yank, then abandoned it, holstering his weapon as he stepped into the hallway. He gave Room 407 a last look. One man was unconscious, the other growing weaker by the minute. No threat there. He poked his head outside the room. Elevator a far distance to the left. Interior stairwell a few feet to his right. Exterior stairs at the end of the hall, also to his right.

Mevlevi chose the safer path and hurried to the exterior staircase. Forget the limousine. It was compromised. He'd skirt the hotel entrance and walk the short distance down the main road to the stand of restaurants he had seen when arriving. From there he could call a cab. If his luck held, he could be in Brissago in less than an hour. And across the border a short time thereafter.

Khamsin will live.

Chapter 65

General Dimitri Marchenko checked his watch, then strode across the hangar floor. The time was 1340 hours. Nearly noon in Zurich, where Ali Mevlevi was arranging the transfer of eight hundred million francs to a government account in Alma-Ata, Kazakhstan. He felt a ruffle at the back of his throat and knew his nerves were acting up. He told himself to be patient. Mevlevi was nothing if not exact. He'd probably call at twelve on the nose. No point worrying until then.

Marchenko walked to a circle of soldiers standing guard around the Kopinskaya IV. He saluted, then approached the bomb. The weapon had been placed on a small wooden table a dozen paces from the Sukhoi attack helicopter. It lay on its side; its inferior lid had been removed. Time to program the altitude at which the bomb would detonate.

The pilot of the helicopter stood next to the table. He was a handsome Palestinian smiling broadly while shaking hands with his Kazakh comrades. Marchenko had learned that there had been fierce competition among the pilots to determine who would receive the honor of dropping "Little Joe," a knock-down-drag-out

848

fight to see who would joyously be vaporized at the moment of detonation.

The pilot described his flight plan to Marchenko. After takeoff, he would keep the aircraft close to the ground to avoid radar, maintaining a fifty-foot ceiling while keeping his airspeed a brisk hundred forty knots. Five miles from the Israeli military post at Chebaa in the hills overlooking the Lebanese border, the chopper would climb to a thousand feet. He would activate the Israeli transponder and pass himself off for one of dozens of routine flights that daily shuttle between Jerusalem and the border outposts.

Once inside Israeli airspace, he would establish a southeasterly course and make for the settlement of Ariel on the occupied West Bank. The distance was short, about sixty-five miles; flying time less than thirty minutes. Approaching Ariel, he would descend to two hundred feet. He had memorized a map of the town and studied dozens of pictures of it. When he had spotted the town's central synagogue, he would bring the chopper down to fifty feet and detonate the bomb.

Marchenko imagined what the Kopinskaya IV would do to the small settlement. The initial blast would create a crater more than a hundred feet deep and three hundred feet wide. Every man, woman, and child within five hundred yards would be vaporized instantly, as a fireball hotter than the face of the sun roasted their bodies. Farther out, the shock waves would crumble most wooden structures and ignite any others that were still standing. In little over four seconds, the entire settlement of Ariel, and every living being in it, would cease to exist.

Marchenko lifted the nuclear weapon, bringing the LCD nearer his eyes. He hesitated for a moment, realizing that he would be directly responsible for bringing death to over fifteen thousand innocent souls. He scoffed at his wounded conscience. Who in our world is innocent? He programmed the bomb to detonate at an altitude of twenty-five feet. He checked his watch. Ten minutes before twelve in Zurich. Where was Mevlevi?

Marchenko decided to attach the weapon to the helicopter. He did not want any delays once his money had been transferred. Besides, he had to do something to keep moving or else he'd go mad. As soon as he had word from Mevlevi, he would activate the bomb, gather his men, and proceed back to Syria, where their aircraft waited to ferry them home to Alma-Ata, and to a hero's welcome.

He ordered the chief mechanic to move the weapon to the Sukhoi and to attach it to its right firing pod. The mechanic cradled the Kopinskaya in both hands and marched to the helicopter. Marchenko himself opened the steel claws that normally held an air-to-ground missile while the mechanic fitted the bomb to the pod. The entire process took one minute. All that remained was to enter the proper sequencing code and the bomb would be primed.

Marchenko ordered the pilot to warm up the engines, then walked briskly from the hangar to the concrete bunker that housed Mevlevi's communications center. He descended two flights of stairs and passed through a four-inch steel door before entering the radio shack. He ordered the soldier on duty to connect him with Ivlov, now positioned just two kilometers north of the Israeli border. A husky voice came on line.

"Ivlov."

"What is your status?"

Ivlov laughed. "I have three hundred soldiers a stone's throw from the border. Half of them are wearing more Semtex than clothing. If you don't give the order to go soon, they'll cross on their own. To their minds, they're dead already. We have a battery of Katyusha rockets pointed at the heart of Ebarach. Rodenko has twice as many aimed at New Zion. It's perfect fighting weather. We're waiting for the green light. What the hell is going on?"

"Hang on for a few more minutes. I expect the okay anytime."

Marchenko ended the communication, then returned to the hangar. The determined young pilot had put on his helmet and climbed into

851

the cockpit of the attack helicopter. A minute later, the turbine engine whined as it came to life. The long rotor blades began to turn.

Marchenko looked at his watch. It was five minutes to twelve in Zurich.

Where the hell was Mevlevi? Where was his money?

Chapter 66

Nick sped down the Gotthardo Pass, thankful for the milder climatic conditions prevailing on the southern side of the Alps. Ten minutes before he had been enveloped in swirling snow. Now, as he passed the mountain auberge of Airolo, the sky was clear except for a general haze that partially obscured his view of the green valley below. The road had also improved. After an initial series of switchbacks, the highway had widened to four lanes and assumed a straight slope downhill. With his left foot awkwardly planted on the accelerator and his right leg propped over the center console, he maintained a cruising speed of one hundred fifty kilometers per hour.

Stall him, Peter. Do not let him leave that room. I'm coming as quickly as I can.

Nick was thankful for the automobile's hermetic seclusion. The hum of the engine was constant, nearly hypnotic. He pushed himself into its center, allowing it to absorb the pain of his injured leg, and if he was honest, the sting of his wounded heart. Sylvia had been Kaiser's spy. At his behest, she had supplied Nick with his father's activity reports. At his command, she had plumbed Nick's innermost thoughts, her promise of love tawdry bait used to lure him out of his protective shell.

I loved you, he thought, wanting to blame her for the frustration, the fury, the injustice that tore at his gut. And then he wondered if he really *had* loved her, or if part of him had always suspected that her affections had been less than genuine. He'd never really know. His view of their time together was permanently tainted by her acts. He feared that suspicion would become a permanent faculty, like sight or smell, a sixth sense that would not allow him to fully unburden himself to another, and so would never permit him to truly love. Over time, it might fade, but like it or not, it would never fully disappear.

And then another voice rebelled at the sentence he had passed on his own broken self. *Trust,* it said. *Trust in yourself. Trust your heart.* Nick smiled as the count robustly joined in, *It's the only thing we have left these days.*

Maybe there was still hope.

An hour later, Nick had crossed through the urban center of Lugano. He drove the Ford at breakneck speed along a two-lane road that mimicked the lake's undulant borders. A sign indicated the town of Morcote. Red tiled roofs passed in a blur. A filling station. A café. A taxi flew by in the opposite direction, horn blaring as it crossed over the center line. Then he saw the Hotel Olivella au Lac and his heart skipped a beat.

A half dozen police cars were crammed into the hotel's courtyard. A steel gray van was parked next to them, its sliding door pulled open. Six policemen in navy jumpsuits rested inside. Their glum expressions attested to the outcome of the operation.

Nick pulled the Ford Cortina to the side of the road and hobbled across the street to the hotel. A uniformed security guard tried to keep him from entering the hotel.

"I'm an American," Nick said. "I'm with Mr. Thorne." He opened his wallet and flashed an out-of-date Armed Forces identification card. But the guard couldn't care less about the card. He was staring at the blood-caked shirt and the torn trousers.

"DEA," Nick said, paying no attention to the guard's disgusted expression.

The guard softened his demeanor and nodded. *"Prego, signore.* Fourth floor. *Camera quattro zero sette."* Room 407.

The corridor was quiet. A single policeman stood guard at the elevator landing. Another waited next to an open door at the far end of the hallway. Miles of blue carpeting lay in between. Nick could smell the cordite even at this distance. Gunshots had been fired. *Who was dead? Who was wounded? Who had suffered from the failure of his ill-conceived plan?*

Nick gave his name and waited while the

policeman walkie-talkie'd for approval to an unseen poobah in the room at the end of the hallway. A two-syllable response blurted from the walkie-talkie, and Nick was allowed to proceed.

He was halfway down the corridor when Sterling Thorne emerged from the room. The drug enforcement agent was wearing a drab green jacket, and his face was streaked with grime. If possible, his hair was more disheveled than usual. All in all, it was an improvement.

"Who do we have here? The prodigal son himself. 'Bout time you showed up."

"Sorry," said Nick, deadpan. "Traffic."

Thorne began to smile, then as if seeing him for the first time, grimaced. "Jesus, Neumann. What happened to you? Looks like you've been in a fight with an alley cat. And lost." He pointed at the bloody shirt. "I'll have to tell the boys to order up another ambulance. How bad is it?"

Nick kept limping toward the room. No point in going into the details now. "I'll live. What happened here?"

"Your buddy took a cap in the shoulder. He's all right, but he won't be pitching in the World Series. Lost a lot of blood."

"Mevlevi?"

"Gone." Thorne pointed to the emergency exit at the end of the hall. "We found some of his blood going down the stairs. Some more in the hotel room. The police have sealed the borders and are searching the hotel and the surrounding towns for him."

Nick was furious. How could Thorne have allowed a wounded man to escape? He had known all along that the Pasha would be at the hotel. Why hadn't he positioned his men here before Mevlevi's arrival? He could already hear Thorne's excuse. *The Swiss police won't move until they have proof of wrongdoing on their own soil. We had to wait for Jester.*

"Was it you that cut him?" Thorne asked.

"We had a personal disagreement," said Nick, checking his anger. "He wanted to kill me. I didn't think it was such a great idea. He had a gun. I had a knife. It was almost a fair fight."

"Tell you the truth, we all thought you were dead. We found the limo you were supposed to have come in downstairs. Chauffeur was in the trunk. Arm near torn off and a bullet in the back of his neck. I'm glad to see you alive." Thorne laid a hand on Nick's shoulder. "That's a treasure trove of financial impropriety you collected. Mevlevi's file from USB, proof of his accounts at the Adler Bank, even photographs with his signature on the back of them. Not to mention his phony passport. Not bad, Neumann. We'll have his accounts frozen in less than forty-eight hours."

Nick shot him a burning look. In forty-eight hours, Mevlevi would have wired every last dime he had out of this country. In forty-eight hours, he would be back in his Lebanese mountain hideaway, safe and sound. *In forty-eight hours, I'll probably be dead.*

Thorne caught his stare. "I know we should have gotten him." He raised a finger. "And that's as close to an apology as you're going to get from me."

"Jester?"

"Alive. The contraband was lost in the arrest. Burned up." Thorne dragged a thumb across his sooty cheek and held it up for inspection. "That's about the only thing left of it. But we have our tie to Mevlevi nonetheless. Thanks to you, we finally managed to get the Swissies' cooperation. Kaiser's going down. Your colleague Mr. Feller says he was here but stopped to take a call in the lobby from a Miss Schon. Must've been a warning because he never came up. We can't find him anywhere. The Swiss won't issue an APB until formal charges have been filed."

Nick let the mention of Sylvia's name pass right through him. He'd have plenty of time later to tell himself what a fool he'd been. "I thought you said they were cooperating."

Thorne shrugged. "In fits and spurts. Mevlevi is one thing. Wolfgang Kaiser another. Right now I'm taking what I can get."

Nick started toward the open door. He felt incredibly sad. The whole plan had fucked up. The police hadn't gotten Mevlevi or Kaiser.

"I want to see my friend."

"Go ahead. The ambulance is on its way, so hurry it up."

Peter Sprecher lay on the floor of the large salon. He was conscious. His eyes were open, darting around the room. Bath towels had been placed under his shoulder. A police officer sat beside him, keeping pressure on the wound in an effort to stanch the bleeding. Nick eased himself to the floor, sure to keep his right leg extended, and relieved the officer of his duty.

Sprecher lifted his head and gave the weakest of laughs. "Didn't get you either?"

"No, he didn't." Nick kept his hand firmly on Sprecher's shoulder. "How are you, *chum?*"

"I may be taking a smaller jacket size. But, I'll live."

Nick was worn out. "Well, we tried."

"I diddled him as long as I could. Had to come up with a dozen excuses. It wasn't easy. I couldn't help but imagine what had happened to you. When he got word his shipment had been taken down, that was that. He wanted out."

"You did good, Peter. Real good."

Sprecher smiled slyly. "I did better than that, chum." Wincing, he lifted himself from the floor and whispered, "I know where he's gone. Didn't want to tell Thorne. Tell you the truth, I never trusted him. Five minutes earlier and he'd have gotten the Pasha."

Nick leaned closer, putting his ear to Sprecher's lips.

"I heard Mevlevi talking on the phone. He didn't know I spoke his lingo. Brissago. Main square in an hour. He's meeting someone there. Pissant of a town, smack on the Italian border."

"It's eleven-thirty right now. When did he leave?"

"Fifteen minutes ago. You just missed him, schmuck."

"And Kaiser? A no-show?"

"Don't know where the Chairman was. Ask Feller. They've already taken him out of here. Mevlevi pistol-whipped the poor chap. Bleeding worse than I was. Don't tell him, but I think he saved my life. Now go on. Get out of here. Find Mevlevi and give him my best regards."

Nick took his friend's hand and squeezed it tightly. "I'll find him, Peter. And don't worry, I'll let Mevlevi know just how you feel about him. You can count on it."

Sterling Thorne was waiting for Nick at the doorway.

"Neumann, before we pack you off to the hospital with your buddy, I wanted to share something we found in Mevlevi's briefcase."

"What is it?" Nick wasn't going to any hospital. At least not yet. And he was in no mood to stand around shooting the shit. Every second put more distance between him and the Pasha. Every second lengthened the odds of his capture.

Thorne handed him a sheaf of papers attached at the upper-left-hand corner by a gold paper clip. Three words in bold Cyrillic script ran across the top of the page. The documents were addressed to Mr. Ali Mevlevi, address a post office box in Beirut. Below Mevlevi's name, written in English, was a devil's lexicon of modern armaments. Aircraft, helicopters, tanks, missiles. Quantities, prices, availability dates.

Despite his impatience, Nick could not help but give the pages his utmost attention. "This list includes a battlefield nuclear weapon. Who the hell is selling this stuff?"

Thorne scowled. "Our new Russian allies, who else? Do you have any idea what Mevlevi can do with this?"

"Didn't you say he had a private army?"

"I said 'private army,' as in half-assed militia. There's a dozen of those already in Lebanon. This here constitutes enough firepower for the First Marine Division. I don't even want to think of what Mevlevi would do with a nuke. I've been on the horn to Langley. I imagine they'll get in touch with the Mossad."

Nick studied the sheets. He could practically feel the tumblers fall into place as his mind unlocked this one last puzzle. Why did the Pasha want to fund a takeover of the

United Swiss Bank? Why had he peopled the Adler Bank with Middle Eastern executives? Why his urgency to get Gino Makdisi's forty-million-dollar prepayment? Why had he come all the way to Zurich?

Nick sighed. Because the Adler Bank wasn't good enough for him. Because the Pasha needed USB as well. Because he required the combined cash and securities held by both banks to buy his Easter basket of shit-hot, state-of-the-art weaponry. God only knew to what use he'd put them.

Nick handed back the papers to Thorne. "Sprecher told me something that might interest you. He thinks he knows where Mevlevi's headed."

Thorne cocked his head, sniffing the air as if he had the scent of his prey. "He didn't mention it to me."

Nick considered telling Thorne the truth, then thought the better of it. If he wanted to pursue Mevlevi, he had to move Thorne out of the way. Thorne would insist Nick go to the hospital directly. Or he'd say that Nick was a civilian, something about how Thorne couldn't allow his life to be endangered. Bottom line: Thorne would do anything to have Mevlevi to himself.

And so would Nick.

"Peter thought you might have been responsible for the screwup. I set him straight. Told him that you didn't know Mevlevi was on to

me." Nick paused, allowing Thorne to dangle a little longer.

"Goddammit, Neumann. Where in the hell did he say Mevlevi was heading?"

"Porto Ceresio. It's east of here, on the Italian border. But don't run off, I'm coming with you."

Thorne shook his head. He was already reaching for his walkie-talkie. "I appreciate your enthusiasm, but you aren't going anywhere with that leg. You stay put until the ambulance gets here."

Nick decided more resistance was needed. "You're not leaving me here. I gave you this information. Mevlevi tried to kill me. It's personal now. I want a shot at him."

"Exactly why you're staying here. I want Mevlevi alive. Dead he does us no good whatsoever."

Nick lowered his head and muttered to himself, as if exhaustion had won him over. He raised an arm in protest, then allowed it to drop.

"Thanks for your help, Neumann, but you're better off getting yourself patched up." Thorne brought the walkie-talkie to his mouth. "We've got word on where Mevlevi is heading. I'll be downstairs in a minute. Get us a couple squad cars as escort. Some podunk town called Porto Ceresio. Call the local authorities. Tell them we're heading over. Ya hear?"

Chapter 67

Ali Mevlevi sat in the backseat of a speeding taxi, furious about the loss of his briefcase. It held everything: his agenda containing all his banking information — accounts, code words, phone numbers; a copy of the weaponry he had purchased from Marchenko; and most important, his cellular phone. He had always liked to think of himself as being calm in the face of danger, but now he knew that was not the case. He was a coward. Why else had he lived his life holed up in a fortified compound in a lawless land? Why else hadn't he chased after Neumann and made sure that he was dead? Why else had he fled the hotel before he wrested the briefcase from that maniac Sprecher's grip? Because he was afraid, that's why.

You're a coward, Ali. For once, he did not try to deny it.

Mevlevi shifted in his seat and asked the taxi driver how much farther to Brissago. The driver said, "Almost there." He'd been saying the same thing for half an hour now. Mevlevi looked out the window. The foothills of the Tessin rose on either side of him. The landscape was a moribund green, similar to that of the Shouf Mountains near his home in Lebanon. Occasionally he caught a glimpse of the lake off to his left. The blue water consoled him. Italy lay on the other side.

Mevlevi sat up straighter and grimaced with pain. His left leg felt as if it were on fire. He lifted his pant leg and looked at the wound. The gash was only three inches long, but he'd been cut deeply, almost to the bone. The blood had tried unsuccessfully to coagulate. He had been moving around too much, first struggling with Peter Sprecher, then running from the hotel to a taxi stand a quarter of a mile up the road. Now the wound had suppurated. The blood had turned a chocolate black and was oozing down his leg.

Damn the leg! Concentrate on how to get yourself out of this mess!

Mevlevi considered what he must do once he reached Brissago. He knew he didn't have much time. The swarm of policemen outside the hotel made clear the involvement of the Swiss authorities. His accounts would be frozen in a day or two. An international arrest warrant bearing his name would be issued any minute. Kaiser was probably already in jail. Who knew what he would tell the authorities?

A curious sense of detachment descended over him. The more he thought about his situation, the freer he felt. He would lose his investment in the Adler Bank as well as his shares at USB and the twenty million in cash he had deposited there only Friday. He was ruined financially. That much was patently clear. He heard his father's voice telling him that if a man had religion he could never be bankrupt; that Allah's love made every man rich. And for the first time in his life, he truly believed it.

Mevlevi had only one thing left to him. The successful implementation of Khamsin.

He drew a deep breath and calmed himself. Ott had promised to credit his account at USB with eight hundred million francs this morning before noon. If he could get the money wired to Marchenko before word of his own escape and Kaiser's arrest leaked out, he could make sure he left the world with at least one lasting legacy. The destruction of the settlement of Ariel. The extermination of fifteen thousand arrogant Jews.

Mevlevi checked his watch. It was twenty minutes before twelve. He set forth in his mind the calls he would have to make. It would be more difficult without his agenda. He would have to improvise. He knew Ott's number at USB. He knew the number of his own communications facility in Lebanon. He just needed the time to make two phone calls.

Mevlevi looked out his window. Despite the terrible pain in his leg, he smiled.

Khamsin will live!

Nick raced the Ford along the winding road.

He squeezed the steering wheel and asked himself where the hell Brissago was. The map he'd found in the glove compartment gave the distance as forty kilometers. He'd been driving for over half an hour. He should be there by now. He held the car tight into a sharp curve. The wheels complained and the engine revved. He almost missed the white sign that flashed past on his right: "Brissago" with an arrow pointing to the left.

Nick took the next turnoff. The road narrowed and descended a steep hill before coming to Lago Maggiore. He rolled down the window and let in a fresh lake breeze. The air was almost warm; the day, peaceful. Fitting, he thought. It matched the reserve that had come over him since leaving the hotel in Lugano. He allowed himself no feelings for Sylvia, or for himself. He did not think of his father. He was powered by a single emotion. A pure hatred for Ali Mevlevi.

The road veered from the lake and passed through a tunnel of elm trees. The town of Brissago commenced at the other side. Nick slowed the Ford and drove along the main street. Small buildings lined the road, all with red tile roofs and whitewashed facades. The street was deserted. He passed a bakery, a kiosk, and a bank. All were closed. He remembered that many smaller towns kept their stores shuttered on Mondays until one o'clock. Thank God. In his perfect blue suit,

Mevlevi would stick out like a sore thumb.

Brissago, Sprecher had said. *Twelve o'clock. Main square.*

Nick looked at his watch. Five minutes to go. He drove to the end of the main drag and followed the road as it turned sharply to the right. The town square opened up to his left. It was a large piazza with a modest fountain in its center. A less modest church sat at the opposite side of the square and next to it, a café. Perfect for those who needed something stronger than Communion wine. The lake ran along the far side of the church. Closer to him, a few old men were playing boccie ball on a small dirt court. He slowed the car, scanning the square for the Pasha. He saw an old woman walking her dog. Two kids sat around the fountain smoking cigarettes. No sign of Mevlevi.

Nick pulled into a gravel parking lot fifty yards up the road. He eased himself out of the car and walked back to the square. His approach provided no place to hide, no buildings where he might conceal himself. He was out in the open without any weapon. He'd be an easy target if Mevlevi caught sight of him. Funny, right now, he didn't really care. He moved as if in a trance, his eyes glued to the wide-open piazza in front of him. Mevlevi might not even be here. He'd left the hotel on foot just ten minutes before Nick had arrived. He hadn't had a car waiting. That meant he would have had to either steal a car or find a taxi.

Nick walked to the fountain and looked around. The place was as quiet as the grave. No cars approached from either direction. The old-timers playing boccie didn't glance in his direction. He could hear the breeze whistling by, and somewhere far off a dog barking.

As quiet as the grave.

He crossed the square to the church and pushed open its massive wooden doors. He stepped inside and leaned his back against the wall. After a few seconds, his eyes grew accustomed to the dark and he looked up and down the nave, seeing if Mevlevi was seated somewhere in the pews. A few women dressed in black occupied the front rows. A priest came out of the sacristy and adjusted his clerical vestments, preparing for the midday service.

Nick left the church. Shielding his eyes from the sun, he walked to his right toward the lake, then stopped at the corner of the church. For a moment he watched the men playing boccie. Another world, he thought. He looked out at the lake, a few feet away. The surface was ruffled by a steady southerly breeze.

He decided he could keep a good eye on any activity in the square from here. He pressed his shoulder against the wall and told himself to be patient. He looked over his shoulder. There was a phone booth about ten steps away, tucked in by the walls that fronted the apse. He returned his attention to the square. A white Volvo drove by, then nothing. He checked over his shoulder again, his interest drawn to the phone booth. A man stood inside it, his back turned to him. Medium height, dark hair, navy overcoat.

Nick took a step toward the booth. The man turned and faced him, eyes opening wide.

The Pasha.

Ali Mevlevi had reached Brissago's main square at ten minutes before twelve. He walked to the fountain and looked to all four corners, expecting Khan to show his face, then realized that his assistant had had to cover a greater distance. The extra time made Mevlevi happy. He needed to find a phone booth and call Ott in Zurich. He made a tour of the square and had just about given up when he spotted a silver booth with a yellow PTT sign pasted to its window alongside the church. He rushed to the booth and called the United Swiss Bank. Several minutes passed before the vice chairman of the bank could be located.

Mevlevi held the phone to his ear, praying that word of the police action in Lugano had not yet filtered back to Zurich. He would know the instant he heard Ott's voice.

"Ott, *Guten Morgen.*" The voice was its usual officious self. Thanks be to Allah.

"Good morning, Rudolf. How are you today?" Mevlevi asked in his most casual voice.

The Swiss could smell desperation miles away, even over the phone. Something in their blood.

"Mr. Mevlevi, a pleasure. I imagine you are calling regarding your loan. Everything is in order. We've credited the entire amount to your new account."

"Wonderful news," said Mevlevi. He realized some small talk was mandatory. "And Konig's announcement this morning, how did your staff take it?"

Ott laughed. "Why, terribly, of course. What do you expect? I've been at the floor of the exchange since eight. Everyone and their aunt is scrambling to get their hands on shares of USB. The professionals seem to think it's a done deal."

"It is a done deal, Rudolf," Mevlevi said confidently, marveling at his own capacity for bullshit. "Rudy, I've had a small problem this morning. My briefcase has been stolen. You can imagine what I had in it. All my account numbers, phone numbers, even my cellular. I've had to get away from this wretched government functionary, Wenker, just to call."

"They can be terrible," Ott agreed unctuously.

Mevlevi said, "I need a favor, Rudy. I had wanted to transfer that entire amount to a colleague first thing, but I don't have his account number with me any longer. I was wondering if I gave him my account number and my password, you know, 'Ciragan Palace,' as always, if he could give you the coordinates of his bank."

"What is his name?"

"Marchenko. Dimitri Marchenko. A Russian colleague."

"Where will he want the money transferred?"

"The First Kazakhi Bank of Alma-Ata. I believe you have a correspondent relationship with them. He'll give you the details."

"How will we know it is him?"

"I'll phone him right away. I'll give him my code words. Ask him the name of his baby. It is Little Joe."

"Little Joe?"

"Yes. And Rudy, make the transfer urgent." Mevlevi didn't dare say more. He heard Ott repeat the details as he wrote them down. Ott's mind was fixed on the chairmanship of the new USB-Adler Bank. He wouldn't let the small matter of a slightly irregular transfer ruin his budding relationship with his new boss.

"I see no problem . . . *Ali*. Have Mr. Marchenko call me in the next few minutes and I'll personally take care of it."

Mevlevi thanked him and hung up the phone. He inserted three five-franc pieces into the phone and dialed a nine-digit telephone number. He could feel his heart beating faster. All he needed to do was to give the general his account number and password.

Mevlevi heard the connection go through and the phone ring once, then twice. A voice answered. He ordered the soldier manning the desk to find Marchenko immediately. He tapped his foot, waiting to hear the Russian's smoky voice.

Marchenko came onto the line. "*Da?* Mevlevi? This is you?"

Mevlevi laughed easily. "General Marchenko. I am so sorry to keep you waiting. We've had a small change in plan."

"What?"

"Nothing serious, I assure you. The entire amount is in my account. Problem is I've misplaced *your* account number at the First Kazakhi Bank. I've just spoken with my bank in Zurich about the problem. They would like you to call them and give them the account information. You'll be speaking with Rudolf Ott, the vice chairman of the bank. He's asked me to tell you my account number and my code words. Please give him your name and tell him your baby is named Little Joe. He'll make the transfer directly afterward."

Marchenko paused. "You're sure this is correct?"

"You must trust me."

"All right. I will do as you ask. But I will not program the baby until the money is in our account. Understood?"

Mevlevi breathed easier. He had done it. He had brought Khamsin to fruition. The flush of triumph warmed his chest. "Understood. Now do you have a pencil?"

"*Da.*"

Mevlevi looked out at the lake. What a glorious day! He smiled, then turned and looked back into the square.

Nicholas Neumann stood ten feet away staring directly at him.

Mevlevi met his gaze. For a second his throat tightened and the number of the account he had acquired Friday from the International Fiduciary Trust escaped his recall. But a moment later, his voice grew firm. The number was etched clearly in his mind. At that moment, he knew that Allah was with him.

"My account number is four four seven . . ."

Nick slammed open the door of the phone booth. He grabbed Ali Mevlevi by the shoulders and threw him into the steel and glass wall, then stepped into the booth and delivered a single hammer-like blow to the stomach. The Pasha doubled over, the phone tumbling from his hand. Christ, it felt good to have a go at this monster.

"Neumann," grunted Mevlevi. "Give me the phone. Then I'll go with you. I promise."

Nick brought his fist across Mevlevi's jaw and felt a knuckle crack. The Pasha slid down the wall, his hands fumbling for the receiver. "I give up, Nicholas. But please, I must speak with that man. Don't hang up."

Nick grabbed the receiver and brought it to his ear. An irritated voice said, "What is the account number? You've only given me —"

Mevlevi cowered in the corner.

Nick looked at him and saw a frightened old man. A large measure of his hate had been spent. He could not kill him. He would call the police, summon Sterling Thorne.

"Please, Nicholas. I'd like to speak with the man on the phone. Just a moment."

Before Nick could respond, Mevlevi was up, coming at him. He'd lost his fragile mien. He held a small crescent-shaped knife in his hand and with it he slashed viciously at Nick's belly. Nick jumped backward, parrying the blow with his left hand, and pinned the attacking arm to the glass wall. With his right hand, he whipped the phone cord around Mevlevi's neck, using the metal coil as a garrote. Mevlevi's eyes bulged as the cord was pulled tight. Still he didn't drop the knife. His knee fired into Nick's groin. Sonuvabitch had plenty of fight left in him. Nick swallowed the pain. He gave the cord a ferocious tug, pulling Mevlevi off his feet. He felt a distinct snap.

Mevlevi wilted. His larynx was crushed, his esophagus blocked. He collapsed to his knees, eyes blinking wildly as he fought to draw in a breath. The opium harvester's knife clattered to the floor. He brought both hands to his neck, trying to dislodge the cord fastened around his neck, but Nick held it firm. Time passed. Ten seconds, twenty. Nick stared at the dying man. He felt only a grim determination to end his life.

Suddenly, Mevlevi bucked. His back arched and in a last mad paroxysm, he crashed his head three times against the wall, cracking the glass. Then he was still.

Nick unwrapped the cord from his neck and brought the receiver to his own ear.

The same irritated voice asked, "What is the account number? You have given me only three digits. I need more. Please Mr. Mev—"

Nick hung up the telephone.

Above him, the church bell tolled the midday hour.

Moammar al Khan drove his rented white Volvo slowly past the town's main square desperately searching for his master's figure. The square was empty. The only people he saw was a group of old men gathered near the lake. He flicked his wrist and checked the time. It was exactly twelve o'clock. He prayed that Al-Mevlevi had been able to reach Brissago. It pained him to see his master in such difficulty. Betrayed by one so close to him. Chased from this country as if he were a common criminal. The Western Infidel knew no justice!

Inshallah. God is great. Bless Al-Mevlevi.

Khan turned the car around and drove back past the square. He continued down the main street hoping to see his master. Maybe he had misunderstood his instructions. Khan arrived at the entrance to Brissago, then decided to drive back to the square and find a place to park. He would go stand near the fountain so that Al-Mevlevi would not miss him when he arrived.

Khan checked his rearview mirror for any traffic following him. The road was clear. He spun the wheel and directed the Volvo back through the small town. He slowed once again as he passed the square, even rolling down his window and craning his neck outside. He saw no one. He accelerated down the straightaway toward a gravel car park about a hundred yards ahead. On the other side of the road, a man was limping slowly toward the car park. Khan turned his head and looked at him. It was Nicholas Neumann.

Khan shot his eyes to the road in front of him, then realized that Neumann had never seen him. Neumann should be dead. If he was here it could only mean that he knew of Al-Mevlevi's plan to escape across the border. But why had he come alone? The Arab's neck grew taut. To kill Al-Mevlevi, of course.

Khan drove the car into the parking lot. The only other automobile there was a red Ford Cortina. He guessed that it belonged to the American. He parked the Volvo at the opposite end of the lot. He watched Neumann approach in the rearview mirror, waiting until he opened the door of the red car and lowered himself into it.

Khan needed no instructions for what had to be done. He opened the door and stepped from the car. He crossed the gravel slowly, not wanting to alert Neumann to his presence. Behind him a black Mercedes pulled into the lot and parked next to his car. He kept his attention on the Ford. If there were witnesses, too bad. He'd kill them too. He unbuttoned his leather jacket and reached a hand inside for his weapon. He felt cold steel and smiling, petted the grip. He lengthened his stride. The world around him shrank to a constricted tunnel. Only Neumann at the end of that tunnel was in focus. Everything else was a blur. A distraction.

Neumann started the engine. The car shuddered and a puff of exhaust came from the tailpipe.

Khan drew his pistol and placed the tip of the barrel against the driver's window.

Neumann looked into the gun. His eyes opened wide but he did not move. He took his hands from the steering wheel.

Khan allowed him a final moment of terror, then increased his pressure on the trigger. He did not feel the bullet that drilled a hole into his brain, blasting away the entire left side of his skull. He saw a flash of bright light, then his world went dark. The pistol dropped from his hand and thudded to the ground. He collapsed against the car, then fell onto the gravel. Dead.

Nick did not move. He heard the pop of a high-caliber pistol and watched helplessly as the gunman's body pounded into the window, then slid to the ground. Ten feet behind him stood Sterling Thorne, gun extended.

Thorne approached the car, holstering his side arm as he walked.

For a moment, Nick sat still. He stared straight ahead of him. He thought the lake was very beautiful. He was alive.

Thorne knocked on the window and opened the car door. He was grinning.

"Neumann, you are one piss-poor liar."

Chapter 68

Nick arrived at the Kongresshaus at ten-forty-five, fifteen minutes before the general assembly was scheduled to commence. The auditorium, which seated several thousand persons, was filling rapidly. Reporters from the world's major financial publications dashed up and down the aisles, speaking to stockbrokers, speculators, and shareholders alike. In the wake of allegations that Wolfgang Kaiser had actively maintained close ties with a notorious Middle Eastern drug lord, all ears strained to learn who would assume control of the United Swiss Bank. But Nick had no illusions. After a spate of apologies and promises of tighter controls, business would continue as usual. The fact that Ali Mevlevi was dead and the flow of heroin into Europe slowed, at least for a little while, did little to console him. Thorne had his victory, but Nick's was tainted. Nearly twenty-four hours after his escape from the Hotel Olivella au Lac, Wolfgang Kaiser had not yet been apprehended.

Nick walked to the front of the auditorium and looked back on the sea of faces streaming in. No one paid him special notice. His role in the affair was unknown — at least for now.

Angry and frustrated, he wondered if Ott and Maeder and all the others would conduct the meeting as if nothing out of the ordinary had occurred yesterday. He imagined what Peter Sprecher would say: . . . *but Nick, nothing out of the ordinary has.* And his anger and frustration grew.

Still, he had half a notion that Kaiser just might show up. Self-preservation would dictate he stay far away from the general assembly, but Nick didn't think the idea of being caught had ever surfaced on Kaiser's private radar. The Chairman of the United Swiss Bank forced to flee Switzerland? Never! Even now he probably believed that he had done nothing wrong.

Nick spotted Sterling Thorne slouching near a fire exit to the left of the stage. Thorne caught Nick's glance and nodded. Earlier, he had given Nick a copy of that morning's *Herald Tribune.* A small article on the inside front cover was circled. "Israeli Jets Knock Out Guerrilla Strongholds." The story said that a renegade faction of Lebanese Hezbollah loyalists had been captured as they massed near the Israeli border, an unknown number killed. A final paragraph stated that their base in the hills above Beirut had been bombed and destroyed. "So much for Mevlevi's private army," Thorne had said, smirking. Though when Nick asked him about the battlefield nuclear weapon, his smile vanished and he shrugged as if to say "We'll never know."

Directly in front of Nick, a yellow rope was strung across ten chairs in the first row. Each chair held a white index card bearing the name of its occupant. Sepp Zwicki, Rita Sutter, and others he knew as residents of the Fourth Floor. Looking to his right, he caught sight of Sylvia Schon making a slow march up the aisle. She was counting heads, spotting how many of her precious charges had attended the meeting. Even now, she was following the Chairman's orders.

He walked toward her, his choler growing with each step. A portion of it was directed at himself — for believing, for trusting, maybe even for loving, all when he should have known better. But most took Sylvia as its target. She had traded on his life for her own benefit, and for that he could never forgive her.

"I'm surprised to see you here," he said. "Shouldn't you be helping the Chairman find the next flight to the Bahamas? Come to think of it, I thought you might even be there already."

Sylvia moved closer to him, trying on a sad smile. "Nick, I'm sorry. I had no idea that —"

"What happened?" he cut in, unable to stomach her false apology. "Did you discover that getting someone out of a hotel is a helluva lot easier than getting him out of the country — especially when the whole world's after him? Or are you planning on joining him after this whole mess cools down a little?"

Sylvia narrowed her eyes, and her face grew rigid. In that instant, any feelings they had shared for each other disappeared forever. "Go to hell," she snapped. "Just because I helped the Chairman doesn't mean I'd run off with him. You've got the wrong woman."

Nick found an unoccupied seat three rows from the stage and laid his cane on the floor. He sat down awkwardly and adjusted his leg. Doctors had cleaned and sutured the wound to his lower thigh. He wouldn't be doing the samba anytime soon, but at least he could walk.

The lights dimmed, and Rudolf Ott rose from the table and walked to the dais. A heckler from the rear of the auditorium yelled, "Where is the Chairman?" His cry was quickly picked up by others. Nick craned his neck in the direction of the catcalls, then after a moment, returned his gaze to the stage. Two rows in front of him, all seats were filled but one. Only Rita Sutter had not yet arrived.

Ott placed a sheaf of papers on the lectern, then removed his glasses and laboriously polished them as he waited for the jeers to die off. He adjusted the microphone and very audibly cleared his throat. The audience quieted and soon an uncomfortable silence filled the room.

Waiting for Ott to begin, Nick couldn't keep

Sylvia's words from playing over and over in his head. *"You've got the wrong woman."* Where was Rita Sutter? he began to wonder in earnest. Why wasn't she attending the most important general assembly in the bank's history? He recalled the photograph of Rita Sutter kissing Kaiser's hand at his father's going-away party in 1967. Had it been more than just a show for the camera? He remembered wondering why Rita Sutter would settle for a job as Kaiser's secretary when she was clearly capable of so much more.

"Ladies and gentlemen," Ott said, finally, "normally, I would open the proceedings with a brief welcome followed by a summary of the past year's activities. However, recent events dictate that I depart from our traditional schedule. I have news of a special nature that frankly, I cannot keep to myself any longer."

Nick sat up straighter, as did every other living, breathing being in the auditorium.

"Following the directives of Klaus Konig, the Adler Bank no longer wishes to present its own slate of candidates for election to the executive board of the United Swiss Bank. Therefore, I am pleased to hereby nominate all sitting members to a term of one year."

A cheer erupted from the gathered employees. It rippled through the hall and spilled into the foyer and washed out onto the street. A string of reporters ran from the auditorium. An orgy of flashbulbs exploded.

With one sentence, the monster had been defanged.

No explanation was given, though Nick figured he knew why. All shares held in the Ciragan Trading account had been indefinitely frozen by the Swiss federal prosecutor's office. The Adler Bank would be prohibited from exercising its proxy on the shares until such time as rightful ownership could be determined — meaning that for the next several years the shares would be without any voting power. When it could be proved that the shares belonged to Mr. Ali Mevlevi, a heroin-smuggling murderer, now deceased, the Adler Bank would file claim to their unfortunate client's assets in Federal Court — as would the United States Drug Enforcement Administration and any other agency that had the least bit to do with the pursuit of Mevlevi. No decision regarding the ultimate disposition of the shares would be made for a decade. The United Swiss Bank could rest easy until then.

Nick remained seated while everyone around him stood and cheered. He told himself he should be happy too. USB was rid of Kaiser and free of Mevlevi. The bank would stand alone as it had for the past one hundred twenty-five years. Its continued independence might be his only victory.

In front of him, Martin Maeder pumped Sepp Zwicki's hands. Ott paraded up and down the dais, patting his fellow board members on the back. *The king is dead,* Nick thought, staring at his pudgy figure. *Long live the king.*

Nick lowered his eyes and found himself staring at Rita Sutter's empty chair. Practically the entire bank was here, but not her.

"You've got the wrong woman."

And then he knew.

Abruptly, Nick rose and made his way to the aisle. He had to get to the bank. Wolfgang Kaiser was there. Now. Forcing his way through the exuberant crowd, Nick ran his suppositions through his mind over and over again. Kaiser had never expected to be a fugitive from justice. Faced with the prospect of an uncertain term in a Swiss jail or flight to a country with lax extradition laws, he would choose the latter. Nick had been foolish to think Kaiser might show up at the general assembly, but he was certain that the Chairman wouldn't flee before learning that Konig had lost his battle for seats on USB's board. Kaiser was too prideful for that. Before leaving, he would need to retrieve some belongings — cash, passport, who knew what — from the bank. And this was the only time that had been left him. The bank would be nearly deserted, with only a skeleton staff on duty. And one very efficient executive assistant.

Nick reached the end of the row and started up the aisle. His leg argued for him to slow. He ignored it and moved even faster, passing through a pair of swinging doors into the foyer. The long, low room was packed to bursting with the overflow crowd. Reporters hovered in every corner, urgently filing dispatches by cellular phone. Nick threaded his way through all of them. He had a strong desire to yell at the top of his lungs for every goddamned person to get out of his way, but somehow he was able to check it, and after another minute he was outside. He rushed down the broad flight of granite stairs. A fleet of taxis had assembled along the curb. He jumped into the first in line and barked his instructions. "Take me to the United Swiss Bank."

Three minutes later, the taxi lurched to a halt in front of the imperious gray building. Nick paid the driver and got out. He hurried up the stairs, noting the uniformed policemen loitering on the pavement nearby.

Hugo Brunner stood behind the lectern inside the lobby, and when he saw Nick, he came forward shaking his head. "I'm sorry, Mr. Neumann. I have strict orders you are not to be allowed into the bank."

Nick leaned on his cane, a little out of breath. "From who, Hugo? The Chairman? Is he here?"

"That is none of your business, sir. Now if you please . . ."

Nick stood up straight and slugged Brunner in the stomach. The hall porter gasped, and as he doubled over, Nick rewarded him with a jab to the chin. Brunner collapsed to the marble floor and lay still. Apologizing silently to the older man, Nick bent forward and dragged him behind the lectern. The bank was so quiet that not a soul had noticed.

The Emperor's Lair was deserted. Lights burned in offices on either side of the corridor, but all were empty. Nick limped toward the Chairman's anteroom, his only company the echo of his own uneven gait. The double doors to the Chairman's office were closed. Nick took a deep breath, then placed his ear against the smooth paneling and listened. He heard a rustle inside, then something heavy hitting the floor. He gripped the handle and turned it slowly. It was locked. He took a step backward, lowered his shoulder, and threw himself at the door. It buckled inward and he stumbled into the room, unable to stop himself from falling to one knee.

Wolfgang Kaiser stood a few feet away, a surprised look pasted on his face. His skin was gray and haggard. Dark pouches supported his eyes. He had removed the canvas of the Renoir oil from its gold leaf frame and was rolling it up tightly. A cardboard cylinder sat on the couch next to him.

"It's the best I can do," he said, in a light tone inappropriate for the occasion. "I haven't put aside any cash, and I imagine my accounts have already been frozen." He motioned with the rolled-up canvas. "In case you're wondering, it belongs to me, not to the bank."

Nick found his cane and pushed himself to his feet. "Of course. I know you wouldn't dream of stealing from the bank."

Kaiser stuffed the canvas into the cardboard cylinder, then popped on a plastic top. "I suppose I should thank you for killing Mevlevi."

"Anytime," said Nick. He was put off guard by Kaiser's collegial tone. He reminded himself that yesterday the same man had wanted him dead. "Where's Rita Sutter? I didn't see her at the assembly."

Kaiser opened his eyes a little wider and laughed. "So that's how you knew I was here? Clever of you. She's waiting for me downstairs. We came in through the gate at the rear. She stuffed me in the trunk of her car. Insisted it was safer."

"I'd say that makes her the clever one."

Kaiser placed the cardboard container on the couch behind him. He took a step away from Nick, absently brushing the end of his mustache. "You have no idea how thrilled I was when you decided to join the bank. Foolish of me, I know, to think you actually wanted a career with us. For a while, I thought you might take my place one day. Call it an old man's ego."

"I didn't come here for my career. Just to find out why my father was killed. He didn't deserve to die so you could leave your stamp on this bank."

"Oh, but you have it backward, Nicholas. I needed the bank to make sense of my life. I always viewed it as something greater than my own ambition, or at least something worthy of it. Your father was a different story. He wanted to shape it in his own image."

"The image of an honest man?"

Kaiser laughed wistfully. "We were both honest men. Just living in dishonest times. Surely you can see all I've done for the bank. We're up to three thousand employees. Think of their families, the community, the country even. God knows what would've happened had Alex taken over."

"At least he would have still been alive, along with Cerruti and Becker."

Kaiser frowned, then sighed. "Maybe. I only did what I had to do. You have no idea the pressure Mevlevi put me under."

Nick thought he knew it only too well. "You should have fought him."

"Impossible."

"Only because you're a weak man. Why didn't you tell my father that Mevlevi was going to kill him?"

"I did. I warned him time and time again. I had no idea things would get out of hand so quickly."

"You had every idea. You closed your eyes because you knew without my father there was no one to challenge you for the chairmanship of the bank."

Nick stared at him, allowing his anger to crest and flow over him. This one man whose actions were responsible for so much in his life. His father's death, his own wandering childhood, the struggle to pull himself from a foundering ship, and when he had, the decision to chuck it all and come to Switzerland. If he wanted to, he could lay every step he'd taken at this man's feet.

"Why?" he shouted. "I want a better reason than your stinking career."

Kaiser shook his head and a look of commiseration saddened his face. "Don't you see, Nicholas? It was the only way. Once we choose our paths, we are committed. You, me, your father. We're all the same. We're true to ourselves, victims of our character."

"No," Nick said. "We're not the same. We're different. Very, very different. You convinced yourself that your career was worth the sacrifice of your morals. Offer me ten million dollars and the chairmanship of the bank and I still wouldn't let you leave this building."

Kaiser started forward, an inner rage darkening his features. He raised his arm to protest and opened his mouth as if to shout, but no sound came out. He took a few steps, then slowed, as if he no longer had the energy to continue. His shoulders slumped, and he walked to his desk and sat down.

"I imagined that was why you were here," he said in a defeated tone.

Nick looked him in the eye. "You were right."

Kaiser managed a weak smile, then slid open a drawer to his right and removed a dark revolver. He lifted it in the air, admiring it, then lowered it to the desk, and with his thumb cocked the hammer. "Don't worry, Nicholas. I won't harm you, though I've plenty of reason. It's you who I have to blame for this mess, isn't it? Funny I'm not more upset. You are a good man — what we all wanted to make of ourselves once."

Nick approached the desk slowly. He twirled the cane once in his hand, tightening his grip on its rubber handle. "I won't let you do this," he said softly in quiet counterpoint to his inner fury. "Please put it down. That's a coward's way out. You know that."

"Really? I thought it was the warrior's way."

"No," Nick said. "When defeated, a warrior lets the enemy decide his punishment."

Kaiser stared at him oddly, then raised the gun to his head. "But, Nick, as you yourself know, I am the enemy."

At that moment, a cry came from the doorway. Later, Nick realized it was Hugo Brunner yelling for Kaiser not to shoot. But right then, it registered only as a distant noise, hardly a distraction at all. Nick was lunging toward the desk, sweeping his cane across its broad expanse, hoping to deflect Kaiser's arm. The cane smashed a lamp and bounced off the computer monitor. A shot exploded in the room, and Kaiser toppled in his chair to the floor. Nick thudded against the desk and fell to the floor.

Wolfgang Kaiser lay a few feet away, motionless. Blood flowed copiously from the wound to his skull. In a few seconds, his face was painted a dark red.

Nick stared at the body, cursing Kaiser for having gotten off so easily. He deserved to spend the rest of his life in a gray concrete cell, eating watery soup and ruing the loss of everything he had held dear.

Then Kaiser coughed. His head lifted a few inches off the rug before banging down again a moment later. His eyes blinked wildly and he gasped repeatedly, realizing at that instant that he was still alive. He brought a hand up to his head and when he pulled it away, Nick saw that the bullet had carved a three-inch furrow across his temple and into his hair. The wound was only a graze.

Nick scrambled across the carpet and pulled the gun from Kaiser's hand. He didn't plan on giving the Chairman a second chance.

"Stop," shouted Hugo Brunner as his boot crunched onto Nick's wrist. He lowered himself to one knee and removed the pistol, then in a kinder voice said, "Thank you, Mr. Neumann."

Nick stared into the older man's gray eyes, and his heart sank. He was certain Brunner would assist the Chairman in his escape. But for once, he was wrong. The hall porter helped Nick to his feet and after mumbling something about his jaw being swollen, phoned the police.

Nick sat on the couch, tired but content. The seesaw wail of a siren sounded in the distance and drew near. It was the sweetest noise he had ever heard.

Outside, the sky was a downy gray. A sharp wind blew from the south, teasing the air with the first intimations of spring. Nick paused on the steps of the bank and breathed in deeply. He had expected to feel happier, freer maybe, but deep inside him a doubt lingered, a certainty that he had somewhere to rush to, someone he had to see, but he couldn't quite remember who or what it was. For the first time since his arrival in his father's country two months ago, he had nowhere to go, no pressing schedule to meet. He was on his own.

A black Mercedes sedan was parked at the curb. Sterling Thorne lowered the window. He was grinning. "Get in the car, Neumann. I'll give you a lift."

Nick said thanks, then climbed into the car. He was waiting for a final comment, something about everyone getting what they deserved, but for once Thorne kept quiet. The car pulled away from the curb and for a few minutes, no one spoke. Nick stared through the window at the sky. He spotted a patch of blue, but an angry gray cloud soon covered it. Thorne shifted in his seat and looked over his shoulder at Nick. The West Virginian was still smiling. "Say, Neumann, know where we can get a decent hamburger in this town?"

Wednesday morning, Nick stood in the departure lounge of Zurich Flughafen, staring up at a massive blackboard that listed all flights scheduled to leave before noon. An overcoat was draped over one arm. His only suitcase sat on the floor next to him. Resting his weight on the sturdy cane, he eased the pressure from his injured leg and allowed his eyes to roam the destinations: Frankfurt, Stockholm, Milan. The names excited him. Cosmopolitan cities offering the chance to start a new life. After an instant, he lowered his eyes and studied the flights bound for more familiar locales: Chicago, New York, Los Angeles.

The departures board fluttered, the twirling of hundreds of aluminum tabs sounding like the shuffling of a giant deck of cards. New letters clicked into the place of old as each flight climbed a row closer to the top of the board, a few minutes nearer to takeoff.

A voice announced, "Swissair flight one seven four, departure to New York, now ready for boarding through gate sixty-two," then repeated the message in German and Italian.

Nick opened his wallet and took out a

square of white paper. He unfolded it and studied the address: 750 Park Avenue, apartment 16B. He smiled. The only way Anna was going to Greece this summer was with him. He thought a ceremony atop the Acropolis might be very nice. Looking up, he found the flight to New York listed on the departures board. He had thirty minutes to make it.